Eileen Townsend is ~~novels~~ *Of Woman Born*, ~~~~
Child, *The Other Woman* and *Child of Fire*. With her
husband, Professor Colin Townsend, she compiled
War Wives, the widely acclaimed story of women in
the Second World War. Of Scottish birth, she is
an MA graduate in Modern History and Political
Science. Eileen Townsend now lives on the banks
of Lough Derg in the West of Ireland.

EILEEN TOWNSEND

DREAMTIME

HarperCollinsPublishers

HarperCollins*Publishers*
77–85 Fulham Palace Road,
Hammersmith, London W6 8JB

This paperback edition 1994
1 3 5 7 9 8 6 4 2

First published in Great Britain by
HarperCollins*Publishers* 1993

ISBN 0 00 647981 2

Set in Linotron Meridien by
Rowland Phototypesetting Ltd
Bury St Edmunds, Suffolk

Printed in Great Britain by
HarperCollinsManufacturing Glasgow

CONTENTS

We are born alone and die alone,
and in the end is the beginning,
and in the beginning is *Dreamtime* . . .

BOOK ONE

Passion's Child

Passion's child . . .
She was one
Made but to love, to feel
that she was his
Who was her chosen:
what was said or done
Elsewhere was nothing.
George Gordon, Lord Byron

CHAPTER ONE

22 December 1841
London, England

Christmas is coming, the goose is getting fat,
Please put a penny in the old man's hat,
If you haven't got a penny a ha'penny will do,
If you haven't got a ha'penny, God bless you!

If Carrie had a dream it was to celebrate Christmas with her father stone-cold sober. It was to recreate the kind of Christmas they had had when her mother was alive.

But the world had been different then, the winters not so long or so cold, and the dragon's breath that rose in white clouds from her nostrils and mouth had been a source of wonder, not the constant reminder of how chill the house would be on her return home from work. Carrie's mother had once told her that life did not begin until you were grown up; before that things just happened to you. And she had often pondered on those words as she neared her twentieth birthday, for the things that had happened to both herself and her young brother Billy over the past few years had brought little happiness to either. Maybe it would be different soon.

'Hot roast chestnuts – penny a bag!'

A small crowd, composed mainly of sailors, had gathered around the stall by the side of the road where nuts were sizzling and popping on the hot grill. Carrie paused and dug hopefully into her coat pocket. She brought out five farthings and handed four over to the man scooping the chestnuts into bags made from twists of grey sugar paper. He accomplished the operation with one deft flick of the wrist and flashed a gap-toothed grin at her as he handed over the tempting fare. 'There you are, Miss!'

Resisting the temptation to open the bag and pop one in her mouth, she smiled to herself as she placed it in her basket. It would be a small treat for her father and brother when she got home. There was bubble and squeak for tea, with cabbage and potato left over from the night before, so the chestnuts would be something special to look forward to.

It was now after seven o'clock and the lamps were lit along the main thoroughfare that was the East India Dock Road. Those that had homes to go to were hurrying on their way to them or crowding into the many taverns that lined the narrow pavements. She passed the usual clutch of prostitutes already plying their trade on the street corners and several drunks reeling their way back to their ships. Carrie knew that many of the women with whom she worked would be too afraid to cross this particular area of London's docklands twice a day, but to her it was simply home and no more or less frightening that any other part of this great city at the heart of the British Empire.

It had seemed a long day, for there were special orders to be finished on gowns being made up or altered for Christmas dances, and everyone in the workshop had been working flat out to keep to schedule. Seamus Casey, the proprietor, prided himself on both the quality of his workmanship and his ability to deliver on time, so no shirking was allowed.

Carrie stifled a yawn and the metal rims on the heels of her boots clinked rhythmically on the icy pavement as she continued the mile walk from Casey's garment factory in East Stepney to her home on Semple Street, one of the warren of winding back alleys that ran along the north bank of the Thames, behind the East India Dock Road.

She and Billy had lived all their lives in the two upstairs rooms of the two-up, two-down brick terrace. They had both been born there, in the same back room where their mother Bridie had died of consumption almost eight years previously.

Bridget Clayton, née Shaughnessy, had been from Kilcormack in County Wexford, and they had all loved her, for Bridie had been the sunshine that lit those two dismal rooms. Dark of hair and bright blue of eye, she had had a laugh that could be heard right down the stairs, yes, and out into the street beyond. And she could curse in both English and the Gaelic – a fact that used to both amuse and infuriate their East End father.

> Auld Granny Gray
> She let me out to play.
> Over the garden wall
> I let the babby fall,
> Then me Mammy came out
> And gev me a clout
> An' knocked me over
> A bottle o' stout!

Carrie did not know why that silly bit of Irish children's nonsense came into her head as she hurried along the frozen pavement, perhaps because she was thinking of how much Billy would enjoy the chestnuts, and wondering if he might even be home before her and have the fire already lit. She always associated that verse with her young brother. It was what her mother used to sing to her as a child, to make her smile whenever she was left with the chore of looking after him.

'Mind you take care o' him now, Carrie *aroon*, or I'll Granny Gray ye when I get back!' Bridie Clayton would warn her daughter with a laughing shake of her fist, as she tightened the black knitted shawl around her shoulders and gave her small son a last cuddle. Little Billy of the fair curls and baby blue eyes had been the apple of his mother's eye. 'He's his father's spit, so he is!' And that was the greatest compliment his mother could bestow, for Bridie

13

had loved her tall, fair-haired English husband with a passion reserved for little else, except perhaps her beloved Ireland.

But Carrie had loved her father too in those early days of childhood, for in the short times he spent ashore with his small family Ted Clayton had lavished more than her fair share of love on his young daughter. Maybe the fact he had nearly lost her in infancy had accounted for the close bond that had existed in those early years. Polio was a terrible thing for any child, but to have it happen to your own firstborn was nothing short of tragic.

By the time she reached young adulthood, the only visible sign the illness had left was a slightly withered left leg and a limp that Carrie had always done her best to disguise. The iron calliper that she had been forced to wear throughout her childhood had long since given way to a specially reinforced shoe, made by Ted Clayton himself on a cobbler's last set up on the living room table. The long candlelit hours he had spent in an attempt to construct something that was not instantly recognizable as a surgical boot were incalculable. Yes, he had been a good father in so many ways. But she had never thanked him for all his work on that hated boot; indeed as a young girl she had often been violently hostile at being forced to wear such an ugly thing. There had been plenty of tears shed over its cumbersome weight and thick ugly laces. And, despite her guilt at her adolescent thoughtlessness, even now she could not look back on those early years without a shudder. Children could be cruel and the nickname 'Peg-leg' haunted her still.

Perhaps because of her handicap, Carrie had always felt an outsider. She had had no special 'best friend' like other girls of her age – no one except Billy. Not being able to run and jump and join in other street games had been a hard cross to bear. In fact, the only fun she could ever remember coming out of her infirmity was when the monstrous calliper was occasionally removed from her leg and her mother would teach her the Irish Jig in the middle of the living room floor. Convinced such exercise would be good for the afflicted limb, Bridie Clayton would spend hours trying to persuade the painfully thin, stubborn little leg to attempt the pointed knee kicks and intricate steps of her country's favourite dance. The memory of those precious hours when, hand in hand, the two of them would clatter around the living room floor in fits of giggles until Mrs Nolan down below was forced to knock on the ceiling in disgust with her broom handle could still bring a smile to Carrie's lips.

She never did master the Irish Jig, nor any dance come to that, but she would revel in watching her mother put on an exhibition especially for the family's benefit. If their father was at home he would sit there beaming, and clapping his hands and stamping his feet in time as his wife tripped the light fantastic on the bare wooden boards in front of the fire.

And it was not only in her feet that Bridie Clayton was talented, for she could sing like a bird and knew all the old Irish rebel songs off by heart. One in particular called 'Father Murphy of the County Wexford' was both her mother's and Carrie's special favourite and tears would flow freely from her eyes as her mother's voice quivered and broke over the last few lines:

> At Vinegar Hill, o'er the pleasant Slaney,
> Our heroes stood vainly back to back,
> And the Yeos at Tullow took Father Murphy,
> And burned his body upon the rack.
> God give you glory, brave Father Murphy,
> And open heaven to all your men;
> The cause that called you may call tomorrow
> In another war for the Green again.

Father Murphy of Kilcormack, her mother's family's parish priest, had led the local people in their fight against their English overlords, and listening to stories of those dramatic days at the end of the last century left the young Carrie with a curiously divided sense of loyalties. She had little doubt, the way her mother told it, her Irish relatives had had right on their side, but accepting that made the English the villains. That was something she knew her father could never accept. As far as Ted Clayton was concerned, the good God Himself was an Englishman and anyone unfortunate enough to be of any other race was blighted indeed. 'You listen to those tall Croppie tales at your peril, Caroline,' he would warn his young daughter. 'Your mother should know better than to fill your head with that nonsense.'

Yes, her mother's family had been what her father always referred to as 'Croppies' — small sharecroppers — who, like so many others in those hard times, could not provide enough to feed even their own family. So the young Bridie, along with several others, had ended up crossing the Irish Sea to England in a desperate bid for survival. Although she herself had married an Englishman and had settled down to London life, from what Carrie could gather, those of her mother's brothers who had come over with her had wasted no time in getting into trouble with the authorities and had ended their days in British jails. 'Politics,' Bridie Clayton told her young daughter. 'That's what it was. They died for the cause, Carrie *aroon*, and we honour their memory to this day.'

Politics was a thing that was rarely discussed in the Semple Street household when the family was all together, partly, Carrie suspected, because her mother was a good deal better informed than the man of the house on the subject, and, much as he loved his wife, Ted Clayton would not have a bad word said against his Queen or Country in his presence.

But Ted Clayton was not always at home, and during the long dark evenings when her husband was safely at sea there had been plenty of time, as they sat before the

16

fire, for Bridie to fill her young daughter's ears with stories of the other great Irish heroes such as Wolf Tone and Daniel O'Connell, and of their brave stands against British oppression. Despite her father's opposition, by the time her mother died shortly after Carrie's twelfth birthday, the young girl had drunk deeply from the cup of bitterness that Bridie, like so many Irish parents, had passed on to her children. For one still so young, it had left her with a distinctly jaded view of British justice towards its own people.

Looking back, it was funny how almost all discussion on not only political issues, but on life in general, had ended with their mother's death. It was as if the light had gone out of life for them all. They worked, ate and slept, in that order, and there was very little else to look forward to.

But Carrie and Billy still loved their father, for he was a good man at heart, despite everything. And everything really meant only one thing – the drink. He had always liked a glass, even as a young man, but when his wife died and left him with two young children to fend for, Ted Clayton had taken to the bottle in a big way, and it had been getting worse of late.

'A jug o' porter, and a tot o' mother's ruin keeps the old dog's tail a'waggin'!' he'd say, as, for the umpteenth time, he raided the old tobacco jar on the mantelpiece where the rent money was kept. And Carrie would bite back her anger and despair as she watched the precious pile of saved sixpences and silver threepenny bits disappear down their father's throat in the form of the 'mother's ruin', clear spirit that was sold in any number of squalid gin shops locally. They should have renamed it father's ruin, she would think bitterly to herself, for there were far more men fell prey to it than ever there were women.

Hearing him staggering his way back upstairs around midnight each night became a familiar occurrence to his son and daughter as they approached adolescence, and then young man and womanhood. Usually he was much too drunk by that time to bother them, but just occasionally he would feel like continuing at home whatever argument he had been having in any one of the multitude of public houses that characterized that area around the docks.

'Ger up outa yer beds, you lazy bleedin' dossers!' he would shout, as he hauled the covers first off Billy, as the youth lay pretending to be asleep at the far end of the straw mattress in the small bedroom adjoining the main kitchen cum living room. Then he would do the same to Carrie, lying curled up beneath a blanket on the ancient day bed against the opposite wall.

'What sort of a welcome home is this for a hardworking fella?' he would demand. 'I've a good mind to take the first ha'penny dip outa here!'

He was always threatening to sign up on the next ship, but never did. Then he would look around him, for drink made him ravenous. 'Not a bite of supper left on the table. You're a lazy pair o' buggers and no mistake!'

Ted Clayton had been in the navy from a boy of twelve, and had remained a seaman throughout the thirteen years of his marriage – right up till his wife had died almost fourteen years to the day from when they first met. It had been a good marriage, and Carrie suspected that her parents having to spend so much time apart had something to do with it. Being separated for several months at a time meant that the few weeks of the year her father spent on shore leave were generally happy ones.

There was no doubt it had been a real love match for the dark-haired, spirited young Irish Catholic girl and the goodlooking, fair-haired English sailor. Neither had had parents or close relatives to consider, so there was no need to stand by formalities once they had decided they were right for each other. They had set up house together in the two small rooms in Semple Street several months before Bridie's swelling stomach made a visit to the local priest a matter of urgency, for the proud father-to-be was due to

18

set sail for yet another voyage at any time. Most of their friends did not even bother to make it legal, but Ted Clayton was having none of that. He wanted to do right by his beloved Bridie, so a ceremony they would have. And he had even taken instruction in the Catholic faith for good measure, although that was something that went by the board as soon as they left the church. Their daughter Caroline, a squalling, dark-haired miniature replica of her mother, was born less than three months later.

The proud father did not set eyes on his new daughter until she was nearly four months old, when, tanned of skin and ebullient of spirits, he returned from a voyage to the West Indies. He arrived with a brown, hairy coconut for the infant sticking out of the top of his kit bag and there was always great hilarity in the small house whenever Bridie recounted her first sight of the gift. Never had she seen such a thing in her entire life and thereafter always referred to it as 'the craetur', for nothing on earth would convince her it was not of the animal species. There was never to be any question of feasting on the flesh of 'the craetur', for her mother would have none of that. To consume 'the puir wee thing' could not be contemplated and it continued to have place of honour on top of the mantelpiece throughout Carrie's childhood, and was to be the first of all manner of exotic oddities that would be unpacked from their father's bag at the end of each long voyage.

After their mother's death, both Carrie and Billy had felt a great sense of guilt that their father had had to leave the life he loved to look after them. Relying on casual labour on the docks, or even occasional work as a mudlark, filching coal from the Thames barges to sell for the odd copper or two, was no substitute for the pride he had taken in being at sea.

Even the difference in his appearance had been dramatic after settling for a life ashore. No longer was he the fair-haired, well-built young man who would arrive home with his kit bag over his shoulder to sweep them up, one under each arm, and swing them round and round in the middle of the living room floor. After their mother's death he seemed to lose all pride in his appearance. Gone was the handsome father they had been so proud of and in his place came this stranger who seldom washed and seemed to lose his hair and grow fat and flabby in the blink of an eye. His once tanned skin became pasty and shot through with red veins, with a scattering of what he referred to as his 'grog-blossoms' disfiguring the neighbourhood of his nose. These unsightly bumps were not the only testament to his love of the drink, for his spreading stomach was forever bothering him. 'Gut rot', he would call it and it could lay him low for days on end. At times like that, in dire pain, he would even take to 'blubbing', as Billy called it, when he had no money either for food for his children or drink for himself, let alone to send for a doctor.

Carrie grew to hate those days when the pain in Ted Clayton's stomach and the despair in his heart grew too much and tears would run freely down the red-veined cheeks and he would turn his head to the wall so they would not bear witness to his misery. He had sunk almost as low as it was possible to sink, and, if Billy often had little sympathy, she understood. She knew what it cost him in pride – and, yes, he had still had some of that left.

'It'll be the work house for us, young 'un,' he would say to her, with real fear in his eyes at such times. That was the ultimate nightmare of the poor, the final degradation. There was nowhere lower. That was it, the very bottom. Unless perhaps one counted Newgate Prison, that notorious hellhole known throughout the Empire for its callous disregard for human life or dignity.

Things improved slightly at home when Carrie and Billy became old enough to go out and earn some money of their own. Their mother had been inordinately proud of her abilities with her letters and numbers, and before she died she was equally proud in having passed on her

20

prowess to her daughter, although her success with young Billy's reading and writing was decidedly more limited.

'The lad's more like me, Bridie love,' her husband would say, by way of consolation. 'More a doer than a thinker, ain't you, lad?' he would declare, playfully clipping the young boy's ear.

Billy would nod enthusiastically. 'Aye, Pa. I'm a doer, all right!'

And Billy became a real doer at eleven, when he was taken on at 'Smellies', the local name for Simmons and Levy's Clothes Exchange, where unredeemed pledges of apparel, consigned there by the local pawnbrokers, were bundled up and sold on, much of it to dealers from Ireland.

Carrie was apprenticed in much the same line of work. Seamus Casey had a garment factory in East Stepney, where Carrie was taken on as a mender. This was not quite as good as being an apprentice dressmaker, but she comforted herself in the knowledge that she was so quick on the uptake that she was very soon as capable of making a complete garment from scratch as any one of the other older women employed there.

Being Irish himself, and having known her mother, her employer had a soft spot for the young Carrie and promised if she worked hard enough she would be allowed on to proper dressmaking before long.

Her father had been so proud of her the day she brought her first wage home. 'Two shillings and threepence, Pa.' She had laid it on the table in front of him – one silver florin and a shiny silver threepenny bit.

Ted Clayton had had tears in his eyes as he looked across at his daughter. He had been laid low with his 'gut rot' and had not worked for four days and it was the only money in the house. 'Your mother would have been proud of you this day, Caroline,' he had said, giving her her full title, as he always did on a special occasion. Then he had gone out and spent the two shillings on drink.

Carrie could not remember when his drinking became

a real problem — so real that they would lie awake in trepidation, waiting for the stumbling feet on the stairs each night. It must have been when she was around fifteen. About five years ago. Just after she became a woman.

Ted Clayton seemed to resent that neither in looks nor attitude was she his little girl any longer. And the fact that with her head of waist-length thick dark hair, bright blue eyes and comely figure, she was becoming even more like his dead wife in appearance by the day, seemed to upset him even more. It was like living with Bridie's ghost. Sometimes it was all that he could do to contain himself, especially on a Sunday when Carrie got all dressed up to go out walking. She would be aware of him looking at her from across the room as she preened in front of the mirror above the mantelpiece, but she could not understand the reason for the change in him. As a child she had been the apple of his eye. It was as if somehow he blamed her for being alive when his beloved Bridie was dead. And sometimes he would get up abruptly and go out, slamming the door behind him, and they wouldn't see him again until nightfall, when the booted feet missing the wooden treads of the stairs would once more bring fear to their hearts.

What would it be tonight, she wondered? It had been almost a week now since he had been on a binge and she hoped fervently he would manage to stay sober until at least Christmas Day was past. Although Billy was now almost a young man, she felt she owed it to her brother to make Christmas that bit special — as much like their mother would have made it as possible.

She glanced longingly into the lamplit stores as she walked the last few hundred yards to Semple Street. There was something about this time of year that made you long for everything to be perfect. The poulterers had plump geese hanging from hooks above the counters, and nuts and dates and all manner of treats were filling the windows, some of which sported the latest fashion of gaily decorated Christmas trees.

22

Most of Carrie's colleagues had been running up little presents for family and friends during their lunchbreaks, and Carrie gave a satisfied smile to herself as she glanced down into the basket on her arm. Inside, just beneath the bag of hot chestnuts, lay a handsome green plaid waistcoat she had sewn over the past two weeks as a present for her father. She could barely wait for Christmas morning to see him in it. He had once taken such care over his appearance that she hoped the gift might encourage him to regain some of his lost pride.

It was with a light tread, despite her weak ankle, that she hurried up the stairs to insert her key into the front door lock. To her relief, Billy was already in and had the semblance of a fire burning in the grate.

'Lord, I'm freezing!' Carrie exclaimed, rubbing her hands together, before kneeling to hold them in front of the meagre flames. She picked up the leather bellows and aimed a few puffs of air at the smouldering coal, then turned to her brother. 'I'm glad Pa's not back yet,' she confided. 'I've got his present in my basket and want to see what it looks like on.'

Billy looked up from the penny-dreadful he was flicking through. 'Don't look at me!' he warned. His sister had used him as a clotheshorse for her creations too many times in the past. It had even been known for him on one never-to-be-repeated occasion to have to don a lady's tea gown!

'Oh go on, Billy-boy!' Carrie urged, getting up and heading for the basket. 'Please! I've spent ever so long on it.' She held up the garment in question in front of him and he eyed it sceptically.

'Well, it's not as bad as that bloody frock, I'll give you that,' he admitted grudgingly.

'Try it on – please!' she coaxed. 'Go on, let's see you in it!'

'Aw, have a heart, sis, it'll be miles too big. Pa would make two of me!'

'Oh get on with you! Go on – just this once, before he

gets back. I've got to see how it looks. Pa'll look a real swell having his Christmas goose in this, I'll be bound!' And she smiled that winning smile she always used on such occasions, knowing she could win him over. He would do it to please her, just as he had done so many things over the years to please her. Billy, with the floppy fair hair, bashful smile and lanky frame. Billy who would one day grow into a goodlooking young man, just as his father had been before him, but who would never believe it of himself. He was far too self-effacing to admit he would ever amount to anything in this life.

But if, like their father, he wasn't the brightest of men, then he was certainly one of the kindest, and all that Carrie really hoped for him was that he would not fall prey to the demon that had blighted their Pa's life. Her secret fear was that one day it might be his feet and not their father's she would hear staggering up those stairs. But now there was no time for such dark thoughts and she smiled indulgently as Billy picked up the waistcoat from the table to keep her happy.

'Well, how do I look?' He made an elaborate, sweeping bow in front of her a minute or so later, then stood up grinning as he stuck his hands inside the gaping front of the garment. 'I reckon I'd have to eat some amount of Christmas goose to fill this lot!'

They were still giggling over the sight of him in it when the sound of the door opening made them whirl round.

'Pa!'

Ted Clayton stood in the open doorway and they could tell at once something was wrong. There was trouble writ large across his coarsened features.

'What is it, Pa?' Billy divested himself of the waistcoat as he spoke and passed it behind him to Carrie, who stuffed it out of sight in her basket as she too looked across at their father in some concern.

'I've had me wages pinched, that's what,' Ted Clayton replied in a bitter voice. 'Bloody well pinched out o' me

24

jacket pocket as I was wearing the bleedin' thing. What do you think o' that, then?' He looked from one to the other as if daring them to deny the awful truth of his statement.

Carrie and Billy exchanged nervous glances. He looked stone-cold sober so there was little chance he had drunk them away. He had to be telling the truth. Both their hearts sank. They had been relying on that money for the goose and the other little extras they had hoped to get for Christmas.

Under his children's dismayed gaze Ted Clayton sat down heavily on a wooden chair by the side of the table and put his head in his hands. Carrie looked at Billy, who raised his eyes to the ceiling, then quietly turned and left the room. She knew he could not bear to watch. He too knew what was coming. Their father's shoulders began to shake. He was going to blub. God, how they hated it when their father cried.

'Don't take on so, Pa,' she pleaded as she headed for the tall wooden dresser. If ever there was a moment to do the time-honoured thing and make a cup of tea it was now. But her heart sank as she peered into the empty caddy. They were out of tealeaves.

'Don't worry, Pa, I'll borrow some off Mrs Nolan,' she said reassuringly, patting his shoulder as she passed on her way to the door. The Irish woman in the flat underneath owed them some anyway.

'Not even as much as a bloody tealeaf in the house and Christmas not two days away!' Ted Clayton's distraught voice followed her out the door.

She hurried down the stairs, the empty tea caddy in her hand, but Carrie had barely uttered the request to their neighbour when they both heard her father's booted feet clattering their way down the stairs and out into the street.

'Where in heaven's name is he going?' Carrie ran to the door and called after him, but no heed was paid as he disappeared into the darkness.

'Don't worry, Carrie love, he'll not get far with empty

pockets, and I doubt they'll allow him anything more on the slate around here,' Billy said, trying his best to console her a few minutes later, when eventually she made the tea with the borrowed leaves. 'With nothing to spend, at least we'll all get some sleep tonight.'

Never did words prove more wrong.

It was a little after midnight before their father eventually staggered into the bedroom where his son and daughter were both half asleep. He remained long enough to knock over the small table with the candlestick, then lurch out again to crash into the dresser and send one of the pair of Staffordshire dogs flying. At the sound of it smashing to the floor, Carrie got out of bed, grabbing her shawl to clasp around the shoulders of her nightgown as she hurried in her bare feet across the wooden floorboards to the open bedroom door.

In the gloomy pool of light from one candle, she stared down at the broken ornament in a mixture of disappointment and anger. 'Oh, Pa, how could you? Ma loved those dogs!'

Whether it was the mention of her dead mother or not, Carrie could not tell. But something in their father seemed to snap at that moment.

'Bloody dog!' he shouted. 'I'll give you bloody dog! You care more for that bloody dog than you do for me – your own father!' And at that, he took a sideswipe at the other one still sitting proudly on the dresser and sent it flying across the room to end up in pieces by the front door.

He then made for the next nearest thing, the earthenware teapot sitting on the table between them, and it followed the dog across the room, spilling its contents as it flew through the air.

That was too much for Carrie as she surveyed the mess with dismay. 'No, Pa, stop it!' She rushed towards him as he began to look around wildly for something else to throw. As he reached for the tobacco jar where she kept

26

the rent money, she grabbed his arm, but he threw her off.

She had never seen him quite like this before. He was going to wreck the place. 'Billy, please! Help me!' she cried in desperation towards the bedroom.

Seconds later her brother appeared in the open doorway, white-faced and apprehensive.

'Come to take me on, have you, mate?' their father jeered, facing up to his son, his fists waving in the air as he attempted a grotesque dance, weaving on the spot like a prize fighter.

Billy stood uncertainly in the doorway. He looked a comical figure in his stained and well-darned woollen combinations, his long lower limbs painfully thin beneath the misshapen legs of the garment. Bleary-eyed, he pushed a hand through his fair hair and looked at his sister, uncertain of how to react as their father pranced before them.

'Come on then, let's be havin' you!' the older man shouted. 'We'll see who's the better man around here!'

'Let's get him to bed,' Carrie said wearily. It seemed the most sensible thing to do.

But Ted Clayton was having none of it. 'Get yer bloody hands off me!' He was flailing out now with both fists and one caught Carrie on the side of her head as she attempted to take his arm.

This was too much for Billy. 'Watch what you're doing there!' he yelled at his father. 'You hit Carrie!'

'I'll bloody well hit more than Carrie, you young whelp!' their father shouted. 'Try to take me on, will you?' He lurched towards his son and aimed a blow at the younger man's stomach.

Billy's thin figure caved in and he bent double, gasping in pain, as the older man's other fist crashed into the side of his head. Carrie looked on appalled as her brother went down on his knees, groaning and holding his middle. She had to do something to help him. She looked around her frantically then grabbed the poker from the fireplace as her father hauled the hapless Billy to his feet again and aimed another blow at his midriff.

'Stop that!' Carrie yelled, incensed. 'Stop that at once! Leave him alone, you great bully!' She aimed a warning, glancing blow at her father's shoulder with the poker, then when that had little effect she shoved it into her brother's hand.

'Whack him one, Billy!' she cried, as their father's fists continued to lash out in his son's direction. 'It's the only thing that'll stop him!' He was going to pulverize the poor lad otherwise. She had never seen him like this before. He was never one to get fighting drunk. Argumentative yes, but never fighting drunk. He seemed to have taken complete leave of his senses.

Half mesmerized by the blows raining down on him, Billy obeyed, prodding awkwardly at his father with the poker. He had no aggression in him and was at a loss as to what to do for the best. Then, seeing that the prodding was only serving to increase the older man's ire, he raised the metal instrument and brought it down with a hefty blow, aiming at his father's left shoulder. But at that moment Ted Clayton moved and the poker met the left side of his head.

'Aaaaahhhh!' A look of shock and pain registered for a second on Ted Clayton's face, then he staggered backwards clutching at his temple, which was now streaked with coal dust from the poker. The weight and immediate effect of the blow seemed to stun all three. Their father stood for a moment, swaying in the middle of the floor, then, as Carrie and Billy watched, he seemed to collapse and fall backwards against the edge of the sofa, before sliding down to land with a thud of his head on the wooden floorboards.

'Oh my God!' Carrie rushed forwards to help him up. There was blood beginning to ooze from just above his left ear, and, as she grasped him beneath his armpits, the older man gave a gurgling sound in his throat.

At first she could barely move him, for he weighed far

more than she anticipated. But, summoning all her strength, she succeeded in pulling him off the bare floorboards.

As Billy watched, too stunned to move, she laid their father gently down on the rag rug in front of the fire and knelt beside him, her hand on his brow. His eyes opened and he seemed to stare up at her for a moment. There was a look of surprise on his face before the stare went blank and a slight tremor ran through his body. Then he was still.

Too shocked to take in what had just happened, Carrie sat staring down at the massive, motionless bulk of the man who was their father. There was complete silence for a moment or two as Ted Clayton's son and daughter gazed at the prostrate body on the floor beside them. Then Carrie turned and looked up at her brother, standing silently watching only a few feet away, with the poker still in his hand. Her voice was awestruck and there was real fear in her eyes as she whispered, 'Dear God, Billy, I think we've killed him. I think we've killed Pa!'

CHAPTER TWO

'My God, Sis, what do we do now?'

Carrie, who was kneeling by the smitten man's side, shook her head as she attempted to stem the blood from their father's temple with her handkerchief. She was as stunned as her brother. 'We'll have to get help,' she said in mounting panic, then her heartbeat quickened even more at the sound of feet on the stairs. With a bit of luck it would be Mrs Nolan. They could get the old woman to run for a doctor.

It was indeed Mrs Nolan, but she was not alone. Behind her stood two uniformed policemen, then behind them peered the small freckled face of her youngest grandchild. All four gazed down at the body on the floor.

'Dear Mary and Joseph! Have ye done for the puir fella good and proper, then?' their neighbour declared, looking askance at Billy, who was still standing with the poker in his hand. She had heard the carry-on upstairs and had got quite alarmed, sending her young grandson to alert the Peelers whose Black Maria was parked outside the public house not four doors down. But never had she imagined anything like this. 'In the name of the wee man, it's bloody murder, so it is!'

Then before anyone else had a chance to say a word, she threw up her hands in the air and backed fearfully out of the room, crossing herself as she went, and grabbing her grandson by the arm. This was not the sort of thing for a child to see.

Somehow Carrie expected sympathy at that moment, but their neighbour's declaration and hasty departure left her totally confused. Then came the enormous shock of having her hands immediately pinioned behind her back and seeing the same being done to Billy. 'Just what do you think you're doing?' she protested. 'What's this for? You can't do this to decent people!'

'Bloody right we can!' the fat sergeant informed her. 'It's not often we catch 'em in the act like this!'

Catch 'em in the act? The words echoed in Carrie's head as they were bundled out of the house and down the stairs to the waiting Black Maria. He had made it sound as if they had done something to be ashamed of – as if they had been responsible for their father's death.

The fat sergeant was quite adamant and well pleased with himself. 'Seems like an open and shut case to me if ever I saw one,' he declared to his colleague.

Stupid man, jumping to conclusions like that, Carrie thought to herself in indignation, but she bit her tongue, determined to set the record straight as soon as they reached the station.

Without the benefit of her strengthened shoe, she banged her lame ankle as they were hustled into the van, but she was far too upset to notice the pain.

Quite a crowd had gathered in the street outside. Domestic disputes were a never-ending source of amusement, and there was a chorus of jeering, whistles and ribald laughter as Carrie and Billy were pushed up the steps of the vehicle, Carrie still in her nightgown and shawl, and her brother a scarecrow sight in his old woollen combinations.

'You'd think they'd have had the common decency to let us get dressed first, wouldn't you?' Carrie commented angrily to Billy, who was being pushed along behind her. 'Typical Peelers!'

Neither of them had even seen the inside of a Black Maria before, let alone travelled in one, and the stench of unwashed bodies packed so closely together was almost unbearable. The already foul air was further polluted by the language of the other occupants collected from the public house down the street, who cursed and swore drunkenly, screaming oaths at their captors as the driver and his assistant, a gauche, pock-faced young constable, manhandled Carrie and Billy into the two empty cells nearest the van door.

The inside of the vehicle had a narrow passage running up the centre with wooden-slatted, individual booths down either side, into which each prisoner was shoved. 'I'm not going in there!' Carrie protested to the young constable gripping her arm, only to be told, 'Yes, you bloody well are!'

'What d'you think we are – rabbits?' she shouted after the officer. 'I've seen ferrets housed better than this!'

It must have been designed for dwarfs, for there was barely room to stand up or to sit down, so all she could do was to shift about in an uncomfortable semi-crouching position as the vehicle rattled its way along the rutted road. Within seconds every muscle in her body was aching, along with her ankle, and she could just imagine what it must be like for Billy with his lanky six-feet frame.

He was locked into the cage on the other side of the passage but it was impossible to talk to each other through the slats because of the noise of the other prisoners and the rattling and creaking of the van. Before the outside door closed, plunging them all into total darkness, Carrie had caught a glimpse of his face and could see he was terrified, for his pale blue eyes stared ahead of him as if in a trance as his lean fingers clutched at the wooden spars. She longed to be able to offer some words of comfort, to tell him not to worry, it would all be sorted out down at the station. But once trapped inside the moving vehicle, with its noise, stench and the painful jolting over the stones, she began to feel they would surely both perish before they even reached their destination.

It seemed incredible to think that less than an hour before they had been safely asleep in their beds, with their father still alive and carousing in one of the nearby public houses. She knew that Billy must be feeling just as upset and confused about this turn of events as she was, but things had happened so quickly they had had no chance to utter a coherent word of comfort to one another. The police had been at the door before they had even had time to gather their thoughts.

The journey to the police station seemed interminable but Carrie tried to console herself with the thought that they would be able to discuss things once they got there. After that it would just be a matter of time until the police were furnished with the full facts and they could go home and see to the proper laying out of their father's body.

Nothing could have prepared her for the shock that awaited them. Once inside the blackened stone building, Carrie and Billy were shoved unceremoniously into different rooms where the questioning began immediately and was to continue relentlessly throughout the night.

'You'd better not hide anything,' a tall, scrawny police inspector warned her. 'It'll be all the worse for you if you do. From what my sergeant tells me that young man you were brought in with was caught in the act with the weapon still in his hand.'

Carrie looked at him in disbelief. 'Oh, no! It wasn't like that at all. It wasn't Billy's fault. Billy wasn't responsible!'

In an effort to save her brother from taking all the blame, she immediately confessed to striking the first blow with the poker herself. Not only was it the truth, but surely they would be more understanding, her being a woman?

But, unbeknown to her, in another cell further down the corridor, Billy was attempting to take all the responsibility on to his own slight shoulders. So intent were they both to shield the other that the word 'accident' was never actually mentioned. But there was no doubt about it, what had occurred back there in their living room had been a pure accident. Neither had even contemplated doing their father any real harm. They had both loved him, despite his faults.

There was no sleep in the police cells that night for the

interrogations went on for hours, with first one officer doing the questioning then another taking over as the night wore on, until neither Carrie nor Billy knew what they were saying or signing their names to when eventually two large, closely written pieces of paper were pushed in front of them. 'This is just a record of the facts – nothing to bother your head about,' the officer told Carrie. 'Strictly for the files.' She wanted desperately to believe him and signed simply to get things over with so they could get back home as quickly as possible.

There was no heating in the cells and neither was offered as much as a blanket or a hot drink to keep out the winter's chill, although the police themselves were well fortified with steaming mugs of tea. But throughout it all, both Carrie and Billy were convinced that somehow, once it was all sorted out, they would be allowed home. The police themselves insisted their cooperation was essential if they wanted to get out as quickly as possible. 'You make it easy for us, and we'll do the same for you,' they were told when they finally obeyed orders and signed the statements. It came as a terrible shock when they eventually got out of the police station to realize that, far from returning to Semple Street to arrange a decent Christian burial for their father, they were heading for the place that had been a byword for horror in every Londoner's heart for generations past. Newgate Prison. Even the very name chilled the soul, for the great granite fortress had been synonymous with hell on earth for seven hundred years.

The sound of the great iron gates clanging shut behind them had a finality about it that would fill the hardest heart with foreboding.

There was an icy wind blowing as they were hustled down the Maria's wooden steps on to the slippery cobbles of the prison courtyard. A thick frost glinted on the ground and on the dirty stone of the buildings that loomed out of the darkness all around them, for it was not yet daylight as the Admittance Officer came marching up with his check list at the ready.

'Follow me!' the man commanded, and befuddled by lack of sleep and shivering with cold, Carrie and Billy were led through the ancient iron and oaken door that had been clanged shut behind the guilty and innocent alike since long before the days of Henry the Third.

The chill and gloom of the place was only slightly less horrifying than the smell that greeted them. The confined stench of centuries had percolated into a vile greenish-grey slime that clung to the walls and infused in their nostrils as they stood barefooted, with chattering teeth, on the ice-cold, stone-flagged floor.

'Got any means, the pair of you?' the man demanded, once they were lined up in front of an ancient oak desk. He was a tall, stooped individual, with a thin, red-veined nose and a grey heavily waxed moustache, well known for his irritability, particularly in the early hours of the morning. Seeing Billy's blank look, he gave an impatient shake of the head, then spelt it out more clearly. 'If you've got the money, it's fifteen shillings for entry to the Masters' Side, with five bob a week on top of that for bed and bedding. There's another fifteen bob to pay the steward for heating, candles, plates and cutlery and the like. Then there's your victuals.'

'Victuals?' Billy repeated dully.

The man became even more impatient. 'Aye, victuals. Are you deaf or just plain daft, lad? The felons' entitlement is naught but a penny loaf a day and pump water to drink – same as you wash down with. If anything more is wanted, you have to pay for it. If you don't have the money then it's the Common Side for you both. And there's no frills there, I warn you.'

Billy looked in dismay at Carrie, who had heard enough. 'It's the Common Side for us both,' she said through gritted teeth. 'And God help us, I'll be bound!'

'Right, Davis,' the Admittance Officer said with some

relief to a turnkey standing nearby. 'You heard. It's the Common Side for 'em both. Take this young fella down first!'

The turnkey marched forward and gripped Billy by the elbow.

Carrie looked on in alarm. 'Hey, wait a minute! Aren't we to be allowed time to talk, for pity's sake?'

'Take him away, Davis!' The officer's patience was rapidly running out. Common Siders were always the most bother.

Carrie felt panic rising in her. Was there to be no time to even say goodbye? No time for a word of comfort? She rushed forwards to the man, only to be restrained immediately by a firm hand behind her. 'Please, officer!' she begged. 'Let me speak to my brother! Just a word or two before you take him away!'

'Shut yer garret there!' the Admittance Officer barked. He was well used to troublemakers. 'You're in Newgate now, not bloody Margate!'

Carrie glared at the man as the sight of Billy being marched away from her in chains brought tears of frustration to her eyes for the first time since their arrest. So great was her concern for him that the full horror of what had happened to their father and of her own situation almost failed to register as she was herded into double file and frog-marched with the other females to the women's Common Side.

The smell, filth and noise of the place seemed at first to pass right over her head as she fretted over her brother's plight. After several minutes, however, she was brought back to reality as she found herself caught up in the reception procedure that would mark her out as no longer a free person, but an inmate of the most notorious jail in the entire British Empire.

A shout of 'Over here, you lot!' had them all turning in the direction of the cry. The admittance formalities were about to begin.

One by one they were strip-searched, then weighed and measured, before being handed a patched blanket each, with which to cover their nakedness on the journey down the dank, evil-smelling stone passageways to the bathhouse.

'You've got a treat awaiting you in there, my ladies,' said one of the turnkeys who escorted them, and there was something about her tone of voice and the smug grin on her face that filled Carrie with foreboding as she struggled to keep up on an already weak ankle that was by now throbbing and badly swollen.

The bathhouse was a long, gloomy, ice-cold room, with lime-washed walls and stone floors where freezing water lay in puddles from previous immersions. The place had a foul stench to it and the whole interior was barely lit by a few small windows high up on the walls, through which the pale light of morning was just beginning to filter.

The baths themselves were two long, narrow, waist-high ditches running down either side of the room, the lower parts of which were coated with cement and covered in a vile greasy slime, pieces of which had come off and had coagulated into a ghastly scum which floated on the murky surface of the three feet of cold water that was ready and waiting for the cleansing of the new inmates.

'If you ain't got the pox when you arrive here,' one of the other new arrivals told Carrie, 'you sure as hell will have when you leave!'

The thought of getting naked into that slime with the other women was appalling, but there was little time for contemplation of the horror as four hefty turnkeys were on hand to make sure all were divested of their blankets almost immediately and manhandled over the sides of the bath, to be totally immersed and scrubbed down with sugar soap.

The icy water caused such a physical shock that it completely took Carrie's breath away and momentarily paralysed her, freezing the scream in her throat.

'Let's be having you, then!' The heftiest of the warders came over and, placing both hands firmly on Carrie's shaking shoulders, pushed her down beneath the filthy surface of the water. As she spluttered to the surface, it was all she could do to stop herself from vomiting, and the cries of distress of the old woman next to her as she too was ducked added to the horror.

Only when their guards were convinced they had been thoroughly baptized into their new life and all trace of the old removed with the harsh abrasion of the sugar soap were they allowed out and each handed a threadbare filthy rag with which to dry themselves.

'Call these towels?' one of the older prisoners muttered in disgust, as they stood shivering violently on the stone flags. 'I wouldn't insult any floor of mine by using one of these things on it!'

'We'll have less lip there, Ma, if you don't mind!' a turn-key warned. 'You lot left your rights to pass opinions on the other side of that wall out there. You're in Newgate now, and if you don't realize it, by God you soon will!'

Somehow, it had not dawned on Carrie that she would be required to don prison garb, and the sight of the pile of stained, coarse clothing that was then handed to her caused her to protest in alarm, 'But I have my own things!'

'Not no more, you don't, my girl. Them's your clothes now, like it or lump it!'

Carrie gazed in dismay at the patched brown serge prison dress and the coarse blue woollen stockings with untidy darns and thick red stripe that were to be held up by two lengths of thick yarn. They had been worn and washed so often the wool had gone hard and matted, and they looked far too short for her legs.

The effect of donning such articles was dramatic. It was as if that bath and these clothes had not only contaminated her, but had robbed her of something infinitely precious – her self-respect. In fact, it had robbed her of her own identity. She was no longer Caroline Clayton; she was simply a felon awaiting trial. A condemned criminal, already found guilty.

A cold anger welled up in her at the injustice of it all. And her heart ached for her young brother and what he must be going through right now. She held her head deliberately high and did her best to choke back the tears as, dressed in her prison clothing, she hobbled painfully along behind the others as they were marched back down the freezing, dark passages on their way to the waiting cells.

Over the next few weeks Carrie waited impatiently for her own case to be heard, because she was certain that her troubles and Billy's would then be at an end and that truth and justice would finally prevail. She could hardly wait to see her brother again for she worried constantly about him and how he was bearing up. He had never had her stamina; even as a child he had been delicate. And he was so easily cowed — wouldn't say boo to a goose, poor Billy. No wonder their mother used to worry so much about him. It was not true that females were always the weaker sex. That was something that both Bridie Clayton and her daughter knew only too well.

When the morning of the trial came, Carrie's first sight of him, standing there in the dock in his drab, ill-fitting prison uniform, marked all over with the hideous black impressions of the Broad Arrow, the 'crow's foot', denoting the articles belonged to Her Majesty, was almost too much to bear. Never well-built at the best of times, he had lost an enormous amount of weight and looked bent and ill. She thought her heart would burst as he attempted a brave smile and held up a hand in recognition.

'Have faith, Billy love!' she called out, only to be silenced immediately by a warder who warned her she would be removed from the courtroom and would be tried in her absence if she spoke out of turn again.

What then followed made no sense at all and she could only listen in horror as the fat sergeant who had been the first on the scene that night read out what appeared to be full confessions by both herself and Billy, admitting to the murder of their father.

Even the poker was produced in evidence, and seeing the familiar household article she had known from birth in such a place had a totally numbing effect on her spirits. Carrie found she could not bring herself to look at it and began to feel quite detached from all the so-called evidence. Despite everything, in her heart remained the firm belief that somehow, at the crucial time, she would be called upon to give her version of events.

But this never happened. And it was only when the presiding judge placed the black cap upon his head and pronounced that both she and Billy had been found guilty of the murder of their father Edward Clayton and would be 'hanged by the neck until dead', did the cold reality of the situation dawn.

Carrie gripped the handrail of the dock, stared at the elderly man who had just uttered the fateful words and screamed at him, 'No! No! We're innocent! You must let us speak!'

She was immediately grabbed from behind by one of the court officials who pinned her arms back and clamped a hand over her mouth. Above the suffocating palm she could just see Billy out of the corner of her eye. He had slumped down in the dock and was being held up by two warders.

She kicked out at the man in whose grip she was held and was immediately bundled out of the courtroom and down a long set of steps into the waiting cells below.

Their evidence would not be required, she was told. They had been all but caught in the act and had signed confessions that same night. There was no more to be said.

They told her the date of her brother's execution a week later, but Her Majesty's Privy Council in its wisdom and

40

charity had agreed to a stay of execution on her part while her appeal was considered. Somehow it seemed the final injustice.

CHAPTER THREE

27 January 1842
Newgate Prison, London

'Please . . . please . . . in the name of God, don't let them do it!' Carrie's voice was hoarse now for she had been screaming like this for hours. But she could not stop, she could not give up, and there was desperation in her agonized pleas as she beat her fists against the hard oak of the cell door until the skin of her knuckles was raw, bleeding flesh. She was immune to her own pain, and her pale face was flushed with exertion, the whites of her eyes red-veined, and the lids swollen with tears. There was no timepiece in her cell to watch the precious minutes tick past, but there could not be long left – an hour at the most – for it was almost daylight. She had to make them understand before it was too late.

'Shut yer mouth in there, you milk-fed trollop! It's no good you making that row. Them as gets sentenced to swing, swings, and hollering your head off like this won't make no difference.' The female turnkey on the other side of the door adjusted the collection of keys hanging from her waist and threw a scathing glance at the peephole through which the prisoner was screaming. 'If I 'ad a brass farthing for all them as claimed to be innocent . . .'

'But he *is* innocent! Dear God in heaven, he *is* innocent!' Carrie's voice was almost incoherent now, her throat choked with tears, as she called after the departing woman. Wouldn't anyone listen? They would be taking him to the scaffold at any minute – murdering him for a crime he did not commit. They would be killing an innocent man and nobody seemed to even care.

She sank to her knees behind the locked door and wrung

her hands. The stone floor was cold and damp, and a cock-roach scuttled across the hem of her skirt, but she was oblivious to everything but the one fact that was beating like a muffled drum inside her aching head: Billy Clayton, her own little brother, was going to die.

They had given her the news only last night: the execution was scheduled for nine o'clock. It would be day-light by then and the piemen, with their laden baskets on their heads, and the shawled and bonneted barrow women selling pigs' knuckles, jellied eels and other delicacies would be in their favourite spots to serve the crowds that were already thronging up Holborn, past St Sepulchre's, to make their way up Snow Hill towards Newgate Street itself.

On this morning of all mornings, Newgate was the place to be. Since 1784, when the old procession to Tyburn was abandoned, this grimy fortress had been the scene of Eng-lish justice exacting her most dire retribution, and such occasions were traditionally ones of great festivity, to be enjoyed by all but the poor unfortunate creature awaiting his fate, and his grieving friends and relatives.

As the time drew nigh, spectators filled the windows of the houses opposite the prison and even squatted on the rooftops for a better sight of the proceedings. Wooden stands had been erected in front of the scaffold to cater for those willing to pay sweetly for a guaranteed view. Already it would be filled to overflowing, such was the public's lust for blood.

From the noise that filtered into the dark cells and dingy passageways of the prison, it was clear that they were already congregating, claiming the best places beneath the dark shadow of the gallows. The scaffold was primed and waiting, jutting out from a small door in the prison wall. The men who erected it had worked through the early hours of the morning, by the light of flaring torches, which cast weird shadows on the grime-blackened walls of this most feared of places.

A three-sided fence had been erected around the

execution site, guarded by a double file of armed soldiers, their fixed bayonets now glinting in the pale grey morning light. Their presence was to protect the condemned creature from the public's wrath, for some executions aroused much excitement in the man and woman in the street – the most sensational being described in particularly lurid terms and sold in penny-dreadful broadsheets for some days before the event.

But not all who awaited justice by the rope were guilty of such heinous crimes. Many innocents had already swung from that blackened noose. Many guiltless hearts had been stilled and others broken in this awful place. Some trembled on their way up the steps, they said, protesting their innocence to the last; some wept and begged forgiveness, whilst others swaggered, looking the world straight in the eye.

When the time came, the black-robed chaplain and his assistant would emerge first, out of the door leading from the prison causeway to the scaffold. Behind them would walk the hangman and his assistant, followed by six uniformed guards.

Carrie knew that the sight of the condemned man or woman always brought a surge forwards and a wave of jeering and shouting from the gathered crowd, for such ceremonies were regarded as outdoor theatre and the poor condemned creature little more than a pantomime villain. She had been caught up in an execution crowd once herself and knew that the hope was always for a declaration of guilt or innocence at this point, for that would add a dash of real drama to the proceedings and give something to talk about as the spectators wended their way home after the deed was done.

As the condemned prisoner prepared to face his God, the voice of the chaplain would ring out, the familiar words imparting a chill into every heart: 'All ye gathered here in the face of God this day, pray for this poor sinner for whom the great bell is about to toll.'

Then he would turn to face the condemned man: 'You who have sinned against your fellow man and are condemned to die; you who stand now preparing to face your God; in His name I ask you to repent your sin. Seek the mercy of the Lord for the salvation of your soul . . . Do so and may the Lord have mercy upon you! May Christ in His goodness have mercy upon you! May your soul not perish in the fires of hell but be raised to life everlasting in the name of Jesus Christ our Lord! Amen . . . !'

Then all would fall silent as the great bell began to toll. The execution bell. The time would have come for the black hood to be pulled over the prisoner's head and the noose tightened around the neck. Throughout the whole throng of milling humanity gathered below, as the sonorous tones of the bell resonated in every head and in every heart, not one sound would be heard between that moment and the awesome seconds of the drop.

Carrie felt physically sick at the thought of it. They said some did not die instantly, but hung there in mortal agony, often taking up to twenty minutes till the last breath was squeezed from the bursting lungs. The 'Newgate Hornpipe' they called it – that final desperate twitching on the end of the rope. And the death struggle was all part of the grotesque, deadly show the crowd was now flocking to see.

But the agony did not end there, for everyone knew the custom was for the dead body to be taken for medical purposes. On a cold mortuary slab it would be decapitated, disembowelled and quartered for further dissection by medical students. Such stuff were nightmares made of, and for weeks now she had been seeing Billy's face, staring up from that marble slab.

Every fibre of Carrie's body ached with exhaustion as she leaned back against the ancient oak door and stared bleakly ahead of her into the darkness of the prison cell. She let out a sigh that was more of a groan and ended in a dry, painful sob that caught in her throat as

45

she contemplated the hell their mother would now be going through were she still alive. 'There is no such thing as justice in this country, child,' Bridie Clayton had once told her daughter. 'Not for the Irish or the poor, at any rate. And, God help us, they usually amount to one and the same thing!'

The most painful thing of all to bear was that Carrie knew she had let her dead mother down, just as surely as she had let Billy down. For she had promised always to look after her younger brother, just as she had looked after him as a child.

'You'll always look after the wee one, Carrie love,' her mother had pleaded, during those last dreadful days when the life blood she coughed up seemed frighteningly red against the white, chipped enamel of the bowl that never left her side, and had to be emptied with increasing frequency. 'You'll see no harm comes to him when I'm gone.'

Carrie had dabbed at her mother's brow and nodded her head, too choked to speak. And the fear would go out of her mother's eyes and she would sigh and lean back on the pillow. She had no need to worry. The wee one would be looked after. Carrie would see to that.

But Carrie had failed. She had failed in a way that would have been impossible even to contemplate then, and was too much to bear now that it was too late. She had been trying to tell them ever since the day that their father died, but they wouldn't listen. Dear God, they just wouldn't listen . . .

She ran a despairing hand through her cropped hair and could feel the hot bitter tears burning beneath her closed eyelids as she leant back against the cell door. A giant clock was marking time in her brain, every swing of the pendulum striking one second off her brother's young life. She could not make it stop. God knows she had tried, but she could not make it stop.

How long she sat there she did not know. Twenty minutes? Half an hour? Perhaps as long as an hour or more. Then it happened. The sound she had been dreading. The sound she had been hearing in her head for weeks now. The dreaded clanging of the execution bell.

At the first note she jumped to her feet as if physically assaulted by the fearful note. Then, placing her hands over her ears, she let out a long, piteous wail of anguish that came from the very depths of her soul.

She sank to her knees on the cold flags, and, raising her face towards the tiny patch of grey sky she could just make out beyond the prison bars, she made a vow: 'I'll get even with this rotten country one day. As long as I live I'll remember what they did to Billy. And I'll get even.'

It was almost an hour later when the door opened and she looked up to see the tall spare frame of the Assistant Governor standing silhouetted in the gloom. He had narrow lashless eyes in a thin consumptive face. His stare was unblinking and there was no compassion in his voice as he looked down at the young woman slumped on the floor in front of him and snapped, 'Clayton, you're wanted.'

Carrie looked up at him. 'Bastards!' she spat at him. 'Bastards! You have just murdered my brother!'

'We'll have less of that Billingsgate language in here, if you know what's good for you. Just pull yourself together and follow me.'

She rose unsteadily to her feet. 'What more do you want of me?' She felt empty, bereft of all emotion. In killing Billy they had robbed her of the only thing she had had left to love. Whatever became of her in the future, she knew she would never again suffer any pain as great as this.

The man yanked her by the arm. 'Straighten up there, it's your betters you're going to see.'

Carrie shrugged off his grasp. 'What do they want me to do, cut my brother down from the gallows?' she asked bitterly. 'Make sure you all get good measure in your pound of flesh.'

'Less lip, madam, if you don't mind. What you're to be

told this fine morning will shut you up for good and all, have no doubt about that.'

The words reverberated in her head as she followed her captor down the long passage that led to the Governor's room. What lay ahead of her she dared not even guess.

On reaching their destination, they found the Governor standing behind his desk, accompanied by the portly, black-robed figure of Father Fowler, the Prison Chaplain. The sight of the clergyman in his official execution robes made Carrie catch her breath and turn away. She could not bring herself to look into the eyes that had just seen her brother die, had just borne witness to his last words, his final breath.

'Prisoner 735358 Clayton, at your request, sir.'

A fug of tobacco smoke hung in the air and a portrait of Queen Victoria gazed down at her from the wall behind the desk as the grip on her arm released.

'That will be all, thank you,' the Governor announced, and with a deferential nod his assistant took his leave.

Carrie stood in silence before the two men who were left, her head held defiantly high. She was not at all sure why she was here. Perhaps it was to tell her officially that her brother was dead and that the date had been set for her own execution. Her chin had a proud tilt to it and her eyes were accusing as they met those of Governor Wedgewood. The elderly man in the black frockcoat stood behind his desk, a piece of vellum in his hand. Overweight and perspiring slightly, he held the document at arm's length and proceeded to study the words with the help of a pince-nez.

The room was hot and stuffy, for a log fire burned in the grate, but, despite her determination not to appear either guilty or cowed in their presence, Carrie suddenly found her teeth chattering as nerves got the better of her. She bit the inside of her cheeks to stop it; the last thing she wanted was for them to think she was worried at what she might hear.

She was in a most peculiar state of mind. One perverse side of her almost wanted to die, wanted it all to be over with. After all, what was there left to live for? Her mother and father were both dead, and now so was Billy. Maybe she would be better off joining them in whatever heaven or hell awaited her rather than go through all this.

She was aware of the Governor's eyes turning from the paper in his hand to her face, but then she began to feel distinctly odd, as if she were standing outside herself observing everything at a distance.

It was the Governor who spoke first, in a voice that had a distinctly irritable edge to it. An early breakfast of bean tansy and sliced turkey's gizzard in the prison canteen had left him with chronic indigestion. He gave a fixed stare over his pince-nez and stated, 'You will be aware by now, Clayton, that your brother has this very morning paid the ultimate penalty for his wrong-doing, whilst you still await the final decision on your own fate.'

Carrie's eyes were now fixed on his face, causing him to glance back down at the paper in his hand as he went on, 'That decision has now been made.'

He paused as Carrie drew in her breath sharply. There was a moment's silence during which the Chaplain by his side cleared his throat and nodded sombrely. Then the Governor continued, 'In its infinite wisdom, Her Majesty's Privy Council has considered your appeal. Its decision on your case was made yesterday and was conveyed to me last night. I felt this morning would be an appropriate time to enlighten you as to the outcome of its deliberations.'

Carrie's heart was now thumping so hard she was sure they could hear it, as he went on, 'No doubt these recent days have not been pleasant ones for you and I dare say you have been fearful that you would follow your brother to the scaffold . . .'

He paused once more to regard her thoughtfully over the top of his glasses. Her face had gone quite white and she appeared to be swaying slightly on her feet. 'Are you all right?'

Carrie nodded, her lips mutely forming the word 'yes'.

He gave a dry cough and after glancing at the Chaplain standing silently beside him, he continued solemnly, 'You are indeed a fortunate young woman. Her Majesty's Privy Council has reconsidered the evidence and the main points of your appeal and in its great mercy it has resolved to commute your sentence from Death by Hanging to that of Transportation for Life.'

Carrie's jaw fell open. She was not to die after all. Transportation for Life. That meant only one thing: The Bay.

'Have you anything to say for yourself in that regard?'

She was struck dumb. Botany Bay. That was the end of the earth. Many did not even survive the voyage, so it was said.

'You will be assigned to the next passage out to New South Wales to have the space available. And here you are again fortunate for I am reliably informed there may be a place for you aboard the *Emma Harkness*, a ship sailing from Portsmouth in two weeks' time.'

But Carrie had no chance to feel grateful or anything else, as the Governor's words grew fainter in her ears and slowly the room began to sway. Her lack of sleep and the heat of the fire became too much, and instead of two, there was a whole sea of faces before her asking for her reaction.

When she came to she was lying propped up on the stuffed leather day bed that stood against the far wall opposite the fireplace, and Father Fowler was offering her a sip of water.

She took the proffered glass and held it to her dry lips with a whispered word of thanks. Then she noticed that the Governor himself was no longer in the room. Obviously he had more pressing matters to attend to than the recovery of a convicted lifer.

The cleric drew up a chair and sat down heavily, spreading his massive thighs across the brocade seat as he flicked his robe and coat tails over the back. 'I've said for long enough the Governor doesn't air this room as he should,' he said.

Carrie took a sip of the water and could not disguise the contempt in her eyes or her voice as she said quietly, 'You have just murdered my brother.'

The clergyman sighed. Her reaction was no more than he expected. His voice was patient but firm as he said, 'The Good Lord works in mysterious ways, my dear, and it is not for us to question those ways. We must accept what we cannot change and place our faith in the Lord Jesus. Your brother had a fair trial. You both did.'

Carrie flinched at the words so piously spoken. A fair trial. Was that what they called it? She shook her head angrily, for she could never accept that verdict. Nothing had made sense since that awful night. Events seemed to get completely out of control immediately the accident happened, with people saying and doing things that she could not associate with what had actually taken place. Words like 'cold-blooded murder' had been used – terrible words, by people she had never set eyes on before or since. Yet they were people who had control over their very lives – and deaths.

'Do you want to talk about it?' the priest asked, bending forwards, with a paternalistic smile. 'Sometimes it helps, you know.'

His breath smelt of whisky and his frockcoat smelt of mothballs. Despite the heat there was a drip at the end of his nose of which he seemed entirely unaware as he disguised yet another yawn and shifted his position. The old bones creaked as he did so. 'Rheumatics,' he muttered. 'Old age, m'dear. Comes to us all eventually.'

'Not to my brother it didn't!' Carrie bit back, then immediately regretted it. She must not take it out on him. He looked tired and old, and she did not envy him his job. 'I'm sorry,' she sighed. 'It's not your fault things have turned out as they have.'

She received a sympathetic smile in return. 'Unburden yourself, child, and I will listen, just as the Good Lord listens to the sinners amongst us as well as the saints.'

Carrie knew exactly what category he had already placed her in. Unburden yourself, he had said. But where did she begin?

As she sat in silence, the clergyman sniffed and dabbed his nose, tucking his handkerchief into his sleeve when he had finished. He had on woollen mittens with the fingers cut out and she noticed his nails were dirty. Cleanliness was obviously not next to godliness in his book. 'Tell me exactly what happened,' he said patiently. 'Tell the truth "and ye shall know the truth, and the truth shall make you free". John 45, verse 39, if I remember rightly.'

'Nothing will make me free of what has happened,' Carrie said bitterly. 'And no telling of your precious truth saved my brother from the gallows, either.'

The cleric gave an embarrassed half smile. 'It is not for us to question the ways of the Lord, my child. But I do know that at a time like this opening one's heart can be of great benefit. Perhaps in talking about that night you will come to accept what you cannot change and it will allow you to go forward in grace from this day on.'

Carrie looked sceptical. Why did men of the cloth always have to sound so insufferably pious? She sighed and closed her eyes as she leant her head against the curved back of the day bed. She could see that scene in front of her as if it were yesterday. Her father's face staring up at their living room ceiling, his pale blue eyes vacant and his mouth slightly open, giving his countenance a rather stupefied look of surprise. Did this mothball-smelling old man really want to know of the pain of having to leave him lying there in the middle of the floor like that? Or of the soul-numbing shock that accompanied his sudden death? That was the man who had carried her on his shoulders as a child and had brought her back all manner of exciting things from his sea voyages. A man who had spent hours fashioning shoes for her lame foot so other children would not scoff and jeer. A man who had given up the sea to care for herself and Billy, at what sacrifice only God would ever know. That man lying there had been her father.

Did this old priest with his dripping nose and pious manner really want to hear what it was like living with the knowledge that they had never been able to give their father a decent burial? Could he understand what it was like not being allowed to even attend the funeral? A pauper's grave they had buried him in, so she had been told. And that hurt. That really hurt.

But Father Fowler's mind had already moved on beyond the actual death. He took it for granted there had been no love lost between the deceased and his children. 'It must have been a trying time – the arrests.'

'The arrests? Oh yes, it was that all right.' She would never get over the shock of being hustled out of the house with Billy into the freezing cold and darkness like common criminals.

And now a month later, with Billy dead, as she gazed, bleary-eyed and exhausted, at the clergyman who sat next to her in the Governor's office she could still barely believe what had happened to them. 'He was asleep, Father,' she said wearily. 'Poor Billy was fast asleep in bed that night and I got him up. I got him out of bed to help control Pa. He got up to do me a favour and today they killed him because of it. They killed him this very morning for coming to my rescue and now they have told me they will let me live.'

The priest smiled across at her. He could not help feeling a personal sense of relief at her good news. He never felt comfortable about the execution of women, particularly young ones like this. 'They will be taking you back to your cell in a moment or two, my dear. This day will have been a momentous one in your short life. It is one you will long remember and reflect upon. Perhaps this is the time now to put our hands together and offer praise and thanks for the great deliverance that God has just granted you.'

Carrie looked sceptically over the rim of the glass as she finished the water, then placed the tumbler on the floor beside her. So God and the Privy Council were as one now, were they? She could really do without these pious words. She felt as drained and empty as that glass and really cared so little for her own fate after what they had done to Billy this morning that they might as well be giving thanks for sending her to the moon.

The man in front of her belched and excused himself immediately. 'Sliced turkey's gizzard for breakfast. Didn't go down too well, I'm afraid.' He patted his mouth beneath the luxuriant walrus moustache as if to ensure no more involuntary emissions and smiled. 'Some wag had added an "n" between the "r" and the "k" of turkey on the menu in the staff canteen this morning. Caused quite a stir when the head warders came in, I can tell you!'

Carrie made an unsuccessful attempt at a smile. She could think of quite a few turnkeys whose gizzards she would quite happily have seen sliced and stuffed down the Chaplain's throat. Then the meagre smile died on her lips. 'Did Billy eat breakfast before they hanged him?' she asked. It was suddenly important to know.

'Can't say as I was informed of that, my dear,' the clergyman lied in some embarrassment. From what he had heard the young man had not eaten for days before he went to his fate.

Her eyes clouded. 'Did you speak to him before . . . ?' She could not bring herself to say the word. 'Did he have any last message . . . ? Please, tell me what he said.' She was sitting up on the edge of the couch now as she pleaded with the cleric. She needed something − just the tiniest scrap of information to cling on to.

Father Fowler frowned. The young man had been in no fit state to say a word, let alone relay meaningful messages when he had seen him this morning just before the execution. Billy had lost so much weight over the past few weeks that the black suit they had dressed him in had simply hung on the skeletal frame, giving him a scarecrow appearance. They said he had refused all food for several days and had seemed barely aware of what was happening around him as he was propelled up to the gallows. A cold-blooded killer was the last thing he looked like. But there could be few crimes worse than the killing of one's parent and the Chaplain knew he could not allow himself to get too sentimental; sympathy had to be saved for those deserving it.

'Did — did he have any word, any last message at all?' Carrie persisted.

Father Fowler cleared his throat and shifted on his chair. 'Well now, if I remember rightly, he did say something. He asked to be remembered to you.' Then seeing the light come into the young woman's eyes, he continued, 'Yes, that's it. He said to tell you he had repented his sin and made his peace with the Lord and begged you to do the same.'

Carrie slumped against the stuffed back of the day bed. He was lying. The priest was sitting there with that crucifix around his brass neck and was lying through his false teeth. Billy would never have admitted to a crime he did not commit. He was no more responsible for their father's death than she was, and he would never have repented a sin he was not guilty of.

Seeing the effect of his words, the Reverend Fowler looked concerned. 'Come now, my dear. I understand you and your brother were baptized into the Roman faith, so you must be aware that confession is good for the soul. I am no Papist, but now you have been spared, I would most strongly advise you to heed your dear brother's last wish and to think most seriously of making your peace with the Lord before you leave our native shores.'

He opened the bible on his lap and regarded Carrie as he would a recalcitrant child. 'You have a long and dangerous journey to the other side of the world ahead of you. Now is the time to turn to Our Lord and pray for his protection and forgiveness.'

There was no good arguing – it was far too late for that. She felt nothing but contempt for people like the Chaplain and the Governor who sat in moral judgement over others. They were the real guilty ones, not innocent folk like herself and Billy, who just happened to fall foul of them and this so-called British justice. Carrie clasped her hands together in her lap and bowed her head. All she wanted now was to get back to her cell as quickly as possible.

Father Fowler had a monotonous voice, tuned to a fine pitch of boredom through three decades of delivering sermons to a captive prison congregation, and his words assumed their Sunday resonance as he intoned: ' "If I climb up into heaven, Thou art there: if I go down to hell, Thou art there also. If I take the wings of the morning, and remain in the uttermost parts of the sea; even there also shall Thy hand lead me, and Thy right hand shall hold me . . ." Australia must not be regarded as an alien land, my dear. God's hand stretches out – yes, even there – to offer deliverance from evil to the poor unfortunate creatures who have so sinned against their fellows that they find themselves banished from all that they hold dear.'

His eyes had a glazed look to them as they fixed on a patch of flaking plaster on the wall above Carrie's head. Then they turned to the bible in his hand. He took hold of the slender red marker ribbon and opened the pages at a selected passage. It was one he always used on such occasions, so that he almost knew it by heart.

' "And as a ship that passeth over the waves of the water, which when it is gone by the trace thereof cannot be found, but the light air being beaten with the stroke of her wings, and parted with the violent noise and motion of them, is passed through, and therein afterwards no sign where she went is to be found . . . Even so we in like manner as soon as we were born began to draw to our end, and had no sign of virtue to shew but were consumed by our own wickedness. For all men have one entrance into life, and the like going out."'

Father Fowler closed the Good Book and clasped it in his two hands as he observed the young woman on the couch before him. 'Our Lord has the power of life and death,' he said solemnly. 'He alone leadest thou to the gates of hell, and bringest thou up again.'

His breathing was laboured as he rose to his feet. 'You have been granted a great dispensation, my dear, and have much to thank Our Lord for. You too have been led to the gates of hell by your own folly and wickedness, but have been saved by the charity of your betters who walk in the footsteps of the Lord. You are going to a new land and are being given the opportunity to redeem your sins. I wish you God speed on your journey.'

He held out his hand and Carrie stood up, a trifle unsteadily, and grasped it. Somehow she could not bring herself to thank him.

But as she sat alone in her cell that night she pondered on those words from the bible about a ship passing over the water and leaving no trace . . . It was like that in life really, wasn't it? You are born and you die, and in the beginning is your end. Life was little more than a dream – a dream that would disappear from your mind like the morning mist from the river. In fact, death was the only true reality in life. It came to us all and it was only the favoured few who left any mark at all of their passing. Who would remember Billy, she wondered, now that he was dead? What mark had he left to tell of his existence? There would not even be a candle lit in church to indicate he had ever lived and died.

Carrie could feel a cold anger deep in her heart for those responsible for snuffing out her brother's young life. And now, in another way, they were trying to do the same to her, by exiling her to the ends of the earth, so all trace of her life on her native soil would be extinguished forever. And she did not know how or when, but she swore that

57

night, as she sat alone in the chill of her cell, that she would not let them succeed. Someday, somehow she would win. She would win for Billy's sake. And for all the countless Billys who had swung from that rope out there on Newgate gallows, or rotted their lives away in cells such as this in the name of British justice.

As she lay quite still on the hard bench that served as a bed and looked up into the inky darkness, she could just make out a small patch of night sky through the tiny window high up in the wall. A star was twinkling there – one solitary star shining just for her. And in that moment, she knew that it was no ordinary star. That was her mother, Bridie, up there and she was saying, 'Do it, Carrie *aroon*, do it. Do it for Billy, and for Father Murphy of County Wexford. Do it for all the poor unfortunate souls of this world who have suffered as you are suffering now.'

'I will, Ma. I will,' Carrie whispered into the silence of her cell, as she closed her eyes, comforted by the fact that her mother was up there watching, and shining just as brightly after her death as ever she had done in life.

CHAPTER FOUR

They'll flog the mischief out of you
When you get to Botany Bay!
The waves were high upon the sea,
The winds blew up in gales;
I'd rather be drowned in misery
Than go to New South Wales!

They arrived on the outskirts of Portsmouth to a day of lashing rain and a grey, angry sea that sent foaming spray up across the road their waggon took along Point Beach. It lashed the dockside, causing the smaller craft moored alongside the convict hulks to toss alarmingly on the white foam, and it put fear in the hearts of the women sitting huddled in the back of the vehicle as it rattled the last mile or so towards its destination. Very soon they would be out there at the mercy of those angry waves. To those who knew nothing of life but the grey back streets of the city, it was an awesome thought indeed.

The two guards sitting in the back of the waggon talked between themselves and the prisoners soon learned that their own transport, the *Emma Harkness*, was moored far out on the Motherbank at Spithead, and that it had already taken on almost its full capacity of convicts. 'Looks like our lot will be about the last to arrive,' Carrie's neighbour commented.

Although well used to the sight of ships at anchor after a lifetime spent around the London docks, Carrie had not expected to find so many vessels in one place. There were masts as far as the eye could see, as well as the enormous, mastless cumbersome shapes of the convict hulks which lay offshore, great floating prisons for a population of felons for whom seasickness was a way of life.

They all craned their necks to get a proper look at the vessels that housed so many unfortunates like themselves. Someone said they were old warships, no longer needed by the navy, but with their bulging oak sides rising high out of the water, with lines of washing hung between the stumps of the masts and from every other possible appendage, and all manner of strange wooden platforms and lean-tos protruding at odd angles from the hulls, they looked more like floating slum tenements.

Nearby were anchored two transport ships, New South Wales bound, but with their peeling paint work and general air of decay they looked little better than the hulks.

'God have mercy!' someone cried. 'Let's pray ours is in better condition than those things. I'll vouch they'll never make it out past the Narrows, let alone all the way to Botany Bay!'

Once they were unloaded from the waggon the relief was enormous, although a freezing cold wind with rain still blowing through it sent them immediately into a huddle by the side of the parked vehicle for shelter.

Every new waggon-load of women transportees brought ribald and often downright lewd comments from the younger men who worked around the docks as they came to cast their eyes over the latest batch of livestock. Many of the women gave as good as they got, but some like Carrie hated being the object of such attention.

'Cattle, that's what they make you feel like,' a dark-haired young Irish woman declared. 'And if it's a cow I am, then, Lord save us, they're a herd of foul-mouthed swine! You'd think they'd never seen a woman before, so you would. If my Eamonn was here today, I swear to God he'd flatten every last one o' them, gawk-ing at decent folk like that!' Her blue eyes took on a far-away look as she added wistfully, 'I can't get over him going on before like that, and that's the God's honest truth.'

Carrie looked sympathetic. 'You mean he's already in New South Wales?'

'God love you, no! He did the Newgate Hornpipe, so he did.'

'Oh no!'

'Oh yes,' her neighbour confirmed. 'You English hanged him last August.' There was a catch in her voice as she said the words, indicating the nonchalance was forced. Then she looked at Carrie curiously. 'Are you married, then?'

'Lord, no!'

'No young man even?' The girl sounded surprised.

It was Carrie's turn to sound wistful. 'No young man either, I'm afraid.'

'And why might that be?'

'I don't really know . . . I expect I had enough to do looking after my dad and brother to get round to walking out with anyone.' Her companion had obviously not noticed her lame leg and Carrie could not bring herself to mention it.

The girl nodded understandingly. 'I expect it's real upset they'll be, you being sent to the Bay and all.'

Carrie looked the other way and made no reply.

But she liked the young woman, whose name it transpired was Molly McGuire. Irish accents always reminded her of her mother. Although she had no wish to get any further into conversation, she also realized that she was far from alone in her grief. Molly's husband had met the same fate as Billy and the knowledge made her look more curiously at the other transportees gathered around them. How many others were nursing broken hearts such as theirs? The vast majority, she had little doubt.

One thing was becoming increasingly obvious the longer they waited there on the dockside: almost none of the huge crowd of distraught humanity that surrounded them was there to sightsee. She reckoned at least a thousand men, women and children were gathered on the foreshore, many gesticulating desperately at the double lines of sailors who, arms clasped, were attempting valiantly to protect the landing stage where barges were being loaded with the last batches of convicts for the next sailing. The majority of the crowd appeared to be women not much older than Carrie, with babes in arms and young children clinging to their skirts. All were beside themselves with grief at husbands being taken from them and sent to the ends of the earth.

'You got anyone to see you off?' the young London woman who had been sitting beside her in the waggon asked, and she got a silent shake of the head in response. There was no one now, not a single living soul left in this country who would mourn her leaving. It was a bitter thought.

But there was little time for sentimentality at saying a final farewell to the motherland as they were helped down into the rolling barge which was to take them to their ship. And for Carrie, with her back to the shore, there was no chance even to turn and watch the land recede behind them as they found themselves heading out beyond the harbour for Spithead.

The *Emma Harkness* turned out to be an enormous vessel, of around five hundred tons, with an uncommonly wide beam and the figurehead of a bare-breasted woman with a crown upon her head protruding from the bow. Her black paint had faded in parts to a silver grey and was raised in large blisters as though her sides were suffering from a severe case of smallpox. The ship sat perched high in the water, looking decidedly top-heavy due to the lofty poopdeck on which several specks of sailors could be seen going about their business.

'She's an old naval transport,' one of the barge oarsmen informed them. 'Fought against Old Boney. Did us proud she did. Was holed at Trafalgar, but made it back home all right. If your eyesight's up to it, you'll just about make out old Captain Griffiths on the quarter-deck.'

All eyes on the incoming barge swivelled in the direction indicated as cramped bodies tried to turn an inch or two for a better view. It was almost impossible to make out anything much of what or who was on board the vessel that was to be their transport into the unknown, for the tiny figures that busied themselves on the various decks looked no bigger than ants. Around the *Emma Harkness* several supply ships were anchored in line, about a cable's length apart, as the last of the stores for the voyage were taken aboard. Beyond them, two old men-o'-war waited; ninety gunners from Nelson's Trafalgar fleet, that were now seeing their days out as convict transports and were awaiting their next duty.

The going had become increasingly rough since they left the sanctuary of the harbour and they made slow progress out towards Spithead, with their oarsmen straining and cursing more as the strain grew with the heaving swell. As the small craft battled its way through the waves the groans of the women on the barge became louder and more desperate with several painfully retching empty stomachs on to the wet boards beneath their feet. Cries of 'At last! Thank God!' went up when eventually they drew alongside the *Emma Harkness*.

The euphoria was shortlived, however, at the sight of what awaited them. 'Dear God in heaven, will you take a look at that! You'll not get me up there. What do you take me for, a blessed monkey?' The young Irish woman echoed the thoughts of everyone as they regarded with horror the slippery wooden ladder that towered above them, clinging to the gunge- and seaweed-covered side of the ship. They were expected to scale that enormous, heaving hull, then clamber on to the deck. 'Sure and you must be mad!'

But climb it they did, all except a sixty-five-year-old from Leicester jail by the name of Betsy. There could be no question it was too much for her arthritic limbs and a boatswain's chair was eventually let down and, to a chorus of cheers from those already safely landed, she was hoisted up and swung inboard.

When Carrie's turn came she was sure she would lose her footing and disappear forever into the churning black waters below. Long tangles of seaweed clung to the copper sheathing around the waterline and to the outer edges of the ladder's rungs. It slapped threateningly around her feet and ankles as she slowly and carefully attempted to work her way upwards one step at a time, her hands grasping desperately at the wet wood. She did not confess to having a lame foot, for the thought of that boatswain's chair was almost worse than that of the climb, but halfway up she knew she had made the wrong decision. She could put no pressure at all on her left ankle and had to end up almost hauling herself up by the arms. She dared not allow herself to look down at the foaming surf below.

'My God, am I almost there?' she gasped at the sight of a seaman's face peering down at her a yard or two above. One last heave and she might just make it. Sweat stood out in droplets on her brow despite the freezing conditions.

'Well done, girlie,' the sailor called out, as he supplied a steadying hand to help her up the last few feet and all but lifted her over the edge of the ship. It was the first words of praise she had had in so long that to her surprise Carrie felt tears of gratitude and relief spring to her eyes as she placed her first tentative foot on to the waiting deck.

She found herself in the middle of mayhem. There was supposed to be no fraternizing between felons, but the mêlée on the deck was such that it was almost impossible to retain order.

The new arrivals were eventually all mustered on the quarter-deck, in varying degrees of excitement and exhaustion, where they were divested of all their personal possessions, including the very clothes they were wearing, and issued with the ship's convict uniforms: two grey blouses each, of a thick, coarse cotton material, two darker grey skirts made out of a canvas-type weave, and a pair of uncomfortable-looking boots.

'They smell,' Carrie protested, as much to herself as to the issuing officer who was still within earshot.

'Mother of God! I'm sorry they ain't come back from the washhouse smelling of roses!' The sailor paused in his doling out of the garments to grab hold of one of her blouses. 'And it's rubbish anyhow. The Captain insists on regular washing. See that there?' he said, pointing an index finger at a large black A inside the collar. 'Well, the other's got a B on it. That means they have to be washed and changed every week, so if you end up stinking you can blame your own smelly skin, not the Navy!'

'Lord, I thought I looked a fright in that prison stuff but this lot takes the biscuit!' a nearby Midlands voice complained, as the new issue was reluctantly tried on for size.

Once all were fully kitted out, they were marched in double file down to the prison decks, which ran the whole length of the well of the ship, with access through the main and fore hatchways. They were informed that these entrances were secured at all times night and day by an armed guard and entry to the prison deck itself was only possible by means of a ladder which was placed in each hatchway and pulled up when not in use.

Next to the hatchways was a narrow passage about seven feet wide which ran the whole width of the ship and this, they were told, was reserved for what little exercise was allowed, along with an area on the upper deck, which was barricaded off with thick oak planks, topped with iron spikes.

'You'd need to be a good 'un to get over that,' their guard commented, and Carrie's heart sank at the thought that the only fresh air she was to be allowed would be taken in the confines of that small fortified yard along with countless others.

Silence reigned save for the clatter of their boots on the

wet planks of the deck as they followed their guard down below to the place from which they knew there would be little escape for months to come.

What they found there was certainly as bad as the worst that Newgate had to offer. The sleeping berths ran along both sides of the well deck in two rows, one on top of the other. These were numbered from one to one hundred, and each convict was allotted a mere eighteen inches of headroom.

'God blind me! You wouldn't have to be fat, would you?' Carrie heard a London voice remark as a berth was tried out for size.

What was even more depressing was that although it was broad daylight outside, inside they found themselves in a gloomy twilight. To provide light and air, scuttle holes had been cut into the sides of the ship. But these were so tiny and securely barred, and so high up, that it was impossible to see anything at all of the sea or sky outside unless you clambered up on to the top bunks to peer out, and this was not allowed. They were also informed that these scuttles would be kept closed in bad weather. 'It's not popular, but it has to be,' one of their guards told them flatly. 'We'd be awash otherwise.' It was not hard to imagine that at times like that the atmosphere down below must become quite unbearable.

Carrie looked in dismay at the bunk that was to be her home. It contained a narrow, hard mattress, a stained pillow long bereft of most of its stuffing, a single patched grey blanket, two wooden bowls and a spoon, all with her allotted berth number of ninety-nine branded on them. If there was a God to be thanked for small mercies, He had at least given her the very end bunk, next to one of the hatchways, so at least she would be spared much of the misery caused by crowding so many sorry examples of womankind into so confined a space.

They learned the ship was also carrying one hundred and twenty male convicts, and along with the crew there was a list of twenty-seven emigrants. What normal free human beings were doing heading for New South Wales Carrie could not imagine, but she had little time to ponder on the matter for their first real meal of the day was about to be served.

Pea soup with bits of pork gristle floating in it was accompanied by a ship's biscuit and followed by a type of suet pudding. 'Eve's Pudding!' the cook announced. 'And I don't give A-dam whether you likes it or not, it's all you're going to get!'

'He cracks that joke to every new shipload,' the old sailor guarding the hatchway told Carrie as she sat back down on the edge of her berth and lifted the half-full bowl to her lips. It was the only safe way to drink, for the ship was swaying so much. She gave the old man a weak smile in response, although from the way her stomach was heaving she was not at all sure she would get as far as the infamous Eve's Pudding.

'I expect you've not found your sea-legs yet,' the old man said with a sympathetic look. 'I wouldn't worry about it, though. Most of us had a miserable time on our first voyage out. You gets used to it in the end.'

Carrie took a tentative bite of the biscuit. It tasted like baked brick dust. 'That's not much help,' she said. 'It's a one-way ticket I've got.'

The old sailor looked surprised – she looked no more than a bit of a girl. 'You're a lifer then?'

'Yes, I'm a lifer.' She squinted up at him. He was sitting on the bottom rungs of the ladder to the hatchway and taking the chance of their mealbreak to light a pipe of tobacco. He had a kind face, she decided. His skin was the colour of tanned leather and covered in a network of fine lines and his eyes had that narrowed, keen look to them from a lifetime of scanning the horizon. 'My name's Carrie. What's yours?'

'Evans,' he replied. 'Dafydd Evans. But you can call me Dai, even if it is against the regulations.'

Carrie smiled. That explained the strange, lilting accent. 'You're Welsh.'

'From Cardiff.' His eyes softened. 'Now there's a fine town for you. Not as big as London, mind, but big enough.'

'I'm from London.' It seemed a funny thing to say. She had never said that to anyone before. There had never been any need to, for she had never been outside her native city, nor had she ever expected to be. 'Down by the East India Dock. Do you know it?'

'I'll say I know it,' her companion replied. 'I've sailed out of there many a day. Know London almost as well as my native Cardiff, I do. You got any family left there?'

Carrie stared into her soup and shook her head. 'My mother died years ago and they've just hanged my little brother for my dad's death.' She looked up at her new friend and said fiercely, 'But he didn't do it. I swear to you he didn't do it. It was an accident. But they wouldn't listen. They just wouldn't listen.'

The old sailor sighed. 'There's been more good men gone to the gallows than have sat in judgement on them, that's for sure.'

He rose to his feet and put a comforting hand on her shoulder. 'Sup up, lass, and take heart. Thou's heading for Botany Bay. There's a new life ahead of you. Make the most of it. Stick in and make a success to spite the buggers!'

Carrie gave her first genuine smile in weeks. 'Dai Evans, you're a nice man – a really nice man.'

The old sailor chuckled as he tightened the belt of his trousers, then spat a mouthful of saliva on to the deck floor. He liked the lass. She reminded him of his daughter. And there wasn't an old salt born who wasn't susceptible to a bit of female flattery.

He stuck his pipe back in his mouth and reached into his hip pocket and extracted a small flask of rum which he uncorked and raised in salute as he gave the traditional toast. 'Here's to you, Carrie *bach*! May your sorrows go

68

drown, now you've left London town and are headed for Botany Bay!'

Poor kid, he thought, little did she know what lay ahead of her even before she set foot on foreign soil.

CHAPTER FIVE

The first few weeks at sea were a nightmare. Both the men's and the women's convict decks took on the appearance and sound of hospital wards as almost all the inhabitants suffered the agonies of seasickness and worse. At least Carrie had the advantage of the end berth and was able to get the occasional breath or two of fresh air whenever Dai Evans was on watch. Totally against regulations, the elderly Welshman took the risk of opening his hatch at regular intervals to allow some of the stale air to escape. But for those unfortunate enough to be housed towards the centre of the deck the suffocating stench was dreadful and their pitiful groans could be heard far beyond the locked doors of the prison quarters.

It was not long before dysentery broke out amongst the prisoners and several members of the crew. Bad meat was blamed, then the drinking water was thought suspect. The situation was made even worse by the fact that the ship leaked. Even in the calmest weather the bedding and mattresses would be damp, and in choppy seas the planks beneath their feet would be awash. For those forced by illness to lie abed all day, it was an unbearable situation.

'Is it always like this at sea?' Carrie asked her old sailor friend in despair one night as she prepared to bed down on the dank, sour-smelling bunk, and Dai Evans ruefully assured her it was.

'Especially when it's an old lady like the *Emma Harkness*,' he said. 'Past her best, she is. Long past her best.'

'But good enough for a prison transport,' Carrie added bitterly. 'They'd probably be quite relieved if we died at sea.'

Their misery was further added to by the vessel's poor drainage, which allowed the accumulation of waste and all manner of filth in the bilges. This was especially bad on washdays, when the foul odours from down below percolated up through the leaky boards. If it was not for the unspeakable smell, Carrie began to feel she might even enjoy Monday mornings, which was the time set aside for the women prisoners to attend to their laundry.

'Show a leg, ladies!' the cry would go up, and, still half asleep, they would tumble from their berths to assemble in the broadways at four o'clock, or first light, where rows of washtubs would be waiting. They would then each be issued with a bar of hard yellow soap and a block of holy-stone for scrubbing. Troughs of warm water for washing and cold for rinsing were put out and six hours was the time allowed to complete the operation.

The women tended to stick to the same tubs which they shared with the same neighbours throughout the voyage, and Carrie was pleased to find herself sharing one with the chirpy, dark-haired young Irish woman, Molly McGuire.

It transpired that the winsome young Molly was as well informed about the Irish political situation with their English overlords as Carrie's own mother had been. The death of Molly's young husband on the Newgate gallows had added to her own burning sense of personal injustice at a legal system that seemed to favour the rich so much over the poor, and even the English poor over the Irish. 'Do you realize just how many so-called offences they can mete out that death penalty for?' Molly demanded of Carrie during one of their first washing sessions together, as she paused to wipe a damp brow and push her sleeves up further above the elbows.

Carrie had no idea and said so.

'Nearly two bloody hundred, that's what!' And she proceeded to reel off several: 'Highway robbery, rioting, perjury, cutting down trees, counterfeiting, concealing the birth of a bastard child, even "breaking down the head of a fishpond whereby the fish may be lost" – whatever that bloody well means!' Molly McGuire's vivid blue eyes were blazing as she grabbed her chunk of holystone and began to scrub with renewed vigour at the clothes in the tub. 'And do you know what one they got my Eamonn on?'

Carrie shook her head.

'Sacrilege, that's what!'

'Sacrilege?' Carrie repeated, incredulously.

'Bloody sacrilege all right. Didn't you know that was a capital offence in your fair land?'

Carrie looked blank. 'You mean they hanged him for sacrilege?' She was not sure what exactly constituted sacrilege. Wasn't it to do with insulting something holy?

'They hanged him for breaking into a church when on the run from the British army, who were arresting all young men in sight. Rampaged right through our village, the bastards, so they did, yelling at the tops of their voices, "Croppies come out!"'

She paused to wipe the sweat from her brow once more with the back of a soapy hand. 'Eamonn and one or two of his pals took refuge in the local church and the army had to break down the door to get at them. So would you believe it, they pinned the broken door on them – sacrilege towards church property!' She gave a bitter laugh. 'I ask you, does that not take the biscuit? They hanged our men for something the bastards themselves did!'

Carrie gazed in a mixture of incredulity and sorrow at her friend. One thing was for sure: she was not the only one with a genuine grievance against the English legal system on this ship.

But washday mornings spent in Molly McGuire's company were not all bitterness and there was as often laughter as sadness in Carrie's eyes when she stood up to her elbows in the soapy water on the opposite side of the tub to her friend. Molly had a clever knack of mimicking voices to perfection and often the whole of their corner of the deck would be in stitches as she entertained them with impersonations of their guards and other members of the crew. She took a particular delight in imitating several of the young ship's officers who hung around the prison deck and the female convicts' exercise yards a lot more than they should. And there was one particular young man that she was especially good at. It was an open secret that from the end of their first week at sea Molly had been making clandestine trips to the cabin of a certain young officer of Scottish birth.

Carrie could not help but feel a certain degree of envy for her Irish friend. The young man in question was quite goodlooking in a redhaired, freckle-faced sort of way. He was from Dundee and went by the name of Ian McFarland, and from the looks he gave Molly if he happened to be in the vicinity when the women prisoners were exercising, he was clearly besotted by her. According to Molly, he was even threatening to jump ship once they had landed in New South Wales, and aid her escape so they could make off together.

We'll go to an island to take special charge,
Much warmer than Britain, and ten times as large:
No customs-house duty, no freightage to pay,
And tax-free we'll live when in Botany Bay . . .

Molly seemed quite fond of 'Mac', as she often called him, and took great glee in mimicking his singing of the popular song of the day, taking off his Scottish burr to perfection. Then she would shake her dark head at the sheer romanticism of it all. 'And just where would we be heading for, I ask you?' she demanded of Carrie as they stood at opposite sides of the washtub one cold March morning. 'Tis not as if the streets of Sydney will be paved with gold, for I sincerely doubt if they even have such things as streets where we're going! The poor lad's never been there himself so he'll be in for as big a shock as us poor sinners, I've no doubt!'

Constant reports of her friend's romance kept washdays interesting, and the sheer relief to be out there in the open

73

air, with the fresh sea breeze blowing the stench from down below from your nostrils, was tremendous. The liberation of being able to gaze out at that unending ocean, where occasionally a sea bird would glide past, would send Carrie's spirit winging its way up into the heavens with it as it rode the wind into blue infinity. Words could not describe her feelings on such occasions, when her own life with its problems seemed as nothing compared to something as wide and vast as the great ocean that had been here since the beginning of time itself. In a strange way it brought comfort, for its beauty was eternal; it was something no government could change. They could condemn their own citizens to death or exile, but the sea went on forever.

But all such romantic thoughts went by the board when the *Emma Harkness* reached the Bay of Biscay and the prisoners experienced their first storm. It began one Sunday night and continued almost unabated for four days. The ship had been set on a south-south-east course when she was forced to run before unforeseen north-west gale-force winds, which then shifted a full ninety degrees into the south-west and began pounding the ship head on.

The winds were accompanied by torrential rain and forty-feet waves which reduced between decks to a swollen river and rushed through every open door and hatchway. Within minutes the forward part of the ship was under water, with the waves crashing in through the bow-ports and hawse-holes, and right up over the knight-heads, threatening to wash away everything in their path.

The first that the prisoners and passengers down below were aware of it was during the night, when the vessel began pitching to such an extent that many were thrown from their bunks and suffered shock and severe bruising as a consequence.

Cries of 'All hands on deck!' and 'Bear-a-hand, lads!' could be heard throughout the ship, as sailors rushed to emergency stations.

It soon became clear that although the vessel had borne away from the headwinds with drastically shortened sails, its aged headstays to windward were now coming under severe pressure. If they gave way, masts and yards would come crashing on the deck causing death and grievous injury to crew and ship alike. It was going to take Captain Griffiths and his men all their expertise to prevent a major disaster.

'If there's one man can be relied on in a situation like this, it's the Cap'n,' Dai Evans assured Carrie and the other terrified prisoners who clustered around him just before daybreak. 'He's survived the worst Cape Horn can throw at him in his day – and they don't get much worse than that!'

The old man's eyes had twinkled as he surveyed the anxious faces surrounding him. 'Why, compared to the likes of Cape Horn, this storm's just a little 'un in comparison! Aye, take it from me, the Bay of Biscay's naught but a china teacup and this little lot a mere ripple on its surface compared to what you meet down South America way!'

But his words were cold comfort to the women who huddled down below, believing their last day on earth had come.

After four days of being buffeted around so badly that even the act of walking upright was impossible, and they thought their trials would never end, suddenly the skies cleared and the winds abated. The sun shone and the ocean that had seen waves of forty feet became a mill pond on which there was barely a ripple to disturb its greenish-blue surface. The hatches and scuttle holes could be opened and once more fresh air was allowed to blow freely into the stifling lower decks. Even those who had never been inside a church in their lives found themselves joining in the prayers of thanks for their deliverance that were being said all over the ship.

When the time came to take stock, no one could quite believe that more harm had not been done. The only real casualties, apart from some repairable damage to the rigging, were a few broken bones when two young sailors were blown off the rigging at the height of the storm, three pigs and several chickens swept overboard, and a totally exhausted crew. For the passengers and convicts alike, the main problems had been those caused by being battened down for so long below decks without fresh air, and the violent cases of sickness caused by the heaving ship.

'Your first storm at sea is always a bit of a nightmare,' Dai Evans told Carrie as he came on the first night watch afterwards. 'But it's like the measles. On a long voyage everyone has to go through it eventually. We can just thank the Lord it wasn't any worse.'

'Like round Cape Horn,' Carrie said, feeling she was learning fast, but not at all sure where exactly it was.

Once the excitement of the storm was behind them, the remaining short run to the port of Santa Cruz passed uneventfully. The few days in harbour to take on supplies, beneath the high conical peak of Tenerife, was a welcome change from the recent drama at sea. And, for the paying passengers, it meant a chance to set foot on dry land once again. Those locked down below could only look on in envy through the slits in the scuttles as the rowing boats set off to explore one of Spain's most exotic colonies.

Once they were underway again, the ship's stores amply stocked with new supplies of fresh water, fruit and vegetables and other essentials, the feelings of envy faded as the prisoners settled down to the familiar routine, and life on board the *Emma Harkness* once more assumed the monotonous round of cleaning, eating, washing, exercise and sleeping. For those not totally incapacitated with seasickness or some other ailment, a certain restless boredom began to set in. Small squabbles between neighbours began to assume giant proportions, leading to physical fights on several occasions.

For the majority of prisoners, having to witness such hostility was not pleasant. 'Scratch each other's eyes out

76

like a pack of Kilkenny cats, some of this lot would,' Molly McGuire commented to Carrie, as two of the worst antagonists were taken away in shackles to cool down after a bout of hair-pulling and name-calling one fine washday morning. 'You're as well keeping yourself to yourself around here, I can tell you.'

Carrie did not demur. She had no wish to become involved in the petty bickering that had become such a feature of life below decks. Nor did she relish the thought of undergoing the usual punishment for such cat-fights: a day spent in the barrel. The unfortunate felon was forced to spend her waking hours incarcerated inside a wooden cask worn like a bodice, with holes cut out for her arms and head. It made sitting or lying down impossible and was one certain way of knocking the fight out of even the worst prisoner through sheer exhaustion.

Some took to their punishment with more spirit than most, with one particular old Irish woman entertaining them all by attempting a jig as she smoked her clay pipe, encased in the wooden barrel. Carrie was immediately reminded of her mother's attempts to teach her the dance, and she smiled wryly to herself for she doubted if her own attempts, with her stiff leg, were much better than poor Mary's. There were quite a few of Irish birth amongst the female prisoners and several of them joined in with the old woman's jerky contortions, until the whole prison deck was convulsed at the antics and the guards were forced to intervene and take Mary out of the barrel to restore order.

Such incidents, however, were the exception rather than the rule and boredom was more often the main cause for complaint. As the voyage progressed Carrie found she was relying increasingly on either Molly or old Dai to keep her spirits up. As Molly was berthed much further down the prison deck, and officially fraternization was not allowed, it proved much easier to talk to her old Welsh friend whenever he was on watch.

In many ways Dai Evans proved to be the ideal companion and his presence brought a calmness and security into Carrie's life that she had not known for a long time. Through the long evening hours, he would sit on the rungs of the ladder to the hatchway door and smoke his old clay pipe, or whittle at a piece of woodcarving – usually a small toy for his grandchildren back in Cardiff – as he told her of days gone by when he was a youngster in Wales.

Carrie would sit dangling her legs off the edge of her bunk, or lie flat out and listen as, in his melodious, husky voice he conjured up scenes of times long gone and loved ones long since dead. 'Memories become more precious than gold, *bach*,' he would tell her. 'When you're as old as I am, you learn that they are something money can't buy.'

She learned that he had first gone to sea as a lad at the tail end of the war against France and he claimed he could even remember the *Emma Harkness* in her first incarnation as one of Nelson's transports. 'A lovely ship, she was then. Nelson had a fleet to be proud of. A sin it was that he didn't live to see final victory.'

But life had been hard in those early days. 'Worked like a horse and treated like a dog we were back then, Carrie *bach*,' he told her ruefully, but with no bitterness in his voice. 'No bigger than a spirit-sheet knot I was, and not strong enough to haul a shad off a gridiron, but by God they made a man of you in double-quick time.'

Half the time Carrie had little idea to what he was alluding in his descriptions of all the goings-on aboard ship, but he had a way of telling his tales that totally captivated the listener, as all the while his gnarled fingers whittled and carved life into the pieces of wood in his hands.

All manner of intricate toys were fashioned with loving care, and, as he put the finishing touches to a monkey climbing a stick, he talked about his family back in Wales and how his father had gone to sea himself as a young lad, but a bad fall from the yard-arm had meant he had had to settle for a life ashore as a clogmaker.

'Best in all Cardiff, he became. Sycamore he used – none of that alder or birch the English cloggers make do with. No, he'd take me with him when he cut the trees in January. Work the wood green, he would, letting it dry out on the wearer's foot. Never had a more comfy pair of shoes in my life than a set of my father's clogs.'

And his keen eyes would shine at the memory of those dear dead days when, if it was a bad winter, they would pull the trunks behind them over the snow strapped on to a special sled. 'He had bells attached to the horses' harnesses, you know *bach*, and I can hear them jingling in my head to this day. Yes, grand days they were. Grand days . . .'

Listening to his stories, Carrie began to feel as if she had known her new friend all her life. Very soon Dai Evans became the father she had lost – in fact, the father she had never really had since her mother's death and the start of Ted Clayton's drinking. She found a great comfort in opening her heart to the old Welshman, who would puff thoughtfully on his pipe as over the weeks that followed he listened to her tell of her despair at the past and fears for the future.

The old man's eyes would cloud with the injustice of it all. 'It's a disgrace, that's what it is,' he would declare, wagging his pipe in the air. 'A young lass like you locked up in a place like this, just when you should be out there in the world enjoying life to the full.'

Then Carrie would feel bad about upsetting him and sigh, 'Oh, it could be worse. Don't you worry about me.'

One evening she was issuing just such reassurances, when her old friend said thoughtfully, 'Tell me, *bach*, what would make a real difference to your life right now? What would really make you happy?' If she'd fancied any particular extra morsel of food, or even something to read, he had endeavoured to do his best to help.

Carrie was taken aback by the question, but gave it due thought. 'You know what I'd really like?' she said eventually. 'I'd really like to be able to escape just for a few minutes by myself now and then. To spend a little while up there on deck, feeling the sea breezes on my face, and breathing the fresh air without a hundred others for company.' Those endless hours spent walking round and round the small exercise space with the rest of the women prisoners had become a penance in itself.

Her companion had looked surprised, but understood. He had that same need for privacy himself now and again. It must be hell for an intelligent, sensitive young woman like her to be locked up down here for most of the day and night and only be allowed to glimpse the sky in the company of all the others. Dai Evans's face took on a contemplative look. Maybe it wasn't such an impossible dream after all. It was an open secret amongst the crew that illicit liaisons were formed between sailors and certain of the women convicts, and that those women were smuggled from the prison deck into the appropriate cabins under cover of darkness. As long as everyone was in place for roll call in the morning not too many questions were asked.

He looked at his young friend as he relit his beloved pipe. 'I don't suppose it would make much difference if it was day or night, would it?'

Carrie laughed. 'A starving man doesn't mind if he's offered bread or oatcake, now does he?' Then she checked herself. 'Although to tell the truth, I'd imagine there's something magic about the night out here on the ocean.'

Dai Evans nodded his agreement. 'Oh, you're right there, Carrie love. Some night the heavens seem to wrap themselves around you and the stars shine so brightly you can almost reach up and pluck one from out of the sky . . . Aye, there's nothing quite like being up there on deck, with the wind in your sails and that best of all sailors' compasses, the starlit heavens above . . .' Then he paused and removed his pipe from his mouth as his seamed face broke into a smile. 'And, if I have my way, you'll know exactly what I mean. Just you wait.'

The following evening Carrie, with the help of her old friend, made her first trip alone up on to the moonlit deck.

Dai waited until most people were bedded down at around ten o'clock, then he lifted the hatch to help her through.

'You'll be all right, *bach*,' he assured her softly, seeing the apprehension on her face. 'There's a new moon and a heaven full of stars waiting for you up there.'

And so she climbed up the steep wooden ladder that took her into the fresh night air and it was as if the breeze that blew into her upturned face came straight from heaven itself. As she stood by the rail of the ship and looked out over the starlit ocean, tears streamed down her pale cheeks for the first time since Billy's death.

There were to be many such trips over the next few weeks, especially when they were passing through the Tropics and conditions down below became so bad that at least one death seemed to occur each day amongst the prisoners.

The sailors, many of whom had become friends with the transportees, had warned them about the Tropics, but experiencing the scorching, endless heat for themselves was quite another matter. With the sun beating down for days on end, the pitch between the planks of the deck melted and ran in bubbling black rivers, and between the inside planks of the prison deck it got so hot that it began to melt and fall from the walls and ceiling in burning globules, scorching holes in fabric and skin alike.

It was such a hot, humid night that on one of her now regular illicit visits above decks, Carrie realized she was not alone as she stood against the rail and gazed out across the inky blackness of the South Atlantic. There was a young woman standing only a few feet away, half hidden by one of the lifeboats. She was crying, and it was that unexpected sound breaking into the soft lapping of the waves that first drew Carrie's attention to her; it was a soft whimpering, like an animal in pain.

She came up quietly behind the figure hunched over the rail and touched her gently on the shoulder. 'Are you all right?'

The young woman gasped and turned round as if stung. 'My goodness, I'd no idea there was anyone else out here!' She had an educated South London accent, with rather a soft, quavering timbre to her voice.

'Please don't be afraid,' Carrie said hastily. 'I only want to help.'

The young woman looked at her curiously as she pulled a lace handkerchief from her sleeve and dabbed at her eyes. Then her brow creased and a look of alarm crossed her face as she noticed the clothing Carrie was wearing. 'You're one of the . . .' She backed away slightly and could not bring herself to say the offending word.

'Convicts. Yes, I'm one of the convicts.' The word almost stuck in Carrie's own throat. Somehow she could not reconcile herself to being a figure of fear to her own kind. 'That doesn't mean I'm not a human being, you know!'

'No – no, I'm quite sure it doesn't.'

'We're not animals, although we're cooped up like them on the convict deck.'

'I – I never thought you were.'

Carrie's indignation abated when she realized there was to be no insult forthcoming. 'I mean you no harm. I heard you crying and just wanted to say, it doesn't do you any good, you know. Life's a swine sometimes, but you've just got to get on with it.'

'I – I expect you're right.' The fear began to fade from the young woman's eyes, although a degree of suspicion remained. She had seen the convicts exercising in their allotted space behind the fortified barricades but had had no actual contact with them before. But this one seemed quite human. There was a moment's strained silence, then she pulled her lace shawl tighter around her shoulders and said, 'I had a terrible headache. I thought a few minutes of fresh air might help. It gets terribly stuffy down there in the cabin.'

'I'm sure the ship's surgeon must have something to help, if it's really bad . . . They take good care of the paying passengers, I believe. Not like us lot. As long as we're still breathing when we land and the Captain gets his money for us, they don't really give a tinker's cuss what shape we're in.'

The young woman ignored the last remarks, for she knew they smacked of the truth. Several of the transportees had already perished to her knowledge. 'I really don't think I need bother the surgeon,' she said. 'I always carry a small bottle of laudanum. It's been invaluable – what with stomach and bowel upsets and all the other delights of life aboard ship!'

Carrie made no reply, but could not avoid a pang of envy. What luxury it must be to have your own cabin and medical supplies on a voyage like this! It was hard not to feel resentment towards those living in the lap of luxury above the prison deck. But she tried not to let her feelings show. 'My name's Caroline Clayton,' she said, extending her hand. 'Carrie for short.'

Her new companion took the proffered hand, still a trifle apprehensively. 'My name's Caroline too. Caroline Cooper.' She gave a tight smile. 'We even have the same initials.'

The two young women stood silhouetted against the ship's rail, regarding each other rather uncertainly for a moment, as the salt breeze whipped colour to pale cheeks. They were about the same height and build, although Carrie guessed her new acquaintance was perhaps two or three years older. She had a pleasant but rather plain face that was partially obscured beneath a straw hat with a black veil covering the eyes. Her hair seemed to be dark and was drawn into a netted bun at the nape of her neck. She removed a stray strand blown by the breeze from across her face with her left hand and Carrie noticed she was wearing a wedding ring.

'You're married.'

Caroline Cooper gave an embarrassed half-smile as she glanced down at the object in question. 'I'm a widow,' she said, then continued a trifle uncertainly, 'in fact, I don't really think I should be wearing this any longer.' And her face took on a decidedly strained look as she added, 'You see, I'm going out to New South Wales to be married.'

'Your husband's already out there?' Carrie said. This woman was travelling out to join her husband. Some people really did have all the luck!

The young woman evaded her eyes and turned and looked out to sea. She took a deep breath of the salty air and a shudder ran through her. 'Not exactly,' she said in a tight voice.

'I beg your pardon?'

Caroline Cooper turned to her new companion and shook her head as she leant back against the ship's rail. 'You didn't mishear,' she said with a sigh. It was a relief to have someone her own age and sex to talk to about it. She had kept herself to herself throughout the voyage, even to the extent of having all her meals in her cabin. 'I'm a widow, and he – my husband-to-be – he's been out there almost twenty years, I believe.'

'You believe?' Carrie was even more puzzled, then realization began to dawn and it was now her turn to look embarrassed. 'You mean you haven't actually met him yet?' No wonder her new acquaintance looked so uncomfortable. It couldn't be that she was one of those infamous mail-order brides, could it? Carrie had only ever read of such goings-on before and had never expected to meet such a creature. There was no direct answer to her question but, intrigued, she persisted. 'You must know a good deal about him, though. I mean, you can't possibly be going all that way to marry a complete stranger.'

'Oh yes, I do,' the young woman insisted, a trifle too

defensively. 'I know a good deal. He's English – from York-shire. A very respectable gentleman, Silas Hebden by name. His father had a farm in the Vale of York which his elder brother inherited. Mr Hebden – Silas – went to sea as a young man and on his second trip out there, to New South Wales, decided to stay and try and make a go of it raising cattle and sheep.' She gave a weak smile. 'It's a great opportunity, so they say, for those prepared to work. I – I expect he's been far too busy to think of getting himself a wife until now . . .' She glanced down at her feet. 'He's almost fifty, or perhaps even a trifle more, I believe.'

'Fifty! But that's old enough to be your father!' Carrie blurted out. Then she immediately regretted it as the young woman's bottom lip began to tremble once more. Carrie laid a comforting hand on her arm. 'I'm sorry, that was really tactless of me. Please forgive me. I'm sure you'll have a very happy marriage indeed.'

To her surprise, the young woman shook her head as she gazed up into the starlit sky. 'I'm not,' she said, with something akin to bitterness creeping into her voice for the first time. 'I'm not sure at all.' Then in a tone barely above a whisper, she confided, 'You see, Miss Clayton, I've already been married to the most marvellous man on God's earth and I know I will never meet the likes of him again.'

Carrie nodded, clueless as to what to say next, as a shower of spray washed over them.

'Yes,' her companion continued, as they moved back from the rail. 'Once you've known real love you don't expect to find it twice in a lifetime . . . I count myself fortunate to have known it at all.'

Carrie's eyes took in the black net of the hat and the black dress the young woman was wearing as they began to walk slowly down the deck. 'He . . . you haven't been widowed long, then?'

Caroline Cooper shook her head as she bit her lip. 'Less than a year. He died just before our first wedding anniversary. I couldn't believe it. We were so happy.' Her brow furrowed as she paused and looked at Carrie for understanding. 'You ask yourself, why you, don't you? Why should something terrible like that happen to you?'

Carrie nodded. She knew the feeling.

'If only I had had a child . . .'

'Have you no relatives left in England?'

Caroline Cooper shook her head. 'No one close. I have an uncle in the Navy, my mother's brother. He is a good man and always showed concern for me, but he's away at sea for months on end. He was my guardian until I came of age, but I could never run to him with my problems as an adult woman. He has no reason to believe that I am going out to New South Wales for any other reason than a wish to build a new life. As for my in-laws, well, both David's parents are dead . . .' Her voice tailed off, then she added faintly, 'It is not easy to be left a widow with no real means of support.'

Carrie nodded understandingly, but at a loss as to what to say to bring comfort to this obviously unhappy creature.

The young woman next to her shivered. She had said far too much already. 'It's getting a bit fresh out here and my headache's much better now,' she murmured, clasping her shawl to her with a lace-gloved hand. 'I'd better be going down below.' She extended her free hand to Carrie. 'Perhaps we'll meet again some other evening. I've enjoyed our little chat.'

Carrie smiled and shook the offered hand. 'So have I,' she said truthfully. To have a real conversation, no matter how short, with a normal free human being was a real luxury. For no matter how much she enjoyed her long chats with Dai, she could never forget that he was a man being paid to guard the likes of her.

She stood and watched her new acquaintance go. Caroline Cooper was a slight figure, with a rather stooped gait, as if she bore far too many troubles on her narrow shoulders for one so young. And Carrie wondered just how she had come to end up travelling to the other side of the world to marry a man she had never even met. As she watched her disappear below decks, there was not total envy in Carrie's heart. Caroline Cooper might have her freedom, but she was not a happy woman. Not happy at all.

Carrie turned and walked slowly back to the rail, leaning her elbows on the smooth wood and cupping her chin in her hands as she gazed out to sea. Was anyone really happy in this life? she wondered as the sea spray blew fresh and cold against her skin. Just a few short months ago she had had so many dreams, just as that young woman must have had when she married her husband. Now those dreams lay shattered for both of them. And what was worse, her new friend seemed to have given up on ever finding happiness again. There was an air of defeat about her, of quiet desperation even, that hardened the resolve in Carrie's own heart not to give in.

She gazed up into the night sky where a star was twinkling brighter than any of the others, and she knew in her heart it was that same star that had twinkled just for her that night in her Newgate cell. 'I'll not fail, Ma,' she whispered. 'I'll not give up.' And she was as sure as there was a God in heaven that Bridie Clayton had heard her.

CHAPTER SIX

Carrie told Dai of her encounter with the young woman when, wet with sea spray but invigorated, she got back to her berth some time later that evening.

The old man nodded sagely. 'Mail-order brides,' he said knowingly. 'I've heard tell o' them all right. Have even seen some on other voyages I've reckoned that were just such poor things.'

'This sort of thing happens a lot, then?' Carrie asked, steadying herself against the back of her bunk as the ship gave a stomach-churning roll.

'Oh aye, in the colonies it does. In fact, anywhere they're flying the British flag and there's plenty of young men defending the Empire, but not enough women to go round.' He gave a quiet chuckle. 'Reckon I'd probably do the same myself if I had to. It's either that or go native.'

'You mean take a native wife?' She knew she should not be shocked, but she was.

The old man sucked on his pipe and confirmed, 'Plenty do, that's for sure. Specially them that have wives back in the old country who can't or won't join 'em. There are an awful lot of little bastards – if you'll excuse the expression – running around far flung outposts of the British Empire with real English blood in their veins.'

He spat out of the corner of his mouth and replaced his pipe between his lips. 'Their Pas can never marry their Mas, you see, lass. Society wouldn't accept it. British men must remember their place. That's why the poor devils have to end up sending for the likes of that young woman you met tonight.'

Carrie gazed up at him from her bunk, where she lay resting on her elbow. 'Do you think they make for happy marriages, then – these mail-order affairs?'

The old sailor chuckled. 'Now you're asking! Is there really any such thing as a happy marriage, Carrie, *bach*?'

'Oh yes,' Carrie said emphatically. 'At least I hope so.' Her expression grew wistful. 'Not that I'll ever get the chance to find out.'

Her companion looked surprised. 'And why not, may I ask?'

'I'm a lifer, remember. Lifers don't get the chance to do anything – except regret what might have been.'

The old man sitting on the steps beside her wagged his pipe in her direction. 'Don't go frettin' your gizzard over that, my girl. Life ain't like that. Not at all. You mark my words. You just take heart you're still alive. Where there's life there's hope. A young chickabiddy like you's not done for yet. You know what I'd do if I were you?'

Carrie shook her head.

'I'd make a pact with myself to succeed to spite the beggars, that's what I'd do!' Then he chuckled, a deep throaty sound that made her smile despite herself. 'That's better!' he said. 'Now go on, say it . . .'

'I'll succeed to spite the beggars!' She felt better already.

But if her own spirits lightened over the next few weeks, that was not true for the young woman she had met on deck. As time passed, Carrie found herself running into her quite frequently during her late evening excursions into the fresh, salty air and sea breezes of the promenade deck. They would always pause and chat for several minutes, mainly about inconsequential things to do with the voyage. Caroline Cooper suffered quite severely with seasickness and Carrie found she could amuse her with the often downright bizarre remedies some of the convicts came up with below decks.

As the weeks passed she got the distinct impression her new friend was pleased they had met and had been longing to have someone to confide in, with whom to share her fears for the future, so Carrie was not at all surprised when one evening an invitation was issued to visit her in her cabin the following night.

'Please, do come in. Don't feel shy.' Caroline Cooper held her cabin door ajar so Carrie could enter, a reassuring smile on her face. It was exactly ten o'clock on one of the warmest late spring evenings they had had on the voyage so far.

Carrie stood hesitantly on the threshold for a moment, then stepped inside the tiny room.

She looked about her in amazement. It was no bigger than a large cupboard, measuring around seven feet by seven. It consisted of a bunk taking up the whole length of the far wall, save for a hanging press at the foot. The porthole was above the bunk, with a row of wall cupboards above that. The only furniture was a small washstand which doubled as a desk-cum-table, and at which the occupant took her meals. A small wooden folding chair sat next to it, which Caroline Cooper hurried to pull out as she indicated for her guest to take a seat. She herself sat down on the edge of her bunk and made an expansive gesture with her hands. 'Welcome to my home.'

'It's not very big, is it?' Carrie said, acknowledging the irony in her friend's voice as she glanced around her. Somehow she had imagined the paying passengers in far more palatial accommodation.

'No, but I shouldn't really complain. I suppose I'm lucky to have it. Single cabins are a rare luxury on board a ship like this.' Caroline Cooper allowed herself a tight smile as the ship heaved and she swayed with it. 'I only got it because I wrote my fiancé and said I couldn't bear to share . . . I've always been a very private person, you see.' There was quite a swell outside and she held her stomach and took a deep breath, letting it out slowly. Then she smoothed the folds in the skirts of her dress and added wryly, 'I didn't really expect him to pay the extra, but he did.'

Carrie sighed. He sounded a considerate man.

'Would – would you care for a drop of Madeira?' Caroline asked, remembering her role of hostess. 'I – I'm afraid I can't offer much in the way of refreshment, but I do have that. I was recommended to bring it by my doctor. He said a glass was good for seasickness and would help me sleep.'

'That would be lovely.' Carrie made herself comfortable on the wooden chair, steadying herself by keeping her good right foot firmly on the floor, wedged against the cabin wall.

As she watched her hostess reach up into one of the top cupboards for the bottle, she could not quite believe she was actually sitting here going through the formalities of a polite social call. But she knew it was the inevitable outcome of their growing closeness. Caroline Cooper really seemed to appreciate the companionship she had found in their evening chats, and although she had never taken much interest in Carrie's own life or asked what mis-demeanour had been committed to deserve such a harsh punishment, she had appeared to be longing to talk about her own plight. But her confidences were to be reserved for the right moment, and as Carrie sat there watching her friend battle with the swell to keep her footing as she searched for the drink, she could not help but think that moment had arrived. This invitation into Caroline Cooper's own private world was her way of say-ing she trusted her. It was akin to being readmitted to the human race.

'Here, let me help.' The ship heaved once more and, sensing her friend was in difficulties, Carrie took the bottle from the other's grasp and set it down on the table, as Caroline sank weakly back down on to her bunk.

'Oh, thank you.' Her already pale face had gone quite ashen as she attempted a smile. 'I really should be careful stretching up like that, I suppose. I get quite faint at times with over-exertion.'

In the light of the oil-lamp, it struck Carrie quite forcibly how alike they looked in certain respects, but she also noted how very thin and frail-looking Caroline was. The young widow had never appeared robust at the best of times, but out there on the deck in the moonlight it had been impossible to observe just how fragile she really looked. The skin was pulled so tightly across the cheek-bones of her face that it was almost transparent, and the lips that were forcing themselves into a smile were quite colourless. 'You're probably not eating enough,' said Carrie in a matter-of-fact voice. 'I know it's difficult, but it's very important to get enough victuals inside you, with so much sickness around at sea.'

'I know, I know. I just don't seem to have the inclination to eat these days – even if the ship didn't roll like this and the food was tempting enough, which it most certainly isn't, I find it difficult to get anything over my throat.'

Carrie made no reply as Caroline summoned up her strength, reached into the press at the side of her bed and took two cups from a shelf in the bottom, into which she carefully poured two fingers of wine. She handed one across to her guest. 'Here's health!'

'And wealth!' Carrie raised her cup in return, and added, 'And here's to a long and very happy marriage for you in New South Wales.'

But at that Caroline Cooper did not raise her own cup to her lips; instead she set it down in her lap and shook her head. 'Not a long marriage,' she said at last. 'Don't wish me that. I couldn't bear it.' Her eyes were full as they met Carrie's. 'I couldn't bear having to spend years as another man's wife. David is the only man I could ever love.' She shook her head in despair at the futility of it all. 'I should have died with him. I prayed to God at the time to let me die too, and I still do. I pray all the time for Him to take me soon so I can join my husband – my *real* husband – at last.'

Carrie listened astonished at the outburst and watched in an embarrassed silence as her friend gulped down a mouthful of the Madeira and a flush came to her cheeks as she pleaded, 'You do understand, don't you? I had to tell you. It's not wicked of me to feel like this, is it?'

'I understand,' Carrie answered, not quite sure if she did or not. She herself had never been in love, let alone had a husband to feel this way about, and, in truth, any husband no matter how old or ugly would be better than the future that awaited her in that prison factory. But her companion was clearly upset and very depressed. 'I do understand, and I don't think it's wicked. We can't help our feelings.'

Caroline Cooper's gaze was searching. 'Can you really understand what it is like to have the whole meaning of your life taken away from you, just like that? When he died I didn't want to live any more. There was nothing left to live for.' She took another gulp of the drink, draining the cup, and gave a shudder. 'For weeks after his death I couldn't bear to go out to face the world. I just stayed in my room, not bothering to get dressed, to eat, or do anything.' Her eyes hardened. 'If a neighbour hadn't intervened and called a doctor, I would have joined him. I would be with him by now.'

Carrie looked down at the drink in her lap, unable to bear the pain in the other's eyes. She had been there once – in that same state of not wanting to go on – when they had hanged Billy. 'What made you answer that advertisement?' she asked softly.

'Poverty.' The word was spoken with bitterness. Then Caroline sighed. 'I knew it was a mistake before the ship even sailed, but I had not the money to go back to where I came from . . .'

She sat up and reached for the bottle on the table and, taking care not to spill, she poured two more drinks. She took a sip of her own, then sat nursing the cup in her hands. 'I've never asked you exactly how you came to be here, in this awful position you're now in. But I guess from the little I know that we come from fairly similar backgrounds. Respectable, but with not two brass farthings to rub together.'

She took another sip of her drink, then drained the cup, as a pink flush crept into her cheeks. 'It's so different for men. They can go out into the world and earn their keep. It's different for us females. We have our good name to think of.'

Her gaze was bleak as she looked past Carrie and stared at the opposite wall. If it had not been for the pawn shop, whose owner agreed to give a good price on the few things of worth David had left, she would indeed have starved in the year between his death and setting out for her new life in New South Wales. Parting with those few items, such as the leather writing case with the brass fittings he had been given for his twenty-first birthday, had been like selling pieces of him, when all she wanted was to cling on to everything that reminded her of their life together.

'It's like an illness, you know, Carrie. This longing for someone who's gone, it's like a slow death of the mind and the body. That's why I can't bring myself to go out on deck during the day, and why I have all my meals right here in my cabin. I can't bear to be part of the outside world any more. He's no longer there, you see. David has gone.'

The bleakness with which those last three words were spoken sent a shiver down Carrie's spine. She reached across and touched her friend's hand. 'I understand,' she said softly. 'And if talking about him helps, then I'm here to listen.'

For the next twenty minutes Carrie did just that; she sat and listened as the ship's timbers creaked and the spray spattered against the glass of the porthole and the young widow talked her heart out about the young man she had married less than two years before. David Cooper had been a shipping clerk, working from an office in Dulwich, whom she had met through a prayer group at their local church. He had been a Londoner by birth, like herself, but had had ambition. For the few months before his death he had been making plans to join the shipyard of Alexander Hall and Sons up in Aberdeen, where he was to be given a chance as a trainee designer on the new clipper ships.

It was to have been a great adventure going to Scotland, and they had both been looking forward to it tremendously. 'David's mother was Scottish, you see, Carrie. From Aberdeen. It was to be almost like going home for him, although he had never set foot north of the border in his life.'

And she spoke with pride of the portfolio full of drawings and plans he had made for the ships which would now never be built – drawings that had convinced the Scottish owner of one of that country's finest yards that the young Englishman deserved a chance. With the tea routes to China and the like proving so highly profitable, and the race being on for faster and faster ships to trade those routes, there was not a yard in the country that was not on the lookout for fresh talent.

Despite her own far more dire situation, Carrie listened with a growing sympathy for her companion's plight. It had been so easy to envy all those travelling out on the *Emma Harkness* in the relative comfort of the passenger deck. But life was never quite as simple as that. 'We all have our crosses to bear, whether we have them tied visibly to our backs for all to see, or whether we keep them well hidden from the rest of the world,' her mother used to say. And from what Carrie was now hearing she knew that Caroline Cooper had indeed a heavy cross to bear. In fact, the longer she sat there and listened to her friend pouring her heart out, the more she doubted if she could ever do or say anything that would help lighten the load of the young woman sitting across from her. Some battles in life had to be fought alone, and hers was one of them.

Over the next few weeks her friendship with the young widow blossomed into one of mutual trust and understanding. Carrie accepted the fact that there was nothing she could say or do that would help make Caroline's life any easier, but neither was there anything the young widow could do to ease Carrie's own problems on the prison deck. Carrie's matter-of-fact cheerfulness, however, seemed to keep Caroline from sinking into too deep a despair and for the first time since that awful night her father died, Carrie actually felt of use to someone.

By the time they were into their fourth month of the voyage most of the attractive young single women were quitting the convict deck after dark to team up with members of the crew. There was quite an exodus from the female felons' quarters on most nights of the week. This was something that the officers appeared to turn a blind eye to for the simple reason that many of their own number were being 'accommodated', as they put it, by their own personal pick of the crop.

At first old Dai Evans was convinced that Carrie too had found a male companion, and that was the reason for her continuing disappearances in the late evening. 'There's nothing to be ashamed of, you know, *bach*,' he told her. 'A healthy young woman like you – why, it's only right and proper you should have caught the fancy of a young man.'

He had seemed quite disappointed when she finally succeeded in convincing him that there was no such sailor Romeo and she was spending all her hours of freedom in the company of another young woman.

'Well, I'll be damned. So my little squab-chick's not a soiled dove after all!'

'Not yet-a-while, Dai, old friend! And I never will be if I have my way!' Already Carrie was well aware that any chance of a decent marriage to an honourable husband was as far beyond her as the moon. And she had no wish to end her days as the plaything of any ship's officer or prison guard, to be cast aside when her novelty value was over.

They were now nearing the end of their voyage and excitement was beginning to run high as gulls and other sea birds were spotted in the skies above them. The wind seemed fresher somehow, the sea a deeper blue. Even the men on the most menial tasks, such as holystoning the decks, seemed to carry out their duties with a smile and a quip for whoever might be passing. Old Captain Griffiths himself actually took to visiting the prison decks at least once a day to see how his human cargo was faring. For most of the early months of the voyage he had neglected this part of his duties, preferring to leave it to his younger officers to report back. But now they were nearing Botany Bay things were very different. Every convict he succeeded in disembarking alive meant more money to swell the company's coffers, so extra attention was now being paid to the welfare of all.

'Aye, it's amazing the difference the prospect of reaching our destination makes,' old Dai commented wryly. 'If things get much more comfortable aboard ship, we'll not manage to persuade any of you to get off, come Sydney Cove!'

'Oh, have no fear of that,' Carrie assured him. 'No matter how bad it is there, it can't be half as bad as this!' She never wanted to hear the creak of timbers, eat a dry tack biscuit, or let her nostrils near the smell of tar again as long as she lived.

Dai Evans made no reply. It was not up to him to disillusion anyone.

Despite the growing high spirits of all on board, the last Sunday service held on deck for the prisoners was an occasion to point out that no bed of roses awaited them on land. In their growing excitement as the voyage drew to an end, it was imperative to make it clear that they were about to be called upon to pay for the sins committed in the motherland, now some twelve thousand miles away.

The ship's chaplain's face was grave as, in a blustery breeze that had the sails moaning and complaining above

97

them, he addressed his wayward flock for the last time: 'I take my text this momentous day from the fifth chapter of Leviticus, the seventeenth verse:

'"And if a soul sin, and commit any of these things which are forbidden to be done by the commandments of the Lord; though he wist it not, yet is he guilty, and shall bear his iniquity!"'

His thin face was serious as he surveyed the congregation and his reedy voice gathered momentum as he got into his vocal stride: 'Each one of you gathered here in the sight of the Lord to pay homage to your God is such a sinner, and as you near your journey's end I implore you to make your peace with your Lord and accept what awaits you with humility and contriteness.'

'Like hell and holy water I will,' Molly McGuire whispered to Carrie. 'They'll not get me into that prison factory!'

'Nor me,' Carrie found herself agreeing. But just how she could escape it was completely beyond her.

On the first day of June, 1842, the *Emma Harkness* made her way northwards up the Tasman Sea towards the east coast of New South Wales and Botany Bay. The wind increased to a fresh breeze, and, as the women convicts took one of their last exercise periods on deck, a sharp downpour occurred, flattening the waves and creating fast flowing streams on the heaving planks beneath their feet.

'Just think, Carrie,' Molly whispered to her friend as they completed their first lap of the enclosure, holding their hands above their heads to shield themselves from the pelting rain. 'In a few days I could be a free woman!'

Carrie could not help but be sceptical as she squinted out of the side of her eye at her friend. 'You really think he'll help you escape and you'll run off together?' she asked, as the rain turned her short crop to rats' tails and ran down the open neck of her blouse. Surely Molly could not really believe that? There was not an officer on board who had taken a convict as a mistress who had not made some such promise.

But Molly was adamant as she wiped the rain from her eyes. 'Sure, it's a suspicious old body you are and no mistake! Of course I believe him.'

'But what if you're caught?'

The question got the look Molly believed it deserved, but not the answer Carrie was waiting for.

'Quiet there, Ninety-nine!' a guard shouted. 'Any more of that and it's the cooler for you both!'

Carrie raised a hand to show she had heard. But both young women knew there would be little chance of being stuck inside a barrel at this late stage of the journey. Even the most unbending guard was assuming a more human face the nearer they got to land.

'All hands on deck!'

Their exercise was cut short by ten minutes as, although the rain had lessened, they were experiencing the sort of heavy swell the old hands referred to as 'the dog before the master'. The wind had become even more troublesome, causing the ship's timbers, especially in the rigging, to creak even more alarmingly than usual and white caps to sparkle on the waves. The Captain knew he could not risk any mishaps at a time like this. All became a hive of industry on board as the order went out for skysails, royals and topgallants to be furled and the topsails double-reefed. But although the convicts complained loudly at having their time in the fresh air curtailed, to everyone's relief the threatened storm came to nothing.

'Thank God that seems to be over. It would be a terrible thing to be shipwrecked within sight of our destination, so it would,' Molly declared, as, still damp but in fine fettle, she sat with Carrie at one end of the communal lavatory some four hours later. With berths at opposite ends of the deck, a visit to the Jake, as the sailors called it, was one of the few times the prisoners could have a conversation in private. The conveniences were four-seaters, but tonight there were just the two of them as they pondered on what lay ahead.

Carrie looked thoughtful in the semi-darkness. 'If you do succeed in escaping, Mol, do you think we'll ever see each other again?' she asked, feeling quite sentimental at the thought of her friend just disappearing into the unknown.

Molly McGuire laughed. 'Sure and we'll make it our business to come back and get you,' she declared. 'We'll spring you over the wall of that prison factory from under their very noses!'

But Carrie was in no mood for jokes. 'You won't try to get back to England, then?'

'England? God love you, no! What in heaven's name would we be going back there for, when they hang inno-cent folk like my man and your wee brother as soon as look at you?' Molly shook her head emphatically. 'Eng-land's the last place we'll be heading.' Then she turned and looked curiously at Carrie. 'You wouldn't fancy going back there yourself, would you?'

It was a question Carrie had never asked herself before. And although she had had no wish to be exiled to the ends of the earth, neither had she any love left for the country that had done this to her – the country that had killed her young brother. 'No,' she sighed, staring at the round peephole in the door, just above their eye-level. 'No, I would never go back. England is the last place on earth I would want to return to.'

Molly beamed. 'You'll stay and let us rescue you, then?'

'You make it sound like a great adventure.'

'But it is, Carrie, it is!'

Carrie's melancholy melted in the sunshine of the other's smile. She only wished she could be so sure.

Morning brought with it a strongish wind, playful enough for the Captain to order the topsails shortened to their last row of reef points as excitement both below decks and above reached fever pitch. The prisoners watched the lads climbing like monkeys up the rigging as they walked their familiar route around the exercise deck for what might be the last time. Even the very air they breathed felt sweeter as their eyes scanned the horizon for their first sight of land. It was official: they were now no more than forty-eight hours from their destination.

Excitement was tinged with apprehension. The voyage had been no bed of roses; quite a few had not survived the trip. In the main, they were the ones who had been pathetic specimens to begin with; barely a month had gone by without one or two ceremonies consigning some poor unfortunate creatures to the waves.

For those who remained, however, there was by now a curious sense of security in the sameness of the routine. Liked or disliked, faces had become familiar, with each person on board knowing exactly what was expected of them and what the following day would bring. But now it was all coming to an end. Soon they would put into harbour and this oddly comforting sense of togetherness would come to an end, and heaven only knew what lay ahead.

For Carrie, as for most of the others, it was with strangely mixed feelings that she viewed the future. Although in some ways she could not wait to be back on dry land, the idea of never seeing her friends again was not a happy one. Apart from Molly and Dai, she knew she would miss Caroline terribly, for the two had grown very close over the past weeks. It was frightening to think that Mr Silas Hebden was probably making the overland journey from his sheep station to pick her up right now. He had a place in the Hunter Valley, Caroline had told her, and they would be overnighting in either Sydney or a place called Parramatta before he returned with her to his farm at Yorvik.

Caroline had talked a lot about Yorvik. Yorvik . . . It was a funny word all right. She said Silas Hebden had named his farm after the old Viking name for York, his home city in England. 'I reckon that when the Norsemen first landed from Scandinavia and set up their farmsteads they must have been pretty similar to my own first attempt at a home out here,' he had written to his bride-to-be, and she had shown Carrie the letter.

'Of course I'm hoping it's improved a good deal since then,' Caroline had added as she refolded the page and placed it in her case. 'We've come quite a way since the Dark Ages, after all.'

'Not in prisons we haven't,' Carrie murmured with feeling. For no matter how primitive Silas Hebden's sheep station was, it was bound to be a thousand times better than the prison factory that was waiting for her on landing at Port Jackson, the harbour in Botany Bay.

It was a strange thought that, depending on the wind, tonight might be the very last night she would see her friend. There was so much still to talk about. Carrie hoped that somehow they would be able to keep in touch once they reached dry land, but they both knew that would depend on the goodwill of the man who would be waiting there on the quayside for his new bride. While some free settlers did not seem to mind the convicts and some even went as far as employing them or even taking convict brides, it was significant that Silas Hebden had done neither. And as far as the latter was concerned, he had sent all the way to England for his. Carrie knew this did not augur at all well for any further contact between herself and the future Mrs Hebden.

Was that why she was feeling so uneasy as the day wore to a close and her thoughts dwelt more and more on her last visit to her friend in a few hours' time? She became more aware of it as the skies began to darken. It was a strange feeling of unquiet, so disturbing that she was almost tempted to break her own rule of waiting until the prison deck had settled down for the night before she made the five-minute journey to Caroline's cabin.

'You look tense tonight, Carrie *bach*,' Dai told her as he came on watch. 'Is anything wrong?'

Carrie shook her head but somehow could not manage her usual smile. 'I hope not, Dai, old friend. I hope not.'

There was a bright moon high in a pale opal sky as the last rays of the sun gave way to night and shafts of indigo blue flooded the heavens. The sea was a gun-metal grey shot with silver and the gangway she always used was quite deserted as Carrie climbed up out of the prison deck to make her way to Caroline's cabin. Any other evening, earlier in the voyage, she would have been happy to just stand there in the quietness by the ship's rail and watch the pink glow slowly fade with the dying day. But tonight was different. Her feeling of disquiet had been growing all evening and she was sure there was going to be some sort of emotional scene that she was not at all certain she would be able to cope with. Her friend had grown more and more agitated as they neared their destination and the headaches that seemed to plague Caroline Cooper's life were becoming daily occurrences. She seemed to be relying totally on Carrie for the emotional support to carry her through this last stage of the voyage and this was proving an increasingly heavy burden for the latter to bear.

As far as Caroline was concerned, the thought of meeting her future husband before the week was out was assuming nightmare proportions. And when Carrie had inadvertently mentioned the planned wedding two days previously, her friend's response had been desperate. 'How can I ever stand before God and pledge myself to another man?' she had cried. 'How can I do it when David is the only one I could ever love?'

And Carrie had had no answer. It was far too late for such questions and they both knew it. They should have been addressed four months and twelve thousand miles ago, not now when they were within hailing distance of their destination.

104

Carrie issued a heartfelt sigh as she picked her way carefully over a rotting plank, then almost tripped over the ship's cat, who disappeared mewing into the darkness. She knew that her friend would have little interest in her own private anxieties about the coming days, yet Carrie also knew she would be called upon more than ever to provide the emotional crutch that her friend so badly needed. But that crutch would be kicked away by circumstances just as soon as the ship docked at Port Jackson. There was no way round it. Caroline was promised to another man and he would be waiting there on the quay to meet her, no matter how much she might now wish it otherwise. She would just have to recognize the fact and make the best of it.

Seldom could there have been a more reluctant bride, Carrie thought to herself wearily as she made her way towards her friend's door. And, sympathetic as part of her was to Caroline's plight, another part had gradually been losing patience over the passing weeks. No matter how bleakly she regarded her future life with her unseen husband, Caroline had very little to complain about compared to the hundred women who inhabited the convict deck below her.

It was with a curious mixture of feelings that Carrie knocked at the closed cabin door. Please don't let us argue, she prayed. Not now. Not so near the end . . .

She listened for a movement inside and the usual call of 'It's open!' When there was neither, she paused, her brow furrowing. Although somewhat calmer now, the boisterous wind had been making the sea increasingly choppy all day. Maybe it wasn't just a headache that was afflicting her friend this time; perhaps Caroline had had one of her regular bouts of seasickness and had taken to her bunk.

Carrie knocked twice more. There was still no answer. Could Caroline be out at this time of night? Puzzled, she tried the handle. To her surprise, the door creaked open and she felt a momentary pang of apprehension. Perhaps Caroline really had been ill, but had fallen asleep and would not want to be disturbed.

There was very little light in the cabin, for the oil-lamp fixed to a bracket on the wall above the table had just about burned itself out and a gloomy glow pervaded the interior. Caroline was lying in her bunk as Carrie had anticipated, and the latter drew back, uncertain whether to disturb her friend or not. It was hard enough to sleep on board ship without being bothered by unwelcome guests just when you had managed to drop off.

But the odd thing was, she knew their meeting tonight was eagerly awaited. It was a funny time to decide on an early night. Carrie paused and looked across at her friend. She must have been feeling really ill to have allowed herself to fall asleep like this and give up their last real chance of saying goodbye.

A trifle uncertain as to what to do for the best, she decided to go in.

She could see at once that her friend was fully clothed, lying on top of the bed, half on her side, facing away from the door, with an arm thrown up over her face. Perhaps she was not really ill but had just nodded off.

Carrie tiptoed over to the bed and looked down. 'Caroline . . .' She whispered the name into her friend's ear. No response. She gently lifted Caroline's arm from her face and laid it at her side. There was still not the slightest sound or movement from the figure on the bed. 'Caroline . . .' She spoke louder this time. But still there was no response. By now Carrie's heart was beating faster as she bent closer and placed her hand on her friend's forehead. It was quite cold and clammy to the touch.

'Caroline!' The name was almost shouted now as Carrie took hold of the other woman's shoulders and attempted to move her over on to her back. It was like moving a lead weight and the face she found staring up into her own made her cry out loud.

'My God!' She jerked back in horror, letting go the other's shoulders as a pair of unseeing eyes stared upwards at the row of cupboards above, the pupils no bigger than pinheads.

Unable to accept the evidence of her own eyes, Carrie took hold of her friend once more and began shaking her. 'Caroline . . . !' The shaking became rougher, as Carrie's voice became more and more agitated: 'Caroline — for God's sake, wake up!'

But Caroline was not going to wake up. Caroline Cooper was never going to wake up again.

'Oh God . . .' Carrie let go the leaden body and slumped back against the side of the bunk. She was shaking, partly from exertion and partly from shock as she stared down into the face of the woman who had become the best friend she had ever known.

The skin of Caroline Cooper's face was grey, but, for some strange reason, both her lips and the tips of her ears were a livid blood-red colour that was just beginning to turn blue. It was obvious she was not long dead.

Carrie groaned aloud. If only she had got here a few minutes earlier! God knows, she could easily have done so. She had felt uneasy about her friend's state of mind all day. But never in her wildest dreams had she imagined it would come to this. She pushed a despairing hand through her hair, feeling both angry and impotent. What a waste! What a waste of a life!

But as the stark reality of the situation dawned and she sat there in the gloom of the spluttering oil-lamp, she knew in her heart that Caroline would not have wanted to be saved. Her friend had got her most fervent wish at last: she had joined her husband. If there really was such a place as heaven she was with her beloved David at last.

Carrie turned in a mixture of helplessness and sorrow from the body on the bed and her eyes fell on the small folding chair that had been moved to the side of the bunk to serve as a bedside table. On it was an empty purple bottle of tincture of opium and an upturned glass.

She glanced at the bottle, then reached over and picked up the glass. Holding it to her nose, she sniffed. She was right: laudanum. Even without the bottle, she would recognize that distinctive odour anywhere. Her mother had used it regularly to combat the terrible headaches that used to afflict her during the last months of her life.

She turned the glass slowly in her fingers as she looked back down at the vacantly staring face of her friend. That Caroline had also used laudanum to combat headaches, she was well aware. But no matter how depressed she had been, it had never crossed Carrie's mind that her friend might use the drug to take her own life.

For a moment she felt guilty at the impatient thoughts she had had on her way here tonight. 'Lord, Caroline, I'm sorry . . .' she sighed. But, wherever she was now, she knew her friend had to be in a happier place than this. And if there was any truth in religion, then she had indeed been reunited with the man she loved. When David Cooper had died so tragically young, he had taken his young wife with him in all but her physical body. Her heart and soul had gone to the grave with him long ago.

But what of the man she had not loved, but whom she was travelling to the other side of the world to marry? What of Silas Hebden waiting there on the dockside at Port Jackson for his new wife? What of him?

Carrie felt a momentary pang of sorrow for the man. One thing was for sure, the fact that his bride-to-be would not now be getting off this ship would be a devastating blow to him. From what Caroline had said he had spent a lot of money he could probably ill afford to bring her over here. What a bitter pill for any lonely man to swallow that his investment had ended up a corpse – killed by her own hand – before he could even set eyes on her.

Carrie looked around her at the few personal possessions scattered around the cabin. Would they give them to him?

Her brow furrowed. How could they? No one would even know of his existence. In fact, she doubted if anyone on this entire ship knew of Silas Hebden, except herself, and of course Dai. But he did not know the man's name or anything about him.

As she sat there in the flickering pool of light from the lamp, beside the dead body of her friend, a terrible thought began to form in her mind – a thought so awful that at first she tried to banish it before it was properly formed. But it refused to go away. The skin of her arms came out in gooseflesh. She could feel the hairs at the back of her neck begin to stiffen with the sheer horror of it.

But was it really so horrific? No matter how much she might wish it otherwise, Caroline Cooper was dead, and she – Carrie Clayton – was still alive. She was still young and the will to live – really live, not just exist behind prison bars – was strong.

She stared at the body, her blood quickening as her gaze took in the slight figure of roughly the same height as her own and the dark hair. They could have been taken for sisters. She had once said as much to Caroline, but the latter had merely laughed and claimed that Carrie was by far the prettier of the two. 'I vouch poor Mr Hebden, waiting out there in New South Wales, would reckon he had by far the better bargain if he saw you stepping off the boat as his bride-to-be!' she had declared.

And now those words said in jest repeated themselves in Carrie's head.

Dare she? Dare she? Could she possibly risk taking the place of her dead friend? Her pulse raced at the very idea. Perhaps – just perhaps – it was not such a crazy idea after all. There could be little doubt she was the first to find the body. And Silas Hebden had never set eyes on his wife-to-be. Caroline herself had told her that she had thought of having her likeness done in miniature to send him but had not had the money to employ an artist. Carrie's mind was a maelstrom of excitement and dread as she gazed down at the lifeless form of her friend. The only real obstacle to her taking the place of the dead woman would be the body. What was she to do with it?

Her eyes turned to the porthole about three feet above the bunk. Caroline was not a big woman. There was surely room enough?

With a furiously beating heart Carrie walked across and laid a hand on the cool glass of the round window. Then her fingers moved down to the snib. She took hold of the metal catch and attempted to turn it. It refused to budge. She learnt over and with both hands twisted the small handle and pushed. Suddenly a gush of fresh air and sea spray hit her face as the porthole swung open. She breathed the salt breeze into her lungs. All her nerve ends were tingling.

Surely it was worth a try? Her friend was dead now, while she was alive. She still had her whole life in front of her. And what sort of a life would it be to spend it as a prisoner all her days? All the injustices of the past welled up within her as she thought of her brother Billy and of her own sentence, which was meant to be a living death. Surely no one would blame her for taking this last chance of freedom?

With shaking fingers she bent down and began to undo the buttons of Caroline's bodice. The body was just beginning to stiffen beneath her hands. Her decision was being made not a moment too soon.

The minutes that followed were some of the most harrowing of her life as she struggled to undress her friend. It would be no good consigning a nude body to the waves, in case it was spotted. If her plan was to be effective they must all believe it was herself – Carrie Clayton – who had fallen overboard and drowned. That meant dressing the corpse in her own convict clothing.

Several minutes later, and trembling in a mixture of fear and excitement, with Caroline's nude body lying on the bunk beside her, she began to undress herself. Ridding her body of the hated convict apparel was akin to cleansing herself of a contamination she had carried with her for over six long months. The relief was enormous. Within minutes she was standing naked in the middle of the cabin.

'Mrs Cooper!'

Carrie froze. This was the last thing she expected. A cold sweat of fear oozed from every pore as she turned towards the door.

Three taps sounded, then again: 'Mrs Cooper!'

Panic-stricken, Carrie moved nearer the closed door and decided the only thing for it was to bluff her way through. 'Yes?'

'I was just passing on my last round, ma'am, and wondered if there was anything more I could get you?'

It must be one of the cabin crew. 'No, no thank you,' Carrie called hoarsely. 'I'm quite all right.'

'Right you are. Goodnight then, ma'am. Sleep well.'

Almost in tears of relief, Carrie listened to the sound of the man's footsteps disappearing into the distance.

But now came the awful task of dressing the body in her own convict clothes. This proved even more difficult and distressing than she anticipated and took all of ten minutes. Tears of frustration and fatigue sparkled in her eyes when, at last, she surveyed the figure of her dead friend now dressed in the garb of one of Her Majesty's transportees. It made a grotesque sight and somehow seemed a terrible violation of their friendship.

But there was no time for contemplation or remorse if her plan was to succeed. That unexpected knock at the door had set her nerves on edge and, for all she knew, Caroline might have seen the ship's surgeon over the past twenty-four hours, and he too might decide to pay a late call.

Carrie took a deep breath as she considered the last and by far the worst and most difficult task in hand. Somehow she had to get her friend's body through that porthole. She gazed at the round window in dismay. It seemed to get smaller and smaller the longer she looked at it. But there was no time to waste.

Clambering up on the bunk, she prised open the window as far as it would go, then bent down to attempt to lift the body. It seemed to weigh far more than it should, but she put that down to her own weakened state as she struggled with her arms beneath Caroline's armpits, clasped the dead body to her breast and got it into an upright position on the bunk.

'Dear God, forgive me . . .' At first Carrie thought it was not going to fit, for it stuck at the shoulders. But five sweating, panicking minutes later saw the body through the aperture.

Now the cabin was empty, apart from herself.

Shocked by the suddenness of it all, Carrie clambered forwards and stuck her head out of the porthole to see the body of her friend in the water below. It was a clear moonlit night and the corpse, already some distance from the ship, looked like a large piece of flotsam as it bobbed around in the waves.

With a thumping heart, she pulled shut the porthole and staggered off the bunk to stand naked and alone in the middle of the cabin. All around her were the scattered possessions of the young woman the world had known as Caroline Cooper, who was about to become Mrs Silas Hebden. But it was not Caroline Cooper who had died in this confined space. It was Caroline Clayton, she told herself. Caroline Clayton had died this night and had just been reborn.

It was an awesome deception she was about to attempt, and if she were to fail and be found out, then not even God could help her now.

CHAPTER EIGHT

The *Emma Harkness* stood off Botany Bay for most of the night, a tall shadow swaying gently in the moonlight as she waited for the turn of the tide and the right conditions to enter the harbour at Port Jackson, on the headland just to the north of the Bay. Conditions had been good over the past three days as the ship steered northwards about twenty nautical miles off the coast of New South Wales, but nothing had cheered the spirits of the crew on the poop deck as much as sighting landfall late last night in the shape of the Five Islands, just offshore of the twin headlands of the Bay.

For those on board the excitement at nearing journey's end was reaching fever-pitch, but Captain Griffiths was too much of an old salt and had enough experience of the tricky cross winds that characterized this last part of the voyage to risk extra sail. One hundred and twenty long days out of Portsmouth it had been, so a few extra hours here and there was not going to make a ha'p'orth of difference. 'The last mile's always the longest,' he said, repeating the old truism to his First Mate, and the seven mile stretch of water from the Heads to Sydney Cove could be troublesome even in a favourable wind.

After days on end without another vessel in sight out on the ocean, since entering and then leaving the Tasman Sea to make their way north up the eastern seaboard, they were seldom out of sight of other shipping and that in itself had been a cause for rejoicing for crew and passengers alike. Fishing boats were passing within hailing distance now and the tall white shape of a barque lay just off their port side, her masts glinting in the first rays of the sun as dawn broke in the eastern sky, turning the heavens into shades of opal, pink and pale blue.

Captain Griffiths stood on the poop deck, his helmsman at his side, the latter's capable hands gripping the polished wood of the wheel. 'I reckon it's time, don't you, Jock?' the Captain said. 'The tide's with us and the wind's as good as we're going to get it.'

He had been up on deck for most of the night, watching the dawn breaking in a clear white light to the east and casting an ethereal glow over the surrounding sea that joined the horizon far behind them in a shimmering silver line. Above them, their wings glinting in the first rays of the sun, seagulls swooped and screamed their cries of welcome. This was the moment he had been waiting for since leaving Portsmouth harbour so long ago. And it was a moment that never failed to excite the old sea dog in him, for in all his years under sail he had never come across another harbour like this, where the white surf broke on to golden sand that stretched for miles around the bays and small inlets which made up this foreign land the English government had chosen for the exile of so many of its citizens.

'All hands on deck! Stand in for the Heads!'

'Aye, aye, sir!' The First Mate disappeared below, then a whistle shrilled and a voice echoed from amidships, 'All hands on deck!'

Within minutes the watch below clattered up from the fo'c'sle and young men and old scattered in all directions, each with his particular task to carry out. The swabbing of the decks began to the accompaniment of lusty singing, even more hearty than usual, as buckets of water were hauled from the sea to sluice down the planks. Other seamen scampered up the rigging to set the sails as the ship prepared to weigh anchor and make for the narrow passage between the twin headlands of Botany Bay and Port Jackson. Smiles were the order of the day for there were girls and grog a'plenty in good old Sydney town, and after so long at sea there was not a man-Jack amongst them who was not looking forward to finding his

114

land-legs again and heading straight for the dockside taverns.

'Want to take over now, Cap'n?' The old helmsman stood aside to let his superior take the wheel. It was a politeness born of more than two decades of working together: the last lap belonged to the man in charge.

'Thanks, Jock.' The Captain gave a signal in the direction of the First Mate some yards away, to show they were underway, as diligently the course was set towards the centre of the mile-wide gap in the cliffs which formed the entrance to the port.

After the silence and stillness of the night, all was now noise and bustle as within half an hour, under only a jib-sail and one top-gallant, the old lady moved slowly upstream on the tide.

Now out of the ocean's swell, her path was steady, sedate even, as the crew threw their greatest efforts yet into their remaining tasks. Several of the paying passengers too excited to sleep had already wandered on to the deck to savour the moment when they would catch their first glimpse of their destination, while down below in the semi-darkness of the prison decks all was in ferment as through the slits in the scuttles the convicts fought each other for their first sight of their new home.

Dai Evans yawned as he hauled open the hatchway to one end of the women's prison deck and let in the first blast of fresh morning air as he had done so many times over the past four months. But as the wooden door clattered into place he yelled something quite different to his usual greeting: 'Muster up there, ladies! Land ahoy! Show a leg there and prepare for landing!'

This time, however, there was not the pleasure in his voice that he had been anticipating only two short days ago. Somehow the excitement had gone out of it all and inside him there existed a deep and abiding ache, which had been there since the night before last when Carrie had not returned to her berth on the prison deck.

At first he had thought little of it, thinking she had been lying to him and she really had a young man amongst the crew as he had once suspected, and they had been making the most of what might be their last night together. Then just after his watch ended he had heard the news.

'Any idea who the poor bitch was, Taf?'

He had looked in surprise at the young beardless youth who had asked the question. The bosun's mate had had no idea of the fear that came into the old Welshman's heart at that moment.

'What you on about, lad?'

'That poor bitch that went overboard last night. Didn't you hear tell about it, then? Spotted she was, about twenty yards off, but dead as a doornail by then, o'course. Weren't no purpose in trying to fish 'er out.'

Dai Evans's heart had stopped. 'No . . . No . . . I never heard o' that. Any idea who she was?'

The lad had shrugged. 'Thought you might know that, seeing as you guard one of the hatches.'

'She was definitely a convict, then?'

'Oh aye, no doubt about that. Those canvas skirts they wear was about the only thing visible. Went up like a balloon in the water, they did. It was the second mate who spotted her. I reckon she's better off where she is now, though, than ending up in that there prison factory.' He had already heard all about what was awaiting most of their human cargo on dry land. 'Better off dead she is, don't you reckon?'

But Dai Evans had looked away, for there were tears in his eyes, which coursed down the leathery skin of his cheeks as he made his way back to his quarters. He prided himself in having grown so thick a skin over the years that nothing that happened on board could get to him any more. But this did. He had grown really fond of that young woman. She had had something about her — a spirit that had not been broken by that accursed legal system back in England, and a determination not to give

116

in. So many did, and they were the ones who went under.

Was it suicide? He could have believed that of almost any of the others, but not of her. In fact, she had been in high spirits as she had made her way up to see her friend that night.

His brow had furrowed as he sat down heavily on his bunk and reached inside his pocket for his pipe. If only he could remember the name of the young woman Carrie had been so friendly with. He had shaken his head as he thumbed a shag of tobacco into the bowl of the pipe. If he could remember, maybe she could tell him something – give him some idea of how the accident could have happened. Not that it was any of his business. But he would like to know all the same. Just for his own peace of mind. She had been a widow, he knew that much. Maybe she was still in mourning. He would look out for that when they were preparing to land.

And now, as that moment came at last, at the rear end of the main deck a young woman ventured into the daylight for the first time in forty-eight hours. She was heavily veiled and dressed in the widow's weeds that had been Caroline Cooper's hallmark for most of the voyage.

Carrie's eyes behind the veil narrowed against the bright morning light as she turned her face towards the majestic rocks of Port Jackson's south headland. Her heart was beating fit to burst. This was the moment she had believed would never come. The moment when, God willing, she would walk ashore a free woman.

She walked further up the deck towards the bow as more and more passengers emerged from their cabins to gain their first sight of their destination. Incredibly no one seemed to give her a second glance. All were far too taken up with what awaited them on shore. Voices became increasingly animated as fingers were pointed at each unfamiliar landmark and the colour was whipped into pale cheeks by the freshening breeze.

Whether it was from being forced to spend so much time below decks or not, Carrie could not be sure, but somehow the clarity of the light seemed so much better here than back in England. It was as if a celestial artist had been generous to a fault with the brightest colours of the palette. The wide southern sky above them was an endless brilliant blue, which was reflected in the deeper blue of the sea where white horses, with foaming manes, rode to shore on the keen breeze. Even the surrounding countryside was a lush vibrant green, which there was no doubt would come as a great surprise to many, who were expecting little short of a wasteland.

There were the masts of other ships visible in the harbour beyond the headland, and as they rounded the bluff and the ship plunged on through the waves heading into the calmer waters of the bay, Carrie was amazed to see quite a settlement along the foreshore. Rows of houses built of a glowing golden stone were interspersed with neat whitewashed cottages. Many had wooden-pillared verandahs, something she had never seen in London, with hedges and bushes marking off individual gardens as neat as anything that could be found back home.

A church spire or two was visible among the collection of houses and huts that were strung out along the banks of what she heard a sailor refer to as the Tank Stream, one of the several small rivers that emptied their waters into the many bays and inlets on this part of the coast. There was also a surprising number of quite impressive buildings around Sydney Cove, their fine-cut stone façades glowing golden in the early morning sunshine. Even a few windmills were to be seen.

Yes, Sydney was already quite a town, she thought to herself, and not at all the barren outpost she had expected. There was obviously a whole community well established here, and it was far from the glorified convict camp it was commonly believed to be.

But even amid the comforting familiarity of it all, as they

118

neared the harbour they could not miss the presence of the 'government men', for gangs of convicts were already visible at work around the landing stages, conspicuous in their white woollen Parramatta frocks and trousers, or occasionally in the older prison garb of yellow jackets with duck overalls, but all branded with the shaming sign of the broad black arrows that marked them out as felons.

Carrie's heart thudded as she looked at them, for that would have been her lot if fate had not intervened. Excitement tingled with apprehension in her veins. Soon she would be amongst them and all the others, the free settlers who made up the population of this place, simply referred to back home as Botany Bay.

But her most testing time was about to come.

The ship was drifting to a standstill now as the cry went up: 'Let go the anchor! . . . Let go the anchor, lads!'

The heavy chain scraped its way along the deck and clanked over the side of the ship and there was a mighty splash at the bow as the *Emma Harkness* came to rest at the Tank Stream side of the dock.

They were about a hundred yards or so from shore when a large rowing boat full of port officials set off from the landing stage and within minutes was alongside. The occupants, led by an elderly stout gentleman in a frockcoat and top hat, clambered aboard to inspect the ship's papers. The Colonial Secretary to His Excellency the Governor, Sir George Gipps, had come to receive the dispatches and inspect the vessel and its convict cargo. He was accompanied by two military officers in full dress uniform and two of his own clerks, and there was much saluting, presenting of arms and shaking of hands as the official party was welcomed on board by Captain Griffiths and his senior officers.

As the Captain and his crew went through the formalities, almost all the paying passengers were lined up along the rails, their eyes scanning the dockside for familiar faces amongst those who had come to welcome the ship.

There must be about two hundred people waiting there, Carrie reckoned, with a rapidly beating heart. And Silas Hebden was one of them.

She thought of Molly and the others still kept below decks. No convicts were to be allowed up on top until the paying passengers had disembarked. And although she longed for a sight of her old friend, she knew that this was just as well, for if anyone was to give her away it would be one of the women with whom she had been incarcerated for these past four months.

Occasionally she caught a glimpse of Dai Evans in the distance and she longed to rush over and give her old friend one last hug. But whilst she believed the Welshman would not give her away, she knew now was not the time to take such risks. Not now she had got this far.

The past two days and nights had been a nightmare. She had almost come to believe that she was somehow responsible for Caroline's death, just as they had tried to tell her she had been responsible for her father's. Trying on the other woman's clothes had been a dreadful experience. Carrie had become so used to the harsh material of prison garb that donning the fine lawn undergarments and the slate-grey dress that she was now wearing had seemed sinful. Luckily everything had been a reasonable fit. She found she had lost so much weight with the meagre convict rations that the frail Caroline's wardrobe could almost have been made to measure. Even the shoes were not the problem they could have been. Caroline had had slightly larger feet and this helped accommodate the awkward twist to her own lame left foot. The heavy booted shoes she had been forced to wear with her prison garb had made no allowances for this and had been a great trial. Perversely though, without the means of support she had been used to in the shoes her father had adapted for her, the withered muscles in her left leg and ankle seemed to have strengthened over the past few months and, with her feet firmly buttoned into Caroline's neat black boots, Carrie could almost believe she was not the partial cripple she had been for so long.

Even having her meals delivered was not the trial she had expected for she had made the excuse of being laid low with one of her headaches so she deliberately faced the wall of her bunk when the steward came in. It was as if the angels were on her side, she thought, as one by one the hours ticked past and they drew ever nearer their destination.

She had packed the cabin trunk with the sticker 'Mrs Caroline Cooper' plastered across it late last night, wondering exactly where and when she would open it again. It now stood on deck alongside all the others of the paying passengers, who fidgeted noisily as they waited for the order to disembark.

It took the best part of an hour for the official boarding party to take their leave, then the rowing boats were lowered for the first passengers to climb into. It was to be done alphabetically and Carrie was lucky enough to be told she would get into the second boat. She was just on the point of joining the small group waiting to be helped aboard when she felt a hand on her elbow.

'Excuse me, ma'am.'

She turned to find herself looking straight into the seamed face of Dai Evans.

She gasped behind her veil, but the sun was in the old sailor's eyes and he was not looking directly at her as he said, 'Begging your pardon, ma'am, but you wouldn't by any chance be the young lady Carrie Clayton was friendly with, would you?'

Carrie froze. 'I – I . . .'

'Dear God in heaven!' The old man's heart lurched into his mouth and the colour drained from his face as for the first time he peered through the veil. Was he seeing a ghost? He took a step back as if he was about to fall into a dead faint. 'Lord have mercy on us!'

Carrie grasped his arm to steady him. 'Please . . .' she

121

begged, keeping her voice as low as possible to avoid being heard by any of the disembarking crowd. 'Please, Dai . . . Please don't say anything!'

The old Welshman half staggered backwards to sit down on a nearby trunk waiting to be offloaded. Carrie joined him, her fingers clutching at the rough wool of his jersey. 'This must come as an awful shock to you . . .'

'Whew . . .' The old man nodded as he exhaled his breath noisily. 'Aye, you can say that again.'

'I . . . She . . .' Carrie fumbled for the right words to explain the inexplicable.

'Then it wasn't you in the water,' her friend said, interrupting her. 'It was yon other lass. The one you were friendly with.'

Carrie nodded dumbly as she released her grip of his arm and clasped her hands in agitation in her lap. She looked up pleadingly into his eyes. 'She was dead – Caroline was dead when I got to her cabin that night,' she said, urging him to believe her. 'She – she had taken laudanum – too much laudanum. She – she couldn't bear it, you see. The thought of the marriage to that man. She couldn't bear it.'

'But you can.'

Was it a statement or an accusation? Carrie's eyes searched his for the understanding she craved. 'It has to be a better option than a lifetime in prison, doesn't it? Doesn't it, Dai?'

The old Welshman took a deep wheezing breath as he slowly nodded his head in agreement. He too had heard of conditions in that prison factory on the headland yonder. 'Aye,' he said slowly. 'Aye, lass, it has to be better than that.'

'Lady – they're waiting to board!' A male voice from the next rowing boat to go called up to her.

Both she and Dai Evans stood up at the same time and looked at one another. 'It's not such a crime, is it?' Carrie pleaded softly. 'To want to live a life not caged up behind bars like some wild animal . . . It's not such a terrible thing, is it?'

The old sailor shook his head. Whatever the truth of what had happened in that young woman's cabin that night, it was over and done with, and he could not believe the young woman before him – the young woman he had come to know as well as his own daughter – had done anything to be ashamed of. 'Nay, Carrie *bach*,' he said wearily. 'It's not such a terrible thing.'

'Lady – *please*!'

Carrie glanced down at the young officer who was quite impatient by now, and raised a hand in acknowledgement, before turning back to the old seaman beside her. 'Thank you for that, Dai, old friend,' she said, blinking back the tears as she attempted a brave smile. 'Thank you so much for that.'

They embraced under the puzzled gaze of the officer and other passengers waiting to leave for the shore. The grey stubble of the old sailor's cheek felt rough to the soft skin of her own, and his jersey smelt of the sea and the rough tobacco of which he was so fond. She knew she would carry those smells with her forever.

'He a friend of yours, then?' the young officer remarked with a knowing smirk, as he helped her into the boat.

Carrie looked up at the young man as she manoeuvred her awkward left leg into position, then smoothed the skirts of her dress. 'Yes,' she answered. 'He's a friend of mine. The very best.'

She turned in her seat and watched the *Emma Harkness* diminish in size and importance as they headed for the shore. The others aboard the boat were chattering amongst themselves in their excitement. Most seemed to be government employees or their dependants, destined for no further than Sydney itself. Her admission that she was headed for the Hunter Valley brought raised eyebrows and a comment of, 'See you don't get eaten by them cannibals, then!'

123

'You wouldn't get me within a mile of those savages!' a stout woman with two young children put in. 'Not likely!'

Carrie was puzzled. 'What savages?' she asked, looking from one to the other.

A hoot of laughter went up. 'The darkies, that's what. Don't tell us you don't know about the darkies!'

Carrie made no reply as she stared fixedly towards the shore. Apparently there was a whole lot about her new home that she knew absolutely nothing about.

The landing stage itself was guarded by a dozen or so red-coated soldiers, or 'lobsters' as she heard them called, and behind them there was a milling crowd gathered on the quayside. The passengers from the rowing boat were helped ashore on to the landing stage, as the boat with their trunks pulled in behind it.

At least three-quarters of the people waiting were male and Carrie found herself deliberately avoiding their eyes as nerves knotted in her stomach. He must be here somewhere amongst this crowd. He might even be looking at her right now.

For the best part of twenty minutes she stood on the edge of the quayside, deliberately looking out in the direction of the *Emma Harkness* as more passengers were offloaded into the rowing boats. She knew if she looked round into the crowd behind her, which was now thinning out considerably, she would come face to face with her future.

Eventually, however, she had no choice. The convicts were beginning to disembark and she could not risk being recognized by one of them.

Taking her courage in both hands, Carrie turned and scanned the faces of the single men still standing around. One man stood out from the rest. He was standing by a two-horse waggon that was parked some twenty yards or so from the end of the quay. He had been standing there ever since she disembarked and was staring at her. It was him. It just had to be him. Her heart sank.

124

CHAPTER NINE

The man was tall and thin, with a long, bony face the colour of lightly tanned hide. His grey hair was sparse and barely covered the crown of his head as he stood quite still, with hat in hand, staring in her direction.

They were no more than a hundred feet apart and as their eyes met Carrie forced a tentative smile to her lips. The man paused, his bony fingers gripping the edges of his hat as he continued to stare, then he too attempted a smile. Slowly he began to walk towards her.

He paused more than an arm's length away, as if afraid to come too close. 'You wouldn't be Mrs Caroline Cooper, by any chance?' An Adam's apple bobbed in the scrawny, grey-stubbled throat as he spoke, and his voice was hoarse and still bore the distinctive north of England accent of his Yorkshire upbringing.

'Yes,' Carrie answered. 'I am. But please call me Carrie. You must be Mr Hebden.'

Silas Hebden's thin cheeks creased into a proper smile as he took a step forward. He had several teeth missing in the front and those that were left were tobacco-stained. 'Well, I'll be blowed!' She was much better looking than he had ever anticipated. And a lot younger into the bargain. He extended his hand with some relief. 'It's right glad I am to have you arrive safely.'

Carrie allowed her hand to be shaken. She had gone quite numb. This creature old enough to be her father was to be her husband.

'You – you had a good voyage?' He still had hold of her hand as if afraid to let go, in case she would bolt.

'No,' she replied truthfully as she extracted her fingers from his. 'It was a terrible voyage.'

Silas Hebden had the good grace to look sheepish as he

remembered his own experiences at sea. 'I reckon that was a daft thing to ask.' He looked down at his feet, then met her eyes shyly once more. 'I have a hotel booked for us in Parramatta.' He could have added that a night's board and lodging was somewhat cheaper there than in Sydney itself, but did not. His precarious financial position was not something he wished to go into yet awhile.

'Parramatta?' Hadn't she heard that strange-sounding foreign name before?

'Aye,' he said. 'It's a small settlement some fifteen miles to the north of here. I reckoned you'd prefer to spend a night in town in a decent hotel before making the journey up country.'

'That was very thoughtful of you.'

'Is that your luggage?' He indicated with his head towards her trunk sitting by the quayside.

She nodded and he called to one of the young dockside workers to load it on to the cart he had standing by. As he supervised the loading Carrie looked curiously at the gaunt, rather stooped figure. He had paid his bride-to-be the compliment of dressing up for the occasion in a well-worn black frockcoat and his trousers, above the dusty boots, were baggy at the knees. It was obviously a part of his wardrobe that had come out of mothballs specially for the occasion. But then, she doubted if there was much call for dressing up at all where he lived.

His farm was situated somewhere in the south of the Hunter Valley – wherever that was – and she had gathered from the few letters and other documents she had managed to read from amongst Caroline's belongings over the past couple of days that it ran to over one thousand acres, but most of it was uncultivated.

Silas Hebden dug deep into his pocket and handed the young man a coin, then he turned to his bride-to-be. 'You'll be ready for a bite to eat, I've no doubt.'

Food was the last thing on Carrie's mind, but she readily agreed with him. 'That would be lovely.'

'Right then, we'll make for the hotel. I've booked us into The Traveller's Rest Inn for the night and I've warned the landlord that we'd most likely be requiring something to eat once we got back.'

He still had his hat clasped in his hands as he indicated for Carrie to mount the waggon. 'We'd best be going, then.'

As so often happened when she was nervous, Carrie was aware of her limp becoming even more pronounced as she walked towards the waiting vehicle.

'You got some sort of a gammy leg there?' he asked as she reached the front of the waggon. 'Or is it just a touch of rheumatics from too long at sea?'

Carrie cringed inside. How she hated it even being referred to. 'I – I had polio as a child,' she said. 'But it doesn't really affect me now.'

'Hmm.' His hand felt rough and bony in hers as he helped her up on to the front board of the waggon, then climbed up to join her, his knee joints creaking as he eased himself on to the seat. No more was said about the leg, so there was no question of her being returned as damaged goods.

He had two fine-looking horses between the shafts and he cracked his whip lightly over their backs. 'On we go, my beauties!'

There was lots of activity around the harbour area and Carrie's eyes and ears could barely take in all there was to see and hear as the waggon started off over the rough road. After four months cooped up in the prison deck, all her senses seemed heightened. The air felt fresher, the sky more blue, the whole world around her more vibrant than she had ever known it.

'So this is Sydney . . .' And by the looks of it, Sydney was quite a town. It had already expanded way beyond its original toll fence boundary. A census the previous year had put the population at almost thirty thousand and more were arriving with every ship that docked. The past few years had seen the completion of the aqueduct from

Botany Swamps which had provided the town with a fresh water supply. Most impressive of all, the previous year on 24 May, the Queen's birthday, the Gas Light Company had supplied the town's main streets and stores with the very latest in illumination. For those religiously inclined, Sydney also boasted two bishops and two cathedrals. But if the godly were generously catered for, then so were those who could keep Bishop Polding of St Mary's Roman Catholic Cathedral inside the confessional for many a long day.

'You'll do well to keep your eyes and ears closed around here,' Silas Hebden warned Carrie, as they made their way through The Rocks – the motley collection of old and new buildings huddled around the foreshore – long notorious for its dens of vice. 'No place for a lady!' This haunt of sailors, criminals and prostitutes already had a name that had spread far beyond Sydney's town boundaries. 'But it has improved a lot on what it was when I first arrived here,' he went on. 'Then there were far more old lags and she-lags than was good for it . . .'

'Old lags and she-lags . . .' Carrie repeated.

'Aye – convicts to you and me. Felons of either sex. And no better than they ought to be.'

Carrie stiffened on the wooden seat. 'I take it you have little time for those unfortunate enough to be transported, then?'

'Unfortunate enough to be transported! Good God, woman – hanging would be too good for the majority! It's just as well this is the last year they'll be allowed to ship 'em in here. They're welcome to them out there on the west coast. Bloody disgrace it is, still dumping felons on us. Decent God-fearing folk don't want the likes of them in their midst.'

So now she knew exactly what Mr Silas Hebden's view of people just like herself was.

'Aye, round here there's as bad, if not worse, than any-thing you'd be liable to find around London's docks, I

128

wager . . . Not that a well-brought-up young lady like you would know about that,' he added quickly.

'Oh yes . . .' Carrie began, and was just about to point out she had been born and brought up within sight, sound, and – heaven help her – the smell of the Thames and its dockyards, when she remembered: she was no longer Carrie Clayton at all. 'I – I've certainly heard tell how rough it can be around there,' she corrected herself. 'And I'm sure it must be equally terrible for anyone who has to live around here.'

'Aye, well, it's not all like this,' Silas Hebden assured her. 'We've got our fine buildings too.' He waved a hand in the direction of some yellow sandstone buildings some hundred yards or so away. 'Aye, some grand public buildings and private houses too. And if you take a look over yonder you'll see great strides being made in the harbour itself. We'll have a town to be proud of before long.'

He was pointing past the gable-fronted bulk of Metcalfe's Bond Store, into which part of the cargo of the *Emma Harkness* was now being loaded, towards the mouth of the Tank Stream, where Carrie had come ashore, and where gangs of convicts were working on the sea wall of the new Circular Quay. Their ant-like figures were fetching and carrying great lumps of hewn rock to and fro, under the gaze of several gun-toting guards.

'They've dug that stuff out of what they call the Argyle Cut,' he informed her. 'They're aiming to join up Sydney Cove to Miller's Point and the Darling Harbour. It's going to be a great port, Sydney is. We've even got gas lighting now, you know.'

'Oh really?'

'Oh yes, indeed,' he assured her as they headed along Lower Fort Street. 'And you should see the Government House they're just finishing out there at Bennelong Point. As fine as anything back home, it'll be when it's done.' Then he gave one of his wheezy chuckles. 'They've even given Woolloomooloo Hill the la-di-da new name of

129

Darlinghurst 'cause so many of the nobs that have settled there didn't care for its native monicker.' He shot her a glance as he added proudly, 'And we've got plenty of your upper crust out here, you know. We're not all criminals; I don't want you to run away with that idea.'

Carrie made no reply.

But there was no doubt about it, Silas Hebden was proud of his new homeland, and wanted to convey the best impression of it to his new bride. Several other notable sights were pointed out, but after so many months at sea, and the trauma of the past few hours when she had lived in a cold sick fear of being found out, Carrie was in no mood to take it all in. Much more interesting was hearing his views on the transportees. She could not be too hard on him, for his strong feelings about the convict settlers must surely echo those of almost every free man and woman out here. But if she had ever imagined he might be sympathetic to her lot if he ever found out the truth, that hope was now well and truly dashed.

As if reading her thoughts, he said by way of his own defence, 'I never did hold with those settlers that take convicts as slave labour. Worked to death, some of them are. Seen it with my own eyes. About half the farms in the Valley have lags on them — aye, and she-lags too.'

Carrie had never come across the term 'she-lag' before and it jarred, sounding sub-human somehow. 'You mean the men and women who get transported out here can work on farms?'

The man beside her on the buckboard nodded. 'About half do, I reckon. Not that I have any on Yorvik, mind. Never have done and never will. I'd rather pay the pound a week to my shepherds and know my sheep are going to be looked after properly.'

'It's mainly sheep you farm?'

'Cross breed Spanish marinos, with some Afrikaner Fat-Tail blood in there for good measure.' He threw a gap-toothed grin in her direction. 'But you'd expect a

Yorkshireman to be into the wool trade, wouldn't you? Made our country great, wool did. Greatest county in England, Yorkshire, and New South Wales will be the same on t'other side of the world one day.'

Parramatta, the small township to the north of Sydney, was a lot bigger than Carrie anticipated, with a main street that was almost gracious in its proportions, and extended from the landing place on the Parramatta River to beyond the higher ground where Governor Hunter had first erected his official residence way back at the beginning of the century.

As the horses trotted the length of George Street, the main thoroughfare, Silas Hebden pointed out a substantial two-storey building of red brick called Euchre House, which he informed her was built by an ex-convict who got his freedom and 'did all right for himself'. 'You needn't be too alarmed at the thought of having so many folks like that around,' he told her, a trifle grudgingly. 'Some make decent citizens eventually.'

The Traveller's Rest Inn stood on the corner of O'Connell and Hunter Streets. Erected some ten years previously, the hotel was a simple single-storey building, with two tall white columns on either side of the front door. Silas Hebden brought his horses to a halt just around the corner of Hunter Street and jumped down awkwardly from the front board of the waggon. As she watched him Carrie got the distinct impression he was trying to appear much more fit and mobile than he actually was, and under any other circumstances her heart would have gone out to him, for he was trying his very best to make a good impression. As she sat there, however, she could feel nothing but a numbing indifference, and a growing horror at the thought that this was the man with whom she was expected to spend the rest of her life.

She thought of Mac, the redheaded young Scotsman so besotted by Molly aboard ship, and of the love felt by the real Caroline Cooper for her beloved David. Then she glanced back at the man now holding out his hand to help her down to the rough road beneath. He smiled up at her, showing his few stained teeth. Life was nothing if not unfair.

The landlord was a jovial Irishman by the name of McInally who greeted them warmly, his whiskery brows rising a good half inch at the sight of so young and attractive a woman on Silas Hebden's arm. 'Well now, it's a pleasure to make your acquaintance and I trust you had a good voyage, Mrs Hebden?'

Carrie's own brows rose at the assumption as to her marital status, but there was an immediate response from the man at her side before she had even time to think of a reply.

'Mrs Hebden had a fair crossing, thanks,' Silas Hebden assured their host. 'She's a mite tired now, though, as can be expected. I trust you have our room ready.'

'I do indeed!' The Irishman turned and picked a key with a label on it stating Room 5 from the board behind him, which he handed to his guest. 'I'll be here if there's anything else you require.' His gaze fell approvingly on Carrie once more. 'You're a fortunate man, if I may say so, Mr Hebden, sir.'

Silas Hebden beamed, his first genuine smile of the day. 'You may indeed, Mr McInally.' He presented his arm to Carrie once more and she took it, feeling for all the world like a prize exhibit lamb on the way to the slaughter.

Her stomach was churning, partly with lack of food and partly with nerves as a few minutes later the key was turned in the lock and the door to Room 5 swung open. Her husband-to-be stood back and allowed her to enter first.

She looked around her at the sparsely furnished room, with its rough oak hanging cupboard and matching chest of drawers with a cheval mirror on top. There was an old etching of the Thames, with St Paul's in the background, on the wall opposite the window, under which was a wash-stand with a ewer and basin. Then her eyes fell in dismay on the double bed in the middle of the floor. It was so high it had a pair of steps at the side to mount it and the bedposts were of iron with brass knobs on the ends. Behind the pillows there was suspended a canopy of faded pink brocade, which even at a distance Carrie could tell would feel and smell as dusty and mildewed as it looked. The bedspread was of a matching material.

'It's their second best room,' Silas Hebden's voice announced proudly from just behind her. 'Some visiting nob from England has the most expensive one, so I'm told. But we couldn't ask for more than this now, could we?' Then seeing the look on her face, he asked, 'Is there something wrong with it?'

Carrie made a helpless gesture with her hands. 'There – there's only one bed,' she blurted out, stating the obvious, and feeling both childish and stupid as she did so.

The colour rose in Silas Hebden's stubbled cheeks as he avoided her eyes and glanced towards the offending article. 'Aye, so there is.'

'But we're not married yet.'

Her husband-to-be followed her into the room and poked a finger into the neck of his shirt to gain more air as he felt his body come out in a sweat beneath his best clothes. 'I – I see you're one to stand on ceremony then,' he said in obvious discomfort. He was clearly put out and more than a bit embarrassed by her assertion.

Carrie walked to the window so they were now facing each other across the bed. 'It – it's a bit sudden, that's all. I somehow thought we'd be waiting a few days, perhaps . . . You know, to get to know each other better.'

Silas Hebden's shaggy brows furrowed. 'Get to know each other better,' he repeated with a frown on his face. 'You've got the wrong end of the stick, lass. Hast thou forgotten – thou's come out here at my expense to marry me.'

'Oh yes,' Carrie agreed hastily. 'I know that . . . It's just . . .' Her eyes glanced back apprehensively at the bed.

'You're not telling me you're a'feared o' that?' he asked incredulously. 'Why, you having already been a married woman and all!'

Carrie gave a start. A married woman. Of course, he was right. Caroline had been a widow. And she herself had never as much as been kissed by a man in passion before, let alone . . .

Silas Hebden moved awkwardly around to her side of the bed and, placing his hat on the brocade coverlet, his bony hands grasped her shoulders. He was a good head and shoulders taller than her so her eyes were level with his Adam's apple as he said testily, 'You have not come all the way out here under false colours, have you, lass? You're not one of those women who can't or won't do their duty by a man?'

He was right to have his doubts, he thought. After all, she had been married before but had produced no offspring from the union. Surely he had not paid out that hard-earned cash to bring a frigid or barren creature all the way out here?

The only reason he had advertised in the first place was because it was nigh on six years since the woman he had really wanted had perished along with one hundred and twenty-two others on the migrant ship *Lady McNaughton*. Charlotte Pearson had been a second cousin on his mother's side; a sensible Halifax lass, who would have made a grand wife and mother, and whose death on the voyage out had been a bitter blow in more ways than one. He had never been back to England since settling here almost two decades ago and there was little chance of finding a suitable wife amongst the she-lag rabble that made up the majority of the female population.

So, abhorrent though it had seemed at the beginning when it was first suggested to him, advertising in the

London *Times* had been about the only way to ensure he would be able to sire a son before it was too late – an heir for Yorvik; someone of his own flesh and blood to inherit and reap the benefit of all his years of hard work. And he had wanted a decent woman. It would have been easy enough to visit the prison factory at Parramatta and choose a bride; hundreds of men did. Lined them up like coconuts on a shy for the settlers to take their pick, they did, or so he had heard tell. The woman got her freedom and the man got his bride. But not for him the dregs of society. He had wanted a decent woman to be Mistress of Yorvik and mother of his son. And, to be fair to her, this one was a darned sight younger and better looking than he had imagined. But while that was all to the good, was she a normal healthy woman in her desires? That was the question.

His whiskery brows knotted as he looked her straight in the eye. He was never one for beating about the bush. 'You're not telling me I've bought a pig in a poke, lass, are you?'

'Oh no,' Carrie assured him. 'I'm no pig in a poke, Mr Hebden.'

The thin lips broke into a smile and the few teeth that remained were stained with years of chewing tobacco and decay. His breath had a peculiar stale fish smell to it and it was all she could do to keep herself from turning her face away in disgust as he said with evident relief, 'Well, thank the good Lord for that! You had me worried there for a minute.'

He relaxed his grip on her shoulders and said in a quiet voice, 'What would you say to you removing that hat and letting me have a good look at you?'

Obediently, Carrie removed the two hat pins that kept the bonnet in place, and raised the black net veil to look up into his approving eyes as she took off the hat and placed it on the bed beside his own.

'That's better!' There was undisguised admiration in his

135

eyes as he gazed down at her. Then one bony hand reached out to touch her hair. 'What's happened to thy hair, lass?' he asked. 'It's not very long, is it?'

After the cropping in Newgate, it now barely reached below her ears. Carrie raised an embarrassed hand to the bare back of her neck. 'I – I'm afraid I had it chopped off in the Tropics,' she lied, mentally congratulating herself on her quick thinking. 'I – I wasn't at all well during that part of the voyage and the ship's surgeon thought it might conserve my strength.'

Silas Hebden nodded in understanding. 'Aye, I've heard tell of that happening,' he agreed. 'A pity though, I'll say that. And you'll not be letting another pair of shears near it as Mrs Hebden, I can promise you. A woman's best feature, her hair can be.' His eyes moved approvingly down over her body. 'Not that you don't cut a fine enough figure as it is, I'll say that for you . . . A bit more beef here and there maybe . . .'

As he spoke, his right hand reached out and clumsily covered her right breast, squeezing it painfully between his fingers. Carrie let out a squeal and backed off as if stung. His face flushed once more. 'What's the matter with you?' he demanded in some embarrassment, withdrawing his hand. 'You're just done with telling me you're no pig in a poke.'

She was standing now with her back pressed hard against the mattress of the bed and could feel the panic rising as he stood over her. There was real irritation mixed with the embarrassment in his eyes as they bore down on her. 'We'll be married within the week, any road. Don't you trust me to marry you, is that it? Do you think I've paid for you to come all the way out here just to have my way with you and dump you – throw you in t'midden?'

Carrie shook her head miserably. 'No . . . no . . .' she whispered. 'That's not what I think at all.'

'Then let's be having you, lass,' he said, his breathing

becoming noisier. 'We've an hour to put in till we eat around here. What better way could we spend it than in getting to know one another?'

CHAPTER TEN

Carrie awoke to a rain-washed window and a wind that rattled the panes and caused the flimsy net curtain to shiver in the draught. There was an empty space in the bed next to her, but the feather pillow was still indented with the shape of its missing occupant's head.

She sat up stiffly between the sheets and glanced down at the few straggly grey hairs that remained stuck to the cotton pillowcase. The sight of them made her shiver.

The bedclothes were half turned back at his side, where he had got out of bed, and the bottom sheet was wrinkled. A tiny black spot moved slightly, then leapt from the cotton to disappear on the pattern of the pink brocade top cover. The place was alive with fleas and she had hardly an inch of skin that had not been bitten into raised red bumps.

Another leapt into view, on the pillow this time, and she pounced on it, squeezing its brittle black body between her thumb and forefinger. She could feel its shell crack and eyed with distaste the spots of blood that appeared on her fingertips. Was it her own or his, she wondered? She would never know.

She wrinkled her nose as she flung back the covers to air the bed. She could even smell him, although he was no longer here, for that stale, fetid odour that permeated his clothes still lingered in the fabric of the sheets and in the very air she breathed. The taste and touch of him seemed to contaminate her every pore. The memory of last night still burned in her mind. His skin had felt ice-cold and rough to the touch, then as his excitement and frustration grew, he had come out in a sweat, a chill, cloying sweat that had turned the mat of grey hairs on his chest into a dark carpet and had brought beads of perspiration to the longer, bushier hairs of his moustache.

But at least Carrie had been spared the ordeal of waking up beside him. He must have gone down early for breakfast, she thought with relief, as she tried in vain to blank out the memory of last night from her mind. She closed her eyes and buried her face in her hands as if physically to blot out the scene now replaying so vividly in her head.

That first sight of Silas standing there at the foot of the bed would have been comical under any other circumstances. He had left his socks on as well as his woollen combinations and had apologized for not having a nightgown with him. 'Never had any need for one before now,' he had said, as he stood there smiling that half-shy, half-leering smile at her. 'These here underthings have seen better days. I could take them off if you prefer it.'

'Oh no – really!' She had barely known what to say or where to look as he climbed up on to the mattress and said with a wheezy laugh, 'I reckon you'll be quite happy to take me as you find me, won't you, lass? It'll have been too long since you last enjoyed a man after supper to care what kind of wrapping he comes in.'

He had made it sound as if he were some rare delicacy to be enjoyed with relish. But it had been the worst kind of nightmare as his scrawny body, still wrapped in his discoloured woollen underclothes, had descended on hers.

With no real best friend as she was growing up to explain exactly what happened between man and wife, she had only the coarse remarks of the other female convicts to rely on, and somehow she could never bring herself to believe the awful things they said. She had thought it was only their foul mouths giving voice to their even dirtier minds. Until that evening.

It was hard to decide what had been worse, his mouth with its bad breath and decaying teeth on hers, his pawing at her flesh with those cold bony hands of his, or that other unthinkable thing he had tried to do below the waist. Whatever it was exactly, she had found it both disgusting and extremely painful and she could only thank God that he had given up after a few minutes and got out of bed cursing under his breath.

She had lain there, too stunned and mortified to move or to speak. She did not even dare to do up the neck of her nightgown for fear any movement might bring him back into bed beside her. How long she lay there she could not tell, for she had fallen asleep as he sat smoking his pipe in the chair by the window, and finishing off a half bottle of whisky he had begun during their meal earlier that evening. She had not expected to sleep, but must have gone out like a light and had slept soundly throughout the rest of the night, until now.

She pulled herself up further on the bed and sat looking around her. There was no clock in the room and she did not possess a pocket watch so it was impossible to even make a guess at the time. The sound of cartwheels splashing through the puddles, the clatter of horses' hooves, and the occasional shout from the street outside told her that the people of Parramatta were already up and about their business, so perhaps she had better make an effort herself.

By the look of it, her companion had not even washed for the ewer on the stand was still three-quarters full of water and the earthenware basin beside it had never been used. If she hurried she might even manage to wash all contact with him from her body before he returned.

She pulled the lawn nightgown over her head and tossed it on to the dishevelled bed before pouring about two pints of the water into the basin. But she was only halfway through her ablutions when she heard feet outside the door and the handle turn. Grabbing the towel she held it to her naked body as she half-turned to see Silas Hebden enter the room.

'You're up then,' he said.

'Yes, I'm up.'

He looked tired and even older than she remembered as he closed the door behind him and sat himself down with a sigh on a chair by the door. 'Don't let me hold you up,' he said.

Carrie felt herself flushing in embarrassment as she clutched the towel to her breast. The bottom of it barely reached the tops of her thighs and she was acutely aware of how exposed her lame left leg was to his gaze. Since childhood she had kept its puny shape hidden from others' eyes and she bitterly resented this type of invasion of her privacy that she knew was now going to be her lot. She deliberately turned so that her strong limb was nearest him. 'I – I'd just finished,' she lied, unable to bear the thought of him watching her perform such private functions, and stark naked into the bargain. 'I was just going to get dressed.'

'Don't let me stop you.' His eyes never wavered from her body and as he looked Silas could feel himself getting hot under the collar as she sat down on the bed, with her back half-turned to him, and reached across for her chemise. He had never seen a woman naked before. His only sexual contacts had been hurried, paid-for affairs in his youth, with women of ill-repute as his father would have called them; one or two back in York and a couple in Port Jackson. But that had been years ago and there had been no question of removing non-essential clothes. Now, to be this close to that expanse of white, naked flesh was almost too much for him. He could see the indentations of her spine as she bent over to pull on a stocking and he longed to reach over and run his hand down that curve of soft flesh. For a moment or two his eyes rested on the withered limb. The sight of it took him aback at first, but it did not unduly bother him. Even the fairest of flowers had some flaw, he told himself. True perfection existed nowhere but in the eye of the beholder.

Silas felt both irritated and frustrated. He had expected Carrie still to be asleep and had intended getting back into bed himself in the hope of completing last night's unfinished business.

He got out his handkerchief and dabbed at his brow. Was it hot in here or just nerves getting the better of him, he wondered? If he were half a man he knew he should ignore the fact she was getting dressed and get up and have his way with her now. After all that's what he had brought her halfway across the world for. But last night's fiasco was still too painfully etched on his memory to make any rash move now. He could still not be sure exactly what had gone wrong last night. Maybe it was those whiskies at dinner. Maybe it had just been too long since he had attempted such a thing. He sighed once more. Maybe it was any number of things . . .

'The old equipment gets rusty if you leave it too long, Silas man,' Geordie Appleby, who ran a neighbouring sheep station, had once warned him. 'You got to keep in practice to play the sweetest tunes.' The ex-Sunderland carpenter was a dab hand at taking his pick of the she-lags all right. He must have gone through at least a dozen or so in his time, wife or no wife.

Silas Hebden shook his head at the memory of his friend's warning. How old Geordie would have laughed to witness that pathetic performance last night.

Not that it was all his fault, mind. Lain there like a lump of lard, she had. Then she had started to bubble like a babby when he had tried to perform. 'You're hurting me!' she had cried. 'Please, Mr Hebden, you're hurting me!'

'I'll give you Mr Hebden!' he muttered under his breath. It was her bloody husband he was about to become.

'Beg your pardon? Did you say something?' Carrie looked up from fastening the ribbon at the neck of her chemise and turned towards him with a quizzical expression.

'Nothing . . . It were nothing.' His eyes remained fixed on her as, shrugging her shoulders, she turned her back and methodically went about her business. She had not made it easy for him. The damned thing was, he could almost swear she was still a virgin from the way she carried on, and not a widow at all. Maybe he *had* bought himself a pig in a poke. She was certainly going the right way about convincing him of that. If his damned equipment hadn't let him down so badly, he would know by now.

Silas scratched the stubble of his chin as he pondered what might have been, just a few short hours ago. If she was still a virgin and determined to remain that way and if, despite all his best efforts, he found he still couldn't do the business, a fine bloody mess that would leave him in, wouldn't it?

'I want a son, lass, you realize that, don't you?' he said, almost angrily, speaking his thoughts aloud. 'I want a son more than I want anything on this earth.'

Carrie glanced up in surprise from adjusting her garter. She turned to look at him, and his face had a fixed, desperate look to it as his eyes burned into hers.

'You do understand what I'm saying, don't you? I didn't pay all that money to bring you out here for the good of your health. I need a son. For Yorvik.'

She looked down at her stocking once more and smoothed out the wrinkle over the knee. There was something about the desperation in his face and voice that chilled her. She was a vessel here to be used, of no more value than one of his beloved ewes who had to produce offspring for the good of that farm he kept on about. Then her lips twitched into a mirthless ghost of a smile. In truth, he was using her just as much as she was using him. Perhaps they deserved each other, she thought bitterly. 'I understand, Mr Hebden,' she said quietly. 'And I will give you your son, I promise you that.'

'Eh — lass!' Relief spread across his thin face as he got up from the chair and strode across to the bed. His hands clutched at the bare flesh of her upper arms as he raised her to her feet and clasped her to him in an awkward embrace. 'Eh, lass, it does my heart good to hear that!'

Carrie's nostrils pressed against the coarse woolcloth of his frockcoat and inhaled the odour that had now become more familiar and more repugnant to her than any other.

'Say that again, will you?' he begged. 'Say that again.'

'I'll give you a son, Mr Hebden,' she whispered. 'I'll give you your son.' And tears stung her eyes beneath the closed lids as the man who was soon to be her husband let out a long, satisfied sigh and pressed her to him even more tightly than before.

The journey along the Great North Road from Parramatta to the Yorvik sheep station at the southern end of the Hunter Valley was just less than one hundred miles, along a main highway that was little more than a rough track in places, and seemed to peter out altogether at times. But what Carrie saw from the buckboard of the waggon filled her with astonishment. For a young woman born and bred in the grey world of the London docks, it was little short of paradise. Never had she seen such a wealth of variety and colour, in either the countryside or the wildlife. Small birds with funny names like kookaburras peered down at them from the branches of the tall red gum trees, and grey, bright-eyed possums chittered from the foliage above their heads as they passed. On the ground small white-pawed mice with uncommonly long legs hopped out of their way as the waggon trundled on along the dusty road, whilst in the air birds of all sizes and different hues kept her enraptured for the best part of the two days it took them to reach their destination. Those little blue budgies were truly adorable, and actually to witness brightly plumed parrots flying free in the treetops, and not the pathetic caged specimens with plucked feathers she had known in the past, was something to behold.

'Aye, they make a fine sight all right,' her companion agreed when she commented on the fact. 'But don't speak too badly of them in cages, for I've one at home myself. Barney, his name is.'

Carrie's interest quickened. 'Does he speak?'

The man beside her chuckled. 'Oh aye. Swears like a

trooper, he does. I reckon I'll have to get him to mind his language now there's to be a lady about the place!'

They made an overnight stop at a farm belonging to a Scotsman by the name of Angus Cameron, whom Silas had known for the best part of two decades.

Angus was a goodlooking man in middle age, with gun-metal grey hair that had turned silver at the temples, and a bushy salt-and-pepper moustache. Amiable, but politically ambitious, he prided himself on being on first-name terms with most of the people who mattered in the running of the colony. When Governor Darling had paid a state visit to the Hunter Valley in 1830, he too had stayed overnight at Cameron Creek.

The current Governor, His Excellency Sir George Gipps, was also regarded as a friend. George, as Angus referred to him, was a Kentish man of the same vintage as the Scotsman who had been having quite a troublesome time of it recently. The colonists of New South Wales were not at all satisfied with the way the land was being governed, and particularly the way it was being divided up. Angus was now in the throes of trying to set up a Legislative Council in the colony, comprising of twelve members nominated by the Governor and twenty-four elected by owners of freehold landed property to the value of two hundred pounds.

'Angus is confident he'll become a Representative on either of those two counts,' Silas informed Carrie just before their arrival on the sheep station. 'In fact, I'd go as far as to say he's already got his visiting cards with Representative Cameron made out!'

Then he had given a sly grin. 'Of course if you're fortu-nate enough to speak the Queen's English with a Scotch accent you'll go far in this place, and with Angus being a distant cousin of Lachlan Macquarie, he's almost royalty!' Having already heard awesome tales aboard ship of the legendary Governor Lachlan Macquarie, now being hailed as the colony's founding father, Carrie little doubted it.

Cameron Creek, it transpired, was almost twice as big as Yorvik, running to just under two thousand acres. From what she could see from the buckboard of the waggon as they drove up the last half mile to the house, Carrie thought the land looked well fenced and cared for. There was a newly planted avenue of cedars leading up to the homestead itself, which was on a grand scale, with Palladian columns on either side of the front door and a verandah running the whole length of the front of the house, with a balcony above.

She remarked on the favourable impression she was forming and Silas informed her that although Angus was prospering now, it had not always been so. He had landed at Port Jackson with very little in his pockets and the station had been bought on the principle of 'Thirds', which Carrie now learned was a practice common to many of the first settlers in the area. It meant the land was purchased with money loaned from a Sydney businessman who thereafter would take one third of the profits.

Although things were bad now, with two pounds of wool selling at only one shilling, Angus Cameron had done well enough before the current slump to buy out his sleeping partner, but the Capitalist was having none of it. 'The shark will see me into the grave before he'll let me get title to all my land,' he complained to his guests over a meal of lamb cutlets, potatoes and cabbage, taken in the beautifully furnished dining room of his six-roomed house. 'You're a lucky man, Silas, to have no other greedy beggar's finger in your pie.'

Silas Hebden nodded in agreement as he quaffed his second glass of port. 'I'll drink to that, Gus. No son of mine's going to be saddled with a burden like that to bear when I pass on. What I work for's my own and nobody else's.'

At the mention of a son, both men had glanced at Carrie, who sat alone at the centre of the table, with the men at either end. She could feel herself blushing as their host raised his glass in appreciation at what his eyes were beholding. 'I'll say this for you, Silas, you old scoundrel, you've picked a fine one here. Why, I've half a mind to place one of those advertisements myself!'

At that, the middle-aged maid who had been standing silently at the back of the room, waiting to serve the next course, turned and fled, slamming the door behind her.

'Looks like you said the wrong thing there, Gus old boy,' Silas Hebden said to his friend. 'Touchy beings, women are.'

The incident puzzled Carrie and later the following day as they sat together on top of the waggon, her thoughts returned to it. 'I didn't know quite what to make of it. I thought she was his wife at first,' she confessed. 'When we first arrived, that is. They seemed so well-suited somehow.' Both had been in middle age and were handsome, healthy-looking individuals. The Irish woman, Mary Ellen, in particular was just how Carrie had expected a settler's wife would be, with a suntanned, clear complexion, a broad bosom, strong forearms and capable hands that had been warm in their welcome as they had shaken her own. The fact that she had served the meals, but not joined them at the table, had been curious indeed.

'Aye, well, that would be the natural conclusion to draw,' Silas agreed. 'But it would not be the right one. Mary Ellen will never be Mrs Cameron. She's a she-lag, you see, lass. Even though they've been together for well nigh ten years now.'

There was that expression again! Carrie grimaced as she threw a glance at the man beside her. 'That does not exclude her from the human race, you know,' she said, finding it hard to keep the anger from her voice.

'Maybe so, maybe so . . .' There was no conviction in his reply.

'But Angus – Mr Cameron – won't marry Mary Ellen.'

'Mary Ellen's a "lifer",' her companion replied, a trifle wearily. 'And an Irish one at that. Angus has got political ambitions, like I told you. The two don't mix. He could never introduce her into Sydney society as his wife.' He gave a throaty chuckle at the very idea. 'Imagine her – a bog-trottin' Croppie lifer – being introduced to Sir George and the other dignitaries at some fancy do at the official residence in Sydney. Why, the Governor would have a fit!'

'It seems to me we English look down on two distinct breeds of our fellow human beings out here,' Carrie said. 'The convicts and the Irish.'

'And not necessarily in that order!' her companion agreed with a wheezy chortle. 'And you've missed one out.'

'Oh?'

'The darkies. Although there's some as would take issue at calling them human beings. Shoot 'em like dogs, some of the new station hands do, when they think they can get away with it.'

Carrie turned to look at him in horror. He must mean the cannibals she had heard of on the ship coming over. Shoot them like dogs! 'But that's terrible. Do you have any of them on Yorvik?'

The man beside her smiled. 'Happen you'd do well to wait and see,' he said with an enigmatic smile. 'We're on Yorvik land already, so we're almost home.'

They had left the Great North Road some time ago, and the land was greener and more domesticated now, with forests of tall red cedars in the distance and clumps of dense brushwood that in patches had had swathes cut through it for the road.

As they rounded a curve in the track, a creature leapt out from behind a tree, sending Carrie into mild hysterics. Her scream brought the waggon shuddering to a halt and she found herself clinging on to the arm of the man beside her as several more of the same species, in varying sizes, leapt into view.

'What on earth are they?' she gasped, almost rigid with

148

fright, as the waggon was surrounded by a herd of nervous coughing and snickering beasts so peculiar in shape that she would have died laughing had she not been so terrified. She had never seen anything like them in her entire life.

Silas Hebden grinned and patted her arm. 'They're only roos,' he said. 'They won't do you any harm.'

'Roos?' Carrie repeated. 'What on earth are roos?' Her eyes darted anxiously from one to another as they jostled around the stationary waggon. Up on their hind legs, they seemed taller than most men, as they dangled their funny little arms and eyed the waggon and its two occupants warily.

'Kangaroos,' her companion said. 'They're native to here, just like the darkies. And neither'll do you any harm if you don't go interfering with them. Tell you the truth, I'm surprised we haven't seen more of them on the way over here. A real plague they can be at times.'

He stood up in the waggon and raised his whip in his right hand then cracked it in the direction of the largest of the beasts, a giant creature it seemed to Carrie, reddish brown in colour, and looking straight at her. 'This'll be the old man wallaroo,' Silas informed her. 'He'll be the boss. If I get rid of the beggar, the others will follow suit . . .' The whip cracked once more. 'Away with you! Shoo!'

The animal in question let out a roar that had Carrie rooted to her seat in sheer terror as, flailing its short arms in a pugilistic fashion, it bounded even closer, making quite alarming warning noises in its throat.

Carrie pressed herself against the back plank of the buckboard and half stood up, as if getting ready to leap into the rear of the waggon. 'Do something – please!' she shrieked.

The whip cracked again and caught the animal's chest. 'Off with you . . . *shoo!*' Silas Hebden roared at the creature and lashed out with the whip again.

Carrie covered her face with her hands, as, with a last look in her direction and a bad-tempered thump of its tail and hind feet, the animal turned and bounded off, disappearing into the scrub at the side of the road. For a second or two the others remained, still snickering and gazing curiously with their black button eyes at the waggon and its occupants. Then with a dozen dust-raising thumps of their heavy tails they too were bounding off after their departed leader.

'Thank God for that!' Carrie gasped, peering through her fingers in the direction of the dust-cloud that had just been raised. 'Let's get out of here, please!'

Silas Hebden had a broad smile on his face as he rattled the reins and flicked his whip over the horses' backs. Handled that nicely, he had, he thought to himself. Saved the damsel in a time of distress. Not that they would have harmed her any, he was pretty sure of that. But this was not the time to enlighten her of that fact.

Carrie breathed a sigh of relief and made herself comfortable once more as the waggon got underway. For a city girl like herself who was a virtual stranger to countryside of any description, this journey had been one incredible spectacle after another. She felt no embarrassment at her fright at the sight of those roos. Back home she had grown up not even setting eyes on a cow until she was quite a young woman. A day trip to Kent had opened her eyes to a whole new world. But out here . . .

She sank back against the wooden plank that served as a backboard and let out a sigh . . . Well, this was something else entirely.

CHAPTER ELEVEN

Home turned out to be a single-storey, whitewashed wooden house, with a verandah running half the length of the front of it. It stood in a clearing surrounded by eucalyptus trees, with several other much smaller, rougher-looking wooden huts at about a hundred yards' distance. For late June, the middle of the winter out here, it was a fine evening and the scene they were now looking upon was far better than Carrie knew she had any right to expect. Perhaps it was the comment Caroline had made about those Viking settlements that had put her off. But this was nothing out of the Dark Ages. This was quite nice. Quite nice indeed.

'Like it?' Silas Hebden asked, as he helped her down from the waggon at a little after six in the evening.

They stood side by side and looked across at the building, its white painted walls gleaming in the early evening sun, and Carrie found herself smiling. No, it was not at all bad, she thought to herself. And a far cry from the prison factory at Parramatta, she had no doubt. 'It's nice,' she said. 'Really very nice.'

Her companion grunted his appreciation of the comment, then added, 'Of course it needs a woman's touch, I'll not deny that. Unlike some, I've never had a she-lag around the place. I just make do the best I can with the help that's available.'

Carrie smiled a secret smile to herself as she began to walk towards her new home. If only he knew . . .

The house contained four rooms: two at the front and two at the back and a middle passage that ran all the way from the front to the back door. 'This here's the parlour, you may say,' Silas informed her as they entered the front room on the left. 'It's where we will do our entertaining and such like.'

The remark seemed rather odd with hardly a neighbour within a day's journey, but she let it pass and cast her eyes round the room. It contained a cast-iron stove, with two armchairs on either side, two more chairs in front of it; a large Jacobean oak cupboard, a day bed upholstered in a blue striped material beneath the window, and, rather incongruously, a baby grand piano. He saw her eyeing the instrument with some surprise and explained, 'I bought it at a house sale in Sydney. Shipped over from England it had been, but the owner died and his possessions were put under the hammer. Scarce things pianos out here, you know.'

'I don't doubt it.'

'Aye. In the time of Governor Macquarie, just before I arrived out here, there were only five in the whole colony, and the best belonged to Mrs Macquarie. When she left it was sold, resold, then exchanged for a piece of land that made £200,000!' He gave a low whistle and shook his head. 'Those days are gone, I'm afraid. So there's little chance of my ever persuading old Geordie Appleby or the likes to exchange even a bit of their scrub for this old thing. Not that I'd want to, mind. Quite fond of it, I am. Do you play?'

Carrie shook her head. 'No, I'm sorry to say I don't. Do you?'

To her surprise he did. 'Mother sent us all to lessons when we were young. To a Mr Bennett in York. Lived in a little house just off the Shambles and used to whack us across the knuckles with his ruler if we got a note wrong.' He glanced down at the back of his right hand. 'I still can feel the sting of that damned thing if I make a mistake to this day.'

Carrie walked over and drew a hand tenderly across the polished walnut lid. Her fingertips made twin tracks in the dust. 'Our son will play,' she said.

Silas Hebden beamed. He could ask for nothing more.

The remaining rooms were a back kitchen-cum-living room, which she recognized immediately as the place where she would spend most of her time, and two bedrooms on the other side of the centre passage. The back one was theirs and the front one awaited the son of whose arrival his father was now sure.

As they stood in the room patiently awaiting the heir to Yorvik, still bare save for a chest of drawers, a wicker chair, and a mildewed etching of York Minster on one wall, Silas Hebden's grey eyes took on a misty look reserved for such thoughts, and he said, 'I'll call him Henry after my father.'

Carrie, who was standing at the window gazing out, turned and looked startled for a moment, then shook her head and, in a voice so firm that she quite surprised herself, she said, 'Oh no you won't. He shall be called William — Billy — after my brother.'

The man who was soon to be her husband looked across askance at having his wish thwarted, but there was something about the set of her features that made him let the matter rest for the moment. 'Aye, well that's a bridge we can cross when we come to it,' he said soothingly. Then he chuckled as he rubbed the day's growth of white stubble on his chin. 'And the sooner the better, eh, lass?'

As he turned to leave the room, he did not see the shudder that ran through Carrie's slight frame.

He had had no chance to repeat the Parramatta performance last night at Cameron Creek, for, true to his Presbyterian morals as far as others were concerned, the Scotsman had put them in separate rooms. But Carrie had no illusions that she would not be so lucky a second night and the thought was not a happy one.

She was left alone as Silas changed from his best clothes into old and set out to check that nothing had gone amiss with the place in the four days since he had left. She watched with relief from the verandah as his tall, stooped frame disappeared around the side of the house. It would give her a chance to have a wash and brush up, collect her thoughts, and have a better look around the house. And on the whole, up to now, she liked what she saw. There was not a great deal of furniture, but what there was was good; the only thing the place lacked was a woman's touch in the soft furnishings and small items of decoration that made a house into a home. Perhaps before long she might get a trip into Sydney to make some purchases from some of the many stores they had passed on their way through the town.

It was already dark when Silas returned and Carrie was standing on the verandah enjoying the night breeze.

'I'll give my face and hands a wipe and join you in a cup of tea in ten minutes,' he said.

Carrie looked up at the night sky, where the stars were all upside down. It took some getting used to, having the sky as well as the seasons back to front. But there was something about this land that breathed freedom – that called you out to glory in its wide open spaces. Even in the moonlight it possessed a magic all of its own. 'I'll just have a breath of fresh air,' she called out, 'then I'll join you inside.'

The air was fresh and clean and pure delight to lungs used to long months of the stale, foul atmosphere of the ship and before that of Newgate itself. She found herself taking long deep breaths as she walked across the cleared land in front of the house and gazed up into the night sky. 'Free at last!' she sang out as, spreading her arms, she did as graceful a pirouette as her left leg would allow.

No matter how old and ugly Silas Hebden might be, she must never forget he was her saviour, she told herself. If it was not for him she would now be in that terrible place they called the prison factory at Parramatta, where the other women were headed.

She thought of Molly and wondered if her dream had come true and her young Scotsman had succeeded in helping her escape. Carrie doubted it. So many young women must have been made just such promises on similar voyages. And so many must have been disappointed. Her heart went out to her spirited Irish friend, for she had not deserved such a fate, any more than poor Billy and countless others had deserved theirs.

But I must not get morbid and depressed, Carrie admonished herself as she walked in a wide sweeping circle around the house. Not tonight of all nights, the first night of real freedom. The first night she had felt really safe.

She glanced back at the house and could see the lamp burning through the kitchen window, and the parrot called Barney in its cage. The whole scene looked so peaceful. After long, storm-tossed months at sea, she had come in to port at last.

Then she stopped and bent her ear to the wind. What was that sound? At first she thought it was the mewing of a kitten in the distance, but as she began slowly to walk on in its direction she realized it sounded like singing. Strange, haunting singing that was coming from somewhere behind that copse of trees just ahead of her.

Taking her courage in both hands, she made for the sound, taking care to avoid the clumps of prickly spinifex grass that seemed to infest the sandy soil. Like a wraith in the moonlight, she slid silently into the trees and walked through their dark foliage to emerge in the shadows at the other side, to a sight that made the hairs on the back of her neck stand proud and gooseflesh cover the skin of her arms. She drew in her breath sharply and hardly dared breathe as her eyes grew wide with wonder.

And all the while the singing went on: '*Mana-manaa, mana-manaa, Manin-yaa, manin-yaa, Ngala-barrai, ngala-barrai, ngala-barrai . . .*'

The strange, spine-tingling song rose into the night sky as, huddled round a brightly burning campfire, the squatting figures swayed in unison. Brown bodies of all ages, shapes and sizes, their eyes and teeth flashing white in the firelight, raised their voices in unison in a plaintive chant.

155

Carrie had seen nothing like them, not even in books. Were these the cannibals she had heard so much about? Somehow they held no fear for her as she stood transfixed and listened.

Under the wide, black velvet canopy of the night sky, with the moon riding high in a silver splendour matched only by the twinkling stars, she gazed in wonder at the sight before her. What were they singing about? Lost loves, perhaps, as young and old did when gathered round the piano in the parlour of an English home? Or were they offering a hymn of praise to their gods? It was a strange, mystical sound that the breeze carried to her, sung in a perfect unison that told of thousands of such evenings going back to time immemorial.

Suddenly one of the group got up: a young man with wild hair, whose lithe brown body was ochre-daubed in shades of red, white and gold. He was joined by two other young men and then two young women. They were totally at one with their nakedness and moved with a fluid easy grace as they danced in the flickering firelight, while the singing grew louder and more rhythmic. Over and over they sang the same strange words, words that were as foreign to Carrie's ears as these sights were to her eyes. She stood quite still in the shadows, beneath the sheltering branches of the tree, and listened and looked her fill.

The music was growing even louder now, as possum-skin drums held between naked thighs were beaten with a greater urgency and the dancing became more frenzied.

Then suddenly everything stopped as if frozen in time. The echoes of the music pulsated in her head. What had happened? Had they sensed her presence?

Before she had time to become afraid, the music and dancing began again, even more frenetic this time, and an old man got up from somewhere in the circle and began to blow on what looked like a long hollowed out branch of wood. It made a monstrous moaning noise like an elephant in pain. The shock made her shiver and pull her shawl tighter around her shoulders.

'That's old Bandicoot and his didgeridu. You're not frightened, are you?'

The male voice from just behind her left shoulder made Carrie gasp and swing round to stare straight into the face of a rather rough looking character, not unlike some of the itinerant swagmen she had already come across on the road to Yorvik. But this one seemed younger than most of them, in his early to middle twenties perhaps, with a deeply bronzed complexion, much darker than she had seen on any of the other settlers of European stock. He stood about a head and shoulders taller than her and was powerfully built. His curly, reddish-brown hair hung down almost to his shoulders, in the style favoured by native-born Australians to keep the sun off the backs of their necks, and although his features could not be described as fine, they were not unpleasant, in a tough, no-nonsense sort of way. He was dressed in a checked shirt beneath some sort of skin waistcoat, with trousers in a rough material, held up by a wide leather belt from which hung a sheathed hunting knife.

His sudden and unkempt appearance, combined with the sight of that lethal-looking weapon, brought a note of tension to her voice as she backed perceptibly away. 'You – you gave me quite a start! I thought I was alone out here . . . Apart from them.' She indicated with her head in the direction of the campfire.

The young man smiled and the act seemed to light his whole face. He had a full, wide mouth and a row of quite the whitest, strongest and straightest teeth Carrie had ever seen. 'You're never alone in the bush,' he said in a quiet, slightly gravelly voice that had a faint drawl to it, peculiar to native-born Australians. 'We're the trespassers here, lady.'

She was about to inform him indignantly that the land belonged to her husband-to-be, but he continued, 'Out here under the sky, it's *their* land . . .' He jerked his head towards the singing Aborigines. 'And although Old Man Hebden might have laid claim to it, it's still theirs as far as they're concerned. Nobody has the right to own the earth, any more than they have the right to own the sky.'

Carrie's indignation abated somewhat as he effectively put her in her place. 'They – they must be the cannibals,' she said, deliberately ignoring his homespun philosophy and glancing back over her shoulder at the campfire. 'I've heard tell of them. They're not dangerous, are they?'

'The cannibals?' the young man repeated, his lips quirking into a smile as he raised his eyebrows at the description. It was quite obvious he had an English, still wet-behind-the-ears, would-be settler here. He gave a derisory half-laugh as he glanced back towards the fire. 'Not half as dangerous to us as we are to them.'

The remark passed right over Carrie's head, but she got the distinct feeling he was somehow gently mocking her, that he recognized she was an immigrant and did not understand how things were out here. The music rose on the wind and seemed to fill the very air they breathed, the quavering voices belonging not to human beings, but to nature itself. They were listening to the sounds of the universe as they stood there watching the red glow of the campfire and felt their spines tingle with a sound unlike any Carrie had ever heard on earth before. 'It – it's quite beautiful really,' she said, woefully aware of the inadequacy of her words. 'Yes, it's quite beautiful in a weird sort of way.'

The young man made no reply but stood gazing out over the scene as he had done so many times before. His face was grave, his eyes gleaming with a strange intensity as he nodded his head, almost imperceptibly, to the distant music.

'Do you understand any of it?' Carrie asked, moving closer for a better view as the plaintive sounds filled their ears, rising and falling like the wind in the sheltering branches of the eucalyptus trees, and the figures in the centre of the circle whirled and bent, bent and swayed in a rhythmic abandon.

'Yeah, I understand it all right,' her new companion said quietly. 'As much as anyone who isn't a genuine blackfella can.' He leant back against the trunk of the tree and squirted a jet of tobacco juice out of the corner of his mouth into the undergrowth as he continued to gaze at the scene before him.

'What is it they're singing about?' Carrie persisted. She could not help feeling he would much rather be experiencing this alone.

He was quiet for a moment as if wondering whether to continue this conversation, then he turned to her and said, 'They've been singing about their *Palanari*.'

'Their *Palanari*? Whatever's that?'

The young man shrugged, then bent his head to one side as he continued slowly chewing his quid and studying her face. Finally, he sighed and turned back to the campfire, 'You white folks can't really understand,' he said dismissively.

Carrie looked at him in some indignation. He obviously did not include himself in that statement and his dismissal of her question verged on rudeness. 'How can we ever be expected to learn if we don't get the chance?'

He sighed once more. 'Do you really want to know?'

'Yes, yes I do.'

'*Palanari* . . .' he mused. 'I guess some of the whites call it the blackfellas' Dreamtime.'

'Their what?'

'Their Dreamtime,' he repeated. 'It's just about the whole basis of their religion, if you want to call it that. But religion would be the wrong word. You Europeans relegate your religion to maybe a couple of hours on a Sunday at most, but to them their beliefs are part of their whole life. *Palanari* – their Dreamtime – it's their beginning and their end all wrapped up in one. It's the time when the earth

159

was first created, and it's also now – the life that they are living today, and will live tomorrow. It's all their yesterdays too, for time doesn't mean the same to them as it does to you white folks . . .'

He scratched the reddish stubble of his chin. 'No,' he sighed, 'it doesn't mean the same at all. Everything we do, everything we say – you and me standing here talking right now, has its roots in our Dreamtime, and it's up to us to respect life in all its forms, and to respect whatever tests it sends us, for that all helps create the person we are. We must never take anything for granted. Every stone, every blade of grass, every grain of sand is part of that same beginning and end . . . Ashes to ashes, dust to dust, we are simply part of a much greater whole, and must never forget that truth . . .' He gave a wry laugh. 'We mustn't let ourselves get too big for our boots, just about sums it up pretty well.'

Carrie was taking it all in. 'Dreamtime,' she said, savouring the word on her tongue. 'I like the sound of that.' And she also liked the philosophy behind what she had just heard from this most unlikely of teachers. It somehow made sense of what had happened already in her life. If it was all part of a whole, then there was no point feeling bitter about it. If there really was a great scheme to things, then surely that gave hope, not despair. What she had just come through was all part of it. Life was bigger than the moment – bigger than individual tragedies – and had to be lived on a much larger scale. One could not afford to let oneself get warped and twisted by events, but must come through them to the other side.

Suddenly she realized the music had stopped. Surprised, she glanced towards the campfire. There was no one there. To her complete astonishment they had all disappeared as if by magic into the darkness of the night. 'They've gone,' she said, stating the obvious as she looked, wide-eyed, from the empty campfire to her companion.

The young man's face creased into a smile at the shocked

160

look on her face. 'You probably scared them off,' he teased.

'Oh no!' Carrie was truly upset at that.

He shook his head and his grin grew wider. 'Don't worry, it was nothing to do with you. That's how they are, that's all. Disappear into the night before your very eyes, they will. But they'll be back.'

For some reason she did not quite understand, Carrie found that last remark quite comforting as she took a deep breath of the scented night air. 'This has all been quite a surprise, I can tell you,' she said. She made an expansive gesture with her hand in the direction of the deserted campfire. 'I – I'd heard about these people of course, but I didn't realize they'd be found quite so near my own home, or that my introduction to them would be quite so . . . well, interesting!'

The young man quirked his eyebrows at that. He was used to seeing some of Old Man Hebden's occasional visitors taking an evening stroll, especially the wives when the menfolk were chewing the fat over wool prices and the like round the kitchen stove. The boss had said he was heading into Sydney on business, when he left a few days ago. And now this young woman had appeared. And she was calling it 'her own home'. His eyes narrowed as he continued to scrutinize her face, his mind working overtime.

The old devil . . . She could not be much more than twenty or so. Young enough to be the old bastard's daughter. 'You – you're not . . . ?' He could barely bring himself to finish the sentence, so improbable did it seem. He had heard tell some time ago that the old man was thinking of getting himself a wife. But he had imagined one of the old former she-lags from the prison factory at Parramatta might turn up. But someone as young and as pretty as this . . . ? 'Jeez . . . !' He let out a low whistle of disbelief.

'Is something wrong?' Carrie asked. 'Didn't Mr Hebden tell you of my arrival?'

The young man shook his head and ran a hand through

the tangle of curls above his brow. 'The boss tells us nothing but what he wants us to know,' he said, unable to take his eyes off her now that the truth was dawning.

'Well, then,' Carrie said in some amusement at his obvious discomfort, 'perhaps he wants me to remain a secret!' Then she relented and held out her hand. 'But just between you and me, my name's Carrie . . . I expect it's a waste of time you knowing my other name for I'll be Hebden in a few days' time, if I'm not mistaken.'

The young man shook his head in a bemused way once more, unable quite to take it in, as he took her hand. The dirty old bugger! 'I'm Sean O'Dwyer,' he said. 'I'm mighty pleased to meet you, miss.'

'You're Irish!'

'That's very perceptive of you, to be sure, but I've never been to Ireland in my life.'

'But your father must have been Irish,' Carrie insisted, extracting her fingers from his. 'Was your mother Irish too?'

Sean O'Dwyer's smile darkened. 'If I told you to mind your own damned business would you take offence?'

Carrie took a half step back at his cheek. 'And if I told you you're an impudent Croppie, would *you* take offence?'

'Bloody right I would.'

They stood facing one another beneath the gnarled branches of the gum tree, then a slow grin began to spread across Sean O'Dwyer's face. Carrie found herself beginning to smile in return. 'Shake again,' he said, extending his hand for the second time, and she took it, feeling that somehow she had met her match.

When she got back to the house Silas was in the kitchen waiting for the kettle to boil. 'You'll have heard the darkies,' he said, as she hung her shawl on the back of the door. 'Bloody racket they kick up at this time of night.'

'There was someone else out there – one of the hands, I expect. Sean something-or-other.' She wondered why she pretended not to remember his name.

'Oh aye.'

'I take it he's Irish, with a name like that.'

Silas reached for the tobacco jar to fill his pipe. 'Bog Irish, I'll be bound. His father was an old lag who came over on the First Fleet with the first batch of convicts. And his mother . . .' he gave a knowing laugh, as he thumbed the wedge of shag into the bowl of his pipe. 'Well, you'll have noticed he has a touch of the tarbrush about him, even though it's dark out there.'

Carrie's brows rose.

'Aye,' Silas continued as he held a spill into the fire and lit it. 'They say his mother was a lubra.'

'A lubra?' Carrie repeated.

'A bloody Aborigine.'

'You mean one of those natives out there?' She glanced in shock towards the window.

Her companion nodded as he sucked the tobacco into flame. 'So they say, but I've no proof of it, mind. He doesn't really look a half-caste – not as much as some at any rate, but he certainly has something of a look of the tarbrush about him, that's for sure. Anyroad, you'll do well to keep clear of the likes of him.'

Carrie paused in front of the now singing kettle and raised her eyebrows at the remark. 'And why might that be?' She had taken rather a liking to the prickly Mr O'Dwyer and resented being told to have nothing to do with him.

"Cause I said so, that's why, my girl. And you'd do well to take heed of what I say before we go any further.'

She turned from the stove to face him. He was sitting in a wooden rocking chair about a dozen or so feet away, puffing on his pipe. It was obviously a case of start as you mean to go on. 'Make your own bloody tea!' she said, with a vehemence that took them both by surprise as she flung the teacloth in her hand on to the table beside him. 'I'm going to bed!'

When she got to her room she found she was shaking.

That had been an incredibly stupid thing to do. They were not even married yet. Her situation was anything but safe.

She could hear his footsteps at the door and she swung round to stand with her back to it as it opened. She could feel his eyes burning into the back of her head. Finally he spoke, but it was not the reprimand she had been expecting. 'I can see you're tired,' he said. 'These must have been a very tiring and trying couple of days for you. For that reason I will excuse this little outburst. We'll put it behind us and pretend it never happened. But I'd better warn you, Caroline, I'll not be so lenient next time. If you're stupid enough ever to make a next time, that is.'

She turned slowly to face him. 'That sounds very much like a threat to me.'

'Take it whatever way you want to,' he said. 'But remember this: we're going to church in two days' time, me and thee, and you're going to make a promise in the sight of God. You're going to promise to obey. I think it'd be a good idea to put in some practice in the couple of days you've got left, don't you?'

She stared at him across the few feet of bare floorboards. She had just heard the date of her wedding and was staring eyeball to eyeball in a trial of strength with the man she was about to marry; a man for whom she had no love and never would have.

He picked his watch out of his waistcoat pocket and glanced down at it. 'It's gone ten,' he said. 'I'm going to have that cup of tea and will join you in there in a few minutes.' He nodded in the direction of the bed. Then he turned and walked from the room.

Carrie stood alone by the side of the bed and watched the door close behind him. She was tired and thirsty, and would have given anything for that cup of tea. But nothing on earth would make her go into the kitchen and eat a slice of humble pie before she could drink it. She sat down on the edge of the mattress and drew her hand across the rough wool of the blanket. She was here for only one purpose, to produce that son he desired more than anything else. And, heaven help her, he would keep on trying until he succeeded, even if it killed her. And the way she felt tonight, it would be no bad thing if it did.

CHAPTER TWELVE

The wedding was held in the Anglican church in New-castle, with a meal after the ceremony in the staid, eminently respectable Colonial Hotel on Hunter Street. The wedding party was comprised of only seven people: the bride and groom, and the groom's friends, Geordie Appleby and his wife Mabel, Angus Cameron, the vicar who conducted the ceremony, the Reverend Mr Hugh Marples, and his wife, Vera.

'You'll make sure you wear something bright and fitting for the wedding, won't you?' Silas said the night before they set off for their journey to the seaport. 'Not that dark thing you've had on since you arrived.'

So Carrie looked carefully through Caroline's meagre wardrobe and settled on the only light dress in the trunk: a dusky pink affair in a fine linen material, with leg-of-mutton sleeves trimmed with fine lace and lace trimmings round the high neck and the foot of the full skirt. Caroline had mentioned on the voyage that she hoped her husband-to-be intended treating her to a new outfit for the occasion once they landed, for she could not afford to bring one with her. He had written her, she said, of 'David Jones', Sydney's fine store on George Street, and of the wonderful materials and ladies' dresses to be found there. No doubt he had wanted to reassure her that she was not coming out to an uncivilized wilderness, and that they had as fine ladies' and gents' outfitters in Australia as any back home. But, quite obviously, a visit to such a place before the actual wedding had been far from Silas's thoughts.

He seemed pleased with what he saw, however, when after supper that night Carrie retired to the bedroom, to emerge half an hour later, dressed for the occasion. She had even put on a cream straw bonnet, tied with a pink ribbon, and cream lace mittens.

'So that's it, is it? My, you look a treat and no mistake!' her bridegroom had declared as he looked up from reading an old copy of the *Sydney Gazette*. 'Let's hope the weather keeps fine for Saturday. We wouldn't want any of that finery spoilt by a shower of rain, that's for sure.'

They had left for the coastal town of Newcastle, the Hunter Valley's main seaport, at just after seven the following morning, with the wedding arranged for Saturday at one in the afternoon.

Carrie's first sight of her husband-to-be in his own wedding attire made her unsure whether to laugh or cry. The suit, it transpired, had been borrowed from Geordie Appleby, who was not only half a head shorter than Silas but was also a good six inches wider around the waist. The bridegroom had attempted to remedy the latter problem by affixing a wide leather belt around his midriff, but this resulted in an unsightly bulge beneath the buttoned jacket, and the length of the trousers he could do nothing about.

'I decided to wear my boots,' he told his wife-to-be, seeing her looking askance at his lower legs. 'That way the fact that the pants are six inches too short won't be noticed so much.'

Carrie could hardly contain herself. He looked like the most grotesque of music hall turns. Even his necktie, which he had unearthed for the occasion from a trunk at the foot of the wardrobe, was badly in need of a wash and iron, and the scrawny neck which poked up from the white paper collar was peppered with small spots of dried blood.

'I reckon I was a bit hamfisted with the razor this morning,' Silas told Carrie, when she commented on it over breakfast. Then he chuckled to himself. 'The old neck's not used to getting so much attention, that's what it is . . . Two shaves in less than a week! God help us, it'll not get over it!'

Carrie made no response as she attempted to get at least a cup of tea inside her rebellious stomach. In a strange way she felt half sorry for this cantankerous, awkward, yet somehow boyishly shy creature she was about to promise her life to. Heaven only knew what sort of marriage it would be. She felt one step removed from it all, as if she were watching some macabre play being acted out on a stage before her. It was something that had to be got through. Whatever might come afterwards was still in the future, and it was quite enough this morning to be simply getting on with the present.

It was a good day's journey to Newcastle, Silas warned Carrie as he watched her toying with her teacup. They could not expect to reach their destination until nightfall, so she had better have a decent breakfast inside her.

But, despite his entreaties, Carrie found she could not eat a thing. While he was tucking into his tea and damper, the curious bread-cake so popular with the settlers, she decided to get a breath of fresh air and take her last walk on Yorvik land as an unmarried woman. 'You don't mind, do you?' she asked him.

'Nay, lass. Just you leave the condemned man to eat his last meal in peace,' he joked, waving her away. The poignancy of the remark was totally lost on him as he turned back to the table.

Five minutes later found her walking past the straggly row of shepherds' huts that lay between the house and a small lake Silas had told her of about a mile from the property. She had not met any of the station hands yet, for, apart from the young Irishman she had run into the other evening, she had been informed they were out on the range.

The huts themselves seemed very primitive, with only shutters and no glass in the windows, and stringy-bark roofs. Some chickens scratched in the earth around the doors and a grey tabby cat sat preening itself beneath a wattle tree. A washing line of sorts was strung between

168

two of the huts over which a man's tartan woolcloth shirt hung limply, its cuffs fluttering in the light breeze.

The door to the end hut was open and, unable to restrain her curiosity, Carrie peered inside. The interior was almost as primitive as the exterior. There was a hard-packed earth floor, a bed of sorts against the right-hand wall, a spindly chair and a large wooden trunk that seemed to double as a table. An ancient cast-iron stove, with a kettle and a pot sitting on top, stood in the centre of the wall opposite the bed. She wrinkled her nose. Not much of a place, she decided, for a human being to call home.

'You looking for someone?'

The question made her whirl round in embarrassment to find herself looking straight into the enquiring eyes of Sean O'Dwyer. He had obviously come from strenuous work, for beads of sweat stood out on his brow, to which wet, dark red curls were plastered beneath the brim of his hat and he had an axe in his right hand. He propped the shaft against the front wall of the hut as she protested lamely, 'Why, Mr O'Dwyer, you quite frightened the life out of me!'

'Well, I'm real sorry about that,' the young man replied, removing his hat and pushing a hand through his tangle of curly hair. 'I just wondered what you were doing poking your nose into my house, that's all.'

'This – this is your home?' Carrie glanced back into the mean little room, feigning surprise to cover her nosiness.

'T'ain't much, is it?' he agreed, reading the distaste in her look. 'But then I'm just a hand around here, not the boss like the love of your life back there.' He jerked his head towards the big house and there was amusement lurking somewhere in those dark eyes as he leant back against the side of the hut and folded his arms as he chewed thoughtfully on his quid of tobacco.

Carrie lifted her chin as she looked him straight in the eye. He was being insufferably rude, as if intent on provoking a reaction from her. 'Mr Hebden's a fine man,' she said

169

stiffly. 'I won't have him talked of in that way – not to me anyway.'

Sean O'Dwyer raised a quizzical eyebrow and shrugged his shoulders. 'I don't know what you find so offensive,' he said, scratching the auburn stubble of his chin. 'Either he is the love of your life or he ain't. Either way, there's nothing to take offence about.' His brown eyes scrutinized her face and there was definite amusement in them somewhere as he continued to chew thoughtfully on his tobacco. 'You can't tell me you're really taken with the old fella – in a romantic sort of way, I mean.'

Carrie's face flamed. 'It's none of your business!' she declared. 'You really are an insufferable man! Is this how all men speak to women out here?'

He shook his head. 'No, just some, I guess. But then I was born and raised out here so never did get the chance to learn any of that double-talk you English call good manners.'

Carrie had no answer to that and did not attempt one as she turned on her heel to leave.

He grabbed her arm. 'Know what I think?' he said. 'I think you're marrying the old bugger for his money. And I can't say as I blame you. But with your looks I reckon you could have done a darned sight better for yourself, that's all.'

He was so serious now as his eyes burned into hers that Carrie was quite taken aback. Inexplicably her anger evaporated as she shrugged herself free from his grasp and said primly, 'I thank you for your concern, Mr O'Dwyer, but, to quote a certain gentleman – it's none of your damned business!'

Then, as she turned to go once more, she looked down at her feet and raised her eyes to meet his as she said quietly, 'By the way, I'm getting married tomorrow, so it's a bit late to be having regrets, isn't it?'

She could not tell if the statement surprised him or not. He thought for a moment then spat a jet of tobacco juice on to the dusty earth behind him, before placing his hat on his head, pushing it to the back of the thatch of reddish brown curls as he said slowly, 'Not if you're a convict, it ain't.'

Carrie's heart lurched. 'What do you mean by that?' A film of nervous perspiration dampened her skin beneath the fine linen of her wedding dress. 'Do I look like a convict?'

Sean O'Dwyer grinned and a row of perfectly straight white teeth, seemingly unaffected by the tobacco juice, gleamed in the morning light. 'Damned if I know. They don't have the government's arrow tattooed on their foreheads, you know.'

Carrie gave a weak smile, but his remark had shaken her. Could he possibly suspect? She immediately dismissed the thought. He was trying to provoke her, that was all. He was that type of person. But somehow she found it impossible to be offended as he stood there smiling at her. 'I – I'd better be going,' she said, glancing back towards the house where she knew Silas would by now be finishing his breakfast. The lake could wait till later. 'I – I wish I could say it's been nice meeting you again but I'm honestly not quite sure it has been.' She picked up her skirts. 'Good-day, Mr O'Dwyer.'

The young man raised a tanned hand to touch the brim of his hat, the smile on his face beneath it just as broad. 'G'day to you, ma'am.'

On the way back into the house Carrie was aware of not having answered his question about being a convict – of not having lied. But *had* he guessed, she continued to wonder. How could he possibly know? She resolved to put the issue to the back of her mind. It was simply her conscience playing her up every time someone mentioned such a thing. Convicts were more plentiful out here than free settlers, so it was natural for people to wonder about every new arrival. And she prided herself in the knowledge that she did not look like the usual specimen of degraded humanity who arrived on these shores to serve their time. But she felt for them all the same, every last one. And maybe she did not have the government's arrow tattooed on her forehead, but she had no doubt it was now deeply engraved on her heart.

The journey to the coast took longer than they bargained for, with one of the horses throwing a shoe and having to be reshod at Hunter's Hollow, the small settlement about fifteen miles out on the Newcastle road. They arrived in the seaport just before midnight and made straight for their hotel, where the night porter let them in.

To Carrie's relief, decorum had prevailed and they had been booked into separate rooms so at least she was assured of a decent night's sleep.

The ceremony in Newcastle's Anglican church the following day went without a hitch and Carrie found the proceedings had a curious sense of unreality about them. The only time she was aware of feeling anything but an emotional numbness was when the moment came for her to promise to obey. The Reverend Marples's voice had a sonorous tone to it that brought memories of those prison chaplains in Newgate flooding back. Why did they all have to sound so sanctimonious? She was aware of the man by her side looking down at her quite intently at that point in the service and her voice deliberately dropped as she said the dreaded word, although the rest of the vows she spoke out in a firm clear voice.

They retired to the hotel immediately afterwards for a meal of roast duck and all the trimmings. As she walked up the steps and in through the foyer on Silas Hebden's arm, the small gold band she now wore on the third finger of her left hand weighed heavy on her heart every time she stole a glance at the man who was now her husband.

Around the table in the comfortably furnished dining room, it was chiefly the men who did most of the talking, mainly of business, the two favourite topics being sheep and coal. The settlement of Newcastle was now New South Wales's biggest exporter of red cedar wood from the great forests of the Hunter Valley and of coal, which was extensively mined in the area. It transpired that the government leased the mines to the Australian Agricultural Company, which had the monopoly over both the coalmines and much of the pastoral land in the interior. Geordie Appleby and Angus Cameron both had done very well out of shares in the company – a fact which had helped them ride out the drastic slump in wool prices over the past few years. What puzzled Carrie, however, was that Silas appeared not to have been so farsighted.

Business was not regarded as something that womenfolk had any right to interfere in, however, so she restricted her curiosity on this matter to tackling Mabel, Geordie Appleby's wife, about it in the powder room at the end of the meal.

Mabel Appleby was a sharp-featured, highly astute woman, who had none of her husband's bonhomie but just as much brainpower. She had joined him out here in the summer of 1824, during the time when half a million acres of the Hunter Valley were appropriated by free settlers. They had been lucky enough to obtain some of the best farming land and had gone from strength to strength over the next two decades. Why Silas down on his thousand acres at Yorvik couldn't have done the same she really was at a loss to understand.

Mabel Appleby shrugged her narrow shoulders at Carrie's question as she dabbed another touch of eau de cologne on to her handkerchief in front of the ornamental mirror. 'If it's a mystery to you, my dear, then it's an even greater mystery to the likes of Geordie and me,' she told her young companion. 'Better off than any of us, Silas was in the early days. We all had to buy our stations on "Thirds" from a money lender down in Sydney, you know, and Silas never had to do that. Came out here with the capital in his back pocket, he did. But where has it got him, that's what I'd like to know? That place of his is just about the most run down in the territory. If he'd invested some of those early profits in shares like we did he wouldn't be feeling the pinch so badly now. And what's more he'd be able to afford decent help around the place. You can't expect to run a farm that size with only yourself and three farmhands.'

'You mean he only has three hands on the farm?' Carrie said in amazement.

'Indeed, that's all he has,' Mabel affirmed, as she dabbed more cologne behind her ears. 'He has two Scotch brothers who work outback with the flock and that Irish fella who tends to the heavy work around the place now that Silas is not so able.'

'You mean Mr O'Dwyer?' Carrie said. 'I've met him.'

Mabel Appleby gave a short laugh as she half-turned from her primping at the mirror to glance at Carrie in some amusement. 'I can't say as I've ever heard him referred to quite like that before,' she said, slicking a kiss curl over her ear into place with a wet fingertip. 'On the contrary, it's usually some quite unmentionable word whenever your Silas refers to him.'

'He doesn't like him then?'

'Oh, I don't think *liking* comes into it. He does the job that he's required to do, that's for sure. If you ask me it's more to do with the fact that the Irishman doesn't give Silas the respect he's due. He doesn't give any of his betters much respect, come to that . . . Oh, and the fact that he's reckoned to have . . .' And at that Mabel Appleby paused, dropping her voice so that two other ladies at the other side of the room could not overhear. Raising a lace-mittened hand to her mouth, she whispered, 'Well, if the truth be known, he's thought to frequent lubras!'

Carrie frowned. Was she talking in code? And lubras — she had heard that word before.

'Darkie women,' Mabel enlightened her in hushed

tones. 'Isn't it disgusting?' She shuddered. 'Doesn't bear thinking about! Although they do say his mother was half-savage herself, or some such thing. At any rate his father was a convict. Came out with the First Fleet, so I heard tell. A real Irish political agitator who got this poor half-caste in the family way in his old age. Is it any wonder the offspring turned out as he did?'

Carrie was silent as she fingered a ringlet into place in the mirror. Suddenly she knew exactly why Sean O'Dwyer was as cussed as he was. But she would lay any bet that he had more brains in that red curly head of his than her own husband had in his.

'Poor Silas has too many principles, that's his trouble,' Mabel Appleby said, harking back to her original point. 'Choke him to death some day they will, my Geordie has said often enough.'

'Principles?'

Mabel nodded. 'Like not using convict labour on the farm. He could have them assigned to him as Master, you know. Ten pounds a year's the maximum it could cost him. All he'd have to do is to provide the minimum in food and clothing.' She gave a strained laugh. 'Mind you, some don't even do that. Work the poor creatures to death, they do, and the government doesn't bat an eyelid. It's just one more mouth off the stores to them.'

Carrie listened and took it all in. She was learning a lot this afternoon. It might not be the ideal wedding in most people's eyes, but just listening to everything that was being said out there in the dining room and now here in the powder room was giving her an insight into her new life that she knew would be sure to stand her in good stead in the years ahead.

They set off back to Yorvik in the late afternoon and did not arrive home until almost midnight. They took several hours longer on the return leg for the journey was completed in almost total darkness and Carrie found the whole experience quite nerve-racking, expecting as she did to find themselves surrounded at any time by another herd of angry kangaroos.

'It's a good job these old mares know the way home by now, moon or no moon,' Silas said as he helped his new wife down from the waggon at their front door, 'otherwise we'd have ended up heading in the wrong direction and finished up fishing ourselves out of Lake Macquarie.'

When they got into the house and Carrie had lit the lamps and got a fire going in the stove, Silas reached into a trunk he kept locked beneath the bed and extracted a bottle of best brandy which he brandished with pride in front of her. 'Kept it all these years,' he said. 'Finest French cognac, it is. Bought it for this very day.'

He produced two glasses from the dresser shelf and with great ceremony uncorked the spirit. 'This is no time to stint,' he declared, pouring two generous splashes into each and handing one across to her. She was sitting in a windsor chair at the other side of the stove from the rocker in which he always took his ease, and he stood over her and reached out to touch his glass to hers. 'Here's to this day, Mrs Hebden,' he said. 'And here's to our son. May he grow up to be as fine a lad as this grand land of ours deserves!'

Somewhat embarrassed by the toast, Carrie avoided his eyes as she raised her glass in return and took her first sip of the golden spirit. It burned its way to her stomach and she forced a smile to her lips as her husband beamed down at her and downed his in one. There was certainly never any pretence as to why she was here.

The mellowness of the drink seemed to find great favour with the man who had been hoarding it for so long. As Carrie watched silently from the opposite chair, one glass followed another over his throat, until some twenty minutes and half a bottle of brandy later, he was lying, head back, snoring deeply and quite oblivious to his new bride sitting less than ten feet away, with a quiet smile of relief on her face.

When he had not awoken after half an hour of sound sleep, she removed his boots and covered him with a woollen blanket, before putting out the lamp in the kitchen and lighting a candle to make her way to bed.

When a few minutes later she slid between the sheets it seemed symbolic somehow that she should be spending her wedding night alone. In no way did she feel part of the man that now slumped snoring loudly in that chair next door. He was using her, just as she was using him. She felt no guilt and knew that he felt none either. Indeed no one would be more amazed than Silas Hebden if it were suggested that he was doing anything that to some might be less than honourable in choosing a bride simply as a breeding animal.

Carrie was now wide awake despite her tiredness from the hectic events of the day. Her mind was relentlessly playing over the last year of her life like some Drury Lane tragedy. Voices from the past were calling to her, their faces peering at her from behind her closed lids as she lay on the stiff horsehair of the mattress and tried her best to succumb to sleep.

But sleep would not come and eventually she gave up trying and got up and walked to the window. The clouds that had been hiding the moon and stars for the latter part of their journey home had now dispersed and the sky was light, sending an ethereal glow over the surrounding countryside. It was a whole new world out there. This was more – far more – than a mere prison colony, a place for the social outcasts of British society. This was tomorrow.

She wanted to be part of it – to breathe the air of freedom on this, her most fateful of nights. She reached for her woollen shawl and wrapped it around her shoulders as she made for the front door. She could still hear Silas snoring fitfully in the kitchen down the passage when she closed the front door behind her and stepped out into the starlit night.

The trees surrounding the house stood out like giant

sentinels in the moonlight and she could hear an owl hooting in one of the eucalyptus trees that stood between the big house and the huts belonging to the hands. As she walked in its direction, it flew down from the tree, its wings whirring past her head as it swooped off into the silver night. There were all manner of creatures here the likes of which she could never have imagined before, but she was no longer afraid. This was now her land as much as it was Silas's and the knowledge made her strong and proud. Never in her life had she owned anything before; even their home in Semple Street had been rented. But this was different. As Mrs Silas Hebden this was now hers.

There was no sign or sound of life as she walked past the huts, and she breathed an inward sigh of relief. She wanted this night – this moment – for herself. Tonight she wore a golden band on the third finger of her left hand. This ring had bought her freedom. But in her heart it was not to the old man she had left snoring in the back kitchen that she had given her life today. It was to this land, whose starry skies now enveloped her like a mother's comforting arms around her lost child. While her own land and its people had cast her out, and had killed her brother, this land had given her sanctuary. It had welcomed her as its own. And her heart almost burst with love for the country that she now knew as home as she walked the last few hundred yards down to the lakeside.

A small copse of overgrown bushes stood between her and the softly lapping waters and Carrie's step was light, her heart singing, as she approached the spot Silas had told her was the most beautiful in all Yorvik's thousand acres.

Then she saw the eyes, white and staring, less than six feet away in the undergrowth. She let out a startled gasp as she stopped dead in her tracks.

CHAPTER THIRTEEN

The lithe black shape slid out of the shadows and pounced with the grace of a cat, sending Carrie sprawling backwards on to the ground. Long fingers were clawing at her face and pulling at her hair, and bare legs were kneeing her stomach, as the being that was far more wildcat than human pummelled her victim on the hard earth.

'Aaaaah . . . ! Help me . . . ! Please . . . !' Carrie yelled for all she was worth as determined hands grabbed each side of her head and thudded it repeatedly on to the path where a few moments earlier she had walked with a light step and such hope in her heart.

Strong brown fingers made for her throat, squeezing the flesh so hard that Carrie could hardly breathe as she thrashed around on the dusty ground to try to rid herself of this demon. She was aware of grabbing at the matted curly hair, then digging her nails into the creature's face – for she could not think of her frenzied attacker as a human being – as her life's breath was squeezed from her.

The face, dark and distorted, was glaring down into hers, and strange guttural sounds were coming from the mouth, the teeth of which were bared in an expression of seething hatred. Those sounds, those bared teeth, those wild, staring eyes, that vile rancid smell . . . all swam before her in a sensory maelstrom . . .

Then Carrie was aware of nothing else as they melded into one terrifying whole and dazzling colours flashed before her, as her lungs fought their desperate battle for air. She could feel her grip on her assailant loosen and her body go limp as she began to float into unconsciousness.

All at once a gasp exploded from her lips as precious air was sucked into her parched lungs and her neck was released from its vice.

With a startled grunt her attacker let go and scrambled off her, a bare brown foot trampling on her face in the hurry to escape. As Carrie struggled back to consciousness, she opened her eyes to see the creature disappearing into the undergrowth, closely pursued by another shadowy figure.

As she lay coughing and gasping on the ground, the second figure reappeared within seconds and knelt down beside her.

'You all right, lady?' Sean O'Dwyer asked, concern furrowing his brow. 'She didn't break anything, did she?'

Dazed, Carrie looked up at the face peering down at her with such concern in the moonlight. 'Only my spirit,' she managed to joke lamely, her voice little more than a hoarse squeak. She made a vain attempt at a smile she did not feel, and her right hand reached up tenderly to touch her aching neck. 'Who . . . ?'

But her rescuer placed a silencing finger on her lips. 'Let's get you out of here first,' he said. 'Questions can come later.'

Carrie was in no position to argue as he lifted her battered and aching body in his arms and made his way back in the direction of his hut, his bare feet carefully avoiding the prickly clumps of spinifex that peppered the ground.

On reaching the hut, he pushed open the door with his foot and manoeuvred her in, taking care not to bang her head on the narrow entrance. He laid her down gently on the crumpled bed and stood looking down at her as she momentarily closed her eyes and tried to calm her thumping heart. 'Just as well I wasn't asleep too soundly,' he said. 'Otherwise I'd not have heard you yell out there.'

Carrie took a deep breath and opened her eyes to give a grateful smile. Even in the darkness of the hut's cramped interior, she could see that he was wearing nothing but a threadbare pair of woollen drawers along with his concerned expression. He must have got straight out of bed to come to her rescue.

'What on earth was that all about?' she asked hoarsely, as he turned to light a candle, before uncorking a bottle and pouring a large splash of gin into a tin cup. She had no idea she already had enemies in this place. The thought was disturbing, to say the least.

'Here, get this down you first,' Sean said, handing her the cup, before turning to pour one for himself.

She winced with pain as she propped herself up on her elbow to sip the potent spirit, then edged herself over on the narrow bed as he sat down at the foot and shook his head. 'That must have come as a fair shock,' he said. 'But thinking about it, maybe it was no more than was to be expected. I'm surprised old Silas didn't warn you.'

'Didn't warn me?' Carrie said in mystification. 'What do you mean, didn't warn me? What's my husband got to do with this?'

'That was Quarra,' Sean told her. 'Silas's gin.'

Now Carrie was truly puzzled. 'Gin?' That was the stuff they were drinking.

Sean O'Dwyer allowed himself a grin. 'Gin,' he explained. 'That's blackfella talk for a brown woman. It's what the Aborigines call their own womenfolk.'

'You mean like lubra?' Carrie said.

He nodded. 'Something like that.'

'But what has Silas got to do with it?'

Sean took a mouthful of the spirit, swished it around his mouth, then swallowed and gave a satisfied 'Ahhh,' as it worked its way down to his stomach. 'She kept house for him before you came,' he told her. 'Made his damper – did some basic cooking and cleaning. Things like that.'

'What exactly do you mean – "things like that"?' Carrie demanded, feeling herself tense. So often people seemed to talk in code around here.

Her companion smiled, his white teeth flashing in the candlelight. 'Oh, I don't think you have much need to worry in that regard, if you're thinking of hanky-panky between the two of them. There's plenty of us men that do, mind – but I'd bet my best shirt that old Silas is not one of them. A man of principle, I think the term is. He'd have no objection to blackfellas or their gins serving him, but they'd better know their place and damned well stay in it. And as far as black women are concerned, that's not in his bed . . . Yes, a man of principle your new husband is all right, Mrs Hebden.' The last statement was delivered with more than a touch of irony.

Carrie winced. She had heard that phrase already today. 'Do – do you think she's jealous?' she asked, her fingers gingerly touching the still tender flesh of her throat. 'Could that gin woman be jealous of me?' It seemed an incredible thought.

''Course she was jealous. Being old Hebden's gin, she was Queen Bee around here, wasn't she? Lording it over the other women in the camp. The only one to be allowed inside the house, even though only as a skivvy. Of course she was bloody jealous when you come along to take her place. Being a dummy doesn't help matters either. It means she often only half understands what's going on. She'd have had no idea you were even coming until you arrived and she was told by the boss to get the hell out of it and not come back.'

He smiled wryly. 'Not that any of the rest of us were notified of your arrival either. Secretive old bugger when he likes, is old Silas. In fact, I reckon the only reason he took her on was because she was deaf and dumb and wouldn't be able to gossip to the others about things inside the house.'

'I – I'd no idea . . . Silas never said anything about having native help in the house.'

'I expect he was waiting to see how you took to the idea once you'd settled in. Some wives actually like having a gin around the place to do all the heavy work, while others wouldn't let them over the front doorstep.' He looked at her curiously as he took another gulp of his drink. 'Which kind are you, Mrs Hebden?'

Carrie shrugged as she stared down into her cup, then looked up to meet his quizzical gaze. 'I – I really don't know,' she answered truthfully. 'But I think after tonight I'd probably fall into the second category.'

'I can understand that. It must have been quite a shock for you. But, if it's any consolation, I don't think she meant to do more than rough you up a bit. I really don't think she intended to kill you or anything like that. Scare you away from here, maybe. If by frightening the living daylights out of you she could send you packing back to England, she'd be happy.'

Carrie felt her backbone stiffen at that. She had never been one to be easily intimidated. If the English legal system couldn't break her, then some poor misguided creature out here in the wilderness certainly wasn't going to. All the same, it was not an experience she would like to repeat. 'Do you think she'll try it again?'

Sean O'Dwyer shook his head as he drained his cup and set it down on the floor by his feet. 'No fear of that. I'll have a word in the right ears in the camp tomorrow and that particular little lady won't come within a mile of you in future. I can guarantee it.'

Carrie gave a relieved sigh. 'Well, that's something anyway.'

They sat looking at one another in the candlelight and finally he said quietly, 'I guess you didn't intend spending your wedding night in another fella's bed, eh?'

Carrie gave a wry laugh and shook her head.

'Wouldn't you rather be back in the big house there with your old man?'

To her acute embarrassment she found herself blushing as she thought the true answer to that question must surely be no. But decorum prevailed and with it came the guilt. What on earth would Silas make of it if he came looking for her and found her here? She sat up further on the bed.

'I — I'd better be getting back,' she said, deliberately ignoring his question as she handed him the half-finished cup of gin. 'I wouldn't want my husband to wake up and find me gone.'

'No, you certainly wouldn't want him to come looking and find you here,' her companion agreed with mock seriousness. 'Not in the bed of a Croppie bastard like me!'

As he helped her down, she half turned to him and said, 'I'd rather you didn't mention this to Mr Hebden, if you don't mind, Mr O'Dwyer.'

Sean O'Dwyer nodded in agreement. 'You're a wise woman, Mrs Hebden.'

'Am I?' Carrie mused, turning to face him. They stood looking at one another, the candlelight throwing long shadows on to the bare walls of the hut.

He reached out and brushed a piece of prickly spinifex from the hair at her brow, then drew his fingers down the dirtied skin of her cheek. The touch of his fingertips sent a shiver through her body. 'You're cold,' he said.

'No, I'm not.'

'You're not frightened of me, are you?' His voice was soft and she could feel herself trembling inside as well as out as he cupped her chin with his right hand and studied her face. He said nothing for a long time, then letting go he shook his head and half turned from her. 'Some bastards have all the luck,' he said in a bitter voice. She was quite the most beautiful woman he had ever set eyes on and the thought of her returning to that crabbit old fella in the house out there was a personal insult to his own manhood.

Carrie could sense the change in him and she reached out to touch his arm. 'I — I want you to know how grateful I am,' she said softly. 'You might have saved my life out there.'

He turned back to face her and their eyes met. A lopsided grin twisted his mouth. 'You offering any reward?' he asked.

She did not realize he was joking. 'I — I don't really have any money of my own . . .' she began.

'There's always payment in kind.'

'Payment in kind?' She didn't quite understand.

'Like this,' he said, moving forwards and cupping her face between his hands.

His mouth was surprisingly soft on hers, but the kiss lasted no more than a second or two when she pulled herself away, her hand flying to her lips as if to wipe away all trace of what had just occurred.

'It's an old Australian custom,' he said. 'Kissing the rescuer . . . You're not mad at me, are you?'

'No . . . no, of course I'm not mad at you.'

'I kinda hoped you'd enjoy it. I did.'

But that was too much. Carrie turned and fled from the hut and did not stop running until she got back to the big house.

Silas was still snoring in the rocker by the kitchen stove, where she had left him barely twenty minutes before.

It seemed like a lifetime ago.

The room was filled with moonlight, but was now quite cold, for the fire in the stove had all but died out. She lifted the blanket that had slipped from his shoulders and covered him up again, before turning to make for the bedroom.

'G'day, you old bugger!'

Carrie gasped and stopped dead in her tracks as she reached for the handle of the door. He had been awake all the time! Her heart was pounding as she turned to face him, as a loud snore followed the outburst.

She stared down at the figure in amazement. His mouth was half open and he snorted again — a wheezy sound that came up his throat to then whistle down his nose. He was still fast asleep.

'G'day, you old bugger! Old bugger! Old bugger!'

Carrie burst out laughing, the first genuine laugh she had had in ages as she walked over to the parrot's cage.

All her tension vanished as she whispered firmly, 'You'd better be quiet, Barney, or you'll waken the boss.'

'G'day, you old bugger!'

'Goodnight to you, Barney,' she smiled, as she picked up an old tablecloth and covered the parrot's cage. 'And a very goodnight to us all.'

She fell asleep within minutes of returning to bed and slept soundly throughout the night. One way and another it had been quite a day.

When she awoke the next morning Silas was already up and about. Nothing was said about him drinking himself to sleep and Carrie tried to put all thoughts of what had occurred between herself and the Irishman out of her mind. It had been an aberration, and such intimacy would not – could not – happen again.

She deliberately avoided Sean O'Dwyer that day, and the following day, and the day after that. If she went out of the house for a breath of fresh air after supper, she kept well within the garden area. Occasionally at night she could see a light burning in his hut and sometimes, if the wind was in the right direction, she could hear the plaintive sound of a penny whistle coming from the candlelit interior. Those fluting notes were something that never failed to stir the blood, for her father had once fashioned one at sea and brought it back for Billy. But it was their mother who had taught the youngster to play those haunting Irish tunes that eerily now, like some haunting spirit of times past, she could hear at night, carrying on the soft air out here, twelve thousand miles away, at the ends of the earth.

There were so many reasons why Carrie could feel herself drawn to the Irishman, had she allowed her heart to rule her head. In some ways he was as tough and hard as the life he led, but in others she could sense a certain gentleness beneath that rough exterior. There was something of the poet hidden deep within. Most Celts had it – that true romantic streak, the hidden flame burning deep within that no amount of foreign oppression or hardship could ever quench. And with it went a certain careless disregard for money, property or material goods. She could never imagine Sean O'Dwyer setting much store by any of those things. He was nothing like the other men around here. There was nothing of the canny, ambitious Scot such as Angus Cameron about him, nor of the astute English businessman Geordie Appleby, and there was certainly nothing of the dour Yorkshireman whom she had married. The Irishman was a free spirit, a wild rover who would not be tied down by possessions or people. And perhaps it was the latter that made a small voice whisper in Carrie's heart that she must never believe there could be a future for her in that direction. Her wild Irish rover would remain just that to the end of his days. And she knew she had not come this far to give it all up to chase a dream.

But common sense was one thing and putting it into practice quite another. Much to her consternation, Carrie even found herself dreaming about him, with some dreams so vivid she almost believed they were real as she awoke in the morning to blush into her pillow and hope that Silas had not detected the bright flush that came to her cheeks on such occasions.

She had little doubt Sean O'Dwyer would welcome a visit from her, but in doing so she knew that she could be starting something over which she might have no control in the end. This was a situation she could not allow to happen. She had been given this chance and had promised herself that she was going to make the most of it. Yorvik was now her home, and, God help her, Silas was now her husband, and she would make the very best of what was hers and seek no other.

CHAPTER FOURTEEN

The winter that year proved long and cold, but not nearly as wet as in previous years. 'I've seen it rain here for weeks on end,' Silas told Carrie. 'So bad that you'd think this house was sitting on an island.' And he waved his hand in the direction of the lake and the river beyond. 'You've never seen floods until you've seen 'em in the Hunter Valley.'

But thankfully, the rains stayed away and there was no fear of the sudden flash flooding that occasionally hit the area with such ferocity, causing widespread damage to livestock and property alike. 'And thank God for that,' Silas said, with feeling. 'We've got enough to cope with, with them damn silly market prices these days.' No one could afford to lose any of their livestock if they were to make ends meet.

Making ends meet had been something Carrie had been well used to in her previous life, but for a young woman born and raised in the streets of London this was quite different. Every day of her life as a farmer's wife was a new experience, some good, some bad, but all part of the learning process she knew she must go through to make the success of things that she intended.

There was so much to take in. As well as the sheep on which the station relied for its main profit, they had a small herd of dairy cattle – no more than six cows – and these she had to learn to milk, and there were a few pigs, geese and chickens to tend, as well as the normal jobs around the house, such as baking and cleaning. It all took so much time and such an enormous amount of energy that sometimes, come evening, she would barely have the strength left to lift her fork to eat the meal that she had just cooked and served for herself and her husband.

The evening meal was perhaps the part of the day that she least enjoyed, for it was the only time she and Silas sat down face to face for any length of time. It took a great deal of effort to be constantly on the alert for the too-probing question he might come out with as she struggled to maintain her guard against anything that might suggest she had been anyone other than the young widow Caroline Cooper before her arrival in Australia. Sometimes she felt that Silas was trying to test her in this regard by asking deliberately searching questions about her past, and the answers she gave had to be as evasive and general as possible for she had no idea exactly how much Caroline had told him about herself in the letters that had passed between them.

In the early days of their marriage Carrie had done her best to search for the letters, but without success. There were only a certain number of places in the house where they could be kept and the most likely was Silas's old trunk in the foot of the wardrobe. Her attempts to plumb its fusty depths were thwarted, however, in a highly embarrassing scene the second week after the wedding.

'What the deuce are you doing in there?' Silas had barked, unexpectedly entering the bedroom half an hour after leaving the house to work on the sheep-pens one morning. 'You've got no business in there, woman!'

Red-faced, Carrie scrambled to her feet, dusting off her skirts rather than look him in the eye.

'Just what do you think you were up to?'

Her mind whirled. 'I — I was looking for that necktie,' she blurted out. 'The one you wore at the wedding . . . I — I noticed you got some gravy on it during the meal and I thought I'd give it a bit of a wash.'

He viewed her suspiciously from across the room, as he pondered on the validity of her excuse. Then, deciding to give her the benefit of the doubt rather than make an issue of it, he grunted, 'If I want summat washing, then I'll give it thee. There's no need for you to go scrabbling about in my things. I'd thank you to remember that.'

Carrie had made sure whenever she made one of her searches in future he was well out of the way. But she still had not succeeded in finding those elusive letters. She even tackled him about them straight out one evening over supper, then wished she had not, for his rejoinder caused her skin to break out in a cold sweat of fear.

'It's funny you should ask about them,' he said, biting a chunk out of the piece of damper in his hand. 'I was just thinking about them myself t'other day.' He looked at her searchingly across the kitchen table. 'And there's summat I can't quite square in my mind.'

Carrie raised her eyebrows as nerves fluttered in her stomach. 'Oh, really?'

'Aye,' he continued. 'Your handwriting, that's what.'

Her insides knotted. 'M – my handwriting?'

'Aye. I thought from your letter you must be cackhanded, for the writing sloped so far to the left, but now you've come . . .'

His eyes narrowed even more as he looked at her. 'Well, the bits and pieces I've seen you write, it goes quite in t'other direction. In fact, even on t'marriage lines, your signature looked nowt like it used to.'

Carrie stared at him as perspiration broke out on her brow and seeped through to wet the material of her dress beneath her armpits. How could she have been so stupid not to think of such a thing? But even if she had, how could she possibly have known what Caroline's handwriting looked like?

'Well?' He was sitting there waiting for a reply – a reason to explain the unexplainable.

'I do believe,' she found herself saying, 'that nerves and anxiety can cause all sorts of funny things to happen to one's penmanship . . . I was terribly anxious when I was writing to you from England and that probably showed in a certain tenseness in my hand . . .' Her voice tailed off as she reached for the teapot to avoid his eyes. 'I'm much happier now. Much happier.'

Her mind was desperately casting around for something else to add that might further boost his ego and take his mind off that wretched handwriting. She knew he was particularly curious about her late husband, David Cooper, and she could usually be certain of bringing a smile to his face by telling him how much more practical he was around the place than the young shipbuilder had been. 'You know how I've always said what a relief it is to have a husband who is so capable with his hands and that sort of thing . . .'

'Aye, a man's got his part to play and a woman's got hers,' Silas said gravely as he accepted the fresh cup of tea she had poured. 'A marriage doesn't stand a chance otherwise.'

And Carrie knew exactly to what he was referring when he made that particular statement. If men could have produced children, she had no doubt her husband would not have a woman within a mile of the place.

But as the weeks wore on and the leaves on the trees around the house burst into leaf and the small coloured birds that gave her such delight twittered in their verdant branches, all worries about different handwriting and the like receded into the background. Carrie did her best to fit into a lifestyle already firmly established over twenty years of hard work turning a thousand-acre wilderness into a viable farm. But, to her consternation, one particular aspect of her past did still seem to concern her husband. This was the fact that she had made no attempt to write to her relatives back in England. He seemed to regard this almost as a personal insult. The subject was brought up yet again one balmy morning in late November.

'You still haven't written to your people back in London yet, Caroline. Don't you think it's time you were doing so? You'll be having them believing I'm ill-treating you or

191

some such nonsense otherwise.' Silas's querulous voice broke the silence as they sat at opposite ends of the table supping the soup that she had made that morning from their own vegetables.

Carrie's heart sank as she looked up, her spoon halfway to her lips. What made him keep on about this so much? Just how much *did* he know about Caroline's family? Too afraid to open up the subject for discussion and be found out for her lack of knowledge, this was something she had never been able to discover.

'That uncle of yours you wrote you were so fond of, he'll be worrying I'm not taking care of you,' Silas persisted. He was always one to look to his reputation.

Carrie could feel herself tense and hoped it did not show as she took another sip of the soup. Had Caroline ever mentioned an uncle in their many conversations? For the life of her, she could not remember. She put down her spoon and reached for the bread to cut herself a slice. Her mind was working fast. 'I – I believe I have something to confess, Silas,' she said, avoiding his eyes. 'My uncle . . . I'm afraid I'm not as fond of him as one might expect.'

'Oh?' Her husband's beetling grey brows rose as he looked with interest across the table at her. 'That's the first I've heard of such a thing.'

'Yes,' she continued quickly. 'It's difficult to explain such things on paper . . . I expect I didn't want you to feel too sorry for me – having no one I really cared for left in England and all that.'

'Hmm . . .' Silas chewed thoughtfully on a mouthful of bread, then took a spoonful of soup. 'Does that mean you don't intend keeping in touch then?' There was a definite trace of disapproval in his voice.

Carrie gave a casual shrug of the shoulders. 'I expect it does. I mean, what would be the point of it? I never really liked the man and we'll certainly never see each other again.'

'But he *was* your legal guardian.'

She gave a light laugh. 'I'm a big girl now, remember! A married woman, in fact.'

Their eyes met, but there was no love in either's glance. She still had to prove herself in that department, and as far as he was concerned that meant only one thing. She not only had to be a wife, but a mother as well.

As the season wore on and the days grew longer and less cold, work around the farm grew more physically taxing, and in Silas Hebden Carrie became even more aware that she had a basically indifferent husband who at times seemed to resent her very presence on his beloved Yorvik. The more she learned and the more capable she became, the less he seemed to like it. Two decades of coping on his own meant any enquiry from his wife into how things might be better run brought sharp words between the pair and a resentful silence on Silas's part which could last for several days.

Carrie did her best to ignore his childish sulks and attempted to take what pleasure she could from the white-painted wooden house that was now home. The floor was swept several times a day, the windows washed, and the furniture polished till it shone. Even the linen sheets that covered the bed very soon returned to their original white after regular boilings in a large tub filled with hot water and washing soda that now bubbled every Monday morning on top of an old stove in a dilapidated shed she had commandeered for a washhouse.

Her solitary labours over the laundry brought back bitter-sweet memories of those washdays on board the *Emma Harkness* with Molly McGuire, and she could not help wondering what had become of her Irish friend. Had her redheaded Scotsman really kept his promise that they would run off together? Somehow Carrie doubted it, but stranger things had happened out here, of that she was certain.

How many years would it take, she asked herself, before the guilt of her past faded? How long would it be before she stopped being so sensitive to every reference, no matter how fleeting, to her previous life? These were questions that she pondered on long and hard as those first months on Yorvik sped past and the wide acres of her new home grew green in the warmth of the spring sun.

One of her greatest disappointments about her new life was that there seemed to be no spare cash for all those little extras that she believed made a house a home. Yorvik's shortcomings in this regard were more than highlighted by the occasional Sunday visit to the Applebys' place, Eden Vale.

Carrie could hardly believe her eyes the first time their horse and buggy rattled up the long drive, for unlike their own modest wooden homestead, the Applebys' home was made of stone – that same warm yellow stone that made the streets of Sydney glow golden in the sunlight. 'I had it specially brought up,' Geordie said proudly when she commented on it. 'I promised Mabel here she'd have a home to be proud of one day, and by God I've kept my word.'

There was certainly no denying that and Carrie's eyes grew wide with wonder at the fine English furniture, Dresden china ornaments, plump tapestry cushions and satin brocade curtains at the windows. There were even original oil paintings of Mabel's native Westmorland on the walls, and above the fireplace hung a watercolour by a Mr J. M. W. Turner of her birthplace near Kirkby Lonsdale. 'My father bought that one from the artist as a wedding present for us,' she informed Carrie. 'Personally Geordie thinks Mr Turner's rather slapdash with his colours, but I rather like it.'

'It's beautiful,' murmured Carrie. In fact, the whole house was quite the most beautiful place she had ever been in, and it made her all the more determined that one day Yorvik too would be a place to be proud of. Not even Angus Cameron's home could compare with this.

On making the observation to Mabel as the two women

sat drinking coffee in the drawing room after lunch, while their husbands lingered at the dining table to smoke cigars and discuss how business was faring, the older woman positively beamed. 'I really do think you ought to have a firm word with Silas,' she advised her young guest with more than a touch of sympathy in her voice. 'He really should have budgeted for you being able to do the place up a bit – make it a fit place for a young wife to do her entertaining in. These things are so important, you know.'

Carrie did not demur as she stirred her coffee with one of Mabel's dainty silver teaspoons, for her own mind was already wondering how she could possibly return the compliment of the visit in a house that did not even possess matching cutlery.

But despite Mabel's comments, and Silas's own assurances on her arrival that 'a woman's touch' was needed around the place, it seemed the budget simply would not stretch to such things as silver teaspoons, tapestry cushions, or even proper curtains.

Mabel Appleby's original warnings on the day of their wedding were proving all too correct and financially things were far from good on Yorvik. Carrie soon discovered for herself that her new husband had little head for business. Although it seemed that his first decade as a sheep farmer had brought some profit, this had soon been frittered away in silly schemes such as grain cultivation that he had neither the labour nor the equipment to carry out. None of his early savings had been invested, so when the recession of the past few years began to bite and wool prices plummeted, he now found himself with no reserves to fall back on. Things had got so bad of late that they even resorted to killing the stock for a decent meal now and again.

Slaughtering sheep, however, was a side of life on the farm that Carrie could not bring herself to take part in. She had quickly become fond of the docile creatures they relied upon so heavily for their livelihood. To her surprise,

Silas himself seemed to hold the animals in contempt. In fact, he had no liking for sheep at all.

'Bloody stupid animals,' he would declare. 'If they're not getting themselves lost, they're getting drowned in rivers or being gutted by dingoes.' Even their inability to raise decent prices at market he would hold against them. 'I should've gone into cattle. I hear they're still making good money up north on the Macleay River with their beef stock. Aye, cows would've been a more sensible bet all round.'

But Carrie knew whatever her husband had gone into, they would be in a similar situation. Silas's bookkeeping left far too much to be desired, and as the weeks went by she became more and more convinced this was something she could make a much better job of than her husband. Silas could not even add up properly and his calculations were often out to the tune of hundreds of pounds. This was a situation that could not be allowed to continue, but convincing him was an altogether different matter.

Silas was distinctly unimpressed when his young wife began advising him how to run his affairs. 'Who's been filling your head with that rot?' he demanded, when she tackled the thorny subject of investment in one of the new stock companies setting up offices in Sydney.

'Why, Mabel Appleby,' Carrie replied truthfully, as she sat with her workbox at her side darning a pair of his socks one late November evening. 'She seems very well informed on business matters out here.'

'Bah!' Silas snorted, taking his pipe from his mouth and looking up from his newspaper. 'Like a barber's cat, that one – all wind and piss! You'd be well advised to steer clear of taking advice from other women round here, Caroline. Talk through their bonnets, they do! Sticking their noses into men's business, indeed! I'll thank you not to bother your head about my financial affairs. They're none of your concern. You know why you're here and I don't think I need remind you of that.' And his eyes burned into hers from over the top of his newspaper, before he gave the pages an irritable shake and engrossed himself once more in an article berating the government on the allocation of the Land Fund.

The Land Fund was something which was of some concern to farmers such as himself right now. It represented the proceeds of sales of Crown lands 'within the Pale of Settlement', and was augmented by licence fees paid by squatters 'beyond the Pale'. The Governor, Sir George Gipps, was under orders from London that the fund was to be used for the provision of border police and the protection of the Aborigines. The cost of the military garrisons and the running of the convict system was also to be met from the fund and this Silas took great exception to, believing that the British government should be responsible for its own troops and its own felons. He also saw red over good money being wasted on blackfellas. 'Why should our money be used to protect savages?' he protested from behind a cloud of tobacco smoke. 'You'll have the blighters breeding faster than the whites, then where will we be?' He eyed his wife over the top of the paper once more. 'I reckon it's up to our women to see to it that the country's supplied with plenty of good breeding stock. Good English blood and plenty of it, that's what's needed!'

Carrie remained silent. How she hated it whenever that particular subject was brought up. It was already becoming a bone of contention between them. Doing her bit in providing good English breeding stock in the form of an heir for Yorvik was not proving the simple task it sounded.

Nights in the small front bedroom of the house that was now her home were becoming almost unbearable. She found the whole business of performing her nocturnal marital duties both painful and embarrassing. In truth, when it came to that aspect of their relationship, her husband repelled her. Most attempts at copulation resulted in him having one of his bronchial attacks. These invariably ended in a paroxysm of coughing, where he sat swaying on the edge of the bed, his face puce and his eyes streaming. Also, Silas rarely washed, deeming it an unnecessary exercise. And bathing the whole body was totally out of the question. 'Weakens the muscles, it does!' he declared when she first tentatively raised the subject once the smell had become too much to bear. 'Take a look at the blackfellas – they never bathe, and strong as oxen they are!'

The comparison with the fish oil and soot-caked bodies of the Aborigines, she thought ruefully, was more apt than he imagined as she watched him don his working clothes every morning with not even a glance at the ewer full of hot water she would have waiting on the washstand. It would be totally ignored except on Sunday, when he would strip to the waist and give his top half a wipe over with a damp flannel before sharpening his cut-throat for one of his few shaves of the week.

The Sabbath was the nearest that they came to a day of rest on the farm, with the occasional trip in the buggy to Hunter's Hollow, the small settlement some fifteen miles out on the Newcastle road that boasted the nearest church. The fact that it was Church of Scotland and therefore Presbyterian by denomination made little difference, although the Reverend Douglas MacKenzie who ministered to the scattered flock of farming families often incurred Silas's wrath by levelling criticisms at the British government's management of the colony. And, even more controversially, he also had a great deal to say on the free settlers' treatment of both the Aborigines and their labourers.

On one particular early summer morning he was especially forthright as only the previous week there had been several members of the Camaraigal and Gayimai tribes gunned down in their own region of New South Wales for no apparent reason. Taking his text from Isaiah 42, Verse 22, Reverend MacKenzie lectured his congregation over both the plight of the natives and the convicts in their midst:

> ' "This is a people robbed and plundered,
> They are all of them trapped in holes, and hidden in
>   prisons;
> They have become prey with none to rescue,
> A spoil with none to say, 'Restore!' " '

This constant castigation of 'fine god-fearing men and women', as Silas put it, never ceased to infuriate him, for the dour Yorkshireman took a dim view of anyone rallying to the defence of the convicts whom he often referred to as 'the scum of the earth'. Carrie knew that if she had originally harboured any hopes of ever being able to confess her own sins to him, they had long since been grounded on the rocks of a prejudice so deepseated that her husband would not even entertain breaking bread with a 'ticket of leave' man who had done his time and was now free to attempt to build a decent life for himself in the colony.

'Polluted the blood of this country for generations, they have,' he muttered under his breath as they sat side by side in the pew.

And she smiled wryly to herself and wondered what he would make of the fact that the son he so longed for would be born with just such contaminating blood in his veins.

But if her husband's wrath was incurred by the Scotsman's liberal views, Carrie listened with growing concern to what the minister was saying. Her own experiences over the past year had made her even more sensitive to injustices meted out to others. There were too few settlers around willing to speak out like this about man's inhumanity to man. Indeed that very phrase, coined by the minister's favourite poet, Robert Burns, was often used in the sermons and caused many a blush to come to sunburnt cheeks when strong words were delivered on the harsh conditions under which many of the farmers kept their convict labourers.

'Do ye unto others as ye would have them do unto you!'

the minister would thunder, fixing each man and woman in the congregation with an unblinking stare of such ferocity that Mabel Appleby, sitting next to her husband Geordie in the front row, would be forced to take out her fan and cool herself down. Eden Vale was known as a farm that got more than its money's worth out of its convict labour.

After the first Sunday service in December, when he had quoted from Isaiah, as Douglas MacKenzie stood at the door of the small church to shake the hand of each member of his congregation in turn, Carrie murmured, 'That was a most inspiring sermon, Reverend. I couldn't agree with you more.'

The young cleric raised his eyebrows a good half inch. He had already been taken to task by Geordie Appleby amongst a good many others. 'Really, Mrs Hebden?' he said in some surprise.

'Oh yes,' Carrie assured him. 'Sometimes it doesn't do to be too meek in such matters. Sometimes we need to be reminded we are all God's creatures, whether or not we wear the mark of the black arrow, or have a brown skin.'

Then as her husband looked on, thunder-faced, she added, 'You know I have always believed the Bible has it wrong in that regard: the meek will never inherit the earth, they will already have been trampled underfoot long before Judgement Day arrives. Don't you agree?'

The minister's mouth broke into a wide grin beneath its sandy moustache, although he forced a certain air of gravitas to his voice. 'Far be it for me to disagree with the Good Book, Mrs Hebden, ma'am, but what you say is certainly food for thought.'

'Food for thought my eye!' Silas broke in. 'Damned sacrilege, more like!'

Carrie's glance was stony as she turned to look at her husband. 'Then I had better watch my tongue, Silas dear, for I believe sacrilege is a hanging offence in our beloved English homeland. It wouldn't do for your own wife to either be put to death or – worse – become a she-lag, would it?'

She held out her hand once more to the minister. 'Good day to you, Mr MacKenzie. A fine service. I look forward to the next one.'

Silas took her roughly by the arm before she could embarrass him further. 'Stubble your whids, woman, can't you?' he muttered as they made their way to the waiting buggy. 'That kind of talk gets around. You'll have me a laughing stock!'

'I think not, Silas,' Carrie replied coolly. 'In fact, I do believe the Reverend MacKenzie quite agreed with me!'

But Silas would not be placated. 'All the same these damned Scotsmen,' he declared as he untied their horse from the fence where it was tethered. 'Them and the Irish – troublemakers, the lot of 'em!' He turned grave-faced to his wife. 'I tell you, Caroline, we don't know how fortunate we are to have nothing but good English blood in our veins!'

She should not have said it, but she could not resist it. 'Oh Silas, my dear, didn't I tell you? I'm half Irish. My mother was from County Wexford.'

CHAPTER FIFTEEN

If Carrie found that her husband's was typical of the prejudice of so many of the free settlers towards their convict fellows, the fact that there were already one or two such broadminded and outspoken people in the territory as the Reverend Douglas MacKenzie was something she found encouraging and helped reinforce her belief in the weeks that followed that this was indeed a country that offered hope for all. Despite the bigots and the self-righteous, there were independent free spirits here determined to make this a fair and just land for every one of its citizens; people who had come out here to the ends of the earth by their own free will, who were actually enjoying it and were determined to make it as fine a land as ever existed, with dignity and justice for all.

But if Sunday morning visits to the Reverend MacKenzie raised her spirits, she was aware they would sink again come evening for she knew only too well what awaited her. Sunday was a day when Silas attempted to go easy on the bottle after supper and that meant only one thing. He would be almost stone-cold sober come bedtime and ready to put all his energies into what was becoming his consuming concern: the siring of a son.

It did not seem to enter his head that his wife found the act of consummating their marriage any less enjoyable than he did. It was only the fact that she was now sure it was an essential part in the production of a child that made Carrie endure it at all. Her sketchy education as to what one did to start a family was enlarged considerably soon after her arrival by chance confrontations with couples from Yorvik's Aborigine tribe. To them the act of copulation seemed as natural as breathing and bore little relation to the fumbled, unbearable five minutes she found herself subjected to every so often. So keen was Silas to sire his son that, had his fondness for the bottle not stood in the way, she knew that it would have become a nightly occurrence instead of the once or twice a week trial it now was.

Sometimes Carrie could scarcely believe that she, who hated drink like no other because of what it had done to her father, could find herself actively encouraging her own husband to partake of the potent white spirit of which he was so fond. She would even set out the bottle on the table by his elbow after supper as he kicked off his boots and reached for his pipe. What bliss was to be found half an hour later when, three or four glasses on, his head would loll back against the wooden spars of the chair and that familiar wheezing snore would fill the kitchen.

It was then she would either take herself off to bed, if she had had a particularly tiring day, or, if the evening was fine, she would take her shawl from the hook on the back of the kitchen door and spend an enchanted half hour walking under the endless stars in a night sky that seemed to go on forever.

'G'day, you old bugger!' Barney would squawk from the table by the window as she made for the door and she would raise a finger to her lips in a futile attempt to silence the bird as she reached for the old blanket to throw over its cage. 'Quiet, you old rogue,' she would admonish, wagging her finger, as it followed her every movement with its beady little black eyes. 'You will wake the Master!' Nothing must be allowed to spoil this magical time when all of Yorvik was hers and hers alone.

At such times, with her husband safely asleep, she was queen of all she surveyed, and the landscape around the house took on a particular mystical glow in the moonlight. In London the patch of sky visible between the rooftops of Semple Street had been as nothing compared to this wide dark blue velvet expanse of the heavens that could still take her breath away every time she stepped out on to the verandah after supper.

The night came quickly out here, cloaking the hills and covering the valleys in a blanket of deepest purple, sequined with silver stars. And before that there were such sunsets as Carrie had never dreamed of, when the heavens would blaze with tongues of crimson. Sometimes as the sun sank down beyond the horizon it seemed to drag the whole sky with it, leaving tattered edges of fire like shreds from a curtain of flame.

In London there had been noise — always noise: the constant clatter of horses' hooves or carriage wheels on the cobbles and the shouting and cursing of late-night revellers on their way home from any one of the dozen or so hostelries on their street. Here there was silence — a silence that touched the soul and brought one as close to infinity as one could ever hope to get on this earth. Who could blame her, she wondered, for finding this such a paradise?

Only the heat became too much to bear at times, and on such evenings the call of the lake became irresistible, but to reach it meant passing the huts where Sean O'Dwyer and the two other hands lived. She knew that the Scottish brothers, Jock and Davie Henderson, were rarely there as Yorvik's flocks were scattered far and wide across the thousand acres and they called back on station only infrequently. But the young Irishman still spent most of his time working around the farm, and Carrie knew that to pass his hut without being spotted was almost impossible. But as the sun set in a blaze of glory behind the tall gums and the green earth slumbered in the heat at the end of the day, despite her original resolve to steer well clear of temptation, she found she did not mind at all if she discovered she was not the only person on the winding path down to the lakeside on a quiet summer night.

Sometimes it took Silas much longer to fall asleep and the moon was already high in the sky when she finally made her way out of the house to steal down the winding path that was now her favourite walk. And often on such nights Sean O'Dwyer too found it impossible to sleep; nights when the moon was full and the stars so bright you could almost reach up and pluck them from the heavens to hold in the palm of your hand. He would lie on his bunk in the cramped confines of his small hut and watch the slim shadow of his Master's wife gliding past his window on her way to the gently lapping waters of the lake.

Sometimes he resisted the temptation to get out of bed and follow her, for the ten minutes or so of conversation by the lakeside that ensued was more a torture for him than a pleasure. She was a woman after all – a young and beautiful woman – and he was a red-blooded man. The smalltalk they indulged in at such times only served to heighten his awareness that this was a person he could not think of as his boss's wife. And the thoughts that passed through his head brought fire to his loins and a deep-seated resentment towards the old man in the house whom he knew for a fact did not appreciate this treasure.

Sean had not meant to eavesdrop over the past months, but he had heard them arguing, often late into the night, when the sound carried through the open kitchen window out into the yard behind. Hebden was a stubborn old bugger, and was never one for listening to advice; that was why Yorvik was now in such a sad state. Carrie had told him herself of the plans she had for the place, if only her husband would say yes, but trying to get Silas to agree to anything was an impossible task.

'He just won't listen, Sean,' she would tell him. 'I've done all the calculations – all the figures – and he just isn't interested. He seems to regard it as an affront to his manhood that I should even concern myself with such things.'

At times like that when tears of frustration would burn bright in her eyes, Sean would try to tell her it was the way of the world. 'You're a woman, remember. His pride won't let him listen.'

Carrie's eyes would flash back at him. 'But I'm brighter than he is. It's so unfair!'

And he would shake his head. 'Who ever said life was meant to be fair?' he would ask her. And she had no answer to that.

Now, on this summer's night, with the air heavy with the scent of the eucalyptus, and hardly a breath of wind to stir the fragrant green leaves, she was out there, her shadow flitting past his open door. She would never turn her head to look in. But somehow he could feel her spirit reach out to touch his as he lay there and wrestled with his conscience over whether to get up and follow her.

'Aw, shite!'

Despite all his noble resolve, he got out of bed and reached for his trousers. He could not sleep anyway, so what was the point in just lying here tormenting himself?

Carrie was immediately aware of someone behind her as she made her way down to the shore. She knew at once whose footsteps were following at a discreet distance, and, as she reached the edge of the lake, she turned and feigned surprise at the sight of the young man behind her. 'Why, good evening, Mr O'Dwyer! Isn't it a lovely night for a stroll?'

'It is indeed, Mrs Hebden, ma'am. It is indeed.'

Carrie made herself comfortable on the grassy bank and smiled up at him as he flopped down beside her and pulled at a strand of dry grass to suck.

'It's such a lovely evening,' she ventured, aware she was repeating herself, but having no practice in the art of smalltalk at a time like this.

'It is that.' Sean gave a quiet smile and twirled the grass between his fingers as he looked at her from the corner of his eye. 'I hope I haven't spoiled your walk.'

'Oh, no!' The reply was too emphatic and she followed it with a rather embarrassed smile. 'Nor I yours, I trust?'

He shook his head. Could she possibly guess, he wondered, how her arrival had added a whole new dimension to his world? He doubted it, for it surprised no one more than himself. He had had few friends throughout his life, save for the Aborigines with whom he felt more kinship than most of the white settlers he had come across in his twenty-five years. But this young woman was different. He could sense something of the free spirit in her that he could immediately identify with, and there was a certain pride about her that could not be confused with arrogance. Arrogance was a trait common to those who believed themselves superior to this new land and its people, but Carrie Hebden was not like that. She was embracing her new life and her new land with open arms and an open heart and was thirsting to know all there was to know about it. And that was mostly what they had talked about whenever they had met up like this in the past. It was a safe subject that let them avoid anything of too personal a nature.

For her part, Carrie knew she was becoming rapidly bewitched by both the story and the teller, as over the past few months Sean O'Dwyer had spun magical tales of her new homeland. There was something about this wild young Irish Australian that both intrigued and excited her. He bowed to no one – no, not even Silas, and she knew that infuriated her husband more than anything.

'I'll give that no-good Croppie bastard his marching orders one of these fine days, you wait and see!' he once told his wife, and Carrie had smiled quietly to himself, knowing he would never carry out the threat. He relied far too much on his young hand for that. Good labour was worth more than gold in the Hunter Valley right now, particularly if, like Silas, you would not employ convicts.

'The only reason your old man keeps me on is because I'm cheap – and, of course, I'm the best there is,' Sean had told her immodestly soon after her arrival. 'I cost him hardly anything in wages and I know more than anyone

207

in the colony about this land we live in – a darned sight more than the whites who have settled here, at any rate.'

Carrie did not doubt it for one second and she noted that once more he referred to the other Europeans as 'the whites', as if denying his own membership of the race.

And now as they sat together in the moonlight and listened to the gently lapping waters of the lake, she found herself unable to contain her curiosity about his background any longer. Despite all her firm resolve not to allow a conversation ever to get too personal, she threw caution to the wind as she watched him reach into the back pocket of his pants and take out his beloved penny whistle, which he began to clean with the reed he had just plucked. 'They say you're part Aborigine, is that right?'

He half turned his head to glance at her, his dark eyes quizzical. He thought long and hard before answering. 'We are what we are,' he said eventually. Then, with an enigmatic smile, he turned back to his whistle, content to let the matter rest there.

But Carrie pressed on, insatiably curious about his origins and what it had been in his past that had made him the man he was – a man like no other she had ever met. 'What exactly do you know of your background, Sean?' she persisted in a quiet voice, as, disconcerted by her question, he put down his whistle to skim a pebble across the surface of the lake.

The dark eyes took on a strange faraway look as they gazed past her out over the dark blue water. There was a long silence, then: 'Do you really want to know?'

'Yes, yes I do.'

He sighed and frowned as he rubbed the reddish stubble of his chin. No one had ever asked him such a question before and he had no practice in answering it. 'What exactly do I know of my background?' he repeated, with a bashful smile. 'Well, my father was a Tipperary O'Dwyer, Joseph by name. But he called me Sean after his younger brother who they hanged in Dublin Castle just before they transported Pa out here.'

Carrie's face darkened. Was there an Irish family on the face of this earth that had not suffered in this way?

But her companion was unaware of the memories his remark had rekindled as he went on, 'The O'Dwyers are Tipperary's oldest and some would say most notorious family. In fact there are few families in all Ireland who can claim our history. But Cromwell's armies burned our castles and scattered our people to the four winds, and those that remained did not feel obliged to tug the forelock to the English government after that. My father was part of a generation of young men who felt it their duty to fight for the freedom of their land, rather than throw in their lot with their colonial masters. They called themselves the Irish Defenders in their struggle against their English overlords.'

Carrie could hear the pride in his voice as as he continued, 'Some say they took their inspiration from the French, for the year 1798 it was, and my father was just a young lad barely out of his teens, but man enough to be part of a couple of fine victories against the English, at Tubberneering and Wexford, before they caught him.'

And at that he took up his old penny whistle and began to play a haunting tune that was strangely familiar to the young woman sitting by his side on the grassy bank.

Carrie's brow furrowed for a moment as the piping notes filled the quietness of the night air. Then a light came into her eyes as memory held the door and those evenings by the fire with her mother came flooding in.

'Father Murphy of County Wexford', her mother had called it. She had said it was a song of Ninety-Eight, and her blue Irish eyes had burned with pride as she'd sung the words to her small daughter in that cramped back room in London's dockside. At that tender age Carrie had had little idea exactly what Ninety-Eight had meant, but now it was becoming clear:

At Vinegar Hill, o'er the pleasant Slaney,
Our heroes vainly stood back to back,
And the Yeos at Tullow took Father Murphy,
And burned his body upon the rack,
God give you glory, brave Father Murphy,
And open heaven to all your men;
The cause that called you may call tomorrow
In another war for the Green again . . .

Her voice rose sweetly and plaintively in the clear air, in perfect tune with the accompanying whistle, and as the last notes died away into silence, Sean O'Dwyer turned to her with an awed look. 'Who taught you that?' he asked in a hushed tone, for he had just heard recounted in a voice of heartbreaking beauty the story of a man and a cause for which his own father had risked his very life.

'My mother,' Carrie replied softly. 'You see, she was Irish too. From County Wexford. Father Murphy was her parish priest.'

He said nothing; his heart was too full. As they sat there under the wide starlit sky, twelve thousand miles from the land whose blood ran red and strong in their veins, they found solace in each other's silence.

On the way back along the path that led to the homestead, Sean went on to tell her of how his father had been transported with the other young Irish rebels on the convict ship *Minerva*. They had hanged his younger brother, but had given him transportation for life.

Sean turned to her at that point and said quietly, 'He felt guilty about that till the end of his days – that they hanged Sean and let him live. I could never quite understand that.'

'Couldn't you?' Carrie said huskily. She could understand it only too well.

They sent him to the notorious hell of Norfolk Island, he went on to tell her, and he had escaped and joined a

210

gang of other young escapees living rough on the mainland, in the territory of New South Wales. 'Bushrangers, they call them now. Although I doubt if they gave themselves such a fancy handle in those desperate days.'

Carrie had heard tell of them. 'They're a sort of Australian highwayman, aren't they?'

Sean nodded and gave a half laugh. 'That makes them sound fine and romantic, so it does, but there was nothing romantic about that life, I can tell you.' Memories of his father's tales of being hunted from pillar to post came rushing back. Tales of living off their wits, with only a burning sense of injustice to keep them going, and, in his father's case, the fervent belief that one day he might return to the land of his birth and to the arms of the woman he loved.

And always till the end of his days there had been the nightmare of Norfolk Island. What they did to men in that place in the name of British justice was beyond anything any man could happily recount to his son. But what the young boy had learned was enough to convince him that true justice and humanity was not to be expected from the English – not if you were Irish at any rate.

'Did your father ever marry?' Carrie asked, wondering when he himself came on the scene.

Sean shook his head, as he pushed a stray branch out of the way. 'No, he never did. I think to the end of his days he harboured the hope that one day he would return to Ireland. He once told me there had been a girl back in Tipperary and he had vowed never to swear his life to another in the sight of God if he couldn't have her. I think he believed she was waiting for him, right to the very end.' He gave a wistful smile. 'Who knows? Maybe she was . . . Anyway, he died with the name Rosaleen on his lips . . .' Then he added softly, 'My mother's name was Maggie . . . Romantic old cuss for a bushranger, eh?'

Carrie felt her sight blur as tears hovered near. 'And your mother – Maggie?'

Sean O'Dwyer shrugged as they continued side by side up the path. 'Oh, she was dead by then anyway, but she never seemed to mind there had been someone else in his life long before her. Most lifers had left wives or sweethearts back in the old country. She was also a lot younger than him and came along when he was well into middle age.'

'Where did they meet?' Carrie's own romantic feelings were stirred by what she was learning.

'Oh, she was a maid on some station further up the Hunter River where he got taken on to do some seasonal work. Part Irish and part blackfella she was, so I'm told.' He gave a short laugh. 'I never did find out which part exactly. She used to tell me that her body was Irish, but her heart was Aborigine, for she cherished all those myths and legends the blackfellas set such store by . . .' And his voice tailed off as he remembered that soft-voiced young woman who had first told him of the Dreamtime and all the other great mysteries of life.

'They lived together for a while on and off. She died when I was about seven or eight, then Pa took me over and I bummed around the country with him until he himself pegged out when I was eleven or twelve.'

'I'm sorry,' Carrie said, feeling genuine sympathy for this strange young man and the even stranger upbringing he had had.

'Sorry?' Sean O'Dwyer repeated in surprise, raising a quizzical eyebrow as he turned to look at her. He had never considered himself an object of pity before.

'About your father and mother, I mean. I'm so sorry they died when you were so young.'

'Yeah, I'm sorry about that too . . .' And his face became pensive, for now he was becoming uncomfortable at being so forthcoming about his past. It all sounded so trite in the telling, much the same story as thousands of other settlers could tell. And there was so much he couldn't tell. He knew he could never disclose to another human being

212

the love there had been between the fifty-odd-year-old Irishman and his young son. And how the hurts and pain of those early years back in Ireland, and in the hell of that prison camp on Norfolk Island, had been passed on to the next generation through the ears of the child, who now viewed authority, especially in the guise of an Englishman, with more than a little contempt. In fact, he hated the English with a passion reserved for little else.

And what of his mother? What of Maggie, Carrie had asked? What indeed. He had surprised himself even talking of the woman who had given him life. It was not something he had ever done before. To the world at large she had been simply a lubra, for her quarter-Aborigine blood had more than outweighed the three-quarters white blood that had run in her veins. To most folks that had meant she was less than human. Not many actually had the courage to say so to his face, but Sean had known. And it had hurt. She had been all right, had Maggie.

She had taught him how the Aboriginal people shared a real kinship with the forces of nature that surrounded them. She had told of how they felt as one with the earth and all its creatures. The sea, the sky, the plants that grew in the ground below their feet, and the wind that blew, and the stars that shone in the heavens, were all part of the whole to which they belonged. The human spirit, she had told him, was in communion with each and every one. 'Knowing', she had called it, that strange state of being at one with the world you inhabit. And 'Knowing' was part of the Dreamtime, which meant the whole of existence; the beginning and the end of life itself . . .

They had walked in silence for several minutes now, and Sean paused beneath an ancient gum as he turned to Carrie. 'My father used to say you had to be a special kind of person to make it out here,' he told her quietly. 'Those that come from the old country have to knock the dust of that land from their boots at the landing stage, he reckoned. You had to leave your regrets on the shores of

Botany Bay or they would just eat you up in the years ahead.'

And the son of that convict looked quizzically at the young woman by his side. 'Can you do that?' he asked, his eyes searching hers. 'Have you any regrets about leaving England?'

Carrie shook her head thoughtfully. 'No,' she answered truthfully. 'I have no regrets about leaving England, none at all. England never did me any favours. I have no yearnings for the old country, believe me.'

Walking on, he longed to ask her exactly why she had left the land of her birth to come all the way out here to be an old man's bride, but his courage failed him. 'I'm glad to hear you say that,' was all he could manage as they reached the door of his hut. 'Despite what my father preached, he could never make that commitment. He could never forget Ireland, and he died a bitter man.'

Carrie looked at him standing there, one of the first true Australians. And she knew she had to make the commitment his father never could. 'I will not die a bitter woman,' she replied softly. 'I can promise you that.'

CHAPTER SIXTEEN

'Do you like him?'

Carrie put down her basket and hoe and eyed the gelding's gleaming chestnut coat and proud head. The animal snorted and pawed the ground with its right hoof as Sean O'Dwyer slapped its flank and looked enquiringly at his boss's wife. 'Well yes, he's a fine looking animal. Is he ours or yours?'

'A bit of both, you could say. Your old man was offered him in part exchange for some work I did on a neighbouring station, but he was nervous about taking him on. He's quite a handful. But he said we'd take him if I could tame him down a bit. I've been working on him for most of the past six months.' He looked appreciatively at the horse. 'I reckon I've just about succeeded.'

Carrie stroked the gelding's nuzzle. Its coat gleamed a reddish bronze in the sunlight and its nostrils flared and it whinnied softly at the touch of her hand. To her surprise, over the past few months she had discovered she had quite a way with animals, especially horses. She had taken to riding as if born in the saddle, and this particular animal was like no other she had come across. He had a proud, wild look about him, rather like the young man who had tamed him, she mused as she ran her hand over the glossy mane. 'What a noble head!'

'Aye, a real aristocrat, this one.'

'Then I'll call him Duke,' Carrie announced, reaching for the reins. 'With that haughty profile he's got a look of old Wellington about him! May I try him? Please, Irish . . .' She had taken to calling Sean that whenever she wanted to wheedle something out of him, or was just feeling particularly friendly.

Sean O'Dwyer looked dubious. 'Sure you can handle

him? I don't want you meeting your Waterloo out there!'

She laughed and shook her head. 'Just watch me!'

Carrie allowed herself to be helped into the saddle, then, beaming a smile at the young man below, said, 'I'll head out on the north road up towards the creek. You can follow me if you want, but I bet you won't catch me!'

With that she was off like the wind, the animal's hooves sending up a cloud of dust into the face of the watching farmhand. Shaking his head, he headed for his own horse to take up the challenge.

The Irishman smiled to himself as he leapt into the saddle of his favourite black stallion. He had never failed to be surprised by this young woman, who responded with spirit to every challenge thrown at her.

Even in mundane jobs she showed enthusiasm. In her first six months here the change she had wrought on the place was incredible, despite lack of encouragement and often downright hostility from her husband. Gone was that rundown appearance, particularly around the homestead, which had been given a fresh coat of paint. A whitewashed picket fence had been erected around the back of the house in an effort to keep marauding animals out of the vegetable garden, which was already producing as fine a selection of fresh produce as could be found in any local market. And it had all been done on a shoestring. 'Finances don't allow me to spend money on fences and the like,' she had told him. 'So we'll just have to make do with what's lying around.' And they had done just that, converting piles of old timber, left over years ago from building the house, into a fine strong fence to protect her beloved vegetables. She had even persuaded Sean to smarten up his own hut and that of the other two hands.

Rumour had it that, much against his better judgement, she had talked Silas into letting her accompany him to one of the sheep markets at Hunter's Hollow, so great was her interest in helping make a real go of the place. But from what Sean had heard, that had not gone down at all well with the other farmers. 'They don't reckon to women pushing their way into a man's world,' Bob O'Brien, one of Geordie Appleby's hands, had told him. 'She should have enough to do in the kitchen and the bedroom without turning up at the sale ring.'

But as Sean O'Dwyer spurred his horse into action he gave a wry smile at the thought that the young woman disappearing into the dustcloud ahead of him could ever be content with that. In many ways she had more spunk in her than most of the men he had met, who were happy to do just enough to keep food on the table and a roof over their heads. Carrie Hebden had ambition – a word that did not go down too well round these parts, especially with her own husband.

Sean had known she would be entranced by the animal on which she was now some half mile ahead of him, heading out north along the banks of a small tributary of the Hunter River. It had been a favourite ride of his for years and it was now one of hers. He would watch her every morning just after breakfast. Like a bat out of hell she would be, urging her mare forwards, her dark hair flying in the wind as she tore up the four miles or so to the watering hole and small waterfall they called Yorvik Force. And now that old mare she had been given by Silas on her arrival looked destined to take second place to the animal that was already far out of sight up the road.

The day, like almost every other day for weeks now, was a scorcher, with barely a cloud in the sky. They had not seen a drop of rain in almost three weeks. But they had been told the drought was much worse out west; there was talk of billabongs and creeks drying up to little more than waterholes. Only those outback stations with river frontages stood any chance of survival. They had been luckier than most here in the Hunter Valley and on Yorvik in particular, for there was no sign of the station's stream drying up as yet. And thank the Lord for that, Sean

O'Dwyer thought to himself as his stallion's hooves sent up a dustcloud on the dust-dry track. How would he survive without his regular dip? A few minutes spent beneath the waters of Yorvik Force beat a douse down in a tin tub any day!

He caught up with Carrie about four miles down the road, when she pulled up the gelding to wait for him.

She sat flushed and breathless in the saddle, the colour whipped into her cheeks and her eyes sparkling, as she gestured in the direction of a tall bank of weeping willows, their filigree branches shimmering green in the summer heat. Behind the willows towered the enormous shape of an old blue gum tree, its twisted roots visible to the naked eye as they snaked right down the bank of the creek to the water's edge.

As Sean approached he raised a hand and was about to shout a greeting when Carrie held a finger to her lips and pointed in a westerly direction to an area of quite dense bush several hundred yards away.

'I stopped because something's going on over there,' she said, keeping her voice low, as he pulled up his panting horse alongside hers. She had seen two or three brown figures with spears in their hands lurking in the greenery up ahead and guessed a hunt might be in progress.

Sean nodded towards their right and they made for the shelter of the trees by the banks of the creek and tethered their horses to a branch on the broken trunk of an ancient silver gum, as they called the eucalyptus. The tree lay half on its side, as if one day old age had got too much for it, and it had simply keeled over. Without a word being spoken, the Irishman shinned up the old eucalyptus and indicated for Carrie to follow him.

'I'm getting quite used to this,' she whispered, her eyes shining, as he leant over and helped her up beside him, then moved along to give her more space.

She adjusted her skirts to make herself more comfortable on one of the great healed oval scars on the trunk, where

218

in years gone by Aborigines had cut bark for their canoes. She took a deep breath through her nostrils and let out an approving, 'Mmmm . . .' These eucalyptuses gave off such a heady scent that just being in amongst them was better than dousing yourself with the most expensive French perfume. Some were thin-barked and lemon-scented, some thick and gnarled like the woolly-bark, and others like the peppermint and spearwood smelt best of all. But perhaps her favourite was the tall silver gum, such as the one they were now perched upon, for their satin-smooth, shining trunks reaching straight up to heaven seemed to symbolize something about this country. Silver gum trees and golden sunshine . . . The old country had had nothing like this to offer. How she loved this land where every day was a new adventure!

'We'll just keep our eyes skinned,' Sean said, shielding his gaze from the glare of the sun with his hand, as he peered in the direction of the hunters. 'If they are preparing for a kill, we'd better not get in the way.'

A small herd of kangaroos was feeding about two hundred yards away on the left in a clearing just beyond a copse of mulga trees. As they watched a tall brown youth, his naked body gleaming ochre in the bright sunlight, stepped out of the undergrowth, scattering a small flock of budgerigars, which flew off twittering into the sun. He held a spear aloft in his right hand and his lean body moved with a lithe grace.

'That's Banoo,' Sean whispered, 'a younger brother of Quarra.'

Carrie grimaced at the gin's name, then tensed and held her breath as the young huntsman made a wide circle of his prey, his weapon poised above his head. Keeping well out of sight behind nearby trees and shrubs, he crept ever nearer to the biggest of the creatures, a huge dark wallaroo who was contentedly feeding, head down on the edge of the group some distance away.

The animals were in a clearing about twenty yards

across, bordered for the most part by dense patches of green and gold wattle that added splashes of brilliant colour to the vegetation.

Only when the tree cover disappeared altogether did the young hunter step out into the open and walk silently towards the feeding animal. When he got within ten yards, the roo looked up and the young man froze, not a muscle moving.

The animal stood erect and powerful on his hind legs. Its ears were pricked, its large bright eyes watchful as its nostrils tested the air for the scent of an intruder.

The young hunter stood motionless for several tense seconds until, its fears allayed, the animal lowered its head and resumed its meal. Stealthily, as if gliding above the parched earth, the hunter gained another few yards, then another, until he was within arm's length of his prey. As Carrie and Sean watched, hardly daring to breathe, the young man paused once more, his spear held aloft, his brown body rigid, every muscle tensed. In one elegant movement, he stepped back, transferring his weight to his left foot, then lunged forwards to sink the weapon deep into the creature's side.

Carrie gasped and turned away as the other roos snorted in alarm before taking flight as the young man's two companions appeared as if from nowhere to finish the animal off.

'I can't look,' she said to Sean, who was watching the operation that followed with a clinical detachment. She could already cope with most aspects of being a farmer's wife, but killing was not yet one of them. She still found it impossible to wring a chicken's neck.

'Just as well, for they're doing the disembowelling now,' her companion replied, his eyes fixed on the small group, as an incision was made in the animal's abdomen and the innards removed. With a few deft movements, the hunters disjointed the hind legs, before binding them along with the tail to the forelegs. The carcass was then tied to a stout straight branch, to be carried between the taller two of the young men back to the camp.

'They'll have a fine feast ahead of them tonight,' Sean mused as they watched the victorious party disappear into the scrub. He was partial to the odd helping of kangaroo meat himself and was making a mental note to pay a visit once the day's work was done.

Carrie gave a weak smile and wondered how she would cope if she had to hunt down and kill her every meal. This was one of the few occasions she knew she would rather be an Aborigine woman than a man. The women's main task was food gathering from the roots and berries of the lush vegetation in the area, leaving the killing to the men. 'It's enough to put you off roo meat for life,' Carrie sighed. She had already developed too great a fondness for all animals to enjoy such a spectacle, but recognized it was as much a part of life out here as breathing.

As they watched the men depart, a flock of shrilling cockatoos flew overhead, their feathers dazzling white, emerald, crimson and black in the bright sunlight. The birds' high-pitched screaming startled the horses who began to whinny and paw the ground below them, the gelding tugging at his reins to be freed from his restraint.

'Let's give the horses a drink,' Sean said, jumping down from the branch and holding up his hands to catch Carrie as she did likewise.

She landed awkwardly on the rough grass, her weak ankle giving way beneath her, and he had to grip tightly to stop her from falling. She looked up at him, flushing in embarrassment, her face only inches from his, and she noticed for the first time that his brown eyes had gold flecks in them as they smiled down into hers.

'Steady on there,' he said. 'You'll have us both over.'

'I'm sorry,' Carrie said, tucking her blouse back into the waistband of her skirt. 'You've probably noticed I've got a kranky leg.' The colour flared even more in her cheeks, for it was the first time she had ever alluded to her crippled limb in front of him.

Sean reached for his stallion's reins to unhook them from the branch and gave a rueful smile. 'If you have, it sure doesn't hold you up any in the saddle!'

They walked with the horses down to a small pool that filtered off from the main flow of the stream, and when they reached the water's edge, they sat down side by side on a flat rock to allow the animals to drink their fill. The summer sun was now high in the sky and causing sparkling golden sequins to form on the limpid surface of the water. A family of ducks were swimming in the tall reeds that fringed the bank just beneath them. Above them in the branches of the willows brightly coloured birds twittered, and the air was filled with the humming and chirping of all manner of bees and insects.

A mosquito buzzed around her face and Carrie flicked at it absent-mindedly as she watched her companion unhook a billycan from the saddlebag of his horse and kneel down to immerse it in the crystal water of the pool. 'Here,' he said, handing it across to her. 'You'll never taste better than this.'

Carrie cupped the can in her hands and drank thirstily, before handing it back almost empty for him to quench his thirst in turn. He wiped the back of his hand across his brow to remove the beads of sweat that sparkled like jewels on the surface of his skin. 'God, it's hot!' he said. 'Hot enough to melt the very marrow in your bones!' Then what appeared to be a rather bashful smile spread across his face. 'Know what I'd be doing if you weren't here?'

'I've really no idea.' Carrie bent down and trailed her fingers in the water as she squinted up at him in the sunlight.

'I'd be ridding myself of these togs and jumping right in there, that's what.'

She quickly drew her fingers from the pool and sent a shimmering shower of water over him. 'Don't let me stop you,' she laughed as he wiped the droplets from his face. 'If I wasn't such a lady I might even join you!'

For a moment their eyes met and held, then, feeling herself colouring, Carrie looked away and sighed.

'Know that small waterfall about a hundred yards away, just beyond the next ridge?' Sean said. 'I usually head for that on really hot days. Beats washing down in a half empty water barrel outside my hut any day.'

He shook his head at the memory, bending down to help himself to another can of water, and as he drank it beads of sweat ran down the sides of his face. Carrie could see that he was itching to cool off. He looked every bit as hot and sticky as she felt. 'Go right ahead,' she said. 'I only wish I were a man, for I'd love to join you.'

'You really don't mind if I take off for ten minutes? I'm officially working, you know.'

She shook her head and smiled. 'Not a bit. Silas is miles away and what the eye doesn't see . . . You have my full permission.'

'Well, thank you, ma'am!' He raised his hand in a mock salute and she watched with more than a touch of envy as he headed north to the cascade of water named Yorvik Force by her husband.

When Sean had disappeared from view Carrie sat for a moment or two gazing into the dazzling water of the pool, then, as beads of perspiration ran down her back and her whole body felt so hot and sticky that she thought she would surely melt into a puddle on the rock, she finally succumbed to temptation and pulled off her boots. The relief to feel the air on her bare feet was wonderful and she wriggled her toes in delight.

Then, leaving her footwear on the rock, she lifted her skirts up to thigh level and, slipping down off the stone, she waded into the water below. Her pale bare legs caused ripples on the surface, which spanned outwards in the sequined web of reflected sunlight as she walked tentatively forwards through the reeds.

223

At first contact, the water seemed ice-cold and quite took her breath away, then as she paddled further along the bank it grew warmer as her skin became used to the refreshing feel of it lapping around her knees. The family of ducks, alarmed to find they had a visitor, headed off, frantically paddling their way across to the other side of the bank. Carrie smiled fondly after them as the beads of sweat continued to trickle down her spine, and she thought with envy of her companion immersing his whole body beneath the cooling shower of the falls just round the next bend.

What made her decide to head for the waterfall, she was not quite sure. Certainly it was not her original intention. Perhaps it was the delicious feel of the soft sand beneath her bare feet as she paddled round the side of the pool and then along the edge of the creek itself, heading all the time for the bend in the stream that led to Yorvik Force. The water felt so cool and inviting compared to the dry dusty land. The summers were so hot here compared to those of the England she had left almost a year ago. Almost too hot for human beings, she often thought.

There was a distinct dip in the ground just above the waterfall and, reluctantly, she had to scramble back up on to the grassy bank and travel the last hundred yards on land to get to the point where the waters fell off the creek to tumble thirty feet down on to the bare rocks below.

She disturbed a lyre bird in passing, which ran across her path, a timid beautiful creature, whose peculiar dome-shaped nest she could see in the uppermost branches of a tree fern to her left.

Carrie paused for breath, half hidden by the trailing branches of a weeping willow, when the falls at last came into view. To her surprise a lump came to her throat as she beheld the foamy waters of the Yorvik stream throw themselves on to the scorched pale grey of the rocks below, sending sprays of sparkling surf into the air, before surging downwards to rejoin the main body of the creek. It was surely one of the most beautiful sights in all New South Wales and to have it on their own land was wealth indeed.

She did not notice him at first, so dense was the white spray, then she was aware of a figure in the centre of the Force itself. She caught glimpses of him turning and stretching between the cascades of foaming water. Her envy knew no bounds, so deliciously cool and invigorating did it look. Then, automatically, she pressed herself against the trunk of the tree for fear of being seen, as Sean O'Dwyer moved out of the waterfall to stand poised, his arms in front of him, preparing to dive into the churning surf of the creek below.

He was standing with his back to her, dressed only in a pair of wet woollen drawers which clung like a second skin to the taut outline of his buttocks and well-muscled legs. As she watched, he raised himself on to the tips of his toes and prepared to dive. The contrast of his bronzed, youthful, healthy body with that of her husband could not have been more striking. Silas looked nothing like this. Feelings began to stir in her than she had not encountered before, strange fluttering feelings that caused her breathing to quicken and perspiration to break on a forehead already damp with the heat of the midday sun, as she gazed upon the young Irishman who had already come to mean so much.

For a moment or two, he seemed suspended in flight, and his figure as it glided through the air had the grace of a bird and seemed as much a part of the natural landscape as any of the creatures she had come to know and love. Then it completely disappeared beneath the foaming surface of the pool, and just as she began to get really anxious, his head re-emerged about ten yards downstream. She moved forwards for a better view, shading her eyes from the brightness of the sun.

Then suddenly he raised an arm. Confusion reigned. He had seen her! She had never intended to be caught spying like this.

Unsure of whether to turn and run or to stay and brave it out, she stood stock still and stared as he stood up in the pool. The water was level with his waist as he pushed his soaking hair back from his brow and his smile was broad as he beckoned to her to come down.

'It's quite safe, believe me,' he shouted.

What exactly he meant by that she could not be sure, and she was not even certain she was doing the right thing as she began to clamber down the grassy bank to reach the pool at the bottom of the falls. She paused when she was about twenty yards from him and he grinned up at her from the water. 'God, this is beautiful!' He glanced at her own bare feet and his smile grew broader. 'My, but we're brave!'

Carrie bridled. 'It doesn't take much bravery to duck yourself in a river!' she called back.

At that he dived beneath the surface and with slow, powerful strokes he swam right up to the edge of the bank nearest her. Only his head and shoulders were above the water as he shouted, 'Can you swim?'

'Don't be silly,' she called back. 'Ladies – or gentlemen come to that – don't swim. That's for fish!'

'Well, blow me, I must be a fish and never knew it!'

She stood laughing down at him from the edge of the bank. He looked up at her and could see the beads of perspiration on her brow and knew she would give anything to change places. Then his voice dropped as he said, 'What's stopping you, Carrie?' It was the first time he had called her by her name.

She shrugged and avoided his eyes. 'Oh, modesty I expect.'

'You could keep your shift on.' His eyes dropped to his waist and he plucked at the soaking wool. 'Look, I've still got my drawers on.'

She had no answer to that.

'You're not scared, are you?'

'Of course I'm not scared!'

'Well then, you can keep your shift on to preserve your modesty while you cool off in the pool, then get dressed in your dry clothes again for the ride home. Nobody'll be any the wiser. Believe me.'

She stood gazing down at him standing there, shoulder high in the cool water. The sunlight on the surface was dazzling and above them the sky was a cloudless blue. There was hardly a breath of air. She had never done such a thing in her life before, but neither had she ever been so hot and sticky. 'My, but it's tempting.'

'Well, we know the only way to beat temptation, don't we? Yield to it, that's what.' He ducked under the water again, as if to show how wonderful it was and offered, 'Look, if it helps any, I'll turn the other way while you get out of your blouse and skirts.'

Carrie was silent for all of a minute, then, 'All right, I'll do it!' she called, amazed at her own recklessness. 'Turn right around and count to one hundred. And no peeking!'

He had reached eighty-four when, clad only in her shift, she held her breath and waded into the blue-green waters of the pool to join him, letting out a muffled scream as the cold water reached her midriff and quite took her breath away.

Sean turned at that and swam towards her. 'Good girl!' he cried, surfacing only an arm's length away. 'Now duck yourself right under.'

'I can't!' she cried, as the cold water caused her linen shift to cling to her legs and thighs beneath the water.

'Yes you can,' he laughed, seeing her stricken face. 'You won't drown, I promise.' He took a step nearer her. 'Look, I'll hold on to you.'

He placed his hands around her waist and she gasped, either at his naked chest almost touching her or at what was about to happen. 'Are you ready?'

She nodded, not at all sure that she was.

'Right then – one, two, three!' And at three he pulled

227

on her waist until all but the very top of her head was submerged beneath the water.

She emerged into the sunlight a second or two later, spluttering and laughing. 'I did it! I did it!'

'You did it!'

Then they were hugging each other and laughing in delight like two happy children.

It was Carrie who broke free. 'Is this a terrible thing I'm doing?' she asked, her face suddenly serious, but certain she had never had so much fun, or known such excitement, in her entire life, as the water from her soaking hair streamed down her face.

'Are you happy?' he asked.

'Oh, yes!' She nodded emphatically as she wiped a soaking strand of hair from her eyes. 'I've never been so happy.'

'Then how can happiness be wrong?'

'You make it sound so simple.'

'It is simple,' he insisted. 'Life itself is simple, if you let it be. People make their own problems, Carrie.' He waved his arm around him. 'This is my idea of heaven. All I ever need of heaven, really. I come down here just as often as I can in high summer and I don't believe there's a happier man on earth at times like this.'

Carrie could believe it. 'But Silas would say you're just wasting time,' she said.

He looked at her, his eyes suddenly serious. 'But time is all I have to waste . . . I'm a poor man remember, Mrs Hebden. All I'll ever have is what I stand up in, but in so many ways I'm a far richer man than that husband of yours.'

She turned from him, embarrassed by the tears that had suddenly sprung to her eyes.

He took hold of her shoulder and gently turned her towards him, tilting her chin with the forefinger of his right hand. 'You're not crying by any chance?' he asked in a soft voice.

She shook her head. 'Teach me to swim, please,' she

said, as the salt of her tears mingled with the droplets of fresh river water on her face. 'Please teach me to swim, Irish. Please . . .'

For the best part of the next hour he did just that, his capable hands holding her afloat as she struggled to emulate his own prowess in the water. They were both aware that the cumbersome weight of her shift was a real hindrance to her progress and she would have loved to have had the courage to totally dispense with it and allow the cool water to flow unimpeded over her body, but decorum prevailed.

Carrie watched in awe as Sean demonstrated the different strokes he wanted her to copy, his sunburnt shoulders glowing freckled and bronze in the sunlight. She found herself longing to run her hands over the smooth skin and wondered if there was anything wrong with her to be having such thoughts. And when he touched her, his hands grasping her body through the clinging wet linen of the shift, she could feel strange sensations, peculiar feelings such as she had had up there on the bank at her first sight of him standing beneath the cascading waters of the falls.

When finally she was too tired to move another muscle, they knew it was time to go and Sean helped her up on to the bank.

They sat side by side for a moment or two to catch their breath. Then he turned to her and smiled that brilliant white-toothed smile of his. Incredibly they were now totally at one with their state of deshabille as he looked at her. 'I'll have you swimming like a fish before this summer's out,' he said reassuringly, proud of the progress she had already made.

But Carrie shook her head. 'I don't think so,' she said, as she averted her eyes from him and gazed out over the pool. 'You know what they say about too much of a good thing being bad for you.'

His brow furrowed above the dark brown eyes. 'You mean you didn't enjoy it?'

'Oh yes,' she said with feeling, still not looking at him. 'I enjoyed it all right. I enjoyed it far too much.'

Puzzled, he shook his head. 'I think you're telling me to get dressed, because it's time we were going, is that right?'

Carrie nodded as the elation she had felt over the past hour suddenly evaporated. 'I expect that's what I'm saying,' she sighed, as she fought to combat those peculiar feelings within her that would not go away. She thought of Silas and of his reaction if he ever discovered what had just happened up here by the creek and she felt trapped by a situation that was of her own making, yet was not one of which she herself could feel ashamed.

She felt churned up inside and not at all in control of what was going on. 'I'm a married woman, Mr O'Dwyer,' she said, deliberately reverting to his full name as if to distance herself from what was undoubtedly becoming far too intimate a relationship between them. Then she made a helpless gesture with her hands as she turned to face him. 'God help me, Sean, I'm a married woman!'

He reached out and touched her cheek with his fingertips as out of frustration and a welling sense of undefinable disappointment, tears formed in her eyes. One teardrop trickled over her lower lashes and rolled down the damp skin of her cheek. Tenderly he wiped it away as his body moved closer to hers. There was real pain in the eyes that looked back into his own. 'Don't cry,' he said gently. 'Please don't cry.'

Then she was in his arms and they were lying side by side on the warm grass as he rocked her body in his and she sobbed all the hurt of the past year into the damp skin of his shoulder. She was no longer crying out of the frustration of this single episode in her life, but for everything that had gone before. She was crying for her mother, for her father, and for poor Billy. And she was crying for herself, trapped in a loveless marriage with no way out. To try to escape would be to risk being exposed for what she had done. Underneath the respectability of being a

230

sheep farmer's wife, she was still a convict in the eyes of the law. 'Hold me,' she begged. 'Just hold me, please . . .'

He was not exactly sure why she was sobbing like this, but he guessed the pain went far deeper than any shame or guilt she might be feeling over their happiness of the past hour. And he knew if he tried he could probably make love to her, and that she could be his for the taking with a little coaxing, a little love, for as he lay there with her in his arms, he sensed that was what she lacked most of all in her life right now. Perhaps that was what she had always lacked . . .

Exactly what made him resist the attempt to make love to her he would probably never know. Maybe it was her plea of 'Help me, Sean, please help me . . .' as she lay there, her damp body clinging to his, like a drowning sailor to a piece of driftwood. And he knew at that moment that that was all he could ever be to her – a piece of driftwood to cling to occasionally, a piece of flotsam washed up on the shores of this alien country in which she had found herself.

Something had happened in her life, something terrible back there in England. It had to be something terrible to make her come all this way, as she had done, to marry a man old enough to be her father. The only way he could help her now was by not complicating her life any further. If there really was something between them and it was meant to be, then there was time enough. He was in no hurry. As he had already told her, time was all he had to waste in this life. She was asking him to help her and he would.

Gently he prised her body from his and sat up on the grass looking down at her. 'I'm going to help you, Carrie,' he said. 'I'm going to help you by getting into my clothes now and back on to my horse and heading for Yorvik.'

She lay gazing up at him and for a moment she felt cheated, then resentful, and disappointed. But when he stretched out his hand and gently wiped the damp hairs from her brow, she knew she had no right to any of those feelings. 'Thank you, Sean,' she said softly, for he was a man and she knew what it must be costing him to say those words.

She watched him as he reached for his clothes. His body was taut and powerfully muscled from a life of hard physical toil, and he moved with the same grace as the black-fellas for whom he professed such admiration. It was an animal litheness and fleetness of foot that had little in common with the native-born European who seemed clumsy and awkward in comparison. Yet there was something distinctly Irish about the tanned, freckled face that smiled into hers as he pulled on his fustian trousers, and shrugged his arms into his familiar checked shirt, pushing it down into his waistband, round which he then fastened a broad leather belt. He stood looking down at her in his bare feet, for his boots were still with hers back on that rock where they had first sat down. 'You would have made a fine fish,' he said. 'A really fine fish.'

Carrie gave a rueful smile as she sat up on the grass and shrugged her shoulders. That was a compliment indeed.

CHAPTER SEVENTEEN

Once Sean had gone, Carrie took off her wet shift and wrung it out before getting into her clothes, then she sat by the bank for another few minutes gazing into the water. Now the elation was over, her mind had gone quite blank. She felt exhausted. She could not begin to dwell upon what had just passed between herself and the Irishman, for thinking brought too much pain. Never had she known such freedom, such pure undiluted happiness, but it had a price, of that she had no doubt.

By the time she had made her way back to where her boots and horse were waiting she knew that this must not be allowed to happen again. Her nerves were still too raw with all the events of the past year to cope with situations such as this. She had too much at stake to risk throwing it all away. She must try to put it behind her, for to do otherwise was to court disaster.

Despite her negative feeling about Silas, there were so many good things to life as the Mistress of Yorvik. Never in her wildest dreams as a young girl growing up in London had she ever imagined she would one day possess her own horse. Horses were for fine ladies trotting out in style on Rotten Row, not for the likes of her. But as she climbed back into the saddle of the gelding, she knew no fine lady had ever known the thrill she felt every day of her new life riding like the wind across the green acres of this virgin land.

She dug her heels into the gleaming flanks of the animal and could feel the happiness wash over her in waves as she turned her mount in the direction of home and set off back towards the farmhouse.

The first three miles she did at a gallop, enjoying the exhilaration of the ride, then with only a mile or so to go, she drew the horse up on the crest of a small hill to look down on the place that was now home.

There was hardly a cloud in the sky. A haze hung over the valley and in the distance she could see the tall gum trees that sheltered the homestead shimmering in the summer heat. Between them and the hilltop where she now paused, the road wound down the valley, running parallel to the river and past the lake, the edge of which she could just make out glittering blue and inviting in the distance.

'Isn't it beautiful, Duke?' she whispered. 'Isn't this the most wonderful place on God's earth?'

The horse whinnied a response as she stroked its damp neck. Carrie's cheeks were glowing with the ride, her eyes shining, and her hair was now quite dry with the warm wind that had been blowing through it. She raised a hand to shield her eyes from the sun as she looked around her. As far as the eye could see was Yorvik land. All those hundreds of green acres, with their streams and gullies, and glorious trees, it was all theirs – Hebden country. This was where she belonged. She had come home at last.

'Yorvik . . .' She spoke the strange Viking name aloud, in a caressing tone, as she would the name of a loved one. For truly she loved this land more than she could any man. What had passed between herself and the Irishman today she knew she must put behind her. No man must be allowed to come between her and her heritage.

As she got within half a mile of home, she could see smoke rising from the Aborigine encampment to the north of the lake. Several brown bodies were bending over the carcass of the kangaroo she had witnessed being killed earlier. The animal had been laid in a trench of hot ashes and sand to cook and a small crowd of hungry, laughing children were gathering round, excitedly anticipating the feast to come. They had obviously just emerged from a dip in the lake, for they were dripping wet, their slim brown bodies gleaming in the sunshine as they darted like fireflies in and out of the smoke from the roasting kangaroo.

As Carrie's horse cantered past, they came racing over and ran behind it for several yards, waving and shouting, 'Missus! Missus!' Their black button eyes sparkled with love of life as wide grins lit up their faces and they waved both hands in the air.

Carrie knew she was a popular figure with them and she smiled and waved back, shouting, 'Hello there!' as she passed. Several she already knew quite well, for she had got into the habit of always carrying a few sweet biscuits in her apron pocket for any small child she might happen upon when working around the place. The result was often a whole collection of young brown bodies congregating around the garden area, pleading, *'Kalparandi!* Biskits! Biskits! Missus!' This type of fraternization did not please Silas one bit, but she refused to give it up, feeling the more friends she could make around the place the better.

As the horse picked up speed once more and Carrie rounded the last bend in the track before the house, she could make out one solitary brown figure walking towards her. As she drew nearer she recognized it as Quarra.

The gin was walking in the middle of the road, and for a moment Carrie thought the young woman was not going to give way and send the gelding careering into the bushes at the verge. But at the last minute, Quarra stepped aside, with her panther-like grace, and for a split second, as Carrie slowed her horse right down to avoid a collision, their eyes met. The brown eyes that looked back into Carrie's had a cool, almost haughty glint to them that left the latter feeling quite uncomfortable as she dug her heels into the horse's sides and picked up the pace for the last half mile of her journey home.

The sight of that particular young woman still made her uneasy although, as Sean had promised, there had been no repetition of the ugly attack that had occurred on her wedding night. In fact, Carrie had got quite used to seeing her around the place, food gathering with the other women or looking after the children while the men were out hunting. But she never could get used to that haughty stare which she was certain was reserved just for her. It was something she would just have to learn to live with. She couldn't expect to be loved by everyone, after all.

By the time she reached the house, she began to believe she must have dreamt the past hour, so incredible did it all seem, particularly when she passed Sean O'Dwyer taking orders for the rest of the day from Silas by the gate to the vegetable patch.

Setting eyes on him again so soon made her catch her breath and the colour rush to her already flushed cheeks. She hoped her husband would not notice her embarrassment as his farmhand raised his hat to her as she passed and bade her a quietly smiling, 'G'day, ma'am'.

She need not have worried, for Silas completely ignored her arrival. It should have been no more than she expected. The sight of the other brought no joy to either husband or wife, and neither really had it in them to pretend otherwise any longer. Theirs was a marriage of convenience, for better or worse.

Despite her resolve to put the swim out of her mind, for the rest of the day Carrie found she could not concentrate on anything else. No matter how much she tried to turn her attention to things around the house, her mind was filled with thoughts of the Irishman. She found herself longing to see him as she swept the verandah and then plucked a chicken for the pot.

She decided to prepare the bird outside in the hope of catching a glimpse of him going about his work around the place, but she sat on the front step in vain. When over their damper and cheese at four o'clock Silas told her he had sent O'Dwyer out back with a message for one of the Henderson brothers, she could barely disguise her irritation. That meant he would not be returning till almost nightfall. Despite all her good intentions on the ride back, she knew she would be able to concentrate on nothing until she saw him again.

Evening could not arrive soon enough and, come suppertime, she made sure that Silas's gin bottle was conveniently by his elbow on the small side table next to his rocker as he sat down for his last pipe of tobacco of the evening.

'Why don't you join me in one for a change?' he asked her, holding the bottle aloft and indicating with a jerk of his head the glasses on the dresser behind him.

'Oh no, really . . . You know I don't care for the stuff.'

'Oh go on, girl – just for tonight. I insist!'

Carrie could hear his bones creak and wished it did not irritate her so much as he eased himself out of his chair and reached for a glass, which he proceeded to half fill. He handed it across to her with a gruff, 'Go on, get that down you. It might put a smile on your face for a change!'

She took the glass reluctantly and gulped down a mouthful of the clear spirit. It tasted like the worst possible medicine and she wondered once again how her own father could ever have developed such a taste for the stuff.

'That's it! Enjoy it!'

Trying hard not to let her distaste show, she downed the rest of the glass in three gulps, feeling if she showed willing he would let the matter rest. But tonight he was having none of it; he was determined she join him in another.

'Please, Silas, no!' she protested.

But he held up a warning hand as he poured another gill. 'Here's to a decent price at the market next week!' he declared raising his glass.

'To the market!' But after downing this glass even quicker than the other, she excused herself on the pretext of using the earth closet in the back yard.

It was a balmy evening, and not yet completely dark, with just the trace of a breeze getting up as she headed immediately for the back of the house, making sure she kept well out of sight of the kitchen window, which overlooked the vegetable garden. She followed the path around the side until she could just make out the shape of the workers' huts in the distance. The sight of them sent the blood quickening in her veins.

As she stood there gazing through the growing dusk, those same disturbing sensations she had felt earlier in the day began to return as she thought of the young man who lived in the end one of those hovels. Was he back yet, she wondered? Was he already here, only yards away from where she now stood? The longing to see him was becoming unbearable.

Her head felt strangely light and a feeling akin to euphoria began to permeate her being, which she put down to the gin, as she turned from gazing at the huts and began nervously to pace the length of the vegetable patch.

Once or twice she glanced towards the kitchen window and noticed that Silas had lit the lamp. But she could not bring herself to go back in yet. Somehow being out here soothed the turmoil within her. If she went inside again the dream would vanish; the Irishman would be out of reach.

She could just imagine her husband sitting there in his chair as he did every night, and she found herself burning with impatience for Silas to drink his fill and do his usual trick of falling asleep over the last glass. When that happened she could hardly bear to look at him, for his mouth would drop open, and his snoring would rise in crescendo, often waking him up with a jerk, to look around with an alarmed, 'What was that?' But tonight she prayed he would not awaken, for once he was fast asleep she knew exactly where she would be heading, and she could hardly wait.

It took less time than she anticipated. It was just after ten o'clock when she left Silas snoring in his chair to make her way in the direction of the huts on what ostensibly was to be one of her frequent strolls as far as the lake. She hoped it would not be too obvious to the Irishman that what she really wanted was to see him again. Just to rest her eyes on him, talk to him, that would be enough, she told herself, to still these restless feelings she had been struggling to contain since returning home from her dip in the foaming waters of Yorvik Force.

As she set off, the moon had risen in a sky of deepest, darkest blue and the slight breeze that ruffled her hair was fragrant with the scent of the eucalyptus that grew in tall splendour around the house. An owl hooted from somewhere in the direction of the laundry shed and in the distance she could hear the faint, spine-tingling sound of singing coming from the Aborigine encampment. They must be well fed on kangaroo meat and happily content by now, she thought to herself. The celebrations would begin. The blackfellas and their families needed little excuse to enjoy themselves. What satisfied, uncomplicated lives they seemed to lead.

There was usually no one else on the track that led past the workers' cabins, but when the wooden buildings came in sight, she was puzzled to see what looked like a tallish figure walking up the road towards the huts from the opposite direction.

At first she thought it must be Sean himself, for she knew the Henderson brothers were not in the vicinity, but as she got closer she could see the figure was much slimmer than the Irishman. In fact, it was not only slimmer, the person was quite naked. What was an Aborigine doing so near the house at this time, she wondered? Then as the two drew nearer she could see it was no blackfella at all, but a lubra, and, by her lithe gait, a young woman at that.

'Quarra!' She gasped the name aloud and froze on the path as she recognized the distinctive face with its challenging dark eyes, flared nostrils and wide mouth. Unsure of whether to continue, or to allow herself to be intimidated on her own land and make for home, Carrie stood uncertainly by the side of the track and stared in some confusion at the young woman.

But the other had no interest at all in the white woman's

239

dilemma. In fact, Carrie was not at all sure whether the lubra had even noticed her, as the tall slim figure turned off the path some thirty yards ahead and, with a light bouncing stride, made for the end hut, and Sean O'Dwyer's door.

'No!' Carrie breathed aloud as, still rooted to the spot, she watched the young woman pause for a moment outside the door, as if to collect herself, then push it open and enter, with a decidedly proprietorial air.

Carrie stared at the closed door without moving. Her heart felt like a lead weight inside her chest. All the lightness, all the euphoria within her evaporated like morning mist over the lake as she continued to gaze at that door. His door.

Her thoughts were in chaos. What on earth was that lubra doing entering his hut like that at this time, as if she had every right in the world to do so? The cold leaden feeling grew as she contemplated the answer.

Then the anger came. Why exactly she was feeling so strongly she could not tell. She felt betrayed somehow. Was it jealousy? But she had no right to be jealous. No right at all. She had no more claim on the Irishman than he had on her. He was a free man to meet with whomsoever he chose, whenever he chose. But the fact it was that particular lubra and at this time of night was hard to take.

Stiffly, as if struck by some peculiar paralysing force, she began to move towards the hut. She did not stop until she was almost level with the open window. Ashamed of her action, but unable to do any other, she pressed herself hard against the wooden boards and listened.

At first there was no sound but the distant, ethereal singing of the Aborigines over by the lake, then she heard a low-pitched, husky giggle from inside the hut that was distinctly female. The sound froze the blood in her veins and her first inclination was to turn and head back for the house. But somehow she could not pull herself away. That giggle and the other sounds that followed had her transfixed.

How long she stood there, she could not tell. Half an hour perhaps? All she was aware of was of the strange incoherent noises that occasionally came from within those wooden walls. Noises of pleasure. Sounds that seemed to twist a knife in her heart. Then suddenly the door opened and Quarra reappeared. She was smiling, but not that haughty sardonic smile she reserved for the white woman she resented so much. This was a warm, smug smile of satisfaction. Her dark eyes were gleaming as she looked around her. Then to Carrie's horror, those same eyes lighted on her, still lurking there guiltily in the shadow of the hut.

The lubra let out a gasp, quickly followed by a strange, strangled, and totally incoherent spate of guttural sounds that took Carrie completely by surprise, until she remembered Sean telling her once that the young woman was deaf and dumb. Carrie straightened up and tried desperately to regain her composure. Should she just continue her walk and pretend she had noticed nothing? She felt like a naughty child caught in the act of some terrible misdemeanour.

The commotion brought Sean O'Dwyer himself to the hut door. 'Mrs Hebden!' His upper torso was bare, and, dressed only in his ancient work trousers, he stared at Carrie in some surprise and confusion.

She avoided his eyes, as she pulled her shawl tighter around her shoulders and fixed her attention meaningfully on the other young woman.

Quarra began to gesticulate towards her in an obviously agitated manner. To Carrie's embarrassment the young woman was trying to indicate to Sean that she had caught her spying on them. The lubra's gestures became more threatening as the sounds emitted from her throat grew more alarming.

Sean O'Dwyer stood there for a moment or two, his

hands on his hips as if at a loss what to do, then he grabbed Quarra by her arm and began to talk to her in some sort of sign language. For a moment or so the two stared at one another, then Quarra, after casting one last indignant glance at Carrie, turned and ran off in the direction of the lake.

'I see I obviously disturbed a very enjoyable time,' Carrie said, with more than a touch of bitterness in her voice.

Sean O'Dwyer shrugged and shook his head, as he leant back against the door jamb and scratched the mat of curling red hair on his chest. 'She was just going anyway.'

Carrie looked at him. There was no embarrassment, no hint of an apology in his voice or manner at what she had just witnessed. But what *had* she just witnessed? 'I didn't realize you were in the habit of entertaining savages,' she said.

It was entirely the wrong thing to say, for the Irishman's eyes flamed as he shot her a look little short of contempt. 'I choose my own friends, Mrs Hebden,' he said in a cold voice. 'And I won't have them insulted in my presence.'

Carrie knew immediately she had gone too far. 'I – I'm sorry,' she said quickly. 'I didn't mean to be rude. It – it was rather a shock, that's all – seeing her coming out of your hut like that.'

He looked at her quizzically, his head turned slightly to one side as he contemplated her remark. What was it she was objecting to exactly? The fact that it was not a primly respectable young English maiden she had encountered leaving his home? 'Not all of us have got your husband's money, Mrs Hebden,' he said quietly. 'Not all of us can have the luxury of *buying* ourselves a young and beautiful English woman. Some of us have to make do with what's available.'

The words, so bitterly spoken, shocked her. He had plucked out her dreams and left them broken and bleeding right here on the rough track outside his door. The pain was almost physical as she gazed into eyes that had now turned to stone as they looked back into hers.

But she knew exactly what he was saying. He was telling her that she had no right to make moral judgements, no right to feel superior if he had to turn to someone like Quarra for companionship, for, by the same token, hadn't she allowed herself to be bought by that old man lying there snoring in the kitchen of the big house?

But he was not quite right in his assumptions. He simply did not know the whole truth. 'You have no right to make judgements,' she said quietly. 'No right at all. Especially when you don't know all the facts.'

He continued to look at her. 'Then neither do you, ma'am,' he said quietly. 'Neither do you.'

A silence fell between them and she could feel her heart pounding as she looked down at her feet, embarrassed to stay any longer, yet unwilling to walk away and leave it like this. He had spoiled everything. Couldn't he see that? Couldn't he tell how shocked – how disappointed – she was? Something special had happened up there by the creek today. A magic spell had been woven that had entrapped them both. Or so she had thought. But now the memory of that enchanted hour would never be the same.

'Why did you come here tonight?' he asked, his tone softer now, and serious.

'Oh, don't flatter yourself it was to see you! I was just passing, that's all. I was simply having my usual quiet stroll before turning in for the night.' She was aware of her voice sounding uncharacteristically high and defensive as she resolved to salvage what pride she could out of the situation.

'I see.'

'No, you don't see. You don't see at all.' She shook her head in frustration as tears began to glisten in her eyes.

He could see she was upset and walked across and placed his hands on her shoulders. 'I'm sorry I said those things,' he told her. 'I thought you were behaving no better than the other white folks around here.' Couldn't she see? He couldn't have allowed Quarra to be insulted. His own mother had been part Aborigine after all.

'I – I didn't mean to be rude . . .' she began.

'I know,' he interrupted. 'It's hard for you, isn't it? Coming all the way out here to live in the back of beyond with a man old enough to be your father. I shouldn't expect you to understand our ways. I can only half imagine what it must be like for you, for I've never known any other life than this.'

'Are we so very different?' she asked, desperate to find common ground again, to re-establish a part of that intimacy they had known such a short time ago.

'Oh yes,' he replied with feeling. 'Do not forget, I've never known what it's like to live in a proper house – to sit down at a proper table with a white tablecloth and cups with saucers. I'm merely a rough farm hand, not fit to live in a proper house like *real* Europeans.'

She could not tell if he was being ironic or not, but there was no mistaking the passion in his voice as he continued huskily, 'Some settlers look down their noses at folks like me, Mrs Hebden. They like to think they're so damned superior. But being born in a stringy-bark hut doesn't make me any less of a man. And having no proper schooling doesn't make me stupid. It doesn't make me any less bright than they are, just because I can't sign my name.' He wanted her to know that. He would not have her sitting in judgement on him just because he did not always submit to her European code of conduct.

'I know that,' Carrie said quickly, desperate to let him know she did not look down on him. It was not simply because Quarra was an Aborigine that she was so upset. It was because she was a *woman*. Colour had nothing to do with it. She did not dismiss him as simply 'a half-caste bastard', as Silas had more than once referred to him. She had never done that. In a way Sean was as much a victim of circumstances as she was. And every bit as proud.

'I know what they say round here,' she said quietly. 'I know only too well how they judge – and misjudge – people. And I want you to know I shall never think of you as any less of a man than any one of them.' She even managed a wry smile at that, for how could she ever regard him as less of a man than Silas? 'Things like schooling and good breeding, as they call it and set so much store by, don't matter a jot to me. It's what you've got inside you that counts, that and what you intend to make of your life. So please don't feel sorry for me either. There's really no need. I'm quite happy in my own way ... I love Yorvik.'

He nodded and gave a half smile. 'And old Silas? Do you love him too?'

She ignored the question as she took a step out of the shadow of the hut to look around her. 'I love Yorvik,' she repeated with passion. 'And I intend to make it into the finest sheep station in the whole of the Hunter Valley, if not in the whole of New South Wales itself.'

The Irishman walked over to join her, standing just behind her as he too viewed the moonlit countryside.

'You've got one thing I haven't got, Carrie Hebden,' he told her quietly. 'You've got ambition. And ambition is a fearsome thing. It can make you or eat you up.'

She turned to look at him, her head tilting upwards in both pride and defiance. 'There's nothing wrong with ambition,' she said fiercely. 'If you haven't got ambition, you're only half alive. I want to get on in this world, to make something of myself. Whatever I do, I want to be the best. And if that means being a sheep farmer's wife, then I want to be the best sheep farmer's wife there is.' How she longed to be able to say simply a sheep farmer, but that was whistling for the moon.

Sean O'Dwyer's mouth quirked upwards at one side, in a semblance of a smile as he said ruefully, 'So you want to be the best, do you?'

'You're making fun of me.'

'No I'm not, I'm just marvelling at all this great ambition that's burning away in that small body of yours. You'll have smoke coming out of your ears before long.'

'You *are* making fun of me!' She half turned to go and he took hold of her arm.

'Just remember one thing, Carrie,' he said quietly. 'There's nobody capable of stooping so low as those who are hell bent on rising in this world.'

Their eyes met and held. He could not – or would not – understand. 'It's time I was getting back,' she said, shrugging herself free of his grasp. 'Silas might have woken up by now.'

Carrie was aware of his eyes on her as she made her way back down the path towards the house. She no longer felt the anger or humiliation she had at the sight of Quarra entering his hut; instead a great sadness filled her soul. She had felt she had met a kindred spirit in the proud young Irishman they called Sean O'Dwyer, but now it was as if they were standing on either side of a great divide that neither could bridge.

But maybe it was just as well, she told herself. Any romantic dreams in her life had to be reserved for what really mattered, and that was Yorvik, the land that she loved far more than any human being.

She pushed open the back door of the house a few minutes later and entered the candlelit kitchen.

'G'day, you old bugger!'

She glanced across at the parrot and gave a weary smile. 'Good day, you old bugger, yourself!' she said, as she bent to take the empty glass from the hand of her sleeping husband.

It had been quite a day.

CHAPTER EIGHTEEN

If Carrie learned anything from that summer she had her first swimming lesson at Yorvik Force, it was that dreams like bubbles will burst and disappear forever in the cold light of another day just as surely as the sun rose and fell behind the tall silver gum trees every morning and night. Such happiness as she had known then could not last forever, but, in truth, she had not expected it to. The Irishman, Sean O'Dwyer, was forbidden territory and there was still enough of the Catholic left in her to recognize a mortal sin when one manifested itself.

So that summer's day merged into another, and that week into another week, and those enchanted few hours in the pool by the waterfall became simply a treasured memory as her first six months on the Yorvik sheep station at the foot of the Hunter Valley gradually turned into a brand new year. And if the year that had gone had been the worst of her life, then the year to come she would work to make one of the best. Yes, 1843, she resolved, would go down in her book of memories as a real red letter year.

As the cropped convict hair grew down past her shoulders and her skin became unfashionably sunburnt through long days of working outdoors, the pale-faced young girl who had arrived on the shores of New South Wales gradually turned into a capable, strong-willed young woman, almost unrecognizable as the physically weak creature who had disembarked from the *Emma Harkness* on to the landing stage at Port Jackson.

If Silas noticed any difference in her as the old year ended and a new one began he made little comment. His private thoughts he kept very much to himself. The only time he let himself go was on the occasional Sunday evening when he would spend an hour playing his favourite old hymns on the piano in the parlour.

> Rock of Ages, cleft for me,
> Let me hide myself in Thee;
> Let the water and the blood,
> From Thy riven side which flowed,
> Be of sin the double cure,
> Cleanse me from its guilt and power . . .

His usual gravelly voice would assume a thin reedy tone as the words rang out and his bony hands struck the notes with as much fervour as the organist in his beloved York Minster itself. At such times Carrie knew better than to join him. Companionship was neither requested nor required. Indeed, companionship was something Silas had managed to get along without very well during his two decades on Yorvik and he was not about to change his ways now. Circumstances had decreed he find himself a wife, but she knew she was there primarily for one purpose, first and foremost: to give him a son. In return she became Mistress of Yorvik and could make of that what she wished.

But not even Silas could begin to guess at the passion for this place that now burned in his young wife's breast. As the old year gave way to the new, perhaps only the young Irishman who tended to the rough jobs around the place recognized the burning desire within her that drove Carrie Hebden to do her utmost to strive to be a good wife to her husband and to make a success of her loveless marriage so that her beloved Yorvik itself could prosper.

At times as Sean worked silently at his tasks and observed how things were, he hated the elderly man who paid his wages for the disdainful way he treated his wife. Silas had never been known for his humour or his optimism, but surely the occasional smile or enthusiastic remark now and again would not go amiss? She was trying so hard to win his approval.

248

'*You* like it, don't you, Sean?' she would ask after getting little response from her husband about some small improvement she had made to the house or garden.

He would nod his approval, then smile as he saw the light return to her eyes. And he would think how, if he were her husband, he would do his damnedest to see that that light never went out, and that indomitable spirit in her was never quenched.

Yes, there was no denying that he felt jealousy at times. Carrie Hebden was the most spirited and physically appealing young woman for miles around; it was bad enough that she was married to a man more than twice her age, but to be unappreciated into the bargain . . . Well, that only went to prove what he already knew. There was no such thing as justice in this world.

Although the attraction between them remained, over the weeks that followed there were no more such intimate moments such as had occurred that hot, breathless day out at Yorvik Force. Perhaps neither had the courage to initiate something both knew might quickly get out of hand. But something else had grown out of that day, an unspoken understanding between the two that seemed to transcend sexuality. They were both outsiders here, and each recognized in the other a certain rebellious kindred spirit. 'We're the type who are going to make this country great,' she once told him. 'Not the likes of Silas and the others who cling to the old ways and values and look down their noses on half the population.'

At times like that Sean O'Dwyer often wondered where exactly her sympathy for the underdog came from. She seemed to be particularly touchy where convicts were concerned and sometimes he couldn't help wondering . . . But then he would dismiss the thought out of hand. Silas had met her off the boat, after all. They had written letters to each other before her arrival. So he resolved simply to be thankful for her coming, for it had wrought such changes in the old place that he thought he would never live to see.

'Oh, I have such plans for Yorvik, Sean,' Carrie would tell him, as she paused in the hoeing of her beloved garden, or in hanging out the washing. 'But plans take money and times are hard right now . . .' Then she would sigh, for there was no denying that.

The cloudless sun-soaked days of the summer that had just gone had had a price and many parts of the country were suffering the worst drought in living memory. With countless rivers and waterholes out west dried up to no more than a trickle, cattle had been dying in their thousands for weeks now, causing frantic farmers to rush to sell their stock. The markets had become glutted and the price of bullocks had fallen from six pounds to a mere six shillings a head. Only those more affluent farmers in the less affected areas, such as Geordie Appleby in the Hunter Valley, could afford to sit it out and hold on to their herds. And on Yorvik too Silas opted for keeping hold of his lowly six beasts. 'I'd rather eat them myself than give them away for those prices!' he declared, and for once Carrie agreed with him.

To add to the misery of the free settler farmers, news had reached them early in the new year of a disastrous fall in the price of wool on the English market. The enormous production of their own Australian sheep farmers had overstocked the Yorkshire warehouses and England's woollen mills could no longer cope. Things were going from bad to worse. Who would ever have predicted a glut of wool? Prices tumbled. So, with sheep fetching barely sixpence a head at market, by the end of the summer New South Wales's sheepmen, as well as cattlemen, were facing ruin.

Every day for months now the newspapers had been filled with heartrending stories of squatters up country abandoning their runs, of farmers deserting their stations, and of some even taking their own lives rather than face disgrace in the bankruptcy court. Just before Christmas, at the height of the heatwave, had come the announcement that the Bank of Australia, no longer able to cope with the unfolding tragedy, was closing its doors.

'Never did trust banks anyhow,' Silas had informed Carrie over their Christmas dinner, as they discussed the latest piece of news. 'Just as well I don't use 'em, isn't it?'

Carrie had stared at him over her plate of roast mutton. 'What do you mean, you don't use them?' she asked. 'Where on earth do you keep your savings, then?'

He looked at her long and hard, then got on with cutting a piece of meat as he swallowed his previous mouthful noisily, his jutting Adam's apple bobbing with regularity in his scrawny neck. 'Happen that's my business for the time being, Caroline,' he said mysteriously.

'But – but what if anything was to happen to you?' How on earth would she know where the money was?

He paused with the fork halfway to his mouth. 'You're not thinking of putting arsenic in the pepper pot or owt like that, are you?'

She had to smile, for by the look on his face he was only half joking. 'Don't tempt me,' she said. 'I might just be driven to it one of these days.'

But despite their own hardships they knew they were not suffering half as much as many of their neighbours who had much bigger herds of cattle and sheep, and so had much more to lose as the situation worsened. Heaven only knew what mental miseries the likes of those folk were going through right now. Even the Applebys on Eden Vale, or Angus Cameron on Cameron Creek would not be immune, for, with their savings amounting to a tidy sum, theirs must have been a miserable Christmas indeed with that bad news about the Bank of Australia.

'We all have to pull together to get through this crisis,' the newspapers were saying, and so with all the impetus of a new year ahead of them, from the start of 1843 Carrie

251

came up with any number of ideas for raising money until Silas finally lost his temper.

'Why can't you just mind your own damned business and let a man get on with the job of running the place?' he demanded in exasperation one evening over supper. Angus Cameron and the like didn't have to put up with this kind of interfering woman, so why should he? Wasn't what he had already made of the place good enough for her? He had ridden out hard times in the past and would do so again. All it needed was a bit of patience.

But patience was not one of Carrie's virtues, and she knew in her heart she could not stand by and see their beloved farm become run down and risk bankruptcy like so many others in the area. Her deep love was as genuine as Silas's own for the thousand acres he had claimed from the wilderness, but she knew he would never understand that.

She had thought when she first arrived here that she would feel like a trapped animal, but instead, for the first time in her life, she knew what freedom was. More than that, she had hope – hope and ambition. Here she could breathe free. For almost twenty years London's smoke and fog had filled her lungs with grime and was an impenetrable horizon to her world. But now out here there was no such grey horizon. In its place there was an endless sky and the air was pure and clean. Who could blame her for wanting to cling on to it? Who could blame her for wanting to fight to protect it?

But although Silas did not share her fears, a sort of truce began to develop between them. Times were hard for everyone and Carrie knew she must not put too much pressure on her husband, who was doing his best to keep the place going on very little. Instead, she decided to concentrate on developing her vegetable garden – the patch of scrub behind the house that was now, with frequent watering, beginning to flourish into an impressive display.

This was an aspect of life on the station that Silas did

not mind her annexing as her preserve. 'More women's work than sheep rearing,' he told her. Carrie did not agree, but went along with the compromise, and very soon the carefully tended garden was not only keeping them in fresh vegetables, but was producing far more than they could ever eat or store. This happy state of affairs meant that extra cash could be earned by offering the wares at the weekly market in Hunter's Hollow.

How she came to enjoy those outings when she would load up the waggon with all the best produce and set off with high hopes for the small settlement out on the Newcastle road.

Instead of dressing in her oldest working clothes like so many of the traders, she would make a point of putting on one of her prettiest dresses and a clean white apron and bonnet, so that she could not fail to attract attention. And attention meant money.

She would put out her stall with the other farmers on the area of common land adjacent to the police station and as the day wore on and more and more people arrived, the place would take on a real air of festivity, despite the depression that pervaded the country as a whole.

After being on the station all week with few people to talk to, Carrie would revel in the banter of the market place, where traders and customers alike shared a laugh and a joke, with black humour over the dire predicament of many being the order of the day. Some farmers and smallholders travelled up to one hundred miles to trade, and the hard times meant all manner of things were on offer. To the people of the southern part of the valley it was very much the social highlight of the week, when news would be passed back and forth about friends and neighbours, and how they were coping with this terrible state of affairs that had befallen them all. It reminded Carrie of the street markets of her native London, and with the mixture of English, Scottish, Welsh and Irish voices around her, if she closed her eyes she could easily have been back there. But as she set to laying out her wares each week, she never ceased to be thankful that she was not. This was her home now.

'I swear I don't know how you can bring yourself to stand there and do it,' Mabel Appleby declared the first time she encountered Carrie in charge of the Yorvik stall. 'Bartering and haggling like that . . . Why, folks will think you're no more than a common trader!'

'But that's exactly what I am when I'm here, Mabel dear,' Carrie replied. 'Trade is not a dirty word, you know. We have to make a living.' It was a waste of breath really, for she knew her friend would never understand. Ladies did not soil their hands in such a public way in Mabel's world, no matter how dire the straits in which they found themselves. And there was no question but life on Eden Vale was now tougher for the Applebys than it had ever been. Rumour had it that they had lost far more than they were letting on over the past few months.

But if Mabel Appleby was less than enthusiastic about Carrie's new role as market trader then, thankfully, Silas was not. In fact, he was becoming quite encouraged by the amount of extra cash his wife's little enterprise was bringing in. 'By God, you're doing well there, Caroline, if I say so myself!'

He even, on occasion, allowed the Irishman to accompany her to the market and for Carrie those were the best days of all. Sean O'Dwyer would do the heavy work of lifting and setting out the stall and then they would sell the wares side by side, his native banter adding to the fun of it all as new friends were made on each trip. Then, tired out but usually with empty crates to show for their hard work, before driving home they would sit in the back of the waggon and share a meal of damper and ale.

Sean would laugh as Carrie insisted on spreading out a clean white cloth on which to lay their makeshift meal, then handed him his damper on one of her best plates. It was while she was busying herself with that that he would take out his penny whistle and play all the familiar old Irish tunes that her mother had taught her back in Semple Street, and to her delight many a new one, such as 'The Wild Colonial Boy': the song that could still get you thrown in jail for singing in any of the Sydney pubs.

He was a wild colonial boy, Jack Donahoe by name,
Of poor but honest parents, brought up in Castlemaine.
He was his father's only hope, his mother's pride and
    joy
And dearly did his parents love their wild colonial
    boy . . .

'I saw him once, you know — I saw Jack Donahoe before they killed him,' Sean told her one bright autumn evening as she sat sipping her mug of ale in the back of the waggon, the empty produce boxes all around them.

'Really?'

'Yeah. Late spring of 'twenty-eight it was, just after he and his bushranger pals had been sentenced to hang. Jack made a break between the courthouse and the condemned cell and soon gathered another gang of escaped Irish convicts around him and headed up the Hunter Valley. He'd done most of his thieving around Parramatta, Windsor and Liverpool, so I reckon he thought he wouldn't be so recognizable up north.'

He gave a rather bashful grin as he admitted, 'I was only knee-high then, but if I remember rightly my Pa put them up in our hut for the night . . . He had served time on Norfolk Island with one of the gang. Once a Wild Colonial Boy, always a Wild Colonial Boy, I guess you could say. At any rate Pa seemed to keep up with most of them as a matter of honour and never failed to help out anyone on the run if he could.'

Carrie listened, soaking it all in. Even she had heard tell of Australia's most famous outlaw of the past generation. The Wild Colonial Boy — it sounded so romantic. 'I bet they looked a fearsome rough lot,' she mused, taking another sip of her drink.

Her companion shook his head. 'Quite the opposite. To tell you the truth I'd never seen the likes. Jack, in particular, was a real swell. A little fella he was, with hair the colour of ripe corn, the brightest blue eyes I'd ever seen, and he wore a black hat with a satin ribbon round it. Oh yes, and a wonderful bright blue coat with a real silk lining and shining black lace-up boots. A real dandy he was and no mistake. I remember my Pa declaring as they left that nobody need tell him that crime didn't pay after that!'

Carrie smiled to herself as she broke off another piece of damper and nibbled at it. 'You were never tempted, though – to make your living as a bushranger?'

Her companion laughed. 'God love you, no! Jack Donahoe himself ended up dead shortly after that, in a shoot-out with a government officer. And I've known too many end up like that or swinging from the end of a rope to risk that end myself ... Not that you'd know much about that side of life. But it happens, you know. It happens all the time.'

Carrie made no reply, but wondered what he would say if only he knew.

As they drove back to Yorvik in the waggon together some ten minutes later, the mention of the hangman's rope brought thoughts of her brother back to mind, and she could not help but wish that Billy could have been there with them as they made their way steadily homewards in the last golden rays of the evening sun. How he would have revelled in this life and loved this land.

But Billy was dead and the man sitting beside her knew nothing of her brother or of her early life. She had buried the memories of those days beneath the blue waters of the Atlantic Ocean. 'I feel so lucky,' she said softly. 'I feel so very lucky to be part of all this.' And she stretched her arms wide as she sat beside Sean on the buckboard of the waggon. The sun was setting and they seemed to be heading straight into a blaze of gold and crimson glory as the horses trotted their way homewards.

'Tell me one of your stories, Sean,' she begged. 'Tell me one your mother told you.'

And once again he obliged.

Her story times, she called those return journeys when he would regale her with the strange myths and legends of his mother's people. And she would listen enthralled and look afresh at this land they both loved.

'Why don't you write them all down?' she asked him that evening. 'They would make the most wonderful book.'

The stricken look that came into his face at that moment made her wish she had bitten her tongue. 'I thought you knew I don't have my letters,' he replied in a tight voice.

'No . . . I . . .' She stumbled on her words. Had he ever told her? For the life of her she could not remember. That he could count, she had no doubt, but the admission that he could neither read nor write made not the slightest difference in her eyes. He was quite simply the strongest, yet the most gentle man she had ever met.

The contrast between the young Irishman and her husband was most marked on those evenings after returning from market. She could not help but compare the two as she sat over supper with Silas in the back kitchen. How old he appeared at times like that. How old and joyless. Particularly when something was preying on his mind and very often, if it was not the price of sheep, that meant only one thing. The main bone of contention between them was still the lack of any sign of a son and heir, about which Carrie knew her elderly husband was becoming increasingly impatient. And the more times were hard and he was having to fight to keep the place going, the more important it seemed. It was as if having an heir waiting in the wings to inherit would somehow guarantee the future.

'It's not natural,' he told his wife one cold wet evening in late June, 1843, just after her return from Hunter's

Hollow. 'A young woman your age ought to be rocking a cradle by now, instead of spending her days behind a market stall or with her back bent in that damned vegetable patch! Why can't you be like other women?'

And Carrie bit her tongue as she had done so many times in the past. She felt like asking him if he ever imagined it might just be his fault there was still no sign of the longed-for child. It was at such moments that she wished desperately for another woman as a confidante, someone who might guide her in the mysteries of conception and birth. She took no pride in the fact that she now knew a lot more about the production and rearing of sheep than of her own species.

Producing a child was something she knew she could never discuss with Sean O'Dwyer, although the young Irishman had become the closest thing to a best friend that she had ever known. And she had no doubt whatsoever that he was more than a little acquainted with the facts of life himself. For all she knew, perhaps not only Quarra but half the young females in the local tribe were still making after dark visits to his hut, and they certainly would not be going there to discuss the weather.

But her friend's love life was something she tried hard to ignore. Passion and desire was an area around which great confusion still reigned in her mind, and so she did her best to stifle the strange feelings she often felt in his presence. There were plenty of other aspects of their growing friendship to concentrate on, she told herself. They found they laughed at the same silly incidents, and laughter was not a frequent occurrence at home with Silas.

But perhaps most importantly, the young Irishman listened with real interest to Carrie's plans for Yorvik. He would smile and run his fingers through that unruly red thatch of his as she told him of how one day it would be the finest sheep station in all of New South Wales. 'Remember what I told you once about ambition,' he would warn her. But she knew he was behind her all the way, and he kept her informed about all sorts of things about the farm that her husband had not bothered to tell her.

It was during a stint of log chopping around the back of the house one afternoon in early July he came out with a question that made her almost drop the chunk of wood she was carefully placing in the stack. 'Could you repeat that?' Carrie asked, her brow furrowing, as she turned to face him.

Sean paused in the act of lifting his axe and glanced across at her. What had brought the sudden testiness into her voice? 'I said, are you looking forward to having your visitors?'

'What visitors?'

He put down the tool and leant on it for a breather as he said, 'Those folks from England. Are you looking forward to their arrival?' Then, seeing her puzzled frown grow even deeper, he added, 'Didn't Silas tell you?'

'It's the first I've heard of any visitors,' Carrie said, wiping her hands on her apron to rid them of the sticky resin from the wood and trying hard to keep her voice calm as she scrutinized his face. 'Did Silas tell you this – about us having visitors?'

Sean O'Dwyer shook his head as he pushed back his hat and wiped his brow. 'I got it from Bob O'Brien, Geordie Appleby's lad, when he brought over that waggon with the sheep earlier this afternoon. He must have overheard Silas telling his boss.'

Carrie was silent. That was possible. Silas had been over at Eden Vale for the best part of the morning and she had not spoken to him since he got back. 'What exactly did Bob O'Brien say?' she asked anxiously.

Sean shrugged as he picked up his axe again and swung it behind his right shoulder. 'Oh, just that he'd had word that some relatives of yours were coming out to Yorvik to see how you were faring.'

As the blade cut deep into the log, sending splinters

flying in all directions, Carrie's heart stood still. She took a deep breath and could feel it pumping in her chest, as if getting ready to break through her rib cage.

'Are you all right?' Sean asked, noting the sudden change in her. He let go the axe and came hurrying across as she took a faltering step backwards to sit down heavily on an old chopping block.

She could feel herself begin to shake inside as she looked up at him. 'You're sure he said relatives of mine?'

Sean scratched his head, as he stood with one foot on the side of the chopping block looking down at her. He had only mentioned it because he thought the subject would please her. This shocked look on her face was not what he had bargained for at all. 'Well, fairly sure,' he said, a trifle uncertainly. 'Bob said he had overheard Silas telling Mabel Appleby, I think it was . . .'

'What exactly did he say?' Carrie cut in impatiently. It was important that he got it right.

Sean sighed, wishing he had never brought the subject up. 'He said that some uncle of yours – a sea captain, if I remember rightly – wanted to come out to Yorvik to see how things were going with you . . . Mind you, he could've picked it up wrong. He didn't mention any dates and for all I know the fella might not have even left England yet. I don't want to go raising your hopes any that it's definitely your relative that's coming. It might very well be Silas's for all I know.'

Carrie felt as if she had been kicked in the stomach by her favourite horse. He didn't want to raise her hopes, he said . . . My God, if only he knew the terror that was now in her soul. 'I – I think I'd better find Silas and get to the bottom of this right away,' she said, rising unsteadily to her feet. 'Thank you for telling me about it.'

Sean O'Dwyer was left looking distinctly puzzled as he watched her hurry off in the direction of the house where Silas was due back for his late afternoon cup of tea at any time. He had expected her to be pleased at the news. It was a rare thing indeed for folks to get visits from British relatives out here. Why on earth was she looking as if the world was suddenly coming to an end?

CHAPTER NINETEEN

Silas was just coming in from one of the sheep sheds when she got back to the house and Carrie could barely contain herself as she waited for him to rinse his face and hands in the bowl of water she had laid out on the kitchen table. He was obviously tired and not in the best of moods after his long ride from the Appleby place. He patted his face dry with the towel and wrinkled his nose. 'What's that I smell?'

'There's a chicken in the pot. I thought I'd boil one as a treat for supper. It'll be ready when you are.'

Carrie fiddled with her wedding ring, unsure of whether to bring up the subject of the visitors now or wait till later. He was always in a better mood with a meal inside him. Finally she could contain herself no longer. 'I was talking to O'Dwyer this afternoon,' she said, taking care not to refer to the Irishman as Sean in Silas's presence. 'He said something about us having visitors. Is that right?'

Silas looked at her sharply. 'How in deuce did he know that?'

'I think Bob O'Brien, Geordie's hand, mentioned it when he came over.'

'There are far too many people sticking their noses in other folks' business round these parts, if you ask me.'

'But is it true?' It was difficult to keep her voice steady and she was anxious not to appear too agitated as she gripped the back of a chair for support.

'Aye, I may have heard something to that effect.'

'But *who*, for heaven's sake?' She was almost shouting now, she was so on edge.

Silas looked at her from out of the corner of his eye as he sat down to remove his boots. 'Happen it's your uncle and aunt, that's who.'

'My uncle and aunt!' Carrie almost strangled on the words. 'My uncle and aunt are coming out here to Australia?'

'Nay, lass, not coming. They're already here.'

She stared across at him in rising panic as, quite unconcerned, he got on with the task of removing his boots, whistling softly to himself through the gap in his front teeth. 'They're out here already?' she repeated in a hoarse voice, so low and desperate it caused him to look up.

'Aye, that's what I said. Sea captains can bring their good ladies with them on long voyages, you know, so happen they've both taken it in their heads to come this trip.'

The words rocked Carrie to the core, but getting more information out of her husband was like drawing teeth. 'And they're coming out here to Yorvik to see me?'

'I never said that.' He gave a sigh of relief as he pulled off the second boot and got up and began to pad out of the room, heading for the bedroom.

Carrie hurried after him. 'Tell me, for pity's sake!' she said, pulling at his arm. 'Tell me everything you know!'

He paused at the door and turned to look at her. What on earth had brought all this on? It was surely nothing to get this het up about. 'There's nowt to tell,' he said, shrugging off her hand. 'When I were in Newcastle t'other day I met a Sydney fella having a glass of ale in the Ship Inn, a Captain on one o' them coal coasters who'd just put into harbour for his next load . . . Anyroad, we got talking and when he heard where I was from he said he'd had a jug of ale with a Captain Bidwell from London who had just put into Port Jackson and was intending to visit a niece he had somewhere up country in our direction. Married to some queer old fella from Yorkshire, he said! Queer old fella from Yorkshire, my eye! And then he had the gall to ask me if I knew of such a fella who'd got himself wed to a young wife last year!'

Carrie would have smiled at the look of indignation on Silas's face had she not been so concerned. 'What did you say?' she asked, as he carried on into the bedroom in search of a pair of more comfortable shoes.

'What do you think I said?' he muttered, feeling under the bed, then rising stiffly a moment or two later, a pair of old brown shoes in his hands. 'I told him that queer old fella he were on about was one of the most upstanding settlers in the Hunter Valley and that he'd be well advised to put that in his pipe and smoke it! That's what I said.'

'But the London sea captain – do you think he'll come? You told the Applebys he would.' How awful to think she did not even know the first name of this uncle of hers!

Silas shook his head as he sat down with a sigh on the edge of the bed to put on the shoes. 'Nay,' he said, bending down. 'He'll not bother making a journey all the way up here at this time o' year, no matter what their intentions on leaving England. T'weather's too bad.' Then his eyes narrowed as he looked at her quizzically. 'You're not that bothered about it, are you – if he does come?'

Carrie looked flustered. She ran a hand through her hair and gave a helpless shrug of her shoulders before turning and making for the window where she looked out and fixed her gaze on some chickens scratching around in the gritty earth at the edge of a puddle. She hoped he could not tell how agitated she was as she said as lightly as possible, 'I'd rather not see him again, and that's the truth. As I told you once before, we didn't get on too well at all, I'm afraid.' Then she turned and looked at her husband imploringly. 'There's no way you could stop him if he wanted to come, is there? There's no way you could let him know he's not welcome?'

Silas was becoming increasingly bored by the whole thing. 'Stop your fretting, woman,' he said irritably. 'The fella would have to be mad to come all the way out here in this weather. You've got nowt to worry about, so let's hear no more about it.' Then he wagged a gnarled finger in her direction. 'But that'll teach you not to write. If you'd just dropped a line or two to let them know there was nothing to worry about and you were doing well, then they'd not have bothered coming, that's for sure. Bad manners that was on your part, Caroline. Damned bad manners.'

Carrie leant against the window sill and stared blankly at the chickens still pecking around in the dirt. If only she could believe him. If only she could believe that the man would not bother travelling the hundred miles or so up to the Hunter Valley in search of his niece. 'I'd better see to the supper,' she said dully. But her appetite had completely gone.

For the next few days she found she could think of almost nothing else but that chance remark by Sean which had panicked her so much. Then her fear began to abate as the normal day-to-day activities once more demanded her attention. By the end of the week she realized she had been worrying over nothing. Silas was right. No one in their right mind would come all this way up country unless they had to. After the prolonged drought of the previous season, the weather had been atrocious over the past fortnight and those that could foretell such things were claiming there was more to come. She could not believe Caroline had been close enough to her uncle to merit such a journey in these conditions. The Great North Road was bad at the best of times, but in weather like this it was almost impossible.

Carrie quickly became absorbed in her daily tasks and put the whole episode out of her head, and certainly it was the last thing on her mind as she rode Duke, her gelding, on her favourite ride out beyond the lake towards Yorvik Force on the following Saturday morning.

For the first time in nearly three weeks there had been no rain overnight and the air felt fresh and invigorating, although everything was still soaking, and there were ominous grey clouds to the north.

She had passed the other side of the lake and was about half a mile beyond the Aborigine camp when she saw the near-naked figure of the young woman. At first she thought it was Quarra, because of the multi-coloured scarf wrapped around the bare waist, but the dark figure was of a much smaller, slighter build, not much more than a child really. She was walking parallel to the road, about halfway between it and the stream that connected the lake to the waters of the creek. What caught Carrie's attention was that her gait was unsteady, not typical at all of the fleet-footed grace of the race. In fact she seemed to be staggering more than walking. Then Carrie noticed she was carrying something in her left hand.

She slowed the gelding to walking pace and narrowed her eyes in the soft light as she looked across the twenty yards or so of scrub. My God, it looked like a child! That object the girl was clutching looked like a tiny infant, but she was carrying it by the neck as if it were no more than a rag doll.

'Whoa, boy!' Horrified at what she thought she had just seen, Carrie brought the horse to a halt and, tethering the reins to a branch of a nearby tree, she dismounted. Throwing caution to the wind, for she had never interfered directly in Aborigine affairs before, she decided to follow.

The girl was obviously making for the swollen banks of the stream. The rains of the past weeks had caused it to break its banks, causing flooding as far as the edge of the road in places. The area was covered by a type of tall, sweet-scented cane grass, which the Aborigines referred to as *nama-nama*, and the knotted roots of which formed a tough brown lace blanket across parts of the ground. As Carrie watched, the girl picked her way carefully across the flooded earth, using the grass roots as best she could to find a dry footing. It took her all of five minutes to reach her destination, a wide bend in the stream, by a low deformed coolibah tree, where the current was particularly strong.

On reaching the water's edge, as Carrie watched from a

safe distance, to her horror the young mother paused, stood quite still for a moment or two as if in contemplation, then tossed the child into the swiftly flowing water.

'Oh no!' This was too much! Carrie gasped and rushed forwards, her feet sinking into the marshy ground.

The young girl, whom she recognized as Miri, one of their own Yorvik tribe, looked quite startled at the sight of her and immediately began to back away in the opposite direction, her bare feet squelching ankle-deep in mud in places. Despite the horror of what she had just witnessed, Carrie's heart went out to her. She could see immediately the girl had blood smeared down her legs and looked all in.

'No, wait! Please wait!' Indicating for the young mother to stay put, she began to battle her way towards the place where the child had disappeared. Her shoes were sliding and sinking into the muddy ground all the way, as she called out, 'Stay there! Just you stay there!'

Incredibly, the small body of the infant was still visible, trapped in the dense clump of bulrushes by the edge of the rushing water. Carrie gazed down at it and her heart sank. It was too far out for her to reach.

By the look of it, the infant was newborn and was possibly already dead, but whether by its mother's hand it was impossible to say. There were also two major things going against it: it was female, and it was far too pale to be wholly Aborigine. Its hair was a fairish red and its blood-streaked skin was a pale creamy colour, not at all similar to the rich tawny brown pigmentation of the young mother.

The girl was still standing within ten yards of the child, visibly shaken by Carrie's presence. It was obvious from the state of her that it could only be a matter of minutes since she had given birth. Had she come out here to get rid of the body before it could be seen because she knew the child's colour would reveal its father was a white man? It was no secret that half-caste children were even more unwelcome to the Aborigines than they were to the white race. Carrie had heard several tales over the past year of such children being destroyed at birth.

'*Unijerunbi minku?*' – What do you want? – The question was muttered sullenly as dark eyes looked from beneath lowered lashes at Carrie. '*Waita koa bag! Mimai yikora!*' – I must go! Don't keep me here!

'I'm sorry,' Carrie said impatiently. 'I don't really speak your language.' Her Aborigine vocabulary was certainly far too limited to cope with a situation like this.

Her eyes travelled back to the pathetic small body caught in the reeds. The sight sickened her; it made the creation of new life seem so cheap. She thought of the times she had prayed for a child of her own over the past year. Surely even a tiny creature like that deserved a proper burial? How could a mother do that to her own offspring?

She had little doubt that the miserable young girl now watching her every move had, in all probability, given birth to a live child and had taken its life only a few short minutes ago before attempting to get rid of the body. A year ago that knowledge would have shocked Carrie, but she was desperately trying to understand these people and their ways that were not her own. If they were to learn at all that such behaviour could not be tolerated, it had to be by kindness and example.

But what of the father? What of him? Her brow furrowed, for white men were not exactly numerous on Yorvik land. But she put that question aside to attend to more pressing matters.

'I must rescue it!' she announced, as much to herself as to the bemused young mother. Her decision was spontaneous and emotional. She knew she could not leave that little human being trapped there to be eaten by carrion. There was enough of the Catholic left in her to know it must be given a Christian burial if at all possible. She must not walk by on the other side and pretend it had not happened.

'Hold on to my arm!' she commanded the mother. 'Hold

on to my arm. I'm going to try to get your baby back.' She was not even sure if the girl understood any English, although she probably knew basic words and phrases.

She indicated what she wanted the girl to do, and two brown hands clutched on to Carrie's left arm as the latter moved closer to the side of the stream, then squatted down as near to the edge as possible, before reaching out for the tiny corpse. 'Drat it!' She was still a good four feet short.

It took all of five minutes and the aid of a long branch to manoeuvre the infant near enough the side of the bank to make a rescue possible. More than once Carrie thought she had hooked it free of the rushes only to have the tiny corpse swept back into the greenery by the foaming waters.

When at last her fingers closed round the infant's wrist she let out a gasp of relief and shouted, 'Pull!' to the young mother anxiously holding on to her other arm on the edge of the bank.

The small body felt ice-cold and slimy to the touch as she clasped it to her breast and scrambled back up the slippery slope, with Miri watching her every move with a bemused look on her face.

There was no doubt the infant was dead and Carrie felt a lump come to her throat as she gazed down into the perfectly formed little face. Laying the child gently on the wet grass, she bent down and removed her petticoat to wrap it in. 'You'll excuse me if I don't stand on ceremony,' she said to the silent watcher. 'But some things are more important than decorum.'

When she had swaddled the dead child in the lace-trimmed cotton, she gazed down once more at the tiny face in her arms. She felt strangely protective towards it. It had a soft down of fairish red hair on its head and perfect features. The small rosebud mouth was pursed into what looked like a quiet smile.

She turned to the girl watching silently a few feet away. 'How could you do it?' she asked. 'How could you do such a thing?'

The girl stared back at her, then dropped her gaze to the ground. '*Eloombra . . .*' she said softly. '*Eloombra-ni-a . . .*' Such a thing was a way of life. How could she expect this white woman to understand? She raised her eyes and made a shrugging movement with her shoulders.

'Who is the father?' Carrie asked, looking straight at her and adopting an authoritative tone. 'You must tell me. Who is the father?'

The girl stared at her in silence, her face inscrutable.

But Carrie persevered. 'Do you understand me? Father – who is the father?'

The girl nodded and took a step or two back from her inquisitor. She understood all right, but was reluctant to say.

'Father,' Carrie pressed further, adopting an even more severe tone. 'Who is the father of this child?'

The girl's brown eyes brimmed with tears as she looked away, wiping them with the back of her hand.

She was clearly little more than a child herself. Carrie walked over to her and placed both her hands on the young mother's shoulders, forcing her to look at her. 'Who is the father of this baby?' she persisted, more softly this time. 'What is his name?'

There was a moment's silence as the two looked at one another, and it was obvious who was the stronger. 'Chon,' the girl said at last. 'Chon – he father.'

Carrie's heart lurched and she stared at Miri as her worst fears were confirmed. The Irishman – Sean. Perhaps in her heart she had already known. Dear God, he had a lot to answer for.

Sick to her soul, she told the bemused mother, 'I shall take the child and see to it that it has a Christian burial.'

The girl seemed not to understand, so Carrie indicated for her to go by making a dismissive gesture with her hand. Miri did not need a second telling. She turned on her heel and, without a backward glance at her dead child, she ran off over the muddy ground, back to the road in the direction of the camp.

Carrie watched her go as she fought to control her own emotions. What she was now experiencing was akin to what she had felt that awful night she had seen Quarra go into the Irishman's hut. How could he do it? Once more she felt personally betrayed. How could he do it? How could he? What was it about men that made them behave in this way?

Clutching the child to her, she returned to her horse and, with some difficulty, she climbed back into the saddle and made off in the direction of home, the small bundle lying wedged in front of her.

It was now almost midday and Sean O'Dwyer was making for his hut for a smoke and mug of tea when the gelding, with Carrie and the bundle aloft, approached, cantering down the road towards him. His smile of greeting was wide and genuine as he lifted his hat and flashed those magnificent teeth at her. 'G'day to you, ma'am!'

But his greeting went unacknowledged and Carrie was tight-lipped and grim-faced as she climbed down from her horse, then reached up and lifted down the dead infant.

The Irishman paused at his hut door, wondering what was coming next, and to his surprise Carrie asked grimly to be admitted. Puzzled, he stood aside to allow her to enter, then followed her in. 'What is it?' he asked, not a little disturbed by her demeanour. He had never seen her like this before.

She looked around for a place to put the baby, and, deciding the chest he used as a table would not be appropriate, she walked over and laid the small corpse wrapped in her petticoat on the bed.

'What the hell's that you've got there?' Sean asked, totally unaware of the contents of the bundle.

'I've brought you the body of your dead child,' she said softly. 'I thought the least we could do was to give her a proper burial.'

'My dead what?'

'Your dead child,' she repeated bitterly. 'Your daughter.'

Sean O'Dwyer frowned, totally unable to comprehend what was going on. 'What the hell's this all about?' he demanded. 'You come in here with a face like a wet Sunday and go on about some dead child. What dead bloody child, for pity's sake?'

'I rescued her from the reeds at the edge of the stream,' Carrie said, tight-lipped. 'It was a miracle I succeeded or she would be carrion for the crows by now.' Then in response to the blank look still on his face, she repeated even more loudly, 'I fished the child out of the stream. Can you understand that? The poor little mite had been tossed in there like . . .' She made a helpless gesture with her hand. 'Like some worthless piece of flotsam!'

Sean glanced across at the small swaddled bundle and took off his hat to push a hand through his hair. 'Look,' he said, pouring himself a mug of water from a can on the wooden trunk by the bed. 'You may be getting some sort of sick pleasure out of acting the role of Pharaoh's daughter rescuing the infant Moses from the bulrushes, but I swear to God I don't know what you're trying to say.'

He drank down the water thirstily then wiped his mouth with the back of his hand before setting down the empty mug and moving closer to take a better look at the infant. Almost nothing was visible inside the wrapping but a tiny nose and a small screwed-up mouth. He rubbed his chin thoughtfully as he shook his head. 'Where did you say you found it?'

'Thrown into the stream by the mother,' Carrie said grimly. 'Tossed there like a piece of rubbish.'

'Well, I'll be buggered. But it's got nothing to do with me.'

'Please don't take me for a fool,' Carrie said, losing patience now. 'I've just spoken to the mother – Miri.'

His brows rose. 'Miri, eh?'

'She named you as the father.'

'She did *what*?' There was real anger in his voice now as he stared at her in disbelief.

But Carrie was in no mood to be intimidated. He had to be made to face up to his responsibilities. 'I have just spoken to Miri down by the stream,' she affirmed. 'It was tough getting it out of her, but she named you as the father.' Her tone was graver still as she added, 'She wouldn't lie about something like that, now would she?'

'Holy Mary and Joseph!'

'Yes, well, I doubt if even the Holy Family can help that hapless little creature now, but the least we can do is to see that she receives a proper Christian burial.'

Carrie glanced back towards the bundle on the bed as she made for the door. 'A small patch of earth with a cross above it isn't too much to ask, I would have thought. And a prayer said for her soul. If you want someone to attend the ceremony with you, I'll come.' Then she paused to add, 'I won't say I'll be glad to, but I'll come.'

And with that she strode out of the door, to leave him standing open-mouthed in the middle of the hut floor.

When she had gone he walked over to undo the flannel wrapping and stare down at the tiny lifeless face. It was a half-caste all right, as he suspected, but, as sure as there was a God in heaven, it wasn't his.

He thought of calling Carrie back and assuring her the child had nothing to do with him, but his pride would not allow it. For his own satisfaction, though, he had to get to the bottom of this.

It was over an hour before he tracked Miri down. The young girl was resting on the edge of a clearing often used for feasting, some distance from the camp. She had fallen asleep inside an old canoe that had been lying on its side in the undergrowth there for years. She looked surprised and slightly alarmed as Sean knelt down on one knee and shook her awake to demand the same question of her as the boss lady had just done an hour earlier.

She struggled to raise herself on to one elbow and

blinked the sleep from her eyes. Why was he sounding so angry? And why was he so interested in the child's father? Her wide mouth was set firm and she looked away, avoiding his eyes as he pressed her to respond to his repeated question. Then as his voice rose angrily, she finally met his gaze and admitted softly, 'Chon . . . Chon . . .'

'Chon?' he repeated. Then realization dawned on Sean O'Dwyer's face. He had seen the younger of the two Scotch brothers hanging around her for long enough whenever he was in the vicinity of the camp. He was like one of old Silas's rutting rams whenever he was on station. Sean shook his head and gave a mirthless smile. How could Carrie know Jock Henderson preferred to refer to himself by his proper name of John?

After patting the reluctant young mother's arm and assuring her the information would go no further, he slowly got up, then turned and headed for home. He would give the child a proper burial all right. It was the least he could do for the poor little mite. But would he tell Carrie she had been mistaken? He had still not decided on the answer half an hour later as he sat down to a very belated midday meal.

When Carrie got back to the house she felt both anger and disappointment at the incident that had just occurred. How could the Irishman deny his own flesh and blood like that? She was almost as disappointed at that fact as at the knowledge that her friend had fathered an illegitimate half-caste child. The initial pain she had felt at the revelation he might actually be sleeping with Quarra or some of the other native women had now eased to a dull ache in her heart, but there was no doubting that this had opened the old wound. How could men be so cruel, she wondered? Did he ever stop to think what hurt he might be causing her? She gave a bitter smile as she opened the back door and paused to clean her muddy boots on the mat. Knowing her Irishman as she did, she was well aware he probably never even gave it a second thought.

She headed straight to the washbowl to clean up, for her skirts and the arms of her jacket were streaked with mud from the bank of the stream.

She had just wrung out a cleaning cloth and was wiping down the navy blue worsted of her skirts when the kitchen door opened from the inside hallway.

'G'day, you old bugger!'

Silas's expression was one of impatience mixed with annoyance at the sight of his wife. He ignored the bird. 'What on earth are you doing in a mess like that?' he asked, looking askance at her muddied clothing.

'Cleaning myself down, that's what!' Carrie answered in no better a mood.

'Well, you chose a fine time to come back looking like a tramp,' her husband told her gruffly, jerking his head back through the door he had just entered. 'A fine sight you are to be greeting your visitors and no mistake!'

Carrie froze. Slowly she straightened up and stared at her husband. 'Wh – what did you say?'

'Your visitors,' he repeated impatiently. 'Captain Edwin Bidwell and his lady wife, Mrs Esther Bidwell. Your uncle and aunt and legal guardians. They're waiting to see you in the parlour.'

CHAPTER TWENTY

'You mean they've come?' Carrie dropped the muddied rag with which she had been cleaning her skirts and her hand flew to her mouth as the moment she had been dreading became a reality. 'M-my uncle and aunt – they're here on Yorvik?' Her first inclination was to turn and flee as she gasped the question, the answer to which she dared not hear. Caroline's aunt and uncle here – in her own home – waiting to meet her. She was living her worst nightmare. 'You are telling me they are here in this house?'

Silas gave a irritated nod. He had not exactly been overjoyed himself to see the pair drive up in that hired buggy some ten minutes or so ago, especially with his wife nowhere to be found. They had stood there on the verandah as if they owned the place, him in his Captain's uniform and his wife dressed for a day out in Sydney rather than a visit to a sheep station up country on a wet winter's day. He had done his best to welcome them though, by offering a glass of his best whisky to the Captain and a glass of Madeira to his wife.

From what he could gather both Captain and Mrs Bidwell were quite concerned at having had no word at all from their niece since her arrival in New South Wales the previous year and were looking forward eagerly to seeing Caroline again.

'It's not like her not to write, Mr Hebden, not like her at all. Caroline was nothing if not a conscientious young woman. Always ready to put others' feelings first, she was. I can't think what's got into her not keeping in touch, to put our minds at rest,' Mrs Bidwell had said, twisting her leather gloves in her lap as Silas poured the drinks.

Esther Bidwell was a large, stout woman with faded fair hair and rather protruding blue eyes that had looked at her host with some anxiety as she accepted the glass of wine. 'One hears so many stories, you know. From what we've been told respectable young women are a precious and extremely rare commodity out here and all manner of things might have befallen her.'

'My wife has had her abducted by white slavers and all sorts,' Captain Bidwell put in from his seat on the opposite side of the room. He was a tall, stout man with a ruddy complexion and rather gruff way of speaking that belied a surprisingly sentimental nature. And he was genuinely concerned for his niece. Caroline had been his only sister's child and was not the most worldly of young women. Had he been ashore when this damn-fool idea of marrying a sheep farmer on the other side of the world came up he would have put a stop to it good and proper. But he had been in the middle of a voyage to the Cape and by the time he got back to London it was already too late; the *Emma Harkness* had sailed. 'Aye, when no word came within a six month, she was convinced white slavers it must be. Weren't you, my dear?'

Silas had given a wheezy cough as he handed the Captain his glass of whisky. 'Happen I haven't come across many of those in my time out here.'

Esther Bidwell had taken a sip of wine in relief at that. 'I trust she's happy here?' she had said, glancing around the room with a critical housewifely eye. There was not much in the way of furniture but the place looked well enough cared for. In particular the piano brought some comfort. Caroline had always been gifted musically. 'We do hope the reason she hasn't written us is not because she's been unhappy, Mr Hebden.'

The two of them had looked at Silas with real concern on their faces, and to save himself further embarrassment, he had been forced into a lie. 'Now then, happen you've been worrying yourselves needlessly,' he had assured them. 'Caroline most certainly wrote you, for I took the letter myself not long after she arrived here and gave it over in Port Jackson to go out with the next ship bound for England. She was most concerned you should not worry . . . I can only venture to suggest it got lost on the voyage. These things do happen you know, as the good Captain here must know only too well.'

Their relief had been palpable, and Captain Bidwell had been forced to acknowledge the truth of what he had just heard. 'Aye, there's been far worse lost aboard ship than mail before London's been reached,' he said gravely. 'Far worse.'

And now Silas advised his young wife of that white lie as they stood in the kitchen some ten minutes later. 'I had to say that, otherwise it looks bad, Caroline,' he told her gruffly. 'Really bad. And I trust you not to embarrass me further. It was not a pleasant experience having to lie like that to cover up your unfortunate omission. Now the very least you can do for the pair of them after their long journey is to make them welcome.'

But Carrie was barely listening to what he was saying. Her whole world was crumbling around her. If she went into that parlour they would expose her for the fraud she was. And worse, they would demand to know what had happened to their niece – the real Caroline Cooper. She would have to tell them that Caroline was dead and then it would all come out. And once they discovered she was in fact a lifer who was being transported for murder when she met their niece on the *Emma Harkness*, they would automatically think she had killed Caroline to take her place as Silas's wife. Dear God . . .

'I can't go in,' she said hoarsely, gripping the edge of the table for support. 'I can't go in there and you can't make me.'

Her husband gaped at her in a mixture of frustration and mounting anger. 'What in heaven's name is that supposed to mean – you can't go in there?' Silas spluttered. 'Good God, woman, those people have driven a hundred miles or more to see you! In fact, your Aunt Esther has come from the other side of the world!' He had flecks of saliva speckling his moustache and he wiped his mouth impatiently with the back of his hand. 'I swear to God I've never been so black-affronted in all my born days!'

Carrie had never seen him so furious and she could well understand why as she began to back away from him until she was pressed hard up against the far wall by the window. Her face was deathly pale and her breathing was coming in short gasps. 'No . . . no . . .' she pleaded. 'Please, Silas, I can't . . .'

But Silas's patience was now at an end. He had had enough of this. She would embarrass him no further. He would stand for her wilfulness – nay, her downright rudeness to these poor people – no longer.

He marched across the room and grabbed her by the arm. 'You'll not get away with making a fool of me like this, my lady!' he shouted, no longer caring if the visitors waiting in the next room overheard or not. She was their blood, not his, and no doubt they were well used to her wilful, stubborn ways by now. 'They're your relations sitting waiting for you through there, my lady, and, by God, you'll do your duty by me and make them welcome. This is *my* house and they are guests under *my* roof and you'll not discredit me one moment longer!'

He attempted to drag Carrie by the arm towards the door, but she stood her ground, digging her heels in and shaking her head vehemently. 'No! No! I won't go through there! You can't make me!'

'We'll see about that!'

A physical struggle ensued that sent the parrot's cage flying off its stand and the terrified bird flapping crazily against the bars of the cage, sending green feathers flying in all directions as it squawked its indignation to the world.

The commotion brought the Bidwells hurrying through from the parlour next door to see what was going on. They stood in total confusion and not a little embarrassment in the open doorway as their host battled it out with a strange young woman.

At the sight of them standing there, Silas dropped his grip of Carrie's arm immediately. The colour rose in his seamed cheeks as he attempted to retrieve a shred of dignity from the situation. He turned to his wife. 'Caroline, I'd be grateful if you could say hello to your aunt and uncle and then perhaps we can behave like civilized human beings and offer our guests a bite to eat.'

Carrie stared at the two faces gazing back into her own. There was utter perplexity in both their expressions.

Edwin Bidwell looked at his wife, then they both looked at Carrie, before turning to Silas standing beside her.

'But this is not our niece,' Captain Bidwell said in a bemused voice. 'This is not Caroline Cooper.'

Silas's mouth dropped open. 'What was that?'

'I said this is not Caroline,' Edwin Bidwell said, louder this time as both anger and confusion mounted in him in equal measure. Was someone trying to pull the wool over their eyes? 'What the deuce is going on here?'

He turned to Silas once more and using all the authority gained from thirty years before the mast with a Captain's ticket, he said, 'I trust we have not been misinformed. You *are* Mr Silas Hebden, aren't you?'

Silas straightened himself to his full six feet so he could almost look the other in the eye. 'That I am, sir,' he replied, in a dignified tone, wondering what on earth the man was on about.

'And this is the Yorvik sheep station.'

'None other.'

'And this young woman here is your lady wife?'

'She is indeed. This is Caroline.' Silas glanced towards Carrie, who was leaning ashen-faced against the window sill, as if her legs might give way at any moment. 'This is my wife.'

'Then all I can say is, she may very well be your wife, but she is certainly not our Caroline. That young woman is not our niece. She is not the Caroline Cooper who sailed out here on the *Emma Harkness* last year to marry you,' Edwin Bidwell continued in his most authoritative tone, and his wife stood open-mouthed just behind him looking as if she were about to faint at any moment.

But if they were confused, Silas was even more so. He bridled at his visitor's tone and assertions and could make no sense of them at all. Were they taking him for a fool? 'Take care there, Captain,' he warned. 'I fear one of us is a mite confused. This young lady is indeed the Caroline Cooper who agreed to come out on the *Emma Harkness* to marry me, for I met her off the ship myself. Good God, man, she has the papers to prove it!'

'She may well have the papers to prove it,' Edwin Bidwell declared. 'But I can assure you this young woman is not our niece. She is not the Caroline Cooper we know.'

He turned to his wife, who was now standing with her hand over her mouth as if afraid she might scream at any moment. 'Tell him, Esther,' he commanded. 'Tell him this is not our Caroline.'

But Esther Bidwell was too shocked to say a word. This was the first voyage in five years that she accompanied her husband on and it was only for dear Caroline's sake that she had agreed to come at all. She had been every bit as alarmed as her husband at having no word from his niece for so long, and she had become quite convinced that something awful must have befallen her. She could only shake her head as she gazed in confusion and mounting anxiety at this strange young woman who was purporting to be Edwin's beloved sister's child. She extracted a lace-trimmed handkerchief from her jacket pocket and held it to her nose as tears began to well in her eyes.

'You can see that my wife's been dreadfully shaken by this whole business,' Edwin Bidwell said, thoroughly upset himself by now and determined to get to the bottom of things as quickly as possible. 'And I can't say as I blame her. She's just travelled to the other side of the world to find an imposter in our Caroline's place.'

His eyes bored into Silas, whom he seemed to be holding responsible for this whole sorry state of affairs. 'Explain yourself, sir! Just who is this young woman – and more to the point, where is my niece? What have you done with her?'

'Done with her?' Silas blustered. 'I'll have you know, my good sir, I sent this young woman, Caroline Cooper, the money for her fare and I personally met her off the boat. And you ask me what I've done with her?'

'But this is not the Caroline Cooper – our niece – who left England to marry Mr Silas Hebden of Yorvik sheep station, we can assure you of that.'

It was stalemate, and now Silas Hebden was just as confused as they were. He turned to his wife, who had been standing silently behind him. Never for a single moment had he doubted her to be anyone but the young woman to whom he had written those letters. Damn it all, she still had them in that trunk she came with. There was something mighty strange going on here and he was determined to discover the truth. He looked at Edwin Bidwell and said ominously, 'Happen, it looks, Captain, as if someone is lying. And that someone is not me, I can assure thee o' that.'

It was time to confront his wife. 'Just who are you?' he demanded of Carrie. 'If you're not Caroline Cooper, just who the deuce are you?'

Carrie stood there as three pairs of eyes bore down on her and three pairs of ears impatiently awaited her answer. What did she tell them? To admit the truth was tantamount to writing her own death warrant, for with her life sentence for the murder of her father still hanging over her nobody would ever believe she did not murder Caroline Cooper and dispose of the body, simply to take her place and gain her own freedom. No – there was no way on earth she could tell them the truth.

'Answer me, woman!' Silas commanded. 'Have you lost your tongue?'

Carrie opened her mouth and her voice was hoarse as her throat contracted with nerves as she looked at the man who was her husband. 'I – I'll explain everything,' she said imploringly. 'I promise you, I'll explain everything. If you just give me a moment . . . I – I don't feel too well . . .'

She began to back towards the door. 'If you put on the kettle for our visitors, Silas dear, I'll just get a breath of fresh air . . . I'll be back in a moment.'

Silas glanced across at the Bidwells, then they all looked at Carrie. There was no denying she looked dreadful. Her face was grey and her lips colourless, and she was shaking.

'Well, it'll do none of us any good if she takes poorly and can't explain herself, that's for sure,' Edwin Bidwell said. 'We've waited this long for an explanation, I dare say a few minutes more won't hurt.' He turned to his wife. 'What do you say, my dear?'

Esther Bidwell looked dazed. She shook her head as she fumbled with her handkerchief. 'I think the young lady should be allowed to get a breath of air if she needs it,' she said in a shaky voice. 'Then perhaps we can all sit down and have a cup of tea and get to the bottom of this.'

'Aye. I'd hate to think the police would have to be brought in,' her husband said ominously. 'But I warn you, Mr Hebden, I'll not shrink from doing so if I'm not satisfied with the answers we get.'

At that Silas Hebden turned to his wife. 'I'd not tarry out there if I were you, Caroline. There are things to be resolved here tonight. Major things, and the quicker we get down to it the better.' He made a move towards the door leading back to the parlour and began to usher his guests out. 'We might as well go back through next door and make ourselves comfortable,' he told the Bidwells. 'My wife won't be more than a minute or two.'

Carrie watched all three of them disappear into the lobby between the two rooms, then, before Silas had a chance to return, she opened the back door and closed it quickly behind her.

Once outside, she paused for a moment to steady herself, then set off as fast as her shaking legs would carry her to the stables where she knew her horse would be waiting.

'Quiet, boy! Quiet!' she implored, as the animal whinnied its delight at seeing her again so soon.

She seemed to be all thumbs as she struggled with the tack, then led Duke out of the mustiness of the stables into the grey daylight. 'Easy . . . easy . . .' she implored the beast as it tossed its head and snorted approval at being in the fresh air once more. Please don't let Silas look out of the back window, she prayed, as she attempted to pacify the prancing horse.

The relief she felt was overwhelming when she was finally on its back and heading off up the north road in the direction of the lake.

She cast only one fleeting glance back at the house that had been her home for the past year. They would be in there waiting for her, wondering what was taking her so long. Then Silas would apologize and go and look for her, and when he did not find her, realization would dawn and he would curse and head for the stables.

He would find the horse gone. But they would never find her. They would believe she had headed south towards Sydney, or east towards Newcastle. Never for one moment would they think she would be heading north into the unknown.

The wind was cold on her wet cheeks as the gelding raced onwards, and she was suddenly aware she was crying. Tears were streaming from her eyes as she thought of what she was leaving behind. Yorvik . . . even the very name was magic to her soul. She had loved this land that would now be hers no more. For she could never return here. She could never again assume the identity of her dead friend. As sure as there was a God in heaven they would arrest her and send her to that hellhole they called the prison factory in Parramatta and she would never breathe the air of this land again as a free woman.

Where she was heading for she neither knew nor cared. She was fleeing for her life and all she knew was that she had to put as many miles as possible between herself and this place she loved so much.

'We'll make it, boy,' she whispered into her horse's ear, as she bent low over the flying mane. 'We'll make it. Just you wait and see.'

But in her heart she was not so sure, as a cold rain began to fall and mingle with the tears that flowed in bitter streams from her eyes.

JINDABARLI – *the Justice of Dreamtime*

The time that followed was what Carrie would look on as the Wilderness Years. They were the long weeks, months and years when she truly believed she was being tested, being made to pay for her sin. She had assumed the identity of a dead woman and had been found out; now she was being made to pay the price.

The Aborigines had a word for it: *Jindabarli* – the Justice of Dreamtime.

When she fled from Yorvik that wet winter's day in 1843 she had no idea where she was headed. Her only concern was to put as much mileage between herself and her accusers as possible.

There followed days and nights of panic, loneliness and fear of the future. For all she knew there might be 'Wanted' notices out for her in every police station in the land. She could be living her last days as a free woman. To avoid the towns and villages, for days she bypassed the roads and well-used tracks, choosing instead to travel only over the roughest terrain, for fear of her guilt catching up with her in the form of a bounty hunter or some sharp-eyed lawman.

At night she slept in ditches, to awake soaked to the skin, still dog-tired, to make her way across waterlogged billabongs and swamps, over a landscape awash with rain, the likes of which had not been seen in the territory in years. The long drought that had caused so much misery had ended in a flooded countryside that made normal travel almost impossible. As she struggled onwards she was faced with rivers breaking their banks and everywhere was the stench of rotting corpses of drowned cattle. Farmers were having their livelihoods destroyed before their very eyes.

The misery of that time was not hers alone. Up and down the territory others were having their lives torn apart. Even the poor were not immune. Those that had begun with little, were left with less as squatters' huts were washed away, and the relentless rain burst through their stringy-bark roofs. Rich and poor alike were suffering as the flood waters claimed all in their path.

Often during those dark days Carrie doubted if she could carry on. Where was she going? She had no answer, for there was none. She was in a strange land amongst strangers. But she pressed on, avoiding the worst areas and urging Duke, her beloved horse, to go that last long mile every night, before bedding down wherever she could find a dry few feet to rest her weary body.

Food she begged or stole whenever the opportunity presented itself, and she was not ashamed to do either. The countryside was full of itinerants such as herself, forced to take to the road for one reason or another. Quite a few were on the run from the law, but the majority were free settlers or squatters forced off their runs by either the flood waters or the terrible depression the country had been going through.

There was a quiet desperation to the people during that year of 1842–3. So many had seen their dreams die along with their cattle, first through drought, then through flood. There seemed no justice to life. Only those who believed in *Jindabarli* could see a reason for their suffering. The debt was now being called in for whatever sins they had committed during their lives. Several old lags she met spoke of going back to Britain, but it was only talk. They had no money to go, nor any money to stay. Life was hard indeed for the new Australians.

For months Carrie lived a precarious hand-to-mouth existence, picking up what little she could in the way of food or money for doing any type of menial work available. For the most part people were kind, for Australians had long had an open door policy towards swaggers and others.

Often it seemed that half the country was on the move, in search of God only knew what. But if a door was knocked at in the outback, whatever food there was within that homestead was shared and a bed made up, if only on the floor.

It was after months of such a life that Carrie eventually came upon a band of men who were to prove her salvation. She was at her lowest ebb when she came across the bushrangers. Originally escapees from the hell of Macquarie Harbour and the new Port Arthur prison in Van Diemen's Land, over the past year they had reached the mainland and had been gradually moving north. After spending some weeks in the Blue Mountains, they had made their way via a drove road over Mount Macquarie down through Hartley and then on to the big cattle market at Emu Plains, some forty miles from Sydney, where livestock from all parts of the territory was sold or bartered. For those who chose to spend their lives as bushrangers, such as 'The Swingers' as they called themselves, even in the hardest of times there were rich pickings to be had, particularly around country markets where a lot of cash was changing hands. By the time Carrie met up with them over a hundred miles north of Yorvik, their swagbags were filled to bursting.

These fugitives from justice who came to her rescue when her horse got trapped in a ditch were, to her surprise, not Irish but native Englishmen, transported from the Shire counties during the infamous 'Captain Swing' riots of the previous decade. Now in their twenties and thirties, all five had been active in their youth protesting against the loss of Common Land due to the government policy of Enclosure, and against the Corn Laws, which protected the rich grain-producing farmers at the expense of the rural poor.

'Fat lot of good it did us,' the youngest, a freckle-faced young man called Dan Hudd, told Carrie. 'Those greedy buggers of farmers have won, haven't they? Families like ours back home got nowhere to graze their cattle now and can't afford bread for their little 'uns' mouths.'

This deep-seated resentment of rich farmers who got richer still at the expense of the small man now extended to their new land of Australia. They had no guilt at robbing those rich station owners they felt could afford it, and were generous in sharing their bounty with those in need.

Carrie was terrified at her first sight of them, for with their brightly coloured kerchiefs covering the lower part of their faces and their wild, unkempt appearance, they looked nothing short of pistol-toting highwaymen. But they proved real gentlemen in a time of need. Once they had pulled Duke free from the mud that entrapped him, they quickly saw her desperation; she had not eaten for almost two days. That night they shared their food and shelter with her, and not one attempted to lay a finger on her. From then on they prided themselves on being her protectors. 'There'll never be anyone come any funny business with you while we're around,' they swore to her. And in the quiet moments of evening, they even told her of their own wives and sweethearts back home, and of how they hoped one day to see them again. But in her heart Carrie knew they never would. Their fair young sweethearts would grow into bitter old women waiting, and their children would have children in their turn. England was a whole world away now. For those sent here under a life sentence, it meant exactly that.

Most of all throughout the weeks that followed, she came to enjoy the camaraderie of sitting around the campfire at night with them, telling each other stories and singing songs. And while all the old English folk songs were sung with great gusto, and sometimes a quiet tear, the bushrangers she discovered had their own roll call of heroes about whom songs had already been written. It was a strangely moving feeling to sit there and listen to such pure-bred Englishmen sing:

Old Ireland lies groaning, a hand at her throat,
By coward betrayed, and by foreigner bought.
Forget not the lessons our fathers have taught!
Though our land's full of danger and held by the
   stranger
– Be brave and be true!
We'll take to the hills like bandits of old,
When Rome was first founded by warriors bold,
Who knew how to plunder the rich of their gold:
A life full of danger, with Jack the bushranger
– The bold Donahoe!

That song, they told her, had become the bushrangers'
anthem, and the fact that she knew someone who had
actually met the bold Jack Donahoe in the flesh considerably raised her prestige in the eyes of her new friends.

'He may have been shot just before we reached these
shores, but we're carrying on his tradition. We're the Australian Robin Hoods of today!' Harry Howarth, a landless
labourer's son from Leicestershire, declared. And they
truly believed themselves to be so. Whether some of the
rich farmers they robbed would have been quite as compli-
mentary, Carrie could not be so sure.

She remained with her new friends for almost four
months, until, weary of constantly moving from place to
place, she reluctantly left them in a particularly beautiful
part of the Macleay Valley to knock on the door of the
finest house she could find to ask for work.

BOOK TWO

The Path of Hope

Build not upon resolve, and not upon regret,
The structure of the future. Do not grope
Among the shadows of old sins, but let
Thine own soul's light shine on the path of hope
And dissipate the darkness. Waste no tears
Upon the blotted record of the lost years.
Ella Wheeler Wilcox

CHAPTER TWENTY-ONE

October 1872
Great Glen cattle station, Macleay River Valley

Carrie got up from the chair and grasped the newspaper to her breast as she walked to the bay window and looked out over the lush green lawn fronting the house that had been her home for the past twenty-nine years. The fine lines etched in the skin around her eyes and mouth creased into a fond smile, for the window was open and she could hear the laughter of her son Billy as he played with Tiger, his pet collie, on the grass. 'William Shaughnessy Gordon.' She spoke the name aloud. It had a fine sound to it. William for her brother Billy; Shaughnessy for her Irish mother, and Gordon for her child's father, the man who had taken her in all those years ago and made her welcome in his home.

A shaft of evening sunlight highlighted the few strands of silver that streaked the head of still glossy dark hair as she waved at her son then turned to let her gaze linger on the fine furniture, the oil paintings of Scottish glens on the walls, the baby grand piano in the corner, and all the other trappings of wealth that she had become so accustomed to over the past two decades. Great Glen was a fine house, grander even than the Applebys' Eden Vale, more elegant than Cameron Creek, and more impressive than just about any other home she could think of in New South Wales. But never was it something that she could take for granted. Never. It had been too sorely paid for.

When she had knocked at the door that day in 1843, she had been at the end of her tether. Tired out mentally and physically from so many months spent on the road, she had held out little hope of being offered a job. After all, who would rush to employ such a scarecrow as she had been then? But the Great Glen cattle station was no ordinary place. It was owned by an elderly Scotsman by the name of John 'Big Jock' Gordon. And Big Jock had been big of heart as well as big of stature, for he had immediately taken pity on the unkempt young woman standing on his doorstep pleading for work in return for bed and board. His housekeeper of twenty years had died not six months before and he was tired of fending for himself, or relying on the goodwill of his hands' wives. It was high time he replaced old Agnes on a permanent basis. But he was still a canny Scot, for all that. 'Can you cook?' he asked Carrie, in that bluff, no-nonsense way of his. If he gave this wretched creature a chance, she would have to prove herself or she would be out on her ear.

'As well as anyone,' had been her boastful reply, for she had nothing to lose.

'Well, then, I'll give you a week's trial.'

That week's trial lasted for almost sixteen years, until her swelling stomach told Big Jock that perhaps it would be more fitting if a visit were paid to the local Presbyterian minister to ensure the child of a name.

The knowledge that she was pregnant had come as a great shock to Carrie, for at the age of thirty-six she had all but given up on ever becoming a mother. She was not even living as Big Jock's common-law wife. Their relationship was more one of affection than lust. They had ended up in bed together only infrequently in their years under the same roof, and usually only when the whisky had given him the courage to pursue whatever amorous thoughts he managed to keep well in check the rest of the time. For the most part, Big Jock's dour Scottish Calvinistic upbringing held sway over such excesses of the flesh, and on the days following the odd occasion when he did fall from grace, he could not bear to look her in the face without a deep flush coming to his already florid features.

This almost boyish embarrassment Carrie found strangely touching, and on those rare occasions when he did pursue her sexually, there was never any question in her mind of refusing him, for Big Jock Gordon was not an obnoxious fighting drunk like so many she knew. Even under the influence, he was a gentle, sentimental man who would quote Robert Burns to her as his blue eyes misted with thoughts of home, and the level of the whisky bottle beside him got lower and lower. In their own ways, she knew they were both lonely people, like so many who had arrived out here to make a new life for themselves, and he had been good to her. How could she refuse him the occasional comfort of her bed, when he had opened his home, if not his heart, to her all those years ago?

It was funny how there had never been any question of them being 'in love'. Carrie guessed, although she had no proof, that there had been a young woman once, back in the old country, but for one reason or another the romance had been ill-fated and Big Jock had come out to Australia to forget her. Only in the sentimental love songs of Burns that he so often played on the piano in the parlour did the ghost of that past return to haunt the blue of his eyes, as he gazed out of the window and left Great Glen's green acres far behind to fly back to that cold northern land. Only when he thought there was no one to hear would his gruff voice echo the words of the poet that he had carried with him in his heart to this far place:

> Till a' the seas gang dry, my love,
> And the rocks melt wi' the sun,
> And I will love thee still, my dear,
> While the sands o' life shall run . . .
> So fare thee weel, my only love,
> And fare thee weel a while,
> For I will come again, my love,
> 'Tho 'twere ten thousand mile . . .

But both he and Carrie, his silent listener, knew that he would never 'come again'. That flame that he had always carried in his heart would never be able to flare up and warm his heart with its glow. Like so many out here, fleeting memories branded on the heart when young would have to last a lifetime. For Big Jock, as for so many others, second best would have to do.

It was funny how well Carrie found she understood, although no words were ever said. And, as for herself . . . Well, if she was really truthful, the only man she ever dreamt about she knew would have been just as ill-fated a romance. The Irishman, Sean O'Dwyer, was not the sort that any sensible-minded female would have ever got herself involved with. But, still, just occasionally, somewhere deep in her soul she gave a silent sigh for that rare free spirit who had touched her life so fleetingly all those years ago . . .

The day that her employer proposed marriage was one of the worst days in Carrie's life. Although she knew she was not in love with him, nor he with her, she had a deep affection for the big, burly Aberdonian, despite his fondness for 'the water of life', as he always referred to his country's favourite drink. His decision to 'do the honourable thing' and ask her to be his wife she appreciated deeply, but she also knew that to marry him would be to become a bigamist as long as Silas was still alive, and she had no proof that her husband back on Yorvik was anything other than still hale and hearty. She had had no choice but to confess that instead of being the widow she had made herself out to be, she was, in fact, a runaway wife. And in order to soften the blow, she had added the fiction that she had also been the victim of several years of physical abuse.

Whether Big Jock was truly upset by the news she never managed to find out, for the Scotsman had made a lifelong virtue of hiding his innermost feelings. The word marriage was never mentioned again, although he did tell her that his lawyer in Port Macquarie had made provision for both her and the coming child in his will. It was more than she could have hoped for, and certainly more than she expected, for, despite their shared parentage of Billy, she knew that she and Big Jock would never actually live together as husband and wife. She was his housekeeper and liked it that way, and so did he. She had made no attempt to seduce him, nor he to seduce her. The few occasions they had ended up in bed together had been more by accident than design, and neither ever imagined his fumbled few minutes of passion would result in the birth of a child. In fact, when it did happen, for several months afterwards Carrie had been convinced she was simply putting on weight. It had taken Big Jock himself to suggest tentatively perhaps it was time she saw a doctor.

When Billy was eventually born his father was captivated. The slightly built, fair-haired youngster was the apple of the old man's eye. He could see generations of Aberdeen-born Gordons in the boy. 'His grandfather's spit!' he declared at his first sight of the child, as he held him up to the light of the bedroom window and marvelled at the perfect features and the head of soft, downy fair hair. But Carrie could see only one person in that small screwed-up pink face. He was her brother Billy incarnate.

When Big Jock died of a heart attack shortly before his son's ninth birthday, Carrie was devastated. The whole of the Valley seemed to go into mourning. The Scotsman had been the bedrock of the community and the gap he left, many said, would prove impossible to fill. He had been one of the first to introduce the Hereford breed of beef cattle into the area and his success had made Great Glen one of the wealthiest cattle stations in the whole of the Macleay River Valley.

That was all of four years ago now and the weeks that followed his death had been an enormous strain until the lawyers finally completed their work and informed her that Great Glen and its three thousand acres was indeed hers and her son's. Big Jock had said he would take care of them both, but this was much more than that. So very much more. Carrie had sat in the lawyers' office and tears had filled her eyes as she signed the title deeds on behalf of herself and Billy.

'He had no living kin back in Scotland, you see, ma'am,' Mr Manners, the senior partner, had told her in his high-pitched voice. 'The boy meant a great deal to him. Especially coming so late in life.'

Carrie had given a quiet smile in response. 'I know. He means a great deal to me too.'

'Will you sell the place, or put in a manager?' the lawyer had asked as she put her signature to the document.

To his surprise, Carrie had shaken her head. 'Oh no, I won't do either of those. Most certainly not. I shall keep it on and run it myself,' she had told him firmly.

'It's a big undertaking for a mere woman you know, ma'am. Running a station the size of Great Glen is no job for the faint-hearted.' He wanted to add 'or the fair sex', but diplomatically held his peace, although his gaze was one of concern as he regarded her over the rim of his spectacles.

'I know,' Carrie had said, handing back the pen. And she had smiled that quiet smile to herself once more, for she knew that this was just what this mere woman had been waiting for all her life: the chance to prove that when it came to running a station she was not only as able as any man, she could be a darned sight better than most.

It was an opportunity she grasped with both hands, sitting up long into the night reading all the literature available on the raising and breeding of cattle. She attended every sale for miles around, whether she intended to buy or not. Just being there and watching and listening – talking to other farmers – all added to the sum of her knowledge, which by the end of her first year in charge had become prodigious.

By the end of the second year Carrie had managed to maintain the growth Jock had scheduled before his death, and by the end of the third she had increased profitability by twenty per cent. Now at the tail-end of the fourth year on her own, the station's profits were over fifty per cent up and still growing. They had the biggest herd of beef cattle in the Valley, and over the past year she had even felt confident enough to indulge her passion for sheep. Her flock of cross-bred Swaledales were the talk of the sales rings and, after more than her fair share of initial suspicion and resentment at a woman interfering in men's work, her opinion was now as respected as much, if not more, as any other station owner's in the territory.

Why then, with all that behind her, was this small advertisement in the *Sydney Gazette* causing her heart to beat so fast?

She turned her gaze back to the newspaper in her hands as she sat down on the edge of the window seat to re-read the lines that had caused her heart to miss a beat:

WANTED

INFORMATION ON THE WHEREABOUTS OF ANY LIVING RELATIVE OF THE LATE SILAS HENRY HEBDEN, ESQ., OF YORVIK SHEEP STATION, HUNTER VALLEY, NEW SOUTH WALES. PLEASE CONTACT: MACAULEY & SON, ATTORNEYS AT LAW, GEORGE STREET, NEWCASTLE, AS SOON AS POSSIBLE.

Carrie looked at the date. It was almost a week ago. She only infrequently saw a copy of the *Gazette*. This one was left by a neighbouring farmer from up near Kempsey, who had called in to break his journey at Great Glen on his way back from Sydney a few days ago.

She stood up and paced the floor, her footsteps soundless on the thick pile of the Persian carpet that had been one of Jock's last acquisitions.

So Silas was dead. Surprisingly she felt no sorrow at the news. There had never been any love between them and it would be hypocritical to pretend otherwise now. In truth she had hardly given him a second thought over the past three decades, so full had her life been here. But she had certainly not forgotten Yorvik. And no matter how much she had come to love Great Glen, it could never match up to her very first Australian home.

What would become of it now? Her heart ached to think of it returning to a wilderness again, or of some callow youth fresh from Britain attempting to make it his own. In that short first year, Carrie had poured her heart and soul into that land and now, with Silas gone, she could not bear to think of it going to someone else. Hidden deep in her heart there had remained the hope that one day she might return. But it had seemed an impossible dream. Until now . . .

She paused in her pacing to glance down at the gold ring still on the third finger of her left hand. Despite everything, she had remained Silas's wife. And she was now his widow. Dare she? Dare she claim her inheritance?

She could barely eat and she slept little over the next few days, as she pondered on the wisdom of re-opening the door on the past. Her main fear was that Silas or Caroline's aunt and uncle might have broadcast the suspected reason for her flight. For all she knew the police might be waiting for her right now, to talk to her about Caroline's disappearance should she return.

But somehow she could not believe that. Silas was too proud a man to make himself a laughing stock over a thing like that. Married to an imposter indeed! No, she told herself, he would not have voiced his suspicions to a living soul. He would have much preferred to make out that his young English wife could not take to life on a sheep station and had high-tailed it back to London. He could have lived with that. And by the same token, he would have done his best to spin some yarn to the Bidwells to pacify them. The last thing he would have wanted would have been for them to make him into a figure of fun in the neighbourhood. What exactly had been said on that day she had fled Yorvik, she would probably never know, and that had been the reason for her inner turmoil in the years that followed. To her dying day she knew she would be looking over her shoulder. That was part of the cross she had to bear.

It was a little after ten in the morning, four days later, when Carrie got up from her seat at the writing desk by the window in the parlour to ring the bell at the edge of the mantelpiece. She had thought about it long enough. The time had come to act.

Two minutes later the housekeeper bustled in.

'Get hold of Will for me, will you, Ellen?' Carrie said. 'Tell him it's important.'

The housekeeper disappeared in search of the head stockman, and Carrie began to pace the floor. Her mind was made up, but was she making the right decision? She had still not come to any conclusion when Will Morton appeared at the open doorway.

'You sent for me, ma'am?'

'Yes, Will, I did.' Carrie nervously fingered the edge of her desk. 'Prepare the best waggon and horses for Newcastle, would you? I'll be going down there on business tomorrow.'

The head stockman looked at her in surprise. There were no special sales or the like on in the area that he knew of. 'Business, is it, ma'am? Will you want me with you?'

Would she? Carrie thought for a moment then nodded. 'Yes, I think that's not a bad idea.' Will might just come in quite useful.

When he had gone she raised her eyes to the ceiling and uttered a silent prayer. If ever she needed assistance from above it was now. She would either come back as owner of her beloved Yorvik or she would not come back at all.

CHAPTER TWENTY-TWO

'Now remember, Will,' Carrie told her head stockman as they stood across the road from Silas's lawyer's office in Newcastle's George Street, 'you only want to find out if Yorvik is for sale, and if so, get details. You must on no account mention my name or where you're from.'

Will Morton stood silently on the pavement and listened. He was a quiet man, more at home with animals than with his fellow human beings, and he had long since given up trying to understand the way his boss conducted her business affairs. But he trusted her, just as he had trusted Big Jock. Great Glen had been more than blessed with its owners. 'I understand, ma'am.' He tipped his hat and loped across the road, his long, slightly bandy stride indicative of a life spent more in the saddle than on foot.

Carrie watched him go from the doorway of a ladies' outfitters, then waited impatiently for his return. She did her best to appear to be concentrating on a selection of the latest hats on offer. She could not risk being seen by anyone inside Macauley & Son, the attorneys, until she had more information.

Will was back within minutes, a disappointed look on his face. 'Bad news, ma'am, I'm afraid. The Yorvik station's not for sale. Not yet-a-whiles at any rate. They're still hoping to contact the heirs.'

Carrie's heart leapt. 'Who did you speak to?'

'The clerk, I reckon it was. The young fella on the front desk.' Then, seeing the interested look on his boss's face, he warned, 'He seemed quite positive in what he said. I doubt if you'll have much luck making an offer there.'

Carrie patted his arm as the excitement within her grew. 'See that coffee house across the street – a few doors down from Macauley's? Go and get a table for two and order coffee and cakes. I'll join you in ten minutes.' Then seeing his dubious expression, she added, 'Just keep eating and drinking till I arrive. I'll foot the bill.'

A smile spread across his lean face. Fancy cakes were a rare treat on station. 'Yes, ma'am!'

She watched as he crossed the road and disappeared into 'Bailey's Coffee House', then she turned to glance at herself in the glass of the dress-shop window. Nerves were fluttering in her stomach as she straightened her hat and adjusted the high lace collar of her blouse, beneath the well-cut maroon jacket she had chosen for the journey. Was she being a fool? Was she risking everything to regain an impossible dream? Many would say so. She had no proof that Silas or the Bidwells had not informed the police about what had happened. For all she knew she could still be a wanted woman. The gamble was enormous. But was it worth taking? All night she had wrestled with the question. But she had always been a creature of impulse, and her heart had told her that this was what she had been waiting for all these years. For three decades she had been treading a path of hope – the hope that one day she would return to Yorvik – that one day Yorvik would be hers.

She took a deep, quivering breath into her lungs and tried to calm her nerves as she waited for a carriage to pass by before crossing the road to the lawyer's office.

The same rather pimply-faced young man was still seated behind the desk as she entered and asked to see Mr Macauley. She could vaguely remember the stout, elderly solicitor with his pince nez and air of gravitas that had so impressed her husband. 'A real gentleman is Mr Macauley,' Silas had declared on more than one occasion. 'Scruples – that's what he's got. Not like some of the sharks that have set themselves up out here. Cheat you as soon as look at you, they would!'

The clerk disappeared through a door behind him and

returned a minute or so later. 'Mr Macauley will see you now, if you care to step this way, ma'am.'

He smelt of the Macassar oil with which his fairish hair was liberally plastered and she noted he had an East End of London accent. The sound of it brought back vivid memories of her origins and only served to increase her nervousness as he ushered her through into an oak-panelled room, then bowed politely and took his leave.

She was left standing in the middle of the floor, facing a middle-aged man with greying mutton-chop whiskers and a balding head, who rose from behind his desk as she entered. He held out his hand and smiled. 'Henry Macauley at your service, ma'am. Please take a seat.'

Carrie shook hands, then perched herself on the edge of the hardbacked chair in front of the desk and clasped the bone handle of her umbrella. She had been expecting Mr Macauley, Senior. This must be the son. 'Your father . . .' she began.

'My father died three years ago,' Henry Macauley informed her. 'I run the place myself now.' He gave a weary half-laugh as he sat back down again. 'Or at least it runs me!' He pressed his fingertips together in a praying motion and leant forward on his elbows on the desk, as he continued in his most confidential tone, 'Now how can I be of help to you?'

Carrie felt her cheeks begin to flush and fought to keep her voice steady. 'It's about Yorvik . . .'

'Ah, the Hebden place . . .' He gave a sorry-I-can't-help-you sort of shrug and leant back in his chair. 'We've had a good few enquiries about that. But it's not on the market at the moment, I'm afraid. Still looking for the heirs, you see. The late owner was married briefly at one time. We've been trying to contact the lady concerned and haven't had much luck up till now.'

Carrie's insides knotted. He certainly sounded straightforward enough. There was nothing in the tone or content of what he said to suggest this was anything other than a normal estate to settle. It was now or never. 'I am Mrs Hebden,' she said, rising to her feet. 'I am Silas's wife.'

Henry Macauley's mouth dropped open and for several seconds he sat silently gaping at her. He had been told he had not a hope in hell of ever contacting old Silas's wife, who had run off and left him thirty years ago. Not that he could blame her from what he could remember of the old boy. Crabbit old fella he had been. Henry stared at the middle-aged woman in front of him, who was anything but old and crabbit-looking. She was not at all bad-looking for her age, in fact, with that neat figure and head of dark hair. 'Well, I never! Well, I never indeed!'

The lawyer stood up and came round the front of the desk to shake Carrie's hand once more. His face was beaming. 'This calls for a glass of something!' he declared, pumping her hand as if he were drawing water. 'Old Silas's wife, eh?' He stood back and looked at her. 'But, if you don't mind me saying so, ma'am, you look so young!'

'I'm a middle-aged woman, Mr Macauley,' Carrie replied with a smile. 'Quite old enough for my liking . . . Although not as old as my husband, I must admit. He — he would have been in his eighties by now . . .' Her voice tailed off. It was difficult talking about a man she had run out on nearly thirty years ago.

But Henry Macauley seemed to have no such scruples as he poured them both a glass of sherry. 'Well I never!' he declared once more. 'Who would have believed it! I've met Silas on several occasions over the past ten years — since I joined Pa in the firm, and, I'll be honest with you, I always took him for a confirmed bachelor. You could have knocked me down with a feather when I learned he had once had a wife . . . Still had a wife when he died, in fact, for I understand you were never divorced.'

Carrie's heart leapt at the news as she twiddled nervously with her wedding ring.

He handed her one of the glasses and said, 'Of course, there'll be a lot of legal stuff to get out of the way, but I can't see that should hinder things too much, once we've established you are who you say you are. Are you staying in the area?'

'Only for a day or so. I now live up in the Macleay Valley.'

He looked interested. 'The Macleay Valley, eh? Nice country up there, so I believe. I had an uncle who sailed out of Trial Bay — Pa's younger brother . . . Do you live on the coast?'

'I run a cattle station some miles up country.'

His brows rose. 'Is that so?'

'And a very successful one at that,' she could not resist adding.

Henry Macauley looked impressed, then gave a rather embarrassed smile. 'I should warn you, Mrs Hebden, ma'am, that Yorvik — your inheritance — has seen better days. Old Silas rather let things go over the past few years, I'm afraid.'

It was no more than she expected. 'To Yorvik!' she said, raising her glass. 'To my beloved Yorvik — for better or worse!'

The following day she made the long journey out to set eyes on her old home for the first time in three decades. She took Will with her, but did not tell him the whole truth of the matter, explaining that Yorvik had belonged to a now dead relative and she was negotiating to buy the old place for sentimental reasons.

'It's not like you to be sentimental, if I may say so, ma'am,' Will told her, as the waggon wheels rolled over the last half mile of rutted track before turning the corner that led to the homestead itself.

Carrie half turned in her seat. 'So I'm a hard woman, am I?'

'No, not hard exactly. Level-headed's maybe a better word. You know what you want and you go out and get it — no messing around.'

Carrie mused silently to herself. It was odd hearing how

others saw you. Often it bore no relation to how you saw yourself. At heart she was still that highly nervous young woman who got off the *Emma Harkness* all those years ago. But even then she had had hopes and dreams. And hopes and dreams did not come true just by wishing. 'Bloody hard work, that's what it's taken, Will,' she said. 'Bloody hard work.'

'Any idea of the state of the place?' Will asked, as they neared their destination. So many stations and squatters' runs seemed run down and needed money spending on them these days.

Carrie grimaced on the seat beside him. 'We'll reserve judgement on that, but I'm not optimistic.'

As soon as they reached Yorvik land she could see immediately that the lawyer's warnings were proving accurate, and even Will had a depressed look on his face as the waggon rolled over familiar territory. The place had an air of neglect about it that was almost palpable. Small disconsolate knots of Aborigines wandered on the horizon, but even they seemed demoralized.

'Not much husbandry been going on around here by the looks of it, ma'am,' Will commented needlessly, as they neared the house.

Carrie could only look on in growing dismay. It was far worse than she had anticipated. If there were still sheep on the place they were nowhere to be seen, but maybe they had all been sold and the hands paid off. She felt herself tense. She had deliberately not allowed herself to think of the hired labour, for to her that meant only one person . . . But it was nearly thirty years ago. Surely the Irishman would have moved on long ago. Wouldn't he?

She frowned into the late afternoon sun as the waggon rolled on over the rutted ground towards the homestead. Sean O'Dwyer . . . She could see him still, for he was as much a part of her dream of Yorvik as the land itself. In many ways he *was* Yorvik, for he was the one who had taught her to love this land and its people. But in his own

307

way he had been as impossible a dream to attain. She had told herself all those years ago that he had betrayed her by fathering that child and then denying his own flesh and blood, but time had eased the pain. He had not betrayed her, for she was never his to betray. He had been merely living the life he had been born to. He was as free a spirit as ever haunted these wild empty places.

'Looks like we're almost there, ma'am.'

Will's voice broke into her reverie and she glanced ahead of her in the direction he was pointing.

There it was, still familiar, but now a distinctly grubby white in the pale yellow light. 'That's it, Will,' she said, her heart beating faster as she raised herself on the buckboard for a better look. 'That's it all right!'

But the excitement in her breast turned to dismay the nearer they got to the single-storey wooden house. The dingy white paint was now flaking and peeling and had worn off altogether in parts, leaving the wood grey and porous beneath. Part of the verandah was sagging and the whole place reeked of neglect and decay.

'Pull the horses up here, will you, please?' Carrie said in a low voice, as they reached the picket fence that ran from the side of the property round to enclose her vegetable garden at the back. 'And you wait here, if you don't mind. I'd rather like to take a look inside by myself first.'

She found her legs shaking as she got down from the waggon and made her way up the rickety wooden steps to the front door. Part of the floor of the verandah had rotted and given way in places and had never been repaired. Silas had only been dead a matter of weeks, but the rotten boards looked like they had been that way for years. She paused with her hand on the rail to look around her as she had done so many starlit nights ago. It was like looking at a graveyard.

It was with a heavy heart that she turned the key the lawyer had given her in the lock of the front door and pushed it open. It creaked on its hinges and the air inside smelt stale as she walked through the hall, making for the kitchen.

She pushed the door open and paused for a moment to pluck up the courage she knew she would need to enter the room where once her world had fallen apart. From the little she could see through the half-open door, it had been left exactly as it was on the day Silas died. There was a fly-ridden, mouldy piece of damper sitting on the table, alongside a cup with no doubt the coagulated dregs of tea in the bottom. Even from this distance, the stink was incredible, and she could well imagine what she would find if she attempted to open the food press.

Standing here in the doorway brought it all back, and in many ways it was as if she had never been away. Taking her courage in both hands, she shoved the door open fully and walked through.

'G'day, you old bugger! Silly old bugger!'

She froze for moment, then whirled round to gape at the black beady eyes looking straight into hers. 'Barney!'

She flew across the room and all but embraced the metal bars of the parrot's cage. 'Barney, you old rogue! Fancy you still being here!'

'Silly old bugger! G'day, you old bugger!'

He must be over thirty by now and his plumage had seen better days, but he actually looked pleased to see her!

She gripped the bars with her fingers and pressed her face against the cage and closed her eyes as tears flooded the surface beneath her closed lids. 'I've come home, Barney old boy . . . I've come home at last . . .'

And despite the decay, despite the neglect, nothing had changed. Nothing . . .

CHAPTER TWENTY-THREE

Carrie opened the back door of the house and narrowed her eyes to scan the area between the homestead and the lake. She ignored the sight of the overgrown vegetable garden and rested her gaze on the part of the stringy-bark roof that was just visible between the tall silver gums.

She made no conscious decision to walk down that familiar path, but walk it she did, as she had done so many times in the past. Halfway between the house and the huts she paused, for this was the distance at which she would be sure to hear the plaintive sound of that penny whistle on the evening air. But now there was only silence.

As she drew nearer she could sense that around the whole area of the huts was an air of depressing sadness. Chickens no longer scratched for food, no dogs barked, nor horses whinnied, and everywhere weeds grew tall and strong where once small patches of vegetables had been cultivated. The doors to two of the cabins hung off their hinges, and by the look of it they had not been inhabited for years. On the third one, the door was still in place, but it looked in no better a state than the others. There was no doubt about it, none of them had known human habitation for years. Her heart sank and her eyes filled. She wiped away the tears with an impatient hand. She would have been a fool — a sentimental fool — to expect anything other than this. It had been nearly thirty years; a whole generation had been born and grown up since she had last been here.

Of their own accord her feet walked the remaining short distance to the hut that had once been home to the Irishman, and her heart was filled with melancholy. How often she had tried to shut him out of her mind over the years, and how often would that broad white-toothed smile and those dark eyes haunt her dreams. They had been no more than ships in the night, passing through each other's lives, then she had moved on. But something of him had remained deep within her, something had touched her soul as no other had done before or since.

The door was ajar, open to the elements. She paused, then pushed it further open and went in.

'Oh my God!'

Two pairs of eyes met across the few feet of the dingy interior. A man was lying on the makeshift bed, his ravaged face looking up into hers.

Slowly she walked nearer, their eyes still locked.

'Carrie . . .' a voice said. 'Carrie . . .' His voice was faint and hoarse. It had been almost thirty years, but he had recognized her immediately. He had always known he would. The years rolled back as their gaze held. It was only yesterday since she had gone.

'Sean?' She whispered the name. The very sound of it sent a tremor through her body. It was the first time she had spoken it aloud in a generation.

A bony hand reached out for hers. Carrie took it and sat down on the edge of the bed.

She shook her head, too overcome to speak, as she gazed into the emaciated face of the man who had once meant so much. 'What happened, Irish? What's wrong?' She would barely have recognized him, he had lost so much weight and the lower part of his face was covered in several weeks' growth of copper-coloured beard. His once dark auburn hair, however, had gone quite grey, but was still as thick as ever as it curled around the neck of his flannel vest. She clung on to his hand and with her free hand reached forwards and felt his brow. It was cold and clammy to the touch. 'You're ill,' she said, knowing she was stating the obvious. 'You're very ill . . .'

He lay there looking up at her; his dark eyes seemed to glow in the dim interior of the hut. 'I knew you'd come,' he whispered hoarsely. 'I swear to God I knew . . .'

'Then it was more than I did,' she confessed, raising his hand to her lips and kissing it. 'I only found out they were looking for me a few days ago ... I had no idea Silas had died until then.' She dropped her gaze from his and looked out of the door of the hut. It was now surprisingly painful to talk of the man she had fled from all those years ago. 'Silas's death ... I presume it was a heart attack?'

Sean O'Dwyer shook his head on the pillow. 'No,' he corrected her, in a tired voice. 'Silas died of the influenza. Gone within five days, he was.'

'Flu?' she queried, aghast. 'Silas died of the flu?' A particularly virulent strain had been sweeping the colony for the past few months, but it had not yet reached as far north as the Macleay Valley and it had never occurred to her it might be the cause of Silas's demise.

The Irishman nodded. 'Wiped out a couple of the older blackfellas and one of the kids, it did. Apart from the natives, there were only the two of us left on the station ... The Hendersons got paid off three years back.' He gave a wheezing attempt at a mirthless laugh. 'I nursed the old bugger – did my level best by him – but it was no good. He didn't have the strength to fight it and he died in his sleep on the fifth night.'

'And you?' Carrie asked. 'You became infected too by nursing Silas?'

He shook his head wearily at the inevitability of it all and closed his eyes. 'Damned if I know if that was the cause, for he wasn't the only one who caught it. I could've got it from several folks round here.' He sighed. 'I was all right at the funeral and I told them – the lawyers – I'd take care of the old place until it got a buyer. They were keen that it didn't get in any worse a state than it was. Then they told me they were putting out "Wanted" advertisements in the local newspapers for you ...' His eyes softened as they looked at her. 'Can't say as I dreamt for a second that they'd find you ...'

'And you became ill yourself sometime after the funeral?'

'Aye, a few weeks after. I tried to keep going for a week or so – feeding the parrot and the few animals that are left and what not – but these past few days . . . Well, it just got beyond me . . .'

'Was there no one to help you?' Carrie began, thinking of Quarra and Miri and the other black women who would once have been only too happy to tend to his every need. 'Was there none of the blackfellas who could look after you?'

'They took off up country after several of their tribe died. Then old Silas himself pegged out,' Sean said. 'I reckon they thought bad spirits were around the place. They'll be back, that's for sure, but not for a while.'

Carrie listened, his hand still in hers. Although she was alarmed he had had no one to look after him, there was almost a perverse satisfaction in what he was saying. She had wondered so many times over the years if he had taken himself a wife. For all she had known he might even have set up home with the likes of Miri, who, after all, had once given birth to his child.

He had sensed the tension in her voice as she asked those questions and his mind too was retracing the years to that terrible day of their last meeting when she had confronted him with the dead body of the child.

When he found out later she had fled from Yorvik that night he had not known what to think. Was it because of the half-caste child? Did the shock of its discovery mean that much to her? He could come up with no other explanation and Silas had been of no help. His employer had never uttered a word over the years that followed that gave any clue about his wife's disappearance. Closed up like a clam, he did. Never mentioned her name. Only on his death bed did he come anywhere near unbending. On the very last night, when he realized he was almost within sight of the pearly gates, Silas had sighed wearily as Sean

313

asked him if there was anything else he wanted. 'Only a son, lad,' he had sighed in that wheezy voice of his. 'Only the son I should have had and never did. Someone to carry on this place after I'm gone . . .'

Then his head had slumped to one side on the pillow and he had closed his eyes. Sean had stood watching him for a moment or two, then walked out and closed the door behind him. Silas Hebden had died that night.

And now Sean O'Dwyer looked into the eyes of the woman who had denied her husband that son. 'Nearly thirty years it is,' he said huskily. 'Thirty years, and you never said goodbye.'

Carrie looked down at his hand still in hers and stroked the calloused skin of his palm.

'Why, Carrie? Why did you go? How could you just take off like that without a word?' It still hurt, even now.

'I can't tell you that,' she said, shaking her head. 'Please don't ask me, Sean.'

'Was it because of me? Because of that dead kid?'

She shook her head once more. 'No,' she said faintly. 'It wasn't because of you, or the dead child.'

He was silent for a moment, then whispered, 'It wasn't mine, you know – that kid – it wasn't mine. I wasn't lying when I told you that.'

She could feel a flush creeping up her neck as she looked up and met his eyes, and she could feel herself tense. Why, after all this time, did that memory still have the power to hurt as it did? 'It – it really doesn't matter,' she said. 'Not any more.'

'But it does,' he insisted. 'And you know it does, just as much as I do.'

They looked at one another in silence. A whole generation had been born and another had died since they last set eyes on each other. There was so much between them, yet so little. They had not been prepared, all those years ago, to commit themselves, yet both had known the glow from that tiny spark either one of them could have ignited would have burst forth into a fire that would have consumed them both. The silence was broken only by the rhythmic wheeze of his breathing as he lay on the bed studying her face.

'You're really telling me the child was not yours?' Carrie asked finally, in a small, tight voice. Her insides were knotting and she almost hated him for bringing it up.

'Yes, I'm telling you that. The father was not me, but Jock. Jock Henderson.'

'Jock Henderson?'

'Yes. Miri was telling you it was John, not Sean.'

'John? The father was called John?'

'That's right. She told me herself. I tackled Jock about it next time he came on station, and he couldn't deny he'd slept with the girl.'

A sigh shuddered through Carrie's body and she pressed his hand even tighter. The assumption that she had jumped to so readily . . . She had never even given him the benefit of the doubt. And it had almost tarnished a memory that, despite everything, had still glowed golden in her mind down through the years that followed. She took a deep breath. 'So you're not a dad after all.'

'Not that I know of, at any rate.'

Impulsively she bent forwards and kissed his brow. A feeling of lightheartedness was bubbling up inside her. 'I'm going to get you out of here,' she told him. 'And I'm going to look after you myself until you're well again.'

Sean merely smiled.

'Then after that I'm going to turn Yorvik into the most successful sheep station in the whole of the Hunter Valley.'

He looked dubious at that.

'I can do it, you know,' she assured him. 'I'm making enough money out of Great Glen – that's my home in the Macleay Valley – to do the necessary to make this place pay again . . . Will you get well and help me, Sean?'

The Irishman's eyes smiled back into hers and he gave

315

a weary sigh. 'That ambition of yours, Carrie Hebden . . . Where will it ever end?'

'When I'm the most successful station owner in the whole of New South Wales,' she said firmly. 'And I will be one day. Will you help me?'

'Do I have a choice?'

She shook her head. 'Not if you want to get chicken broth and all manner of goodies brought to you to help you get well, you don't!'

He smiled. 'Ah, so it's blackmail, is it?'

'You do like chicken broth, don't you?'

It was months since such a delicacy had touched his lips. He sighed. 'It looks like I'm going to have my work cut out, doesn't it?'

'You'll stay with me? You'll stay on and help me?'

For the first time he summoned all his strength and gave a grin that showed his teeth, and they were still as straight and strong as they had been all those years ago. 'I reckon I could be persuaded.'

Carrie beamed as she leant over and hugged him.

'Ehmm . . . Excuse me, ma'am . . .'

They both looked round to the doorway to see it filled with the tall, lean figure of Will Morton.

'Good God, Will, I'd quite forgotten about you!'

The head stockman looked somewhat embarrassed as he took off his hat and said, 'Begging your pardon for butting in like this, ma'am. I was getting a trifle worried, that's all.'

'And you had every right to be,' Carrie assured him, slipping down from the edge of the bed and straightening her skirts. She half-turned to Sean lying beneath the old grey blanket. 'I just ran into a very old friend, Mr Sean O'Dwyer. He's been here on his own and has been very ill for some time now. But he's going to get better. I'm going to see to that.'

Neither of the two men doubted it for one moment. If Carrie Hebden said something, she meant it.

She remained at Yorvik over the next week, sending Will back to Great Glen with the waggon, while she tended to her patient. She moved into the house, but Sean refused to be moved from his hut. 'This has been my home too long to be making changes now,' he told her. So she rode out to Hunter's Hollow and stocked up on all manner of provisions and left a message for a doctor to come out as soon as possible.

Slowly the Irishman began to gain strength, and the difference was visible within a few days. On the fourth day Carrie brought a tin bath from the house and placed it in the middle of the hut floor, where she filled it with hot water.

'You want me to get into that?' he asked, eyeing it suspiciously. He had never used one before. If the weather was fine he would bathe in the lake or the creek, and if not . . . Well, he made do with a sluice down from the rain barrel outside.

'I do indeed. You'll feel a new man after it.'

'You volunteering to scrub my back?'

'Really! Behave yourself, Mr O'Dwyer!' But she was smiling as she said it.

Sean rubbed his three-week-old beard and propped himself up on one elbow on the bed as he looked down at the steaming hot water. 'I guess I must be smelling like an old pole cat by now,' he mused.

'Like ten old pole cats!' Carrie corrected him, then held a towel out towards him. 'You can use this to cover your modesty until you get in.'

He took it a trifle nervously as she turned her back. Then he sat up and pulled his old vest over his head and slipped his legs out of his drawers. He slid out of bed and, after testing the strength in his legs, took a few shaking steps in the direction of the tub.

'God, I'm like a skinned rabbit,' he commented at the sight of his shrunken body, easing himself over the edge of the bath and letting out a yell as the hot water hit his foot. 'What are you trying to do to me, woman, boil me alive?'

'Just get in there!' Carrie commanded, still with her back turned. 'Don't be such a baby!'

The baby continued to curse and mutter under his breath as he lowered himself down into the steaming water, yelling most loudly when it met his private parts. 'Holy Mother of God!'

'Are you in?'

'I'm in!' he gasped, placing a flannel modestly between his legs.

Carrie turned to face him and armed herself with a bar of soap. 'Don't look so wary, you're going to enjoy this,' she told him soothingly, as she picked up a full ewer of warm water and held it over his head.

'Aaaah!'

'Don't be such a baby!' she scolded him again as she lathered the soap into his soaking hair. 'You'll never recognize yourself after all this.'

'That's exactly what I'm afraid of!'

The battle went on for a full ten minutes, until, dripping wet but squeaky clean, the Irishman stood up in the dirty water and wrapped a towel around his midriff. 'Come here,' he commanded Carrie, who had turned away momentarily to protect his modesty.

She walked over to where he was standing and he held out his hands. She took them and stood looking up into his face. There was not a trace of dirt and it was pink and glowing as it smiled down into hers. 'You should keep that beard,' she told him. 'I like a man with a beard.' It was funny how it had kept its colour although the hair on his head had gone quite grey.

'Ever been kissed by a man with a beard before?'

Carrie shook her head, her colour rising.

He bent forwards, then paused his mouth only inches from hers as his eyes met the startled gaze of someone in the doorway.

'Oh, my goodness me!' Mabel Appleby's hand flew to her mouth at the sight before her. She began to back away from the open hut door, then turned and fled.

The Irishman looked down at Carrie. 'Seems like we shocked the neighbours,' he said with a smile. 'Do you mind?'

'Not a bit. Do you?'

He shook his head. Then he carried on where he had left off. 'They say kissing a man without a beard is like eating a meal without salt.'

It was just as well she had always liked her food well salted.

CHAPTER TWENTY-FOUR

Mabel Appleby's mouth pursed as she stood alongside her husband Geordie on the Yorvik verandah and listened to Carrie tell of her finding the Irishman, Sean O'Dwyer, in a sorry state, but who was now recovering from what could have been as fatal an illness as Silas's. 'In fact, had he not been half Silas's age and twice as strong, he probably wouldn't be here now.'

But the Applebys were not impressed by what they regarded as her excuses for quite indecent behaviour. Standing there in that hut helping bathe a naked man . . . Well, it didn't bear thinking about! But bad behaviour was no more than they expected of a woman who had run out on her marriage thirty years ago.

'I told you that Irishman was at the bottom of it!' Mabel had exclaimed to her husband not ten minutes before, after rushing back to the house to find him. 'Haven't I said all along that O'Dwyer character was the reason she ran off in the first place?'

There was a undeniable sense of satisfaction mixed in with the expression of shock at what she had just witnessed. She had been convinced for the past three decades that Carrie had left because Silas had discovered her having an affair with his station hand. It had been no surprise to anyone in the Valley that it was the woman who had gone and not the guilty man, for Silas was just the type to set more store by a good station hand than a flibbertigibbet of a young woman no better than she ought to be.

There had been much shaking of heads and wagging of tongues when their wedding had first been announced, for although it was never actually admitted the Hebdens' was a mail-order marriage, no one had any doubt about it, least of all Mabel. The fact that it lasted no more than a year came as no surprise to anyone. But although all sorts of ideas were put forth as to why Carrie ran off, there was not a soul in the Valley who knew the truth of the scandal, for Silas would not discuss it. If anyone even dared to mention his missing wife's name in his presence, he would silence them with a frosty, 'I'll thank you to say no more in that regard, if you don't mind.' He had totally banished all trace of her from his life. And now here she was back, large as life, to claim her inheritance. And cavorting with a naked Irishman into the bargain. Was there no shame in the woman?

'I'll be honest with you, Mrs Hebden,' Geordie Appleby told Carrie in his gruff, no-nonsense northern English way. 'I didn't reckon on you turning up again like this – none of us did. We all thought you'd gone for good and that the place would be sold. I even went down to Macauley's in Newcastle to give them a reasonable offer on it t'other week. I spoke to Henry Macauley himself at the funeral and told him I was interested in the place and he seemed to think along the same lines I did – joining Yorvik with Eden Vale would be good for the whole area.' He cleared his throat and adjusted his necktie. 'I fancy you'll not be considering living here again – under the circumstances – so that offer still stands. The lawyer has it in writing.'

'Yes,' his wife put in quickly. 'Considering the state of the place, it's a very reasonable offer indeed.' She patted the bun at the nape of her neck and cast a disparaging eye around the verandah on which they were standing. This place was not fit for pigs now. But she must not think ill of the dead, she told herself. 'Poor Silas. It was the drink that did it, you know. After you left him it went from bad to worse. Sometimes he wouldn't be sober for weeks on end. Many's the day Geordie had to ride over and sort things out. At their wits' end, the workers were sometimes.'

'Aye, I'm surprised his hands stuck by him as long as they did,' Geordie Appleby added. 'Those two Scotch lads

321

– the Henderson brothers – good workers they were, but they hadn't seen a penny piece in wages for weeks when they finally left. I told them often enough they were being fools to themselves sticking by him like that, but they'd been on Yorvik since they arrived out here as young lads and were loath to leave ... Anyroad, they saw the light in the end and got fixed up with Angus Cameron over at Cameron Creek a few years back. As for the Irishman ...' His voice tailed off and he shook his head. 'Well that bugger's always been a law unto himself.'

Carrie listened in silence. It amazed her to find them still alive. Geordie must be well into his eighties by now, and his wife not that much younger. They appeared much smaller than she remembered them, shrunken by age, their skins dried out like shrivelled walnuts by half a century beneath the Hunter Valley sun. Mabel had developed a dowager's hump that made her head poke forwards, giving her sharp bird-like features an even more belligerent, accusatory look than before. Carrie felt they were talking at her, not to her. She was standing behind an invisible wall of disapproval that would prove impossible to climb. Not only had she committed the unpardonable sin of running off and leaving their old friend Silas to turn into an alcoholic, she had sinned still further by coming back and claiming her inheritance. That she had been caught in such an embarrassing situation with Sean O'Dwyer simply added fuel to the flames.

Geordie Appleby took out his pocket watch and glanced at it, before making a move towards the steps leading down to where their buggy was waiting. 'Aye, well, like I said, the offer's in writing and you'll not get a better one, I'll vouch for that ... I'd be obliged if you could let me know by the end of the week if you've accepted it or not.'

'I'll let you know now,' Carrie said before he got any further. 'I'll not be accepting that or any other offer. You see, I intend to return here to Yorvik and make something of it. It may not look much now, but Yorvik will come back from the dead before long, you wait and see. And I'll be running it myself.'

Mabel Appleby was halfway down the steps behind her husband and her mouth dropped open as she turned to look at Carrie. 'You'll be coming back here to live?' she said in a shocked voice.

'Yes. Is there any reason why I shouldn't?'

'I . . . Well . . .' Amazed, Mabel turned to her husband for support.

Geordie Appleby was just as taken aback, but, as an astute business man, was determined not to show it. 'I fancy what my wife means is, it'll not be the plain sailing you might imagine. It'll take a good deal of money to put this place to rights.' He glanced around him at the broken verandah and general air of dilapidation. 'Aye, a good deal of money indeed.'

'I have a good deal of money.'

Husband and wife looked at one another. There was an awkward silence, then Geordie Appleby unhooked the reins of the buggy. The wind had been taken completely out of his sails. 'We'd best be going,' he said abruptly. It had been a mistake to ride over here in the first place. They had heard that Silas's wife had been seen in the area but could not believe their ears. And so, always priding himself in getting straight to the heart of the matter, he had suggested that they come and see for themselves. The shock of finding Carrie as large as life and determined to keep the place going with herself in charge was immense. It was almost like a personal insult. It was akin to telling him that the success he had had over the years in running his own station was nothing to shout about; it was mere child's play. Worse than that – a woman could do it! Geordie's face was set in grim lines as he helped his wife up on to the seat.

Determined to part on good terms, Carrie came down the steps and shook hands with them both, but the smiles were strained all round as the Applebys took their leave.

She watched the buggy disappear back down the track, then turned and walked in through the front door. In a way she had had the last word, but she got no satisfaction from it. Friends were hard to come by in life, especially out here, and both Applebys had been friends of a sort throughout the first year of her marriage. She could well understand their disappointment. They had obviously thought they were going to pick up Yorvik for a song and make it part of one of the biggest stations in the territory. Her return had put paid to that particular dream. She would not be easily forgiven.

Carrie sighed as she made her way through to the kitchen, now cleaned up and almost unrecognizable from the way she had found it. She would make a cup of tea, she decided. She could certainly do with one.

While she sat sipping her tea some ten minutes later her gaze fell on the old wooden chest by the side of the stove. She had barely noticed it before, but as she sat there idly taking in its dusty exterior, tied round with a length of old rope, curiosity got the better of her. It had certainly never sat there in Silas's day. Wherever he had kept it, it must have been well hidden, and probably with good reason. Hadn't she wondered as a young wife where exactly her husband had kept his money?

Placing her cup on the table, she got down on her knees in front of it and undid the rope. She could feel her heart beating in anticipation as she prised open the lid. Then her heart sank. It was not money at all inside the musty interior, but piles of old letters and personal documents.

At first she closed the lid quickly on the past, unable to confront the years that had gone. It was akin to consorting with ghosts. But something made her change her mind, and before long she was reading the words of the eager young bride-to-be Caroline Cooper as she wrote to her intended from England that she 'could not wait to get out to Yorvik and meet him at last'. It was all there, all the hopes and dreams, all the fears . . . How she would have loved to have found this treasure all those years ago when she was struggling day to day to convince the man she married she really was the young widow he had sent for.

Then just as she was on the point of closing the lid on those unhappy memories, she saw a letter addressed to Silas in quite another hand. This one too bore the head of Queen Victoria, but it was not from Caroline. Carrie scanned the words it contained with a furiously beating heart.

> . . . So you can imagine with what sadness we read of your poor wife's death. We shall never know now of the mystery of the disappearance of our dear niece, but we choose to believe that it was her own wish to rebuild her life as she thought fit. It is our considered conclusion that the poor girl met with a young man on the voyage out, with whom she chose to spend her life, and to spare your feelings arranged for a travelling companion to take her place. An offer of marriage from such a successful gentleman as yourself would be eagerly sought after, we have no doubt . . .

The signature at the bottom was that of Captain Edwin Bidwell.

Carrie replaced the letter in its envelope with shaking fingers. So there she had it. Silas had salvaged his pride by telling the Bidwells his wife had died in an accident, and they had come to their own conclusions about poor Caroline. Certainly it seemed the most likely explanation – especially after meeting the old man with whom their niece would have had to spend her life. Who could blame her for preferring a young sailor or fellow voyager to the elderly suitor she knew awaited her?

'Poor Caroline . . .' Carrie sighed, as she let the lid of the old chest fall with a clatter, to guard its secrets once more. Those years had produced so many ghosts that walked with her still. The past was ever present. It was not something she could ever escape; it remained with her. All those people, long gone, were as much a part of her as the air she breathed.

She got up from her knees and walked to the window to gaze out over Yorvik's green acres. She had met the living as well as the dead from her past today, and a strange peace descended on her heart as she stood there breathing in the pure Valley air. In a strange way she had confronted her ghosts by coming back here; she had stood up to the past, and in so doing could now look forward to the future with less fear in her heart. It was a good feeling.

News travelled fast in the Hunter Valley that week, and before she made the journey back to Great Glen, much to her surprise, she had a visit from Angus Cameron. The Scotsman had also heard that Carrie was back on Yorvik and rode over to make an offer on the place in person. He too was taken aback at the revelation that she was not selling, but intended to run it herself.

'Running a station's no easy job, my dear,' he told her, with all the authority vested in a Representative of the Legislative Council, as well as forty years as one of the most successful station owners in the territory. 'Damned hard work it is, even for someone like myself who's been at it for decades. I take it you'll be looking for someone to take charge of it for you?'

Carrie topped up his cup of tea, then poured herself another from the brown earthenware pot. 'No, as I said, I'll be running it myself,' she said, replacing the teapot on its stand and sitting back down on the rocker.

His shaggy brows rose a good half inch. Unlike Geordie Appleby he had not shrunk with age and, if anything, he was an even finer figure of a man than when Carrie had first known him. His hair and brows were pure white, beneath still keen blue eyes, and his solid figure was unbowed. 'Have you any real experience of this type of work?' he asked, eyeing her with more than a little scepticism. Living here as Silas's wife for a mere twelve months thirty years ago hardly qualified her to put herself in charge of a place like this. There were a thousand acres out there. A thousand acres that had almost reverted to the wilderness they had been before Silas came near the place. The woman had taken leave of her senses.

But Carrie was adamant. 'Oh yes,' she assured him, as politely as possible. 'Don't worry about that. I've run a three-thousand-acre spread in the Macleay Valley for the past few years. Great Glen — maybe you've heard of it?'

Angus Cameron almost choked on his cup of tea. 'Great Glen! But that's Big Jock Gordon's place!' His brows quirked and his eyes narrowed. 'He died some time back.'

'And he left the station to me.'

The Scotsman let out an audible gasp and replaced his cup in its saucer for fear of spilling the contents, so astonished was he. He had known Jock Gordon for donkey's years. They had met at sales up and down the country as well as the occasional social gathering; he was one of the most respected men in the colony. Angus's brow furrowed, as he tried to figure how this state of affairs had come about, for the big Aberdonian had never married to the best of his knowledge. 'You — you were a friend of Big Jock's?' he queried, hoping that was a diplomatic enough way of putting it.

'I was his housekeeper.'

'Ah . . .' The reply brought a meaningful silence. Mary Ellen had been his own housekeeper for the past forty years, but she still had no wedding ring on her finger. And he had certainly never even considered leaving her the station. Jock Gordon must either have been out of his mind or he must really have thought highly of this goodlooking woman, who, although no longer young, still had a vitality about her that was far from common amongst females out here. It was a hard life for women on the whole, no matter how much money their husbands might have. He had been impressed by her that very first day Silas stopped off at Cameron Creek after her arrival at Port Jackson. A definite cut above the usual, she had been. It had come as no surprise to him, though, to hear that the marriage had run into trouble after a year. Silas could be a cussed old bugger. No head for business either. Not like himself, or Jock Gordon, come to that. And now he looked at Carrie curiously, wondering just how much she and the big Scotsman had meant to each other. And, more importantly, was she telling the truth? Was she really capable of running a station on her own?

'I know what you're probably thinking,' Carrie said hesitantly. 'You're probably thinking I'm either mad or just plain stupid to even consider such a venture. I can assure you I'm neither. I intend to make a success of Yorvik. This country needs success stories, Mr Cameron. There have been too many of the other kind for far too long.'

The elderly Scotsman looked across at her and nodded sagely. He could not agree more. Between drought and flood and God knows what else there had been bankruptcies aplenty over the years. 'You're right there,' he said firmly. 'And, by God, I'll be the last one to stand in your way.' He admired backbone in a person, and all the more so when it was manifesting itself in the shape of an attractive woman like this. The fact that she was a female muscling in on a man's world might bother some, but not him. He had known one or two over the years, particularly amongst the wives of the Legislature, who would make far better *men*, never mind Representatives, than their husbands. 'I wish you luck, my dear,' he said with feeling. 'And if there's anything I can do to help, you only have to ask.'

He gave a wry chuckle as he rose from his chair and held out his hand. 'I'm a formidable enemy, Carrie Hebden, but a bloody good friend. I hope you'll always regard me as the latter.'

Carrie took his hand and shook it warmly. 'Thank you,' she said, deeply touched by this unexpected support. 'Thank you very much. I'll remember that.'

She related her conversation with the owner of Cameron Creek to Sean O'Dwyer later in the day and the Irishman listened quietly as he lay on his bed in the hut.

'He's a good ally to have,' he confirmed gravely. 'And you'll need all the friends you can get if you come back here, for there are those who for their own reasons, like the Applebys maybe, will want to see you fail. It's not the done thing for a woman to run a station, Carrie. A woman's place is in the kitchen and in the bedroom, not out on the range or in the sales rings. You'll be away out there on your own trying to prove them wrong.'

Carrie gave a quiet smile. She had been alone for most of her life, so it would be no hardship to go on standing on her own two feet. 'You'll be here, won't you?'

'Oh yes, I'll be here all right . . . If you want me.'

She sat looking at him in the failing light. His face, still ravaged by illness, was comfortingly familiar. The tanned skin was paler now and deep lines grooved the broad brow beneath the shock of curling grey hair, but the eyes remained the same, dark and penetrating, as they looked into hers. 'I want you, Sean O'Dwyer,' she said in a quiet voice.

Then slowly she rose from the end of his mattress where she had been sitting and smiled down at him. 'You know I've never said that to anyone in my life before.'

He nodded but made no reply and he gazed up at her and held out his hand.

She took it and held on to it. They would make a good team, the two of them. 'Just you and me against the world,' she said quietly.

'Just you and me.'

Sean's eyes followed her out the door. It was evening and a silvery glow was filling the sky through the open window opposite his bed. A few short days ago he had almost given up the will to live; there had been nothing left to live for. Then she had returned to him in a dream one hot, sticky night, and he was twenty-five again. It had been so very real. When he awoke he was awash with sweat, but the fever had abated, and later that very day the door of his hut had opened and she had been standing there.

He could hear her footsteps pass his open window and for the first time in longer than he cared to remember, he felt a deep peace in his soul. He leant across and lifted his penny whistle from where it was lying on top of the wooden chest. He held it in his hands and ran his fingers over the smooth surface of the wood, with its carefully gouged holes. It had been a long time, a very long time since he had bothered to pick it up. He had never felt like it before. Maybe he would play a tune, he told himself. A good Irish tune.

Carrie had gone no more than a few yards when the plaintive notes floating on the evening air stopped her in her tracks. A tingling sensation ran through her and gooseflesh covered her skin. It was funny how so cheap a musical instrument could thrill the blood like no other.

Her heart was beating faster as the notes of the old Irish tune danced in her blood. She looked around this place that was home. Every inch of it she loved, every blade of grass, every leaf, every stone. If there really were such a thing as *Palanari*, as the Aborigines called it, a Dreamtime that was the past, the present and the future rolled into one, then this was hers. Yorvik was her Dreamtime. Dreamtime was here and now . . .

To her left, over on the far horizon beyond the lake, she could just make out a line of naked figures silhouetted against the evening sky. The blackfellas were coming back. The evil spirits had surely left Yorvik at last.

CHAPTER TWENTY-FIVE

Carrie left Yorvik at the end of the week to return to Great Glen. It was a wrench, but Sean was now well on the way to recovery and she had left him well supplied with food bought from the market in Hunter's Hollow.

Revisiting all her old haunts had brought untold joy, and, unlike her old neighbours the Applebys, the few local people who recognized her did not seem to hold any grudges for what had happened in her marriage. Amongst the ordinary settlers out here there was little satisfaction to be had from sitting in judgement upon their fellow men and women. Too many had come through too much in their own lives to worry about how others conducted theirs.

There were days, Carrie decided, when you just knew things were going to go your way, and she had felt that immediately her horse and buggy had entered the settlement that had blossomed into quite a small town over the past thirty years.

Hunter's Hollow had looked green and pleasant, with its long main street ending in a grassed area, surrounded by trees, where they still held the weekly markets, and where she had taken a special delight in filling her basket with all sorts of goodies she thought might appeal to a recovering invalid's palate.

She was on her way back to where she had parked the buggy when she came face to face with one of the first people to recognize her: the Presbyterian minister, the Reverend Douglas MacKenzie. He stood stock still on his way across the Common, as if he had seen a ghost. He even took his spectacles out of his pocket and placed them on his nose to make sure he was not seeing things as she loaded the vegetables into the back of the vehicle. 'Well,

I do believe I'm right! It *is* Carrie Hebden, isn't it?' He snatched off his hat and rushed forwards, his hand outstretched.

Carrie still had not come to terms with how much everyone had changed in appearance in the past thirty years. In her mind's eye they had remained the same as the day she left, but now the young became old overnight. But it took her only a few seconds to place the clergyman, now well into his sixties and distinctly stout. Despite the extra weight, that righteous square jaw and the blue-eyed intensity of that gaze was still the same. 'Why, Mr MacKenzie!'

Douglas MacKenzie's once good head of sandy-coloured hair had all but disappeared, save for a few greying tufts over his ears, but his face still shone with the same integrity it had all those years ago. 'My, but it does my heart good to see you back!' he said, pumping Carrie's hand. 'And back for good, I hope?'

'Indeed I am. I'm taking over Yorvik and am determined to make something of it.' Carrie allowed herself a modest smile. 'Some folks round here seem to think it's no job for a woman, but I'm determined to prove them wrong.'

The cleric looked dubious. 'I've heard tell that'll be quite an undertaking, my dear, for the place is in a fair state of disrepair, so they say. But I wish you well.' He replaced his black hat on his head and gave an encouraging smile. 'I'll even go as far as to say a special prayer for you.'

Carrie returned his smile. 'Well that's very thoughtful of you . . . We might as well enlist the help of the Almighty as anyone else, mightn't we? In fact, I think I'll need all the help that's going over the next few months!'

And help, she knew, was going to be her main preoccupation in the weeks and months ahead. She would have to employ new hands for Yorvik, that was for sure. But she would make do with men borrowed from Great Glen for the immediate future, until she saw exactly what was needed. They could come back with her to Yorvik when she returned with Billy the following week.

She could not wait to get back up north to Great Glen and tell her young son of the place that had once meant so much to her. She had already written him a long letter about it, but actually being here and seeing it for himself would be wonderful. Part of the joy in taking pleasure from something was to share it with others.

Carrie had felt quite guilty recently over the small amount of time she had been able to spend with her son. Since his father died the station had consumed almost all her time and energy, so the boy had been more or less left to his own resources when he was not in the school-room.

His education too was posing a problem, for Mr Bardon, the elderly tutor who had provided his lessons over the past few years, was finding it increasingly difficult to cope with the child now he was reaching adolescence. 'It's not that he's indolent exactly, ma'am,' he told Carrie. 'But he needs his interest stimulating. He needs other boys around.'

Carrie knew only too well what was coming after that. Barnaby Bardon was convinced the boy should be sent back to England to complete his education. 'You have the money, if I may be so bold, ma'am, and there's no finer thing to spend it on than your child's future. A place like St Cuthbert's would do him the world of good.'

St Cuthbert's, the York public school where Barnaby Bardon had spent his own schooldays, was renowned for its high academic standards and sporting prowess. Both were areas that Carrie felt could certainly do with being encouraged in her son. Billy, with his fair good looks and dreamy blue eyes, was a child who needed backbone putting into him, as his father had once said. Jock Gordon had loved his son, but he too, before he died, had been concerned that the youngster did not have enough companionship from boys his own age. 'He needs some rough and tumble in his life. Mooning around this place talking

333

to adults all day isn't healthy.' He had even written in his will that he hoped Carrie would see to it that Billy received 'the best education that money can buy'.

'I take it Mr Gordon means a Scottish or English education, ma'am,' the lawyer had said. 'But of course the ultimate choice of school will be down to you.'

Carrie's heart had sunk at the words. But as the summer progressed, the thoughts of Big Jock, the lawyer, and Mr Bardon echoed more and more in Carrie's mind. Was she being selfish denying Billy the chance to mix with his own age group, and get the first-class education into the bargain that his father had regarded as so essential? The last thing she wanted was to make a mother's boy out of him. And there was no denying that over the past few years Billy had missed the presence of a father figure in his life. Jock had been a man big of heart as well as stature and she knew she could never assume the role of both parents. In fact, if she was really honest with herself, she had barely had time to do full justice to her role of mother since she'd taken over the running of the station. And if she had had little personal time to spend with the boy in the past, she would have even less now that she had Yorvik on her plate.

But before making any decision on her son's future she must first show him her old home. She knew that having received her letter, he would be really excited to see everything for himself. And seeing it for himself was indeed the first thing on the boy's mind when she returned home at the beginning of the following week.

'When can we go and see it?' Billy asked, already impatient to get on with things, as together they mounted the steps of Great Glen. 'When can we go there – to Yorvik?'

'We'll return in a few days,' Carrie promised him, reaching out a hand to tousle his hair. 'We'll get one or two of the men to take some implements over and make a start at getting the place in order, and you can help. I've got

334

such plans for the old place, Billy dear. Such wonderful plans!'

Her excitement was contagious, for over the next couple of days the youngster could not wait to get started on the journey that would take them to the wonderful place his mother had told him so much about. He listened with growing anticipation as she related to him all the plans she had already sketched out in her mind.

'Will you really build a grander house than Great Glen there?' he asked over supper on the night before they set off. His young mind could not comprehend a better house than the one in which he had been born and brought up.

'We'll build the most beautiful house in the whole of New South Wales,' his mother told him. She had already designed it in her head. It would be made of that lovely golden stone that she had first admired on her arrival in the colony and it would have Palladian columns on each side of the front door and balconies from all the upstairs rooms, to take full advantage of the most wonderful views in the world.

'But what will you do with the old one that's still there?'

Carrie was for a moment at a loss for words. 'Just you wait and see,' she told him as she spread her bread and butter to go with the goat's-milk cheese they were enjoying. It had already crossed her mind what she might do with the wooden homestead where she had lived with Silas Hebden, but exactly how her idea would go down in a certain quarter she was not quite sure.

When they arrived at Yorvik two days later, however, to her great disappointment Billy's reaction was not at all as she had hoped.

'But it's old and falling down!' he cried, disappointment writ large across the childish features of his face, as he stood outside the homestead, with its flaking paint and sagging verandah. 'Oh, Mama, how can this place be so wonderful?'

Carrie hugged him to her. 'But it is!' she told him, her own heart sinking at the realization he was not seeing it through her eyes. 'And if you can't see it yet, then you will. Believe me, you will. The old place will be beautiful again, Billy dear, I promise you. Just wait and see.'

But Billy was not willing to wait and see. He could find nothing to attract him in this awful place, with its rotting wood and tumbledown fences. He could not wait to get back to Great Glen, with its fine lawns for playing on and its marble floors, so good for bouncing balls. Even his mother's special friend that she told him about in the waggon on the way over did not live up to expectations.

'Why is your beard red and your hair grey?' he asked Sean O'Dwyer, as the two shook hands in the Irishman's hut.

'Well now, that's a good question,' Sean replied with a smile, then parried with one of his own. 'Do you always ask such good questions?'

The boy thought for a moment. 'I think so,' he said solemnly. Then he looked about him at the interior of the hut, with its scant possessions and dirt floor. 'You don't actually live in here, do you?'

Sean affirmed that he did. 'I've lived here for almost four times as long as you've been alive.'

'But it's a pigsty!' the child exclaimed. 'In fact, our pigs live better than this, don't they, Mama?'

Carrie's cheeks flamed. 'Billy, really!'

But the Irishman merely smiled. The child, with his fine upbringing and fancy clothes, was as far removed from his own life as any human being could be. But he was Carrie's child and for that reason, if no other, Sean would be tolerant.

Despite Billy's disappointment, he and his mother spent many weeks at Yorvik over the next few months, and before long she had her grand house built, just as she promised him she would. A firm of builders from Newcastle was employed, using only the finest stone brought up all the way from the same quarries that had provided the materials for Sydney's gracious dwellings.

The new house had ten rooms in all, including a forty-feet drawing room, a dining room with a crystal chandelier that held fifty candles, and an entrance hall with a veined marble floor and a staircase made out of polished red cedar that swept up to the first floor in as graceful a curve as any in Sydney or Newcastle. It was built on the hill about a mile north of the original homestead, with glorious views for miles around. But most magical of all was the view from the master bedroom balcony, from which the sparkling blue of Yorvik Force, like a sapphire set in emeralds, could be glimpsed in all its dazzling splendour.

During her visits, Carrie continued to live in the old house whilst the new one was being built, and on the day the key was finally handed over and the last tradesman left, she asked Sean to accompany her and Billy on a ride over to have their first official look around.

Her own excitement knew no bounds, but she tried to keep it in check. This was the very first time in her life she had had a place that was one hundred per cent her own. Both Great Glen and the original Yorvik homestead had belonged to the men she had lived with, but no longer would that be the case. Every stone of the new Yorvik was hers and hers alone.

The air was autumnal and the trees dazzlingly gold amid the green, and it was like a thousand dreams come true as Carrie mounted the wide stone steps and walked in through the front door. Pride and elation tingled in every nerve in her body. This was it. She had come home at last. Her heart was singing.

But the Irishman by her side was disconcertingly silent as they walked from room to room, their footsteps echoing on the uncarpeted floors. Eventually she could contain herself no longer. 'Well?' she asked, as Billy played outside and they stood together on the balcony of the main bedroom, looking out on the scene she loved more than any other. 'What do you think of the place?'

Sean O'Dwyer's face was pensive. He had no wish to offend. He knew only too well what this place meant to Carrie. She had poured more than money into it; she had poured her whole heart. But it was no place for the likes of him. He felt uncomfortable here. Hemmed in by luxury, suffocated by marble pilasters and ornate ceilings that would look more at home in Sydney's George Street or in London than here. 'It's a grand house, Carrie,' he told her. 'A grand house for those who like such places.'

'But you don't.'

He shrugged his shoulders and sighed. 'I'd be like a fish out of water in a place like this.'

She turned from him and stared fixedly out across the green rolling landscape towards the waterfall in the distance, feeling her eyes mist. His lack of enthusiasm had poured as great a deluge of cold water over her as ever came from Yorvik Force.

The feeling of disappointment almost choked her. She so much wanted both him and her son to love this place as much as she did. But Billy had no interest in it and now this . . .

'I've hurt you . . . I'm sorry . . .' Sean O'Dwyer reached out to touch her arm, but Carrie shrugged him away.

'You don't have to apologize,' she said stiffly. 'There's no reason why you *have* to like it.'

He looked at her standing there, her hands gripping the white-painted wood of the balcony rail so tight the knuckles showed white through the tanned skin as she gazed out over the rolling green and gold countryside. Fine lines fanned up from the corners of her eyes and the early autumn sunlight picked out the strands of silver that were shot through the dark brown of her hair. So much had happened in her life since they were first together, so much that he could never share. She had moved on so far in those thirty years, and not just in distance. Once they had been two young people thrown together by circumstances whose lives had touched for one brief moment. Flotsam on the river of life, they had been. But too much water had flowed between them since then. It would be wrong to try to go back to recapture the past. He might have remained the same, but she was a different person now. She was an independent, successful woman. He recognized that and admired it, but he would not pay homage to it. He had his own values, and they could never be hers.

'I – I didn't really expect you *like* this place,' Carrie said haltingly, still not looking at him. 'I guessed it would be . . . well, a little ostentatious for your taste . . . But I thought it might let you see that you can't go on living in that awful hovel of a hut you've lived in for so long . . . Dear God, Sean, life has moved on in the past generation. Progress has been made!' She was looking at him now, her eyes pleading with his.

'What are you trying to say, Carrie?'

She made a helpless gesture with her hands. 'I suppose I'm trying to tell you that you can't go on living in that awful place any longer. Billy was right, it's only fit for pigs. You must at least move into the old Yorvik house.'

'You want me to move into Silas's place?'

'Yes, that's exactly what I want.'

'I'm sorry.'

'I beg your pardon.'

'I said I'm sorry, I can't do it.'

'What do you mean, you can't do it?'

'Exactly what I said. I can't move into Silas's old place. It's not me.'

'What do you mean, it's not you?' she demanded, her voice rising. 'Does *being you* mean living in a pigsty for the rest of your life? Is that what *being you* means?' She was shouting at him now. 'Isn't it about time you paid yourself a little self-respect? Isn't it about time you climbed out of that mire and made something of yourself?'

'Like you, you mean?'

'Yes, like me! Why not like me?' Why was he trying to do her down like this? Why was he spoiling what should have been the happiest moment of her life? No one had ever done her any favours. Everything she had, she had had to fight for, against all the odds. 'I'm not ashamed of the success I've made of my life,' she told him, her blood rising as she fought to keep her voice in control. 'But ambition's always been a dirty word to you, Sean, hasn't it? Well, it isn't in my book. This country needs people like me . . . People with guts who want to make something of themselves!'

Sean's face was immobile, betraying no emotion as he turned from her and began to walk back into the bedroom. Carrie ran after him and pulled on his arm. 'I'm sorry,' she cried. 'Please forgive me. I didn't mean to imply . . .'

'That I'm just a fella with no guts, content to live in a pigsty?'

She dropped her grip on his sleeve and looked away, as embarrassment coloured her cheeks.

'But I am, Carrie,' he said quietly. 'You're right. That's exactly what I am.'

He reached out and tilted her chin round so that her eyes met his. 'Maybe it's the blackfella in me, I don't know. But all this . . .' He made a sweeping gesture with his hand around the palatial room. 'This type of thing doesn't mean a thing to me. I don't need all this stuff to live – to be a better human being. Look at the blackfellas . . . All right, they're despised and looked down on by white folks like old Silas and the others, but they're happy. By Christ, they're happy. They don't even need a roof of any kind over their heads to find their *Palanari*.'

She could feel the hot rush of tears to her eyes as they looked back into his. *Palanari* . . . The Aborigines' Dreamtime. What was he trying to tell her?

'This may be your Dreamtime, Carrie, but it's not mine. And never could be. I'm happy in my hut, pigsty though it may be to some . . . If you want me to move out, then

I will. But I'll never move into Silas's house. Never. I don't want your charity and I don't need it.'

They stood looking at one another, the few inches between them as wide a gulf as the ocean.

'I love you, Sean O'Dwyer,' Carrie said, tears streaming down her cheeks.

'And I love you.'

Neither had ever said those words before.

She rushed into his arms, and clung to him, as the tears flowed from her eyes. 'Damn you . . .' she whispered. 'Damn your stubborn pigheaded blackfellaness to hell . . .'

Billy was enrolled as a boarder at St Cuthbert's College in England's ancient city of York for the beginning of the autumn term of 1873. He was fourteen years old, tall for his age and slim, with an unruly quiff of fair hair that flopped over his brow, above blue eyes that still had that same dreamy look to them that his mother had known all those years before in her beloved brother after whom he had been named.

As he prepared for the long voyage to England, trying on his new suit of travelling clothes for the first time, Carrie observed wistfully that her son looked quite the young man. Her little boy had grown up in the twinkling of an eye. He had crossed over the threshold from childhood into adolescence and she had not even noticed. The sight of him all dressed up in his first real grown-up suit of clothes tugged at her heart, for there were so many similarities between the two Billys. In both looks and manner, Carrie knew that in her own son she had his uncle incarnate. And never more so than now as he prepared to leave her, for it was during these adolescent, gangly, awkward years that she remembered her brother the most.

Even their characters were similar. She herself had been a child with an enquiring lively mind and a quick intelligence, but her brother had been a more soulful, contemplative personality who found it difficult to raise any enthusiasm for learning, or much else come to that. But he had been a loving child, always eager to please, and not one you could remain mad at for long if he did commit any misdemeanour. He had had a disconcerting way of hanging his head and balefully looking up at you from beneath girlishly thick lashes, and this was a trick at which her son Billy had been particularly adept. It never failed to work, and at such times Carrie would wonder if he would ever know the memories that such a small act rekindled. Then a great sadness would envelop her, for she knew she could never tell him of the tragedy that had befallen his uncle. The pain went too deep and it was too intertwined with her own story to make for comfortable recounting. Whoever said that time healed all things had never gone through what she had.

But it was a story that she would replay and replay in her mind, for the older she got, the more sure she became that the past, the present and the future were inextricably linked. The Aborigines knew this and had tried to encapsulate that knowledge in the meaning of Dreamtime, a concept that seemed to have very little relevance to the modern world. To that ancient race time had no meaning; the past, the present and future were as one. Every living thing was a part of a whole that encompassed every wind that blew, every blade of grass, every ripple of the ocean. To understand yourself you had to accept your past as part of your present and part of your life to come . . .

It was a philosophy that appealed greatly to Carrie as it was the nearest she could get to understanding her own life. So much of what had gone before was with her still. Even the very act of giving birth had been touched by a past still achingly vivid; a past that would not let her go.

It had been a long and severe labour and she had lain in her bed at Great Glen all day, then watched the creeping shadows of twilight outside her window brighten to a star-lit night. By midnight, just before her child was born, the sky was ablaze with constellations so brilliant they seemed to dazzle her eyes as she gazed up at them. But in all that shining splendour, one star had shone brighter than the rest. One star up there in the glittering heavens was shining for her and her alone. She had seen it a lifetime before, that night in the Newgate prison cell when it had shed its light on the darkness of a soul bereft of all hope. It had brought her the faith to go on. And she was seeing it again on the other side of the world as she heaved and struggled on the dishevelled sheet in her bed at Great Glen. She was not alone any more. Her mother was with her. Bridie was there watching over the birth of her first grandchild.

That knowledge had brought a great sense of peace to her heart, and when finally she had held the squalling little red-faced bundle in her arms Carrie knew there could be no question as to his name. She had always intended to call him after her brother, but seeing him lying there nestled close to her breast had made that decision absolute. She was no longer in that large, comfortable bedroom, she was back in that bleak room where they had all slept in Semple Street and her own mother was holding just such a squalling puce-skinned child. Both infants were long and slim, with perfectly formed features, and had heads as bald as coots. 'That means he's going to be fair like your daddy's side of the family,' Bridie Clayton had told her small daughter with a smile when the child had pointed it out. 'He's not going to be a dark Irish bog-trotter like his Mammy and wee sister!'

And now that wee sister was watching her own child leaving for that same country she herself had been born in but banished from all those years ago. Carrie had no love for England, that was for sure. It had taken from her the brother she had loved, and now she was sending her own son back to those hated shores. Was she mad? Had she quite taken leave of her senses?

She had wrestled long and hard with her conscience over this. But in the end she had decided, why not? If that hated place could offer the best education that money could buy, why not make good use of it? Why not take all it had to offer and use it in the service of this new land she was helping build? One day Billy would come back a fine educated young man, eager and willing to take over Great Glen and Yorvik. He would be ready and able to take up the burden at a time when she herself would be only too willing to lay it down. Then and only then could she feel she had done her duty, done her best by both her beloved son and her beloved land.

The actual separation involved, however, was infinitely more difficult to rationalize. With England a four-month voyage away, she knew she would not see her son for several years, for even long school holidays could not accommodate such extended periods of travelling time.

'But he won't be the only one by a long chalk, you know, ma'am,' his tutor, Mr Bardon, reminded her. 'There are parents just like yourself living at the farthest ends of the British Empire who all have this dilemma to face. England's public schools are full of just such sons of the Empire. Education must come first. To deny him the chance of the best the mother country has to offer would be a great tragedy. You would be refusing him the greatest gift a parent can bestow on a child.'

No matter how much it hurt, Carrie knew that to be true. Barnaby Bardon was a sensible, good man and when he then volunteered to travel with Billy and see him safely deposited into the safe-keeping of St Cuthbert's, she knew she could stick her head in the sand no longer. Her son was at the age when he needed a proper education and she would have to get used to the idea of parting with him, despite the pain it involved. So thank God for Barnaby Bardon.

Even the holidays would no longer pose a problem. The elderly man had decided to return to spend his retirement with his unmarried sister at her cottage on the Yorkshire coast, near Scarborough. This would place him in the ideal position to keep a fatherly eye on the boy. And he was at great pains to assure his employer that her son would be well looked after, both at school and during the holidays, when he would personally see to it that Billy spent the time at home in Scarborough with him and his sister.

'Don't you worry, ma'am, my sister Alice will fuss over the lad like a proper mother hen. And St Cuthbert's is a fine school. You'll be as proud as anything once they've done with him. Make a real man of him, they will!'

Carrie listened as he did his best to put her mind at rest. But parting with one's only child was akin to severing a limb. Although undemonstrative by nature, she loved Billy with a passion, and now her very heart was being torn from her at the prospect of his leaving. Her only consolation was that the boy was excited at the prospect of going. To him the voyage was to be a great adventure at the end of which he would have lots of playmates and 'learn to be a gentleman', as Mr Bardon put it.

Carrie saw him off from the quayside at Sydney harbour one bright, breezy morning in late April of 1873, his arrival in England timed to coincide with the start of the beginning of St Cuthbert's autumn term some five months later. As planned, he travelled in Barnaby Bardon's care, his lanky adolescent figure in the new tweed overcoat already towering a good head and shoulders above the stooped, elderly tutor as the two walked side by side up the gangplank of the ship.

'Don't worry about me, Mama,' Billy told her, as they embraced for the last time. 'I'm going to love England, I know I am!'

'Are you, Billy?' Carrie murmured, clasping her to him for the last time.

'Oh yes! Just as much as you do!'

How little the young understood . . .

She wept as the tall ship sailed out on the tide, its white sails gleaming in the early morning sunshine. Despite the sun, a light rain was beginning to fall; the type the Aborigines called *mudi meechi* – kind rain – but Carrie was unaware of the raindrops as they mingled with the tears streaming down her cheeks. Billy stood at the ship's rail, his arm raised in a final goodbye, until his hand was lost in a sea of other waving hands.

She stood on the quayside and waved her white handkerchief until she could wave no more and the vessel was merely a speck on the rushing blue tide, as it made for the twin headlands that guarded the entrance to the open sea. It was her son's childhood she was waving goodbye to, standing there on the rain-washed cobbles, for when he came back he would be a young man.

As Carrie turned to make her way back to her carriage, she was aware of a shabbily dressed middle-aged woman staring at her from a distance of some twenty yards. Even among a population where the majority were far from affluent, she was poorly dressed, in a frock of a dark checked material beneath a black woollen shawl, which she wore over her head as protection against the falling rain.

Was she simply admiring the new mulberry velvet jacket and the latest bustled skirts she had worn specially for the occasion, Carrie wondered? At such times she was acutely aware of the quality of her own clothes and the poverty of others. She deliberately averted her eyes as she lifted her skirts above a puddle in the cobbles and continued hurriedly across the quayside towards her waiting transport.

To her consternation, the woman followed, and grabbed hold of her arm before she had gone more than a few yards.

'Excuse me . . .'

Carrie turned, her face still wet with tears, to meet the other's quizzical gaze.

The bright eyes looking into her own narrowed as if to ascertain that her suspicions were well founded, then came the exclamation. 'Jesus, Holy Mary and Joseph – it *is* you!'

Carrie's heart began to beat faster. If this was someone from her past, she would rather not know. She was still far too upset over her leave-taking of Billy to feel like making polite conversation, and furthermore she had no wish to be recognized by anyone from her early years. Those days were dead and gone and she had no intention of resurrecting them here on the quayside on such a momentous day. 'I'm sorry, I'm in a hurry!' She retrieved her arm and made to continue on her way, but the woman had other ideas.

'Don't you recognize me?' she demanded. 'Don't tell me I've got that old that you can't tell it's me!'

That voice. Those bright blue eyes. Carrie felt she was going to pass out. 'Molly?' she queried faintly. 'You're not Molly McGuire, are you?'

'Molly McFarland now,' the woman corrected her, with a wide smile. 'And what would your name be these days?' she asked, glancing down at Carrie's wedding ring.

'Carrie Gordon-Hebden,' Carrie answered, a trifle self-consciously. Since taking over Yorvik she had added Big Jock's name to her own for the sake of her son and realized it was quite a mouthful.

A ring of laughter came from the smiling lips opposite. 'My, but that's high-falutin' and no mistake!' Then Molly grabbed Carrie by both hands. To heck with names and formalities! 'How are you, Carrie love? It's so good to see you!'

Carrie's own lips had great difficulty in forming a smile. How she had got through the past thirty years without being recognized she had never ceased to wonder, but it had always been a fear lurking at the back of her mind that one day there would be a repeat of the Bidwell incident that had turned her life upside down. One day, just like this, someone would stop her in the street and recognize her — expose her for the liar and the cheat she had been for all these years.

'We thought you had drowned, you know,' Molly was saying, her still bright eyes shining as she kept hold of her friend's hand. 'They told us you had gone overboard just before we entered harbour . . . I shed tears for you, you know!'

'Did you, Mol?' Carrie said, looking at the once pretty face, now weather-beaten and marked with the poverty that had been her lot.

'Aye, that I did . . . But don't you worry, I'll not ask you how you got away if you don't ask me!'

But how Molly escaped the waiting prison factory was obvious by her name. 'I don't have to ask, with a name like McFarland. I take it your Scottie really did jump ship and spring you?'

'He did that!' Molly grinned, showing several missing front teeth. 'In fact, he's over there right now and will be delighted to see you again after all this time. Come and meet him!'

So Carrie was hustled across the dock to meet Ian McFarland, whose red-haired good looks she found were virtually intact, and who, apart from a little weight around the middle, was still instantly recognizable as the young ship's officer who had taken such a fancy to the high-spirited Irish convict girl.

After seeking out her driver to tell him she had met up with old friends and would be making her own way back to the hotel, Carrie accompanied her two friends to a dockside tavern, where ale and cakes were ordered, and she listened as they told her of their lives over the past three decades.

After jumping ship and bribing a guard to allow Molly's escape from the notorious women's prison factory at Parramatta, they had made for Woolloomooloo where a branch of the McGuire family had settled on the Riley estate. Accommodation was eventually found and this hundred acres of scrubby land bordering the shores of Woolloomooloo Bay proved to be an ideal hideaway for the young couple, who were soon joined by a family of four sons. Unlike the toffs who were building their grand houses on top of Woolloomooloo Hill, the McFarlands' cottage was more shanty than desirable dwelling, but the slab hut, with its shingle roof and earthen floor, had had more than its fair share of laughter amongst the occasional tears over the years.

Ian, John, Seamus and Robert, they had called their

boys, and they had all had their father's red hair, but their mother's lively character. Too lively at times.

'They can never say they didn't have a good childhood,' Molly said, sentimentally shaking her head as she downed the remains of her second jug of ale, paid for by Carrie. 'Ian here – staunch Presbyterian though he is, God bless him – let me enrol them in Cosgrove's Catholic School in Castlereagh Street, but the rascals were never there. If they weren't hanging around the Quay, they were prowling the market to see what they could scrounge, or hanging around the toffs' houses on Woolloomooloo Hill, and up to no good wherever they got to. The priests were forever expelling them, only to take them back again after I pleaded with them. Lord, my knees were fair worn out by the end of it all!'

'And what are they doing now?' Carrie asked in all innocence.

Molly and Ian McFarland exchanged glances. 'Aye, well, not any occupation that we'd care to boast about, that's for sure,' Ian said cagily.

Then, less inhibited than her husband, Molly leant forwards across the table to confide in her friend. 'You've heard of the likes of Ben Hall and his gang, I've no doubt.'

Carrie affirmed indeed she had. Up to his death eight years ago there had not been a more wanted outlaw in all of New South Wales than Ben Hall. 'They were bushrangers, weren't they?'

Molly nodded. 'My cousin Jacky McGuire – the boys' uncle – was Ben's best mate. Both married Walsh girls of good Irish stock. In fact, Jacky's wife Helen was Ben's Biddy's eldest sister, and we were all guests at Ben and Biddy's wedding in Bathhurst back in . . . I think 'fifty-six it must have been.' She turned to her husband for confirmation.

'A right old shindig that was, I can tell you!' Ian McFarland put in. 'Jacky was best man and told some right stories once he'd had a few! I had to put my hands over our four lads' ears at times, I can tell you!' He grinned and shook his head at the memory. The Irish certainly knew how to enjoy themselves when they got together. It was just a pity young Biddy had to go and upset the applecart by running off with that no-good ex-policeman Jim Taylor, taking Ben's young son Harry with them.

'Jacky and Ben were partners in business as well, sharing a leased run of 16,000 acres at Sandy Creek . . .' Molly continued, then her voice faltered. '. . . Aye, it was a real shame when Biddy ran off with that Taylor fella. Ben, the poor lad, went right off his head. Wanted nothing more to do with farming and took to the road, bushranging. He rode with Darkie Gardiner and his gang for a time, and then set up in business on his own, so to speak, with my cousin Jacky and a few others.'

Then Molly had the good grace to blush, as she added quietly, 'Our four lads seemed to reckon their uncle was a bit of a hero. They used to listen to his stories over the years, so when they were finished with school . . . Well, they took to helping him and Ben out as part of the gang.'

'You couldn't have been too happy about that,' Carrie said in some concern. As far as the police were concerned, the only good bushranger was a dead one.

Ian McFarland, sitting across from her, nodded and looked thoughtful. 'It was the gold that did it, back then in the early sixties. Turned a lot of folks' heads, it did – including the lads'. Get rich quick was the thing. Farming was for fools when there was money like that to be had . . .' He fell silent as he contemplated the state of affairs out west that had caused such havoc in their own family amongst so many others back in those heady times, when fortunes were made and lost on a daily basis.

Gold-digging was nothing new to the colony, but the discovery of unusually productive seams about two hundred miles west of Sydney in the early sixties had led to rich pickings being there for the taking. Diggers had flooded into the goldfields in their thousands and, for those who did not fancy getting their hands dirty but did not mind robbing a mail coach or two, like Ben Hall and his gang, there was plenty of money to be had. They said millionaires were being made overnight in the best fields and a drunken digger was easy prey, especially at night when carousing in one of the riotous new gold towns such as Forbes or Young.

A new hundred-mile-long road now wound through the Weddin Mountains linking the two towns, and over the past decade this particular highway had become the province of the Wild Colonial Boys, despite the best efforts of Inspector Sir Frederick Pottinger and the Western Division of the new combined police force to combat the crime wave.

Carrie, still numbed by her farewell to her own son, did not know quite how to react to this revelation about the McFarland boys as she looked from their father to their mother sitting at the table beside her. Their sons were not only bushrangers, but part of the notorious Ben Hall gang to boot. There was hardly a major robbery in the whole of New South Wales that hadn't been laid at their door. The newspapers were always full of stories of their exploits and the final capture and death of the outlaw in early May of 1865 had made headlines all over Australia. She felt a shiver run through her. All of a sudden she was back in convict territory once more and her own past was looming larger than it had done in years. She glanced towards the door and wondered how soon she could make her escape.

'I know what you're probably thinking,' Molly said. 'And it — it's not something we're particularly proud of, them being bushrangers and all . . . But the way I see it, the law wasn't exactly fair to us in the past. The lads were brought up on stories of how their uncles were hanged, or imprisoned, and their own mother transported for no crime at all . . . You can't really blame the young ones for not having any respect for the law after that.'

Ian, who had been sitting quietly supping his ale as his wife spoke, nodded as he took out his tinder box. She had not been half as upset at the boys' decision to join their Uncle Jacky and Ben Hall as he had been. But the dour Calvinistic Scot had never been one for taking risks like his lively Irish Molly. Sometimes he wondered at the twist of fate that had made him give up a good life at sea to risk everything by helping her escape, then marrying her. The years that had followed in the heart of Sydney's poorest Irish community had been colourful, that was for sure, but sometimes – just sometimes – he could wish for a little less excitement, a little less heartache. The Outlaw Act that had been resurrected by the Legislature now allowed the police, or even bounty hunters, to shoot bushrangers on sight. His eyes were serious as he looked across at Carrie. 'You don't bring children into this world to see them go before you,' he said softly. 'That is the greatest cross of all to bear.'

'You mean . . . ?' Carrie was not sure how to put it.

'I mean Ian and Bobby, our eldest and youngest, were killed in that same shoot-out that killed Ben himself,' Ian McFarland said, avoiding her eyes. His own were full of the pain as they gazed unseeingly into the far corner of the bar room. 'The sixth of May, 1865, near Billabong Creek, a few miles north-west of Forbes, it was. When they shot Ben, they paraded his dead body through Forbes lying across his horse like a bloody swag, and the townsfolk tore the clothes right off him for souvenirs. Undignified it was . . . Thank God, our own lads were spared that.'

'I'm sorry,' Carrie said. 'I'm so very sorry.'

Ian McFarland shrugged. 'They were grown men. They knew what they were getting into.'

'And the other two?'

'Well now, that's a sore point and no mistake,' Molly interjected. 'They're still plying the same trade, but we want them to give up.' Her voice fell to a whisper as she said wearily, 'God knows, since their brothers' deaths we've tried to persuade them often enough . . . But you know what young folk are like.'

Carrie nodded and thought of her own son whom she had just seen off on the boat to England. She would have fought to the death to keep him from ending up like Molly's boys. 'You would like Billy,' she told them. 'He's been a real joy to me over the years.' And Molly and Ian listened in astonishment as she told them of her life as Mistress of a large sheep station at the foot of the Hunter Valley, and of her plans for the future. She talked for all of ten minutes without interruption, then Ian finally spoke up, his voice as serious as his face as he said quietly, 'That old farmstead you mentioned — the one you no longer need because you've built the big house . . .'

'Yes?'

He struggled with the best way to put it. 'You wouldn't consider letting it out in return for some work around the place, would you?' His heart was beating faster as he looked across the table at her. Thirty long years they had lived in that shanty on the old Riley estate. Now here was a chance — just the ghost of a chance — to get out.

'I don't quite understand . . .' Carrie's own heart began to race, and she prayed inwardly she was not about to hear what she feared she might.

'I'm not as young as I once was,' the Scotsman admitted, with a wry smile. 'But there's still some strength left in these old hands yet. And I'm certainly willing, that's for sure.' He said no more but looked at Carrie in a mixture of expectancy and embarrassment.

'You — you're asking me to let you have the old Yorvik homestead?' She let out a breath, as if she had been hit in the stomach. 'I — I . . .'

Molly, who had been sitting silently by, had warmed to the idea as soon as her husband had come up with it. Noticing Carrie's indecision, she added quickly, 'You needn't worry about us being any embarrassment to you. We'd know our place and wouldn't presume.' She clasped her hands together in mounting excitement as she glanced at her husband. 'Oh Ian, with a place like that we might even persuade the lads to leave the road . . . I'm sure Carrie here would have plenty of spare work for them around the station.'

Two pairs of eyes turned on Carrie, who had gone quite pink. Why had she been so stupid as to go blabbing her mouth off like that? No matter how fond she had been of Molly, and however genuine a person Ian was, there surely could be no question of having them come and live on Yorvik. Couldn't they see she had spent thirty years trying to undo the past and make something of herself? To invite that past right into her own home was surely to place a viper in her bosom. Who knew when one day or night, the worse for drink perhaps, one of them might let her secret out? She looked from one to the other as the colour flared in her cheeks. There was so much hope in their eyes. So much hope.

'I'm sorry,' she began. 'I'm really sorry . . .'

'You mean you don't want us near you?' Molly said, her voice tightening. 'We're not good enough for you now, is that it?'

'No . . . No, that's not it at all!' Carrie said quickly, her mind searching frantically for an excuse that sounded plausible. 'It's just that I've already promised the house to a worker on the station . . . He – he's due to be married shortly . . .'

Molly and Ian exchanged glances.

'That's quite all right, Carrie,' Ian McFarland said. 'There's no need to explain. We understand.'

Shame filled Carrie's soul and a silence fell between them. Suddenly it had all turned sour.

After a minute or so she could bear it no longer. She pushed her drink from her and rose to leave.

Ian McFarland got to his feet and held out his hand. 'I'm sorry if I've embarrassed you in any way,' he said, with real understanding in his eyes. 'I really didn't mean to.'

Carrie took his hand and shook it gratefully. He was a nice man. A genuine man.

She looked down at Molly and held out her hand, but her friend turned her head the other way and pretended not to see.

Carrie and Ian exchanged glances. The hurt had been done. There was no more to say.

The rain was still falling when she got back outside. Beyond the harbour wall the sea had gone from blue to a leaden grey, and the heavens above were overcast and heavy. Almost as heavy as her heart.

She turned and glanced back at the tavern door. Two sailors were brawling on the front step.

She put up her umbrella and made for one of the cabs that were standing at the rank about fifty feet away.

'Not a very nice day, ma'am,' the cabby said, as he helped her into her seat.

'No,' Carrie replied with feeling. 'Not a very nice day at all.'

CHAPTER TWENTY-SEVEN

With her son at school on the other side of the world, Carrie threw herself into the job of managing her two stations, Great Glen and Yorvik, but it soon became obvious she could not remain torn in half forever. One would have to go. Her decision to sell Great Glen was made over Christmas 1873, her first without Billy.

'You're sure you're not just feeling depressed because the young lad's over there in England?' Sean O'Dwyer asked her, as they sat over a billycan of tea in his hut on Christmas Eve.

Carrie shrugged and swatted at one of the countless small flies that infested the hut on hot evenings such as this. She flicked the tiny carcass off her forearm with a satisfied grimace.

'They do say women can turn funny when their kids leave home, you know.'

She rubbed the small spot of blood off her arm. The Irishman often seemed to know her better than she knew herself. 'Maybe that comes into it, who knows?'

There was not a breath of air. The weather had been sultry all day – conditions that did peculiar things to one's mood. It was headache weather and one had been threatening ever since she got up this morning. Thinking of Billy only made it worse. God only knew how she was going to get through Christmas Day tomorrow.

They lapsed into silence, and Carrie sat motionless on the rickety wooden chair, staring out through the open door of the hut as she sipped her tea and thought of Billy at school in far-off York. The pain she had felt that day they had said goodbye on the Sydney quayside was with her still; it had turned into a dull ache that would be there until he returned.

She had already had three letters, one from her son, one from the headmaster, and one from Mr Bardon, Billy's old tutor, reporting on their arrival in Britain back in August. A whole term would have gone by now, and at the end of it Barnaby Bardon had promised to take the boy to Scarborough to spend Christmas with him and his sister. They would be kind to Billy, Carrie had no doubt of that. The tutor had said in his letter his sister was already baking special treats to store away for the boy's arrival. He would be the child their home had never known. Cosseted and doted upon, the festive season would be one delight after another by the sound of it. He might even experience his first English snowfall. That was something she knew he would be thrilled about. Christmases ought to have snow and blazing fires, with roasting chestnuts, stuffed goose and plum pudding, and all the good things the growing middle classes were taking for granted back in the old country. Even now, after all these years, she could not get used to having Christmas in high summer, with soaring temperatures and little appetite for the sizzling roasted bird she insisted the cook still prepared.

One of the station cats yawned, stretched, then got up from where it had been lying at the open door of the hut and wandered inside, arching its back and purring contentedly as it rubbed itself against Carrie's skirts. She absent-mindedly stroked its fur as she let out a heartfelt sigh for the festive idyll she had never been able to share with her son, and now never would. By the time he came back he would be a young man.

'You can't go on living his life for him, you know,' Sean said quietly. 'You have to let go sometime. All parents do.'

'I know. I know.' She leant back in her chair and, resting her cup on the nearby wooden chest, she waved a cooling hand in front of her face as the cat moved on to Sean. 'God, it's hot . . .' Then she was pensive for a moment or two before assuring him, 'I haven't been spending all my time mooning about my son, you know. I really have been turning my mind to other things recently.'

'You're quite serious, then, about selling one of the stations?'

Carrie nodded as she reached for her tea and took another sip. 'One place is enough for anyone, man or woman, to manage these days, with all the extras the workers are demanding. It takes more than money to build schools and houses and all the other things that people expect. Sometimes I feel I can barely keep up with the demands of modern life . . . I suppose what I'm saying is that I've come to the stage when I feel I can't do both places justice. If I'm in Great Glen I feel guilty about not being here in Yorvik, and vice versa. I'm dividing my energies as well as my time. I feel torn in two, Sean. One will have to go.'

'And that one's Great Glen.'

'And that one's Great Glen.'

He gave a quiet smile as he sipped his own tea from the battered tin mug and regarded her thoughtfully over the rim.

'You never doubted that, did you?' she queried.

He scratched the hair on his chin. He had not shaved since his illness, and now with his head of shoulder-length greying hair and copper-coloured beard, Carrie constantly pulled his leg about looking like the old man of the woods. 'No, I can't say as I did,' he answered slowly. 'You and me, we're tied to this old place, Carrie girl, God help us . . . It's in our blood.'

They looked at one another and Carrie gave a wistful smile.

'This place meant freedom to me once, when I first arrived,' she sighed. 'No one can ever know what riding over these wide open spaces came to mean after being cooped up in . . .' She was about to say a convict deck and checked herself. '. . . In a ship for four months.'

The Irishman put down his mug and felt inside his

pocket for his clay pipe. He pressed a plug of tobacco into the bowl, then reached for his tinder box. In all the time he had known her she had never spoken about her life before she arrived in the colony and, never one to probe, he had never asked her. But that had not stopped him being curious. What on earth had brought a young girl all the way out here to marry that crotchety old coot Silas Hebden? He puffed the tobacco into life and looked at her fondly through the smoke. 'You were a good-looker then, all right. You must have set many a young man's heart a'beating before you ever reached these shores.'

Carrie could feel herself colour beneath the sunburnt skin of her cheeks. 'No, I can't say as I ever did. Not that I knew of at any rate.'

He looked surprised. She was a secretive one all right. He gave a pull-the-other-leg sort of smile, then admitted, 'Well, you surely made mine miss a beat or two in those days, I can tell you!'

'Did I? Did I really?' She was surprised at the wonder in her voice and the faint leap her blood gave as she looked at him.

He puffed on his pipe and smiled that easy smile she knew so well, and his teeth were still as straight and white as they had been all those years ago. 'Aye, that you did.'

His words hung between them in the stifling air of the hut. For a moment their eyes held, then, with an almost girlish embarrassment, she dropped her gaze to the cup in her lap. She felt closer to him than she had felt to any man, and even after thirty years he could still make her heart miss a beat with a certain word or look. Yet there remained a gap between them that could not be bridged. He had tried to tell her that day they had visited the new Yorvik together for the first time, but in a way she had always known it. Even as a young woman she had sensed he would not be owned, could not be tied down, or belong to any one woman. For all she knew he had had many native wives over the years, and might still have. And perhaps that was what cut deepest of all in her heart. Perhaps that was what had ensured that that gap between them remained as wide as it did.

They sat in silence as he puffed contentedly on his pipe, his eyes resting on a face still beautiful despite the passing years. He had visualized it so often, lying there on his bunk, over the three decades that had gone. There had been other women in his life since then; one or two former she-lags he had run into over the years, and of course Quarra and a couple of others from her tribe. But none had compared with the woman who now sat beside him and had once sent the blood coursing through his veins like no other.

'There should be a good market for a place like Great Glen, wouldn't you say?' Carrie asked, interrupting his musing, and getting the conversation back to safer ground.

'No doubt about it. You won't have much trouble finding a buyer these days, not with all these rich squatters around that we hear so much about.'

Steadily rising wool prices over the past few years had led to some squatters beginning to rival the old, well-established station owners in the colony. Their newly built palatial houses were now surpassing even the likes of the new Yorvik and Great Glen in their splendour, boasting such unheard-of things as ballrooms and billiard rooms. In fact, some stations were beginning to resemble small villages, with their own general store, post office, church and school. This new, growing breed of successful squatter even seemed to be immune from the natural disasters that had plagued so many settlers' lives in the past. The succession of droughts and floods that had brought ruin to hundreds of hard-pressed farmers over the past decade had been easily ridden out by most of the richer squatters, whose credit-worthiness was sufficient for any of the banks to loan them more than enough funds to see them through the bad times. Now with prosperity on the way again, many were looking to increase their holdings. Great Glen would be a prize indeed.

So, after much thought and not a little regret, the Great Glen cattle and sheep station was put on the market two weeks later and sold before the end of January, 1874, to one of the very squatters Sean had spoken of when the subject was first mooted in his hut that Christmas. The sale, to an elderly Irishman by the name of Patrick Molloy, caused much talk, for the Dubliner was a ticket-of-leave man, an ex-convict who had worked his way up from nothing twenty years earlier to become the owner of one of the biggest spreads in New South Wales, before putting in his bid for Great Glen.

Although she had certain regrets, for she knew how much Big Jock had loved it and their son had been born there, Carrie felt no real guilt at parting with the place. In her heart Yorvik had always been home, and now with the extra money from the sale she could really begin to plan for the future and make it into the thriving business she had always dreamed of.

Several of the workers chose to remain on Great Glen and work for their new employer, but those she relied on most, such as Will, her head stockman, chose to come with her to Yorvik, and she had new cabins specially built for them on the flat land between the old huts and the lake. She offered one of the new buildings to Sean, but it came as no surprise when he refused. He was happy in his 'pig-sty' as he had referred to it ever since Billy's remark, and there he would remain.

So with papers to be signed and furniture and implements to be moved to Yorvik or sold, the year of 1874 passed quickly, and by the start of 1875 the additional money spent on the station was turning it into one of the best husbanded in the Valley. Almost all the land was now fenced and Carrie threw herself into experiments with new cross-breeds of sheep. To help her in this task she made enquiries about the Henderson brothers and discovered that the younger one, Jock, had left to try his luck down in the Victorian goldfields at Ballarat, but his elder brother Davie was still at Cameron Creek. To her delight he agreed to return to Yorvik for a substantial increase on the wage Angus Cameron was paying him and, with him at the helm, the Yorvik station began to gain a country-wide reputation for the quality of its wool and mutton.

Before long, their breeding experiments had resulted in a sturdy cross-breed comprised of Lincoln Longwool, Ryeland, with more than a dash of Scottish Blackface, and the Yorvik sheep as it became known brought even more money into the station's coffers.

On the beef and dairy cattle front, Will Morton, determined not to be outshone by the Scotsman and his sheep, had done a fair bit of experimenting himself and as healthy a herd of finest Illawarra beasts as could be found anywhere in Australia was being built up. This part Ayrshire, part Shorthorn, with a dash of old mixed breed, brought Carrie enormous pride and pleasure, and from their growing dairy herd she succeeded in setting up quite a profitable butter and cheese producing business, the results of which were sold not only at the weekly market in Hunter's Hollow but also further east in some of Newcastle's finest food stores under the tempting name of 'Yorvik Gold'.

But the decade of the seventies did not bring prosperity or good luck to all the stations in the Valley. In the spring of 1877 Mabel Appleby died, to be followed twelve months later by her husband, Geordie. The latter suffered a heart attack on his way back from Newcastle after instructing his lawyer to instigate a law suit against Carrie for what he saw as encroachment of Yorvik land on to that of Eden Vale during the massive fencing operation she had put in train. The exact boundaries on the outer reaches of both stations had always been a contentious issue as no proper maps were available, but she trusted Davie Henderson to make an honest assessment of what was hers. The fencing of the land was part of the reason she had enticed him back on to her payroll, for along with his brother he had spent more than half his life shepherding Silas's flocks across those far-flung acres and would know better than anyone what was Yorvik land and what was not.

It was with a heavy heart that Carrie attended Geordie's funeral. Despite all their differences over the years, she had respected him as a farmer and as a man, and was sorry he had gone before their legal dispute could be resolved. She was sorry too that he had not attempted to settle it out of court first. But his immediate recourse to law was symptomatic of the way things were going in the colony. The successful sheep and cattle stations like theirs were becoming big businesses, impersonal affairs where the human factor was in danger of getting lost.

So the elderly settler joined his wife beneath the good earth, in a sheltered corner of their flower garden at Eden Vale, and at the beginning of the summer of 1878 the station was put up for sale. Despite her decision to sell Great Glen, Carrie toyed seriously with the idea of buying it. Great Glen had been over a hundred miles away, while Eden Vale bordered her own land. Combining the two stations would make her the biggest landowner in the lower half of the Hunter Valley — bigger even than the redoubtable Angus Cameron who still farmed Cameron Creek when he was not away in Sydney, leading his busy and increasingly successful political life.

But, in the end, Carrie decided against the purchase. Yorvik was taking up so much of her time that she was loath to take on any new venture that might jeopardize its continuing prosperity. Instead, all her energies remained concentrated on her sheep and cattle, and into making the amenities on the station as good as possible for her workers. In that same summer of 1878 she had a small one-room schoolhouse built for the workers' children, who were now eighteen in number, and a middle-aged spinster from Newcastle, by the name of Miss Matilda

Chapman, was engaged to din the basics of letters and numbers into their unwilling little heads.

As she watched them troop into school each morning Carrie realized that a whole generation had been born and grown to man- and womanhood since she had first set foot on these shores. The country itself was growing up. New South Wales now boasted six towns, apart from Sydney, which had a population of over two thousand people, and the railways were pushing outwards into the hinterland, domesticating more and more of the bush. There was even talk of installing kerosene street lighting in Hunter's Hollow, and the town now boasted a theatre that had seen music hall turns all the way from London. One particular young woman had given a version of the Lola Montez spider dance one hot December night in 1878 and caused a near riot, forcing the Reverend MacKenzie to warn from the pulpit against the importation of vice from the mother country.

'Aye, we've managed well enough to manufacture our own up to now!' one wag had called out from the back of the church. And although there had been a good quota of askance looks in his direction, amongst the titters, no one could deny the truth of it. In the bigger towns prostitution and drunkenness were rife, while in the smaller settlements such as Hunter's Hollow, young men known as 'Larrikins' were now roaming the streets in quarrelsome gangs known as 'pushes', wearing such fancy apparel as tight-fitting elephant-footed trousers, and French boots with fashionable corkscrew heels.

'It makes me feel a real country bumpkin to see them,' Sean commented to Carrie on his return from town one day in early 1879. 'And to think most of them are even younger than your Billy!'

Those words hit home, for, with the seventies gone, Carrie was only too aware that her beloved son was a child no more. While she had been so taken up with affairs on Yorvik, across the world in England he had been growing to manhood without her. His whole adolescence had gone in the twinkling of an eye. Letters had had to take the place of conversations, each one eagerly awaited. Her own four pages were diligently posted once a week, along with regular hampers of tuck, containing rich fruit cakes and biscuits specially baked for the midnight feasts he wrote so entertainingly about.

From what she had heard not only from her son, but also his old tutor and his sister, the Bardons' small Yorkshire cottage had become as good a second home to Billy throughout his schooldays as she could ever have wished. The elderly couple corresponded with her regularly, giving news on all the things that Billy himself would never dream of commenting on, such as his height and weight, and now the fact that he was regarded by the young ladies of their Scarborough neighbourhood as quite a 'looker'. This information Carrie read with a wistful sigh. Surely it was the very last nail in the coffin of childhood innocence; her little boy was now an object of female desire.

At the end of July, in the last English summer of the decade, Billy Gordon-Hebden matriculated from St Cuthbert's in York with indifferent grades but with the goodwill of his tutors who, along with his mother's substantial financial means, proved successful in pleading his case for admittance to Oxford. He got word of his place at Trinity to read Divinity and Philosophy just before he set out on his first voyage home to Yorvik at the end of August 1879.

The weeks leading up to his arrival Carrie could think of nothing else but her son's return. She had decided to keep his room at Yorvik exactly as it was when he left it, but a few more manly touches were soon added, such as a new set of silver-backed brushes engraved with the initials W. G.-H. for his dressing-table, and a new dressing-gown in burgundy silk followed them, which she hung on the back of the bedroom door. And one by one the new gradually replaced the old, even to the extent of a brand new bed ordered specially from one of Sydney's finest furniture stores.

'I wouldn't buy too much if I were you,' Sean O'Dwyer advised her. 'Young folk have their own ideas and likes and dislikes these days.' But Carrie would not be deterred and by the time she was due to set off for Sydney to meet his ship, the room was hardly recognizable as the one he had left six years previously.

To his surprise, Carrie asked the Irishman to accompany her to meet Billy on his arrival, and at first he refused the request with an apologetic shake of the head. 'I'm afraid I haven't got the clothes that would do justice to accompanying a fine lady like you on a trip to town.'

Carrie coloured. 'What does that matter?' she declared. 'If that's what's stopping you, then I shall buy you some!'

'You'll do no such thing! And if you do then you can wear the darned things yourself. I'll only put on my back what's bought fair and square with my own money.'

'But *your* money, as you call it, is *my* money anyway!' Carrie protested, as disappointment welled up in her. 'I pay your wages, remember.'

The look she received chilled the blood. 'Can I ever forget it?'

They looked at one another across the few yards of brown earth in the vegetable garden. In her dismay at his refusal to go with her, she had touched the most raw nerve of all. 'I'm sorry, Sean,' she said quietly. 'I didn't mean it like that . . . I – I'd really like you to come with me, that's all.'

He shrugged his shoulders in the red plaid shirt as he picked up a hoe. 'You don't need me with you,' he said. 'I'm the last person you need in a fancy place like Sydney.'

'No, you're wrong there. You're so very wrong.' Why was he doing this to her? Why was he making her plead like this? 'You're the only person I could possibly want with me . . . It's important to me, Sean, really important.

I haven't seen Billy for six years . . . Say you'll come . . . Please.'

Sean rested his folded arms on the shaft of the hoe and squinted at her through the midday sunshine. Then he tipped his hat up on the springy grey curls as his eyes creased at the corners in a wry smile. 'You're a strange one, Carrie Gordon-Hebden. You're a strange one indeed.' She did not need him. She did not need anyone. She was one of the strongest, most self-sufficient people he knew. But he was man enough to feel his masculine pride flattered by her words.

Sensing his resolve thawing with the smile in his eyes, Carrie's heart quickened. 'You'll come, then? You'll come with me?'

'I'll come.'

CHAPTER TWENTY-EIGHT

'You're sure you want me waiting here with you?' Sean O'Dwyer asked as they stood on the quayside and watched the small boats offload the first batch of passengers from the great ship that now lay at anchor just off the headland.

Carrie gripped his arm and jumped up to see over the heads of the gathering crowd. She could barely contain her excitement. 'Of course I want you with me!' she insisted. The Irishman had been a tower of strength, calming all her nerves and apprehensions over the past two days of the journey from Yorvik to the bustling town that Sydney had now become.

He was the first to recognize Billy, some ten minutes later, as the young man appeared head and shoulders above a knot of newly decanted immigrants who stood in some bewilderment on the cobbled dockside. 'Look, there he is!'

Carrie's gaze followed his pointing finger and she caught her breath at the sight of the tall, well-dressed young man who was her son. He stood several inches over six feet and his fair hair was fashionably coiffured with Macassar oil; a pair of sandy-coloured mutton-chop whiskers adorned the pale skin of his cheeks, and, most startling of all, he appeared to have the makings of a moustache. His frame was still slim, but elegantly attired in a well-cut, waisted, fine wool jacket, beneath which was a dark green plaid waistcoat and matching trews.

'He looks quite a dandy,' Sean observed, as Carrie did her best to compose herself. 'Quite the young man about town.'

'Yes . . . Yes, he certainly does,' she breathed, gazing in some awe at the tall figure who was now a heart-tugging combination of his father, Big Jock, and her own brother Billy. There was almost nothing left of the winsome young boy who had left these shores six years ago, except perhaps in his heart, for she prayed so often that he had remained an Australian in spirit beneath those cold grey English skies.

Carrie let go Sean's arm. 'I – I must go to him,' she whispered, tentatively raising her hand to catch her son's attention. 'Oh, Irish, I can hardly bear it!'

The Irishman remained where he was, a wistful smile playing around the corners of his mouth, as he watched her rush across the cobbles to where Billy Gordon-Hebden was standing. The smile became a shade more wry as the two embraced. He wished he could take to the lad, but something in his heart told him that he would care no more now for the young man who had returned to their midst than he had for the callow youth who had left six years ago.

'Billy darling, you remember Sean – Mr O'Dwyer . . . He very kindly accompanied me from Yorvik,' Carrie told her son a few minutes later as the two men came face to face.

The Irishman held out his hand. 'Nice to have you back, lad.'

'Good day to you,' Billy replied, as his gaze took in the shoulder-length grey curly hair and the grizzled red beard. With that bronzed skin and those shabby clothes, Sean looked every bit the itinerant digger or wild and woolly bushman he had remembered. He could not imagine what his mother was thinking about still cohorting with the fellow and he made no secret of his displeasure as they walked back towards the waiting carriage. He deliberately ignored the Irishman as his mother chattered nervously about the voyage and how wonderful it was to have him back.

'I can imagine how excited you must have been at the prospect of coming home,' she told him as they settled side by side into the carriage. 'No matter how marvellous another place may be, there really is nowhere like home.'

'Oh I don't know about that.' The rejoinder was given with a laconic sigh as the young man gazed out of the cab window.

'You quite took to English life, then?' Sean said, breaking the awkward silence that followed.

'It's civilized at least,' Billy replied. 'People have more on their minds than sheep and cattle.'

Carrie glanced at Sean, who was sitting across from them, and she could see his lips tighten beneath the bristles of beard. Perhaps this homecoming was not going to be quite the ecstatic time she had imagined. Billy even sounded like an Englishman now, and that was something she had not accounted for. Hearing the cut-glass accent coming from her son's lips for the first time came as quite a shock.

She had booked them all into the fashionable Clarendon Hotel overlooking the bay. They had three single rooms on the second floor and a table was reserved for dinner at seven.

Billy was only too pleased to be able to don his fine woolcloth bespoke dinner suit for the occasion, but when he entered his mother's room at just after six-thirty he was unable to disguise his horror at the sight of the Irishman already standing there. Sean O'Dwyer, possessing nothing remotely resembling a dinner suit, was attired in a grey, collarless cotton shirt, beneath a light worsted jacket the colour of cow dung, and the same shapeless pair of grey trousers that he had worn that afternoon at the quayside. It was a wonder he did not still have that battered old bushman's hat on his head. 'What in heaven's name type of outfit do you call that?' Billy asked, in undisguised contempt, as his mother's heart missed a beat.

'My clothes, that's what,' the reply came. Then with a steely look, 'Are you lodging some sort of objection?'

Billy looked at his mother for support, but Carrie

371

deliberately avoided her son's eyes as she busied herself pulling on her gloves. 'Well, if you can take the embarrassment, I dare say I can,' he replied with a shrug. 'I do think you could have made an effort, though, for my mother's sake.'

'Don't bring your mother into this,' Sean O'Dwyer warned. 'She knows me well enough by now. And she knows I don't give a fart for the pretensions of folks round here who imagine themselves a cut above the rest of us — or for brats still wet behind the ears who should know better than to show disrespect for their elders.'

'Please, you two!' Carrie begged, scooping up her beaded evening bag from the bed. 'Let's not spoil everything by this stupid bickering. What does dress matter anyway on a red letter day like this?' She slipped the chain strap of the bag over her wrist, then linked her arm into that of her son as she threw a pleading glance at Sean. 'Let's just go downstairs and enjoy our supper.'

Sean O'Dwyer walked behind them down the two flights of stairs to the dining room. With Carrie in a new salmon-pink, shot silk creation, with an enormous frilled bustle, and her son in quite the smartest piece of tailoring he had ever set eyes on, he felt like some sort of circus freak as he stepped out in their wake, and he cursed the day he had ever been talked into this.

This whole place, with its plush carpets, crystal chandeliers and whispering, cringing flunkies was not his style at all. All this ostentation suffocated him. He had felt this same sense of dislocation the day Carrie had shown him round the new Yorvik. His heart had gone out to her, so desperate was she for him to approve of it, but he could not hide his distaste then and he was finding it almost as impossible now. And his discomfort was increased considerably by the look of surprise and displeasure on the face of the head waiter as he entered the plushly furnished dining room as a member of the Gordon-Hebden party.

The meal itself proved to be every bit the ordeal that the

Irishman had anticipated. His every move was scrutinized with ill-disguised contempt by the younger man, who made a point of totally excluding him from the conversation whenever possible.

Carrie could not help but notice the behaviour of her son towards her friend, but her delight at having him back again took precedence over the hurt she felt. She told herself Billy was obviously tired from the long voyage and a few days of rest back on Yorvik would restore him to the best of health and spirits. 'Just think, darling, you'll be sleeping in your own bed within a couple of days!'

Billy gave a quiet smile but made no comment and she found herself prattling on. 'What were you looking forward to getting back to most?' she asked, eager for any indication that something about her beloved Yorvik had been sorely missed. 'What did you miss most about the old place?'

He thought for a moment than answered, 'Tiger. I was looking forward to seeing my dog again.'

Carrie caught her breath and glanced across at Sean. The animal had died all of three years ago and Billy was as well aware of the fact as they were.

When the meal was over at a little after nine, Billy declined the invitation to join his mother and her friend for drinks on the terrace and preferred to take his ease with the younger society in the bar, which included quite a few fashionably dressed young ladies over from England with a dancing troupe, who were about to open in a show in one of the local theatres.

Seeing the look of disappointment on Carrie's face, Sean put a comforting hand on her shoulder as they walked with their drinks through to the open verandah. 'Don't take it too hard,' he said. 'They're more his age in there, and you'll have all the time in the world to talk when you get back to Yorvik.'

But Carrie found it hard to be pacified. 'He's changed,' she said, sitting herself down on one of the fancy wrought-iron seats, and moving her skirts along a bit so that the Irishman could join her. 'He's not an Australian any more, Sean. And it's not just his accent. Those years have turned him into a real Englishman. It's a terrible thing to say but I honestly get the feeling he isn't even all that happy to be back.'

'Come on now, he's tired, that's all. And maybe he does miss the friends he's made back in England. It would be mighty funny if he didn't, wouldn't it? Surely that would be much worse. If he couldn't wait to return here and see the back of them, then you'd know he'd been unhappy and hadn't settled down over there.' He bent forwards, forcing her to look at him. 'Well, wouldn't you?'

Carrie managed a wan smile. 'I expect you're right,' she sighed. 'But you can't help imagining how it's going to be beforehand – the homecoming and all that – and somehow life has a nasty habit of turning round and kicking you in the teeth when you least expect it.'

She looked out over a bay of twinkling lights, the sweeping coastline below dark and glittering like scattered diamonds on a bed of darkest velvet. Was she being selfish? Was she asking too much wanting everything to be perfect? By asking Sean to accompany her today she had somehow hoped that after all these years her son would appreciate what the Irishman meant in her life and that his delight at seeing her again and being back on his native soil would spill over into, if not exactly pleasure at seeing Sean again, at least a comfortable acceptance of the way things were. But none of that had happened, and worse, she almost believed that Billy was not happy to be here at all. It was as if she had dragged him back into a past that he had left behind and wanted nothing more to do with. A shudder ran through her, despite the warm evening air. It was her own life in reverse.

As if reading her thoughts, Sean said quietly, 'You know there are all sorts of reasons why he might not have been so keen to return. For all we know he might even have a young lady back there in York. Your handsome young son might have fallen in love. Young men do, you know.'

Carrie looked at him sceptically. That was a fine one coming from him. 'Not all young men,' she reminded him. 'You didn't, did you?'

He had no answer to that.

Curious, she pressed the point. 'Did you ever, Sean? Did you ever fall recklessly, passionately in love with anyone as a young man?'

His mouth quirked into something resembling a smile as he sighed and leant back against the seat. 'My Pa once said that love is like a well – fine to taste, but bad to fall into. I reckon he had a point there.'

'But he loved a woman, you once told me – back in Ireland – a young woman that he never forgot.'

The Irishman nodded. 'The O'Dwyers never do things by halves. If they fall in love, they fall in love for life . . . It's too bad that in Pa's case and so many others it's not always with the most convenient woman.'

Their eyes met and held, and in their look they were speaking the unspeakable. 'Let's have another drink,' he said, lifting the half-empty wine bottle from the table in front of them. 'We're a funny old pair, you and me, Carrie girl. A right funny old pair.'

They retired just after ten. It had been a long and wearying day, exhausting on the spirit as well as the body.

Outside her room, to Carrie's astonishment, Sean paused then lifted her right hand to his lips and kissed her bent fingers. It was an immensely touching gesture from a man far removed from such romantic notions. 'Sleep well,' he said softly. 'And don't blame the lad too much. We were all young once, and have all made our mistakes.'

She watched as he disappeared into his room, two doors down, next to Billy's. Then she opened her own door and closed it behind her, shutting her eyes as she leant back on the panelled wood. She could feel tears forming, hot and prickly beneath her closed lids, but was not quite sure why she was crying. Perhaps it had just been too long a day.

For his part, to Billy the night was just beginning. The relief at being able to escape that uncouth Irishman's company was tremendous and his displeasure at being back in this godforsaken country was tempered by the bevy of attractive young English women he found himself surrounded with. His mother had opened a bank account for him in York several years previously and he had plenty of money in his wallet to enjoy himself. Champagne was the order of the day, and by midnight it was flowing so freely that several of the company had already passed out.

It was then that the management intervened with a helpful, but insistent, hand on his arm, ushering him back to his room.

'There we are, sir,' the portly manager said, as he deposited his charge into the nearest armchair then went across to light the oil-lamp by the side of the bed. 'A good night's sleep is what you need now. If there's anything else you require, don't hesitate to ring. The night porter will be downstairs to see to your requests.'

Billy waved him away with an elaborately dismissive gesture of his arm as he slumped into the chair, still clutching a bottle to his breast. 'Spoilsports, that's what you are!' he declared. 'Packing people off to bed like children . . . When is this country ever going to grow up?'

The door closed, quietly but firmly, and he sat staring at it for a moment or two, then reached over to a small bedside pot cupboard on top of which sat the oil-lamp and a decanter of water and a glass. He splashed a good measure of the Champagne from his bottle into the glass and quaffed it thirstily, before belching loudly into the silence of the room. Then he yawned, a long, loud, gaping yawn that brought him staggering to his feet and weaving the few steps across the floor to the bed.

Before lying down he attempted to pour himself another drink, but more Champagne was spilled over the top of the pot cupboard than landed in the glass. 'Damn!' he groaned as it ran over the sides and trickled down on to the polished wood of the floor beneath.

Billy put the bottle down by the side of the lamp and pulled a handkerchief out of his trouser pocket to dab ineffectually at the puddle. Then with a grimace he realized he could not stuff the soaking linen square back where it came from without soaking his trousers. Instead he tossed it on top of the wicker basket of logs and kindling that stood on the other side of the pot cupboard.

Why was life so bloody difficult? He threw himself down on the satin coverlet and let out a groan. The effect of his head hitting the pillow made his senses reel in a kaleidoscope of whirling, swirling, dazzlingly colourful patterns. What he needed was another drink. He reached for the Champagne bottle only to push it away from him with a heartfelt 'Damn!' The bloody thing was almost empty!

He got to his feet to make for the door and head downstairs in search of another one. The almost empty bottle lay next to the overturned oil-lamp that it had hit when it was discarded in disgust a moment or two before.

As the door shook on its hinges from the slam of the departing occupant of the room, the burning oil began to drip down the sides of the pot cupboard on to the contents of the wicker basket below.

It took almost ten minutes for the fire to take hold and spread to the dividing wall against which the blazing basket was sitting.

Carrie was fast asleep on the other side of the lath and plaster partition. She was dreaming she was at an Aboriginal feast on their land at Yorvik. The tantalizing aroma of the kangaroos roasting in the ground was almost extinguished by the acrid smell of the smoke from the fires. It was everywhere in her dream, great grey swirling masses of it, obscuring the view and making her choke and splutter as she tried desperately to watch the proceedings from her favourite vantage point.

Then, almost blinded and choked by the smoke, she could feel the heat. Her face and arms were being scorched by the sheer intensity of it. She tried to back away, but it seemed to follow her. Her lungs were full of those terrible fumes and her skin was beginning to fry in the intense heat. She was coughing and spluttering now, and sitting up in bed, her clogged lungs silently screaming for air as she opened her eyes, and before her terrified gaze realized that her nightmare had become reality.

The whole room was ablaze.

CHAPTER TWENTY-NINE

Sean smelt the smoke before he saw it creeping insidiously in long wraith-like fingers beneath the door of his room. He sat up in bed and tried to focus his eyes in the darkness. It caught in his throat, causing him to cough and his eyes to smart. What the hell was going on?

He leapt out of bed, stubbing his toe on the chamber pot in the darkness, and, cursing, he made for the window, where he tore back the curtains. There was just enough moonlight to distinguish the dark shapes of the furniture in the room, and, most sinister of all, the grey sea that swirled around his ankles.

It was now almost impossible to breathe and his eyes were streaming. He pulled on his trousers and shoved his feet into his boots, then grabbed a neckerchief he had worn on the journey down from the top of the dresser and plunged it into the ewer of water on the marble-topped washstand by the window. His hands shook as he tied the sodden cloth around his neck, pulling it up over his nose and mouth, before making for the door.

The corridor outside was already filled with smoke, and flames were engulfing the door to the room next to his – Billy's room. 'Dear God!' he gasped. If the lad was still in there he was beyond help, that was for sure.

His thoughts immediately turned to the woman in the room on the other side of the flaming door. 'Carrie!' Panic enveloped him.

Fighting his way past the flames, through the billowing smoke, he made his way to Carrie's door and grabbed the handle. Luckily it was not locked. Momentary relief flooded through him as he threw it open.

At first he could see nothing for it seemed the whole room was filled with rancid black smoke. Tongues of bright orange flame flickered through the dense clouds, mainly on the side of the room that shared a wall with Billy's. As he wavered uncertainly on the threshold, he could feel the heat scorching his skin. His eyes were streaming as he tried his best not to breathe in behind the makeshift mask.

Then through the inferno he saw her. She was lying sprawled across the bed, as if making a last desperate attempt to reach the window, where the curtains were still drawn and already aflame along the hems.

Like a madman, with no heed for his own safety, he plunged through the swirling smoke and made for the bed.

He tried to scoop her up into his arms, but she seemed to be clinging on to something – he could not tell what. She could not be moved. Panic overwhelmed him. Flames were licking around the edges of the bed and the drapes above the bedhead were already ablaze, the edges of the bedding that skirted the floor smouldering. She was lying face down, her arms spread-eagled above her head. Time was running out. He was not even sure he would make it back to the door. He could not leave her here, yet he could not move her.

Taking his courage in both hands, he grappled her around the waist and pulled with all his might. That did it. He staggered backwards under the weight as the body moved and, clutching it to him, he backed blindly in the direction of the open door.

Carrie seemed to be pulling half the burning bedclothes with her, for her hands were closed fast around the top counterpane.

Sean's lungs were at bursting point as, after what seemed an eternity, he backed into the corridor. He could no longer see where he was going and he had found the doorway purely by instinct. Smoke was swirling around him in the corridor as he stood there bent over, coughing and spluttering, with Carrie's lifeless body slumped in his arms.

In the distance there was a shout of 'Fire!' Then, much closer, a yell of 'Christ Almighty!'

The voice that broke into his consciousness belonged to the hotel manager, who had reached the top of the stairs and now stared in horror at the sight that met his eyes. He had just left the bar, after failing to persuade 'that uppity young Englishman', as he referred to Billy, to go back up to his room. He was on his way to report the recalcitrant guest to the night porter, when he had spotted smoke coming down the stairs.

His portly figure made a dash for the man standing there coughing, with the body of a woman clasped in his arms.

Then all hell seemed to be let loose as other guests on the corridor, either awakened by the noise or the smell of smoke, threw open their doors and added to the confusion. A woman began to scream nearby.

'Give me the lady!' the manager ordered Sean, who appeared completely dazed by events.

But the Irishman would not give her up. Clasping Carrie tighter to him, his face and upper torso perspiring and blackened by the smoke, he staggered his way towards the staircase, to be helped down the wide carpeted steps by two of the other guests.

They sank on to the relative sanctuary of a plush-covered chesterfield at the foot of the stairs and, pulling the neckerchief from his face, Sean wiped his streaming eyes and gazed down in desperation at the woman beside him.

Carrie lay motionless on the deep cushions, her eyes closed and her singed hair spread out over the arm of the couch. Sean groaned out loud as he bent over the beloved face, the skin of which was now painfully blistering in parts. Her lips were swollen, the area around them puckered and distorted. It was impossible to tell if she was breathing or not.

'Is she a goner, Mister?' one of the onlookers asked. 'Is she dead?'

'No!' Sean almost screamed at him. 'No! She can't be dead! Dear God, she can't be dead!'

He bent over Carrie once more and tried to focus eyes now almost completely blinded by a mixture of tears and smoke irritation. He needed some sign, some indication that she was still alive. He grabbed hold of her shoulders and began to shake her and shake her, until at last something resembling a quiet, wheezing breath was exhaled from her lungs. 'Breathe, Carrie! Breathe!' he sobbed. Genuine tears were streaming down his cheeks now. Hot bitter tears of desperation as he gazed into the face of the woman he loved. 'Live, Carrie . . . Damn you . . . Live!'

Then all was pandemonium and the air was filled with the clanging of bells and shouted commands as fire appliances arrived from town. Ladders were being erected on the front of the building, and hoses dragged through the entrance lobby and up the stairs, while guests, most still in their nightclothes, ran with buckets of water, passing them from one to the other in a long human chain reaching right up the stairs.

Through it all Sean sat on the sofa fighting for breath, with Carrie's prostrate body in his arms. It felt as if his lungs were on fire and someone was squeezing his chest in an invisible vice. Every inhalation was agony.

Two doctors arrived on the scene, and, despite his protestations, Carrie was taken from him and lifted on to a stretcher to be taken to the local hospital.

'Don't you worry, sir,' he was told. 'Your wife will be in good hands.'

They wanted to take him too, in the second waggon, telling him he was suffering from smoke inhalation and burns to his hands and forehead. But he was having none of it. He was only half listening to what they were saying, for someone a few feet away was telling him that the woman's son had been drinking in the bar and was still there. He must have started the fire, they were saying, for the manager had taken him back drunk to his room some minutes earlier and the fire had started in that same room shortly after he had left it to return downstairs.

'The bastard! The young bastard!' He should have known that young idiot was to blame! A blind anger boiled up inside him, as, pushing aside the medical men who were intent on tending to his injuries, Sean staggered through to the bar on the other side of the hotel. Here all was quietness as the life-threatening smoke had not yet penetrated that far. It was difficult to believe it was part of the same building.

He paused for breath, wheezing painfully at the door, and wiped his eyes. There were still one or two lamps burning and in the gloom he could just make out the slumped shape of Billy in the far corner of the room. It was quite obvious he was in a drunken stupor and had been for some time.

The sight of him lying there so oblivious to the havoc and destruction he had caused, not to mention the injury to his own mother, incensed the Irishman even more. Every step was an effort as he crossed the room. 'Wake up, you bastard!' Tugging at his lapels, he pulled the semi-conscious young man to his feet, then pushed him back down on the padded bench. 'Wake up, damn you!'

'Wh . . . what the hell?' Billy Gordon-Hebden gazed bleary-eyed into the irate, smoke-blackened face of the man glaring wildly down at him through red-rimmed eyes. 'Wh . . . wha'd'you want?'

'You, you bastard!' Unable to contain himself any longer, Sean aimed a blow at the side of the younger man's jaw. It made contact, but in his own weakened state, it did more damage to him than to the recipient as it sent him sprawling across the bench.

Wheezing painfully for breath, he staggered to his feet and glared down through swollen, red-veined eyes at the young man looking up at him with a bewildered air as he nursed his painful jaw.

'Steady on there!' Billy said in an aggrieved voice, rubbing the tender skin. Had the Irishman had too much to drink, and was this his way of getting back at him for some imagined slight dealt out earlier this evening? 'What the hell was that for?'

'You've killed your mother, you bastard! That's what it's for!' Sean stood there wheezing noisily, clenching and unclenching his fists. He wanted to beat the living daylights out of the young bugger, but he found himself shaking from head to foot. All energy had drained from him. He felt useless – impotent. And suddenly tears were coursing down his cheeks once more. He was standing there in front of this sanctimonious little swine and he was bawling like a baby.

Billy blinked his eyes. 'What the hell's going on?' he demanded, attempting to straighten himself up on the seat. 'Where is Ma? What do you mean, I've killed her?' It was as if he was being forced to witness some crazy pantomime. But one thing was obvious, he was not the only one the worse for drink around here. 'You're drunk!' he told his tormentor, slurring over his own words, despite his attempt to appear sober. 'You're drunk out of your stupid head!'

'I'm not bloody drunk,' Sean hissed at him. 'I've never been more sober in my life. And your mother is not here, for your information. She's on her way in a hospital wag-gon right now – to a bloody mortuary slab for all we know!' He waved a hand in the direction he had just come from. 'The place is on fire, Billy boy, and it started in your room! You've burned your own mother to death!'

Billy attempted a protest and tried to get up, but tripped and fell forwards on to his face and Sean left him lying there as he walked slowly towards the door. What lay ahead of him, or anyone else in this hotel – in this entire bloody world – he could not care less about. They had taken Carrie away. That was the only thing that mattered. They had taken Carrie away and he might never see her again.

He had no recollection at all of collapsing at the door of the Clarendon a few minutes later, or of the helping hands that picked him up and laid him on the stretcher which took him to the waiting hospital waggon.

When he came to, he was in a hospital ward and being tended by two women dressed in white peaked caps and large white aprons. 'You've not died and gone to heaven, if that's what you're thinking, and we're no angels,' a broad Irish voice said. 'So just be lying still, will you, while we do our best to tend to these burns.'

One was dabbing at his face and the other at his body with some creamy solution on cotton wool, and for the first time that night he was aware of pain. He winced and tried not to cry out loud as they tended the scorched flesh.

How long he lay there while they did what they had to do he had no idea. 'Carrie, I must see Carrie,' he kept repeating.

But the nurses had no idea who Carrie was. Far too many people had been brought in here tonight to remember individual names. Quite apart from those injured in the fire at the Clarendon, there had been a brawl at one of the more notorious public houses in The Rocks and the admittance wards were full to bursting with injured sailors, a handful of prostitutes, and several unlucky citizens who had got caught up in the fracas.

Sean had no idea that the drink they gave him on admittance contained a sedative powerful enough to knock him out completely till mid-morning the next day, and when he awoke there was one of the doctors who had attended to him at the hotel standing by the bed.

'How are you feeling, sir?' the physician asked. He was a tall, stooped man with a tired look to him as he bent over and felt the patient's pulse.

'I'm fine,' Sean answered automatically, not at all used to being addressed as sir. 'I have to get out of here . . . I have to find Carrie.'

'Carrie?' the doctor queried.

'The woman I was with . . . The one they took away

first in the first waggon from the Clarendon.' There was a note akin to desperation in his voice.

'Ah, that one . . .'

'You know where she is, then? You know what happened to her?'

'Not exactly,' the answer came. 'But I can find out.' He turned to one of the nurses standing at the foot of the bed. 'I'll let Nurse Connolly here know and she can convey the message to you.'

Sean murmured his thanks as he sank back on the pillow. 'You won't forget?'

'I won't forget.'

It was two o'clock in the afternoon before the young Irish nurse appeared again, and this time she was pushing a bathchair in front of her.

'What's that thing for?' Sean asked, as she neared the bed.

'It's for you,' came the reply. 'You wanted to see what had happened to that lady friend of yours.'

Sean's heart quickened as he painfully tried to pull himself up on the pillows. 'You're taking me to see Carrie?'

'That I am.'

He could feel his heart beating fit to burst beneath the white hospital nightgown he wore as she helped him from the bed into the bathchair, then wheeled him along what seemed like an endless succession of bleak, tiled corridors that smelt of disinfectant, until at last they came to a large double door. It had a notice with several letters in black across it and he cursed the fact he could not read. Swallowing his shame, he asked the nurse, 'What does that say?'

'It says "Mortuary",' she replied in a matter-of-fact voice, as she pushed open one side of the door and carefully manoeuvred the chair through.

'Mortuary!' Sean gasped, throwing himself round in the wheelchair to face her. 'Carrie's not here, is she?'

'Sit down, will you!' the nurse commanded, pushing

him back into the chair. 'Sure and you'll have this thing over and then we'll both be for it!'

They were on the other side of the door now, in a long, cold room with rows of tables running down either side. At least half of them had bodies on them, covered in white sheets.

'No . . . No . . .' he kept repeating as he was wheeled down the middle, expecting any minute the chair to stop beside one and the shroud to be pulled back to reveal what he dreaded most of all.

But Nurse Connolly did not stop; instead, on reaching the other end of the room, she pushed open another door and they entered a much smaller room with only six beds.

The wheelchair rattled over the stone-flagged floor to stop at the bed by the opposite door.

'Your friend was brought here last night because the main admittance ward was already full,' the young woman told him.

'Wheel me closer!' Sean begged hoarsely, half standing in the chair for a better look at the motionless figure on the bed.

Then he was right next to her, his eyes taking in the fearfully bandaged face. Nothing of her was visible except the spaces left for her eyes, nose and mouth.

'Carrie,' he whispered, forcing himself out of his chair to stand, leaning over her. 'Carrie, it's me . . .'

'I'm told the patient's not liable to waken up for some time,' the Irish voice behind him said.

'Carrie, sweetheart, it's me . . .' Never had such an endearment passed his lips to a living soul before, but he felt no shame, no embarrassment as he continued to plead softly for some sign, some flicker of life that would give him hope.

'I wouldn't tire yourself, if I were you,' the young nurse persisted. 'She can't hear you.'

'Carrie, my love . . .'

Slowly, like the fluttering of a fledgling's heart, her

eyelids beneath the bandages began to tremble, and she was looking at him. 'Hello, Irish . . .' she whispered, in a voice so faint it was heard only by him.

He raised her bandaged hand to his lips and began to sob like a baby into the mummified palm. He turned his tear-stained face to the young woman at the foot of the bed. 'She's alive,' he whispered. 'She's alive . . . Dear God, I'm so happy . . .'

Nurse Mary Rose Connolly raised a sceptical eyebrow. He could have fooled her, standing there blubbing like a baby.

CHAPTER THIRTY

It was almost two months before Carrie was released from hospital; two painful months in which the skin of her face began to grow back shiny and transparent across the burned flesh. She had the bandages taken off one week before her release and she grimaced in shock at her first glance in the mirror the nurses held up for her. She hardly recognized the face that stared back at her, for the skin of her cheeks was still painfully tender, although, happily, her eyes were virtually back to normal and the swellings around her lips had gone down.

'It won't always be like that,' she was told reassuringly as she tentatively touched the healing flesh. 'The redness will fade in time. In another couple of months you'll hardly be aware of the injuries.'

Carrie raised her eyebrows in some scepticism and just prayed they were telling the truth. She had never been a particularly vain person, but every woman cared about how she looked, and this was not a pretty sight. She listened in concern as they explained that burns were the worst of all injuries to heal, but luckily her skin had been scorched rather than burned and so there was a fair chance she would be left with little or no scarring once nature had taken its course. The clear, tanned skin of her cheeks before the fire now had the texture of crumpled tissue paper, but that would not always be the case.

'I'll just have to turn Muslim until the redness disappears,' she joked to Sean as he visited her on the day of his own release. 'At the moment, it looks like there's nothing for it but to take the veil when I get out of here!'

He shook his head and gave a rueful smile as he sat on the side of her bed, his hat in his hands. At least some of that old indomitable spirit was still there. She could still joke about it. 'You'll not find anyone on Yorvik who will even notice,' he told her soothingly. 'And it won't affect your running of the old place at all. You'll still manage to keep the gang in order as well as you ever did.'

'Will you come and fetch me?' she asked. 'When they let me go, will you come and get me?'

But he shook his head. 'You know that won't be possible,' he told her. 'Billy wouldn't stand for it.'

Carrie's lips hardened. Sean was right, of course. His relationship with her son had been positively volcanic since the fire. On the few occasions they had met at her bedside they had almost come to blows. Sean still could not forgive Billy for causing the fire that had done this to her, and, for his part, Billy was still adamantly denying any such responsibility. The Fire and Police authorities had been of little help in apportioning blame, for by the time their experts got to work the inferno had left little evidence to go on; that whole part of the corridor had been reduced to ashes.

'He hates having to stay on here in Australia, you know,' she told Sean. 'My being here has meant he will have to miss the start of his first term at Oxford. He'll never forgive me for that.'

'Forgive you!' Sean exploded. 'The young bugger had better not complain in my hearing, I'm telling you!'

Carrie sighed. Things could not have gone more wrong since her son's arrival back in his homeland. She had sensed at the outset that he had resented having to come all the way back to Yorvik out of some sort of filial duty to her, and spending all those months at sea to return to a country for which you retained no love must have been hard to bear. She was trying her best to see it through his eyes. And the knowledge that Billy was now at daggers drawn with her old friend was one of the worst things to come out of this whole sorry mess. 'Please do your best not to fall out with him when you get back to Yorvik,' she pleaded. 'For my sake, Irish. Please . . .'

Sean nodded grimly as he reached out and touched her hand. 'I promise,' he sighed, stroking the still tender flesh. 'Though, God knows, it'll be hard.'

He had heard from Davie Henderson, on the head shepherd's last visit, that Billy was already throwing his weight around at the station, playing the boss man while his mother lay helpless in hospital in Sydney. Neither had mentioned it to Carrie for fear of troubling her, but already there had been two workers leave and others were threatening to go. Only Davie and Will Morton's pleas for them to remain for Carrie's sake made them think twice and agree to try to stick it out until she came home.

And so, pacified by Sean's promises to keep the peace with her son, Carrie parted reluctantly with her friend and the Irishman set off for Yorvik after granting another promise that there would be no special celebrations for her return. 'I want everything to be as normal as possible,' she told him. 'It's going to be hard enough facing the world after all this without setting myself up like a new Aunt Sally stall for everyone to come and gape at.'

Once he had gone, she could hardly wait for her own release. She had ordered a new dress and jacket from David Jones, Sydney's best outfitter, for the journey home and she was particularly pleased with the hat that came with it, a feathered creation with a very pretty veil that did much to obscure her healing cheeks.

When the day came and Billy arrived punctually to collect her, it was the first time he had seen his mother without her bandages. But even behind the carefully arranged veil, there was no disguising the pain she must have gone through as the healing process took its course. Carrie was determined to play down her suffering, however, as she greeted him with her usual fond smile.

'Hello, darling.' She held out a gloved hand and he took it, his eyes riveted on the pink shiny skin of her cheeks. Her eyes were bright with unshed tears, for she had been keyed up about this moment for so long. She felt for him and hated to see him embarrassed like this. She had so wanted things to be different for this, his first return home.

Billy took her hand by the tips of her fingers and paused awkwardly in front of her. Try as he might, he could not lean forwards and put his lips to that still painful-looking flesh, although in some ways he was very relieved it was not worse. Looking at it now, he could actually believe the doctors when they assured him the redness would fade in time. 'Hello, Ma,' he said tightly. 'Nice hat you've got there.'

The journey back to Yorvik was a difficult one, for they were thrown together for the best part of two days. There seemed to be little choice but to discuss the future and the matter of Oxford was the first to be raised. Billy was adamant he could not begin his degree by missing a whole term. The university simply would not agree to it, no matter how genuine the excuse. 'I'll have no choice but to stay here,' he told her in a flat voice. 'No doubt you'll be delighted to hear that.'

Carrie sat silent for a moment. They were facing one another across the carriage so it was impossible not to notice the pained expression on the other's face. 'I don't want you to be forced into anything you don't want to do, darling, you know that.'

'Do I?' Billy gazed out of the carriage window as his fingers tapped impatiently on his knee. A group of kangaroos were grazing by the roadside and set off in some commotion as the vehicle approached, but they made no impact at all on the young man. His thoughts were much too bound up with his future to notice anything of the countryside they were passing through. 'Are you telling me you're not expecting me to come back to Yorvik eventually?' He gave a derisory smile. 'To inherit the family estate?'

The venom with which the words were said came as a shock and Carrie did her best not to let it show. 'Well, *eventually*, perhaps, yes . . . But not until you're ready. I want you to get as full an education as possible, you know that.'

'As full an education as possible – to raise sheep!'

Carrie tensed, but was determined not to allow herself to be riled. He was young, and the young knew it all. Their parents' values were never their own. But things changed with time; the young grew up, grew more tolerant. 'It's what your father would have wanted,' she said quietly. 'He was an educated man,' she went on. 'He spent a whole year at Aberdeen University before deciding he'd rather try his luck on the other side of the world.'

'My father's home was Great Glen and Great Glen's not there any more for me to inherit.'

Carrie stared at him. The words were spoken with some bitterness. It was the first time he had ever expressed any resentment or disappointment at her selling the Macleay Valley station. 'You mean you would rather you were coming back to Great Glen and not Yorvik?' she asked, already afraid to hear the answer.

Billy shrugged. 'At least that damned Irishman would not be there.'

An alarm bell rang in her head. She had hoped to avoid this particular subject and at first decided to ignore the remark, but the ominous silence that followed made that impossible. 'You don't like Sean, do you?' she said at last in a tired voice.

'Like him?' Billy gave a hollow laugh. 'What is there to like, for heaven's sake? He's ignorant, uncouth and far too uppity for his own good. I can't for the life of me understand what you see in him. But it's very obvious what he sees in you.'

Carrie bristled at that. 'Oh, is it now? And what might that be?'

'You're the boss, that's what. And you're a woman.'

'Oh, so he's not only after my land, but my body as well?'

Billy flushed and moved uncomfortably on his seat. 'There's no need for that sort of talk.'

'But that's what you meant, isn't it?' she demanded. 'But you're wrong, Billy, so very wrong. Sean O'Dwyer isn't like that, he's . . .'

'Please!' Billy held up his hand to silence her. 'I really don't want to know. I don't want to hear how wonderful he is, and what an incredible support he's been to you, et cetera, et cetera. If you believe that, then fine . . . Only don't expect me to feel the same way when I don't. I can't like the man, Ma, I just can't. And God knows I've tried.'

Carrie's expression softened. 'I know, darling,' she sighed. 'I know.' He would come to appreciate the Irishman in time, when he was older and not so judgemental of other people whose lives he could not understand.

They lapsed into silence, and, as she sat there looking at him as he stared sullenly out of the carriage window at the passing countryside, Carrie realized more than ever how big a gap was opening up between herself and her son. It was something she had known in her heart ever since their first meeting on the Sydney quayside, but dared not admit. There was too much emotion invested in their relationship for that, too much guilt in her heart for ever having sent him away to school in the first place. The things that never ceased to delight her about this landscape they were passing through – the forests of fine red cedars, the sweet-scented gum trees, the birds and animals – none of that seemed to touch him. Any little exclamations of delight she made at a passing flight of colourful parrots or budgerigars went ignored. 'Do you still feel like an Australian, darling?' she found herself asking. 'Do you still regard this as home?'

Billy's mouth quirked at the side. 'An Australian?' he repeated with a feigned half-laugh. 'What on earth is an *Australian*? There isn't even a country called Australia, so how can I feel like an Australian, for heaven's sake?'

'What do you feel like, then?' Carrie asked, her heart sinking at the response.

He thought for a moment. 'Well, my father was Scottish, you are half English, half Irish, and I was educated in England, so that makes me as British as they come, I suspect . . . Yes, that's what I am,' he said emphatically. 'I'm British and proud of it!'

'The perfect young British gentleman.'

Billy beamed a genuine smile across at her, completely unaware of the irony in her voice. 'It's what you've paid out for all these years to make me, Ma, isn't it?'

Carrie sighed. 'Yes, darling, I expect it is.'

The first few weeks back at Yorvik turned out to be just as difficult as she'd expected. Although her injuries were healing, Carrie found she tired a lot easier than before and, worst of all, people seemed to regard her as an object of pity, offering sympathy at every turn, that she neither sought nor appreciated. She wanted to forget what had happened back there in the hotel that night and just get on with life. She knew Sean still blamed Billy for the accident and to Carrie that seemed terribly unjust. There had never been any direct proof he had been responsible and it was most upsetting to attempt to make him feel so guilty about it.

Thankfully, however, the question of her son's guilt or innocence over the accident was not an issue that was ever discussed on Yorvik. Only sympathy and love were ever expressed by the workers and their families, and Carrie was deeply touched to find the schoolchildren had even made their own special little cards, with messages for her, expressing their hopes for a speedy recovery. To Miss Chapman, the schoolmistress's embarrassment, however, some of her pupils had taken great pains to draw rather lurid pictures of their fathers' employer being engulfed in what looked like the flames of Hades.

For her part, Carrie was delighted with the offerings. The children's vivid and unsentimental imaginations made a refreshing change from the outpourings of sympathy she normally had to put up with from the grown-ups. 'Don't worry,' she told the blushing teacher. 'When it comes to the next Bible lesson and you're telling them if they don't do what they're told they'll go down into the fires of Hell, you can now use me as an example of what they'll look like if they survive! That'll be enough to keep them little angels for life!'

The cards themselves were proudly displayed on the drawing room mantelpiece as a constant reminder of everyone's concern. The parents and grandparents of the children too seemed to feel that they must also offer their sympathy at every turn, and, although irritating in a way, to Carrie their solicitude was nevertheless touching. 'We were all so upset when we first heard, ma'am,' Will Morton's wife told her. 'It was as if the bottom was about to fall out of our world. And it would have, if you hadn't recovered like you did.'

Carrie never knew quite how to respond to such confidences. Their obvious love for her and their dependence on her made her feel a great love and responsibility in turn towards all those who lived and worked on Yorvik. They were *her* people. And how she wished Billy could feel the same about them, for each and every one was almost as much a part of her family as her own flesh and blood.

But, thankfully, as far as the little Aboriginal children were concerned, the fact that she had come through a difficult time seemed to matter not one jot. They were simply delighted to have her back again to resume her habit of carrying sweetmeats around in her pockets for them. She was still the Pied Piper to the dozens of little brown bodies who followed her around the yard shouting 'Kabbarli' – their word for grandmother – in those sing-song voices of theirs. 'Tucker, Kabbarli . . . !'

But, amongst all the comments made about the accident after her return, it was perhaps the reaction of the adult blackfellas that gave her most cause for thought.

'They think it's *Jindabarli* – some sort of Justice of the Dreamtime – what has happened,' Sean told her one evening as they sat in front of his hut over a mug of tea. 'There's talk in the camp of *Jimardi* – that it's nature's law of retribution.'

'You mean they think I'm being punished for something I have done that has offended against the laws of Dreamtime?' Carrie asked in a quiet voice.

Sean nodded, grave-faced as he puffed on his pipe, then immediately tried to reassure her. 'But that's just blackfella talk. You don't have to take any notice of that.'

'Oh, but I do,' Carrie told him. 'I certainly do, for it could be true. They could be right.'

'What's that supposed to mean?'

She sat silently by his side, looking out across the moon-lit landscape to where a campfire sent a red glow into the growing darkness of the heavens. 'Things happened in my life before we met, Sean, lots of things. Things I'm not proud of. Not proud at all. If there is a God, maybe this is his way of getting back at me.' She was honestly beginning to believe that. Things like her father's death, and taking Caroline's place . . . Living a lie for all these years. Such things had to be paid for eventually. Perhaps the fire, and Billy's resentment of his homeland, perhaps that was all part of it – of paying her back for past sins.

'But that's stupid talk!'

Carrie turned to face him. 'Is it? You don't scoff at the rest of the blackfellas' beliefs, do you? Why should this one be so different? Why should it be wrong?'

He shrugged. 'Because I know you, that's why. You couldn't do anything awful if you tried. You're as honest and straightforward as the day is long.'

As honest and straightforward as the day is long . . . Carrie gave a wry smile as she stood up and laid a hand on his shoulder. 'Dear Irish,' she said softly. 'Dear loyal Irish . . . If only life were so simple.'

He watched her as she walked slowly back in the

direction of the new Yorvik. Her left leg, something that had not bothered her in years, had stiffened during her weeks in bed, and she walked with a slight limp now. She was heading back to the new home that she had built with so much love, for a life that once had so much to offer. But apart from Billy and Ellen the cook, she was alone in that great house, just as she was alone in life. All her wealth, all her success had not brought her the happiness and contentment he knew she so badly craved. The black-fellas had a saying that when life gave with one hand it took away with the other. It had done that to her all right.

Sean sighed and stood up, his bones creaking with the first stages of rheumatics as he did so, and, as he turned to make for his hut, he was aware of a shadow moving in the doorway. It was one of the younger gins. His eyes clouded . . . Not tonight. Dear God, not tonight. Even the thought of such indulgences at a time like this when Carrie was going through so much brought feelings of shame. He made a dismissive gesture with his hand and the young woman disappeared into the undergrowth behind the hut. There were times in this life when it was right to be alone, and tonight was one of them.

CHAPTER THIRTY-ONE

Billy remained on Yorvik until the following May. It was 1880, the beginning of a new decade and, Carrie hoped, the start of a clean slate in their relationship which had been anything but easy in the year just gone.

He had taken full advantage of her inability to function as effectively as she might have wished in the early months of her return from hospital by introducing his own ideas into the running of the station. Many, such as the attempt to train some of the young cattlemen in the art of sheep-shearing, were hare-brained schemes that she did not hear of until the damage had already been done, but more often they were simply rather petty orders that irritated more than angered her, such as insisting upon everyone calling him 'Sir'.

'It seems to me you actually encourage familiarity and lack of respect around the place, and it's got to stop,' he told his mother firmly when she challenged him about it over dinner one evening in early January. 'People take advantage when there's a lack of firm leadership. They take liberties both with their actions and their tongue – some more than others, I hasten to add. I've told that Irishman he's on his last warning.'

'You've done *what*?'

'O'Dwyer – I've told him he's got to toe the line and remember his place or he's out.'

Carrie found it difficult to keep her voice level. 'And when exactly did you tell him this?'

'This morning,' Billy replied, reaching for the pickle jar and spearing a small onion. 'The fellow had the cheek to contradict me in front of one of the other men. I had no choice but to put him in his place. You get complete anarchy otherwise. If they see one getting away with it, they all try it.'

It was then that Carrie realized that both her son and Yorvik really would be better off with him on the other side of the world. There would be anarchy all right, but not for the reason he had just given.

Yes, several years beneath the dreaming spires of Oxford would surely see a big difference when eventually he returned to take over Yorvik. He would be a fully mature man by then. At the moment she could only close her eyes for so long over his interference. And it was time she admitted it, Billy was never going to be another Big Jock. He was too wrapped up in appearances and status to make a really effective employer. He enjoyed giving orders but she could not remember an occasion when he had actually rolled up his sleeves and got down to some hard physical work himself. In truth he was far more a Clayton than he ever was a Gordon. Looking back now, with the benefit of hindsight, she could see that both her father and her brother Billy had been rather ineffectual men in their own way. Some, more cruelly, might even say shallow. They had been unduly impressed by outward appearances, but were not really able to cope with the everyday stresses in life. Her father had combated this by turning to drink, and her brother, well, he had been still too young for that to become a real problem. She could see the similarities surfacing already in the new generation, even in the fact that her son would not sit down to a meal without a bottle of wine on the table, and would insist on polishing it off in one sitting. 'No use leaving it for the servants to get their hands on,' he would tell her. 'That's a dangerous habit to get into.'

And Carrie would find herself agreeing. Everything he said, he said with so much authority. His impeccable, educated English accent carried all before it. There was no arguing with him. Even she found it difficult, despite knowing she was in the right most of the time.

'But you've never shirked from putting anyone in their place before,' Sean protested, when she went round to his hut later that same night to apologize on behalf of her son. 'You've successfully run two stations and been boss to dozens of men, why should you find it so impossible to put a young lad like that in his place when you know he's overstepped the mark?'

'Because he's my son, that's why!' Carrie said wretchedly. 'Can't you see, Sean, all my adult life I've had no one — no one to really call my own. Until him. All my hopes, all my dreams have been vested in him. He's my past, my present and my future all rolled into one . . .'

The Irishman let out a low whistle. 'That's a mighty heavy burden for any youngster to bear,' he told her. 'Maybe it's no bad thing he's heading back for England come May.'

Those words came back to haunt Carrie several months later as she stood on the quayside for the second time and waved goodbye to Billy as he set out once more for his beloved England.

Had she put too much pressure on him to conform to the son she had always wanted — the one who would love Yorvik as much as she did? She knew such questions would torture her in the weeks and months ahead.

They had parted with expressions of love on both sides, but Carrie could not help feeling they were both going through some sort of charade. She doubted very much if Billy would miss her half as much as he said he would. His spirits had gradually been improving for weeks now, the nearer he got to his return to England, while her own had sunk into a dull, aching despair where her son was concerned. No matter how much she might wish it otherwise, he did not feel the same about Yorvik as she did and probably never would.

Why were relationships so difficult, she wondered? All she had wanted out of life was security, and someone to love and a family. Was that too much to ask? The world

seemed full of happy families. Everywhere she looked —
even on this windswept quay — there were husbands and
wives with their broods of offspring. How did they manage
it? How could they get it so right, when she always seemed
to get it so wrong?

Even her relationship with the Irishman, Sean O'Dwyer,
was fraught. Her son hated him, and she had little doubt
the feeling was entirely mutual. Neither could bear the
other's company for even a few minutes, although Sean
took great pains not to let her know the full extent of his
hostility towards Billy.

As for her relationship with the Irishman himself, well,
she had no doubt they both loved each other in their own
ways, yet there had been no real physical intimacy ever.
Perhaps if she had remained longer on Yorvik as a young
woman, things might have been different. Perhaps the hot
blood of youth that had once pulsated in both their veins
might have proved too much and she could have ended
up giving herself in body as well as soul. But that had
never happened, and to return half a lifetime later with
the passions of youth all but spent ... Well, that was
another story altogether.

She had raised the matter with him once, in a joking
sort of way, just after she built the new Yorvik. They had
been part of the small crowd throwing rice outside the
station chapel at one of the young stockmen and his new
bride. There had been the usual selection of ribald comments from the crowd about the night to come, and as they
had walked away Sean had given a half-envious backward
glance at the pair as they made off in a ribbon-festooned
buggy. 'I bet there's many a young fella around here today
would give a month's wages to be in his shoes,' he had
said ruefully. 'Aye, and the not so young into the bargain!'

Carrie had had no doubt he was referring to himself, for
the bride was an extremely pretty young woman, and she
was disturbed to find a pang of jealousy pierce her heart.
It had been many years since she had known that same

bloom of youth. 'Don't you think as one reaches middle age our desires change?' she had asked him. 'Don't they lessen with age? Do we not reach a stage in our lives when such things cease to have the importance they once did?'

Sean had looked at her in some surprise out of the corner of his eye as he wiped the palms of his hands together to rid them of the floury residue from the rice. He thought about what she had said for a long time, then just when she was convinced he was going to ignore the question, he replied in a quiet voice, 'The blackfellas have a word for it – what you're talking about. They call it *Matunga* – the time of one's life when the blood cools . . .'

Then he had half shaken his head and given her a look that was almost pitying as they walked on. '*Matunga*,' he had repeated with a sigh. 'Some, they say, are born in that state and for them I reckon we must feel only a great sadness . . .'

Carrie did not know why, but she felt he was talking not only to her but about her at that moment. A chill had crept into her heart. Perhaps he believed she had been in a state of *Matunga* all her life, that her blood had not merely chilled in middle age, but that she had been born cold-blooded where physical love was concerned. Nothing could have been further from the truth. And more than ever now as old age crept gradually upon her she felt the need for the type of warmth and physical intimacy that she had never known. Physical love in the past had either been a repulsive torment with Silas, or a duty she felt she had to comply with for Big Jock after all his kindnesses to her.

She had glanced at the man by her side as they walked back towards the main station buildings to resume the day's work. If anything he had grown even more attractive with the passing years. All that weight he had lost during his illness had returned and his build was strong, his muscles hard beneath the still taut flesh. With his head of wiry grey curls, bristling copper beard, and those dark eyes with their golden glints, he had a presence about him that made all other men she had ever met pale in comparison.

He had his enemies, certainly and those who had nursed resentments for one reason or another over the years would refer to him scathingly as 'The Darkie' because of his Aboriginal blood. In truth his deeply bronzed skin was little darker than most of the others who had spent their lives outdoors in these parts, but she knew such supposed insults cut no ice with him. Sean was just as proud of the blood of that ancient race that ran in his veins as of the rich Celtic strain inherited from his convict father. He was a real Australian all right, as true a one as ever walked this earth, unlike her own native-born son who could not wait to put as many miles between himself and his native shores as possible, and who preferred to regard himself as a 'real British gentleman'.

Perhaps the reason she had been so deeply hurt over the Irishman's relationship with Quarra – and who knew what other gins – was because in her heart she too had longed for that degree of intimacy. She knew she could never have asked for any commitment from him, for he was not that kind of man, he was too free a spirit ever to be tied down. But if she had given herself freely, asking for nothing in return as the native women did, and she had found herself pregnant, what would *their* son have turned out like? Certainly nothing like Billy, that was for sure. And despite the deep love she felt for her son, she knew she would keep on asking herself just that. And the question was even more poignant now that he was a grown man, for she could not help but compare him with the Irishman – the man who still meant far more to her than his own father, Big Jock, had ever done.

Carrie gave a deep sigh as she turned from the departing ship that was taking her son from her. There were so many aches in her heart that sometimes it felt like a gaping wound; a wound that was far more painful that any physical ones she had had to bear. A deep sadness filled her soul, only partly due to her son's leave-taking, and she automatically pulled at the veil that half-covered her face as she began to walk slowly back across the crowded quay.

Although she had become quite used to being around people since her accident, it still took courage to face the world at large in a growing city such as Sydney, with her cheeks still bearing traces of the fading scar tissue. The quayside was crowded with people, and except for the occasional pitted complexion of a former smallpox victim, all seemed to have such healthy countenances. A carriage and pair were parked a few feet away and she caught sight of herself in the glass of the cab window. She seemed to be drawn to her reflection now like a moth to a flame. But in so doing, she too risked being burned, for there was no ignoring it, she was no longer the young, attractive woman she had once been. Father Time, and the fire, had seen to it that whatever secret hopes she might have retained of reversing that state of *Matunga* the Irishman believed her to be in had now gone forever.

She threw herself into her work on her return to Yorvik and the months that followed were not unhappy ones. Slowly she found her old energy returning and she recovered most of the use of her hands. She even found herself accepting with pleasure all the social invitations that came her way from friends and neighbours in the Valley. Her favourite place of call, however, remained the home of her old friend and neighbour Angus Cameron, who made a point of inviting her to every function he held at Cameron Creek for his illustrious Sydney political friends throughout that winter. He, above all, accepted her for the successful station owner she was. The fact she was a woman no longer came into it. 'You know as much as anyone in this territory about running a profitable sheep or cattle station,' he told her. 'It does them good to listen to somebody else plead the farmers' case apart from me now and again.'

The past decade had seen great changes in their country. By 1880 their own land of New South Wales could no longer be regarded as an immigrant colony, for at least two-thirds of the population were now native born and proud of it. Although amongst Angus Cameron's peers in the Legislature Britain was still looked upon as the mother country, to be emulated and admired, amongst the workers themselves there was no such forelock-tugging. In fact, in some quarters, particularly amongst the large population of Irish stock, there was downright hostility towards the Old World, with its unfair class privileges and socially prejudiced justice system.

Carrie felt a growing pride and sense of excitement for the future of their country as she listened to the talk around Angus's dinner table of social reform and 'Australia for the Australians'. She often wished that Billy could have been with her on such occasions, for he would see for himself that his country was not all rough diggers and swagmen as he seemed to think. There was an educated, literate and politically conscious class here who had a real pride in their land and wanted to see it prosper and who were dedicating their lives to that end.

But by the tone of his letters home, Billy had no burning desire to return to the land of his birth. On the contrary, he was writing that after graduation he might well consider settling down in England for the foreseeable future:

> . . . I know you won't be too happy at the prospect of this, Ma, but I also know that most of all you want the best for me. I truly feel a spell working in the 'real world' of London would do me a power of good and make me far better fitted for managing Yorvik when the time eventually comes . . .

Exactly how he came to that conclusion remained a mystery to Carrie, but she could not fail to get the message. Billy did not want to come home directly after graduation. And 'when the time eventually comes' could mean anything.

Her decision to allow him to stay on in England after

graduation and actually support him to the tune of five hundred pounds a year was met by hostility from Sean, who felt she was giving in far too easily. 'You're laying up trouble for yourself, Carrie girl,' he told her. 'When he does come back, he'll have an even bigger grudge than before.'

'Then that's a risk I shall just have to take,' Carrie said. 'If I forced him to come back immediately after he got his degree, he'd never forgive me, so either way, I just can't win.'

The private heartache she felt, however, she kept well hidden from her son. In her letters she tried hard to be amusing and she kept him well informed with all the political and social happenings of the day. And in the latter half of that year she had plenty to write about, for the news was almost totally dominated by the trial of Ned Kelly, the country's most notorious bushranger, who was being prosecuted at the Central Criminal Court in Melbourne for murder. Australians everywhere were following the case avidly as Ned had become something of a folk hero to many, and even Sean, who usually took no interest whatsoever in happenings outside their own part of the country, was keen to follow what the newsmen were writing.

'Just listen to this,' Carrie told him with a smile, one balmy morning in early November as she stood at the gate of a sheep pen and held open a copy of their local newspaper, which was carrying the story in all its lurid detail. 'Someone asked Kelly the other day what he thought of the police and he reckoned they were "a parcel of big, fat-necked, big-bellied, magpie-legged, narrow-hipped, splay-footed sons of Irish bailiffs"!'

'I'd say that just about sums them up pretty well,' Sean agreed with a grin, as he looked up from paring a ewe's hoof. 'All the ones I've met at any rate.'

They were still standing there in the sunshine discussing the case when Davie Henderson rode past, and, doffing his hat, called out, 'Begging your pardon for interrupting, ma'am, but I've just ridden past the big house and met Ellen on the way down here looking for you. Seems you've got a visitor. I told her I'd let you know.'

'Thank you, Davie,' Carrie called back, then she threw a puzzled glance at Sean. 'I wasn't expecting anyone today,' she said, folding up the paper. 'I just hope it's not that Hopwood girl back.' Sarah Hopwood was a maidservant from Angus Cameron's place who had managed to get herself in the family way by one of Yorvik's stockmen and the girl had already been over twice begging her to intervene and persuade the young man in question to do 'the honourable thing'. In Carrie's opinion that really was asking her to act above and beyond the call of duty, no matter how sorry she felt for the young woman.

She was still working out what she would say to convince the girl there was really nothing she could do to organize wedding bells on her behalf when she hurried up the steps of the big house several minutes later, to be met by Ellen in the hall.

'I've put the woman in the drawing room, ma'am,' the housekeeper said. 'Do you want tea brought in?'

'No, don't bother, Ellen,' Carrie said in a weary voice, dismayed that her suspicions were confirmed. 'Whatever's to be said won't take that long.'

Placing the newspaper on the hallstand, she opened the drawing room door with 'Good morning, Miss Hopwood' ready on her lips. But the words remained frozen on her tongue.

Standing in the middle of the Persian carpet was Molly McFarland. 'Good God!'

'It's good to see you again, Carrie,' Molly said, rushing forwards, extending her hand. 'I – I just hope you don't mind me travelling up here to find you like this.'

'No . . . no, of course not,' Carrie lied, her insides churning. She had something akin to that sinking feeling she had experienced all those years ago when she had returned home to the old Yorvik homestead to find the Bidwells in her front parlour. To be forced face to face with your past like this in your own home was not a comfortable situation; it had been bad enough running into the woman at Sydney docks. 'How – how did you know where to find me?' she asked, distancing herself slightly by moving behind an easy chair so there was a good ten feet between her and her old friend.

'Oh, that was easy, Ian was reading the *Herald* the other day, and there was a bit in it about a dinner party that politician fella Cameron had given for some big-wigs on his place in the Hunter Valley and it gave some details of the guest list. From what you told us when we last met, Ian said the Mrs Caroline Gordon-Hebden it mentioned was almost certain to be you.'

'Oh.' It was as simple as that.

'You're probably wondering why I'm here,' Molly said, already aware that her welcome had not been exactly effusive up to now.

'Well, yes. It is rather a long way to come for purely a social call.'

A shaft of sunlight was streaming in through the big bay window to the side of them and falling on Molly's face. It looked pinched and old, the pretty, pert features almost unrecognizable. It was the face of poverty that Carrie had seen so often throughout her life. The only difference between it and those wretched faces of the London slums was that here the shrivelled skin had a brown, weather-beaten look to it. The greying hair tied back in an untidy bun at the nape of the neck was stringy in texture and Molly passed a smoothing hand over it, then adjusted her shawl as she assured her old friend, 'Oh, this is no social call. We need your help.'

Carrie's fingers gripped the back of the chair. 'My – my help?'

'Yes,' Molly said, her fingers nervously toying with the fringes of the shawl. 'I wouldn't have come, wouldn't have bothered you, but you're our last chance. Our last chance to save Seamus.'

'I don't understand.'

'You're obviously well connected,' Molly insisted. 'You have friends in high places. You're our last chance to save our lad from the gallows.'

Carrie stared at her, inwardly shrinking from what she might be asked to do. From what she could recall of that meeting in the public house at Sydney harbour, Molly's lads probably deserved most of what was coming to them. Nobody became a bushranger without knowing the risks they were running.

'You may have heard of that Ned Kelly trial that's going on down in Melbourne just now,' Molly continued, as Carrie's eyebrows rose with interest. 'Well, our Seamus was part of the gang . . .'

As Carrie caught her breath, her friend wrung her hands, trying to think of the best way of putting it to gain some sympathy for her son. 'Of course we only have the police's say-so that Seamus was involved, and you and I both know what police evidence is worth . . . Not that I'm trying to whitewash him, mind, that would be the pot calling the kettle black with a vengeance. And I don't deny he was there, but I don't believe he was responsible for any killings . . . Anyway, he managed to escape during the carry-on that surrounded the burning of that Glenrowan Inn all the fuss was about, and he was nowhere near Ned or any of the rest of the gang when the law eventually caught up with him. In fact, the poor lad's been holed up in our outhouse for the past week or so – until the bastards came and got him four nights ago.'

Her face, old far beyond its years, seemed infinitely weary as did her voice as she whispered hoarsely, 'They're charging him with the same offence as poor Ned. Murder.'

'And you want me to try to do something to get him off?' Carrie said in a flat voice. Her mouth had gone quite dry.

'You're our last chance. You've got on, Carrie. You're a rich woman now with friends in high places.' Then her face hardened. 'Not that I've come to beg, mind you. I'll not have you think that. But I said to Ian no matter how high and mighty you might have become these days, you would never be one to forget your roots. You'd not be one to forget that you came here in chains like the rest of us. You'd not see one of your own kind go to the gallows if you could help it.'

Carrie could feel her jaw tighten as Molly was talking. There was an underlying threat in there somewhere, she was sure of it. It was as if her old friend was telling her that she still had the measure of her, that despite all the riches and success, all the fine connections, she was still a convict at heart like herself. She had not the shadow of a doubt that should she refuse to help, the real threat would be uttered, the threat to expose her for what she had been all this time – a fraud.

'You will help, won't you?' Molly persisted, worried now by the silence from across the room.

'I'll do what I can,' Carrie replied in a tight voice. 'I'll have a word with Angus and pressure will be brought to bear in the right places. On one condition.'

'And what might that be?' Molly asked, her face brighter now as she saw a glimmer of hope at last.

'That you don't ever breathe a word of this to anyone – anyone at all. That you tell no one that it's me who has helped you – if help I can.'

Molly's dark brows rose. 'Sure I'll not say a word, if that's what you want. Although it's always good to give credit where it's due.'

'I don't need that kind of credit,' Carrie said quietly.

'Ahhh . . .'

Carrie studied her old friend's face from across the room. Molly was as fly as they came, as sharp as a needle, and nobody's fool. Carrie did not have to spell it out. Her friend knew well enough she wanted no more part of that

411

criminal fraternity that Molly herself was still so bound up in. But whether she would keep her promise to say nothing was impossible to tell.

Carrie walked to a Georgian writing desk on the far wall and, opening it, pulled out a drawer. Inside was a wad of notes: at least fifty pounds. Without even counting, Carrie handed them to her old friend. 'Take these,' she said, 'and see that your son gets the best lawyer in Melbourne to defend him.'

Molly looked down at the bundle of money in her hand. She had not expected this, but she was far too sensible to refuse. Pride did not come into it. 'God bless you, Carrie love,' she said. 'I'll not forget this . . . And you'll not forget your promise. You'll speak up for Seamus in the right places? You'll not let the bastards hang him?'

Carrie put an arm around her old friend's shoulders and walked her towards the door. Into her mind flashed an image of two young women laughing and giggling, to the annoyance of the guards, as they paraded side by side round the exercise deck of the *Emma Harkness*. 'Don't worry,' she told her. 'I'm sure things will work out.'

She stood on the front step and watched as her friend made for a spindle-legged horse tethered to the ornamental lamppost and hoisted herself aloft. She had travelled for two days to beg for this favour and had not been given as much as a cup of tea. Carrie felt shame wash over her that she had not even been able to bring herself to offer her even that most common of courtesies. But fear was a terrible thing. It ate into your soul and lay there waiting, sometimes for a lifetime, to spring up and devour every principle you held dear.

'You'll not forget now!' Molly called as she raised a hand in farewell.

'I'll not forget!'

And Carrie knew she was not lying, she never would forget. As long as she lived she would remember the day she bought her friend's silence with fifty old pound notes.

And she knew in her heart as she turned back to the front door that she would never breathe a word to Angus Cameron, or anyone else for that matter, in Seamus McFarland's defence. She had come too far and had paid too high a price already to risk everything by doing that. Caroline Cooper would never have consorted with a she-lag such as Molly McGuire. Only Carrie Clayton would have done that. And Carrie Clayton was dead.

'You'll be wanting that cup of tea now, ma'am,' the housekeeper said as Carrie closed the front door behind her, leant back against it and shut her eyes.

'Yes, Ellen, I'll be wanting that cup of tea.'

CHAPTER THIRTY-TWO

Billy Gordon-Hebden graduated from Trinity College, Oxford, in July 1884 and to his mother's great sorrow did not travel back to New South Wales immediately afterwards as she had hoped, but took a flat in London's Bloomsbury and set about living the life of an English gentleman of means.

The letters that passed between mother and son during the months that followed his leaving Oxford and settling down to London life were amicable but strained, with Carrie determined to do everything in her power not to become the nagging parent across the sea with whom he eventually cut off contact altogether.

Her disappointment at not having him home was moderated, however, by her pride in his gaining a degree. From what she could gather it was an unclassified one but, as Angus Cameron assured her, a degree was a degree, and it would not fail to impress the right circles when eventually he did decide to return. 'We need good educated Australians like your lad,' he told her over dinner at Cameron Creek one evening. 'This country will be united one day, you mark my words, and the likes of your Billy will be running it.'

He had said it with such conviction that Carrie had no choice but believe him. In fact, her heart had quite swelled with pride, for, after all, Angus was now looked upon hereabouts with the greatest respect, and practically regarded as one of the founding fathers of the colony, spoken of in the same reverential hushed tones reserved for the great god Lachlan Macquarie himself.

The news of Billy's graduation from Oxford was carried in all the local newspapers, and even the *Sydney Herald*, who went as far as to carry a woodcut picture produced from a head and shoulders portrait Carrie had had painted of him before he had left for university. He looked so like her brother Billy in the finished oil, resplendent in its gilt frame, that she had never had the heart to put it up on the wall after he left, and it was ironic now to see it plastered all over the press.

'You must be so proud of him,' was the comment she received from everyone who spotted the picture and read the piece, and many even went as far as to say the extra time he was spending in the mother country could only benefit his own homeland whenever he chose to return. For her part Carrie almost came to believe it, and told herself that she had been extremely selfish in expecting him to return right away. The university of life in a country such as Britain could be as formative and useful as the actual subjects he had spent those four years studying.

The news that arrived by post some seventeen months later, with his card for Christmas, 1885, came as a real shock.

Carrie had been taking breakfast in the morning room, still in her favourite satin-quilted dressing-gown, when the housekeeper brought the post.

'Thank you, Ellen,' she smiled, putting down her teacup and reaching for the bundle. Several items she recognized by their distinctive red wax seals as bills, which she ignored and pushed to one side, pouncing instead on the envelope bearing the stamp with Queen Victoria's head on it and the familiar handwriting on the address. She always went to Billy's letters first, no matter what else might be waiting.

Inside the envelope was a Christmas card with a snowy coaching scene, and inside that a letter. Carrie opened it eagerly, spreading the page out on the white damask cloth of the table. But the expression in her eyes changed from one of keen anticipation to disbelief as she read then reread the words in his familiar elegant scrawl. Her breath caught in her throat and she could feel her insides knotting. 'Oh no . . . !'

She had to find Sean!

Letting the envelope and card fall to the floor she clasped the letter to her breast and rushed from the house, her long hair streaming behind her back, for it was still early and she had not yet put it up.

At last she found him hoeing the vegetable garden and whistling to himself in the bright morning light. He looked up in surprise at her hurrying figure.

'What the hell?' His brow furrowed as he pushed his hat back on his head. She was still in her dressing-gown, with her hair everywhere and her face was flushed from the exertion. What the deuce was going on? He put down the hoe and came over to meet her. 'What is it, old girl?'

'Listen to this!' Carrie panted, leaning against the fence to catch her breath. She waved the card in front of him. 'Just listen to this!'

Holding it at arm's length, for her sight was no longer what it used to be, she began to read:

Dear Ma,

I realize this may come as a bit of a surprise to you and may not be quite the Christmas present you've been expecting, but the fact is I got married the other day to the most beautiful girl in the world. Her name is Helena, but she is known as Nella, and her father is the Honourable Richard Foston-Strutt-Smith, and the family hails from Northamptonshire. Nella is very keen on the idea of seeing Australia and the family home and all that, so we will be sailing for Yorvik on the St Bede *out of Southampton, on the fourth of November – a sort of delayed honeymoon. You can expect us around the end of February. We do hope you don't mind us landing on you like this. We expect to stay about three months.*

Enjoy Christmas!

All love,

Your devoted son

Billy.

'Well, what do you make of that?' Carrie asked, her face glowing with perspiration and her eyes shining.

The Irishman looked thoughtful. 'What was her name again?'

'Helena Foston-Strutt-Smith,' Carrie replied. Then they both burst out laughing. 'Oh, Sean, it's not funny!' she protested, wiping the tears from her eyes as he grinned at her.

'So the little bugger's gone and done it, has he?'

'It certainly looks like it . . . I – I don't know quite what to think.'

'Then don't think anything,' Sean replied, clasping her with both hands on the shoulders. The animosity he still felt towards her son counted for nothing at a time like this. She had come to him to share her excitement and confusion at the news and he would be right behind her as always. 'Just look forward to it,' he told her. 'Who knows, she might even be quite human, despite her name!'

When Carrie had gone, however, the encouraging smile died on his lips. Billy was coming home . . . His heart sank at the thought, for as long as he lived he would never forgive that young man for what he had done. In truth, there was no room on Yorvik for the two of them, for he could scarcely bring himself to breathe the same air as the young blighter. But he had made the effort before and would try to do so again for Carrie's sake.

As he turned back to the job in hand, Davie Henderson passed by and called out, 'Good day to you, Sean!' Then as the Scotsman paused to lean on the fence and take a swig from the water bottle on his belt, he said, 'I've just passed the boss – she looks pretty happy with herself this morning.'

'Billy's coming back,' Sean said in a deadpan voice.

'You're kidding!'

'I only wish I was, mate!'

The Scotsman let out a groan. 'Made my bloody day, that has!' He looked quizzically at the Irishman. 'Do you think the old lady knows how much the young bugger gets up our noses?'

Sean shrugged. 'It wouldn't make any difference if she did. He's her son, Davie lad, so the sun rises and sets on that young so-and-so no matter what he does or says. The best thing we can do is grin and bear it.'

The Scotsman gave a dubious 'Hmm', as he pushed the stopper back into the water bottle and wiped his mouth. 'If he comes any of his high falutin' ways with me, I might not be quite so tolerant as I was in the past when he was a lad.' Then seeing the Irishman suppress a smile at the comment, he added with feeling, 'I was a bit of a dab hand with the old fists when I was younger, I'll have you know!'

Sean looked at the gangly frame, now stooped with advancing age, and the thin, sinewy arms, and shook his head as he gave a disparaging laugh, 'Well, if you need a referee, Davie mate, then I'm your man – guaranteed to be completely partial where any opponent of that young bugger's concerned. But I reckon an old man roo would stand as good a chance in a one-to-one!'

The dismay of her two longest-serving hands at the news, however, was lost on Carrie as she hurried back to the house to begin all the preparations that would be necessary for the newly-weds' arrival. She was already in a state of eager anticipation at the news and any initial indignation she had felt at Billy marrying without her knowledge was soon lost in the flurry of activity that followed. That very morning the best guest room was set aside to be specially done out for their stay. New drapes were ordered from Newcastle and a brand new Indian carpet in a Tree of Life design. And it was with some wistfulness three weeks later that she surveyed the newly delivered double brass bed with its gleaming knobs and thick horsehair mattress. Her little boy married, she could scarcely believe it . . .

She was on her way downstairs after doing some final titivation to the newly-weds' bedroom when she heard a commotion coming from the kitchen. Puzzled, she made her way there, to be confronted by an agitated Ellen busy shooing out one of the older gins who occasionally helped her around the place.

'What's going on, Ellen?' Carrie asked as the kitchen door slammed behind the departing old woman. 'What was that all about?'

'I don't rightly know, ma'am,' the housekeeper sighed. 'That was Jeeba. One of the other women from the tribe had been speaking to her outside and she came in wailing something about *Karani Bunpi* – women's business – and moaning the name of Marika.'

'Marika,' Carrie said sharply. 'That's Quarra's daughter, isn't it?' Even after all these years she found it difficult to say that name. But she certainly had nothing against the daughter, for Marika herself was a pretty young woman and very popular with the young men of the tribe.

'Aye, it is.'

'Do you think there's anything wrong with her?' When she came to think about it, she had not seen Marika around for quite some time. She went to the window and looked out into the morning sunshine. '*Karani Bunpi* . . . women's business,' she mused, toying with the lace curtain. 'You don't think she's giving birth, do you?' That was certainly what the phrase often referred to.

Ellen gave a dry laugh and shrugged her ample shoulders as she continued kneading the dough on the floured baking board. 'If she is they'll not want us interfering, that's for sure. As far as they're concerned, it's not only women's business, it's black women's business, and they'll not thank us for poking our noses into it.'

The incident continued to play on Carrie's mind, however. Why would women's business be such a cause for wailing? Eventually the sense of responsibility she felt for her blackfellas got the better of her, and later that day she made a point of riding over in the direction of the camp.

To her amazement she found it totally deserted. There

419

was not a soul in sight, although pots and pans and other belongings were still lying around. Usually this meant only one thing, a death in the tribe. She knew that the *kuran* – or soul – of the newly dead was greatly feared by the blackfellas, who could not accept that death could come by natural causes. To them it was always due to a hostile spirit conjured up by an enemy, or the most dire retribution meted out by the spirits themselves for some wicked act.

Sean had told her how they believed that the spirit of the dead man or woman would seek vengeance for the untimely ending of its earthly life, and that was the reason why so often she would find the blackfellas' camp totally deserted. They would all have been forced to flee, often for as long as three months, until they felt it safe to return.

There were so many such strange beliefs to be contended with that a white man or woman had to tread carefully for fear of offending the living, and this Carrie had no wish to do. The welfare and goodwill of those whom she regarded as *her* Aborigines were paramount.

Climbing down from her horse, she looked around her with a feeling of growing disquiet. The silence was positively oppressive. There had to have been a death, there was no other explanation for it. The last time anything like this had happened was almost a year ago when one of the older gins died. They had all just vanished into thin air, to reappear just as silently some three months later.

Tentatively she prodded at the deserted utensils and implements with the toe of her shoe, all the time her eyes and ears tuned for any sound that might indicate a human presence other than her own. Nothing stirred. There was no sound but her own footsteps cracking a broken twig here or there.

Finally, when she had all but decided to go home, she came to a quiet hollow on the outskirts of the camp. It was late afternoon by now; the air was heavy with the scent of eucalyptus and there was no wind; the type of day when even a sigh could be heard from afar. She had on a wide-brimmed hat, which she pushed back on her head, and looked about her. It was far too hot to be messing around, not even sure what she was looking for. She was just about ready to admit defeat and head for home, when she heard it. It sounded like one of the station kittens at first; a faint mewing sound, almost indistinguishable from the gentle whispering of the grass.

It sent a shiver down her spine. Slowly she walked in its direction, towards a shallow trough between two tall gum trees. Here the ground was covered with scrub and an assortment of leaves and other ferns and broken branches. And there was that sound again!

Her heart was beating faster as she knelt down and brushed at the heap of leaves and branches with her hand.

'Oh God!'

She drew back as if stung. There was someone in there! She had touched a human hand!

Carrie rose unsteadily to her feet, her heart pounding. If there really was a dead body, then she surely had found it. She looked around her in rising panic. But there was no one within a mile.

Then the sound came again. That faint mewing. A cold sweat broke beneath the fine lawn of the chemise under her cotton blouse. The sound was coming from down there in those leaves. From that dead body.

The Irishman had told her all sorts of tales in the past about the blackfellas' beliefs and about the different spirits that inhabited their world. So vivid was his telling that she almost believed the *kuran* was still here, sitting at the head of the grave, watching her at this moment. She shuddered, then let out a scream as some of the leaves beneath her gaze moved and as she stared, two tiny fingers poked into the fresh air.

'Dear God in heaven!'

Immediately she was on her knees, brushing at the debris for all she was worth. Within seconds the face of a young Aborigine woman stared up at her, her brown eyes gazing vacantly heavenwards into the canopy of green foliage above, her generous lips apart, as if uttering some silent cry of protest. It was Marika, Quarra's daughter. Ellen had been right. And lying beside her, half covering her left breast, was the tiny form of a newly born infant. As the leaves were brushed off, it squirmed slightly and waved its right arm in the air.

'Oh, you poor little mite!'

Carrie bent over and scooped up the child. It was the smallest human being she had ever seen and weighed no more than a couple of pounds. The minute limbs floundered and a pathetic squeak was emitted from its mouth as she held it to her breast. It was no bigger than a newly born kitten and its quivering little frame was streaked with blood.

'You poor little soul,' Carrie whispered into the screwed-up little face. They had left it here to die with its mother. What on earth had possessed them to do that? What had this tiny creature ever done to deserve that fate? If she had come half an hour later it would probably have been found and devoured by a dingo or any other wild creature that happened to be roaming hereabouts.

Re-covering the corpse of its mother with the leaves and debris, Carrie took off her hat and placed the infant inside. It curled up in the felt womb and she hung the unlikely cradle around her neck as she made for her horse.

On getting back to the big house, she took her fragile cargo immediately into the kitchen and laid it on the table to the astonishment of Ellen, who gazed at it, dumbstruck. 'What in heaven's name is that?'

'It's the reason for all that hoo-ha earlier this morning,' Carrie replied. 'The mother's dead and they have all disappeared in terror of the spirits and left this poor little thing to his fate.'

Ellen gave a 'wouldn't you know it' raise of her eyebrows. She was well used to the ways of the blackfellas over the years; nothing surprised her any more. She had had several cases of infant mortality brought to her notice since first joining Big Jock's employ on Great Glen over fifty years ago. She had even known several newly-borns to be devoured by their own kith and kin, particularly the female ones who had far less worth than their brothers. And that had taken some coming to terms with. 'What are you going to do with him?' she asked, reaching out to tentatively touch the tiny fingers.

'We'll have to give him a wash and some milk,' Carrie said with more practicality and resolve than she felt. 'We've got some of those tiny droppers we use for the weakest lambs, haven't we?'

'Oh aye, they'll be in that dresser there.'

'Right, then, we want them boiled up and filled with some sterilized milk. Our first task is to get something inside him until I can find an Aborigine wet nurse in the area to take over.'

Ellen paused on her way across the room and turned to shake her head. 'You'll not get any blackfella wet nurse to take care of that little lad,' she told her in an emphatic voice.

Carrie looked up, extracting her little finger from the curled-up fist of the infant. 'Why not? Because his mother's dead, you mean?' Surely that couldn't be any reason for allowing a child to die?

'Worse than that, ma'am. He's half white. This little fella is a half-caste. Didn't you notice?'

Carrie stared down at the curled-up body of the tiny child, whose life was in their hands. 'No . . .' she breathed, shaking her head in some bemusement. 'How stupid of me . . . I didn't notice that at all.'

Ellen went to look for the glass droppers and when she came back, Carrie was still standing protectively over the child. 'Who do you think the father can be?' she asked. 'Do you think it's one of my men – someone on Yorvik itself?'

The housekeeper raised her brows and gave her employer a pitying look across the table.

'Well, yes, I suppose it must be,' Carrie said. 'That's certainly the most likely answer . . . But who can it be?'

Then her mind flew back to more than a generation ago when she had been faced with a very similar situation to this. Young Jock Henderson was the offender then, but he had left years ago, first to join Angus on Cameron Creek, then to try his luck in the goldfields. But there were plenty of other young, red-blooded lads still around and it was an unacknowledged, but tacitly accepted fact of life that fornication between the single white workers and the younger gins occasionally took place. Many of the black-fellas even offered their women to white men in payment for some special favour, or as a simple act of friendship, but there had never been a real, long-lasting relationship between black and white on Yorvik to the best of her knowledge.

'Have you any idea who could be responsible for this, Ellen? You get to hear much more of the gossip about these things than I do.' There had been quite a change-over in stockmen and young shepherds of late so Carrie was becoming out of touch with the workforce for the first time in her long years as boss. 'I mean, it has to be one of my men, doesn't it? Can you think of a name offhand?'

Then, to her surprise, colour flared in Ellen's plump cheeks and she deliberately avoided her employer's eyes. Carrie was quite taken aback, for she had never seen her housekeeper blush before. 'Well?' she persisted in some bemusement. 'Have you any idea?'

'That's not for me to say, ma'am,' Ellen answered primly, going about her work. 'And I'd be obliged if you wouldn't embarrass me further by pressing the point.'

'But that's stupid! If it's one of my men, then surely I have a right to know?'

'That's as may be, but it's not up to me to tell you . . .'

Anyway, I'd just be repeating hearsay, and you know I've never been one to go in for that sort of thing.'

'Aye, that's true,' Carrie sighed. Her housekeeper was one of the most straightforward people she had ever come across. She could not penalize her now for a trait she had always admired her for in the past. 'How do you suggest I find out, then?' she asked, in an ironic voice. 'Do you suggest I go round interviewing them all individually?'

Ellen shrugged as she put on a pan of water to boil the droppers. 'That's up to you, ma'am, you're the boss, not me.'

'Yes, I'm afraid I am,' Carrie sighed, looking down at the hat with its precious contents. 'Just who *is* your Pa, little one? I suppose we'd better try to find out.'

Carrie did not discuss the disappearance of the Aborigines from their camp with Sean or the finding of the child. She was aware that he knew about it, but was equally conscious of the fact that when she attempted to raise the subject on the evening she found the baby, he seemed reluctant to talk about it, muttering something about 'bringing bad spirits to the place by yattering about things that don't concern us'.

'You don't mean to tell me you believe all that stuff about the *kuran* of the dead body still lurking about round here?' she had asked sceptically.

But he had been adamant. 'There are some things it's best to steer clear of, that's all.'

This was strange, for although Quarra herself was no longer alive, having died of blood-poisoning after a snake bite some years previously, she knew that he had been fond of her daughter Marika. It was as if her death was being deliberately ignored, but for what reason she could not be sure.

If he knew that Marika's child had survived and she was looking after him in the big house he certainly did not let on, and Carrie herself did not broadcast the fact. Even their most enlightened white neighbours could turn peculiar when it came to the mixing of the races and becoming too involved in blackfellas' affairs. So rather than risk offending either side, she kept her secret to herself, knowing it was only a short-term measure anyway. She and Ellen were diligent in their care of the infant, feeding it on demand, first with droppers, then with a feeding bottle, until within four weeks it had almost trebled its birth weight and, despite their resolve not to become emotionally involved, they were inordinately proud of their charge.

For those first weeks the infant had lain on a blanket, in a large wicker basket covered by a net to keep off the flies, on a small table by the side of the stove, whilst Carrie agonized over what to do with him. She and Ellen had endless conversations on the subject, and at last decided there was only one thing for it. No matter how fond they had become of him, they were both too old to be surrogate mothers to the mite; he would have to go into a foundlings' home. There was talk of one opening in Newcastle, but failing that he would be taken through to Sydney, just as soon as they were convinced he was strong enough to survive the journey.

Carrie decided that moment had just about arrived one quiet evening in mid-February. But she also knew she could not go on forever keeping her secret from her friend. Perhaps now that she had made the decision about the baby's fate it was the right time to show him to Sean.

Wrapping the infant in one of Billy's old shawls, she set off for the Irishman's hut just before sunset. When she got there he was sitting on a chopping log outside the door playing on his penny whistle. Even after all these years it was a sound that never failed to send a thrill down her spine as it drifted towards her on the evening air.

He looked up and stopped playing as she approached with the child in her arms. Wiping the end of the whistle he rose up and stuck it in his hip pocket. 'What's that you've got there?' he asked, eyeing the bundle in her arms with some suspicion.

'Why don't you take a look?' She held the bundle out towards him and, frowning, he peered into the lacy woollen cover. She could see his jaw tighten beneath the copper of his beard as he stared at the child.

'It's a half-caste.' There was a look akin to accusation in his eyes as he took a step back as if to distance himself from the child. 'Where did you get it?'

'I got it from a grave last month,' Carrie said, trying to keep the emotion from her voice.

There was a long silence, and his dark eyes became darker still as he looked at her in the golden glow of the setting sun. 'It's not Marika's kid?'

'It is.'

His jaw visibly tightened and he took a deep breath and let it out noisily as he scratched his head.

'Don't tell me you didn't know I've been looking after him for the past few weeks,' she said.

He shook his head as he continued to scratch the wiry thatch. His face looked strained and a thin film of perspiration had appeared at his temples. 'I swear to God I didn't,' he said with feeling. 'I did hear something a couple of weeks back about you looking after some kid but I figured one of the workers' wives had probably been under the weather and you were doing your good fairy act, and it certainly couldn't be any long-time thing or you'd have mentioned it.'

'You didn't hear about him, then?'

'I didn't even know it survived the birth – let alone what sex it was.' Then his eyes narrowed. 'What do you intend doing with him?'

Carrie sighed as the infant began to fret and she moved him on to her shoulder. 'I haven't got much choice really,' she replied, rubbing his back. 'I haven't any idea who the father might be and the mother's dead; he'll have to go into the orphans' home in Sydney.'

'No!' The word was exclaimed so loudly that she jumped.

'You have a better idea?'

Sean was staring at the child in her arms. 'He can't leave here,' he said. 'It wouldn't be right. This is his home.'

'But his mother's dead,' Carrie persisted. 'And with no father to look out for him.' She gave a helpless shrug of the shoulders as she continued to rub the baby's back. 'No white couple will take him in, that's for sure. And who does that leave – no one.'

The Irishman's face was pensive. 'I know someone,' he said finally. 'Yes, that just might work . . .'

'Who?'

'Old Bandicoot's gin, Jeeba.'

'Jeeba!' Carrie shook her head in disbelief. She was the old woman who had first alerted her to the situation. Age was almost impossible to tell with the Aborigines, but she must be all of seventy and her man old Bandicoot was just about the oldest blackfella on Yorvik land. He and his wife took little part in the life of the camp and, either out of old age or indifference, they had not joined the mass exodus after Marika's death.

'But Jeeba's far too old!' Carrie protested. The only reason she allowed her to hang around the kitchen so much was out of a sense of charity. She was certainly not up to any real work.

'Age doesn't come into it. She's as capable of looking after the kid as anyone else round here.'

Carrie looked at Sean strangely. She had never seen him so adamant about anything. She could feel a cold feeling creeping into the pit of her stomach. There was a strange sensation of history repeating itself, but in a quite different way. 'You – you wouldn't happen to know who the father is, by any chance?' she asked in a quiet voice.

There was a long silence. Then, 'I might. Do you really want to know?'

They were looking into each other's eyes, and the unspeakable was being spoken in the silence of their gaze.

'No,' Carrie said at last. 'No, I don't think I do.'

Clasping the child to her, she turned and headed back

for the big house, half running, half walking, her left leg suddenly a lead weight now, as it always seemed to be when she was agitated. She was totally oblivious to the greeting of Will Morton, who was on his way homeward after his day's work.

'What's wrong with the boss?' he called to Sean, still standing at the door of his hut.

The Irishman shrugged and sat back down on the wooden block with a sigh. He took out his penny whistle and began to play. The tune that came out was 'Father Murphy of County Wexford'. He did not choose it, nor did he choose the tears that sparkled in his eyes by the time the melody died on the soft evening air.

CHAPTER THIRTY-THREE

'Begging your pardon, ma'am, but you'd better come down and sort this out.'

'Sort what out, Ellen?' Carrie asked, looking up from her desk where she had been going over the accounts for the best part of the morning. 'Can't it wait?'

'No, I'm afraid it can't, ma'am.'

Carrie took off her reading spectacles and sighed as she pushed back her chair. She could do without this sort of interruption when she was trying to balance the books.

She followed the stout figure of the housekeeper downstairs to the kitchen, as muttered utterances about 'some folks around here getting too big for their boots' reached her ears from an obviously disgruntled Ellen.

To her surprise, when they arrived at their destination, Sean was standing by the kitchen table, hat in hand, and with a determined look on his face. He half raised the hat at Carrie's appearance, but there was no trace of his customary smile.

'Sean!' Carrie exclaimed. 'I didn't expect to find you here.' He seldom, if ever, crossed the threshold of the big house. She turned to Ellen. 'Just what is this all about?'

Ellen's double chin quivered with barely suppressed rage. 'Mr O'Dwyer came breezing in here not five minutes ago and demanded I hand over the child,' she stated with undisguised indignation. She glanced at the makeshift crib in the corner by the stove, as if to reassure herself the object of the dispute was still there. 'He claimed he had permission to take him. But I told him I'd heard no such thing and certainly wasn't going to hand over the baby until I'd seen you and we'd sorted this thing out.'

Carrie looked at Sean, who said nothing, but his fingers

were drumming on the felt brim of his hat. 'Is this true?' she demanded. 'Did you try to take the child?'

'You make it sound like a bloody accusation!' he declared. 'But yes, I don't deny I came for the boy. I told you I would. I said I'd find a home for him – that you couldn't let him go into an orphanage.'

'A home for him!' Carrie scoffed. 'With old Bandicoot and Jeeba, you mean? You really think that decrepit old pair would make fit parents for the child? You really think they'd be able to look after him at their age?'

'Yes, yes I do,' Sean replied firmly. Then his voice became more halting. 'And . . . Well, it wouldn't just be them. I'd be there to do my share.'

The two of them looked at each other across the kitchen table. 'You – you'd be there to do your share,' Carrie said quietly.

'Yes, that's right . . . I'd be around to teach him things – do things with him that they're not up to any more. That kid's not going into any orphanage, not if I have anything to do with it.'

Ellen, who was standing silently by the stove, arms folded across her ample bosom, looked from one to the other. There was a battle of wills going on here.

'But you don't have anything to do with it, do you?' Carrie said in a quiet voice as she walked across to the cot and looked down at the sleeping infant. 'He's going into a foundlings' home, because that's exactly what he is – a foundling. And *I* found him, remember. If I hadn't gone looking that afternoon, he'd be dead by now.'

'And that's exactly what he'll be if you put him into that orphanage,' the Irishman told her in a heated voice. 'The kid'll not survive five minutes in there. He'd have a much better chance staying here on Yorvik.'

Carrie looked down at the tiny tawny-coloured face and the two small clenched fists poking out from the light cotton sheet that was covering him. In the few weeks since his birth a fuzz of dark reddish-brown hair had begun to appear on his head; the sight of it never failed to twist a knife in her heart. Could she spend the rest of her life looking at this child as it grew from infancy to childhood, from childhood to adolescence, then from young manhood to adulthood in front of her very eyes? 'And if I do?' she said at last. 'If I do go ahead and take him to Sydney?' Her chin tilted upwards as she looked at the man standing across the table from her. 'What then?'

There was steel in Sean O'Dwyer's voice as his eyes met hers. 'Then I'll go and get him back.'

They stood looking at one another. There was absolute silence for several seconds, then Carrie turned to the housekeeper. 'See that everything the child needs is packed, then hand him over to Mr O'Dwyer, Ellen,' she said stiffly. Then she hurried from the room.

She did not stop until she reached her bedroom. She made straight for the balcony and threw open the door to stand in the sunshine, gazing out over the scene she loved more than any other. In the far distance the green of the land was shot through with the blue ribbon of the Yorvik river, and she could just see the tall trees that guarded the spot where it threw itself off the rocks to tumble down the thirty feet of Yorvik Force. Memories crowded her mind, as tears sparkled in her eyes. She made no attempt to wipe them away as they trickled down her cheeks. Then she thought of her own son, and of the love and pain in equal measure he had brought into her life. She had not asked to become a parent, many did not, who nevertheless found themselves with children to care for. But, after a child's birth, that did not stop the feelings that almost overwhelmed one at the knowledge that you were responsible for the very existence – the fate – of another human being.

She was still standing there on the balcony five minutes later when the Irishman reappeared down below, walking round to the front of the house, with the infant in his arms and a bag containing its essentials swung over his shoulder. He walked off in the direction of the old homestead where

Bandicoot and his wife had taken up residence some years since in the disused washhouse.

Carrie watched until he was almost out of sight. He looked a solitary figure as he strode on into the sunshine; but then he had been a loner all his life. Like the child in his arms he had been born an outsider. There were many round here who disliked him, finding the rough exterior and lack of camaraderie hard to take. But she knew different. The hard man had as soft a heart as could be found anywhere. The thought that that small scrap of humanity in his arms would end up miles away in a foundlings' home had been too much to take. Old Joe O'Dwyer, his father, had been faced with much the same problem two generations ago and he had not turned his back. Could his son do less?

'Forgive me, Irish,' she whispered, as his image faded into the dazzle of the morning sun. Then she blinked her eyes and turned back into her bedroom. She had been less than generous in her attitude down there in the kitchen. But then she had never claimed to be perfect. 'But I'm trying,' she sighed, as she sat down heavily on the edge of her bed and stared at her reflection in the mirror opposite. 'I really am.'

Carrie deliberately avoided any contact with her old friend over the next ten days, partly out of embarrassment at her own reaction and partly because she was so keyed up about the imminent arrival of Billy and his new wife. She was determined that everything was going to be as perfect as possible for their welcome to Yorvik, and as far removed from what had happened last time as was humanly possible.

Their ship was due into Sydney on the twenty-seventh of February and she made sure she arrived in the city in good time, booking into the Grand Hotel and reserving the best suite in the place for the newly-weds.

Her dress she chose with special care, opting for a simple, but elegant creation in pale grey voile, with a fashionable bustle and matching hat and veil. On her hands she wore a pair of pale grey kid gloves, with ornamental buttons which she found herself fiddling with nervously as the passengers disembarked, exactly to schedule, on the Circular Quay.

She spotted Billy and his wife almost immediately. They were amongst the first down the gangplank and she caught her breath and gave a gasp of joy at the sight of the good-looking young man, with the elegant young woman on his arm.

He had changed not at all, save for a few extra pounds around the waist perhaps. The moustache was thicker too, and waxed and twirled at the edges; it gave him a rather roguish appearance, but, with his well-cut, bespoke-tailored three-piece suit, the overall effect was certainly dashing and Carrie could quite understand what had attracted the young English woman to him. And Nella herself was quite a head-turner, with her tallish, slim figure and corn-gold hair, which she wore piled up on her head with a curled fringe over the brow, in the style favoured by Alexandra, the Princess of Wales.

Billy gave a rather bashful smile and embraced his mother awkwardly on the quayside, then he turned to his wife. 'Ma, I'd like you to meet Nella . . . Am I not the most lucky man imaginable?'

Carrie clasped the young woman's hands warmly in hers. 'Welcome to Australia, Nella dear. It's so lovely to meet you at last!'

The younger woman smiled and, being well versed in the situation from Billy, took great pains not to let her gaze linger on the still tender-looking skin of her new mother-in-law's cheeks as she returned the compliment. 'It's wonderful to be here,' she replied in a startlingly cut-glass English voice that quite took Carrie aback. 'It makes me feel I really am a Gordon-Hebden now I'm on colonial soil!'

To Carrie's delight, her new daughter-in-law's initial

enthusiasm for all things colonial seemed to continue unabated throughout their stay at the hotel and on their journey back to Yorvik. Nella had been charmed by Sydney, which was now quite a cosmopolitan city, and seeing the young woman's pleasure and excitement at her first contact with the native wildlife of the countryside as they travelled north brought back bitter-sweet memories to Carrie of her own first journey to the Hunter Valley, all those years ago with Silas. Never could she have imagined in those far-off days just how dramatically her life would change after she stepped on Australian soil. Even the very home she now lived in would have been undreamt of in Silas's time, and two days later her heart swelled with pride at the squeal of delight Nella gave at her first sight of the big house.

'Why, it's beautiful!' she exclaimed, gazing at the Palladian columns and gracious balconies, which immediately reminded her of the pictures she had seen of the fine colonial mansions of America's Deep South. This was far more civilized than she had been led to expect and came as the most wonderful surprise. She turned indignantly to her husband. 'Oh, Billy, you never told me it was so beautiful!'

The young man by her side gave a wry smile as he puffed on his cigarette. 'Really?' Beautiful was the last word he would have chosen. In fact, with its ornamental pillars and balconies, he regarded it as rather vulgar. Yes, there was a real look of new money about it. *Nouveau riche*, that's what it was all right. But he was pleased with his wife's enthusiasm nevertheless, although he could not resist adding, 'It's decent enough, I suppose, but Great Glen was even better. Wasn't it, Ma?'

Carrie winced inwardly, but it did not show as she agreed that Great Glen was indeed a fine house.

Nella's enthusiasm was further increased by an invitation from Angus Cameron to a dinner given in their honour, in which he made a point of introducing the newly-weds to several of his political friends from Sydney, whom he felt could be of great use to Billy, should he eventually choose to follow in his own footsteps by combining a challenging political life with running a successful sheep and cattle station.

'He really seems to believe that Billy can go straight to the top of the political ladder out here, should he choose to,' Nella confided to Carrie the following morning. 'He said that while many were talking of cutting their roots with the mother country, such things as a good British education still counted for something with those who matter. Oh, Mother, it's all so exciting!' Nella clapped her hands together in delight as she continued, 'And from what I've heard, the social life in Sydney is quite wonderful. It's not at all like I imagined before we arrived out here!'

'Oh, and what did you imagine?' Carrie asked, looking up from her newspaper as they sat together in the morning room drinking their first cup of coffee of the day.

Nella's finely arched brows rose a good half inch as she toyed with the handle of her cup. 'Oh, a somewhat rougher place, I think . . . Yes, not quite so civilized really. Even Daddy had warned me the country has been founded on convict labour and is populated by people with actual convict blood in their veins.' She gave a shudder at the very thought. 'You haven't actually come across any, have you?'

Carrie deliberately kept her attention fixed on the paper. 'One or two.'

'Really?' Nella's blue eyes widened and she gave a theatrical shudder. 'How exciting! But I sincerely hope I don't encounter any. My Uncle Henry, Daddy's elder brother, was a judge who sentenced quite a few to transportation, you know.' And her eyes brightened. 'Oh, the stories he tells! You couldn't imagine! He's always in demand to give after-dinner talks and the like, even now he's retired. He's had the whole family in stitches at Christmas with his tales, especially of the tall stories that were told by the convicts to get out of transportation . . . It never worked, though. And exile was no more than they deserved. Ridding the country of its vermin, he called it.' Then she giggled. 'Of course he's never actually been here himself, but I can't say he was too happy at the thought of me coming to a vermin-ridden land! What a pity he's never seen Yorvik! I'm sure he would be quite happy now if he could come here and meet all the wonderful people I've already met.'

Carrie listened as she sipped her coffee and smiled across the table. 'I'm very glad to hear it, my dear. It's always nice to know we're living up to expectations.'

But the irony behind the smile was totally lost on Nella, who was suddenly looking very pensive. Then a slim hand rose to her mouth and her cheeks drained of colour. For a second or two she sat quite still, then she got up with a hurried, 'Excuse me, please!'

Puzzled, Carrie watched as her daughter-in-law rushed from the room, to return five minutes later, ashen-faced and with a film of perspiration shining on her forehead. 'Are you all right, my dear?'

Nella nodded. 'I shouldn't have had that coffee,' she said, glancing accusingly at the silver coffee-pot still sitting on the table. 'It doesn't seem to agree with me these days.'

Carrie looked at her quizzically. She had noticed her daughter-in-law had been looking distinctly seedy on several occasions since her arrival. And, most worryingly, usually first thing in the morning. Her gaze took in the fine-boned face and delicate features, with just the slightest hint of haughtiness to the demeanour, as Nella settled herself on a chaise longue by the window and, with a sigh, rested her blonde head on the backrest.

'Nella . . .'

'Mmmm?'

'Please tell me to mind my own business if you wish, my dear, but I can't help wondering . . .' She paused, considering the best way to put it, then decided there was no use beating about the bush. 'You wouldn't be — well, in the family way by any chance?'

Nella's eyes sprang open and she sat bolt upright on the chaise. 'What ever makes you say that?'

Carrie gave a placatory smile. 'Now, don't go getting agitated. I just wondered, that's all . . . You've been looking rather under the weather occasionally.'

Nella made a face, her rosebud mouth pursing, then she let out another heartfelt sigh. Her gaze moved to her stomach and she gave a desultory pat just below her waistline with her right hand. 'It does rather appear that way, I'm afraid,' she said. 'Not that I know a great deal about such things.' Then, as she looked across at Carrie, tears sprang to her eyes. 'It's so unfair,' she cried. 'We've hardly had time to enjoy ourselves — and now this!'

Carrie wasted no time. The doctor was called immediately from Hunter's Hollow. Dr Archie Fraser was an Edinburgh-trained physician who had seen it all many times before. It was not at all unknown for young women to go right to the moment of birth without realizing that motherhood was nigh. The fact that Carrie's daughter-in-law had at least another four months to go was definitely in her favour. 'But don't you go over-taxing yourself, mind!' he warned Nella. 'You may be tall enough, but there's not much of you as far as weight's concerned, and it's not too late for things to go wrong!'

He turned to Carrie, who was standing by. 'You see that she gets enough rest and doesn't go doing anything daft.' He glanced back at the young woman on the sofa. 'No dancing till dawn or any such high jinks from now on!' he told her, for he too had been at that evening at Angus Cameron's house and had noted how the young couple had made the most of the accordion and fiddle band that had been supplied for the entertainment.

Nella made a face when the doctor had gone and flopped back on the sofa. 'This is truly dreadful!' she wailed. 'I'm

438

to become a virtual recluse and all because of this wretched condition!'

For his part Billy was every bit as dismayed as his wife at the confirmation of the news of approaching parenthood, not least because it meant that Nella would be confined to Yorvik until after the birth in mid-July. All his plans to return to England by then were falling to pieces before his very eyes. 'This is terrible,' he told his mother, when out of earshot of his young wife. 'Can't anything be done about it?'

Carrie gaped at her son, aghast. 'Of course not!' she exclaimed. 'What a thing to suggest!'

But Billy was unrepentant. 'You needn't sound so shocked, Ma,' he insisted. 'It happens all the time, you know. Hot baths, bottles of gin, that sort of thing. And you can't blame people either. Dashed inconvenient, babies can be, when they come along at all the wrong times.'

'Well, inconvenient it may be,' Carrie told him. 'But it's happened, and there's an end to it. I'll have no more talk of hot baths and gin in my house, thank you very much! You'll give that girl all the support she's going to need over the next few months and you'll rejoice in the fact that before the year is out you'll have brought a brand new Australian into the world!'

She did not even bother to wait for the expletive that was released under his breath as she swept from the room to check on the new consignment of cattle.

As she approached the shed usually set aside for new arrivals, there was no sign of Will nor of any of the young lads who assisted him, although two unfamiliar steers were feeding from a trough just inside the door. She turned and was just on the point of leaving when two legs appeared from the trapdoor to the hayloft above. Seconds later Sean O'Dwyer dropped at her feet and both looked in surprise at the other. The two had not exchanged words since that day he took the foundling away, although she had seen him from afar working around the place often enough.

They stood staring at one another in silence for a moment, then the Irishman spoke. 'That's a fine-looking young woman Billy's got himself. I trust they're enjoying their visit?'

Carrie nodded, already uncomfortable at the small-talk. They were standing here like employer and employee. It was not a good feeling. 'Nella's a very nice girl,' she said, avoiding his eyes. 'Billy's a lucky young man.'

'Are they staying on here for long?'

'Until after the birth.' She did not mean it to come out, for she had promised both of them she would say nothing to anyone for some time yet, and she could have kicked herself as his brows rose in surprise.

'So you're to be a grandmother, are you?' He made a whistling sound through his teeth, then his face broke into that familiar grin. 'Well, congratulations! That's quite something!' His smile softened as he mused, 'Looks like you'll really have earned that name the blackfellas call you.'

Carrie gave a strained smile. 'Kabbarli', their word for grandmother, had been a backhanded compliment she had had to put up with for years. 'Speaking of blackfellas,' she said pointedly, 'How is the baby these days?'

Sean O'Dwyer's brown eyes hardened. To the best of his knowledge Carrie had been nowhere near the child since he had handed him into Bandicoot and Jeeba's charge weeks ago. 'Is that a pleasantry, or do you really want to know?'

'Of course I want to know!' Carrie declared, the colour creeping into her face, for she was only too aware that her behaviour in that department left a lot to be desired. No matter how caught up she had been in Billy and Nella's arrival, she should have gone round to check on its welfare. Her guilt made her all the more defensive. 'I have every right to know, after all. Don't forget the child wouldn't even be here if I hadn't saved it!'

'Oh, of course, how stupid of me! How could I forget!

And I expect the poor little bugger's got to remain grateful to the end of his days, is that it? The Great White Mother saved him to live a fate worse than death!'

The outburst took Carrie by surprise. She had rarely seen Sean like this; there was real anger there as he continued bitterly: 'Poor little bastard growing up neither fish nor fowl on the fringes of both worlds. This is a wonderful life that you saved him for, isn't it, Carrie? When your grandchild gets that silver spoon shoved into its mouth, that little fella's gonna be grubbing around in the dirt for crumbs from the rich lady's table.'

His words hit home, more painful than any physical blow. As she reached out a hand into the space between them, he ignored it and turned to go. 'Just don't expect him to be grateful, that's all, Mrs Gordon-Hebden,' he threw back over his shoulder. 'Just don't ever expect gratitude – from either of us!'

CHAPTER THIRTY-FOUR

Despite Nella's pregnancy and the warnings from Dr Fraser, to Carrie's alarm her son and daughter-in-law threw themselves into a hectic round of social engagements for the remainder of the autumn, accepting invitations to functions as far apart as Sydney, Newcastle and Forbes. Within a matter of six weeks their social circle had widened to include most of the young up-and-coming politicians of the day, drawn from what Nella referred to as the 'best' families in the colony.

They were invited too, along with Carrie, to the special party given by Angus Cameron to celebrate his acceptance of the CMG from the Queen. The Companion of the Order of St Michael and St George was an honour much coveted in the circles in which he moved, and the old Scotsman was justly proud. But he was also an old enough hand to realize that many of his younger political friends felt he was selling out by accepting such a thing from the British. 'St Michael and St George are both dead and buried,' one told him. 'And to be companion to two corpses is about the same as being brother to a load of stale fish, or uncle to an ancient egg!' Angus recounted this tale with great glee to Carrie, Billy and Nella over his glass of whisky, much to Billy's disgust. Nella, however, was greatly amused and listened with some sympathy to all those who had come to resent her own country's 'meddling' in Australian affairs.

But while his wife was continuing her love affair with Australia, for his part Billy was growing increasingly impatient with the company in which he constantly found himself. Their concerns frankly bored him. He really could not care less about the great social and political reforms that were being passed through the Legislature, or of the worries being expressed about the growing trade union movement, or the immigrant Chinese problem. Nor could he get excited about the talk of the different colonies uniting into one Australian entity. The very word Australia and the term Australian meant nothing to him; he even took a perverse delight in declaring his allegiance to the English cricket team whenever the occasion arose. He actually seemed to revel in recounting to his new Australian friends how he had been present at the Oval for Australia's momentous victory over the old country in 1882, but had been waving the flag of St George.

On such occasions even Nella found it too much to take and she would apologize profusely for her traitorous husband.

'You really should be more proud of your country,' she told him firmly, when they were discussing the matter over breakfast one morning in late May. 'This is a marvellous place to live, and the people are so friendly . . . But they're not going to remain friendly for much longer if you keep going on about how superior England is!'

'The people!' Billy scoffed, pushing aside his tea cup. 'You haven't met "the people". You've only met the top layer of society. Scratch beneath that and they're all a load of old lags and she-lags − or at least they're descended from them!' He made a face as he sat back in his chair and lit a cigarette. 'You can vouch for that, can't you, Ma?' He shot a look at his mother sitting at the other end of the table from him. 'They must have been much more obvious when you first came out here.'

'You really shouldn't refer to people like that, Billy,' Carrie told him. 'Lags and she-lags − it's quite offensive. They're human beings, all of them, despite their origins.'

Billy gave a quiet smile, then blew a perfect smoke-ring, which he watched with satisfaction as it drifted slowly to the ceiling. 'That may be your opinion, but it certainly isn't the attitude most decent people take round here. Why do you think people like Nella and me are so fêted and sought after? Why is everybody so keen to see us stay? It's because they need leaders with pure blood, uncontaminated by convict stock. They don't want a society based on a convict heritage.' He wagged his cigarette in her direction. 'Do you honestly believe, for example, that if you were a sheila we'd be getting half these invitations? Not on your life! We wouldn't even get one!'

Carrie winced inwardly. His fashionable diminutive for the name she-lag made the horror of the word no less painful. 'I – I can't really say,' she answered haltingly, to be interrupted by Nella.

'Billy's right, Mother. And that's the only aspect of this place that disturbs me, really – its convict heritage – and the fact that there are so many blackfellas, as they call them, around.' She threw an impish grin to her husband across the breakfast table as, her morning sickness well behind her, she reached for a piece of toast. 'Now that really would be something to keep quiet about, wouldn't it? Even worse than your mother or grandmother being a sheila would be if you had black blood in your veins!'

Billy's eyes were on Carrie as his wife finished her statement. He could see the tenseness creep into the fine lines of her face. He was silent for a moment, then said in a pointed voice, 'Ma's got a darkie friend. Haven't you, Ma?'

Carrie's fingers tightened around the handle of her cup, which was halfway to her lips. She replaced it in the saucer without drinking. 'If you mean Mr O'Dwyer, then yes. Yes, I do.'

'Mr O'Dwyer!' Nella hooted, covering her mouth to stifle the giggle. 'You mean he's half darkie and half Irish?'

'And old-lag Irish his father was for good measure,' Billy added.

'Good heavens!' Nella's blue eyes widened at the thought of this poor benighted creature. 'Such a fellow is really a friend of yours, Mother?'

Carrie looked from one to the other, then dabbing her mouth with her napkin, she rose from the table. 'My best friend,' she answered simply. 'Now, if you'll excuse me, I have work to do.'

Billy watched her go, then turned to his wife. 'That's a sore point with Ma,' he told her. 'That O'Dwyer fellow, he's a really uncouth character but she won't hear a word against him.'

'Have I met him yet?' Nella asked, intrigued.

'I shouldn't think so. But you may have seen him around. He's the walking scarecrow with the bright red beard that lives in one of those pigsties round the back of the old homestead.'

Nella said no more on the subject, but resolved it might be quite interesting to meet this undoubtedly awful character that her husband thought so little of, yet her mother-in-law called her best friend.

Later that day she told Billy she was going to take a short stroll, but there was only one thing on her mind. She would do her best to seek out this curious half-breed Irish blackfella.

It took her twenty minutes to find him. He was in one of the sheep-pens, administering some sort of medicine to a sickly ewe by means of a drenching horn down its throat.

'Hold still, you bleeder!'

Nella heard him before she actually saw him and her ears were assailed by even more choice language before he realized he was being watched.

The animal was proving more obstreperous than anticipated and, as she stood nervously behind the fence, the Irishman wrestled it into a restraining yoke, made from a sturdy fork cut from a tree and driven into the floor of the pen. Sitting astride its back, the muscles of his forearms stood out like knotted rope beneath the bronzed skin as with some difficulty he pushed the ewe's head into the V of the fork, then shoved a wooden pin through two holes at the top.

'Hold this!' he barked at her, thrusting the drenching horn – a hollowed-out cow's horn containing the medicine

– into her hands as he struggled to open the animal's mouth.

Quite taken aback, she obeyed, holding the evil-smelling substance at arm's length, from behind the safety of the pen bars.

'Give it here!'

Again Nella obeyed immediately, only too glad to get rid of it as he reached across and grabbed it from her outstretched hand. She watched in a mixture of fascination and revulsion as the medicine was then poured into the prised-open jaws of the reluctant animal.

The whole operation took about five minutes and beads of sweat were trickling down the sides of the Irishman's face when he had finished. He wiped them away with the back of his hand and looked curiously at his observer, who was wiping her own hands with a lace-trimmed handkerchief. 'You must be Billy's wife,' he said in a matter-of-fact voice.

Nella lifted a quizzical eyebrow as she sniffed her fingers and grimaced, before tucking the handkerchief back into her sleeve. 'Yes, I'm Mrs Gordon-Hebden,' she said pointedly. 'And I take it you must be O'Dwyer.'

Sean grunted as he pulled the stake from the ground and tossed it into a corner of the pen. 'How are you liking the place, then? A bit different from England, I reckon?'

'A bit,' Nella replied noncommittally as he came out of the pen and closed the gate. Billy was right, she thought. He was a rough-looking character and no mistake. Quite fearsome, actually, with that wild, grizzled grey hair and shaggy red beard. 'I hear you're a friend of my mother-in-law.'

The Irishman's eyes narrowed as he pulled his hat back on his head. 'You could say that.'

'Have you known her long?'

'Long enough.'

Nella gave an embarrassed smile. 'I don't mean to sound so inquisitive,' she said quickly. 'It's just that she doesn't talk much about her past and neither does my husband.'

'Not many of us do round here,' Sean informed her. 'You see, it's not the past that matters, young lady. It's now and the future that counts. People come here to bury their past, not drag it around with them like some great millstone round their necks ... Now, if you'll excuse me ...'

'I know, I know – you've got work to do!' Nella watched as he gathered up his gear and set off in the direction of the shearing shed. Cutting her off like that was insufferably rude of him. She had only wanted to find out something more about this family she had married into and he seemed the best person to tell her. All she really knew from Billy about the Gordon-Hebdens was that his father had died when he was quite young and his mother had sold their station in the Macleay Valley to buy Yorvik because she had lived here in her youth.

But her mother-in-law still had the traces of a quite distinct East End of London accent. The two things did not quite tally. In fact, although she had not let on to her husband, Nella had been quite shocked to hear his mother's voice. Perhaps having been born out here he was not aware how much accents mattered. Heaven only knew what her own parents would make of it if they ever heard her mother-in-law open her mouth. Her own mother would probably pass out on the spot.

She could not quite make up her mind if she liked Carrie Gordon-Hebden or not. There was something distinctly private – distant almost – about her mother-in-law. Even that awful accident with the fire she had had she would not discuss, other than to say that it was just that – a pure accident – and no one was to blame. Billy too was tight-lipped on the subject. There seemed to be so much that people would not talk about around here ... On the one hand, her welcome could not have been warmer, with every comfort being provided, but on the personal front there remained a barrier which she had no permission to cross.

. Finding out more about her mother-in-law became one of Nella's private passions over the next few weeks. She could not share her resolve to dig deeper into his mother's past with Billy for her husband would not have approved at all, but as he seemed quite content to spend his afternoons with his feet up in the library, in the company of a bottle of gin, she had plenty of time to herself to pursue her quest. She had little success, however, in digging around in chests of drawers and the like for anything that might provide some clues to the Gordon-Hebden family tree, so it looked as if she would have to turn to people.

One of the first she approached was Angus Cameron on their next invitation to supper at Cameron Creek. The opportunity came when after dinner Billy became involved in a card game, and the old man asked if she would care for a stroll in the moonlight to see an ornamental waterfall he had just had installed in the Japanese garden he had had planted at the side of the house.

Even at his advanced age, the elderly Scotsman was more than a little taken by the delicate gazelle-like creature young Billy had fallen for, who still managed to retain such an appealing presence despite her growing waistline. He gave her his arm as they walked through the beautifully landscaped gardens to the spot where specially diverted water from a nearby stream had been made to tumble off a rocky outcrop bordered by imported Japanese cherry trees. The whole effect was quite stunning and Angus was obviously very proud of his latest success story. All things Japanese were high fashion both in the old country and Australia at the moment and it meant a great deal to him to hear approval voiced by the young English woman.

But Japanese water gardens were the last thing on Nella's mind as they stood beneath the cascading waters, and as soon as she had murmured the obligatory words of admiration, she came straight to the point. 'You've been here a long time, haven't you, Mr Cameron?'

The old Scotsman gave a wry smile. 'There's nobody been here longer, I can assure you of that, my dear ... Aye, only old Silas could claim to have been farming here in the Valley as early as I was.'

'Old Silas?'

'Silas Hebden, Carrie's first husband.'

Nella's heart missed a beat. He obviously thought her better informed than she was. 'Carrie and Silas – you knew them both back then, did you?'

Angus Cameron's mouth creased into a smile beneath the white whiskers. 'Och aye, but old Silas and me – we were here a good twenty-odd years before he decided to take himself a bride and Carrie came on the scene.' Then he gave a throaty chuckle as he confided, 'The old blighter was over fifty, if I remember rightly, before he placed that advertisement for a wife in the London *Times*. And I remember well the time he picked Carrie up from the ship in Sydney harbour to take her back to Yorvik, for the pair of them stopped off here on the way home ... A right bonnie young thing she was too, I'll say that for her.'

Nella listened dumbstruck. Was he telling her that her mother-in-law had been a mail-order bride? She could feel her stomach churning at the very thought of it. Did Billy know? Her brow furrowed as Angus changed the subject to point out the fountain he was so proud of.

But the more she thought about it, the more convinced she became that her husband did indeed know, and that might help explain his underlying dislike of this country. Perhaps, deep down, he felt ashamed. And quite rightly so, for to become a mail-order bride was tantamount to prostituting yourself, wasn't it? To have that sort of skeleton in your family cupboard was almost as bad as having convict blood in your veins!

Over the next two months finding out more about her mother-in-law's past became an obsession. She was even beginning to doubt if Carrie had ever been married to her husband's father, for when she had dared to enquire when her mother-in-law's wedding anniversary had been, the older woman had changed the subject abruptly, then got up and left the room. When she enquired the same thing of Billy, her husband had become quite annoyed. 'What do you need to know all that stuff for?' he demanded. 'Why all this need to know about the past, for heaven's sake?'

'Because it matters, that's why!' Nella told him heatedly. 'Our own family tree goes right back to the Domesday Book, and you only have to look up *Burke's Peerage* to see all the branches of the Foston-Strutt-Smiths' pedigrees going back for generation after generation. When our child is born it will most certainly matter that the Gordon-Hebden line is as well documented. Papa would be quite horrified otherwise.'

Billy listened as he always did when his wife got het up about anything, and he had to admit she had a point. He nodded thoughtfully, then said soothingly, 'If it really means that much to you, darling, I'll ask Ma myself to make sure it's all down on paper well before then.'

His family tree was something that had never really bothered him before, but since marrying Nella he was becoming only too well aware how much store was set by such things. She had told him herself that her family would never have approved of the match had she attempted to marry into 'trade'. The fact that she could tell them that Billy's father had been a big landowner in New South Wales counted for a lot. Landed money was old money, and that was all important, even in the colonies.

For her part, Carrie was blissfully unaware of just how much her past was under discussion between her son and his wife. Her main concern was the meagre amount of time Nella was giving to obeying doctor's orders to rest and consider the baby. She was still accepting invitations and going out with Billy at least one evening a week, and, much more worrying, when Billy retired to the library in the afternoons, she would see Nella out on the range on horseback, of all things.

Carrie had already remonstrated with her several times about the wisdom of continuing to ride this late in her pregnancy, but she had got nowhere. Nella had been a keen huntswoman before marrying Billy and was determined not to let a little thing like expecting a baby stop her from pursuing her favourite sport.

Despite her fragile blonde looks, Carrie knew her daughter-in-law was a very determined character, and, in truth, was already showing far more backbone than her husband when it came to taking an interest in Yorvik and things Australian. She seemed to pick up information quickly and could often be found talking to the men around the place, enquiring about different breeds of cattle or sheep and the latest methods of animal husbandry.

Nella, in fact, was in her element. With the coming of the Australian winter, the temperature was now much more like that of home and she got real pleasure from doing all the sorts of things that, quite unbeknown to her, had meant so much to her mother-in-law when she had first arrived on Yorvik as a young woman.

Although Nella's favourite ride was to the lake, and Yorvik Force beyond, she often avoided that area, for no matter how much she tried she could not overcome her instinctive fear of the blackfellas who inhabited that part of the land. Instead, for her afternoon ride, she took to cantering her favourite mare to the south of the property, to the spot where the track that led up to the station joined the main road to Sydney. And it was there one bitterly cold afternoon in early July that she came face to face on the road with another rider.

Nella pulled up her horse as the old woman approached on the back of an animal that looked only fit for the knackers' yard. By the looks of her, the bedraggled-looking creature certainly did not belong on Gordon-Hebden land, and she must have strayed by mistake from the main road. 'Are you aware you're on Yorvik property?' she called out.

The old woman nodded as she brought her horse to a stop. 'Oh aye, it's aware of that I am,' she replied, eyeing Nella curiously, 'for haven't I been riding all the hours the Good Lord sends to get here?'

The creature was obviously Irish and, by the looks of it, tinker stock into the bargain. 'Well, you'll be aware this is Gordon-Hebden land, then,' Nella said crisply, 'and as I'm Mrs Gordon-Hebden, perhaps you'd like to inform me why you're here?'

'So you're Mrs Gordon-Hebden, are you?' the woman said in some surprise, as two deep furrows appeared in her brow. 'And what, pray, has happened to my old friend Carrie?'

Nella stared at her. 'You – you're a friend of my mother-in-law?'

'I am that,' Molly McFarland assured her. 'A very old friend indeed, for we came over on the boat together.'

Nella's heart quickened. 'You were a mail-order bride as well?'

'God love you, no!' Molly laughed. 'I never had the luxury of one of them passenger cabins. I remained one of the poor blighters suffocating down below in the convict deck, and Carrie had the berth next to mine before she made her escape.' Since Nella knew all about the mail-order thing, Molly presumed that Carrie's family were well aware of her past, even if she was not so keen on the world and his wife knowing. The thought of keeping such a thing secret from your own kith and kin for a lifetime was beyond credibility.

Nella's face paled visibly as she stared at the woman. This could not be true. Please God, she prayed, let this not be true! But the woman was sitting there atop that old nag smiling at her, as if it was all some great joke. At all costs she must not let her know how shocked she was by what she had just heard. 'If – if you and my mother-in-law arrived together as convicts you must be very old friends indeed,' she said, trying to keep her voice steady.

'Oh aye, we're that all right, and we've managed to keep in contact fairly well over the years. Carrie was very good to me and my family some time back and that's why I've travelled up here myself again to see her just now. I've got some news for her I know she'll be quite delighted with.'

But Nella was barely listening any more. Despite an almost desperate need to disbelieve this poor creature, she could come to no other conclusion than that she was speaking the truth. God only knew what her news was or how far she had travelled to deliver it. One thing was for certain, Nella had to get back to Yorvik before the old woman did. She could not have her running into Billy and telling the same story she had just heard, for she was absolutely convinced her husband knew nothing about his own mother being a she-lag. Oh God . . . The very word brought her skin out in gooseflesh!

'You must excuse me,' she told the woman. 'I – I have to get back. There's something I must attend to and I'm already late . . .'

Then she was off like the wind, riding for all she was worth back towards the big house, intent on only one thing, to put as much distance between herself and this old hag as possible.

So distracted was she by the chaotic thoughts churning in her mind that she failed to see the group of kangaroos grazing by the roadside, just beyond the last blind bend before the big house came in sight. The old man roo that leapt out in front of the mare gave neither the animal nor its rider any chance. Nella was thrown from the saddle like a rag doll, catching her booted foot in the stirrup, to be dragged a good fifty yards before the panicking beast came to a full halt.

It was several minutes before Molly McFarland caught

up with her, and the sight that met her eyes made her gasp in horror.

'Dear God in Heaven, save us!'

The perspiring animal was standing by the side of the track, with the broken body of the young woman lying half on the muddy verge beside it. She was obviously still alive for she was groaning faintly, although her eyes were closed.

Shocked, Molly clambered down from her horse and knelt down beside the injured girl. Blood was trickling from the side of Nella's mouth and she was holding her stomach.

'Can you hear me?' Molly asked, placing a hand on the young woman's brow.

The blue eyes flickered open and a deeper groan was emitted from the parted lips.

'I'll better go and get help,' Molly said, her panic rising.

'No . . .' the young woman whispered. 'Please . . . don't leave me . . . The baby . . .'

Then, for the first time, Molly's eyes turned to the young woman's stomach. 'Oh, dear God!' She was not only pregnant, but heavily so.

'The baby . . .' the young woman groaned again, as one hand clutched at her stomach. 'Don't leave me . . .'

Then the scream came, so long and harrowing that it brought tears of anguish and frustration to Molly's eyes as she began to pull off her petticoat in a frantic attempt to aid the impending birth. She had attended several confinements in her time, but none quite like this. And it was all happening so fast . . .

The blood was flowing more freely from the young woman's mouth as her body writhed on the muddied ground. It had rained heavily during the night and her fair hair was lying in a pool of dirty water. God only knew what internal injuries she had received. But they were of secondary importance now.

Nella's waters had broken in the fall and the contractions

were becoming more powerful and agonizing with each passing minute. Molly did what she could to make the mother-to-be as comfortable as possible and continued kneeling by her side, offering what little comfort she could as Nella gasped and groaned beside her.

It seemed to take a lifetime for the baby's head to finally appear. 'Push!' Molly kept imploring, as over the next twenty minutes the young woman passed in and out of consciousness. Why didn't someone pass by? Molly kept looking around her in desperation, praying inwardly for assistance as she implored the semi-conscious girl, 'Please, please don't faint ... Push ... Please push! One more time!'

But the young woman could push no longer and it took several heart-stopping minutes more, and all of the Irish woman's experience and skill, to manoeuvre the infant's skull from its bloodied prison into the cold light of the winter's day.

In the end it came with such a rush that the small body slithered through Molly's hands and, missing the crumpled petticoat, landed on the muddied ground between its mother's legs.

Molly was in tears of relief as she picked it up and held the squirming child in triumph over the prostrate body of its mother.

'It's a girl!' she exclaimed, as the tears streamed down her face. 'Mrs Gordon-Hebden, you've got a lovely daughter!'

And she could swear she saw a smile of recognition on Nella's lips as the young mother gave a deep sigh and closed her eyes.

CHAPTER THIRTY-FIVE

Carrie's face turned ashen as she looked up from her paper-work to see the dishevelled figure of Molly McFarland standing in the doorway, with a squalling, red-faced infant in her arms.

'Begging your pardon, ma'am,' an anguished Ellen blurted out. 'I tried to stop her, but she insisted on follow-ing me up here!'

'What's going on?' Carrie demanded, her mind already working overtime, and dread coming into her heart as she got up from the desk. 'What are you doing here? And who is that child?'

'This is your grandchild!' Molly announced proudly, stepping forwards to place the infant into her old friend's arms. 'I swear to God when I set out for here the other day, I never thought I'd end up being given such a task to perform!'

Carrie was speechless as she gazed down into the pink, screwed-up face, then back at Molly. 'But where's Nella?' she demanded in a choked voice. 'Where's its mother?'

At that Molly's smile vanished and an anguished look came over her face as she made a gesture in roughly the direction of the accident. 'The young lady had a bad fall from her horse not a mile or so down the road,' she said. 'You'd better get help out to her quick, for I believe she could be quite badly injured. She seemed to have passed out when I left. I certainly couldn't move her.'

Carrie gasped as her worst fear was confirmed. How many times had she pleaded with Nella to give up her riding? It had been sheer madness to carry on at this late stage in her pregnancy. 'Ellen, get one of the men to fetch Dr Fraser immediately,' she commanded. 'I'll ride out there to Nella right away.'

She pushed the crying child back into Molly's arms. 'Look after it until I get back, would you?' she said, in mounting panic. 'Where did you say the accident happened?'

'Not a mile down the road, heading south towards the main Sydney carriageway.'

Stopping only to grab a satchel containing rudimentary medical aids from a shelf in the pantry, Carrie rushed to the stables to saddle her horse, then changed her mind, and to save time commandeered a stallion already saddled belonging to one of the cattlehands.

It was soft going, along a track deep with puddles and mud, but it took her less than ten minutes to reach Nella. She had no difficulty finding her, for the young woman still lay sprawled half on the track, half on the dank grass of the verge. The lower part of her clothing was not only muddied, but badly stained and dishevelled from the birth, but Carrie ignored that to stare at the bloodless face as she clambered down from her horse.

'Oh Nella . . . Nella . . .' She almost threw herself to the ground beside her daughter-in-law. The long fair hair had come out of its riding net and was lying in a pool of dirty rainwater. Carrie gently turned the blonde head towards her. Nella's eyes were closed and the blood that had oozed from her mouth was congealing into a dark red stain that had run over her shoulder and collected in a small pool in the curve of her neck. The sight of it struck fear into Carrie's heart. Whatever injuries the young woman had sustained in the fall, they were not all visible, that was for sure. 'I'm here, Nella darling . . . Help has come . . .' she whispered, stroking the pale skin of the young mother's brow.

But Nella was beyond help, and in her heart Carrie already knew it as she lifted her daughter-in-law's wrist and felt in vain for a pulse. 'Please don't let her be dead. Oh please God, don't let her be dead . . .' But in the twenty minutes since Molly McFarland had delivered the child and ridden for help, the life had ebbed from Nella Gordon-Hebden's young body, and no amount of praying was going to bring it back.

It was a totally stunned Carrie who remounted her horse five minutes later to return to the house. On the way she met Will Morton and two other hands riding out to help, pulling a wagon behind them in which to carry Nella back.

'How is she, ma'am?' Will called. 'Is it bad?'

Too distraught to speak, Carrie nodded, then called out in a choked voice, 'Bring her home, Will, please. Don't let her lie there any longer.'

There was a small crowd gathered outside the house when she finally reached Yorvik, in the middle of which was Molly with the newly-born infant still in her arms. All eyes were riveted on Carrie's face as she dismounted from her horse and tossed the reins over a nearby post. But, too overcome to speak, Carrie walked past them all without uttering a word and carried on up the steps and into the front door. It was then that she thought of her son. No one had even given Billy a second thought. Where the devil was he?

The library! He spent most of his afternoons closeted in there. Keeping up with his studies, he claimed he was, but she was only too aware of the empty gin bottles piling up in the midden behind the big house. The grief she felt was multiplied a hundredfold at the thought of what this would do to him.

She barely had the energy to drag herself up the stairs and once more felt that old familiar weakness in her left ankle that had made her young life such a misery. Her legs were shaking beneath her by the time she reached the library and pushed open the panelled cedar door.

Billy was there, sitting in the far corner by the fire, a glass in his hand, a book in his lap, and his feet resting on a small beaded footstool. He looked up in surprise as his mother entered and raised the hand with the glass. 'Ma! What brings you here?'

Carrie's heart sank even further. There was something about the tone of voice and the gesture that told her immediately he was the worse for drink; not drunk exactly, but certainly not sober.

She hovered in the doorway for a moment, then slowly entered the room, closing the door behind her.

He looked puzzled. 'Is anything wrong?' Then seeing the pain in her eyes, he added quickly, 'It's not Nella, is it?'

He rose unsteadily from his chair, spilling part of the drink on the rosewood tabletop as he put down the glass and came towards her. 'What is it? What's happened? She's not gone into labour, has she? The baby . . . she hasn't had it?'

Carrie nodded dumbly. 'You've got a . . .' Then she came to the absurd realization that she did not even know the sex of the child.

But Billy did not seem to notice. The child was the least of his concerns. 'Nella . . .' he insisted. 'What about Nella? How is she?'

There was no way round it. No easy way of putting it. 'She's dead, Billy,' Carrie told him softly. 'Nella's dead.'

'No!' He gaped at her in disbelief. 'No! No! No! She can't be! . . . I – I saw her only a hour or so ago . . .'

He took a few staggering steps towards his mother then fell to his knees. She rushed to him and threw her arms around him as he buried his face in her skirts and sobbed his hurt into her encircling arms. For Carrie this was the greatest pain of all, as she stood there stroking his hair and murmuring meaningless words of comfort. She would bear any agony rather than see him suffer.

She led him by the hand to the sofa and they sat down side by side. 'It was an accident,' she told him gently. 'She fell from her horse and went into labour immediately . . . She was found by an old friend of mine who was arriving on a visit. Molly delivered the baby, but it must have been too late to do anything to save poor Nella.'

He listened in silence as the tears ran from his eyes but,

459

strangely, Carrie found she could not cry. It was as if all emotion had been washed from her. Life had dealt too many blows in the past for her to give way now that Billy needed her so much. There was no pain that she would not gladly bear for him, no unhappiness that she would not shield him from. But at this moment when he needed her the most, there was nothing she could do or say that could ease the agony he was going through. This was his own private grief that not even a mother's love could assuage.

When at last his sobs began to subside, 'Stay here,' she told him quietly. 'I'll go and find out what's happening downstairs.'

He half rose to follow her, but she put a restraining hand on his shoulder. 'No, please darling, you stay. There's nothing you can do by coming with me.' It would do him no good at all to see poor Nella's body in the state she herself had witnessed it. 'I'll be back just as soon as I know what's going on.'

Billy nodded and took a deep breath as a silent sob shuddered through him. His head ached and his eyes had trouble focusing. What he needed more than anything was another drink. He nodded dumbly in reply to his mother. He was only too happy to let her take over.

The cart with Nella's body was standing by the front steps when Carrie got back downstairs and she instructed Will to see to it that her daughter-in-law was taken up and laid in the bed of the guest room overlooking the lake. It was the brightest and best of the spare rooms and it seemed only right somehow.

'You'd better wait before seeing to the laying out of the body until after Dr Fraser's been, but you can begin preparing hot water and things now,' she told Ellen, and was surprised to hear how calm and collected her voice sounded.

As the group dispersed to carry out her instructions, she was suddenly aware there was only herself and Molly left.

The latter still had the newly-born infant in her arms.

Carrie shook her head wearily as she looked across at the child. 'I – I never even asked what sex it is,' she said in a tired voice.

'It's a girl, Carrie love. You've got a granddaughter.'

'Oh.' To her shame she felt a momentary pang of disappointment at the news. A son would have been so much better. An heir for Yorvik. Then the ghost of a smile flickered at the corners of her mouth and, seeing her old friend look quizzically at her, she confessed, 'I was just thinking how like my late husband I must be getting.'

But yes, she thought, as she walked across to take her first peek at the infant, an heir for Yorvik would have been so much better. Her own son had no love for this place, but perhaps a grandson might have made up for that, the greatest disappointment of her life.

'Let's go inside,' she told her old friend.

She took the infant from Molly McFarland's arms and the two women walked back into the house. Ellen was busy seeing to the preparations for laying out Nella's body, so Carrie put the child in the cot they had used for the foundling some months earlier and set about making a cup of tea. 'The good old English answer to every crisis,' she murmured, with an attempt at a mirthless smile, as she put the tea things on to a tray with some biscuits and beckoned on Molly to follow her as she walked with it through to the drawing room.

She felt as if she were acting out some dreadful nightmare in which the world was going to pieces around her, but she had to remain calm. Although devastated by what had just happened, she felt curiously numb. Her daughter-in-law was dead, her son was going to pieces upstairs, but she had to be strong. Whatever happened she had to keep control of her own emotions.

Her face showed the strain as she sat down at one end of the drawing room sofa and placed the tray on a small table in between herself and her old friend, whom she

461

gestured to sit down opposite. 'Poor Molly,' she said. 'What a shock all this must have been for you.' She shook her head. 'What a shock for us all.'

Molly sat silent, her hands clasped tightly in her lap. The good news she had come all this way to share now seemed of such little consequence.

Sensing her discomfort, Carrie resolved to do her best to put her friend at her ease. 'Do forgive me,' she said, with a distracted air. 'I've never even bothered to ask what brings you all this way to see me.' Her voice dropped as she leant forwards to pour the two cups of tea and asked, 'It's not more help you're needing, is it?'

Molly shook her head. 'Oh no,' she assured her. 'It's not more help. On the contrary – it's to give you this.' She reached inside her blouse and extracted a small cloth bag hanging from a drawstring around her neck. Pulling it open, she took out a wad of banknotes. 'There's fifty pounds there,' she said, reaching across and laying them in Carrie's lap with a proud smile. 'Our debt of honour's repaid at last.'

Carrie looked down in astonishment at the money. She had all but forgotten the gift she had made all that time ago. 'But I didn't ask for repayment,' she said, shaking her head. 'Nor did I expect it.'

'Sure, and I know that,' Molly replied, shoving the empty purse back down her neck. 'But it cost me a lot to come begging like that, I can tell you . . . I – I wouldn't have done it for myself. But when it's one of your children whose life is in danger . . . Well, I think you understand what I mean . . .'

Carrie knew exactly what she meant, and as she sat there listening with glistening eyes, she felt very small. They were both mothers who would kill to defend their own. There was no height that would not be scaled, no depths that would not be plumbed for one's child. 'Did it work?' she asked softly. 'Did you manage to get Seamus a decent lawyer for his trial?'

Molly nodded, her heart full as she remembered the agony of those days. 'Not only that,' she told her friend, her own eyes now shining. 'But he got off. There were no witnesses willing to testify to him being there at the time they set fire to that inn, so they let him go . . . Oh, Carrie, if we hadn't been able to afford one of the best lawyers in Melbourne he could have swung. They could have killed him, just like they killed Ned and the others. As it is, that close shave convinced him he'd used up all of the nine lives his father always maintained he had, and he took the twenty pounds that was left over to set himself up as a carter in The Rocks.'

As Carrie listened, Molly allowed herself more than a hint of mother's pride in her voice as she added, 'He earns good money ferrying goods to and fro, from the warehouses to the ships. It's taken him all this time to save that up to repay you – and it was his idea to give it back, not ours.'

Carrie looked down at the pile of notes in her lap. They were dirty and well-thumbed and all the more precious for that. 'I – I don't know what to say,' she said, shaking her head. 'I really don't.'

'Then don't say anything,' her old friend told her. 'I'm just so sorry my mission, which should have been such a happy one, has had to turn out like this . . . That poor young woman . . . '

Carrie let out a deep sigh as her thoughts flew back to Nella. Sitting here for these past few minutes, sharing in Molly's pride in her son, she had almost forgotten the tragedy that had befallen her own. 'Poor Billy . . . Heaven only knows how he's going to get over this . . . How any of us are going to get over it.'

'You will be strong for him,' Molly told her. 'It's part of our job.'

Carrie attempted a weak smile. She had been trying so hard to be strong all her life. 'We haven't exactly had it easy, you and me, have we, Mol?'

Molly had finished the tea in her cup, and she carefully brushed the biscuit crumbs from her lap on to her plate, before rising to go. 'It's been a long road, and a hard road from that landing stage at Portsmouth docks. But I wouldn't wish myself back in the old country for all the gold in the Bank of England.'

She made a move towards the door. 'I won't detain you any longer,' she said. 'This is a terrible day for you, so it is. The last thing you need is other people intruding on your grief.'

'Oh no!' Carrie protested. Her friend had travelled many long, hard miles to repay this debt. 'I so much appreciate your coming here to tell me. And I'm glad, so very glad, for all your sakes . . . As for what's happened out there today, well, it could have been much worse if you hadn't been there. The baby could have died too.'

She got up herself and took hold of her friend's arm. Memories of Molly's last visit and the summary dismissal she had inflicted still brought pangs of guilt, she had to make up for it. 'But don't imagine you're going out there to get back on that horse. You're going nowhere today. We've got plenty of room here. You'll stay the night at least.'

But Molly was adamant. This was no time to be bothering her old friend and she said so. She was on the point of holding out her hand to bid farewell when the drawing room door opened and Billy came in.

His eyes were bloodshot, the lids swollen with tears. He had just come from seeing the dead body of his wife and needed his mother now more than ever. 'I – I'm sorry,' he said, looking in confusion at the two of them. 'I had no idea you had a visitor.'

Carrie led her friend across the room to where her son was standing. 'Billy love, I know this is hardly the time . . . But this is a very old friend of mine, Molly McFarland . . .'

Billy held out his hand and shook the visitor's in a mechanical fashion. 'How do you do?' he said in a dull voice.

'I'm so sorry, son, about what's happened,' Molly said, clasping his hand much longer than was needed.

'Molly found Nella and delivered the baby,' Carrie informed him. 'If she hadn't been there your daughter would have died too.'

Billy looked bemused. 'The baby . . .' he began, then shook his head. He had never even given it a second thought. 'I have a daughter?'

'You certainly have,' Molly assured him. 'I delivered the little mite right there in the mud, by the side of the road.' Then, seeing the grief still writ large on the young man's face, she added by way of consolation, 'You know we have a saying in Ireland that a child born on a bed of mud will go further in life than one born in a feather bed.' She gave a wry smile, 'But you don't want to be listening to an old biddy like me . . . May God bless you, son, and your little one, and may the saints walk with you through this life.'

Carrie beckoned to Billy to sit himself down and, after assuring him she would be back soon, she walked with Molly to where her friend had tethered her horse round the side of the house. The animal had been given food and drink by one of the hands, and Carrie slipped it one of the sweetmeats she always carried in her pocket.

'You'll keep in touch,' she told her old friend. 'You'll let me know how things are going.'

Molly nodded and clasped Carrie's hand in both of hers. 'Sure, it's the least I can do. And you take care of yourself now. You'll be needed more than ever after this. God bless you, Carrie love. God bless all three of you.'

All three of you . . . The words sounded strange to Carrie's ears as she helped her friend into the saddle, then stood watching as Molly set off back down the long track towards the Great North Road. She seemed a small, vulnerable figure atop the horse's back, but Carrie knew that within that frail body was a backbone as strong as any man's. She watched until horse and rider were almost out of sight, a mere dot on the horizon, and then turned to make her way back inside. As she did so, she was totally oblivious to the man watching her from the door to one of the stables, some fifty yards away.

Sean O'Dwyer had just heard the news and could scarcely believe it. He had got used to seeing the young blonde-haired woman around the place and had even grown to have a grudging admiration for her curiosity and enthusiasm for station life, even if she did object to getting her own hands dirty.

He paused for a moment, uncertain of whether his presence would be welcomed at such a time. Words had been said when they last met, harsh, bitter words, but that could not stop them from feeling each other's pain.

Carrie saw him and she too paused in her tracks.

They began to walk slowly towards each other, then over the last few yards Carrie began to run. She flung herself into his arms and clung to him, as a drowning sailor to a life-raft. It was weeks since they had spoken and the words that had passed between them then had been washed away by too many tears to still have their sting.

But no words were needed now. He just stood there rocking her in his arms. She could feel his strength pouring into her. He was her rock, her salvation.

'Thank you, Irish . . . Thank you . . .' she whispered. Then, without another word, she pulled herself free and ran back into the house. Her son needed her. Her son and that small child still lying in the makeshift crib by the kitchen stove.

She made for the kitchen first, to find that Ellen had already washed the infant and attended to the cord. She now lay in the basket wrapped in a large clean towel. Jeeba was standing by the cot making cooing noises at the fretting child.

Carrie walked over and, looking down at her granddaughter, remembered what her old friend had said. 'Our little child of the mud,' she sighed. 'What's going to become of you?'

The old gin looked up at her and in a hoarse voice gave a cackling smile. '*Noora-nee-nurran. . . Noora-nee-nurran . . .*'

Carrie looked puzzled, but Ellen, who had worked with the old woman for years and had picked up more of the language than most, merely smiled. 'That's blackfella for "Child of the Mud", ma'am,' she told her.

'*Noora-nee-nurran*,' Carrie repeated, bending to pick up the whimpering child. She liked that. Somehow it suited this little mite who had been thrust into the cold world so brutally this day. 'Noora-nee-nurran,' she murmured softly into the tiny ear. 'Let's go and meet your father, little Miss *Noora-nee-nurran* – Child of the Mud.'

BOOK THREE

Dreamtime

I loved you, I love you, for this love have lost
State, station, heaven, mankind's,
My own esteem,
And yet cannot regret
What it has cost,
So dear is still the memory of that dream . . .

George Gordon, Lord Byron

CHAPTER THIRTY-SIX

October 1901
Yorvik

The clouds that scudded across the southern sky were a dazzling white against the blue. It was one of those golden mornings that made one feel glad to be alive. Spring had a special magic in this part of the Hunter Valley, and the breeze that blew across the wide acres surrounding the big house carried with it a promise of the long days of summer that lay ahead. Green buds, as tight as a newborn baby's fist, were preparing to uncurl, and day-old lambs were taking their first tottering steps in the lush grasslands that stretched to the far horizon. Even the children who made their way reluctantly to the schoolhouse each morning had a lightness to their step. Soon it would be summer, school would be over and the season of happy hours would be here; happy hours spent helping with the animals and swimming in the lakes and billabongs that made this such a special place to all who lived here.

But today was Saturday, the favourite day of the young; a day for doing the chores, then finding time to do a million and one more important things, such as chasing the gaily coloured butterflies that darted between the sweet-scented blossoms of the fruit trees and amongst the wild flowers that embroidered the long grass bordering the path leading to the river.

All around the station, childish laughter marked this day as one on which no slates would be scratched with tiresome sums or letters. Today there had been no school bell tolled on the stroke of nine to end the freedom of two of the oldest pupils to grace those rough-hewn benches from Monday to Friday. This morning Noora Gordon-Hebden,

Carrie's fifteen-year-old granddaughter, and her friend Joe-boy, had spent the early hours fishing in the lake and had then presented the best of their catch – a small, silver-scaled beauty – to one of their oldest friends in the Aborigine camp behind the big house.

The old woman who received their offering was known as Kambu, which meant 'skeleton' in blackfella language. She was a solitary creature who sat apart from the life of her tribe, her bony frame the colour of the brown earth where she squatted tending the ashes of the fire on which she was now cooking the gift from her two young friends. Joe-boy had taken a butterfly he had caught in his net to show her – a prize bright blue specimen, with black-and-yellow striped wingtips. But the old woman was not amused. To capture such creatures was to commit a great sin. She told them of the *Nimma-gunta*, the butterfly fairies, who were abroad in the land at this time of year, and of the *Doowullen*, the small gnomes, who were their best friends, and of how together they guarded the newly born and the very young. What they had done in catching such a being was terrible indeed.

'Them look after you, l'il yella-fella,' she told Joe-boy, the tawny-coloured youth who sat cross-legged and repentant on the dirt beside her. 'We done hab no *Nimma-gunta* and you'm be longtime dead. Kabbarli – she follow dem *Nimma-gunta* and done find you, l'il yella-fella piccaninny.'

Joe-boy glanced at Noora, the girl by his side, in some embarrassment. Talk of his earliest beginnings, of how he was left to die as a baby, before being found by Carrie Gordon-Hebden, the Mistress of Yorvik – the one the black-fellas referred to as Kabbarli – was always a source of pain to him. But Noora was nodding sagely; every word gleaned from these ancient lips was to be cherished for it filled in the multi-coloured jigsaw that was her life and her heritage here on Yorvik. And there was still so much to learn.

Kambu's gnarled hand grasped the stick to rake the

dying embers around the bark-wrapped morsel that would make up her only meal of the day, and she sighed as she closed her eyes, already half blind to the modern world in which she now found herself. She had talked too much for one day. She was tired. So very tired. Already they were gathering, the spirits of the nether world, waiting to lure her the last few paces down the road of no return. She could see them sometimes, shadows from her childhood of those who had gone before, beloved memories of another time when she and the world were young, and she would dart like a little dark shadow through days such as this, wreathed with sunshine and the incessant chatter and laughter of friends.

Even now in old age, with the spirits of the dead gathering to claim her, she could still remember how it was to be the age of the young girl and tawny-coloured youth who for the past half hour had sat enthralled by her side as she talked of butterflies, and of those dear dead days; days long gone when young men and old would woo her, but she had only eyes for one. The laws of the tribe decreed she belonged to another, but her heart knew better, and together with her beloved they would escape the disapproving eyes of their elders to run into the bush; two fleeing figures in a warm dusk lit by fire-flies, as the crimson rising moon turned to silver and bathed them in its glow.

The old woman sighed. It was all so long ago, so long, long ago. And she was tired now. Tired of talking. Tired of life. Her eyes closed once more and, as if of their own accord, her hands returned to the rhythmic tap-tapping of her *woolwa* sticks that brought her comfort and contact with the spirit world of which she would soon be a part.

Then her lips opened and in a weary voice she addressed the two young people sitting cross-legged next to her. 'Ol' woman done yabber-yabber long time. Ol' woman tired. Ol' woman makem tucker. Her eat now. You savvy?'

Noora glanced at Joe-boy. It was time they were leaving. They got up as one and both bent to touch the old lubra on the shoulder. The old woman laid down one of her sticks and raised a hand in farewell, and Joe-boy dug into his pocket to extract a handful of witchetty grubs which he pressed into her upturned palm. These soft, creamy creatures, as thick as his little finger, which tasted of almonds and were as fat and juicy as the most luscious fruit, he knew were a special favourite, and he had extracted them himself from the trunk of an old gum tree on the way here.

Both he and Noora loved to stop by the blackfellas' camp on days such as this and listen to tales of life in the days long before they were born. The old woman could even remember Old Silas, who was the first white man to attempt to build a station out of the wilderness. 'Him cranky ol' bugger,' she had told them, with a knowing cackle, and they had no cause to doubt it. They knew that Carrie, Noora's grandmother, preferred not to talk about the man to whom she had once been married more than half a century ago and the old lubra was about the only other person left on the station who could remember those days. To the two young people who now left the fireside to let their old friend enjoy her meal in peace, hearing such stories merely added to the mystique that was Yorvik, this land they both loved so much.

'What do you fancy doing now?' Joe-boy asked, as they mounted their horses and left the blackfella camp behind.

Noora shrugged her shoulders and tossed her mane of fair hair. 'Head into the bush, I reckon. If I stay around here I'll only get hauled in to help out in the house.'

They headed out past the lake, where a few of the younger women from the tribe were fishing, whilst their elders dug for roots to feed the army of children that seemed to grow larger by the day. For more than a decade now Carrie had instigated a policy of keeping tally of the number of pregnant lubras on station, and attempted to make sure there was not too great a difference between infants actually born and those who survived. The apparently callous behaviour of some of the native women to their newly-born offspring had never ceased to appal her and she remained determined to stamp out this needless cruelty where at all possible.

But her granddaughter had no such noble thoughts on her mind on this loveliest of days as she urged her horse forwards, determined to keep ahead of the mount of her companion. Noora's laughter rang on the wind as they left the encampment far behind and headed for the wide open spaces that made up Yorvik's thousand acres.

They had gone less than five miles into the bush when both pulled up their animals to walking pace. There was some kind of encampment ahead, for smoke could be seen spiralling up from behind a copse of ancient coolibah trees.

'What do you reckon's going on there?' Noora asked, turning in the saddle to shout to Joe-boy, who was some thirty feet behind.

Joe-boy's dark brows knitted as he pushed a hand through his shock of reddish-brown curls. Then a troubled look came to his eyes as he gazed at the scene ahead of them. The slim figure of a boy a few years younger than himself was visible at the edge of the trees. He was standing alone, looking towards the fire where, no doubt, several elders of his tribe would be gathered. Joe-boy was pensive for a moment longer, then, 'Come back, Noora!' he called. 'We've got to get out of here!'

He jerked round his horse's head and dug his heels into the animal's sides. He had recognized that young boy as Jamba, one of the youngsters from the camp, and he could guess exactly what was going on in this lonely spot. The boy was being prepared for manhood. Joe-boy had heard talk of it in the camp for some time now. No wonder the poor little blighter looked so apprehensive. As he stood there, naked save for his hair belt and bandicoot tassle, the tribal fathers were preparing the sacred ritual that would admit him to the world of men, setting his feet on the path where, with head held high, he would step out proudly to the nameless tune that pulsated through all blackfellas' veins. They would be directing him down the road to his personal Dreamtime.

'Noora! For God's sake!'

Reluctantly Noora turned her own horse's head away from the scene ahead to follow her companion back down the road they had come. 'Why can't we go on?' she demanded when alongside her friend. Indignation throbbed in her breast, for she was keen to continue. It was a day for riding forever, with the fresh breeze in your face and the scent of summer in your nostrils. She was not ready to go back; she was enjoying this ride and hated being thwarted. 'Why do we have to turn back now?'

'Because you're a female, that's why,' Joe-boy told her, with that troubled look still in his eyes. 'Can't you guess what's going on? They're getting ready to circumcise that kid back there and if he sets eyes on a woman or girl before that happens, they'll kill him.'

'They'll what?'

'They'll kill him,' Joe-boy confirmed, then added impatiently, 'Don't you know they're not allowed any type of contact with a female at a time like this?'

Noora frowned, the clear skin of her brow puckering beneath the fair fringe, as their horses trotted side by side in the direction of Yorvik once more. 'I didn't know that,' she said with some scepticism, for she was not sure she fully believed it. She often suspected Joe-boy of exaggerating blackfella lore and practices to make that part of his own heritage seem more mysterious than it actually was. 'In fact I've never even heard of that before and I've lived here almost as long as you have.'

'Well, you don't know everything, Clever-clogs, although you like to think you do!'

Noora ignored the remark, her frown deepening. This circumcision stuff was never really discussed by anyone, and it was certainly not a subject about which questions were actively encouraged at home; consequently she had only a sketchy idea of what exactly they did to a boy at a time like this to allow him to become a man. 'I don't see what's so terrible about that kid setting eyes on a female,' she said. 'It sounds crazy to me. Is it supposed to make him unclean or something?'

'Yeah, that's right,' Joe-boy replied, ignoring the irony in her voice. 'That's exactly what it means.'

'But that's absurd!'

'No, it's not. Not to them at any rate. They believe he has to keep himself totally pure – and that means no contact at all with the female sex – so he's in the right state to learn all the sacred words and signs – all the totems and things known only to the men of the tribe. He's not even allowed any food gathered or prepared by a woman. He must eat only from the hands of the tribal elders before the ceremony is performed.'

The Irishman had told him all about the mysteries of circumcision when he had first become aware of his young blackfella friends being taken from the camp at intervals to undergo the ritual. Sean O'Dwyer had explained how at that special time the spirit *Goondabuduri* would come and take the soul of the boy so that that of the man could enter into his body. But the whole process would be ruined if the boy were to have sight, sound or smell of a female during this sacred time.

'Well, I think it's a stupid, uncivilized carry-on,' Noora said, casting a backward glance in the direction of the copse. 'In fact it's an insult to women and I've a good mind to ride right back there and tell them so!'

She pulled up her horse and looked defiantly at Joe-boy. 'I really do, you know. I think it's high time someone showed them women are just as important in this life as men!'

Joe-boy paled beneath the tanned skin of his cheeks. 'You wouldn't dare!' he breathed. Even someone as hot-headed as Noora couldn't surely be *that* stupid? 'Even you wouldn't dare do a damned fool thing like that!'

That was enough for Noora. 'Just watch me!'

To Joe-boy's horror she turned her horse and set off back in the direction of the trees, throwing up a dustcloud from the dry track behind her. Her action filled him with panic for he knew it would result in the almost certain death of the boy who was being prepared for the ceremony. But he also knew Noora and, as her grandmother would put it, she had her paddy up now. It was the Irish in her coming out with a vengeance. Whenever she came across something she believed to be unjust or just plain stupid she did not hesitate to say so. He had to stop her.

'Come on, boy!' With a sharp slap on his mount's flank, Joe-boy dug in his heels and urged the animal forwards in hot pursuit.

It took him several minutes to catch up with her. As their horses galloped side by side she threw him a defiant glance, her eyes gleaming as her hair streamed out behind her. Her smile was broad as she called out, 'You won't stop me, Joe-boy!'

But Joe-boy was determined. He knew the boy's life depended on it, whether she believed it or not.

There was only one thing for it. When his horse was half a neck ahead of hers and the animals were stride for stride, taking his courage in both hands, he leant across to grab her from the saddle.

Her yell of shock was painful to his ears as he hauled her across the horse's back and attempted to pull her on to his own steed. But there was not yet enough strength in his youthful arms to cope with the weight and they toppled to the ground in a tangle of flailing arms and legs as their startled horses came to a snorting halt some distance ahead.

'You pig, Joe-boy! You could've killed me!' Noora gasped and lashed out at the young man lying panting painfully on the grassy verge by her side. 'You could've killed me, do you hear? I could be *dead* because of you!'

Joe-boy put up an arm to shield himself from the blows.

'That's just what that poor kid would've been if you'd gone showing your face over there!' he yelled back at her, indicating with his head the copse of trees a half mile ahead. 'They'd have killed him, Noora. I swear it. That poor little fella would never have had the chance to grow up to be a man because of your damned fool interference!'

Noora's blue eyes glared across at him, but her face became more pensive. 'I don't believe you,' she said, beginning to dust herself off. 'I don't believe you, Joe-boy. It's just one more of your stupid lies.'

Joe-boy scrambled to his feet and glared down at her as she wiped the dirt from the sleeve of her dress. 'I don't tell lies, Miss Clever-clogs. Just because I happen to know more things about what goes on around here than you doesn't make me a liar. But it does make you a silly, hot-headed little bitch!' With that he turned and made for his horse.

'Don't you dare call me a silly bitch, Joe-boy!' Noora blazed, scrambling to her feet. 'A bitch is a female dog — and if I'm a dog then you're a pig ... You're a ... a ...' She searched for a vile enough adjective to satisfy her rage.

'A black pig? Is that the word you're after?' Joe-boy looked down at her from the saddle of his horse, a quizzical smile quirking the side of his mouth. His skin was the colour of light golden hide and the brown of his hair glinted red in the midday sun. 'Don't ever let me forget I'm a blackfella at heart, Noora, will you?'

Carrie's granddaughter stared up at her best friend with tears of indignation sparkling in her eyes. 'Get out of here, Joe-boy!' she yelled back. 'Just get out of here and leave me alone!'

Noora watched sullenly as he rode off, with a toss of his curly hair and a laugh that proclaimed his victory: one minor victory in a friendship that thrived on such battles. 'I'll teach him,' she promised herself as she made for her horse. 'You're a pig, Joe-boy! You're nothing but a big-headed pig!'

But Joe-boy was long out of earshot, his laughter riding on the wind that whipped through his hair as he bent low over his mount and urged it ever faster on the road back to Yorvik.

CHAPTER THIRTY-SEVEN

Carrie sat in her favourite chair by the drawing room window in the soft light of evening, her tapestry in her lap, and looked at her granddaughter as Noora lay sprawled on the chaise longue totally engrossed in the pages of a book. As her restless fingers absent-mindedly twirled a strand of long fair hair, the young girl had that dreamy look in her eyes that her grandmother knew so well. She had had that habit since a small child and it was hard now to reconcile the memory of that placid, apple-cheeked toddler with the athletic, spirited young woman she had become. It was well-nigh impossible to believe that she was now all of fifteen years old. Almost a woman.

So much had happened in the decade and a half that had gone, and now here they were just over the threshold of a new century. It was just as well, Carrie mused, that she had not nurtured secret hopes of putting her feet up on becoming a grandmother, back then in the mid-eighties when Noora was born. How disappointed she would have been! She had never worked so hard in all her life as she had during these past fifteen years on Yorvik.

The nineties had seen the boom years of the eighties replaced by years of strife and hardship, during which even the biggest and most successful station owners had witnessed their profits slashed and increasing unrest amongst their workers. In the growing trade union movement, the sheep shearers had been amongst the most militant activists, with their declared aim to prevent a bale of wool leaving the country unless it was shorn by union shearers. This had enraged many of the station owners, who declared they would not be dictated to by men whose wages they paid.

Up and down the country woolsheds had been burned

down and many a heated meeting had taken place that had ended in fist-fights between masters and servants, and by the end of the first year of the nineties the trouble had spread far beyond the stations themselves.

There had been a taste of things to come in November of 1891, when on Sydney's Circular Quay an angry crowd of unionists and their sympathizers, some ten thousand strong, created general mayhem and overturned vehicles that were being used to carry blackleg wool to the ships for transportation to England. Molly McFarland's son Seamus's waggons had been amongst those involved and he himself had suffered a broken leg and other injuries in defending his vehicles.

Although there had been no Yorvik wool in transit on that particular day, part of that consignment of non-unionist wool bore the stamp of Cameron Creek, for Angus, the old Scotsman still in charge there, was adamantly opposed to anyone telling him whom he could or could not employ to shear his sheep. 'I'll shear the bloody things myself rather than have them dictate to me what men I can and can't use on the job,' he told Carrie. And, for her part, Carrie had more than a little sympathy with her old friend's stand. Although she paid her own men above the recommended rate, and had agreed to her own hands joining the union, she too was not so keen to see it made obligatory.

The demonstrators that day were eventually dispersed by a police cavalry charge, but the marker had been laid down for what was to lie ahead, and there was not a sheep station owner in the country who did not have many a sleepless night over the issue in the years to come.

Carrie was convinced that the constant trouble with the unions that marred the last years of Angus Cameron's life was ultimately responsible for the fatal heart attack he suffered. For her and for most of those who had known and loved him, Angus's death on the twenty-second of January, 1901, really did appear to signify the ending of an era, much more so than the death of the old Queen Victoria who died on that same day, back in England.

One thing that proved of some consolation to Carrie, however, was that her friend had lived just long enough to see the fulfilment of his political dream. He too had felt a real pride in this land that they had spent a lifetime helping to build, and he had longed more than anything to see it standing proud and free. It could not remain tied to the apron strings of the motherland forever. Their shared joy was immense when the first real step towards that goal was accomplished. Nothing could have been more symbolic or filled their hearts with more happiness than when on the first day of January, this very year of 1901, the Commonwealth of Australia had been born.

Carrie had travelled down to Sydney with Angus and her granddaughter Noora to join the half million others who thronged their great city in the sweltering heat, to hear the proclamation being made and to witness the grand procession wend its way from the Domain to Centennial Park. Sydney had seen nothing like it before. It was as if the biggest carnival in the world had come to town. But all over Australia it was the same as the people rejoiced. Bunting garlanded every street and brass bands played, flags were waved, and old and young alike marched in triumphal procession through every city, town and village.

Although there were to be celebrations in nearby Hunter's Hollow, Carrie had felt it was important to be in Sydney, at the very heart of things. It would be a day to remember, a day that would live on in their country's history, and one that she had been determined not to miss. Their beloved land had come of age and she wanted her granddaughter too to retain this day as one of the lasting memories of her own young life that would remain with her throughout the coming years.

'This will be something you will tell your grandchildren about in fifty years' time,' she told Noora as they stood side by side on Sydney's George Street and waved their flags in the boisterous, jostling crowd that cheered the marchers to the echo. 'We're entering a new era, Noora darling. The old world is giving way to the new, and we are privileged to be part of that process.'

Great bonfires were lit throughout the land and one of the biggest of all had been on the hill overlooking Yorvik. The station children had collected for it for months, and none had gathered old jumble and firewood with more gusto than Noora and Joe-boy. The stack had reached twenty feet in height before the torch was ceremonially put to it by the Master of Yorvik, a none-too-sober Billy Gordon-Hebden, and it was still smouldering when his mother and daughter returned home three days later.

Yes, Carrie thought to herself, there had been many experiences she had shared with her granddaughter over the years; unforgettable ones that would remain writ large in the young girl's book of memory long after she had passed on. Some would say she had been trying to make up for the loss of Nella, the mother the child had never known. But it was much more than that. She could see so much of herself in the high-spirited youngster. They had even bought their first Singer sewing machine together, and, putting all her early experience at Casey's garment factory to good use, Carrie had taken great pride in showing her granddaughter how to create a whole variety of new outfits for the array of dolls which decorated the window sill of her bedroom.

Whether it was being present at the birth of a new breed of sheep or cow, learning to dive off the sun-bleached rocks of Yorvik Force, or simply showing her how to grow her own tomatoes from a plant in the kitchen window, the two had been inseparable. And, best of all as far as Carrie was concerned, there was still so much to do, so much to discover together. With her granddaughter's birth, life had become a whole new journey of discovery, one that she still took pleasure from with each new day.

Perhaps, in a way, she was compensating for the sense of estrangement she felt with her own son. The gulf that had grown between them during Billy's schooldays in England had continued to widen over the years, to now appear almost unbridgeable since his wife's tragic death. Billy now withdrew more and more into himself, seeking solace from neither his mother nor his child, but from the bottles of clear potent spirit which he had consumed with increasing frequency since his wife's funeral.

Although she had only just come into their lives, Nella's death had come as a terrible shock to everyone on the station, and it came as no great surprise to his mother that Billy had never quite got over it. His drinking, which was already becoming a worry to Carrie before Nella's accident, got much worse after that, with at least a bottle a day being poured down his throat. He seemed to completely give up on life. He had no interest at all in the running of the station, nor did he feel inclined to accept social invitations from people he referred to scathingly as 'backwoodsmen', although most were highly respected and successful citizens in their own right. Instead, he moped around the house, often never bothering to get dressed from one day to the next, and talked longingly of England and of how one day he would return there. The only thing that was stopping him was his daughter, for his mother had made it clear that his place was with her. If fate had decreed that Noora should grow up without a mother's love, then Carrie was determined she should not also do without a father's.

Carrie sighed as she thought of how much Billy still seemed to resent the child at times. It was as if he actually blamed her for her mother's death. Her whole upbringing he had all but turned over to his mother right from the start. Even the choosing of the name he had left to her, stating only that Helena had to be in there somewhere, in remembrance of his beloved wife.

So the tiny infant had been christened Noora Helena Gordon-Hebden, by the Reverend Douglas MacKenzie in

485

the Scottish Presbyterian Church in Hunter's Hollow; the old man came out of retirement specially for the service.

Carrie had held the child in her arms throughout the blessing, but she had insisted that her father carry her out of the church. On the steps outside, however, Billy had handed the infant back to her, with a bitter-sweet smile on his face, and said, 'It's over to you from now on, Ma . . . Just love her, that's all I ask.'

At that moment Carrie knew he could have added, 'for I can't', and a chill had passed over her heart. This squalling, blue-eyed infant had taken his beloved wife from him, and nothing was ever going to change that fact. The passing years had only served to add to the pain as the pink, featureless little creature began to turn into a beautiful young woman who would one day be the living image of her dead mother.

'I think I'll go and say goodnight to Prince, Moo darling,' Noora said, interrupting her grandmother's musing, as she put down her book and rose with a sigh from the chaise. She had called her grandmother by the affectionate Aborigine name of Moo-Choo-Choo since early childhood, but over the years this had been shortened to the more familiar Moo. There was no disguising the affection between the two as Noora bent to kiss the old lady's silver hair.

'I swear that horse gets more cosseting than is good for it,' Carrie chastised, but there was no rancour in her voice. She too remembered the love she had felt for Duke, the first animal she could call her own.

Noora's steps were light as she ran down the passages and out the back door of the big house, to make her way to the stables. It was a calm, balmy evening and the indignation she had felt over her fight with Joe-boy earlier in the day was now a fading memory. Who could possibly remain in a bad mood in such surroundings? The ivy that her grandmother had planted on the house walls was uncurling fresh green shoots that would soon form a

486

verdant canopy over her bedroom window, and the old magnolia tree by the balcony was shedding its blossoms in scented clouds that drifted past on the breeze each night as she lay in bed dreaming of the year to come. So many exciting things were happening in her life just now, making the beginning of the new century seem symbolic somehow. She felt special – really special – for her very country was growing into adulthood at the same time.

'You and your generation *are* the new Australia, Noora darling,' her grandmother had told her that momentous day in Sydney and those words were forever engraved on her heart.

She cast her eyes heavenwards and breathed deeply on the pure evening air. There was a particular stillness about this time of day. Most of the hands had gone home to supper and the work horses were enjoying their well-earned rest. It seemed as if the whole of Yorvik was at peace with itself, and if all Yorvik was at peace, then so was the world.

As she passed through the tack room, she paused to glide her hands over the well-oiled leathers of the saddles and harnesses. Brightly polished ornamental brasses hung from nails in the wall. These were the ones used by the great shire horses when they were done up for the shows. This place had a smell and an atmosphere all of its own. It was one that she loved more than almost any other; only her grandmother's library with its cedar wood panelling and rows of leather-bound volumes could compare. If someone offered her a million pounds she could not choose which she loved the more, her beloved Prince or her precious books.

Her father could not understand this passionate love for things equestrian. Animals bored him almost as much as human beings. Even his own fondness for the written word was not what he claimed it to be, and from a tender age his daughter had realized that he used the library for his drinking much more than for its original purpose. The fact that Noora often disturbed his peace there to search out yet one more book to devour never failed to mystify him as he sat, glass in hand, and pondered on the fate that had decreed he spend his life in this godforsaken place.

But books were the last thing on Noora's mind as she picked her way over the hay-strewn cobbles to reach the end stall where her horse was kept. To her surprise she found she was not alone.

'Joe-boy!'

The tall, tawny-skinned youth turned from brushing the flank of the animal in the next stall and straight white teeth gleamed in the broad mouth as he grinned in recognition and some surprise. 'Noora!'

'I didn't expect you to be here. I just came by to say goodnight to Prince.'

A shaft of evening sunlight broke through the dusty panes of the window, making particles of dust dance in the still air as he continued brushing the animal's chestnut hide and humming softly to himself. Noora's blue eyes narrowed as she squinted across at him. Should she keep up the fight? She sighed. It would take far too much effort. 'I kind of thought you'd have gone fishing tonight,' she said at last.

'Be-anga's busy,' the boy replied with a shrug. Be-anga, the Aboriginal word for guardian, was the name by which he called the man who had been father, uncle, brother and friend to him ever since his foster parents, old Bandicoot and his wife Jeeba, died. Even his name Joe-boy had been chosen by the Irishman himself, in honour of his own father Joseph O'Dwyer, one of the very first Irish Australians; a real hero whose tales of valour the boy knew better than any fairy tale. 'Real busy, he was. He told me to bugger off!'

'Joe-boy!'

But Joe-boy's grin only grew the wider, for he loved to shock her. Not that he believed for a moment that she was really shocked. Noora could swear as well as Be-anga at times, and certainly as well as he could himself. They had had regular swearing contests when they were younger and most of the time she had won hands down. But that was before she started to refer to such things as 'childish', which she seemed to do all the time these days whenever he suggested one of their favourite childhood pursuits. He put down the brush and gave the animal a satisfied slap on its flank. 'That'll do you for tonight, mate!' Then he turned to Noora. 'Do you fancy a ride?'

Noora looked doubtful as she swung on the gate to the stall. Would it end up in another argument? She was really in no mood for such a thing. Anyway, it must be almost nine o'clock and she had to be in by then at the latest. A growing girl needs her beauty sleep, her grandmother insisted, and Moo could be very insistent indeed about her rules being obeyed, even at weekends. 'Oh heck, I don't know about that . . .'

'Just a short one?' Joe-boy coaxed, gathering up the brushes and comb to return them to the tack room. 'Your grandma won't really mind and, for sure, your Dad'll never know.' They were both well aware that by now, Billy would be too far gone to have any idea of the time, or of even what day it was.

Noora looked into the pleading eyes. They were a dark walnut brown with golden glints. He had on his sick spaniel look as she called it, but it had a curious way of melting her heart.

'Please . . . Pretty please . . .'

She sighed, still doubtful.

A quite different look came into Joe-boy's eyes. 'You're not chicken, are you?'

That was the most hurtful of all questions. She swung back fiercely on the gate and with a hefty shove pushed him into the feeding trough. 'You're a pig, Joe-boy! I told you that this morning and it's true. And that's exactly where you deserve to be!' she shouted, as, covered in grain and swill, he struggled to get out.

489

'You bitch!'

'I'm not a bitch! I told you before, a bitch is a female dog, stupid!'

'Well, if I'm a pig, then you're a dog!'

They looked at one another in mutual indignation, then both burst out laughing.

There was a moment's hesitation.

'You'll come?'

'Oh, all right then, I'll come!'

They set off together on the lakeside road and on up the hill to the point where they had built the great celebration bonfire earlier in the year; the remnants of it still lay in a charred circle on the dry ground. From here they had a wonderful panorama of the main parts of the station, including the big house and all its outbuildings. Behind them the sun was just beginning to go down in a searing splash of crimson across the heavens, causing the waters of the lake in the distance to dance with fire.

Noora's breath caught in her throat as she gazed at it. Diving in there would be like diving into the molten heart of the earth itself. Memories of last summer swam into her mind and of cool water washing the cares of the day from her skin. 'I'm going for a swim!' she announced, tossing her long mane back from her shoulders and setting her horse's head in the direction of the lake.

'You can't,' Joe-boy protested. 'It's too late. You have to be back by nine, remember.'

But such silly rules had no relevance at a time like this. 'Just watch me!' she called behind her. 'Who's chicken now?'

She took off like the wind, her heels digging into the animal's soft flesh, urging it on, faster and faster, as her long hair, caught in the dying rays of the sun, flashed gold in the slipstream behind her.

For a second or two he watched her go. Then, unwilling to be left behind, with a cry of 'Come on!', Joe-boy raced off in pursuit, his bare feet pressing on the stirrups, egging the animal to catch up. He knew exactly where she was heading. They had a part of the lake they called their own private pool, in a bend in the stream, just before it reached Yorvik Force.

By the time he got there Noora had already dismounted and was stepping out of her dress. 'Don't sit there staring!' she called up to him. 'Get down and hurry up! Last one in is a scared rabbit!'

He obeyed as he always did, slipping down from his horse, hurriedly tethering it to a nearby tree, his eyes darting back to Noora all the time as the excitement grew within him. She had got down to her chemise now and was undoing the drawstring at the lace-trimmed neck.

She looked up and caught his eyes on her, and she smiled in recognition of his admiring gaze. Poor Joe-boy, she always could read him like a book. 'You'd better hurry up, or you're not gonna win!' she warned.

He began to peel off his shirt, revealing a young supple body the colour of lightly tanned hide, the broadening shoulders already hinting at the physique to come. He tossed the garment over a branch as he ran a hand through the mop of auburn curly hair above the broad, pleasant face. Although they had swum together all their lives, just as they had played together, fought together, laughed and cried together for all of their fifteen years, this was the first swim they had taken together for over a year. Somehow other things had always seemed to intervene. When he had complained to her about it, Noora had told him not to be silly, they were growing up, that was all. They couldn't always be playing around like silly kids.

She was pulling her chemise over her head now and he caught his breath at the sight of her small white breasts in the golden light. She had not had those last year. Not at all. And he could feel his heart beating faster as she turned from him and began to climb out of her drawers.

Then with a triumphant shriek of delight, she tossed the lacy undergarment high in the air and ran laughing down

491

into the cold waters of the pool. She did not bother to wade, but dived off the edge of the bank, to disappear like a silver dart beneath the glittering surface as he climbed out of his trousers.

As he ran down to join her, she resurfaced, squeezing her soaking hair back from her brow with a yell of 'Scared rabbit! I won and Joe-boy's a scared rabbit!'

Not to be outdone, he dived in to join her, his head bobbing up only a few feet from where she was now floating on her back, her eyes closed, her fair hair spreading out on the surface of the water like a golden halo around her head.

Joe-boy stared at her as if transfixed, his feet treading water. Despite the coldness of the pool, he could feel himself begin to sweat and his heart was thudding in his chest. She was so painfully beautiful. He had never thought of her as beautiful before and the shock of the realization mesmerized him.

Noora opened her eyes and, seeing him watching, began to laugh as she rolled on to her front then ducked beneath the surface once more. 'You're even staring like a scared rabbit!' she taunted. Then her smile softened, as she took his dumbstruck expression for disappointment. 'Poor Joe-boy! You can't bear to lose, can you? Race you to the far bank!'

He obeyed automatically, and they set off almost in a line, but this time his more powerful arms had the edge and he got a fingertip touch to the grassy embankment just before she did.

'Who's the scared rabbit now?' he grinned, his pride returning. She was right, he hated to lose just as much as she did.

But Noora too was determined not to end the escapade as the loser. 'Beat you up the bank!'

Before he had time to reply she had hoisted herself out of the water and had begun to scramble up the grassy slope, only to lose her footing and come slithering back down again, landing almost on top of him. He caught her in his arms and the feeling was electric.

Her arms twisted around his neck and she struggled to regain her footing as the soft mud of the water's edge crumbled beneath her tread.

He pressed her body close to his and buried his face in the wet curve of her shoulder.

She gave a small cry as wet flesh touched wet flesh, then she fell silent, and at that moment they both knew that childhood was over.

This time it was different; things had changed forever between them. They had played naked together all their lives, whether building castles in the mud as toddlers, or stripping off out of sight of the prying eyes of the adults, to do as the blackfella kids did and dive into the creeks and billabongs of Yorvik's green acres, as they grew up.

But their bodies were no longer the hard, wiry frames of childhood. The year that had gone had seen to that. Both were taller and firmer, yet softer and stronger. Sensations were happening now as skin touched skin. Sensations that had never occurred to either before. And it felt good. So very good.

The dying rays of the blood-red sun sent flashes of fire across the surface of the pool as they stood there, their bodies entwined, rocking backwards and forwards in the water.

No words passed between them as they scrambled out of the water and up the bank to lie side by side on the dry grass. For what seemed like an eternity they lay there gazing up into the heavens, seared with red and gold, but already darkening with the coming night. Then Noora's hand reached out to touch his arm.

Joe-boy turned his head to see her eyes, dark and luminous in the fading light, burning into his. They had not been this close for so very long. Her fingers were gently stroking the soft damp hairs of his forearm. Her touch covered his skin with gooseflesh. He moved closer, then rolled on top of her as he had done so many times as a child, when they had wrestled and fought with all the competitiveness of young lion cubs. But both knew this was very different.

They gasped in unison as the damp flesh met. Then their arms entwined and they were rolling backwards and forwards on the soft earth. When she cried out in pain a few minutes later, it lasted only seconds. A soft breeze filled their senses with the heady scent of the eucalyptus trees, caressing their naked skin, and above them the night sky was rent with blood, as the sun disappeared below the horizon of the far hills. As they lay there in the shelter of the bank that edged the fire-spangled waters, they were as much a part of Nature's eternal plan as the grass that grew and air they breathed. Their bodies seemed to be moving with the rhythm of the universe itself.

Beneath them the waters of the Yorvik river flowed on to join the great Hunter River, then on into the ocean beyond. But they were beyond time and tide; they were at one with the life force itself. Others had made love on this green grass, countless others, who had been born, loved and died in this fair land. They were all part of that great scheme of things that had no beginning and no end. Eternity was theirs at this moment. Dreamtime was here and now . . .

Then as suddenly as it had happened, it was over.

'We shouldn't have done that,' Joe-boy told Noora, breaking the silence, as they got dressed some five minutes later. 'Only grown-ups are supposed to do that.'

Noora's chin tilted upwards at the words as she tightened the drawstring at the neck of her chemise. Why did he have to spoil everything by bringing feelings of guilt into it? 'Haven't I told you a million times this summer, Joe-boy, *I* am grown up now!' Why did he think she had lost so much interest in their normal childish games this past year? Grown-ups simply didn't act like children any more. And she knew that for absolutely certain she was no longer a child, for hadn't her grandmother told her so several months ago, when she had begun the strange monthly agony known as 'the curse'?

Joe-boy's dark eyes never left her as he tightened the belt of his trousers. How he hated it when she adopted that superior tone. She had used it for months now whenever he suggested they do any of the things they had loved to do together in the past, such as play bushrangers in the woods, or hold boomerang or spear-throwing contests with any of the black kids who might be around. 'Well, if you're grown up, then I must be too, for I'm older than you.'

That made perfect sense to Noora, who smiled indulgently. 'Then if we're both grown up, we can do what grown-ups do without feeling guilty, can't we?' They had both watched blackfella couples doing this for years and there was certainly no sign of guilt amongst them.

'You mean we can do this again sometime?' His heart really was beating fit to burst now.

'If we feel like it,' Noora told him, giving a teasing little smile as she bent down to pull on her shoes. 'And if you promise not to get mad if I let you into a secret.'

She really was teasing him now. 'What secret?' he demanded.

Her shoes buttoned, Noora leant back against the trunk of the tree next to her and studied his expectant face for a long time. Too long.

'What bloody secret?' he demanded, louder this time.

She had not really intended telling him so soon, but what had happened tonight made it seem somehow right that he should know. He was still her very best friend, after all. In fact, more than that – he was her blood brother, for hadn't they cut their wrists and mingled their blood with promises to be 'true unto death' under this very eucalyptus tree she was now leaning against?

She had laughed as the red blood ran and they pressed their open wounds together. But there had been no laughter in his own eyes as he explained to her how this was no ordinary blood, but *kuranita* – the very essence of life itself – that they were exchanging. And he had told her that from that moment their destinies would be as one. They had pledged their unity before the spirits of their Dreamtime and what was done could never be undone in their lifetimes.

'Well, tell me!' His gaze was troubled now as he studied her face.

'Pa wants to send me away to England to get educated,' she said at last, carefully avoiding his eyes as she spoke.

'England! But that's miles away!' Joe-boy was not sure exactly how far, only that it took months to get there. And what was more, Be-anga didn't reckon much to the place at all. 'What does he want to do that for?' he demanded. 'What does your father want to go doing a bloody stupid thing like that for?'

Noora looked down at her feet, and made a semi-circle with the toe of her shoe in the dry sandy ground. 'It's not only Pa,' she said quietly. 'It's me too. I quite fancy the idea.'

Joe-boy looked at her aghast. 'You mean you want to leave Yorvik?' The very idea was unthinkable.

Noora shrugged. 'It – it's not exactly that I want to leave Yorvik, more that I want to see England . . . I want to get a good education, Joey, can't you see that?'

But Joe-boy could not see. 'You're getting a good education right here, for heaven's sake!' Her grandmother's school that they had both attended for the past ten years had a reputation second to none as far as station schools went. 'What does the old lady think of this?'

Noora shrugged, her face darkening at the mention of her grandmother. 'Moo's not too happy about it,' she confessed. 'And I didn't really expect you to be either.'

They stared at one another beneath the darkening sky. 'Is that why you let me do that to you tonight?' he asked in a choked voice. 'Is that what it was all about?'

'I didn't *let* you do anything to me tonight,' Noora answered hotly. 'What happened tonight happened . . . Well, because it did, that's all.'

'Because that's what grown-ups do. Isn't that right, Noora? You had to prove to yourself that you're really not a little kid any more, and this was the best way of doing it. Just like that young fella we saw preparing to undergo his initiation into manhood out there in the bush, you knew you couldn't let them send you to England still feeling a kid at heart, so you used me to make you a woman.'

A deep flush crept up Noora's neck and suffused her cheeks. It sounded so plausible, but he had it all wrong. It wasn't like that at all. 'I didn't plan this to happen tonight,' she protested weakly. 'I didn't even know you'd be in the stables . . . I only went there to say goodnight to Prince . . . This wasn't planned, Joe-boy. I told you, it just happened, that's all . . .'

'And now that it's happened, what then?'

Noora shrugged. 'It doesn't make any difference.'

This was too much. He grabbed her by the shoulders. 'What do you mean, it doesn't make any difference? Damned right it does! It means you've given yourself to me. That's what it means. You're mine now, Noora, whether you realize it or not. We belong together after this. And you're right, it *has* made you a woman. It's made you *my* woman!'

Now it was Noora's turn to get angry as she threw his hands from her shoulders. 'I'm not *your* woman or *any-body's* woman!' she cried. 'I'm my own woman and always will be!'

And with that she pushed him aside and strode over to where her horse was waiting. 'I'm my own woman, Joe-boy!' she called back to him from the saddle, as her heels dug into the horse's sides. 'You can never own me – no one can!'

And as she jerked round the animal's head and set off at the gallop back to Yorvik, she did not hear the whispered,

'You're wrong, Noora. You're so very wrong,' from the young man she had left behind.

Whether she realized it or not, they were more than blood brothers now. They were man and woman. She had given herself to him tonight. They had given their bodies to each other, freely and unasked, just as they had given their souls with the mingling of their blood all those years ago in childhood. One day she would realize that.

CHAPTER THIRTY-EIGHT

Noora entered the house by the back door, making her way quietly up the servants' stairs to her bedroom on the first floor. She felt both exhilarated and disturbed by what had just taken place between herself and Joe-boy. On the one hand she revelled in the knowledge that they now shared an even more special secret than their blood-brothers rite; tonight they had initiated one another into the coveted state of adulthood and it had been only right and proper that it should happen with each other. But his claim that she was now 'his woman' was absurd and she dismissed it as an understandable reaction to her news that she was considering finishing her education at an English school. It was simply emotional blackmail to stop her from leaving him.

If her confession that she was thinking of leaving Yorvik had not got off on such a wrong footing and he had not got mad like that, she would have explained to him that going to England would not be such a terrible thing after all. It was all part of her own steps towards the Dreamtime. Surely he would have been able to understand that? After all, they had talked about it often enough in the past. They both knew that leaving one's home and family to test oneself in the unknown was all part of growing up, of attaining that wholeness of spirit that would ultimately lead to *Palanari*.

In some ways, she thought, the blackfellas' beliefs made so much more sense than the whitefellas'. She loved the concept of *Palanari* – of Dreamtime – and how the coming of age of the spirit was as important as the physical changes that signified adulthood. The idea that one had to leave the comfort of one's tribal home and people to go out and test oneself in the world at large was a concept that appealed greatly. The more she had thought about it over the past few months, the more convinced she had become that England would be her perfect testing ground. To go Walkabout to the other side of the world, to the old country itself, would be the best preparation for attaining her eventual Dreamtime that she could possibly imagine.

But, on the other hand, somewhere deep inside her, she also felt a certain degree of guilt, for Joe-boy would never have such a choice to make; his horizons were limited to the thousand acres of Yorvik land and a roof shared with the old Irishman who set no store by books and learning anyway. Joe-boy had no one to encourage him to better himself. His personal Walkabout would be a poor thing in comparison.

Noora had often wondered over the past few years if Joe-boy would have had more interest in book-learning had he been brought up in a proper educated white family. In some ways she knew that he was every bit as bright as she was. He seemed to have an intuition about life and people that went far beyond anything you could learn from a book. And his athletic prowess was far greater than that of any of the white kids on the station. He could climb trees like a monkey, swim like a fish, and run as fast as any of the blackfella kids of his own age. And perhaps it was this fondness for the great outdoors that made his attention wander so much in school. From her own seat at the other side of the room she would see that dreamy look come into his eyes and his gaze would stray to the window. Then in spirit he would be gone. Mentally school would be over for the day although lessons might have only just begun. There would be notes home, of course, official protestations that Joe-boy was not paying proper attention and fulfilling his potential. But she knew that these went straight into the stove, for not only could the Irishman not read them, but he had every sympathy with the boy. Who in their right mind would want to concentrate on arithmetic when the world was beckoning you with every sunbeam that glinted through the glass, every breeze that blew through that schoolroom prison window?

But even Noora did not completely understand the full impact Sean O'Dwyer, Joe-boy's beloved Be-anga, had had on his life. Although he could neither read nor write, the old man had a wisdom that went far beyond the written word. He had taught the young boy all he knew about so many things other than book-learning, both about his white Australian heritage – from a distinctly Irish perspective – and he had also spent long hours instilling in the child a deep love and understanding of his mother's people, the Aborigines. Spiritually, childhood in that small stringy-bark hut had been a unique combination of the white and the black, and physically it had been a small boy's heaven; a time of unremitting joy in learning to hunt and fish; to track goannas and bandicoots; to tickle fish in the streams and pools; to master throwing the boomerang or practising to throw his own specially made spear at the *djuta*, the small bark disc blackfella boys used to test their marksmanship, and to ride bare-back across Yorvik's wide acres, and pity the poor white kids like Noora whose parents made them attend school every single day.

'Sloping off,' her grandmother would call it, whenever Be-anga allowed Joe-boy to skip school to join him fishing in the creek. 'You're doing no good encouraging that child to slope off like that,' the old lady would call out to the Irishman if they happened to run into her on their way to the lake.

But Sean O'Dwyer would merely smile and wave, with a cheery 'G'day to you, Carrie love!'

He was the only one on station to call the boss by her first name and it was still something of a mystery to Joe-boy exactly what the relationship of these two such important people in his life had been. That they were closer than mistress and servant there was no doubt, and even as a very young child he had been aware of the visits made by the old lady to his guardian's hut, where the two of them would sit and talk for hours, late into the night.

'Yon's the finest woman that ever walked God's earth,' the old man had told the boy on more than one occasion, and Joe-boy had had little cause to doubt it, for Carrie Gordon-Hebden seemed little short of a deity herself to all those who lived and worked on Yorvik's thousand acres.

If Joe-boy stopped to think about it, which he did now and then, he realized it was strange indeed how entwined his own life had been since birth with the two females in the big house – the grandmother and granddaughter. He could not include the master in the equation, for Billy Gordon-Hebden had made no secret of his total disregard, even outright animosity, towards both the Irishman and his young charge. But the fact that Carrie had been the one to save his life at birth and then for him to be brought up of late by the man who seemed to matter more to the old lady than any other except her own son, seemed to Joe-boy to make him some kind of kin with the Gordon-Hebdens. Certainly it had made him regard Noora from a very early age as far more than his Mistress's granddaughter; in fact, they had been far more than friends – more like sister and brother. The pride he had taken over the years in walking side by side with her down the dusty path leading to the small clapboard schoolhouse was very real. She was without question the prettiest girl in the place, with her long fair hair reaching almost to her waist and those blue eyes of hers that could look so innocent one minute, yet fill with devilment the next.

There was no doubt in Joe-boy's mind that he loved Noora. He could not remember a time when she was not there, when it was not his duty to protect her. The fact that she lived in the big house and he had to make do with first Bandicoot and Jeeba's shanty and then the Irishman's tumbledown cabin had made no difference. That special relationship had made itself clear from the very start. And despite her family's wealth, and their power over the inhabitants of Yorvik, he had never felt inferior to her in any way, for the outdoors was his real home and just as he bowed to her sovereignty around the big house and the station itself, out there in the bush it was a different matter altogether. That was a place where he knew he was king. He merely smiled when she told him that the land all around them belonged to her grandmother and would one day belong to her, for, like the blackfellas, he knew that that was just stupid whitefella talk. No one could own the land any more than they could own the air you breathed.

But most of the time he humoured her, and throughout their childhood he had let her follow him and even take part in some of his activities as he pitted his wits and growing strength against the animals and the elements that made up their own personal part of this great land.

As they had grown older Joe-boy had become aware of the need to dream up new ways to win her admiration, invent new tokens of his love. One of the most impressive had been his success at persuading the elders of the Yorvik tribe to admit her to their Dream Circle – a rare privilege indeed for any white person. But as the grandchild of Kabbarli, their revered Whitefella Missus Boss, Joe-boy suspected that Noora's place round the campfire was almost assured without his intervention.

But the memory of that day would live on in his heart, as he knew it would live on in hers.

He had held tightly to Noora's hand as together they had taken their places opposite the elders of the tribe, across the gleaming embers of the campfire. As the crimson and opal autumn sky of their tenth year began to darken and, as the breeze blew the faint but heady scent of the eucalyptus trees to fan the flames of the fire, softly in the dying light the chanting had begun. Their own childish voices had joined in the incantations directed towards the heavens and the spirits of the moon and stars now preparing to shine down upon them.

On the breeze the spirits had come, their sacred voices

whispering through the leaves of the tall fragrant gum trees that surrounded their gathering. If they listened hard, they were told, they would hear their spirit voices informing them that the spirit of *Monkeemi*, the dawn wind, had been reborn into the soul of the white child in their midst; a white child with hair the colour of the morning sun and eyes the colour of the heavens themselves.

When at last the chanting was at an end, the Father of the tribe had handed Noora a branch of the bauhinia tree, the sacred symbol of the Earth Mother, and along with the newly broken branch, he took a small, delicately made spear of the same wood, and this he held into the flames of the fire.

When the point was glowing he bid her stand up and stretch out her left wrist, then he touched the burning tip of the spear to the white flesh.

At that fateful second Joe-boy thought he would burst with pride, for Noora neither flinched nor uttered a sound as the old man told her that from that moment on she had been admitted to their sacred Dream Circle, and the spirit of *Monkeemi*, the dawn wind, would protect her all the days of her life.

From that day to this Noora had been proud of the small shiny spot of scar tissue that was all that remained of the ceremony — that and the memory they both shared. And there had been so many such memories over their fifteen years together.

But things were no longer as they had been. This past year had seen a difference to the closeness there had been between them since birth. For months now Noora had been insisting it was all part of growing up, this unwillingness to join in their contests and games any more. Her blue eyes often seemed distant as they looked disdainfully on the things that had given them so much pleasure in the past. She had taken to speaking more and more of a world beyond Yorvik, 'a world that is waiting there for us to explore'. It was a world of big cities, cities beyond the seas, with names like London and Paris and Rome. There was something called Culture that she told him was very important, and that one could not become a complete human being without it. And Culture could not be found in their own land. 'Australia is not old enough yet, Joe-boy, can't you understand?'

But Joe-boy knew he would never understand. This land was all that he ever wanted out of life. Here he was happy, just as she had been happy. Why go searching after things in other folks' backyards when you had so much in your own?

For months now he had been fretting over the change in her. But tonight all that had changed; tonight he felt elated as he made his way back to the hut he shared with the old Irishman, for, despite all her threats to leave here and go to England, Joe-boy knew that things were better now than they had ever been. She had given herself to him as a woman, and, as a man, he had accepted. She was his and would remain his till the end of their days. They would walk through this life towards their *Palanari* – their Dreamtime – together. And nothing and no one on earth could ever change that destiny.

It was right that she should have been thinking of her road to the Dreamtime tonight, for they had talked together about it often in the past, as he handed on to her the teachings of his Aborigine people taught to him by Be-anga, whose own part-blackfella mother had instilled in him those same sacred beliefs as a small child. And he had also remembered with love and recounted to Noora the stories told by old Bandicoot and his wife Jeeba, before they died. As a small child he had grown to love those two old people who had had such a fund of myths and legends to pass on – stories that went back to the beginning of time itself. And although he sometimes attended the small chapel here on the station, or the big Presbyterian kirk in Hunter's Hollow, he knew the whitefellas' church had nothing like it – these beliefs that had been passed down to the blackfellas from the Ancients since time immemorial. The Christian bible was nothing but tales from Jewish history, while his mother's people had all the living world as well as the dead to draw on for its spiritual fulfilment.

But in a strange way tonight, the more he thought about it, the more Joe-boy felt he understood Noora's need to go to England, for soon he too would be forced to go Walkabout. Before true adulthood could be attained, he knew that the young must go out and prove themselves. This was something taught to him by both Be-anga and old Bandicoot. They must leave those they loved and go out to seek their true selves by testing themselves in the unknown. This they must go forth and do before they could become completely whole adult human beings. To do otherwise was to become merely a piece of human driftwood, a dead soul within a human body. And he knew that with the death of the spirit came the death of that body, for one could not exist without the other. Old Bandicoot of the kind, wise eyes had first taught him that, as they had sat together by the campfire at night, beneath the wide, starry sky. And he remembered how the old man would puff on his pipe of memory and tell him of times past, and of how he too had gone forth as a young man into the bush: for three full moons he had lived by his skill as a hunter and fisher. Then, and only then, did he return to claim Jeeba for his own.

Perhaps, Joe-boy pondered, if Noora insisted on going to England it would not be the end of the world, for one day she too would return, just as Bandicoot had done. And that day he would claim her back as his own. His heart leapt at the thought.

And the old Irishman, who had been watching him from his seat by the window of the stringy-bark hut, puffed on his pipe and smiled fondly at the boy who was no longer a boy, but not yet a man.

Joe-boy caught his guardian's glance and smiled self-consciously, as if the old man was reading his thoughts.

'Have you never thought of getting yourself hitched, Be-anga? Was there never anyone in your life that you wanted to settle down with?' It was a question that had often passed through the boy's mind over the years, for there was no doubting that the Irishman must have been a good-looking fella in his youth and had no more vices than most.

Sean O'Dwyer was taken aback, and shifted uncomfortably in his seat. 'And what kind of a damn-fool question would that be to be coming out with?' he asked. 'Have I not done my duty by you well enough, and can we not cope as well as the next body without having the need of an interfering woman around the place?'

'Oh yes,' Joe-boy assured him. 'You've done that all right. But sometimes I can't help wondering if . . .'

'If there was any biddy who'd taken my fancy in my younger days, is that it?'

Joe-boy nodded and smiled. 'Aye, that's it. Was there ever a sheila you fancied settling down with?'

The old man placed his pipe back in his mouth and sucked deeply. 'Aye, there might have been,' he said at last.

'Then what happened?' the boy asked, surprised by the truthfulness of the admission.

The Irishman gave a wistful smile and a wry half-laugh. 'Nothing happened, Joey lad. Nothing at all. And that was the trouble.'

'You mean you never asked her to marry you – or even to share your hut?'

Sean O'Dwyer gave a weary shake of his head. 'I reckon she had better things to do than to consider either of those two options, lad,' he said, turning to look out of the window where the rooftops of the big house were just visible above the distant treetops. 'And the secret of happiness is to recognize you can't always have what you want most in this life and settle for the next best thing.'

Joe-boy pondered on the words, then shook his head. 'I could never do that,' he said truthfully. 'I know what I want and I'm going to get it.'

The old man turned from the window and looked at the boy in some surprise. There was a determination in his voice that he had never heard before. 'Is that so?'

Joe-boy got up from his seat and walked to the door. He too could now see the outline of the big house's tall chimneys, and he thought of the girl who would now be under that roof. What were her thoughts at this moment? Did she realize that they were now one, that no one else could ever be allowed to come between them, that they belonged to each other to the end of their days?

But Noora knew nothing of the thoughts that were going through Joe-boy's head as she made her way upstairs to her bedroom. Her main concern since leaving her friend had been to get back into the big house without being seen. No matter how easy-going her grandmother was in some ways, she knew that Moo did not like to be disobeyed.

The relief she felt when she closed her bedroom door behind her was enormous. But she had been in her room only a minute or two when there was a tap on the door and her grandmother's voice called, 'Noora darling, are you in there?'

Noora's heart stood still as she caught a glimpse of her still damp hair in the dressing mirror. 'Just a moment, Moo!'

Dashing to open her wardrobe, she slipped her dressing-gown over her outdoor clothes, then rushed to open the door.

'Oh, there you are, darling! You had me so worried! I guessed you'd gone out on your horse, but didn't hear you come back and thought you must have had a fall or something.' At the back of Carrie's mind was always the tragic fate of her granddaughter's mother, for Noora had inherited that same passionate love of riding – and, worse,

508

she often went out bare-back, which was something Nella had never done.

'Poor Moo – I didn't mean to worry you. I've been back for ages. I've been washing my hair.' Noora was surprised to find how quickly the lies tripped off the tongue as she pushed a hand through her long fair locks, then twisted the lot on top of her head as she looked this way and that in front of the dressing mirror on the chest by her side. 'I'll have to start thinking of wearing it up soon,' she mused. 'Especially if I go to England like Daddy wants.'

There was a moment's silence, then Carrie quietly closed the bedroom door behind her. She had been meaning to bring the subject up for weeks now, but had always put it off, fearing what she might hear. 'Is that really what you want?' she asked her granddaughter. 'Really and truly?'

Noora forsook the primping to turn and face her grand-mother and, seeing the troubled look in her eyes, she gave a sigh. 'I honestly don't know,' she said. 'Part of me hates the thought of leaving Yorvik – and you. And the other part of me agrees with Daddy that I should take the chance to further my education – meet different people and find out about life outside a sheep station.'

'But you do meet different people already,' Carrie pro-tested. 'You go to lots of parties and we go to Sydney and Newcastle regularly, and places like that.'

'And places like that,' Noora groaned. 'That's just the point. There's more to life than "places like that". Can't you see, Moo darling? If Daddy sent me to one of those special English schools he's been telling me about to finish my education, I would have a whole new outlook on life when I came back in two years' time.'

'And that's what you'd really want?' Carrie found it impossible to keep the disappointment from her voice.

'Yes . . . Yes, I think it is. And I'd come home after I matriculated, of course. I wouldn't want to stay there.'

Now it was Carrie's turn to sigh. She seemed to have heard all this a generation before. She had hoped it would be different with Noora. She had felt for all these years she had had a kindred spirit in the young girl, someone who loved this golden land as much as she did. Someone who would no more trade it for dismal, grey old England than fly to the moon. But Noora had been reading too many books and magazines of late, and listening to her father too much. And England seemed far from the cold grey country of her grandmother's memory. And would she really be so keen to come back after she matriculated? She was a bright girl – very bright – and if she did well enough there might even be the temptation of university. Her father had talked to her so often about Oxford that it seemed to be an enchanted place where she could have her fill of all the great books of the world and meet other young people whose minds thirsted for knowledge as much as hers did.

'Have you told Joe-boy you're thinking of leaving?' Carrie did not know why she asked that question at this moment, for the Irishman's charge was part of the reason she believed her son was so intent on sending Noora away. Quite apart from Billy's own desire to return to England, Carrie knew he had been growing increasingly concerned about the amount of time the two young people were still spending together. It had not seemed to bother him when they were children, but now they were well into adolescence he was becoming quite disturbed about the friendship continuing at the same level of intimacy.

He knew as well as Carrie did that they had hardly spent a day apart and had grown up together as close as any brother or sister. Closer than most, in fact, for they were true companions, not simply siblings thrown together by fate. 'Well, have you? What do you think *he*'ll say about it?'

Noora felt her cheeks flush at the mention of her friend's name. Her own feelings about Joe-boy were too confused to attempt to put into words. He had simply been there all her life. He had been her shadow – the dark *doppelgänger*

510

that was always there. He was her mirror image turned inside out: she the blonde-haired, fair-skinned, blue-eyed female — he the dark-haired, dusky-skinned, brown-eyed male. She told him wonderful tales of her European ancestors that she had culled from the books in her grandmother's library and he educated her in the ancient ways of his Aboriginal forebears. He was her guide along the secret paths into *Palanari* — their own special Dreamtime.

Noora walked to the window and looked out towards the lake where they had taken another important step along that path this very night. 'I don't think Joe-boy will understand,' she said softly. 'I don't think he will understand at all.'

Then her brow furrowed as she turned to face her grandmother. 'Why does Daddy not approve of him any more?' She could not even mention Joe-boy's name any longer in her father's presence, but he would mutter something about 'that damned darkie'.

As her granddaughter's troubled eyes studied her face, Carrie found herself at a loss for an answer. The truth would not do, for that she could never tell. Her son now hated the youth with almost the same passion he had reserved all these years for the man whom the boy called Be-anga. Joe-boy, like the Irishman Sean O'Dwyer, was guilty of two cardinal sins in Billy's eyes: one, he was part Aborigine, and two, his daughter Noora loved him, just as she, his mother, loved the Irishman. But more than that, he was terrified that the childhood love the two youngsters felt for each other might any day become much more than that.

'Your father's worried, darling,' she said, trying to find the best way to phrase it. 'You and Joe-boy are growing up. It — it doesn't do for young people of your age to be alone together any longer.'

'Why ever not?'

Carrie began to pace the floor, her hands clasped in front of her as she struggled hard for the best way to put it. 'You

– you remember when that thing happened to you last summer, how when you saw the blood you thought you were ill – dying even – and I explained to you that you weren't ill at all, it simply meant you had become a woman at last.'

Noora nodded, remembering well that terrible day.

'Well, now that you are a woman there are certain things you must not do – or at least you must save for the man you love,' Carrie went on.

Then, seeing the puzzled frown on her granddaughter's face, she thought of a better explanation. 'You remember a year or so ago when on one of our walks by the lake we stumbled on that young blackfella couple lying in the grass together and you asked me why they were acting like that?'

'I remember.' She had witnessed dozens of such incidents of lovemaking with Joe-boy over the years, but never with her grandmother present before.

'And do you remember what I said?'

'You said that's what men and women did together when they were grown up. You said that they were showing that they loved one another.'

'That's right, darling . . . And that's what your daddy's now so frightened of happening when you're alone with Joe-boy, now that you're both practically grown up.'

Noora's face lightened. 'Is that all?' She gave an enormous sigh of relief. 'Well, you can tell him that he doesn't have to be scared any more because Joe-boy and I have already done it.'

Carrie stopped pacing and whirled round, her mouth dropping open. 'I beg your pardon?'

Noora shrugged, relieved the fuss was all about so little. 'You can tell him he doesn't have to worry about us not knowing what to do or any of that stuff any more. We had both seen it done dozens of times anyway.'

'And . . . ?' Carrie prayed she was not quite understanding the way this conversation was going.

'And you said that was what grown-ups did when they loved each other. And Joe-boy and I love each other, so we did it.'

Please God, let me be dreaming this, Carrie prayed as she gaped open-mouthed at her granddaughter. 'You – you're telling me that you and Joe-boy have made love?' The last two words were so faint as to be barely audible.

'Sure we did.'

'When, for God's sake?'

'Tonight.'

'*Tonight!*' She was almost screaming. 'The pair of you made love *tonight?*'

Noora began to back away, alarmed at the reaction her matter-of-fact statement had produced. Why was her grandmother looking at her like that? There was nothing wrong with it, was there? The blackfellas did it around the place all the time, and she herself had said it was what grown-ups did when they loved one another. Was she trying to tell her she shouldn't love Joe-boy any more, was that it?

'I don't know why you're getting so het up,' she said defensively. 'There's nothing to get mad about.' What exactly was going on here? Even Joe-boy himself had turned funny afterwards and accused her of only doing it because she wanted to be grown up before she left for England. But what was wrong with that, for heaven's sake? She had wondered what it would be like for years now, and this was the first time they had had their clothes off together since she had become officially 'grown up' last summer.

Carrie was looking as if she might faint at any moment as she made for the edge of the bed and sat down. 'Now listen to me, Noora,' she said, ashen-faced. 'Listen hard, for this is serious – very serious . . . This – this thing you did . . . It was exactly the same as that young couple was doing that we saw the other day?'

Noora nodded. 'I expect so.' What a silly question! How could she possibly be sure? Her grandmother had hustled her away within seconds of them stumbling on the pair.

'Well now,' Carrie persisted. 'It couldn't have been *exactly* the same, could it, because – well, because they were naked.'

'So were we.'

'Lord have mercy!'

'We – we did it after a swim,' Noora added quickly. 'So we had to be naked for that, anyway.'

Carrie was looking at her granddaughter as if she had just confessed to murder. She was going hot and cold at the same time. This was too much, far too much, to take in.

For her part Noora was feeling both confused and betrayed. As far as she was concerned they had done nothing wrong. The only thing she had had to feel guilty about tonight was staying out an hour later than was normally allowed.

'I think you'd better get to bed,' Carrie said, rising with difficulty from the foot of the mattress. 'We'll talk about this in the morning.'

'But there's nothing to talk about!' Noora protested. 'We only made love, for heaven's sake, and you know we love each other, so what's wrong with that?'

Carrie shook her head. Perhaps it was her own fault this had occurred. Maybe she had neglected her duty that day out by the lake. Maybe she should have told her then that white folks' moral values were different from blackfellas'. White folks – decent white folks – waited until after they were married before indulging in such intimacy. 'I – I can't answer that, Noora dear. Not yet, anyway. I – I am far too shocked, far too shocked by what I have just heard to say anything right now.'

Noora flopped down on her bed and glared at her grandmother for what she considered a ridiculous reaction to a very normal occurrence. 'Where are you going?' she demanded sullenly. 'You're not going to blab to Daddy, are you?'

'No, darling, I'm not going to tell your Daddy – not yet, anyway. There's someone else I'd rather talk to first.' With that she opened the bedroom door and, feeling sure her legs would give way beneath her before she reached her destination, she made her way slowly downstairs and out of the back of the house to begin the quarter-mile walk to the Irishman's hut. If ever there was a matter that concerned them both, this was it.

CHAPTER THIRTY-NINE

Sean O'Dwyer looked in some surprise at the breathless figure of Carrie silhouetted against the night sky in the doorway of his hut. 'What the heck?'

'I – I must talk to you, Sean . . .' Carrie peered anxiously over her old friend's shoulder to where Joe-boy was hunched over a supper of damper and tea laid out on the wooden chest. 'But not here. I must talk to you alone.'

At that Joe-boy turned and looked quizzically at her. Carrie avoided his eyes and put an imploring hand on the Irishman's arm. 'Please, Sean, it's important. Very important.'

Sean O'Dwyer gave a shrug and glanced to the youth behind him. 'I'll be back in a few minutes,' he said gruffly. 'Make sure you clean up before turning in.'

He closed the door of the hut behind him and took Carrie's arm, giving it a placatory squeeze. 'Now what's this all about? What can be so dashed important it brings you hurrying down here at this time of night?'

She paused to turn and face him, before they had gone more than a few feet. Her face was distraught. 'It's terrible,' she said, wondering how to begin. 'Just terrible. And it's probably all my fault. I should have warned her . . . Oh Sean, I should have warned her!'

'Warned who about what, for pity's sake? What are you talking about, Carrie. Has something happened to Noora? Is that it?'

'That's exactly it,' Carrie said wearily, chewing at her bottom lip, her hands clasped in front of her as if in prayer.

'She hasn't had an accident, has she?' At the back of their minds was constantly the thought of her mother Nella's tragic fate.

'Oh no, she hasn't had an accident. Well, not exactly.'

'Then what is it? What's "not exactly" an accident? What has happened to her that's so bad it brings you running down here at this time of night?' Seeing how upset she was, he was trying very hard to be patient.

'Joe-boy's happened to her, that's what,' Carrie burst out, her voice rising. 'Your precious Joe-boy's ruined my granddaughter!' Then seeing the puzzled look on his face, she repeated, 'Ruined her, Sean . . . Do you hear? Ruined her! You know what I mean . . .'

'Ruined your gra . . . !' Then his face broke into a grin as realization dawned. 'Well, I'll be blessed! The little bugger!' The dark eyes beneath the shaggy white brows widened in a mixture of disbelief and admiration. 'You don't mean young Joey back there has had it away with Noora!'

'That's exactly what I mean,' Carrie replied, tight-lipped, her anger rising to boiling point at this totally inappropriate reaction to her news.

'Well, I'll be blowed . . . The young devil!' The Irishman slapped his thigh and laughed out loud. 'The saucy little blighter!' Then he shook his head, 'Well, I'll say this for him, he's got more spunk than I had as a young fella, that's for sure!'

'And what's that supposed to mean?'

Sean O'Dwyer's eyes softened, but glistened still, with both pride and amusement as he confessed, 'Oh Carrie . . . How long is it since we first met? Sixty years, as near as dammit . . . Sixty years and not one of them has passed without me regretting that I didn't have the guts – or whatever it took – to do that same darned thing with the woman I loved!'

Carrie felt her colour rising. 'I swear I don't know what you're talking about.'

'You know what I'm talking about all right.' Then his voice softened, along with his expression. 'You're a bright woman, Carrie Hebden, always have been. You don't need me to spell it out to you.'

517

Was he deliberately trying to embarrass her? 'That's not what I came here to talk about,' she protested. 'And you know it. I came here expecting . . .'

She paused just long enough for him to interrupt. 'Sympathy, is that it? You wanted me to throw up my hands in horror and shout, "What a terrible thing – a most dastardly thing! I am totally shocked and heartily disapprove!" Is that what you expected? Then if so, you've figured wrong, Carrie love, for I don't disapprove. Not at all. Heck, how can I?' He gave a throaty chuckle. 'Bloody hell, I envy the lad!'

'You *what*?' Carrie blazed. This really was too much.

'Well, not like that!' he put in swiftly, before she really went off the deep end. 'Not with young Noora . . . I'm far too long in the tooth for that sort of thing. But I envy him his courage in accepting his feelings for the girl and having the guts to do something about it. That way he won't have to live the rest of his life with thoughts of what might have been.' And his eyes were serious as they looked into hers in the moonlight. 'Oh Carrie, Carrie . . . Who are we to sit in judgement on the young? Look at us – two decrepit old codgers with one foot in the grave! We were young once, remember – you and me. We wanted each other too, didn't we? . . . Well, didn't we?'

She looked away, feeling the embarrassment burn in her cheeks. Why was he doing this to her? For sixty years they had skirted around their own personal feelings for each other. Why bring them up now of all times?

Sean took hold of her shoulders. 'Look at me, Carrie,' he commanded, his voice gruff with emotion. 'Look at me.'

Slowly she turned her head and looked at him. In the soft silver of the moonlight her eyes took in the grizzled grey head and beard, and the skin, creased and wrinkled, the colour of newly tanned hide. Only his eyes remained the same, walnut brown with flecks that still glinted gold in the light. They could look deeper into her soul than any man's alive. And they were looking at her now, urging her to understand.

'We still love each other, don't we?'

She nodded, unsure exactly where this was leading.

'And we wanted each other once, when we were young . . . In those far-off days before the blood cooled and *Matunga* claimed us for these dried-up old wrecks of ourselves we've now become. We too wanted to make love back then. And we never had the courage. Neither of us. Did we? And we've regretted it ever since. Isn't that true? Isn't it, Carrie? Isn't it?'

'I – I don't know . . .'

'But you do know. You do. You know just as well as I do.'

Her eyes remained locked with his, and as she stood looking at him the years were rolling back, to the time long before their hair had lost its colour, to a time when their bodies and their hearts were young, to a day more golden than any before or since, when they stood together in the sparkling waters of Yorvik Force, then lay on the soft grass, their hearts beating as one . . . Oh yes, she had wanted him then, all right. It was true. Just as she had wanted him so many times throughout the years that followed. She had wanted him in body as well as soul, and she had never until this moment had the courage to admit it to him. 'Yes, yes, it's true,' she whispered. 'You know it's true . . .'

He took her in his arms and pressed his face into the white hair of her head, and suddenly she was crying, sobbing quietly into the rough cloth of his shoulder. If she was crying for herself or for her granddaughter she did not know, or how long she stood there in the comfort of his arms. But when she had finished, she prised herself gently from his embrace, then dabbed her eyes and shook her head.

'Be happy for them,' Sean said softly. 'Rejoice in their courage to do what we never did.'

But she could no more rejoice in what had happened than he could understand the gravity of the situation. 'What if she has a child?' she found herself saying. 'What then?'

'Then we will rejoice even more and bring it up together!'

He did not understand. He really did not understand. 'No, Sean,' she said quietly. 'That can never be.' She knew that Billy would never allow it. He would kill both Joe-boy and the child rather than see that happen.

The Irishman's brown eyes darkened as slowly his expression changed. 'Because Joey's part blackfella . . . Is that it?'

Carrie nodded bleakly and reached out and touched his arm. 'I did not make these rules,' she said softly, pleading for him to understand. 'Nor Billy. Society made them.'

'No, you did not make them,' Sean replied, tight-lipped. 'People like you never make them. You only carry them out.'

He turned from her and looked out over the moonlit landscape they both knew and loved so well, but a coldness had entered his soul. 'So who is the more guilty, Carrie, tell me that? The people who make those rules that divide others into different classes by their background or the colour of their skin, or those who give them validity by carrying them out?'

She had no answer to that. He was asking her to choose between his own morality and that of her son. His was the natural morality that sprang from a life born and raised in the freedom of this new land, where such things as class or caste had no place. He judged a man or a woman by other criteria than those so important to the Anglo-Saxon caste who still ruled this country. But Noora's father did not. Billy had been brought up to accept and uphold the morality of the British gentleman. And she herself had been instrumental in seeing those values instilled in him.

'I'm sorry, Sean,' she said in a defeated voice. 'So very sorry . . .'

He knew exactly what she was apologizing for. 'Not half as sorry as I am,' he said quietly. And, as he stood there looking at her, he knew the wheel had come full circle. That gulf he had detected between them all those years ago — a whole lifetime ago — was still as wide today as it was then. 'Go home, Carrie,' he said in a tired voice. 'Go home to your big house, and your lily-white grand-daughter, and your fine English gentleman of a son. Go home to them all and leave us in peace . . .'

And with that he turned and walked slowly back into the hut, closing the door behind him.

Joe-boy was still sitting finishing his tea and he looked up in some concern as the old man sat down heavily on his favourite chair and shook his head. 'Something wrong, Be-anga?'

Sean O'Dwyer looked at the young man now regarding him so gravely with those walnut brown eyes of his, and he sighed. 'Not as far as I'm concerned, Joey lad. Not as far as I'm concerned.'

'But the boss — she must have come to tell you something pretty important at this time of night.'

'Aye, that she did.' He reached inside his pocket and extracted his pipe which he began to fill from an old baccy tin sitting on the empty stove. Joe-boy watched in silence as the old man held a light to the bowl of the pipe and puffed the golden shreds into life. He sucked deeply on the pungent smoke before saying in a tired voice, 'She came to tell me about you and young Noora . . . What the pair of you got up to out there tonight.'

Joe-boy's eyes gleamed, then he looked puzzled. If that was all she came to tell him, what was Be-anga looking so miserable about? 'You mean about us becoming man and woman?'

Sean looked at him and gave a half smile. 'If that's how you want to put it.'

Joe-boy drained the last dregs of the tea from his mug and placed it on the top of the chest. 'I reckon I'm a real lucky fella,' he said, with not a little pride in his voice. 'For Noora to become my woman is . . .'

But before he got any further Sean interrupted him. 'Look, son, I'm a mite too tired to go into this whole business with you right now, but let's just say we'll have a bit to talk about, you and me, before this week's out . . .' He searched for the right words, but none would come.

'What exactly do you mean, Be-anga? You're not mad at me, are you?'

The old man shook his head. 'No, Joe lad, I'm not mad at you, but this man-woman business . . . Well, that's blackfella talk. White folks go about such things differently. I reckoned you knew that by now.'

Joe-boy looked at him, his dark eyes grave. This had been the trouble throughout his whole life, sorting out what were blackfella and what were whitefella ways of doing things. Sometimes the two got so mixed up in his head he thought he would never understand where to draw the line. 'But white folks – they believe in that too, don't they? They get married and stuff.'

'Aye, they do that all right.'

'Then Noora and me, we can do it their way too. We can go to church and get married and all that.'

The old Irishman looked at the young man who was as dear to him as any legitimate son could ever be and a deep sigh welled within him from the very depths of his soul. How could he tell him he would never marry the girl he loved, and had loved all his young life? How could he tell him that in the eyes of the world he would never be regarded as good enough for the likes of Noora? How could he cut out his heart? 'We'll talk about it another time, Joey lad,' he said quietly. And he cursed the coward in him for not having the guts to tell the truth.

It was two days before Carrie had the courage to call Dr Fraser from Hunter's Hollow to examine her granddaughter. The old man arrived mid-evening and listened with barely disguised horror as she told him of what had occurred between the two young people, and she felt ashamed of herself for making it sound more like a rape than it actually was.

The doctor's face was grave, when he emerged from Noora's bedroom ten minutes later, after completing the examination.

'Well?' Carrie enquired, not quite sure exactly what she was querying.

'The harm's been done all right,' the old Scotsman said, fastening up his jacket, then adjusting his shirt cuffs. 'But it'll be some time before we know if her life is completely ruined.'

'You mean . . . ?'

'I mean if there's a baby on the way.'

The mere uttering of the word made Carrie gasp. 'Oh dear God . . .' Noora was not yet sixteen. A mere child.

'She tells me her father has not yet been informed,' Archie Fraser said. 'Don't you think he ought to know?'

Carrie's mouth went quite dry. She had been totally unable to tell her son. She shook her head and made a helpless gesture with her hands.

'Do you want me to tell him?'

Did she? Carrie looked at the old man. He had known Billy since her son was a child. 'Perhaps it might be best,' she admitted softly. 'He might take it better coming from you.'

Nothing, however, prepared her for the fury that followed the physician's leaving. She was in the drawing room when Billy burst in, his face puce and his eyes wild. He was almost incoherent with rage as he made for the credenza and poured himself a large Scotch. He seldom drank whisky, preferring the clear potency of gin, and the mere act made Carrie tense even more as he strode to the window and looked out after the doctor's retreating buggy.

'Billy darling . . .' She rushed across and laid a comforting hand on his arm. 'I know just how you must be feeling . . .'

'Do you?' He whirled round to face her. 'Do you really?' he demanded in a voice more bitter than she had ever known it. 'Can you really imagine what it was like to stand there and hear that my own mother was responsible for the ruination of my child?'

'What?' Carrie stared at him, aghast.

'Oh yes, Ma . . . Don't stand there all innocent and pretend you don't know what I'm talking about. You know exactly what I mean.'

'I swear to God, Billy . . .'

'Oh, you know all right. You know, for you were the one who insisted on allowing that black bastard Irishman to remain on the station, knowing what I've thought of him all these years – knowing I had the measure of him, if no one else did.'

He took a swig of the drink and continued, 'You preferred to close your eyes, didn't you? For all those years you just closed your eyes and ears to those tales of his womanizing with the gins . . . While he strutted like a cock on his own particular dung-heap you continued to idolize him, as one little black bitch after another went to and fro from his hut, and one little half-caste bastard after another was conceived and born, to be got rid of at birth like so much garbage. And all the time you continued to call him friend.'

He downed the remainder of the glass in one and pointed it at her as his voice rose. 'You even brought his own bastard child into this very house – still pretending you didn't know who the father was. Still playing the wise monkey who sees all and hears all but says nothing. But you were no wise monkey, Ma . . . You were a bloody fool. There are none so blind as those who simply refuse to see. All those years you were looking the other way, he was laughing at you behind your back. While you were continuing to call him your best friend he was having every bloody gin on Yorvik!'

He strode back to the credenza and splashed another measure of the amber spirit into his empty glass. 'That little darkie bastard of his – that Joe-boy – should never have been allowed to remain on this land. God dammit, Ma, he should never have been allowed near my child!'

Billy was crying now, the tears running down his cheeks, and the hand that held the glass was shaking as he contemplated the full horror of what he had just been told. 'I knew something like this would happen . . . No, for Christ's sake, I knew *this* would happen! I was waiting for it, Ma . . . I've spent years waiting for it! And all the time you couldn't see . . . You just couldn't see . . . Worse – you didn't *want* to see.'

He sank into the nearest armchair and stared straight ahead as his voice continued dully, 'You didn't want to see, did you? You didn't want to see. Just as you closed your eyes for all those years to what the Irishman was doing with those black women, you closed your mind to what his son might do with a white one . . . your own granddaughter! God help us, we were never even allowed to call the little bastard the Irishman's son in your presence. The whole damned station knew the truth but no one was ever allowed to say it because of what it would do to "the boss" . . . You've been a laughing stock, Ma! Do you realize that? All these years you've been a laughing stock – that bloody Irish darkie has seen to that!'

The words fell on Carrie in a relentless torrent, chilling her very soul. They were not spoken in hate. Much worse – they were spoken in love. They echoed in her heart as they would echo in her head forever. Once uttered they could never be reclaimed. His eyes were looking at her in a strange mixture of anger and pity.

'You're wrong, son . . . So very wrong . . .' And Carrie was weeping now, the tears spilling down her wan cheeks as she looked at her only son and begged him to

525

understand. 'It wasn't like that, Billy . . . Please believe that . . .'

'But it was, Ma, it was . . . I could see it, just as everyone on Yorvik could see it. And for your sake I kept quiet. For all these years I've kept quiet. And where has it got me? Answer me that? I've been proved right, that's what . . . My worst fears have been confirmed. That little black bastard has defiled by own daughter. He's ruined Noora, Ma . . . He's ruined Noora . . .'

The glass fell from his hands to spill its contents on to the soft pile of the carpet as his shoulders shook with silent sobs. 'My little girl . . . My little girl . . .'

Carrie stood looking down at him. He was in agonizing pain and she could do nothing, for she was the cause of that pain. 'I – I'm sorry, son,' she whispered. 'I'm so very sorry . . .'

CHAPTER FORTY

Billy Gordon-Hebden's tall, bulky figure weaved a precarious path along the narrow track that led to the Irishman's hut. It was less than an hour since he had had the harrowing conversation with his mother after the doctor had left and he could contain his wrath no longer. Two people were responsible for this tragedy that had befallen his daughter, two half-caste bastards no better than they ought to be who had the brass necks to remain living on his own land.

His florid face was blotchy and tear-stained, his eyelids swollen, and a half-empty hipflask of Scotch bulged from the right-hand pocket of his jacket. Every step of the way he muttered to himself, building up his courage for the confrontation that lay ahead. 'Little black bastard! Dirty black Irish bastard, I'm coming . . . I'm coming!'

He did not bother to knock when he finally reached the Irishman's cabin, but threw all his weight against the flimsy door, which burst open, propelling him into the single-roomed shack where Sean O'Dwyer had spent the best part of his life.

Billy had never been inside the hut since his first visit as a child with his mother. He had compared it to a pigsty then and the memory of that day came flooding back to him as he stood panting in the middle of the floor. He had been right, it was a pigsty, and pigs still lived in it – two of them!

The old man himself was lying on his bed and he half raised himself on one elbow and gasped in astonishment at the sight before him. 'What in heaven's name?'

Ignoring the Irishman for the moment, Billy's head swivelled from side to side as, wild-eyed, he located his main quarry. He let out a grunt of triumph at the sight of Joe-boy sitting frozen to his chair in the far corner of the room. He lurched towards the boy, who leapt out of the seat and avoided the flailing arms of the intruder. Joe-boy's eyes were wide with fear as he pressed himself against the wall of the hut.

'Just what the hell do you think you're doing?' Sean O'Dwyer cried, rising with difficulty from his bed. Dressed only in his woollen combinations, he stood unsteadily on his bare feet and looked contemptuously at the man before him. 'Leave the kid alone! If you've any bone to pick, you pick it with me, Billy Hebden!'

Billy turned and glared at the old man. 'Just you keep out of it, O'Dwyer! It's none of your bloody business!'

'Oh, but it is! Don't you forget, it's my home you're in!'

This was too much! Billy pointed a wavering finger in the Irishman's face. 'You're wrong there, old man – just as you've been wrong about everything else! This is my bloody hut – not yours! Never has been yours and never will be! Every stick of this old shanty belongs to me, just as the land it's built on is mine and all the rest of the land within a day's ride of here. You have no claim to a thing on Yorvik. Not a bloody thing. You and your little black bastard here – you're parasites, that's all. Bloody parasites!'

Joe-boy, who was now standing ashen-faced behind his chair, made a move towards the door, but Billy saw him out of the corner of his eye and whirled round. 'Where do you think you're going, you little rat?'

He made a lurch towards the youth that brought an immediate response from Sean, who made a grab for Billy's arm. 'Leave the kid alone!'

With a roar like a wounded bull, Billy turned and lashed out viciously with his free arm and caught the old man in the mouth with his fist, knocking one of Sean's front teeth backwards on to his tongue. Doubled-up with the pain and coughing, he spat it out and wiped his mouth with the back of his hand. The blow had made his eyes water and a smear of blood covered the age-mottled skin. Seeing it,

Joe-boy let out a shout. 'You bastard, you've hurt Be-anga!'

'I'll hurt more than bloody Be-anga!' Billy growled, reaching out and grabbing Joe-boy's vacated chair.

Sean and Joe-boy watched in silence as he held it threateningly in front of his chest, its four legs pointing at each of them in turn as he jabbed it in front of him.

'What have you come here for?' Sean asked in as controlled a voice as possible. He could taste the blood on his tongue and could feel his insides shaking, but was determined not to let it show.

'You know bloody well what I've come for,' Billy said, and there was no mistaking the menace in his voice or in his look as he glanced towards Joe-boy. 'I've come to get even, old man, that's what I've come for. I've come to destroy the animal who destroyed my daughter's reputation. I've come to see justice done in this land tonight!'

Total fear filled the old Irishman's heart. Billy was drunk, dangerously so, and there was no arguing with a man who was not in control of his own senses. 'Get out of here, Joey!' Sean commanded.

'I will not!' Joe-boy protested. 'I'm not leaving you alone with him!'

Sean O'Dwyer's eyes burned into those of the boy. 'Get out of here, damn you, Joey. I'm not asking you — I'm bloody telling you! *Go!* And *go now*!'

'You're going nowhere till I've finished with you, you little bastard!' Billy made a move towards the boy, jabbing the air between them with the upturned chair.

'For Christ's sake, Joey!' The Irishman shouted the words across the few feet between them.

Uncertain what to do for the best, his glance darting between the old man and Billy, Joe-boy made a tentative sideways move towards the door.

Billy took a staggering step in the same direction, lurching against the edge of the wooden chest in the middle of the floor. Drunk as he was, he was sober enough to know

529

that if the lad had a mind to escape there was no way on earth he could catch him. Not tonight at any rate.

His eyes narrowed as they met those of the youth. 'If you run out of here, you little black bastard, you'll never set foot on my land again. I'll see to that. For if you do there'll be more than the legs of this chair and my fists waiting for you. There'll be the barrel of a gun.'

Joe-boy remained frozen to the spot. Never had he seen such hatred in another man's face. He glanced across at Sean.

'Get out of here, Joe-boy!' the old man pleaded. 'Get out of this house, for Christ's sake! I'll handle this. It won't be the first time I've tangled with *Mister* Gordon-Hebden here, and I've no doubt it won't be the last.'

Joe-boy could see from the old man's eyes that his patience was at an end and he would brook no argument. He had never been in the habit of disobeying a direct order, but would he be a coward to run off and leave him alone with a drunk like this? Be-anga was an old man and the sheer hatred in the glare of the other man chilled him to the core. He had always known that Noora's father had never cared for him, but this was something quite different. There was real loathing in the ice-blue of those eyes.

'Please, Joey . . .'

There was no mistaking Be-anga wanted him to go, so reluctantly Joe-boy began to edge towards the door, glancing nervously as he did so at the pronged legs of the chair still pointing so threateningly at him.

As Billy watched the boy make his way inch by inch towards freedom, he began to have trouble focusing his eyes and was feeling disconcertingly detached from what was going on. It was as if all of a sudden he was watching a play taking place on a stage so distant he no longer had any real interest in it. The effect of the long walk in the night air had done the opposite of clear his head, and the bottle of spirits he had consumed over the past hour was having a most peculiar result. Both his hearing and his sight seemed to be getting increasingly muzzy and his whole body felt as if it no longer belonged to him.

The door closed behind the departing youth with a resounding thud and the two men who were left looked at one another. There was a trickle of blood from the Irishman's mouth and, staring at it in an attempt to focus his gaze, Billy felt a wave of nausea sweep over him.

He put down the chair and pulled open the neck of his shirt, for perspiration was standing out on the skin of his face and he could feel it begin to dampen his armpits. As he stood there gasping for breath shiny droplets trickled down the sides of his nose and glittered on the waxed surface of his moustaches.

'You're a bastard, do you know that, O'Dwyer?' he said through gritted teeth. 'A slimy Irish-Abo bastard. And I'm going to get you for this, you wait and see. I'm going to get you and that little yellow-skinned bastard of yours into the bargain. You won't get away with it, either of you. I'll get even for what you've done to my family. I'll get even, just you wait and see!'

And with that he stumbled towards the door, almost throwing himself into the cool of the night air, where he slumped against the side of the shack. Then, as the old man watched silently through the window, he began to throw up on the small patch of green peas that had been planted beneath the sill.

Inside, Sean O'Dwyer shook his head and turned away in disgust.

The night the doctor confirmed 'the rape', as Billy insisted on calling it, was one that Carrie knew would remain in her memory to the end of her days. The knowledge of the brawl that took place between Billy and Sean hurt her deeply and was described in graphic detail by Billy when he first appeared just after breakfast the following morning, grey-faced and dishevelled after a night spent on the library sofa.

'I showed 'em,' he informed his mother, after a lurid blow-by-blow account that bore little resemblance to what had actually occurred in the Irishman's hut. 'You need have no fear of that, Ma. I showed 'em what I thought of them!'

Carrie, who was sitting at her desk, remained silent throughout, only to say quietly at the end of the heated tale, 'I just hope you left Sean's home with more dignity than you appear to have arrived with.' To hear that he had simply burst into the hut and read the riot act before physically threatening Joe-boy filled her with despair.

Billy glared at his mother. It was more than he could expect for her to understand. 'You need have no fear of that,' he told her. 'I left with my head held high and theirs hanging in shame.' The truth of his departure would never be admitted. If there was one thing he was proud of, it was being able to hold his liquor.

'Have you spoken to Noora yet?' Carrie asked.

Billy shook his head. 'I can't face the girl. I swear to God I couldn't be responsible for my actions if she said anything in my presence to defend that . . . that . . .' He could not even refer to the boy without going red in the face.

He looked about him for his cigars and lit one with shaking fingers. 'I'll leave you to deal out whatever punishment you deem appropriate in that regard,' he said, drawing deeply on the pungent smoke. 'A woman is far better than a man when it's a young girl that's concerned anyway.'

When there was no response from his mother, he queried, 'You don't mind, do you?'

Carrie shook her head. 'No, I don't mind,' she said in a tired voice. After all, she had been taking on his responsibilities in that regard for the past fifteen years.

She found it almost impossible to concentrate on her book-keeping after that and was just on the point of giving up when, to her surprise, Billy returned several minutes later to announce that he had thought it through and, all being well, he and Noora would leave for England in six weeks' time, in the first week of December 1901. They would remain on Yorvik just long enough for Dr Fraser to verify that his daughter was not pregnant.

When his mother protested that perhaps the decision should not be made in such haste, Billy would have none of it. He was adamant that Noora had to be removed from further danger at the first opportunity. His loathing for those he believed responsible for what had happened was beyond bounds and he informed Carrie it would be impossible for him to breathe the same air as 'that pair of half-caste bastards' for one day longer than necessary.

Carrie went immediately to inform her granddaughter, and Noora took the news of her father's decision to remove her to England as soon as possible in total silence. She merely turned her face to the wall and signalled for her grandmother to leave.

Feeling totally inadequate and unable to think of anything to say which might possibly relieve the situation, Carrie left her to make her way to the kitchen where she knew Kate, her daily help, would be in the middle of bread-making. There was a comfort to be gained from the familiarity of the routine tasks of the house that went on regardless of the traumas of the family itself.

The young woman was up to her elbows in flour and she looked up with a faint air of embarrassment as her mistress walked in. Carrie was well aware it was impossible to keep anything from the servants and almost everyone on the station must know by now what had happened, although none had had the temerity to make any comment to her face.

'Any chance of a cup of coffee, Kate?' Carrie asked, seating herself in her favourite rocker.

'I thought you might be down around now so the pot's on the boil,' Kate said, wiping the flour from her hands.

Carrie watched as the young woman went about preparing the brew. She was a plump, comfortable-looking mother of two, in her middle twenties, the kind who would remain the mainstay of her family for the next two generations; a down-to-earth, practical sort who could be relied upon to take the common-sense view on whatever life threw at her. Carrie took her courage in both hands. 'You – you have probably heard something of what's happened regarding Noora,' she began haltingly.

Kate froze, the spoonful of ground coffee beans halfway to the pot. 'Well, yes . . .'

As Carrie wondered how to go on, the younger woman turned to her and, the colour rising in her ruddy cheeks, she blurted out, 'I – I'd just like you to know, ma'am, how much we all feel for you during this terrible time . . . There has even been talk amongst the men of getting a posse together to hunt down that little beggar, Joe-boy, and I'd have a good mind to join it if they did.'

Carrie was totally taken aback by the vehemence of the outburst. It was not at all what she expected. 'Folk really feel that strongly around here?'

'I'll say they do! Why, in all the years I've lived here I've never known feelings run so high. You see it's not just what he did, ma'am – heaven knows other young couples get into that sort of trouble now and again.' She gave an embarrassed half smile. 'In fact I reckon almost as many babbies are conceived out of wedlock as in . . . No, it's not that so much as the fact that . . . that . . .'

'That Joe-boy's a half-caste.'

Kate nodded, then turned back to finish spooning the coffee into the pot. 'That type of thing's maybe been all right in the past, out in the bush say, where men have had no hope of setting eyes on a white woman for years, but decent folk won't tolerate it on their own doorsteps. Especially not the other way round, when it's a blackfella and a white woman.'

She shuddered visibly. 'The idea of that lovely young girl being molested in that way doesn't even bear thinking about! I tell you, ma'am, if that lad as much as shows his face anywhere near Yorvik again, he'll get what's coming to him, make no mistake about that.'

Carrie felt a lead weight on her heart. Somehow she had not expected this type of reaction. Shock perhaps, that the two young people should have got themselves into a mess like this. And perhaps a certain amount of indignation at Joe-boy, for the girl was never thought of as the instigator in these things. And after all they had all known that Noora and Joe-boy had grown up as close as brother and sister.

But as Carrie sat sipping her coffee and pondering on the younger woman's words, she realized that perhaps that was the trouble. However much she herself might have wanted it otherwise, it had never been accepted here on Yorvik that the boss's granddaughter could have such a close relationship with a half-caste. It had never been accepted just as her own relationship with the Irishman had never been accepted. To many Sean would remain to the end of his days 'that damned darkie' and Joe-boy was no better in their eyes.

'I hope it helps to know that we're all behind you in your time of sorrow, ma'am,' Kate said, as Carrie finished her coffee and rose to go upstairs to tend to Noora.

Carrie forced a reassuring smile to her lips. 'I much appreciate everyone's concern, Kate,' she said wearily. 'I'm sure it's genuinely motivated, but somehow I can't help feeling retribution is not what's needed right now.'

Kate looked distinctly puzzled as her mistress left the room. The Bible taught an eye for an eye and a tooth for a tooth, and there was no gainsaying the good book. If that young blackguard Joe-boy as much as set foot on Yorvik land he'd live to regret it, she had no doubt of that, and not even Carrie Gordon-Hebden's charity would be able to save him. He had done more than sin against her granddaughter. He had sinned against every white woman on the place and there was not a God-fearing husband and father who would let him get away with that.

It was with a heavy heart that Carrie made her way up

the main staircase to her granddaughter's room. Suddenly she felt her age more than she had done in years. Every bone in her body seemed to ache along with her heart.

Noora had taken to her bed after the doctor's visit and not got up – partly, Carrie believed, because she did not wish to go downstairs and confront her father.

The young girl was lying motionless beneath the covers, her face against the white pillowslip pale and drawn as her grandmother entered the room. Carrie looked down at her with compassion. 'Is there anything I can get you, my dear?'

Noora shook her head and, despite her resolve not to break down in front of anyone, she could feel the tears begin to well and did her best to blink them back.

'It's all my fault, Moo,' she said despairingly, as Carrie sat on the edge of her bed. 'Daddy got mad at Joe-boy last night, but it wasn't really his fault. It just isn't right to put all the blame on him. It wasn't really his idea. It wasn't either of our ideas. What happened between us out there at the lake wasn't something we planned and neither of us imagined the trouble it would get us into . . .'

She sighed deeply and shook her head as she raised her eyes to the ceiling, 'If only I hadn't blabbed to you like I did, none of this would have happened.'

'Now darling, that's a silly thing to say. You were right to tell me and you must never reproach yourself for that . . . If it was anyone's fault it was mine for not warning you in the first place that such behaviour was not allowed. That it is just plain dangerous.' Carrie gave a weary shake of the head and stroked imaginary creases from the folds of her skirts as her mind raced ahead to the consequences if they found her granddaughter was pregnant. That really would put the cat among the pigeons.

Noora saw the deep furrows that marked the old lady's brow and reached out a hand to touch her grandmother's arm. 'Don't look so sad, Moo darling. It's really not the end of the world.'

Carrie forced a smile to her lips. Of course she was right.

'I'm sorry, my dear,' she sighed. 'And you're right, of course. All this passing the buck won't get us anywhere, I'm afraid. The damage is done and can't be undone. If things were different, you would be obliged to marry the boy, but obviously that's quite out of the question.'

Noora did not have to ask why. She was well aware that people from her background did not marry mere station hands, particularly ones with black blood. But she would never have dreamt of marrying Joe-boy anyway. It would be like marrying her own brother. What did trouble her, however, was the fact that she had heard from one of the maids that Joe-boy had run off into the bush 'like the little yellow-bellied coward that he is', and she was concerned that he might not come back before it was time for her to leave Yorvik. 'I must see him, Moo. I can't go to England without saying goodbye to Joey. You do understand that, don't you?'

Carrie reached out and patted her granddaughter's hand. She understood completely. 'Don't worry, darling, I'll see to that.'

But exactly how she had not the faintest idea.

CHAPTER FORTY-ONE

Carrie kept her promise to her granddaughter, even though it meant swallowing her pride one evening and making her way to the Irishman's hut, a journey she had not made since the night of the so-called 'rape'.

She waited until the week before Noora and her father were due to sail before she went to plead with her old friend, to beg him to try to get in touch with Joe-boy. She knew it was not an easy favour she was asking, for the boy had not been seen around the place since the night of the fight. But just to ensure that the youth knew he would have nothing to fear any more, she added, 'You can also tell him that I will have no objection to him returning to work on the station once Noora and her father have gone.'

The old Irishman raised his brows in surprise. 'You really expect him to do that? You expect him to return here?'

'I don't see why not,' Carrie replied, indignant that her magnanimous gesture should be met with such a response. 'His home's still here, isn't it? And he makes quite a decent living for a kid his age working around the place. I don't know where he's been for the past few weeks, but I expect he'll be glad to see his old friends again.'

Sean O'Dwyer gave a disparaging laugh. 'The fact that they'd string him up as soon as look at him doesn't come into it, I suppose?'

Carrie stiffened. Memories of that conversation with Kate, her daily help, came rushing back. She had put it completely out of her mind as the preparations for the voyage had consumed her attention over the past few weeks. 'What are you talking about?' she asked, knowing full well what was coming.

'Don't tell me you know nothing about the bile old Billy-boy has been spilling around here?'

Carrie averted her eyes. So Billy had been doing his share of stirring things up. She might have known. 'I swear I don't know what you're talking about.'

'Well, I suggest you ask that dear son of yours, for there's not a man-jack around here that hasn't heard of Joey's "frenzied attack" on Noora, as he put it, and they're all gunning for the poor little blighter, I can tell you! Practically queuing up to have a go at him, they are!'

Carrie's heart sank. There really was to be no forgiveness, even with Billy safely on his way to England. 'If that really is the case then I can well understand why he doesn't want to show his face on Yorvik,' she said in a quiet voice. Kate had been right. Feelings really were that strong. Even without Billy's interference they would most probably still be running as high. Noora was the favourite of all the station hands. There was not an older man who did not regard her as his own daughter, or a younger one who was not half in love with her. Joe-boy's continued closeness to her now they were growing up had obviously been bitterly resented and gossiped about on Yorvik even before this.

A silence fell between them as Carrie pondered on what to do for the best. She should have realized she was asking the impossible. But somehow she had convinced herself that if she generously extended the hand of friendship to the boy once Billy was safely out of the way no one would really object too much, and he would be only too glad to return. 'I – I realize if what you say is true then it could be dangerous for Joe-boy to return right now, but I promised Noora I'd arrange for them to meet before she leaves. She'll be devastated if she doesn't see him.'

The Irishman nodded. He believed her, just as he knew Joe-boy would be equally upset at Noora leaving without having the chance to say goodbye. Hell, it wasn't the young folks' fault this had blown up out of all proportion, or for the disastrous consequences for the pair of them afterwards. He blamed himself in a way, for he had not had time to explain the half of it to Joey before he had made off into the night like that. God only knew what he must be going through. Nevertheless, he had a good idea where he was staying and it should not prove too much of a problem getting in touch if the information he had picked up was correct.

'Have Noora round here after dark the night before she leaves,' Sean told Carrie. 'I'll do my level best to see to it that Joe-boy's here.'

When Noora heard the news she could hardly wait. Her excitement at leaving for England had been completely tarnished with the knowledge that her friend had been banished from Yorvik, the only home he had ever known. She blamed herself completely for what had happened. Had she known the scandal that was to ensue, she would never have breathed a word of their lovemaking to anyone, and she knew she would carry the guilt of what had happened all the way to England with her.

Because of what had happened with Joe-boy, she had been distinctly cool with her father of late, but Billy was doing his best to win back his daughter's affections by telling her of all the exciting things they would do together in England.

'Don't forget we'll be living in the very heart of the Empire, darling. And with your grandparents' connections you'll meet all manner of well-to-do people. Why, there's even a chance you'll run into the new King himself at one of their weekend house-parties!'

Such talk had quite the opposite effect it was meant to have on Noora, who felt faintly repelled by the sight of the corpulent monarch with so many scandals attached to his name. She really had no interest in the middle-aged members of the aristocracy, who seemed to fascinate her father so much; she was much more intrigued by the young people she was going to meet. While life here on Yorvik had been wonderful in many respects she had often felt of late the lack of a wide selection of friends of her own age with whom to swap ideas and talk of her hopes and fears for the future, and of all the exciting things happening in the world right now.

There seemed to be so many preparations involved in leaving home. All manner of new items had to be ordered from Sydney or Newcastle. 'Hunter's Hollow won't do,' her father had decreed. 'Far too homespun in their goods and chattels. We can't have her English grandparents commenting on her clothes or other belongings as not being up to standard.'

Noora was well aware that the opinion of her mother's parents mattered a great deal to her father, who could get quite hot under the collar at the thought that they might refer to anything of his or his daughter's as 'rather colonial', which he knew was simply the polite way of saying 'second rate'.

By the time the great day of their departure drew near, however, most things had gone according to plan, and by their last full day on Yorvik six large trunks stood waiting for collection in the hall. Noora was so caught up in all the excitement and last-minute preparations that when her grandmother reminded her on the penultimate morning that she was due to meet Joe-boy that evening to say goodbye, to her shame she had quite forgotten. She attempted to disguise the fact, but the old lady knew the girl too well to be fooled.

'Does this mean we'll all be forgotten in the blink of an eye once you get to England?' she teased, with more than a touch of sadness in her voice as she watched her granddaughter sort through her jewellery drawer for the last time.

'Oh Moo, you know better than that!' Noora dropped the necklace she was holding and rushed to give a reassuring hug. 'Nothing and no one could ever matter as much to me as Yorvik and you. You know that, don't you?' Her blue eyes searched her grandmother's face. 'You know I'm only going to England to give myself, as Pa puts it, "a final polish".'

Carrie sighed. 'I can't say that I ever found you dull enough to need any kind of polishing. But you know I'd never stand in the way of anything you felt you really wanted to do.'

'I know that, Moo darling.' Then, taking her grandmother's hands in hers, Noora continued, 'You know, there's another reason why I'm so looking forward to getting to know London, and that's because it's your own city.' She was aware her grandmother never talked about her past, but there was no way she could disguise her roots as a Londoner born and bred. She was not prepared, however, for the reaction to her words.

'No!' Carrie said, withdrawing her hands and walking to the window to look out over the far hills. 'London was never my city. I was born and brought up there, yes, but that's all. If a chicken lays an egg in the cat's basket, it doesn't make it a kitten.'

She turned to face her granddaughter. 'My mother was Irish,' she said. 'And if I feel any affinity with any land other than Yorvik, then it would be with the people there in County Wexford, although I've never been across the Irish Sea.'

Noora gave a fond smile as she walked across to put her arm around her grandmother's shoulders. 'Dear Moo,' she sighed. 'Always on the side of the underdog, and I love you for it.'

Then without another word being said, both broke into one of the songs that Noora had learned at the old lady's knee before any nursery rhymes:

> God give you glory, brave Father Murphy,
> And open heaven to all your men;
> The cause that called you may call tomorrow
> In another war for the Green again . . .

Both had tears in their eyes as the last note died and Carrie dabbed at her nose with the edge of her handkerchief. 'Away with you, Noora love! We're a daft pair and no mistake!'

Carrie walked with her granddaughter to the Irishman's hut after supper that night and Sean O'Dwyer was waiting in the darkness outside as they arrived.

He took hold of Carrie's arm. 'Let's you and me take a stroll, Grandma,' he said quietly. 'I'm sure the two young people have got plenty to say to each other.'

Carrie and Noora looked at one another and Carrie gave a reassuring smile as Sean pushed open the door. Noora tentatively entered the hut to find a serious-faced Joe-boy sitting in the candlelight. Her initial reaction was one of shock, for his face looked drawn and he seemed much thinner than when they last saw each other. He got up as she came in and for a moment they stood silently looking at one another. Then she rushed into his arms.

Despite her resolve to remain calm and grown up, Noora could feel the hot sting of tears beneath her closed lids as she clung to him. Suddenly it all came rushing back, all the pain and the hurt he must have gone through. 'Oh Joey, I'm so sorry . . . so very sorry for what's happened . . .'

He held her close, his lips pressed into the soft cloud of blonde hair. 'Don't cry, Noora,' he pleaded. 'Please don't cry.' Desperate though he had been to see her again, he had been half dreading this moment. He had already been warned by Be-anga that her father was taking Noora away to England with him and the knowledge gnawed at his insides like a physical pain.

They sat down side by side on the edge of the bed and Joe-boy's eyes were wide and troubled in the candlelight as he looked at her. 'Be-anga tells me you're leaving tomorrow,' he said in a thick voice. 'You're really going.'

Noora nodded guiltily. 'I — I expect so . . .' It was a stupid thing to say, but he looked so sad.

'Don't you want to any more?' he asked, with just a hint of expectancy in his voice.

She gave a hopeless shrug. Didn't he realize it was all fixed? Didn't he know of the weeks of preparation that went into something like this? But how could he? His life was so very different. 'I – I wanted to go,' she confessed in a voice little more than a whisper. 'I told you that before. But not like this. I never wanted it to be like this.' She raised her eyes to meet his. 'I'll miss you, Joe-boy. I really will.'

He took hold of her hands, his heart aching at the pain in her eyes. Seeing her so sad was worse, far worse, than any pain he had had to bear. 'There is no turning back?'

'There is no turning back.'

'Then I will go with you, Noora. Wherever you go, you will never be alone. In spirit I will always be there. You are my woman, remember. Until the end of time. We belong to one another.'

Noora bit her lip. She disliked that sort of talk. It made her feel like a thing that could be owned. But now was not the time to go into that sort of argument again. She forced a smile to her lips as she nodded in agreement. 'I know.'

'You will come back,' he told her, his voice soft and insistent. 'You will come back and we will be together forever. All the days of our lives we will walk the path to *Palanari* – our own Dreamtime – together. I love you, Noora – my woman – and I will wait for that day. I will wait for it all the days of my life . . .'

She could feel her eyes swimming with tears. This was not the goodbye she wanted. She loved him. Yes, she loved him. But as a brother, not as the intense lover she now sensed him to be. There was an urgency about his gaze and his voice that made her uncomfortable. Things had changed between them, but for her it was not how it was for him. She withdrew her right hand from his and reached out and touched his lips. 'Don't say any more,' she pleaded. 'Don't make it worse for us.'

He took her hand in his and pressed his lips into the

palm. It felt soft and moist to the touch. Passions were rousing in him as they had every moment of every day that had passed since their lovemaking on the banks of the Yorvik pool. Her father could banish him from her presence, but he could never banish her from his mind. Waking or sleeping, she was there. He carried her with him, her beauty, her sound, her taste, her smell – they were as much a part of him as the very air he breathed. 'I will be waiting, my love. I will be waiting here to claim my own . . .'

Carrie and Sean O'Dwyer saw Noora run from the hut a few seconds later. Carrie made to call out and hurry after her, but the Irishman held her back. 'Let her go,' he said softly. 'There is a time when even the young need to be alone.'

'She will be a woman when she comes back from England,' Carrie said, already grieving for the child that had gone.

'And we will be old.'

She gave a wan smile in return. 'And we *are* old,' she corrected him.

'We have come through a lot together, one way or another.'

'And it's not over yet.'

He laughed. 'No, it's not over yet.' Then the smile died on his lips as he turned to her. 'Can I ask you something, Carrie?' he said haltingly.

She was puzzled. 'Of course. Anything.'

He looked down at his feet, then gave an embarrassed half smile as he lifted his eyes to meet hers. He never complained in her presence. His physical aches and pains were his own affair. But these past few weeks, since Joe-boy had left . . . He sighed . . . What else could he expect at this age? But there was something that had been preying on his mind, something he had been meaning to ask her for a long time. 'When it is over,' he said haltingly, in that husky voice of his, 'when it's all over and I finally go to that last round-up for old station hands in the sky, can you do me a great favour?'

Carrie tensed and gave an imperceptible nod.

'Could I ask you to see me buried on that grassy bank overlooking Yorvik Force . . .' His voice tailed off as his eyes met hers.

She did not need to ask exactly where, for there was only one place. 'Only if I can join you there,' she whispered.

He held out his hand and she clasped it. Their eyes misted over as they gazed at one another. It was a deal.

Carrie felt a strange peace descend as she turned and left him to walk back to the big house.

Her leave-taking of Billy and Noora at the end of the week was not half as painful as she had imagined it would be. Her granddaughter had regained most of her spirits and could barely contain her excitement at the thought of what lay ahead. They were to be staying at one of London's best hotels until Billy got fixed up with an apartment, and the final decision had been made as to exactly what school Noora would attend. And of course there were her Foston-Strutt-Smith grandparents to visit. Billy had already written to both their country home in Northamptonshire and their London address to inform them they would be heading for the mother country, due to his decision to have Noora prepare for her matriculation from one of the best English girls' schools.

Good girls' schools were quite thin on the ground, even in England, if one wanted one's daughter more than simply 'finished' in all the social graces. But Billy had no fear that with a little string-pulling by Grandpa Fizz – so nicknamed because of his illustrious initials – the problem could be solved in double-quick time.

'You'll not recognize her when you next see her, Ma!' he declared proudly on the quayside, as they took their leave. And there was no disguising the lump that came into Carrie's throat at that remark.

'That's just what I'm afraid of,' she murmured, clasping

her granddaughter to her for the last time. 'Take care, darling . . . And come back to us still the same beautiful young woman you are now.'

'I will, Moo, I will!'

Then they were off, walking side by side up the gang-plank of the great ship that was to take them to the other side of the world – back to England.

Carrie had specifically asked them not to stand and wave, for at three score years and twenty she no longer felt up to the strain of such an ordeal. She had had more than enough such farewells for one lifetime.

She glanced at the small gold fob watch hanging from her lapel. It was one hour before the ship was due to sail. Time enough to share a glass with an old friend before the anchor was weighed and the final chapter closed on her granddaughter's childhood. When Noora returned she would be a fully grown young woman.

Carrie's mind went back to two other young women who, sixty years ago, had done that same journey in reverse. Molly McFarland, née McGuire, would be waiting for her now in the dockside tavern. And she found herself humming softly under her breath as she made for the open door.

There was a Wild Colonial Boy, Jack Donohoe by
   name,
Of poor but honest parents he was born in
   Castlemaine,
He was his father's only hope, his mother's pride and
   joy,
And so dearly did his parents love the Wild Colonial
   Boy . . .

Did they still arrest you here in Sydney for singing that song she wondered, as she crossed the quayside? Some-how she doubted it. Sydney had come of age, as they had all done who had arrived here in convicts' chains.

'Mrs Gordon-Hebden, ma'am?' A pleasant-faced, middle-aged man, with a head of bright red hair, was offering his arm. 'My name is Seamus McFarland. My mother is over there waiting. May I escort you?'

He indicated a tiny figure standing by the door of the Rose and Crown, and Carrie raised her hand in recognition to her old friend.

'You look very like your father,' she said, smiling up into the face beneath the soft felt hat.

Seamus McFarland laughed. 'I don't know who would be most offended by that observation, me or the old man!'

'I take it your mother and father are keeping fine?' Although she had dropped a note to her old friend suggesting their meeting and the time and place, there had been no time for a reply.

'Oh yes,' Seamus replied, with a broad smile. 'I keep telling the old buggers, if it's true the good die young, then Lord knows what the pair of them got up to in the past to be around this long!'

Carrie gave a wry smile in return. 'You could say the same goes for me, for I'm no spring chicken. And from what I heard from your ma about your early exploits, it looks like you'll be heading for a ripe old age too, doesn't it, Seamus?'

Molly and Ian McFarland's third son grinned as they made their way across the cobbles to where his mother was standing. He might well act the respectable gentleman he now was, but your past travelled with you down life's road, and his had been no better than it ought to have been. 'I reckon you're right there, ma'am. I should be around for a fair while myself!' There was no putting one over on this old lady.

Unlike the last meeting in similar circumstances, the hour she passed with her old friends did Carrie the world of good, and she left their company with a lighter heart to watch the great ship begin its journey to the other side of the world. She lifted her hand to wave as it sailed out on the tide, hooting its farewell to those left standing on the shore. Tomorrow there would be another ship on another tide, more hails and farewells. For life went on and all the tears in the ocean could not stop it. It would be pointless to weep for those now setting sail for the old country, for they would have hope in their hearts, just as Carrie knew that she had had hope in her own when her feet first stepped on to this foreign soil.

'Are you ready for home now, ma'am?'

She turned to see the expectant face of her driver, Will Morton's eldest son.

'Yes,' Carrie replied. 'I'm ready for home.' It was a good feeling.

CHAPTER FORTY-TWO

It was several weeks after her son and granddaughter's departure for England that Carrie had her first real heart-to-heart conversation with Sean O'Dwyer. Her own pain at the separation from Billy and Noora, and her knowledge that her old friend must be feeling exactly the same way about Joe-boy, had kept their exchanges to purely small talk about the happenings on the station itself. However, when eventually the ice was broken over their own personal heartaches, what the Irishman had to tell her disturbed her greatly. Joe-boy had once more disappeared completely from Yorvik during the night following his last meeting with Noora and, despite the old man's entreaties for the boy to keep in touch, he had not seen or heard from him since. What little he had picked up had upset him more than he liked to admit. Joe-boy had been seen drunk and making a nuisance of himself around the public houses of Hunter's Hollow, and had even spent at least one night in jail.

'It's not like the lad at all,' the Irishman told Carrie, as they stood outside his hut. 'You know that as well as I do. He was never one for the drink or hanging around bars. When he was here with us he barely touched the stuff.'

His voice was infinitely weary as he pushed back his hat and wiped a hand across his sweating brow. He had been hacking fence posts before she arrived and the perspiration was running in rivulets down his seamed cheeks and into the grizzled grey of his beard. 'That to-do back then over Noora has taken a mighty toll in more ways than one, I can tell you.'

Carrie had rarely seen him so depressed. He looked old and tired and she could understand his worry. Joe-boy had never been a lad to get himself into any kind of trouble before this happened and knowing he was out there some-where, perhaps mixing with the wrong people or getting into all sorts of scrapes, didn't bear thinking about. 'I did ask you to tell him he was welcome to return here,' she said in a defensive voice. 'I would have seen to it that no one took it out on him on the station. We can't blame ourselves, Sean. It's not our fault that he didn't take up the offer.'

'Come on now, Carrie! Did you really expect him to?' Sean said, seating himself wearily on a chopping block. 'No matter what you say about not letting folk take it out on him, you couldn't possibly be there all the time to pro-tect him, any more than I could. He knew better than anybody that the rest of the workers wouldn't stand for it. He wasn't stupid. The poor little bugger knew he had no future here after they all got wind of what happened.' He shook his head and swatted listlessly at an insect buzz-ing around his head. 'But now he hasn't a future anywhere by the looks of it. Not unless he pulls himself together.'

He lapsed into thought, the lines on his seamed face deepening. 'The rape', as they were all calling it, had blighted his own life as well as Joe-boy's. He really felt for the kid. Sean believed him that there had been no attack and that what had happened between Joey and Noora had been as much her idea as his. The kid wouldn't have lied about a thing like that, not to him. There had been com-plete trust between them all his life. Old Bandicoot and Jeeba had died at the stage when the boy had needed a firmer guiding hand, and he had provided that. He had given him the same 'tough love', as he called it, as his father had given him.

In so many ways he could see himself in the young man Joe-boy was now becoming. As his own mother Maggie had taught him of his rich Aborigine heritage, and old Joe O'Dwyer had instilled in him a knowledge and love of his Irish past, so Joe-boy had had the blackfella tales of old Bandicoot and Jeeba to balance the Irish lore he himself had spent long hours relating to the child. It was a heady mixture for any kid to take in. 'Poor little bastard,' he murmured, half to himself. 'He was born to be an outsider, walking that lonely no-man's-land between the two worlds.'

Carrie looked down at him. He was talking about Joe-boy, but she knew he could just as easily be talking about himself. He had taken this whole thing very hard. Old age was not a time to have to bear such pain. She could feel for him, for she too had been an outsider, and perhaps that was what had bound them together over all these years. But she was not branded like he was, or Joe-boy; her own skin was lily-white beneath the sun's tan. To those who barely knew him, Sean O'Dwyer would be 'the darkie' to the end of his days, just as Joe-boy had been in his turn. And while she had been able to bury her past, they were forced to face up to it every day of their lives. She was as aware as he was that that was why the wrath felt here on Yorvik over what had happened between the two young people had been so strong. It had been more than a worker violating the boss's granddaughter, it had been black violating white. And that would never be forgiven. Never.

'Do you want me to send someone down to Hunter's Hollow to try to sort things out?' she asked.

'What the hell for?'

'Well, to . . . to . . .' Her voice tailed off, for she had no answer.

'To rescue him?' Sean queried, his broad mouth quirking into a grimace of a smile beneath the white whiskers. 'Forget it, Carrie. There's nothing you or I can do. There's nothing anyone can do to help the kid now. He's the only one who can do anything. I just hope to God he's got the guts to pull himself together, that's all.'

They both knew what the alternative was; it was seen on every street corner in the country: blackfellas, young and old, the worse for drink; flotsam floating on the tide of life between two different shores, acknowledged by neither.

There were to be several such conversations in the months that followed; bleak exchanges that tortured the soul of the old man and made Carrie return to the big house in despair. As tales of Joe-boy's vagrancy and drunkenness in the neighbourhood filtered back to Yorvik, the effect on the old Irishman was visible. It was becoming increasingly unbearable for her to see a friend in so much pain and yet be helpless to ease his suffering. As the months passed, it became easier to avoid the subject altogether, but the spectre of Joe-boy was always there, a sad, lonely shadow hovering on the edge of their lives.

The real tragedy was that in many ways Joe-boy had given Noora just as much as he had taken from her. Carrie had had several heart-to-heart conversations with her granddaughter in the days before she left for England and she had been left marvelling at the spiritual enrichment gained from the different cultural values the two young people had shared. Noora had talked with feeling of all Joe-boy had taught her of each individual's search for his or her true identity, of how one had to go out into the world and test oneself to enable one to become a whole human being and therefore worthy of the final attainment of Dreamtime.

'To deny your own true identity,' she had said, 'would be to base your life on a lie, and remain throughout eternity a lost soul forever seeking what can no longer be found. Dreamtime is truth, Moo darling. And we are all searching for the truth.'

Those words, so innocently spoken, had cut deep into the old lady's heart, for had not her whole life been based on a lie, on a denial of her true identity? Perhaps, she thought, that was why she was now going through that terrible state of being the blackfellas called *Jindabarli* – the Justice of Dreamtime. Perhaps that was why even in old age there was to be no peace in her soul. Perhaps the divine justice at the heart of things was wreaking its revenge, and it was no more than she deserved.

But despite the doubts and fears she was going through on Yorvik, from England there came only joy. The letters that arrived at the big house from both Noora and her father were full of enthusiasm for life in the mother country. The new Edwardian Era, as the newspapers were calling it, was making London the most exciting city in the world to be living in, and Billy had managed to rent a comfortable four-roomed apartment in Bloomsbury, just off Bedford Square. It belonged to friends of Nella's parents, who had left for India, and the rent was more than reasonable.

Billy and Noora had spent most of their first month in England at Hamberley Hall, Sir Richard and Lady Margaret's Northamptonshire home, and both took immediately to the leisured country lifestyle. 'I've actually ridden to the hounds, twice this month,' Billy wrote to his mother. 'And you know what I think of horses!'

From Noora too came letters bubbling with excitement. She adored, and was adored in return by, Grandma and Grandpa Fizz, and the old couple had used their influence to obtain her a place at one of the country's most exclusive finishing schools for young ladies: Mabberley's, in London's Bayswater. Noora was to board there during the week and return to her father's apartment, should she wish, at weekends, with the last weekend of every month to be spent at Hamberley Hall – and as many in between as her father would allow. Her grandparents, it seemed, could not see enough of their granddaughter. They had even bought her a whole new trousseau, which merited two full pages of description and made Carrie wonder what would happen to the three chests of new, specially tailored clothes she had taken with her.

To her relief, the abiding ache and black periods of self-doubt she had felt after the departure of her loved ones gradually disappeared with the passing months, as she immersed herself once more in the running of the station. The past few years had seen not only her sheep, but also her cattle winning prizes at all the best shows, and she was as keen as ever to keep up her reputation as one of the best breeders in the country.

Her only regret was that so many of those responsible had not lived to see the complete fruition of all their years of hard work. Will Morton, her head stockman, had passed on two years previously, and although he had left two fine sons equally determined to devote their services to the station, it was not the same. In the house too things were different; Ellen, her long-serving housekeeper, had retired shortly after Will's death, to keep house for her invalid sister in Newcastle. She had been replaced in the kitchen by Kate, but it was not the same. And Carrie found she could not forget the conversation the two of them had had after Joe-boy's initial flight. Kate, like so many others, had believed she was showing her loyalty to her mistress and Yorvik, but to Carrie she had instead shown only the prejudice that still blighted so many lives around here.

And as the weeks turned into months and the months into a whole year, Carrie decided to make the coming Christmas a special one for herself and her old friend, as they would both be missing loved ones on that day.

'I'd like you to pack the best picnic hamper ever, Kate,' she told her daily help. 'Cold roast goose, one of your special trifles, and as many little treats as you can cram in.' *Kalparandi*, Sean would call such treats: the equivalent of the blackfellas' sweet roots. Even at his advanced age, Carrie knew her old friend was a child at heart when it came to such delicacies. He had one of the sweetest tooths she had ever come across, but was rarely able to indulge it. Yes, she decided as she watched the hamper take shape, it was time he had something to cheer him up.

With homemade sprigs of red-berried holly stuck to the horse's bridle and dressed in her very best summer frock

555

and bonnet, she turned up outside Sean O'Dwyer's hut at ten o'clock on Christmas morning, with the large wicker hamper containing the goodies strapped securely to the back of the buggy.

'Well, what have we here?' Her old friend was outside feeding his family of stray cats when Carrie clattered up over the rough track. He straightened up, squinting into the sun as he looked enquiringly at the loaded buggy. 'You planning on going places this morning?'

'We both are,' Carrie told him with a smile. Then seeing his puzzled look, she added, 'You're not busy, are you? You've nothing special planned for today?'

He gave an ironic half laugh as he tossed the last of the stale damper at the mewing animals. 'You know me – my social calendar is booked up weeks ahead!'

'In that case, cancel everything,' she told him firmly. 'You're eating out. And I mean out, Mr O'Dwyer . . . We're going for a picnic, you and me.'

'A picnic!' He grinned as he rubbed his bearded chin and looked at the buggy. 'In that?'

Carrie patted the empty place beside her on the buckboard. 'Indeed in this. But there's one condition.'

'Eh?' He continued to squint up at her through the sunlight. 'And what might that be?'

'You bring your penny whistle.'

'My . . . !' He shook his head. It was months since he had even seen the thing.

'Please, Irish,' she pleaded. 'Go and find it.'

So he did. It was sticking out of his back pocket as he climbed up beside her some five minutes later. She smiled at him as she shook the reins and urged the horses into action. 'It's been a long time since I've listened to a good old Irish air,' she told him.

They spoke little on the way to their destination, and he did not need to ask her where they were headed. There was only one place. The waters of Yorvik Force had never looked more sparkling or inviting as Carrie pulled up the stallion to a halt beneath an old gum tree and turned to her friend.

Sean clambered down first, his aged joints a painful reminder of the days when he would have leapt the few feet to the ground. He rounded the vehicle and held out his hand to aid her own descent, then, as Carrie fastened the reins to a gnarled branch of the tree, Sean untied the hamper and lifted it down on to the warm grass.

'What have you got in here, bricks?'

'I've got your favourite tucker in the whole world in there,' she told him proudly. 'And you don't leave here till you've eaten fit to burst!'

'You're a determined woman, Carrie Hebden.'

'And you're a cantankerous old man who doesn't get nearly enough treats in this life.'

They sat down side by side, overlooking the cascading waters. It was their favourite spot; there was no place like it on earth.

'You chose well,' she told him in a quiet voice.

He knew just what she was referring to. He would rest happily here through eternity. These waters, the wide sky, the warm, sweet-smelling grass, this was all part of his own personal Dreamtime. And it was hers too, he knew that. And he knew too that time was running out. He had not been the same since Joe-boy had left. The old bones seemed even more reluctant to get out of bed in the mornings and riding a horse was becoming a thing of the past.

But most worrying of all was the persistent pain in his chest. Sometimes it was worse than at others, squeezing the very breath from him in its burning grip. At times like that he would sit alone in his small hut and wonder about the life that he had led. Folks round here would probably say it had not amounted to much. Most of it had been spent under the same stringy-bark roof – that 'old pigsty' as Billy had referred to it as a child. But for the most part he had been happy there; as happy as he had had any right to expect. And in the later years there had been Joe-boy.

The old man's gaze misted as he rested on the banks of the waterfall and thought of the small boy who had once sat at his feet and looked up at him with brown eyes wide with wonder. There was nothing like the trust of a child to make you feel special. And Joe-boy had made him feel special all right. He had been a good kid – the best – and that had made it all the harder to bear.

'Happy?' Carrie asked him.

He glanced across at her and sighed. 'As happy as you, most probably,' he replied.

She gave a wistful smile in response. They both knew what that answer meant.

He reached across and took her hand. It was something he had never done before, not once in sixty years. She was still wearing the ring that Silas had placed on her finger that very first week she arrived here.

She saw him looking at it. 'I never could bring myself to take it off,' she said quietly. 'In a way I owe everything to him . . . All this . . .' Her eyes scanned the far horizon, and the green acres in between, all of it Yorvik land.

'If it hadn't have been for him we'd never have met,' Sean said, then gave a wry half laugh. 'I suppose I should be grateful to the old bugger.'

'If it hadn't been for him, I might still be in that prison factory.'

Their eyes met. She had said it. She had told the truth.

'I think you always knew,' she said softly.

He gave a sigh as he shook his head. 'I dare say it crossed my mind over the years, but I reckoned if you wanted me to know you'd tell me in your own good time.' Then his mouth broke into that familiar grin. 'Mind you, sixty years was a fair while to wait!'

Then, as if to assure her that neither the confession nor the length of time he had had to wait for it were of any consequence, he raised her hand and pressed it to his lips. As their eyes met she was sure she could detect the hint of a blush beneath the bronzed skin of his face.

'Why, Mr O'Dwyer, I do believe you're human after all!'

He let go her fingers as if stung and began to search in his pockets to cover his confusion. 'Now, where the devil did I put that penny whistle?'

Carrie laughed as she reached for the bottle of wine. 'I haven't given up on making you into a romantic yet,' she told him, as she carefully filled two glasses and handed him one.

They lifted the drinks in unison and she began, 'Here's to . . .' when he interrupted her.

'Here's to us, Carrie girl,' he said, as the crystal rims touched. 'For once, let's be selfish and wish ourselves all the best!'

'To us, Irish darling!'

'To us, Carrie *aroon*!'

It was a whole lifetime ago since she had heard that endearment and as she sipped the wine, the tears ran unashamedly down her face and into the glass.

'We're a couple of old fools,' he told her, and she smiled back at him through her tears.

There were no fools like old fools, but she wouldn't have it any other way.

CHAPTER FORTY-THREE

The ball given at Hamberley Hall by Sir Richard and Lady Margaret Foston-Strutt-Smith in celebration of their granddaughter Noora's first Christmas in England was quite the talk of the county. The cream of Northamptonshire society was joined by 'everybody who was anybody' from all the home counties and the Midland shires, and many more from great houses far beyond. An invitation had even been extended to King Edward and Queen Alexandra, but as the Queen was unwell the invitation was reluctantly turned down, much to the disappointment of all concerned.

The absence of the new monarch and his beautiful Danish wife made no difference to Noora, however. Her excitement knew no bounds as the great day approached. Although officially she was not yet of an age to be presented at Court, the occasion which marked every wellborn young lady's debut into society, her grandparents could not exclude her from their Yuletide festivities. Both Sir Richard and Lady Margaret were immensely proud of the young woman who in looks at least was their beloved daughter Nella incarnate, and they could not wait to show her off to their friends and neighbours. For her part, Noora was enchanted by her Grandpa and Grandma Fizz, who were everything she had hoped and more.

She had spent her first Christmas away from Yorvik at sea, and their arrival in England had been to a land awash with rain and gales, nothing like the Christmas card scenes she had been expecting. It seemed as if her happiness was now truly complete when Christmas week of 1902 saw the whole country covered in the deepest snowfall for decades. Even in London the pavements were piled high and part of the Thames was frozen over as the temperature plummeted.

. . . If only you could be here to see it, Moo darling,

Noora wrote to her grandmother in Australia.

It's so very different from home at this time of year. Everything looks just like a scene from a Christmas card. It really is a dream come true. It's just a pity there's a price to pay for all this beauty. It's really freezing and I swear I don't know if I'll ever get used to this bitter cold. But thankfully Grandma Fizz has been more than kind and presented me with a beautiful fur muff that once belonged to my mother, with ear-muffs to match. All I need now is one for my nose, for it remains a bright cherry-red with a permanent drip!

Mabberley's allowed their young ladies the whole of December off, and the heavy cold that dogged Noora's first few weeks of the holiday seemed to abate as Christmas Day drew nearer. This was an immense relief as her grandmother had arranged all manner of outings and appointments for her in the run-up to the festive season. If Noora was to be introduced into Northamptonshire society, then only the best clothes and accessories would do.

Two weeks before the Christmas ball, the old lady accompanied her granddaughter to the Mayfair salon of Madame D'Arcy, her favourite dressmaker, to have a ballgown specially designed for the occasion.

'I think white organza would be most appropriate,' Lady Margaret announced on sifting through the fabrics on offer.

Madame D'Arcy heartily concurred. 'Innocence with a touch of sophistication, your ladyship – the perfect combination!'

Noora was highly delighted with the result when they

attended for the final fitting seven days later. She twirled in front of Madame D'Arcy's cheval mirror. On a festive note, deep red velvet sashes at the waist and hand-embroidered clusters of red holly berries sprinkled over the full skirts had been added. These, she was told, it would be possible to remove for future occasions when diamanté clusters could be substituted, or any other decoration that happened to take her fancy.

'No alteration is too much bother,' the dressmaker insisted as she helped Noora out of the gown.

Madame D'Arcy, it transpired, had a whole team of ladies who beavered away behind the scenes turning out all manner of beautiful clothes for just such occasions. 'And every seam hand-stitched into the bargain,' her grand-mother assured her.

This piece of information came as a great surprise to Noora, who quickly pointed out that she and her Grandma Moo back in Australia were much more advanced. They had been making their clothes with a Singer sewing machine for years.

'Gracious, child, you mean to tell me you actually *wear* things you make yourself?' Lady Margaret asked, askance.

'Well, what else would we do with them?' Noora countered in surprise.

But the look on her grandmother's face precluded any further discussion on the subject, and not for the first time Noora had the distinct impression she had unwittingly shocked the old lady to the core. This was indeed a strange country, she decided. Whereas her grandmother back home had positively encouraged her to do things for herself, here it was considered the mark of the ill-bred. One simply did not soil one's hands performing any kind of manual work whilst there were servants to do it for you.

Noora found she was learning fast and knew she must try to temper her initial impulses to blurt out the simple truth on every occasion. In order to fit in, she must learn to curb her tongue and listen to the received wisdom of those around her before venturing an opinion on just about anything.

Even at school during the week her fellow boarders seemed so much more worldly wise than she was. Although they looked no older, there was a sophistication about them born of an upbringing in what they all regarded as the very epicentre of the universe itself – London. People Noora had only read about in magazines – members of the aristocracy, the acting profession, famous singers and writers – were all old friends and acquaintances to most of the young ladies of Mabberley's. Listening to them all made her own little world of Yorvik seem very narrow.

The favourite topic in the Common Room, however, was most definitely Romance. And Romance, with a capital R, appeared to be the object of all female longings. Everyone dreamt of falling in love and could hardly wait for their debutante year when this blissful state of affairs was expected to come about.

In her bedroom at night, which she shared with two others, the exchanged confidences usually ended up with much heart-searching about how far one would be expected to encourage a young man before being considered 'loose'.

There were thirty girls in all, most of whom like Noora went home at weekends. Returning on the Monday morning, most were full of tales of the beaux they had met when visiting friends or relatives in the country or elsewhere. Such exciting goings-on seemed a far cry from the closely chaperoned weekends Noora had been experiencing over the past year.

She had seen very little of her father since their arrival in England, for he spent a good deal of time at his Club. This ideally suited her grandparents, who were only too delighted to take their granddaughter under their wing and make up for all the lost time when she had been growing up without them in Australia.

Her grandparents' town house was only ten minutes by cab from Mabberley's and, to Noora's consternation, almost immediately she enrolled, her grandmother began turning up in the evenings during the week to request from Miss Harcourt, the headmistress, that her grand-daughter be allowed out to attend whatever concert or social occasion took her fancy.

'One must understand how deprived the child has been up to now. We have sixteen years of neglect to make up for in so short a time,' Lady Margaret informed the owner of the establishment. 'We can't have the poor girl "coming out" totally ignorant of all that others in her position take for granted, now can we?'

Miss Harcourt could not argue with this, for Noora knew that she too regarded her new charge's Australian upbringing with deep suspicion.

But for her own part Noora had little doubt that she learned as much from her school companions in the evenings as she did from occupying a box at one of the popular West End shows. It was after lights out, in the privacy of their rooms, that the young ladies of Mabberley's really let their hair down and discussed subjects that had little to do with the Three R's. After Romance, the subject talked about with most awe and much giggling was a three-letter word called Sex, which it seemed was something reserved exclusively for after marriage. To have partaken of the forbidden fruit before then was to place yourself firmly beyond the pale of decent society.

It did not take Noora long to realize that perhaps her father and grandmother had had a point in the fuss that had been created over her confession in that regard, and she also knew that this was a secret she must share with no one here in England, no matter how trustworthy they might seem. To admit she had freely surrendered what now appeared to be a girl's most priceless possession before she had even arrived here would be tantamount to

564

committing social suicide. Yes, life was very different indeed from the carefree world she had left behind back home.

It was at times like that when her thoughts would turn to Joe-boy and she longed for news of him, but she knew that in deference to her father her grandmother would never commit her friend's name to paper in a letter.

Her room-mates, Amy and Rebecca, seemed quite fascinated by her previous life on the other side of the world and were keen to know if she had left a beau behind there. Not to disappoint them, Noora found herself talking about her special friend 'Joe'. But to her shame she did not tell them he was a half-caste, or that he was brought up in a stringy-bark shack on their land.

As she lay in bed at night after such a conversation, she often asked herself why she could not tell the truth about him. Was she ashamed? The thought of being ashamed of her friendship with Joe-boy had never entered her head back home. He was simply her best friend and always had been. But here even the name Joe-boy seemed wrong somehow and, feeling sure they would laugh if she used it, she had shortened it to the more acceptable Joe.

In fact, if she thought about it, there was much about her life on Yorvik that they just would not understand. Here her new friends moved in a highly privileged, very exclusive circle that simply did not associate on a social level with those deemed to be below them. To most of the population, and indeed in the past to herself as a young girl reading about such people back on Yorvik, their lives were such stuff as dreams were made of and she was aware she must try very hard to keep her feet on the ground and not allow herself to become too dazzled by the sheer opulence of her new life.

Even the preparations for her Christmas debut at Hamberley Hall seemed quite extraordinary. All the fitting and fussing for ballgowns, or day gowns, or every other sort of gown deemed so essential for the well-dressed young lady, was perfectly normal for the other young women she met, but to Noora it was all quite incredible. Even at school during the week they were allowed to change out of the regulation white blouse and navy skirts and into their own gowns for supper and there was much competition to compare the latest in fashions and fabrics. Each of her new friends seemed to possess a different gown for every night of the week.

'And to think I used to make two dresses do me for the whole of one school term back home,' she unthinkingly told the startled Lady Margaret on one of their regular visits to the dressmaker.

'Good gracious, child, how absolutely frightful!' The elderly lady's brows had risen a good half inch. But she had then bitten her tongue. From what she could gather, life in the Antipodes must have been spartan in the extreme! That type of thing would most certainly never have occurred had poor Nella lived, but Lady Margaret was well aware she must never be seen to be passing any type of judgement on her Australian opposite number, Carrie Gordon-Hebden.

She knew very little about Noora's paternal grandmother, so goodness only knew what sort of an upbringing the poor girl had had out there. She could find no trace at all of the Gordon-Hebdens in either *Debrett's* or *Burke's Peerage*, so she could only conclude that they must have been a family of little social standing here in the old country. It looked like Nella had married into 'new money' after all, despite all her late daughter's assurances that Billy's family came from good landed stock.

But Lady Margaret's suspicions about the Gordon-Hebden pedigree, or lack of it, made her all the more determined to show her only grandchild just how ancient and illustrious her maternal English forebears were, and her efforts had been well rewarded by Noora's reaction on being taken round Hamberley Hall for the first time.

The young girl's eyes had been wide with wonder at the multitude of well-connected ancestors who gazed down at her from the ancient walls. And most intriguing of all was the amazing resemblance she found in many of the pictures to herself. Those same wide blue eyes, and that same high forehead and distinctive flaxen hair seemed to appear in every generation, dating right back to the earliest portrait to grace the oak-panelled walls of the main hall. That particular picture was of a certain Lady Helena Strutt, reputed to be an illegitimate daughter of King James the Second. 'But as he mainly preferred young men to young women, the accuracy of that story, sadly, must remain in doubt,' her grandfather had commented wryly.

With so much personal history around the place, the difference between Hamberley Hall and Yorvik could not have been more marked. Back home they had nice furniture, it was true, but none of it had had any real family connections. None was inherited. In fact, her Grandma Moo had made it clear one must not ask questions about the past, and so her granddaughter had grown up in almost total ignorance about her father's side of the family tree. And, with her mother having died in childbirth, Noora had known next to nothing about her maternal side. But now that was being rectified with a vengeance. Here there did not appear to be a stick of furniture or even the most humble household item that did not date back several hundred years, and almost everything had a story attached to it. The whole house seemed to be a personal monument to the generations of Foston-Strutt-Smiths who had inhabited its ivy-covered walls.

Both the Fostons and the Strutts had been old landed gentry stock who had added the name Smith to the signature of family members when the impoverished heiress to Hamberley Hall, a certain Helena Isabella — known to all as Nella-Bella — married into Victorian 'trade money' in 1842. This was in the ample form of a certain William Herbert Smith, who had made his fortune in installing some of the first indoor water closets into the county's finest houses. Rumour had it that Nella-Bella, then a rather plump, retiring young woman of thirty-two, had gone to the unheard-of extravagance of having a total of five of these new-fangled contraptions fitted in the Hall over a period of two years before 'Bertie' finally got the message.

'I daresay they did each other a favour,' Sir Richard informed his granddaughter with a smile, as Noora stood looking up at their portraits on the morning of the Christmas ball. 'For neither Mother nor Father were what you could call great catches as far as looks were concerned, but between them they had all that really matters in this world, child – breeding and money, in that order. Without them you're lost.'

Then he had turned to her and added with pride, 'But that's something, thank God, you'll never have to worry about. You've not only got both of those two essentials, but you've got looks into the bargain. I tell you, Noora my dear, all the eligible young men of the day will be queuing up to pay their respects when you finally "come out" in two years' time. But you can afford to be choosy. It's not every young woman who is sole heiress to a place like Hamberley Hall, you know.'

Noora stared at her grandfather in amazement as the words sank in. It had never crossed her mind that one day all this might be hers.

Seeing her blank expression, Sir Richard looked puzzled. 'You did know your mother had no brothers or sisters, didn't you?'

Noora shook her head, then nodded in confusion. 'Well, yes, I suppose I did know I had no first cousins or anything like that over here. But somehow it never dawned on me that I'd actually inherit all this . . .' Her voice tailed off as she looked about her at the magnificent furnishings and antiques collected over generations from all corners of the globe. 'I – I don't know quite what to say.'

Sir Richard put his arm around his granddaughter's shoulders. 'Then don't say anything, except that you'll take as much pride living in this great house over the next fifty years as we have over the last. I'll rest easy in my grave, when the time comes, knowing that.'

Noora looked up at the pale blue eyes smiling down into hers and a cold hand passed over her heart. But what of Yorvik? Her grandfather was really expecting her to take over as mistress of Hamberley Hall when he and her grandmother passed on, just as her beloved Moo back in Australia wanted with all her heart for her to take over Yorvik.

'And who knows,' her grandfather was continuing. 'At the ball tonight you might just meet the young man who will eventually join you here!' His eyes twinkled at the thought. Their granddaughter might still be only in her sweet sixteenth year but already his wife had paid close heed to the guest list, making sure that young men from only the very best families were sent invitations. If only half of them turned up tonight, young Noora would have a fine crop to choose from indeed.

It was a rather stunned young woman who climbed the stairs to begin her preparations for the night to come. Her grandfather's words had given her much to think about. Too much.

Noora's bedroom in the Hall overlooked the front of the house, where snow-covered lawns stretched into the distance, disappearing into the moonlit night. Although none had fallen since afternoon, it still lay crisp and even, sparkling beneath a sky lit by a galaxy of brightly shining stars.

The wide drive that led up to the house was lit by dozens of lanterns, and from around eight o'clock, as she allowed one of the maids allotted by her grandmother to assist in the last-minute preening and pampering before she made her way downstairs, Noora was amazed at the number of carriages and motor vehicles that were arriving, to deposit their elegantly attired passengers at the main steps.

'We've had over six hundred in here some evenings,' Sarah, the maid informed her. 'And I wouldn't be at all surprised if we have near enough that number tonight.'

Noora listened in growing apprehension as she sat in front of the looking glass and the girl brushed her long hair into the fashionable Watteau-style upswept coiffure, adding a cluster of red holly berries held in place by a comb on top.

As the maid chattered on about the illustrious guests whom she had served here in the past, Noora prayed she would not let her grandparents down by finding she had absolutely no conversation when introduced to any of the names that were tripping off Sarah's tongue. Already she was well aware she had none of the clever tittle-tattle of her school friends, who seemed to know the latest gossip on all the famous personalities that made up London high society.

'I'm afraid I shall seem an awful Australian country bumpkin to everyone,' she confided to her grandfather, as Sir Richard took her arm at the bedroom door some ten minutes later and prepared to escort her downstairs.

'Nonsense, my dear! You'll be like a breath of fresh air blowing through their closeted little lives. Why, I've got no doubt you have seen and done things back in New South Wales that they could never even dream of over here.'

Noora found herself giving a wry smile, despite her nerves. Just how true those words were he would never know.

But there was little time to dwell on the past as she descended the main staircase on her grandfather's arm, for the banqueting hall below was a sight to behold. A large Christmas tree covered in dozens of small gaily wrapped parcels, which would be the prizes for the games that followed, dominated the right-hand side of the old minster fireplace, in which a huge Yule log burned brightly. Specially designed Christmas bunting was strung around all the walls, and from the chandeliers hung garlands of mistletoe and holly. Already the floor was full of chattering, laughing guests partaking freely of the mulled wine that was on offer on the heavily laden trays circulating in the hands of black-coated waiters, and at the opposite side of the fireplace to the tree, a five-piece band was ready to strike up.

To Noora's great embarrassment, her grandfather paused six steps from the bottom of the stairs and indicated for the band to strike a drum roll, after which he held up his hand to ensure silence for what he had to say.

'My lords, ladies and gentlemen — gathered friends — before the festivities begin I would like to take this opportunity to introduce you to the most important lady in my life, next to my dear wife.'

He turned to beam at Noora and raised her right hand in his and kissed it. 'This is my beautiful granddaughter Miss Noora Helena Gordon-Hebden — Hamberley Hall's next mistress. I know you will all take her to your hearts just as we have done.' Then he turned to Noora once more. 'Welcome home, my dear,' he said. 'Welcome home!'

As one, the assembled crowd below raised their glasses and joined in the greeting. Shouts of 'Welcome home' resounded throughout the hall as Noora stood there by her grandfather's side and gazed about her. Out of the corner of her eye she caught sight of her father standing to the right of the bottom of the steps. His florid face was beaming with pride as he looked up at her and he too held his glass aloft. Then, as the massed faces of the gathered crowd swam before her, she thought of her grandmother back on Yorvik, and of Joe-boy, and she wondered what they would be doing at this moment. What would they think if they could see her now? For a second or two her smile of thanks faltered, but then her grandfather was clasping her elbow and propelling her downstairs into the body of the hall.

'This is all for you, Noora my dear,' he told her with pride. 'Let it be the happiest Christmas of your young life!'

571

Hamberley Hall had seen nothing like it for years as the ancient walls echoed with music and laughter and guests toasted one another and the year to come.

Noora had little doubt that this would be a Christmas to remember as young men jostled one another to ask her to dance. She could scarcely believe that the laughing, chattering creature who was whirling around the floor in the arms of one young man after another, in this exquisite gown, was actually herself.

The revelry had been going on for less than half an hour when she was aware of someone watching her intently from the side of the floor as she danced a breathless Gay Gordons with her grandfather. This particular young man had not joined the others in the initial rush to take the floor with her. He was tall and rather goodlooking, with fair curly hair and an open boyish face, despite the reddish, curling moustache. He stood a good head above his two male companions and he seemed to be watching her every move as the dance proceeded. When the music ended he forsook his friends to march across the floor and present himself to the object of his interest.

Sir Richard's face broke into a wide smile of recognition as the young man strode up and held out his hand. 'Why, Lex old boy, so glad you could make it!' the older man said, grasping the proffered palm and pumping it warmly. 'Your dear mother is still down with this dratted 'flu, I believe, but she did say in her letter she hoped you would manage to come.'

He turned to his granddaughter. 'Noora, my dear, allow me to introduce the son of a very dear friend and neighbour of ours, Lady Mary Foynes. This is her much-travelled younger son, Alexander, who I understand has just arrived hot-foot from his father's place in Ireland . . . Lex, dear boy, my granddaughter, Noora!'

The two young people shook hands and Noora was instantly attracted by the easy smile on the other's face and the strong, open features. There was something about the generous mouth and row of white, even teeth that immediately tugged at her heartstrings, they reminded her so much of Joe-boy. But she banished the thought as soon as it came. This was no night to look back to the past. The present was far too much fun.

Once the formalities were over and her grandfather had diplomatically excused himself, she allowed her curiosity to get the better of her. 'Grandfather said your mother is a neighbour of theirs, but your father lives in Ireland, is that right?'

The young man nodded. 'My parents have discovered the recipe for a very happy marriage – they never see each other.' Then he grinned.

'You mean they live apart?'

'Uh-huh.'

'Oh.' She was quite at a loss for words, but intrigued nevertheless. The habits of the English gentry were a never-ending source of fascination. 'I see . . . Don't they get on?'

'Oh, their marriage could have been very harmonious, as long as Pa agreed to play second fiddle. But he wasn't very good at that I'm afraid, so now he tends his cows in the Golden Vale and Ma spends her days over here, playing bridge with her chums in her old family seat just outside Kettering.' He made bit of a face. 'I prefer Pa's place, personally.'

'The Golden Vale . . . ?' Noora began.

He smiled. 'Sounds romantic, doesn't it? That's what the travel writers are calling our own little bit of heaven in the south west of dear old Ireland. Our estate of Ballymore is mainly in County Limerick, but spreads into Tipperary here and there. No one pays much attention to county boundaries over there.' He sighed. 'I only wish I could say the same about our compatriots in the North.'

'You don't look much like an Irishman,' Noora commented, thinking of her grandmother's dark colouring and bright blue eyes, and of the once red-headed Sean O'Dwyer. To her they both typified the two distinctive breeds of Celtic people.

Alexander Foynes gave a rueful smile, then said in a very pronounced burr, 'Sure and you would be right there, my girl. We're of that strange hybrid breed, the Anglo-Irish – fish out of water on both sides of the Irish Sea.'

Noora smiled. 'Is that why you travel a lot?' she asked, remembering her grandfather's remark. 'Because you don't really feel you belong to either country?' She was beginning to understand the problem in her own life.

'Well now, that's a good question!' His natural cut-glass English accent returned and Lex Foynes paused to think. 'Just why *do* I travel so much? Some people claim they travel to broaden the mind, but for the majority it only serves to lengthen their conversation at the dinner table. They become the most frightful bores. I meet them all the time, both here and in Ireland. In fact, my old man, God help him, falls into that category. He travelled quite a bit in America as a young man and has about a dozen stories all told – and told – and told . . . I don't ever intend to make that mistake.'

Noora smiled. 'I'm sure you won't.'

'Mulled wine, madam . . . sir?'

They both accepted a glass from the silver tray held out by a waiter and an interested smile played around the corners of Lex Foynes's mouth as he sipped the sweet warm brew. 'Mother told me you were Australian,' he said. 'You're not at all what I expected.'

'Oh really? And just what did you expect – someone still in convict chains, dragging a kangaroo behind her?'

He laughed. 'Something like that. Are you over here for long?'

'To finish my education, then I plan to go back.' Noora gave an anxious glance in the direction of her grandfather. 'But don't tell Grandpa that, for goodness' sake. He fully expects me to remain here and ultimately take over the Hall.'

'Aha . . .' Lex Foynes looked thoughtful. 'You're the only grandchild, I take it?'

'I'm afraid so.'

'My dear girl, *afraid so* doesn't come into it! Why, most people would give their right arm to inherit a place like this.'

Noora nodded miserably. 'I know,' she sighed. 'That's just the trouble. I'm not *most people* and I actually like it out there in Australia. Heaven knows, I *am* an Australian and I don't ever intend to give that up.'

'Then you've got a problem.'

'I know.'

Their eyes met and they smiled in unison. Then he took her elbow and, as another dance was beginning, they had to move out of the way. They began to walk towards the window where beyond the glass and ancient mullions the snow was now falling in thick white flakes. 'Pretty, isn't it?' he said.

'It's beautiful.'

'You don't have that in Australia.'

'No, but we've got lots of other things.'

His interest was aroused for, despite his wanderings throughout Europe and the Americas, he had never been south of the Equator. 'Such as?'

Noora gave a quiet smile. 'Why don't you go out there and see for yourself sometime?'

'Is that an invitation?'

She looked a trifle surprised, then nodded her head and grinned. 'If you like.'

They sipped the end of their wine in silence for a moment or two, then he took the empty glasses and placed them on a passing waiter's tray.

'Care to dance?'

Noora glanced towards the floor where couples were waltzing to a familiar Strauss melody. She had only had the most rudimentary dancing lessons at Mabberley's. 'I – I'm not very good, I'm afraid.'

'Come, come, dear girl, that's twice you've used that word "afraid" in as many minutes!' he chastised, taking her in his arms and whirling her on to the floor. 'Australians are meant to be intrepid, fearless characters who break new frontiers at the drop of a hat. Your family must have been of a pioneering spirit to go out there in the first place and I'm sure your English forebears were of the stuff that made this country great. Have your grandparents introduced you to them all yet?' He indicated with his head the array of gilt-framed likenesses gazing down at them from the oak-panelled walls.

Noora sighed and nodded her head. 'Oh yes. It seems we can trace our family tree way back to when our ancestors were actually living in it!' She gave a wry smile. 'Or at least it certainly seems like that from the stories I've been hearing . . . Is your own family very old?'

'Old yes, blue-blooded too, on both sides of the blanket, but not as well-heeled as yours, that's for sure. Poor as the proverbial church mice, we are now. In fact the family pile in old Ireland is almost just that. There simply isn't the money to maintain it. Dear Father, bless his heart, has now gone through the last of the legacy of umpteen generations of rogues and vagabonds and now claims to be living on his wits.' Lex smiled ruefully and gave a heartfelt sigh. 'My mother says it's remarkable how a person can survive on so little capital!'

He swung his partner gracefully out of collision's way with another couple and continued, 'It's sad really. He tried so hard over the years to make some money – invested in all sorts of schemes. "Always keep one jump ahead of the next fellow" he would tell us, and he really did try to live by that maxim. The trouble was he was always off at a tangent and headed in totally the wrong direction. It's a real gift to be so disastrously bad at making money, you know . . . Poor Pa, you'd like him, I have no doubt. He has charm by the bucketful, like most of the Irish. The only trouble is, he's a mite too fond of the whisky these days. Says he only drinks to steady his nerves. The only trouble is he often gets so steady he can't move!'

Noora had to smile. 'And your brother? Grandfather said you were a younger son?'

'Ah yes, dear Harry, the son and heir! He's in the Irish Guards, actually.'

Noora was already acquainted with the habit of the aristocracy to insist on their eldest sons having early officer training. 'So Harry is a leader of men.'

'More a follower of women, I'd say.'

Noora glanced up at him and laughed out loud. His family certainly sounded fun. 'He's not here tonight, I take it?'

'Good Lord, no! And thank heavens for that. I'd never get a look in otherwise.'

The comment pleased her immensely. It was quite a novelty to be taken seriously by a young man such as this. And for him to think a Guards officer would also be interested in her! Well now, that would be something to make her room-mates at Mabberley's go absolutely green.

Noora began to hum to herself in time to the music as they continued to whirl around the floor. He had obviously taken to her, and for her part she was certainly enjoying herself. He was even making her believe she was a passable dancer, so nimble was he on his feet. He had not stepped on her toes once.

When the time came for the dance to end she felt a real pang of disappointment as she accepted his thanks. 'It's been a great pleasure,' he told her. 'Perhaps I can call sometime in the new year?'

Noora shook her head reluctantly. 'I don't officially "come out" for another eighteen months.'

'Good Lord, we might all be dead by then!' he exclaimed in surprise. Then added on reflection, 'But if we're not, perhaps you might like to see me again?'

'Perhaps . . .' Noora murmured, with what she hoped was an enigmatic smile, knowing perfectly well she would be only too delighted to see him again. If the past ten minutes was anything to go by, she was going to enjoy the rest of her stay in the old country very much indeed.

In fact, the whole evening proved to be one of the happiest she had ever known. The people she met turned out to be quite delightful and not at all the stuffy creatures she had anticipated. The older couples were full of all sorts of amusing anecdotes and the young ones so full of fun and energy, she began to feel quite worn out by all the games and dancing by the time eleven-thirty came round and the company broke up to take part in the Midnight Carol Service in the local church.

To her disappointment she did not dance again with her new Anglo-Irish friend, for her time was totally taken up with the score of other young men who presented themselves, then tried their best to impress her as they partnered her in the games and dances. Almost all she took to immediately, although none could dance quite so well as the charming Lex Foynes.

The only one to come near was a red-headed, kilted Scotsman by the name of Gregor McGregor, who sang in accompaniment in a fine tenor voice to the popular tunes the band was playing, and went out of his way to win her one of the presents off the tree. To his great disappointment he did not succeed, so made up for it by presenting her with the spring of lucky white heather he wore in his buttonhole.

'May it bring you every happiness this world has to offer,' he told her, as he pinned it to the bodice of her dress. 'It has certainly brought me luck tonight, for I've met you.'

Noora's eyes sparkled as she walked back to where her grandparents were seated.

'We're so glad to see you having such a good time, darling,' her grandmother said. 'You're quite the belle of the ball!'

Noora could feel her cheeks flush, for she almost believed it to be true.

When the festivities finally came to an end, most of the guests joined their hosts in the local church for the Midnight Service. The twelfth-century church was less than half a mile from the Hall and, along with many of the younger guests, Noora chose to walk the few hundred yards in the softly falling snow.

She was warmly wrapped up in a long red fur-trimmed cloak and matching muff and there was no need for lanterns to light the way, for the moon was high and bright in the starlit sky. The whole world seemed clothed in a glittering white mantle. Never had she imagined anything so beautiful and it seemed almost sinful to do as many of the young men were doing, dashing into the fresh virgin drifts to gather snowballs which they aimed with devastating accuracy at each other, sending many a hat flying into the path of those who came behind.

There was much laughter from all concerned, and many of the company sang Christmas carols as they wound their way down the drive to crowd into the small stone building where generations of Foston-Strutts, including Nella-Bella and her beloved Herbert Smith, were buried in the family vault.

The vicar was waiting to greet them at the door as they stamped their boots on the stone steps to get rid of the snow. Inside, the choir was already in place and a clear young male voice was singing 'Silent Night' as they took their places in the ancient oak pews.

As Noora sat down, threw back the hood of her cloak and looked around her, out of the corner of her eye she spotted Lex Foynes sitting two rows behind. He caught her

579

glance and smiled, winking his left eye before turning to look piously ahead. She found herself smiling as she turned her own attention back to the choir now in full flow beneath the pulpit, the stairs of which the vicar was climbing to begin the service. In the belfry above, the bells began to toll.

'Happy Christmas,' the whisper went up as neighbour greeted neighbour.

Noora returned the greetings and discreet handshakes of those seated on either side, then as the music swept over her and the choir sang the most beloved of all Christmas carols, she closed her eyes. This was her first Christmas in the old country. It had been a lovely evening. A magical evening, like none she had ever known. Hamberley Hall had opened its doors and countless friends and neighbours had opened their hearts to her tonight. Outside, beyond the ancient stone walls of the church, the snow was falling, and in this very building generations of her family had been christened, married and finally laid to rest. If she opened her eyes she could see her family crest on the wall of the north transept, and her great-grandmother had hand-stitched the altarcloth on which rested the bible another ancestor had presented to the people of the parish of Hamberley. She was surrounded by warmth and love and a sense of belonging that reached back through countless generations. Why then, oh why did she suddenly feel so sad?

Beneath her closed lids she was seeing not softly falling snow, but clear sparkling water that cascaded off a rock at an enchanted place called Yorvik Force. There on Christmas Days gone by she would be taken by her grandmother, her darling Moo, to spread out their food and drink on the warm grass, then spend the day lying in the sun, or swimming lazily in the blue waters. More often than not, if her father was not with them, they would be joined before the day was out by the Irishman and Joe-boy. And there too there had been love and warmth aplenty as they toasted the birth of the Christ Child in Moo's home-brewed wine.

'Happy Christmas, Moo darling,' she whispered beneath her breath. 'Happy Christmas, Joe-boy and Be-anga . . .'

And in her heart she was back there with them now as she joined the congregation to rise and sing the age-old hymn, 'Oh Come All Ye Faithful'.

She had come a long way in a few months and heaven only knew how long a road she would have to travel before it took her back to those she had loved and left behind on her beloved Yorvik.

CHAPTER FORTY-FIVE

With the success of the Christmas ball, the new year of 1903 got off to the best possible start at Hamberley Hall, leaving Noora to enter her spring term at Mabberley's determined to do her best to shine academically and make her father, her Grandma Moo, and her Grandpa and Grandma Fizz even more proud of her.

She was also aware, however, that she had to continue to merit that pride, and as the preparations began to pack her trunks for the return journey to London, the dreaded word 'matriculation' could now be heard on the lips of both her grandparents and her father.

'We know you have it in you to do well, darling,' her grandmother told her as she kissed her goodbye on the steps of her school on the second Monday of January. 'And just remember we are all right behind you ... Do you realize you will be the first on either your grandfather's or my own side of the family ever to get this far academically?'

Noora had not known that, and it did little to ease her trepidation about what lay ahead. She was more aware than ever now that so many hopes were vested in her. She could not let them down.

In some ways returning to school and the youthful companionship of her friends came as a relief, despite the hard work she knew lay ahead. There was lots of gossip to catch up on, as many budding romances had developed over the Christmas season, and Noora found she was able to join in with embellished accounts of her own new friendships with Lex Foynes and the other young men she had met at the Hall.

Outside school, the only real cloud on her horizon was her father, who she knew was still drinking far too much.

Although he had spent most of the Christmas holiday with them at Hamberley, over the past year she had seen very little of him, for he spent most of his time at his Club. With her grandparents preferring her to spend her weekends with them, left to his own devices she knew he had had just the excuse he needed to pursue his favourite occupations of drinking and gambling. Soon after their arrival in England, he had joined a card circle which met most nights of the week, often at his flat, where the stakes would mount in keeping with the empty spirit bottles that piled up in the small kitchen.

From Billy's point of view the situation could not be more convenient. He had had no bother settling into London life once more. Many of his old school and university friends were still living in the capital and they welcomed him back into their midst with open arms. Most like him had no occupation, but were 'gentlemen of means' living off their investments, with plenty of time for their most favoured leisure pursuits. For most this included gambling, whether at the races or over cards, and they were in good company since the King himself counted this as his own favourite pastime, when he was not womanizing.

Because her father had succeeded in keeping his drinking within bounds whilst a guest of her grandparents, Noora had nurtured the hope that this improved state of affairs might continue once they returned to the capital after the holiday. But her hopes were soon dashed. Over the weeks that followed she found plenty of evidence of what was going on in her occasional visits to Billy's Bloomsbury flat.

Often she would arrive on a Saturday morning to find he had never been to bed, but would be sprawled in a drunken stupor in an armchair, with the remains of the previous night's card game scattered all around him.

Sick at heart, Noora would attempt to tidy up and dispose of the empty glasses and bottles, the overflowing ashtrays and the other remnants seemingly so essential to a successful game, for she could not face the embarrassment of either one of her grandparents, or even the daily help, finding both her father and the place in such a condition.

As the dark days of winter gradually turned to spring, she grew increasingly concerned not only about his health, but also about the amount he was spending, and where that money was coming from.

'It's none of your damned business,' Billy countered angrily, one Saturday afternoon in early March when she happened to drop by to wait for her grandmother. She had found him unshaven, unwashed, and totally unmoved by the effect this had on her. 'Just keep your young nose out of my affairs, young lady. Just as long as your school fees are paid, you have nothing to worry about.'

'But I do, Daddy, can't you see?' Noora implored him. 'Do you think I can really close my eyes to all those empty gin and whisky bottles around the place every time I stop by? And do you really think I don't know that all those interminable card games you get involved in must be costing you a fortune?'

'What do you expect me to do?' her father countered sullenly. 'Sit around the flat by myself every night drinking tea?'

Noora looked down at him, slumped in his usual armchair. His necktie was undone as was the top button of his trousers, over which his stomach spilled. He had put on at least twenty pounds in weight since their arrival in England and he looked like a man twice his age. His once-handsome face was now bloated, and the alcohol had extended the blood vessels of his nose to make it a highly coloured caricature of the fine feature it had once been.

Before they had left for England her grandmother had confided to her that he was rapidly turning into the image of her own late father, who had also had a drink problem. Did alcoholism run in the family? Noora knew almost nothing about the Londoner who had been her great-grandfather. Although Moo had told her stories at great length about her own Irish mother, she had never really talked about her father except in regard to his liking for his liquor, commenting once, 'He was the nicest man on two feet – if only he could stay on them!'

Now, as Noora looked down at that man's grandson, she realized that the craving to escape into oblivion through the bottle might indeed be inherited, and that no matter how much she nagged or worried she was probably not going to win this particular battle, for drunks could see no further than the glass in their hand. 'I don't really expect anything of you, Pa,' she said in answer to his question. 'Except that you remember that both Moo and I love you and hate to see you doing this to yourself. If you carry on like this much longer, life won't be worth living.'

Billy looked at his daughter and gave a bitter laugh as he lifted his glass to his lips. 'Not worth living, eh? My life hasn't been worth living since the day your mother died. If I drink too much and hasten the end, what of it? All it means is I'll bring closer the day we can be together again. That can't be such a bad thing, can it?'

Noora felt the sting of tears in her eyes as she turned from him and walked to the window so he would not see her pain. 'No,' she told him softly, gazing down into the passing traffic. 'Not if that's what you really want.' And she knew for certain at that moment what she had suspected all her life. He had never really loved her, just as he had never really loved his mother. There had only been two people he had cared about in his life, himself and his wife, probably in that order.

Down below in the street she could see her grandmother's cab drawing up and the old lady getting out. As usual Lady Margaret was immaculately turned out and, with her tall, straight carriage and still flawless complexion, she could pass for someone half her age. She looked up to the window and raised her ebony cane at the sight of her granddaughter, who motioned to her to stay where she was.

'Grandma Fizz is here,' Noora said, composing herself with difficulty. 'I'll go down and meet her, it'll save her climbing the stairs.' She could have added, and it'll save her from seeing you in this state so early in the day. But she didn't. Instead she leant over and kissed the top of her father's balding head.

'Goodbye, Pa,' she said. 'Take care.'

'I will,' he assured her. It was all a charade but neither had any option but to continue playing it.

But her worries over her father receded somewhat as the days flew by and the dreaded examinations drew ever nearer and the staff of Mabberley's impressed upon their pupils just how important matriculation was in the world today.

'Not that you should have too much to worry about, Noora,' her form teacher told her. 'Your work has been consistently good for some months now.' For the past term she had been receiving some of the best marks in the class for her essays and the elderly spinster was particularly pleased with her Australian pupil's diligence, which was in stark contrast to that of the majority of the girls, who did not give a fig about passing examinations. The encouragement gave Noora real hope that the many hours spent poring over her books in the library might not be in vain.

Since being at Mabberley's she had become aware that, if not all things were possible, then at least some were, and there were real opportunities to be had in the outside world if one worked hard enough at school to be awarded a place at university. She could become a teacher, or even a doctor, for a few fortunate women were now qualifying in medicine. This new century was seeing all sorts of advances by the female sex. There had even been a friend of the headmistress's who came and gave a talk to the girls on the topic 'Votes For Women', and that had been a great success, even with those who wanted nothing more than to marry a rich husband and have babies.

Noora's grandparents listened to the reports of her scholastic work at Mabberley's with great pride. Neither Sir Richard nor his wife had gone to a proper school, nor pitted their wits alongside their fellows in a national examination. Private tutors had been their lot and they watched with not a little astonishment how well their granddaughter was progressing.

'I hope you're keeping your grandmother in Australia informed about all this,' Lady Margaret commented as they took coffee in their favourite West End restaurant one Saturday morning after Easter, a few weeks before matriculation. 'I expect she will be just as excited as us to know the final outcome of all this hard work.'

'Oh, don't worry,' Noora said, biting into a chocolate éclair. 'I write every single week.'

And she was speaking the truth, for the letters that came on the mail coach at Yorvik arrived with a clockwork regularity and were eagerly devoured by an anxious Carrie, who even after all this time had not quite come to terms with her granddaughter's departure.

Although she could forget for a while during the day when the outdoor life of the station absorbed her interest, after work in the evenings the big house seemed cold and empty with her granddaughter and son both gone. It was as if most of the joy had gone out of life as she walked through the empty rooms, often ending up in Noora's bedroom which, apart from regular dusting, remained just as she had left it. But the worst part was when Carrie settled down in her favourite armchair in the drawing room after supper and found she had no one to discuss the happenings of the day with. That she found very hard.

But despite the pain of separation, life moved on, and on as successful a sheep station as Yorvik this was particularly true. There were sheep to be reared, kept healthy then sheared, and their fleeces packed for transportation to England, and all the hundred and one other things that made up the station owner's year.

Every month brought its own familiar routine, and when the long-awaited letter eventually came that summer telling Carrie that Noora had not only passed her matriculation with flying colours but might even be accepted for a place at Oxford, her grandmother was momentarily stunned. She had put the real reason behind Noora's preparation for matriculating completely out of her head, and to be suddenly jolted back to the reality of the situation was hard to take. She had just come in from attending the putting down of one of her favourite horses after an accident on the road back from Newcastle and the two things combined, for a moment, proved too much.

Whether it was the upset at the shooting of the horse or the news in the letter she could not tell, but as Carrie stood there in the sunlight of the morning room window and read, then re-read the words in the familiar scrawling script, she was aware of tears running down her cheeks.

She wiped them away impatiently with the back of her hand and stuffed the letter into her pocket. Why on earth was she standing here blubbing like a baby at her age? She should be proud at this moment. Noora had done incredibly well to get this far in so short a time. The whole school here would be so proud of her, for her achievement spoke volumes for the quality of the teaching that had come out of such humble surroundings.

Amongst the pile of post handed in from the mailcoach, Carrie received two letters that same day informing her of the momentous news, for both Noora's and Billy's arrived together. Both were brimming over with excitement. Billy especially seemed to regard it as a foregone conclusion that his daughter would not only be offered a place at Oxford in the very near future, but she would accept, and he would remain in England with her whilst she completed her degree. Carrie's heart sank as she read that bit, for she knew it was just the excuse he had been hoping for to prolong his stay in the old country.

Not even the information that the two of them would be travelling home to Yorvik for 'a short holiday' to discuss the future could revive Carrie's spirits as she relayed the news to Sean O'Dwyer later in the day. In her heart she feared the future was already a foregone conclusion. The visit was merely a placatory gesture for her behalf. Their minds were already made up. They would be returning to England, perhaps forever.

'This is worse than I ever expected, Sean, far worse,' she told her old friend. 'A degree takes years to complete and I haven't got that sort of time left.'

'You can't live other people's lives for them,' the Irishman told her, leaning on his pitchfork at the door to one of the barns. 'You should know that by now, Carrie love. Your dreams might not be theirs.' He too had been waiting for this news for months and had known exactly what it would do to her. His heart ached for her, but it was no more than he expected.

'You think it's selfish to want them to return for good? You think it's too much to expect them to come back to live on Yorvik forever more, to help me run the place and take over when I'm gone?' Carrie's voice was tight as she fought to keep the bitterness from showing, for it had always been her greatest fear that they would both go to England and not come back, that there would be no one here to take up the reins when she was no longer able. And that day was not too far off.

'No, I don't think it's selfish,' Sean told her. 'But I don't think they're being selfish either in doing what they want to do. We're all individuals, Carrie old girl . . .'

He gave a rueful smile as he tossed a forkful of hay into a nearby cart. 'If you remember there once was a time you wanted me to become something I wasn't.'

She looked across at him, but there was no rancour in the affection of his gaze. 'You're right,' she said, in a resigned voice. 'But that doesn't make it any easier.'

'When exactly are they coming?'

She did a mental calculation. 'They should be arriving around our mid-summer, sometime just before Christmas, I think. Noora's taking this coming year off to make up her mind.'

She folded the letter and slipped it back into her pocket. 'It'll be so good to see them both, despite everything. I doubt if Billy will have changed much, but she'll be quite the young lady by now.'

The news that Billy's hopes were to be fulfilled and Noora had indeed been offered a place to read English literature in the old university town of Oxford came in a letter posted just before they left England to return home to Australia. It arrived on Yorvik only a few days before their ship was due to dock in Sydney harbour.

The information came as no great surprise to Carrie, for by then she had had time to come to terms with what she believed to be the inevitable, and, despite her personal reservations, she was immensely proud of her granddaughter's achievements. In a strange way it was a relief to have her greatest fear finally confirmed. It had been the uncertainty that had been so hard to live with.

Now the place at Oxford was a fact, she got in touch immediately with the local papers to broadcast the news. Within forty-eight hours Noora's success was emblazoned in headlines on every paper in the area, and the local Hunter's Hollow *Courier* carried a woodcut picture, taken from a special graduation photograph that Carrie had received the previous month from England. In it Noora looked the living image of her dead mother: a delicate beauty, with her long neck, fine features and blonde hair done up in elegant coils. The local shop sold out within half an hour of the newspaper delivery and throughout the day Carrie received congratulations from young and old alike.

'I do believe I'm beginning to believe it's me that's passed that examination!' she told Sean, after taking a copy down to his hut after supper that day.

When she had finished reading the article to him, he looked up fondly from the chair where he was thoughtfully puffing his pipe, and added, 'Aye, well, given the chance sixty years ago, it could easily have been you, Carrie love.'

Carrie made no reply, but got up from her own chair and walked to the open door of the hut to look out. The sky beyond the copse of gum trees was filled with the crimson glow of evening. 'Things were different then,' she said in a quiet voice, as she took a deep breath of the soft evening air. 'Things like universities – they weren't meant for people like you and me. The world was different then. The poor were supposed to know their place and stay in it.'

'But you didn't.' He looked at her thoughtfully through the tobacco smoke.

'No, I didn't . . .' If ever there was a time to unburden her heart it was now.

She turned to face him.

As if reading her mind, he said softly, 'I've never asked any questions, Carrie love.'

It was true, he never had. They had shared sixty years of life together and he had asked nothing of her or about her. Yet he had given her his all.

'The past is dead, Irish, my old friend, and we have troubles enough in the present to go digging it up now.'

She looked out at the blazing sky and shivered slightly in the breeze blowing across the green acres that were so beloved by them both. The thought of Billy and Noora preferring the old country to all this was something she would never understand.

She sighed as she turned back to smile fondly at the man she loved. 'As to the future . . . Well, for once that can take care of itself.'

CHAPTER FORTY-SIX

Billy decided that, because of her age, he did not want his mother to make the long journey to meet them off the boat from England, so instead Carrie waited impatiently at Yorvik for the great day to finally dawn.

Their arrival in the Hunter Valley was met by a spell of the hottest December sunshine they had had in those parts for several years and it was a distinctly perspiring Noora and Billy who tumbled out of the carriage to greet her when the long-awaited day finally came.

'Moo darling!' Noora was across the cobbles in three bounds to embrace her grandmother, who was standing nervously at the foot of the steps to the big house.

Carrie had tears in her eyes as she clasped her grand-daughter to her, then held her at arm's length and shook her head. She had been right about Noora being quite grown up by now. There was almost nothing of the child left. The face that beamed back into her own was clear-skinned and quite beautiful, every last vestige of puppy fat gone. 'My, but you're quite the young lady!' she exclaimed. 'The very image of your poor mother!'

At that Billy gave a wry half smile and nodded his head in agreement as he came forward to greet his mother with a hug and a peck on the cheek. 'A daughter in a million,' he affirmed as he put his arm around the old lady's shoulders. 'Nella would have been so proud.'

Carrie and Noora climbed the steps into the big house together, their arms entwined, while Billy gave orders as to which rooms the travelling trunks were to be deposited in. He felt no real elation being back here and could not share the excitement that Noora had experienced as they travelled the last few miles over familiar territory. The extra weight he had put on during his time in England was telling on him, and this had been an exceptionally tiring journey. Perspiration glistened on his bald crown and forehead and he paused to dab his brow with a handkerchief as he climbed the stone steps behind his mother and daughter.

The two days that followed were ones of non-stop talking. There was so much catching up to do, and to Noora's surprise her grandmother had arranged for her to be personally interviewed by the local press on her return.

'You have become quite a local celebrity, darling, since they did that last feature on you,' Carrie told her.

The story that appeared two days later about her arrival in her old home made front-page news in two of the area's papers and caused the young woman in question to hoot with laughter as she read out the article to her father and grandmother over breakfast on her first Saturday morning at home.

MISS NOORA GORDON-HEBDEN IS WITHOUT DOUBT ONE OF THE FINEST EXPORT PRODUCTS THE HUNTER VALLEY HAS PRODUCED IN MANY A LONG DAY. WITH HER FAIR GOOD LOOKS AND ASTUTE MIND, IT IS NO WONDER THE ENGLISH ACADEMIC ESTABLISHMENT HAVE DONE HER THE GREAT HONOUR OF ALLOWING HER TO BECOME ONE OF THE FIRST NATIVE-BORN AUSTRALIANS TO GRACE ONE OF THEIR MOST HALLOWED SEATS OF LEARNING . . .

'One of the Valley's finest export products!' her father grinned, dabbing his mouth with his napkin. 'They make you sound like a side of beef!'

'As long as it's one of *our* sides of beef!' his mother put in. 'That really would be a compliment to be compared to!' Carrie glanced fondly across the table at her granddaughter. 'The whole Valley's so proud of you, my dear. Especially our own workers here on Yorvik . . . You'll have to try and get round to see them sometime soon. They're all dying to congratulate you themselves.'

'Well, not this morning, Moo, that's for sure,' Noora replied emphatically, as she folded the newspaper and laid it on the table beside her. 'I'll talk to them all in good time, but right now it's far too hot to go traipsing around shaking hands with everyone.' There was only one place to be on a morning as hot as this. And it was something she had dreamt of for so long beneath England's cold grey skies. But seeing the disappointed look on her grandmother's face, she added quickly, 'But I might get round to it later on this afternoon, if it cools down a bit.'

Carrie listened in sympathy and did not press the point as she spread her toast. The daytime temperature had not dropped below one hundred Fahrenheit for the best part of a week now, and this morning seemed even hotter than usual. 'Well, your father and I are going over to Hunter's Hollow for some shopping later this morning but should be back just after lunch. I'll be happy to come round visiting with you then, if you feel like it.'

Noora got up from the table and bent to kiss her grandmother's cheek. 'Thanks, Moo darling. I'm sure that'll suit me fine.' She replaced her napkin on the table and murmured, 'Now if you'll excuse me . . .'

Carrie and Billy beamed at each other as she left the room and Carrie felt a strange peace descend on her as she took another sip of her tea. No matter what the final decision as to where their futures might lie, she felt enormously proud of this small family that was hers.

As Noora bounded up the stairs, in a fashion she knew would not be at all approved of at Mabberley's, she felt a real elation in her being. The sun was streaming through the tall window on the half-landing and bathing a large oil painting of her mother in a shaft of golden light. She paused in front of it and looked up. 'Thanks for coming here,' she whispered to the perfect likeness of the parent she had never known. 'Thanks for giving me Yorvik to come back to.'

Her room was awash with that same golden light as she

pushed open the door and rushed in. She ran to the window and looked out across the wide rolling acres, past the blackfellas' camp, to where the waters of the lake glittered in the distance. It had been so long, so very long . . .

It took her less than half an hour to saddle her horse and set off on her favourite ride. Being back atop the gleaming chestnut's back felt completely right. 'I'm home, Prince . . . I'm home . . .' She almost sang the words into the animal's ear as she stroked the flowing mane and cantered on through the station.

It was wonderful just feasting her eyes on even the most mundane things, such as the old shearing sheds, and all hands stopped what they were doing to wave to her and call out their greetings as she passed.

Most of the faces were familiar and she called back to them by name. Some, however, were strangers to her and her grandmother had told her she had taken on around thirty new hands over the past two years.

There were many more people about in the area of the lake as she made her way along the winding track. Over the past year part of the land had been given over to grazing and sheep were dotted about, many of them wandering on to the path itself, causing her to pull up her horse and shout at them to get out of the way. It was always a losing battle, for they took their own time to get where they were going.

She was relieved, however, to find there was no sign of either animals or people down by the waterside itself. This, above all others, was her own special place and it would have been terrible to find the life of the station encroaching on what she considered to be her own personal bit of paradise.

She tethered her horse to a nearby tree and ran down to the bank of the lake, throwing her head back and her arms wide as if to embrace the whole of this beloved landscape. How often had she dreamt of this whilst closeted in that small room with her two schoolfriends back in

Bayswater, she wondered as she breathed deeply of the heady brew that was Yorvik air. As much as she loved London, this was freedom. This was her home. 'I'm back!' she called into the silvan silence. 'I'm back!'

She slipped out of her clothes as if in a dream, and gasped in pleasure as the warmth of the sun and the slight breeze caressed the bare skin of her body. Big city fetters had no place here. The constrictions of corsets were thrown aside, the pins were out of her hair and it was flowing free. She was a child again. A child of nature in a place that was hers and hers alone.

As she waded into the blue water, past the floating waterlilies, she was totally unaware of the dark eyes watching her from the depths of the green foliage on the opposite bank; or of the pain that was in the gaze that followed her every movement as she swam slowly and luxuriantly in the limpid waters of the pool.

He had walked all night from Hunter's Hollow and had been waiting here since daybreak. Ever since he had seen that first picture of her in the newspaper in the bar a few days ago, he had known he would have to come back. The news that she was due to return to Yorvik so soon had come as a shock so painful that he had got roaring drunk that very night. But this morning's paper had said she was now home. No matter what the danger, he had had to come. Just to be near her was all he asked. He knew she would come here. It was just a matter of waiting. This was their place and she was his woman.

'Noora . . .' he breathed. 'Noora, my love . . .'

Then he could wait no longer. He was casting off his clothes and running blindly down the bank to dive into the beckoning waters.

Noora, who was facing the other way, screamed and turned round at the splash just behind her. She stood up, the water lapping around her waist as she saw the figure swimming towards her. All she could see was the dark head and the powerful arms and shoulders as they cut their way through the surface of the pool. She screamed again, much louder this time. Then the cry died on her lips as the figure drew up just in front of her and raised his head.

'Joe-boy!'

'Hello, Noora . . .'

She gazed in astonishment at the young man standing in the water beside her. He had grown since they had last met and was a good head and shoulders taller than her. His frame had filled out, but there was a strange haunted look to his face that she did not recognize. His eyes were burning into hers.

'How – how wonderful to find you like this,' she found herself saying, but was not at all sure whether it was true. Automatically her hands moved to cover her naked breasts. Her time in England had seen the death of the wild, free child she had once been. She was a woman now. And he was a man.

'Is it, Noora? Is it really wonderful?' He was moving closer, his eyes devouring her.

She backed away, her feet slipping on the sandy bed of the pool. 'Have you been waiting for me?' she asked, wondering if he had come here specially to find her.

'Yes, I have been waiting. I have been waiting so long. So very long . . .' he told her, his voice huskily low. His dark eyes were lustrous in the sunlight as they took in every inch of her. He had dreamt of this moment for so long. Every day, every hour, every moment spent without her had been an agony for him. They had been together all their lives, until she had been taken from him. But he knew it could not be forever. That summer's day before she left, right here on the banks of their beloved pool, she had given him *Wee-iga* – the finest personal gift and greatest honour she could bestow. She had given him her virginity. She was his woman and he was her man. And now she was back and he was here to claim his own . . .

His heart was pounding and the fire within him was

searing his loins. He wanted her as he had wanted no other, and would want no other as long as there was breath in his body. 'I love you, Noora,' he said. 'You are my woman . . . I knew you would come back to me . . .'

He took hold of her arm and pulled her towards him. Her feet slipped on the bottom of the pool and she half fell. She screamed and lashed out. 'No, don't touch me!' Memories of that last encounter and its consequences burned in her mind. They had caused so much pain to everyone, especially to those they loved. In their innocence they had sinned, she knew that now, even if he didn't. Such a thing could never be allowed to happen again.

'Don't touch me!' she screamed as his arms reached for her. 'Don't touch me, Joe-boy!'

But Joe-boy had to touch her. Couldn't she see that his whole body was on fire? His whole being was aching for her. They were not meant to be two separate souls, but one. The gods of Dreamtime had decreed it. 'I need you,' he cried, his fingers digging into the soft flesh of her upper arms. 'You're mine, Noora . . . You know that . . . We belong together, you and me . . .'

Then he was pulling her towards him, as his lips clumsily searched for hers. They half fell into the water and she began to scream as she struggled to get free.

Her scream filled the silence of the late morning, startling the gaily coloured birds that flew up in a rainbow cloud of twittering indignation into the sun. And it was heard not only by the wildlife that basked in the golden warmth of the hollow, but by one of Yorvik's younger stockmen who was astride his horse on the track that led past the lakeside.

'Noora, my love!' There were tears in Joe-boy's eyes as he fought to cling on to the squirming body in his arms. Why was she doing this to him? Was it all part of some terrible game to make him lose his mind?

'Let go of me!' she panted. 'Let go of me, Joe-boy!'

But Joe-boy would not let go. He could not let go.

Couldn't she see that? He loved her. How could he let her go again? His grip became more fierce, his lips more urgent as they pressed into the soft flesh at the curve of her neck.

She let out another scream, long and piercing. It was her only weapon left as his greater strength was overcoming hers.

The young man who rode up could scarcely believe his eyes. He recognized that long blonde hair immediately. There was only one sheila with tresses like that on Yorvik. That was the boss's granddaughter in there being mauled by a bloody blackfella! What the hell was going on? Was he trying to kill her?

'Help me . . . ! Help me . . . !' Noora screamed again, her piercing cry sending shock waves down the spine of the young cattlehand on the bank. There was only one thing for it. He hesitated for a second, then raised his gun and took careful aim.

The shot rang out on the summer air.

There was a moment's silence, then Noora felt the blood run warm and free between her fingers as Joe-boy gave a gasp and his body slipped from her grasp into the blue waters of the pool.

She turned in horror to look in the direction of the shot, but her eyes would not focus on the black blur of the young man on the horse, as he stood in the bright golden glare of the sun, his gun still upraised. There was a story going round in her head as she clung on to the limp body of the one who had been her blood brother.

As she sank her face into the wet hair of his head, in her mind she could hear his voice telling her still . . .

He was telling her of how long, long ago in the original Dreamtime, when the world was newly born, there had lived a young woman of exquisite beauty: a fertility goddess, the daughter of the most powerful tribal chief in the region. She was as lovely as the fair waterlilies that were the glory of the billabongs and lagoons of their beloved land. Her slender body was as lithe as the lizard and her eyes, as blue as the skies, could be as dark and mysterious as the deepest rock pools in which they had swum together all their young lives.

And there was one who desired her above all others. Desired her more than life itself. Without her he was nothing, an empty shell. He thought at first that she loved him too. But she turned him away, for their tribal laws disallowed such a match between those of different totems.

Then one day he chanced upon her bathing in the still waters of their sacred lagoon. When she saw him watching, she begged him to go away, but this only made his desire for her the stronger.

His whole being aflame, he waded into the lagoon and caught hold of her. Sensing what might follow, she cried aloud and called upon the great spirits to help her.

Her cries were answered. And as they echoed in the clear summer air, an exquisite waterlily floated by on the surface of the water, while unseen by the two struggling figures, from the mud at the edges of the pool there slithered Death in the form of a giant crocodile to devour them both.

From that day to this, he had told her, the lagoons of their fair land have been adorned by the beautiful blossoms of the waterlily. But so often nearby Death is lurking in the shadows, waiting for its chance to swoop and claim its own.

He had told her so much about this land and its people. He was as much a part of this place as the very air they breathed. He had been her lover, her brother and her friend. They had been everything to one another once, before she had left to find her Dreamtime in another place, a place very different from this land they loved. Around them the sun was shining from out of a cloudless heaven as tears filled her eyes and her beloved Joe-boy's blood dripped red through her fingers to spread slowly on the sunlit surface of the pool, staining the pale petals of the waterlilies.

I loved you, I love you, for this love have lost
State, station, heaven, mankind's,
My own esteem,
And yet cannot regret
What it has cost,
So dear is still the memory of that dream . . .

EPILOGUE

There is an old Aboriginal saying, '*Ar-ree-koori-an-yan-a-atninga*' — the sins of the fathers are visited upon the children unto the third and fourth generation. And those were the words whispered by Joe-boy's beloved Be-anga, as the old Irishman sat down on the chair in his hut and heard the news that his son had been shot at and wounded on Yorvik land.

Carrie alone stood with him, her hand on his shoulder. She had insisted she be the one to break the news, and she had shielded him from the terrible circumstances of the affair. He had suffered enough already. To hear that Joe-boy had been winged by the bullet in an attack on Noora, and had then made off into the bush like a hunted animal, would have been too much for him to bear.

Noora herself had saved his life, screaming at the station hand to lay down his rifle as Joe-boy struggled to reach the other side of the pool. She had been in shock ever since, as they all were.

When the old man had composed himself, at his request, Carrie left him alone with his grief.

He walked out into the sunshine and along the path he had walked so often, holding the hand of the small child that had been his only son. Memories came flooding back, and he could hear once more the voice of his father, old Joe O'Dwyer, and of his mother, Maggie, and over all came the childish imploring voice of the infant who had come to mean everything to him. 'Tell me another story, Be-anga, please . . .'

But all those stories were now at an end. In his heart he knew it. He had waited long for this day. The end was not as he would have chosen, but neither had been the beginning. Yet he would do what he had always done and make the best of both.

From afar the woman who loved him watched as, a solitary figure now bowed with age, he went back to his hut to sit quietly in his chair and make his peace with himself over what had happened out there today.

They found him still sitting there the following morning.

The cry went round the blackfellas' camp first. *'Teeri-yeetchbeem* – the red-headed one – is dead!'

His hair had not been red for many a long year, but Carrie knew immediately what was meant as she hurried down that familiar track to the old stringy-bark hut that had been his home.

Part of her own world died with him. She would allow no one else near the body. Only she must touch that beloved flesh, now hard and wrinkled with age.

She laid him out with infinite tenderness and buried him beneath the green grass of their beloved spot on the banks of Yorvik Force where she knew she herself would join him.

The rays of the setting sun were casting webs of gold on the waters of the pool and on the pale petals of the waterlilies as she stood by the grave with Noora by her side.

But despite the heartache, the world today seemed a softer, greener place. There would be no special stone, for the sweet-scented eucalyptus beneath which she buried the man she had loved for over half a century was surely the most noble of all memorials. Never could a spot be more hallowed.

Noora reached out and took her grandmother's hand. 'This is my land too, Moo-choo-choo,' she said softly. 'I was born here and like Joe-boy's Be-anga, I will die here.'

Then out of a clear blue sky, a gentle rain began to fall: the sort the blackfellas called *mudi meechi* – a kind rain. But it was no longer raining in the old woman's heart. The great dark cloud had lifted. She knew now her beloved granddaughter would never return to England.

Noora had tears in her eyes as she raised her face to the heavens and let the soft rain run down her cheeks. She realized now that the old world with all its pretensions and prejudices was no place for her. Her place was right here on Yorvik, building the New World of tomorrow.

She bent and tenderly kissed her grandmother's cheek, then turned to leave the old lady to say her last goodbye to the man she had loved for a lifetime.

Carrie watched her go with a full heart. A great weight had gone from her shoulders. She had found peace at last, for Yorvik would pass into safe hands. It was all she had ever asked.

Then she knelt and raised her eyes to the heavens. He was up there somewhere, watching her, or his spirit – his *kuran* – was sitting right there at the end of the grave listening to her. Most probably smiling that broad smile of his. She was not alone.

'*Impara munna poora, wudgja weeri ni-a*, my darling,' she told him softly, in the language of his dead mother. 'The gods are calling, Irish, my love. The spirits have spoken . . . We come . . .'

And the gentle *mudi meechi* that was falling on this beloved earth where he lay was not rain at all; it was tears of happiness, for one day soon she would join him here. They would make the long last journey to *Palanari* – their Dreamtime – together.

The Other Woman
Eileen Townsend

An unforgettable evocation of love and betrayal stretching from the 1880s to the First World War.

With *Of Woman Born*, *In Love and War* and *The Love Child*, Eileen Townsend has carved a place for herself as a remarkable dramatic novelist. Now with *The Other Woman* she evokes her most vivid and memorable world yet.

The Other Woman is the story of the orphan Mhairi McLeod, born on the mystical Isle of Skye, and of her quest for fortune and her heritage over forty turbulent years. An extraordinary heroine of her time, her happiness will be overshadowed by her illegitimacy, and by the rivalry of a woman whose blood ties bring both pain and pleasure.

ISBN 0 586 21277 9